The Trouble
with
Brides

Books by
Deeanne Gist

A Bride Most Begrudging
Courting Trouble
Deep in the Heart of Trouble
The Measure of a Lady
A Bride in the Bargain
Beguiled
Maid to Match

The Trouble with Brides

THREE NOVELS IN ONE VOLUME

DEEANNE GIST

BETHANY HOUSE PUBLISHERS

Minneapolis, Minnesota

Published by Bethany House Publishers
11400 Hampshire Avenue South
Bloomington, Minnesota 55438

Bethany House Publishers is a division of
Baker Publishing Group, Grand Rapids, Michigan.

Printed in the United States of America

Library of Congress Cataloging-in-Publication Data

Gist, Deeanne.
    The trouble with brides : three novels in one volume / Deeanne Gist.
        p.   cm.
    ISBN 978-0-7642-0893-5
    1. Historical fiction, American.   2. Love stories, American.   3. Christian Fiction, American.   I. Title.
    PS3607 .I55 A6   2011
    813' .6—dc22

                                                                        2010037209

A BRIDE
MOST
BEGRUDGING

Deptford, England
April 1643

SAINTS ABOVE, GIRL. WHAT are you *doing* here?" the shackled man hissed.

Lady Constance Morrow rushed those last few steps across the upper deck. "Please, Uncle Skelly, don't scold me. I couldn't let you leave without saying goodbye."

"It's only for seven years. Now get off this blasted shallop."

She touched a hand to her throat. How could she leave? He'd been much more of a father to her than the earl. Perhaps he felt shamed by the shackles clamped tight around his wrists and ankles.

Her heart squeezed inside her chest. He looked as if he'd aged ten years since she saw him just three short months ago. She might not have even recognized him had he not spoken out.

An unhealthy gray pallor replaced the rosy glow she had grown so accustomed to seeing in his cheeks. And his pride and joy—the pure white beard and mustache he'd kept meticulously trimmed and groomed—grew in great abandon about his face.

But his green eyes were still crystal clear and, at the moment, absolutely furious.

"But *America*," she exclaimed. "It's so far away and wild and heathen."

"It's better than being dead," he growled. "For love o' the king, girl, this ship is not interested in men only. Those colonists need breeders, and the captain chained a whole store of female felons in the hold for that very purpose. You have no business being on board. Where is your maid?"

"I easily escaped from her. Besides, the captain would not dare allow a member of his crew to touch an English gentlewoman."

"He'd dare that and more. All the other well-wishers have long since left, so there is no one on board that can check his actions." He swiveled to look behind him and when he turned back, near panic lit his eyes. "Quick," he cried. "He has seen you!"

Who, she thought. *The captain?* She grabbed the front of her skirts, poised for flight, yet did not move. Releasing the expensive silk, she clasped Skelly's hands in hers. His irons clanked.

"Oh, Uncle. I can't bear this." Her eyes pooled with unshed tears. "I will not let the submissions to your *Diary* go unanswered. I will keep the publication going while you are away. It will be ready and waiting for you upon your return. You have my oath."

"Have you not heard a word I've said? You must leave *this instant.* The captain of this ship is a villain and a coward. It will go the worse for me if he catches us together, and I'd just as soon avoid a flogging. Now, *go.*"

She paled. "Oh! I'm sorry. I had no idea."

She glanced across the upper deck. The captain's huge silhouette advanced, his crisp stride unaffected by the sway of the vessel. Her hairs stood on end. "I love you, Uncle," she whispered frantically. "My prayers are with you."

Picking up her skirts once again, she turned and hustled toward the gangway.

The captain whistled. An unkempt sailor posted just feet from her took two long steps. He grabbed her forearm.

"Release me at once!" she demanded.

The man's dark leathery face formed a grotesque imitation of a smile. "I think not, maiden."

She increased her resistance. He grabbed her other arm. She tried to jerk free. He tightened his hold. She slammed her heel onto his booted toe. The heel broke off.

He snarled, grasped her around the waist, and hauled her clear off her feet, slamming her against his side.

"What's this, Cooper?" The deep voice barely registered in her panicked mind. She could not believe they would be so bold.

She squirmed. Nothing happened. She kicked. Nothing happened. She bit his arm, gagging at the repelling taste of his sleeve.

His grip loosened. Encouraged by this tiny bit of success, she bucked and kicked with increased vigor. He swore. The air suddenly quit reaching her lungs.

The shallop lurched. The rigging creaked.

"What have you?"

"I'm not sure, Capt'n," her captor responded. "A little bird trying to fly the coop, looks like."

The captain fingered her hair. "And a red bird, at that."

She yanked her head away from his touch. "You'll hang for this!" Her threat came out pathetically weak. She struggled for air. "I cannot breathe."

The sailor's pressure did not let up. She labored to stay conscious as her vision began to fade.

"Arman!" the captain shouted.

She jerked her eyes open at the command.

"Sir?" Another voice filtered up the gangway.

"What conveyances are on the dock?"

Her lungs were on fire. She opened her mouth, gasping. A thimbleful of air entered. She needed more. Much more.

"A hired hackney, sir." This, again, from the gangway.

"Anyone in it?"

"Just the driver, sir."

Her eyes refused to stay open. Icy prickles bombarded her fingers, toes, arms, and legs. Yet her hearing still functioned perfectly.

"Take her below with the others."

The captain's quiet words produced seconds of pure terror before blackness overtook her.

CHAPTER ONE

Virginia Colony
Two Months Later

THE GOWN THEY GAVE her fit too closely. It displayed her figure with humiliating clarity, but perhaps that would work to her advantage. She had lost so much weight, she couldn't imagine any farmer wanting to invest in such a sickly looking woman.

Several tobacco planters had been on board already to examine the "cargo." The men stood chained on one side of the upper deck, the women on the other. The men were being sold as indentured servants for seven or fourteen year terms, depending upon their sentence.

But the women were to serve a lifetime sentence. They were to be purchased as brides. One bride in exchange for 120 pounds of tobacco leafage, the colony's cash crop.

All except Constance, that is. She had been placed alone up on the half deck, her wrists and ankles shackled, the first mate standing guard behind her right shoulder. The captain was asking two hundred pounds of tobacco for her. Ridiculous.

Her gaze drifted over the indentured men. Uncle Skelly was not among them, of course. How could he be?

Only twice during the voyage had the captain allowed the women onto the upper deck for fresh air. The first time up, she'd passed Uncle Skelly on the mid deck. With a collar and padlock about his neck, they had chained him not only to a board but to three of the most abominable creatures she had ever seen. Jail fever consumed one of those creatures.

The second time up, she had found Uncle Skelly's place on the board eerily vacant. The first mate, Cooper, had confirmed her fears. Skelly Morrow was dead.

Constance swallowed the rush of tears that even now accumulated in her throat at the memory.

"Look lively, maiden. Here comes a'one," Cooper snarled.

She stiffened as a young farmer of but a score or so years approached the half deck. He looked at Cooper, nodded slightly, then turned to her.

She jerked back when he captured some strands of her hair between his long work-roughened fingers. The captain had not allowed her to wear a headcloth this morning. He'd insisted on having her hair loose and uncovered around her shoulders and back.

This display was nothing short of blasphemy. A woman's hair was sacred and a recognized symbol of her maidenhood, only to be worn free while speaking wedding vows.

She'd never felt so naked in her life. Her hair wasn't soft and silky like other women's. It was wild and thick with tightly coiled ringlets that seemed to multiply when unbound.

The bay breeze picked up, causing her hair to swirl around her face. She tried again to free herself from the man's grasp.

"Easy, miss. I'll not hurt you," he said.

His voice was kind, as were his eyes. He did not rake her with an offensive look nor handle her roughly. If he asked to see her teeth, though, she'd be most uncooperative.

Below, two men captured her attention. One was a dark-haired farmer with a straw hat in his hand. The other was blond and had been on board the ship during the passage over. He'd not been a prisoner, nor had he been a crew member. She'd learned he had paid an extraordinary fee for his passage to the colony, a place he claimed as his home.

The pair singled out Mary, the woman who'd been chained next to Constance the entire voyage over. They spoke with Mary, checked her teeth, and had her walk the length of the deck and back.

The captain approached them. More words were exchanged. The bargaining had begun. In a few minutes, Mary's fetters were removed and she left the ship with the blond man, while the dark-haired farmer signed a voucher for the captain.

Constance tapped down her panic. Mary was more than a fellow prisoner. She was Constance's only friend.

Of a sudden, the captain pointed to Constance and the farmer turned in her direction. He narrowed his eyes, finished his transaction with the captain, and headed to the half deck.

She returned her attention to the young man in front of her. He still had hold of her hair, but he was focused on Cooper.

" . . . a gen-u-ine lady, she is," the first mate was saying.

"Then why was she transported?" the man asked.

"Oh, we didn't ask questions. Not our job to ask questions."

She rolled her eyes.

"You have papers for her?"

"No, he does not," Constance replied.

Cooper grabbed her arm. "Keep quiet, missy, or you'll be the sorrier for it."

"Looking for a bride, Gerald?" The dark-haired farmer had reached the half deck.

The man who must have been Gerald released her hair and jumped back. "Drew! No, not at all."

"Is she for sale?" Drew asked Cooper.

"Aye, mate."

"As a tobacco bride?"

"Aye."

Drew turned back to Gerald and raised an eyebrow.

"Now, Drew, it is not what it appears. I was merely curious."

"You gave up the right to be curious the moment you married my sister."

Gerald's face filled with color. "Actually, it was you I was thinking of," he sputtered.

Drew lifted both brows this time.

Gerald swallowed. "I, uh, just thought if you found someone of an, uh, acceptable nature, you might be interested."

"And you deem this female acceptable?"

Gerald paused. "They say she is a lady of the realm, Drew."

"She has red hair, and I absolutely abhor red hair."

She stiffened. Gerald's face suffused with color. Although her hair was more auburn than red, Gerald's hair was almost orange, it was so bright.

"Your pardon. I did not know."

"Well, well, well. What have we here? Looking for a bride, Master O'Connor?" A scrawny, slovenly man with more teeth missing than not swaggered onto the half deck.

Tension bounced between the three men. Drew put on his hat, shifted his attention to Constance, and tipped his brim. "If you will excuse me, miss." He, along with his brother-in-law, moved past her, past the man with the missing teeth, and past two other farmers now approaching the half deck.

The scraggy man watched them leave and ejected tobacco-colored saliva onto the wooden planks as he followed their progress.

"Emmett," greeted one of the advancing farmers. He and his companion both had great bushy black beards, jolly faces, and rounded bellies. Perhaps they were kin.

"Woodrum," Emmett said, then turning to her, grabbed her cheeks and squeezed until her mouth gaped open. "Well, would you look at all them teeth. Why, she's got a mouth full of 'em. How's the rest of her, Cooper? You patted her down?"

She reared back, trying to grab his arm, but the chains around her wrists and waist restricted her movement. He tightened his grip. The rank smell of him took her breath away, and if he'd had any fingernails at all, they'd have cut half-moons into her cheeks.

"No damaging of the goods, matey, until after you buy her," Cooper said. "Pat all you want, but don't be leaving any bruises."

She stiffened. Emmett released her with a shove, and she would have fallen backward if the big man called Woodrum hadn't caught her elbow. Once she was steady, he relaxed his hold, then let go of her completely.

Emmett raked his gaze up and down her frame, rubbing his hands against his puny chest. "Why's she up here away from them other brides?"

"She's one of them ladies of the realm, she is," Cooper responded. "And she'll cost you a few more tobaccy leaves than them others."

"What proof you got fer yer claim? I say she's nothing more than a quail plucked right off them London alleyways." He eyed her again. "She shore got what it takes to do the job, and I ain't gonna be paying out a bunch of sot weed for used goods."

Woodrum scratched his cheek. "How much are you asking for her?"

"Two hundred pounds," Cooper answered.

Emmett harrumphed. "Of tobaccy? You'll not be gettin' two hundred pounds for a light skirt."

"She's a gen-u-ine lady, mate, but no bloke's a forcin' you to claim her. We already got us a bid for her, we do."

Emmett furrowed his brows. "From who?"

"Drew O'Connor."

Woodrum and his silent companion looked at each other, caution evident in their expressions. Emmett's eyes took on an unnatural brilliance. Constance didn't know what game the first mate was playing, but she would hold her tongue for now.

"O'Connor, you say?" Emmett asked. "How much did he offer?"

"Two hundred."

"Then why's the maid still here?"

"She has to be paid for in tobaccy only. No vouchers. The capt'n wouldn't release her or take her off the block before collecting payment. O'Connor went to collect his sot weed."

As far as she knew, that was an outright lie, but she couldn't be certain.

The merciless sun beat down upon them. Sweat trickled down Emmett's face and into his snarled beard. "Well, ain't that interesting." He wiped his hands against his backside, then looked to the first mate. "May I?"

"Help yourself," Cooper replied.

Emmett reached for her.

She leaned away from him. "Touch me, and I'll see you flogged before the morrow's sun appears on the horizon."

Emmett's eyebrows shot up to his hairline. "Ho, ho! Would you listen to that? A saucy one, ain't she?" Cackling, he rubbed his hands together.

Constance tensed.

"Leave off, Emmett," Woodrum said, grabbing Emmett's arm. "It's clear that she is healthy and there is no padding beneath her garment."

Emmett's lip curled. "What's it to you, Woodrum?"

"Either up Drew's wager or keep your hands to yourself."

"I ain't makin' no bid till I test the goods."

Without taking his eyes off Emmett, Woodrum handed his hat to his companion, removed his coat, and relinquished that as well. He slowly began to roll up his sleeves.

The man's belly may have been round, but his arms and chest appeared to be solid rock. "You'll not touch her unless you pay for the privilege."

Smelling a fight, the farmers on the upper deck had begun to crowd close.

Emmett slowly lowered his hands. "Two hundred twenty, Cooper. I'll give you two hundred twenty pounds for her."

"Two twenty-five," Woodrum countered.

It was time to speak up. "Gentlemen," she interjected, "this is really all quite unnecessary. I am not a tobacco bride. I am the daughter of an earl. The captain kidnapped me and is trying to sell me unlawfully. As soon as the governor comes aboard, I will have an audience with him and will then be freed and on my way back to London."

Her statement, made during one of those unfortunate moments when every person in the crowd, for whatever reason, is silent all at once, carried across the entire breadth of the ship.

The quiet that followed her pronouncement was fraught with shock. On the heels of that, a huge swell of laughter and guffaws from the whole company of men rose to alarming levels. Even Woodrum was amused.

"Oh, she's a wicked one, she is," Emmett cackled. "Where's the capt'n?"

The crowd parted, and the captain took the steps two at a time. Woodrum and his friend receded into the crowd.

Emmett grasped the captain's hand. "I'll give you a whole hogshead for her, capt'n, and while my field boy rolls it down here, I'll be celebrating at the meetinghouse."

The captain pursed his lips for a moment, then broke into a grin. "Three hundred pounds it is, then. Gentlemen, Goodman Emmett here has purchased himself one high-born bride."

The men roared their approval and surged forward, encircling Emmett. He put an X on the voucher and exchanged it for a receipt from the captain. The excitement escalated and the crowd pulled Emmett off the half deck and further away from her. He twisted around. The depraved promise in his eyes projected itself into her very soul.

Bile converged in her throat. She was going to be sick. Forsooth, she was going to be sick right here, right now.

Help me, Lord, help me. Where is the governor? Where are you, Lord? Please, please. Help me.

As one, the company moved from the ship to the shore. And on, she supposed, to the celebration.

Chills from within shot through her body, causing a series of bumps to erupt along her arms and legs. Then an all-consuming anger at the incredible injustice of it all made her blood surge. Her resolve solidified and she focused in on the captain.

"How *dare* you!" she cried. "You will not get away with this. Mark you, if you do not arrange an audience with the governor at once, I will create a commotion of such magnitude they will write legends about it."

The captain did not even bother to acknowledge her. "Throw her back in the hold, Cooper," he said over his shoulder as he descended the steps.

She filled her lungs with the intention of letting out a scream the likes of which would not be ignored. Before she could release it, the first mate squeezed a band of skin between her neck and her shoulder.

Debilitating pain cut off her scream and buckled her knees. She crumpled to the ground. Cooper did not let go but followed her to the floor. She whimpered, trying to pull away from the torturous vice his fingers created.

His hot, foul breath invaded her ear. "Not one sound, dovey. Not one."

CHAPTER | TWO

CONSTANCE LAY SHIVERING AND alone belowdecks. Darkness entombed the hold. Midnight had passed, but morning was still more than a few hours away.

She felt certain the men's celebration was over, for the balance of brides had been picked up long ago. All except for her.

She tried not to let desperation fill her. If the governor had put in an appearance, it was after Cooper had forced her back into the hold and secured her to the wall. With that opportunity gone, she knew there would be no other. At least not anytime soon. And by the time she did see the governor, it would be too late.

She would belong to a man. An odious, vulgar man who inspired revulsion, loathing, and horror. A man who, in the eyes of this colony, would have complete dominion over her. Who would have the right to do with her as he saw fit.

Her stomach clinched and she pushed herself up off the rough planks and heaved once again. Nothing left.

She'd managed to hold her fears at bay until the last bride had been led to her doom. When the trapdoor had closed behind that poor woman, it was the first time in over eight weeks that Constance had been completely alone. And it terrified her. The dark, damp, malodorous deck that had felt so cramped and hemmed in now loomed over her with a soundless assault.

The irons around her waist and wrists weighted her down. Collapsing onto the slats, she vaguely heard the scurrying of a rat echo off the walls of the hold. A fresh rush of tears spilled from her eyes.

Have you heard my cries, Lord? Have you destroyed my enemy? Is that why I am still here?

As if in answer, the squeak of the trapdoor reached her ears just as light from a lantern reached her eyes. She covered her eyes with her arm, the clanking of her chains ricocheting around her.

The heavy tread of the mate clomping down the steps sent her heart into a terrible gallop. She curled into a tight ball. *Please. Please. Spare me, Lord. Rescue me. Please!*

The crewman's smell reached her before he did. "The call to reckoning has come, wench. Up with ye, now. Yer man's arrived and it's anxious he is to take possession of ye."

In a pig's eye, she thought. A great calm settled upon her. She slowly unfurled, pulled herself into a sitting position, and looked up to see who had the late night watch. Arman. A beastly excuse of a man.

He removed the lock attaching her to the wall and pulled the chain from around her waist. Grabbing the irons around her wrists, he yanked her to her feet. The room swirled round, but Arman gave her no time to gain her sea legs.

She stumbled. He shoved her forward. She fell hard on her knees, pain shooting up her legs to her back and neck.

"Get up," he snarled, jerking her back to her feet. "You'll not be playing yer high-and-mighty games with me, missy. Ye might work yer wiles upon Cooper, but yer nothin' more than a hen to that struttin' rooster on the uppers, and if ye think to be givin' him or me any troubles, it'll go the worse for ye."

She kept her face expressionless, but she would not cooperate with Arman or the rooster. And she was prepared to do whatever it took to free herself from the knave.

When they made the upper deck, she scanned the area for the despicable Emmett man that had purchased her. He was not there. Instead, Arman led her to stand in front of the dark-haired farmer they called Drew O'Connor.

What was he doing here? Was he to take her to Emmett? But, no, it had been clear those two were not on friendly terms. Confusion clouded her thoughts.

"Remove the fetters," O'Connor said.

"I wouldn't advise it, sir. The dove has been a bit of a trial."

O'Connor scrutinized her. "A strong gust of wind would knock her over. From what I hear about the victuals you serve the felons, I would imagine she's too weak to put up much of a fight."

Arman stiffened. "She was fed."

"Um. Let me guess. Pease and loblolly?"

"Once a day."

"Remove the fetters," O'Connor repeated.

"You remove 'em."

O'Connor snatched the keys from Arman's hand and reached for her wrists. She jerked them back.

He paused. Moonbeams glanced off the ship's metal bell, throwing his features into dark relief. "Do you not want to be released?"

"I, of course, want to be released, but not only from these irons. I want to be granted my freedom. The captain of this ship kidnapped me. I did not come here voluntarily as a tobacco bride, nor am I a felon."

"Then how is it you stand before me bound with shackles?"

The irons surrounding her wrists rattled as the wooden deck shifted beneath her feet. "My uncle was a prisoner on this ship. I came to bid him good-bye—"

"Lies," Arman growled.

"Hold, man," O'Connor snapped. "I'll hear what she has to say."

A whisper of hope flickered within her. "My uncle was sentenced to seven years of indentured servitude for not subscribing to the king's supremacy. By the time I learned of his sentence, he was already on board the *Randolph*. I hastened to this vessel. No sooner had I located Uncle Skelly than the captain grabbed me and threw me in the hold."

"What of your escort?"

She hesitated. "I escaped from my maid's watchful eye. Had she known of my destination, she never would have permitted it."

"And the other visitors on board? Surely someone saw this atrocity occur?"

"The last of the visitors were leaving by the time I arrived and boarded."

"Did not your driver notice you failed to return?"

She sighed. "I hired a hackney. My own driver is loyal to my father and would not have brought me to see Uncle Skelly. I'm sure the captain saw to my hired conveyance for me."

O'Connor arched a brow. "You were alone?"

Looking aside, she nodded.

"On the docks?"

The disbelief in his tone brought her chin up. "Uncle Skelly was like a father to me. He'd raised me since my mother's death. I was hardly more than a babe. My real father didn't bother to make an appearance until he needed me for a marriage alliance. An alliance I refused to accept."

"Who's your father?"

"The Earl of Greyhame." The tackle creaked and whined against the water's pull but held the slaver fast to the dock.

O'Connor glanced at Arman. "I'll speak with the prisoner she calls Uncle Skelly."

Arman snorted. "There ain't no such person."

"He's dead." The words fell flat from her lips. She still couldn't quite believe it. Forcing down the lump in her throat, she contemplated the vast watery cemetery beyond the dark horizon. "He didn't survive the passage over."

O'Connor scratched the back of his head, knocking his hat askew. "Let me make sure I understand this. You came to the docks *alone* and boarded a ship of felons just to give your uncle a peck on the cheek? An uncle who is, for all practical purposes, nonexistent?"

She jerked her focus back to the matter at hand. "He died!"

"How convenient." O'Connor straightened his hat, his narrowed gaze quickly sluicing up and down her body before resting upon her face.

She returned the favor. His bronzed skin was too dark, his blue eyes too pale, his jaw too square.

That jaw tightened. "I suppose you will now tell me peers of the realm no longer dress in the manner they used to."

She fingered the lacings digging into her waist. The bodice was ridiculously tight. "This gown is not mine."

"No? You mean you wore someone else's clothing when you came on board to visit your notorious *uncle*?"

"Certainly not."

"Then where are your clothes?"

A good question. Before they docked yesterday, all prisoners were expected to bathe. On the upper deck. In the open. She had resisted, of course. But with the help of another sailor, Arman had stripped her of her clothing, shoved her into a filthy barrel, dumped a torrent of salt water atop her, then yanked her out by her hair.

She had kicked and bit and clawed until the captain shoved an unfamiliar bodice, skirt, and headcloth into her arms. No chemise. No stockings. No shoes.

Clutching the items to her frame, she had questioned the absence of the undergarments and the soiled condition of the clothing. In response, the captain threatened to take them back and leave her with nothing.

It was then she had demanded the return of her diary. It lay in the pocket of her old skirt. The captain's eyes had narrowed. The diary would be returned to her in exchange for a more satisfying sport with the men, he had said, starting with him.

She was shrewd enough to know when to retreat. Remembering that retreat fed her anger. She tipped her head toward Arman. "Ask him."

O'Connor turned to him. "Where are her clothes?"

"Below."

"Bring them to me."

"They're rags, matey, and not fit for man nor beast, they ain't."

"The clothing, if you please."

"I want my diary back too," Constance said.

Arman's black eyes impaled her.

"I'll review any belongings she brought on board," O'Connor interjected.

Arman spun around and headed toward the companionway. O'Connor stopped him. "Tell your captain I'll have a word with him as well."

The rhythmic lapping of the water against the shallop accentuated their sudden silence. O'Connor did not look her way. Standing with his head bowed and shoulders slumped, he rubbed his eyes. His sleeveless leather jerkin covered thick, broad shoulders. Its laces opened at the chest, revealing a well-worn shirt underneath, while a cloth pouch hung from the leather belt at his trim waist. Full breeches fastened just below his knees, where long stockings hugged muscular calves. Unadorned braid laced up the square shoes on his feet.

At the sound of Arman's return, O'Connor lifted his head and straightened his shoulders. The sailor handed him a wad of fabric.

Stepping closer to a lantern, O'Connor unfurled and examined the once-beautiful silk dress she had worn that long ago day of her kidnapping. His hands, massive and strong, explored the hollows of the garment, gliding over the soft curves custom-made for her alone. The faded green bodice fluttered beneath the ministrations of his adept tanned fingers. An unwelcome burning crept up her neck and into her cheeks.

Finally, he allowed the dress to slither from his hands to the deck. Dragging her attention from the bundle of silk pooled at his feet, she watched him shake out her chemise. Another inspection of seams and construction followed.

He held up the undergarment by its shoulders and squinted over at her. "Are these your things?"

She nodded.

"Did this fit you when you boarded the ship?"

She blushed anew. "It did."

Cocking his head to the side, he scrutinized the chemise again. "You have lost a considerable amount of poundage."

She said nothing. His strapping frame dwarfed the chemise, hanging limp within his grasp. Even so, he was right. The only fullness left on her body was that across her chest, and even that had diminished in size a bit.

As if reading her thoughts, he regarded the area in question. She resisted the urge to shield herself. She had worn gowns at home cut every bit as low as this one without a moment of self-consciousness.

In time, he retrieved the dress from the deck and fingered its finely woven fabric. After checking the pockets, he shoved the clothing beneath his arm. "The diary?"

Arman handed O'Connor a small, worn book. O'Connor spent several minutes studying the publication. "Where is her diary?"

"That's all we found," Arman answered.

"That is the diary I spoke of," Constance said.

O'Connor looked at her. "This is no diary. This is a collection of nonsense."

She bristled. "It is an almanac containing many delightful and entertaining particulars."

He snorted. "For what purpose?"

"It provides me and a great number of other ladies with a wealth of scientific information."

He opened the volume and turned to one of the leaves. Holding it up to the lantern, he read an entry.

> "At London one morning 'neath the sun's shining glow,
> I found my cane's length in its own shadow,
> As I held it upright; 'twas the tenth day of May:
> Now tell me exactly the time of the day?"

He looked at her over the rim of the book. "You must be jesting."

"Can you provide the solution?"

"Nine hours, thirteen minutes, and sixteen seconds into the morning."

She rolled her eyes. "You saw my answer."

"*Your* answer? These are your figures scribbled in the margins?"

"They are."

He threw back his head and laughed. The deep, warm, rich sound of it chafed her ears. She took a deep breath and met his gaze square on.

"O'Connor," the captain shouted. "Back again from this morning?"

Snapping the almanac shut, O'Connor shoved it under his arm with the clothing. He held out his hand. The captain grasped it.

"Good evening to you, Captain. This wench says she comes unwillingly."

The captain glanced at her. "You're here to claim her, then? I'd heard Emmett lost her in a game of chance this afternoon, but I couldn't quite credit it. You have the receipt?"

O'Connor handed it to him.

Her mouth went slack. A game of chance? They bartered for her in a *card game*?

She snapped her mouth shut. *Was this your answer, Lord? This is what you consider being released? But that's not what I meant and you know it! I want to be freed!*

The captain scanned the piece of parchment, then cackling, handed it back to O'Connor. "By trow, Emmett must be sorely vexed. Particularly since he paid out so much sot weed to purchase her." He clapped O'Connor on the back. "What took you so long to fetch her? All the other men have long since collected their brides."

"I had things to attend to."

A suggestive grin spread across the captain's face. "Ah, yes. I'd almost forgotten. You purchased a bride of your own this morning, didn't you? Were so desperate for one, in fact, that you sent your brother clear to England to handpick one for you." He gave a low coarse laugh. "And you're just now coming up for air? Decided you'd like to try this one on for size? Ho, ho! Emmett's going to throw bung by the cartload when he recovers from his drunken stupor!"

Constance's mind whirled. Was the captain referring to Mary? Mary had left with the blond man, but it was O'Connor here who had signed the purchase papers. Oh, poor Mary! Still, O'Connor couldn't very well try and force Constance into a marriage contract if he was already wed to Mary.

"I've not married the woman my brother recommended but merely purchased her," O'Connor said.

Constance's breath caught.

The captain howled. "Oh, that's even better! By my troth, but I can't wait to see Emmett's face when he hears."

O'Connor's nostrils flared. "Where are this female's papers of transport?"

The captain's expression sobered somewhat. "She came on board the vessel with fraudulent letters to the prisoners in an effort to procure their escape. We seized her before her plan could be carried out."

She gasped. "That is untrue!"

She caught a glimpse of suspicion on O'Connor's face. Surely it was the captain he doubted, not *her*?

By heaven, she must locate the Crown-appointed governor of this godforsaken place haste, posthaste. Only then could this unconscionable injustice done to her be righted.

A sinking sensation began in the pit of her stomach. What if she finally managed an audience with the governor and he didn't believe her? She was no more than a warm female body in a colony desperate to be fruitful. What if the governor refused to believe her simply because it suited his purposes, and the Crown's, to have her here?

This overgrown provincial American might be her only chance at freedom. After all, he evidently owned her. So if he believed her story, wouldn't it be within his power to set her free?

The captain regarded her through half-closed lids. "We were given an order from Lieutenant-Colonel Windem to keep her. She is such a rebel as not to be permitted to stay in the mother country."

"How dare you!" she cried. "My father—"

"May I see the order?"

The captain returned his attention to O'Connor. "The order came by word of mouth."

O'Connor tightened his lips. He handed the keys to the captain. "Release her. I am ready to take her home."

The captain moved to unlock the fetters. "By all means. I almost hate to see her go, though. It's a mighty feisty wench she's been, and she can certainly put on the airs. Too bad I didn't join you in your gaming. Maybe Emmett would have lost her to me and I could move to the next port and sell her all over again!"

Stiffening, Constance squared her shoulders. She and O'Connor stared at each other over the captain's bent frame. Sighing, she held her peace and watched the fetters come off.

"Miss Morrow?"

"*Lady* Morrow."

O'Connor offered her his elbow.

"Do you believe I am who I say I am?"

He said nothing. Merely shifted the straw hat resting atop his long sable waves, then once again extended his elbow.

"I need to speak with the governor. Will you take me to him?"

He gave a brisk nod. "Of course."

She looked at his elbow, then back up at his eyes. "When?"

"It's the middle of the night," he said, a touch of impatience flickering across his face. "Not a very good time to ask the governor for a sympathetic ear."

She bit her lip. He was right, of course.

Lifting her chin, she said, "I'll not marry you until I've spoken with the governor."

O'Connor raised a brow. "Have I asked you to marry me?"

"Well, no, but I assumed—"

"Don't assume."

She studied him for a moment, then hesitantly placed her hand upon his arm and accompanied him off the ship.

"We are going to your home?" she asked.

He nodded.

Leaving the shore behind, she and O'Connor zigzagged through a forest of trees growing, at every footfall, larger and nobler than the last.

The sheer number of trees held her speechless. She had heard the colonies held a wealth of timber, yet she hadn't expected such profusion. Even the moon, resplendent in its full phase, seemed to blaze in an unprecedented fashion, providing them with an abundance of light.

At length, they entered a natural alley lined with trees whose circumference hinted at ages of two hundred years or more. Blending together with the shrubs, they arched overhead, forming a bower. Beams of moonlight filtered through its leafy roof, illuminating the pathway hemmed in by the lush foliage and trees.

Closing her eyes, she inhaled. Sweet smelling scents she could not identify filled her. She savored the pure and delicious aroma just before stumbling across a root.

Her eyes flew open as O'Connor grasped her elbow in support.

"Thank you," she said.

"You are all right?"

She flexed her ankle. "Yes."

Carefully placing her foot on the ground, she looked up. Their gazes caught and held.

An owl searching for dinner used his dense downy plumage to fly close to them without making a sound. He hooted his irritation at their intrusion of his domain. Constance squealed, jumping toward the American and away from the piercing screech. O'Connor emitted a grunt of amusement.

She tightened her lips. "When can I see the governor?"

"As soon as I can find the time to take you to his plantation."

"When will that be?"

"Probably in November."

Jerking her elbow out of his clasp, she took a step back. "November! That's five months from now. I can't wait that long. I have to see him tomorrow."

"Impossible."

She gasped. "I demand it!"

"Demand all you want. I've a tobacco farm to run. That takes precedence over running around the countryside on some wild goose chase. Meanwhile, I suggest you acclimate yourself to the fact that by the law of this land, I own you and I will do as I please."

"But, the ship," she sputtered. "The captain. You said, I thought, my lack of papers and . . . Well, you *must* let me speak with him tomorrow."

"Talking with the governor will do you no good. He won't free you without my consent."

"Then give him your consent. Or leave him out of it all together. Pray, just free me and be done with it."

He shook his head. "I am not a fool, little Lady of the Realm. I will send a message to your so-called father. If and when I hear from him will be time enough to release you."

She stilled. She'd hoped for something a bit more expedient than the time it would take for a missive to reach her father. If a message was sent back with the ship, however, her father, even displeased, would send someone as soon as he received word. "You want not to marry me?"

He snorted. "I assuredly do not."

"Will you send a message on the *Randolph* before it sails?"

He gave her a long pointed look before acquiescing. "I will."

He will? *He will.* She smiled. Really smiled. It was the first time she'd done so since this whole ordeal began. Lifting her hands above her head, she leaned her face toward the heavens and twirled in a circle. The kerchief around her head slipped off.

Closing her eyes, she stopped spinning and offered up a word of prayer and thanksgiving. She opened her eyes to find O'Connor frozen in the pathway.

"Thank you," she whispered. "I am truly grateful."

He gave no indication of having heard her.

She searched the ground for her kerchief. She would have a devil of a time cramming all her intractable hair back into it. Scooping up the limp piece of fabric, she hugged it to her chest. Her throat filled. Lord willing, she'd be home for Christmas.

With her arms hiked up to replace the kerchief upon her head, she moved toward O'Connor. When he eyed the uncovered expanse of her neck, her steps slowed.

He remained still, his focus riveted on her person. She surreptitiously tried to adjust her bodice, peeked through her lashes at the man, then winced. The boor's stare held a most unsettling mixture of mortification and fascination.

She stopped.

Studying her intently, he took two hesitant steps toward her, closing the distance between them.

Heavy, moist air pressed against her, smothering her with its warmth. She took a deep breath. "Are you all right, sir?"

"How many years are you?"

"Why, ten and nine."

"You have red hair."

Blinking in confusion, she lifted a hand to the wisps of hair escaping the kerchief's confines. "It's auburn."

"It's red. And you have freckles as well."

She gasped and covered her cheeks with her hands. A pox on those wretched freckles. Even in the shade, she had simply to be touched by a warm breeze and out they'd pop like fireworks exploding in a starless sky. Still, even the sailors hadn't been so uncouth as to mention it.

His brows drew together in a frown. "They're even on your hands."

Jerking her hands down, she straightened. That he could see them by the light of the moon alone made her humiliation all the worse.

He looked from her face to her shoulders to the bare expanse above her bodice. After an almost imperceptible pause, he shook his head and turned back to the path.

She released the breath she hadn't realized she'd been holding. *Of all the ill-bred, audacious, uncivilized individuals,* she thought.

She watched him disappear around a bend in the path. He wasn't as filthy and openly crude as Emmett had been, nor did he fill her with disgust and trepidation the way Emmett had. But the truth was, she knew absolutely nothing about this O'Connor person. Was he trustworthy? Would he really send Father a missive or was he simply humoring her?

Maybe she should go back. Back to the captain and Arman. Back to pease and loblolly. Back to the damp, dank hold that was now deserted.

She shuddered. She couldn't. She wouldn't. And for what? For the off chance the governor would come on board and hear her pleas? The pleas of a runaway bride and possible felon?

What if the captain did indeed simply take her to the next port and sell her once again for a hogshead of tobacco leafage?

She scrutinized the path from whence she had come. Maybe she should try to slip away. The bower-covered alley would be easy enough to follow, but beyond that, she wasn't sure. Where would she go? What kind of wild creatures lurked in these forests? What of the savages she'd heard so much about?

She stood for several more moments in indecision. *What do I do, Lord? What do I do?* No answer was forthcoming.

The croaking, hooting, and howling of the night increased tenfold. A twig snapped a few yards away. There was nothing for it. Raising her chin, she lifted her gown and followed the path Mr. Drew O'Connor had tread.

C H A P T E R | T H R E E

DREW EMERGED FROM THE natural bower into the sudden burst of moonlight. Flooded with a sense of gratification for what his father had accomplished before him, Drew looked upon the one-room cottage where he'd grown up. He took a deep breath, relishing the rush of love and well-being the home induced. Built in the old wattle-and-daub style, it nestled in a clearing amidst a handful of tall girdled trees.

A hint of smoke swirled out of the clay chimney on one end, while a large pile of firewood lay neatly stacked against the other. A hairless rabbit skin stretching across the square window provided a screen, of sorts, for those sleeping inside.

His brother sat on the oak chopping block in the yard, resting his elbows on his knees. Drew smiled to himself. An incurable optimist, that was Josh. If a thunderstorm came, Drew would anticipate a flood, Josh a rainbow.

Drew thought back to how inseparable they'd been as boys, one the perfect complement of the other. As men, their bond made a natural progression to partnership in the tobacco trade. Drew farmed with passion and voracity, while Josh exploded on the factoring market with a natural ability others merely dreamed of. It was good to have his brother back home after this last bout in England.

Josh removed the toothpick from his mouth. Beneath his hat, dark blond hair curled down beyond his shoulders. "Where is she?"

Drew shrugged. "A few lengths back."

Josh frowned. "Did you tell her to stay on the path? Even though it's dark, snakes still frequent the area."

"What's the point? Her chances for survival are next to nothing."

"Not that bad, surely."

Drew dropped Constance's clothing and diary on the bench by the cottage door. "You've forgotten. Not many women make it once they're sold. Only one out of every three. Only the heartiest. Only the strong. More often than not, only the orneriest of the lot."

Returning the toothpick to his mouth, Josh clamped down on the slender piece of wood. "Just because Leah didn't survive here doesn't mean every woman will meet the same fate."

Drew stiffened. "Leah has nothing to do with it."

"That's an out-and-out lie, and well you know it. It's been nigh on three years since her death, well past time you got over it."

Drew picked up Constance's diary and thumbed through it. It was too dark to read, of course, but no matter, for visions of Leah infiltrated his thoughts. Her quiet beauty transformed into a stark lifeless form, pale against the corn-silk color of her hair as they sealed her in a pine box and lowered her six feet into the ground.

A great knot formed in his stomach. He hated to see the spark and vitality snuffed from the redhead as well. With staunch resolve, he closed Constance's diary. All he need do was keep his distance, and perhaps the cessation of yet another life wouldn't affect him. He'd made that mistake once. He wouldn't make it again. "The wench will be dead before one season's passed."

Josh rolled his eyes. "You don't know that."

"Care to place a wager on it?"

"All right," Josh agreed. "If she's still alive after her seasoning, I win and you have to marry her. If she's dead, you win and I'll have to marry her."

Drew tossed the diary back on the bench. "Very amusing and very safe, considering your betrothed is breathlessly awaiting your return to England."

"So she is." Josh rubbed the stubble on his cheeks. "Well, are you going to marry her or not?"

Drew scowled. "Not. She'll just have to be our servant."

"But she's not a servant, not according to the terms for this shipload of women. The women on the *Randolph* were sold as tobacco brides, not as indentured servants, and well you know it. But you didn't want a bride, did you, Drew?" Josh's eyes snapped with annoyance. "No, you've sworn off women forever, so you say, and because of it you sent *me* on some hair brained mission to scour the prisons until I found a woman who wasn't a hardened felon, was being deported, but would be unable to wed." He spit the toothpick out, watching its arched flight to the ground. "Well, I did that, big brother. I found one Mary Robins, just for you. Wasted weeks upon weeks doing so, in fact."

Drew refused to look away from the anger in Josh's expression. He deserved it and more. His brother had followed his directives with no questions asked, but now all would be voiced and, in fairness, Josh had every right to do so. Therefore, he'd stand here and take whatever his brother dished out—at least for a while.

Josh tightened his jaw. "Then what do you do the first blasted day I get back?" A silence frothed with tension encompassed the glade. "You play recklessly at cards and end up winning a bride. A *marriageable* bride. Now you have two women while others have none." He shook his head, all the bluster and anger seeming to leave him with a whoosh of his breath. "The council won't stand for it, Drew. You're going to have to marry this new one."

Drew stared at his brother with passionless eyes. "No."

Resting one elbow on his knee, Josh searched the wood shavings for a fresh toothpick. "Why not?" Fingering one sliver, then another, he decided on a third. "Aren't you tired of being a virgin? Don't you think a man of twenty-eight years ought to have long since—"

"Enough!" Drew whipped off his hat. "My convictions run a different course from yours. Playing the town bull when you reach England may seem like the ultimate freedom to you, but not to me."

Josh averted his eyes. "I'm not judging you. I'm merely vexed with your pining for Leah. She wasn't your wife—she was your betrothed." He rubbed the back of his neck. "She's dead, Drew. Dead. Why can't you get over it?"

Drew slowed his breathing. "Have you forgotten that we used to be a family of nine? Have you forgotten the death rate in this settlement? Have you forgotten we're parentless, with only Sally and Grandma left?"

"Don't forget Nellie. She's still alive," Josh said softly.

"True. But she's married now and no longer under my care."

"You haven't answered my question."

Drew tunneled his fingers through his hair. "Would I like a woman to call my own? Of course. But from what I've seen, they aren't worth the trouble."

Unwanted images of Constance bombarded him. He hated red hair, and she was a walking beacon. Yet, heaven help him, when he'd seen her on deck and again when her kerchief slipped off, he'd felt the impact clear to his toes.

And those unsightly freckles. They were everywhere. Still, he'd stood staring at her like a woodcock. By trow, when she'd adjusted her bodice he'd not been able to move, much less breathe.

He glanced at Josh. "I don't want a woman if I have to helplessly watch her, and then our offspring, die."

"Then if not for the benefit of an heir, why are you so set on building a grand plantation home?"

"What would you have me do with all that timber Father had us split last year? It's seasoned now and ready to be used."

"There are plenty who would purchase it from you."

Setting his hat back upon his head, Drew stared at the forest of trees just beyond the clearing. "Father made me promise him I'd build it. Not just any home, mind you. He made me promise to build the one he had drawn up. The one he'd purchased all those nails for. The one with three levels plus a brick cellar."

After a moment of speechlessness, Josh snapped his mouth shut. "When did he extract that promise from you?"

Drew heaved a long sigh. "While you were away. He was on his deathbed, writhing in pain. I couldn't deny him."

A soft breeze grazed his face while stirring the fuzzy leaves of the mulberry tree on his left. He plucked a cluster of dark purple fruit from amongst the sheltering heart-shaped leaves.

A tiny stream of sweet juicy nectar trickled from his lips. Wiping his sleeve across his chin, he popped another berry into his mouth. The vibrato of a nearby frog suddenly ceased, leaving the clearing strangely quiet.

Josh slapped his hands on his knees and indicated the bower with his head. "Shouldn't she be here by now?"

Drew shrugged.

Focusing on the worn pathway, Josh squinted his eyes. "What did you think of her red hair?"

Drew's jaw tightened.

Josh's eyes lit with amusement. "Would you like to know what she's like?"

He offered no response.

"Spirited. She's very spirited."

Drew flipped the stem of the berry cluster away.

"Of course, throughout the voyage the men and women were kept on separate decks so I didn't spend as much time with them as I did the men. And the men—well, you'll be right pleased with the men I recommended. With them, your house will be constructed before a year's passed."

Drew refused to give in to the baiting. Where was she anyway? She should be here by now.

"Still," Josh continued, "I slipped down to the lower deck fairly often to ensure one Mary Robins was fed." He stretched out his legs, crossing them at the ankles. "They were chained next to each other, you know. Mary and your redhead."

Drew glared at his brother.

"It's true. So, I'm in a uniquely qualified position to know exactly how spirited she is." He pursed his lips. "Actually, she's a bit more than spirited. Indeed, she's a regular hoyden. But I like her. Truly, I do."

At that moment, Constance trudged into the clearing. Drew allowed his gaze to travel from her partially covered hair to the tips of her bare toes. Her faded tunic was coated with layers of grime and far too snug to provide decent coverage.

His brother stood and offered a slight bow. "How do you do, Lady Constance?"

She collapsed onto the stump Josh had vacated, glancing between the two of them. "You are relations? But of course. I should have realized. Well, how do you do?"

The corner of Josh's mouth tipped up. "Fine, my lady. And you?"

"Don't encourage her, Josh." Scowling, Drew turned to her. "We do not use titles here in the colonies. You will be addressed as all the other servants until we hear from your 'father,' if we ever do."

He watched her struggle to tuck an unruly bundle of curls back under her kerchief. "How am I to be addressed, then?"

"Constance."

She gasped. "You cannot be serious. I will not allow it."

"It is either that or wench," he said, eyes narrow. "If you do not respond to your Christian name, rest assured I will call you by the other."

She compressed her lips. "And what, pray tell, are you to be addressed as?"

"Master Drew."

"I will call no man *master*. I have only one master and He resides up above."

"Well, you have two now."

The cottage door opened and closed. Drew looked back. The woman Josh had contracted for him stood illuminated in the moon's refulgence.

"Mary," Constance breathed.

Jumping to her feet, Constance hurried to the other woman's side. What an incongruous picture the embracing women made. One tall with an aura of strength, the other petite and painfully feminine.

"I'm so glad to see you!" Constance cried.

"Whatever are you doing here?" Mary responded.

Josh cleared his throat. "We've a bit of a problem, ladies. Seems my brother has acquired two women instead of one."

Taking two strides, Drew grasped his brother's arm. "Josh . . . ladies, why don't we step away from the cottage so we don't wake Grandma and Sally." He tightened his grip. "Shall we?"

At the edge of the clearing, he released Josh with a little shove. "Now that you've wagged your tongue, you may explain it to them."

"Explain what?" he asked. "That you accidentally won Lady Constance in a wager? That everyone present, other than our little redhead, knows you never had any intention of wedding Mary from the start? That the menfolk in the colony are going to hang you by your toes when they hear? Or that Grandma will do even worse?"

Drew gritted his teeth. "Never mind. I will explain it to them."

Josh rounded his eyes. "By all means."

"Ladies," Drew began, "I won Constance in a wager and have no intention of marrying either one of you."

Josh burst out laughing.

"Joshua!" Drew hissed. "Lower your voice. Grandma might waken, and I have no desire to deal with her tonight over this mishap."

"Certainly," he allowed. "I wouldn't dream of waking Grandma. Especially not after you went to the extent of leaving Lady Constance in that hold half the night simply to ensure Grandma would be well and truly asleep when you brought her home!"

"Enough!"

Josh clamped his mouth shut, but mirth lurked within his eyes. Drew gave his attention back to the women. "Have you any questions?"

"I'd like a bath now, please," Constance said. "You do have a sponge and bowl I presume?"

Drew tightened his lips. "All the captives bathed before the ship docked."

"In salt water. It was most unpleasant. Besides, the boat . . . well, it had a particular stench to it. I thought once I disembarked the odor would take leave. It didn't. Unless, of course, it's you I'm smelling and not me."

His face warmed by several degrees. "As it happens, Miss Lady of the Realm, my dear mother, God rest her soul, had a peculiar penchant for cleansing one's person on a regular basis. Josh and I wash every day."

Constance gasped. "Every day! Surely you jest. Why, it's unhealthy to bathe so often. It will extract the oils from your skin and . . . and . . . I don't know what all."

"I'll tell you what all. It extracts the livestock from one's head and the layers of grime from one's person. My mother's been gone nigh on three years, but I haven't missed a dip in the creek any day during the warm weather or any Sunday during the cold."

"Dip in the creek?" she squealed. "You *submerge* yourself in the water?"

"I do."

"That's, that's . . ." She crossed herself.

"We expect the same from our servants."

Josh's eyebrows lifted. Mary fanned herself with her hand.

Constance blanched. "Absolutely not. Under no circumstances will I submerge myself in a creek or in anything else for that matter. I've no objection to bathing. But a sponge and bowl will serve. I will *not*, however, descend beneath water of any kind."

He gave her a parody of a smile. "Care to place a wager on it?"

She looked frantically at Josh. "Is he serious?"

Josh shrugged. "He looks it to me."

Drew held back his smile of satisfaction. "Do you still wish for a bath, little Lady of the Realm?"

She took a slow deep breath. After a moment of silence, she inclined her head. "Yes. But, a bowl and sponge will more than suffice."

He glanced at Josh. "Take Constance to the creek so she can wash her face and prepare to retire."

Stepping forward, Josh offered her his arm. "My lady?"

Drew scowled. Constance hesitated.

"No dunking tonight," Josh whispered. "I give you my word."

Studying his eyes for a moment, she accepted his arm and followed him to the creek.

Drew turned back to Mary. "Did Grandma give you a blanket to bed down on?"

"Yes, sir."

"Good. You'll need to fashion some sleeping ticks haste, posthaste."

"Yes, sir."

He removed his hat to scratch the back of his head, then replaced it. She stood with head bowed, hands clasped. A kerchief hid most of her dark brown hair.

"Why is your head bowed?"

She lifted her face, keeping her eyes downcast. "It's disrespectful to be looking you in the eye, sir."

The moonlight softened features grown old before their time. She probably wasn't more than one score, yet lines creased her forehead and the corners of her mouth.

"Here in Virginia, you needn't worry over formalities such as those. You may look at me, Mary, whenever you please."

Slowly, she swept up her lashes. Huge brown eyes focused on his hat, not quite meeting his eyes. The round pecan-colored orbs were by far her best feature.

"You know I have no need for a bride," he said, then blew a puff of air from his lungs. "I am in need of a woman, though."

Her gaze moved from his hat to his eyes. "I see," she whispered.

He felt the heat creep up his neck. "No, no. You misunderstand. I mean I need a woman to cook, keep my house, keep my garden, and take charge of my young sister."

She lowered her chin. "That will pose no problem, sir."

By troth, he had embarrassed her. "You did know I purchased ten men and plan to pick them up in the morning? They'll be quite hungry."

"I will see to it, sir."

"Thank you, Mary," he sighed.

"Certainly, sir."

"You may return to your slumber."

"Thank you, sir."

He watched her walk to the cottage. Though somewhat gaunt, her tall, straight form gave the overall impression of a woman built from staunch and hardy stock.

He nodded. She'd do just fine. Turning his attention to the well-worn trail, he headed toward the creek.

———

"Ah! If it isn't the lucky bridegroom," Josh exclaimed.

Drew growled.

Sitting on the bank, Constance twisted around to see if the men would come to blows. Drew looked willing enough. Josh, however, propped his shoulder against a tree.

"Easy, Drew. I was just wondering when the marriage would be performed."

"Vex me no more, Josh, else I'll knock out your brains."

"You last did that when I was only a lad. You wouldn't have such an easy time of it now."

Constance turned back to the creek. Fringed with trees and a variety of other foliage, the contour of its indented bank dipped and swelled at random. A crudely formed raft moored several feet away bumped against the shoreline.

Nudging her sleeves up, she trailed her fingers through the still water. The night light shimmered across the ripples she'd created. Leaning forward, she splashed a bit of water onto her thirsty skin, relishing its cool tranquillity.

"All I see is a man who needs to be unbuttoning his doublet after supper," Drew sneered.

"Me? Ha! If you're not careful, your guts will surely come tumbling about your knees."

"You impudent, hairy nothing. I've a Herculean stomach."

"Herculean! What rubbish."

Casting a quick glance back at the men, Constance judged the distance separating her from them. Not too close, but not very far either. She shrugged. It would have to do.

Turning her back to them, she loosened her bodice, perched on the bank, and cupped handfuls of the cold, refreshing water into her palms. With care, she poured the water over her face and neck, running her hands across them. It was absolutely divine.

"Consider, you walking gorbelly, I still top you by a good three inches."

"True," Josh agreed. "But what I lack in height, I make up for with nimble feet."

Sighing, Constance began to retie her bodice. Their sparring would surely come to a close soon and she didn't fancy being caught with an open gown. She pulled at the laces with all her strength. She hadn't realized how difficult it would be to do without Mary's help. She pulled again, holding the laces together with one hand and trying to retie the bodice with the other.

"Drew, you're still upset. I would have you at an unfair advantage."

"Humph. Your wit is as fat and lazy as your belly."

Constance heard a chuckle, then a playful whack. She could not close the gap. Frantically she pulled, willing the fabric to come together. "Oh!" she gasped.

One of the laces broke. She stared in horror at the limp piece of cording in her hand, then closed her eyes in mortification. The other half of the broken lace fell out of its housing.

"Lady Constance?"

"Josh, do not address her that way again."

There was a moment of silence.

Biting her lower lip, she tried to pull the bodice together with her hands. In the process, the rest of the lacings loosened. She choked.

"Constance?" Josh asked. "Are you all right?"

She heard a stirring behind her. "Constance?"

"No!" she whimpered. "Stay back!"

The movement stopped.

"What is it?" Drew asked.

She pulled with her hands. It only worsened the dilemma.

"What are you doing?" Drew's voice sounded right behind her.

Crisscrossing her arms, she tucked her chin and hunched over. "Go away." Her plea was muffled.

She heard his knees crack when he bent down beside her, then felt him tentatively place his hand upon the small of her back. She very nearly fell into the water from the shock of it.

"Are you in pain?" he asked.

"Yes. Go away."

He stayed where he was. "What ails you?"

"Oh, you big oaf. Just go away."

"Constance?" This from Josh, now kneeling on her other side. "Is it your woman's pains?"

"Ohhhhh," she cried. And here she thought the situation could not get any worse.

"Joshua!" Drew cried. "You overgrown puke stocking. Have you taken leave of your senses? Use a little discretion, if you please."

"Oh, a pox on it. She's your blasted bride—you take care of her."

Constance heard the unmistakable sound of Joshua's retreat, then silence. If it had not been for Drew's palm burning a hole through her back, she would have thought he'd gone as well. No such luck.

"Are you in great pain or just a little pain?"

She peeked out from above her arm. "Are we alone?"

He looked disconcerted. "Are you planning on doing me in?"

She smiled despite herself. "Not right now."

"We are alone."

She breathed a sigh of relief. "I have need of your jerkin."

His eyes widened. "I beg your pardon?"

"May I please wear your jerkin?" she asked, lips tight.

"Wear my jerkin? Whatever for?"

"My bodice seems to have fallen apart." Sneaking out one hand, she wiggled the broken lace between her fingers.

He jumped up and back. "By trow, woman."

Before she could blink, he dropped his jerkin in front of her and turned his back. She stayed still for a moment to assure herself of his intentions. When his back remained turned, she snatched the jerkin off the ground, slipped it on, and stood.

The sleeveless jerkin swallowed her whole. The deep V in the front, however, provided no cover. She turned the garment around. Much better.

The surprisingly soft leather brushed against her. It smelled of sunshine, sweat, and the great outdoors. It smelled of the man who wore it.

"Thank you," she whispered.

He glanced over his shoulder before facing her. "You have it on backward."

Heat flooded her face. "Yes."

His Adam's apple bobbed nervously. "Your laces broke?"

She did not think her face could burn any hotter. Still, she refused to explain to this barbarian her compelling need to wash away all vestiges of her dreadful ordeal. She nodded.

His attention fell on everything but her. He raked his fingers through his hair. "It's too late for a thorough washing tonight. You may have one in the morning, though."

She chewed on her lower lip and wiped her hands on the jerkin. "With a sponge and bowl?"

His gaze settled on her face. "With a rag and bucket."

She took a deep breath. "Thank you. That would greatly please me."

A waft of air swept the path, strewing a few curls across her face and rustling the underbrush around them. A weeping willow's long tassels swayed gently behind him as he rubbed his eyes, muttering, "What folly."

After a moment, he peered at her wearily. "I have no need for a bride. I especially have no need for an additional woman. You'll simply have to make yourself useful as best you can. For now, help with the cooking and upkeep of the cottage."

"I don't know how to cook."

His eyes narrowed slightly. "And why is that?"

"I never had reason to do so."

"No need for food, have you?"

She tipped up the corners of her lips. "On the contrary, I'm quite fond of food."

"But not of cooking."

"It's not a matter of fondness. It's a matter of know-how. I know not how to cook."

"What do you know?"

"Stitching."

"Nothing else?"

"I'm rather talented with numbers."

"Well, praise be. And here I've been worrying you were worthless."

"Quite so."

Drew contemplated the enigma before him. She couldn't possibly be telling the truth. No gently bred woman would allow her hair to flow with such abandon from her kerchief. No gently bred woman would loosen her bodice with two men mere feet away. No gently bred woman would have survived the passage over. If she was an earl's daughter, he was a king's son.

Still, no common born female would know how to read and write. No common born female would speak in such a refined manner. No common born female would have asked for a washbowl instead of a bucket.

"Are you, by any chance, the *illegitimate* daughter of an earl?"

She gasped. "How dare you! Why, you wouldn't know the queen of England if she were staring you in the face!"

"Answer my question."

"I shall not dignify that question with an answer."

Brushing her skirt to the side, she swept past him and set off down the path—in effect, dismissing him. Well, by trow, he was the master here. The sooner she understood that, the better.

Tightening his lips, he took several great strides, hooked his arm around her waist and lifted her up off the ground. She reacted with vehemence—shrieking, struggling, kicking, scratching, and biting. He wasted no time in releasing her.

She whirled around, crouched and ready to spring. "I have been torn from my homeland, chained in a hold with fifty female felons, sold as a bride, and bartered for in a card game. Suffice it to say I am not in the most tolerant of moods. Touch me again and I'll not be held responsible for my actions."

"You most certainly will. I am your master in all things. How you fare here will be the direct result of how I decide to treat you. Because the majority of the women in this settlement are former criminals, the means by which we control them are somewhat barbaric. Before, I never advocated such treatment, but at this moment, I am rapidly reassessing my stand. Do not ever walk away from me when I've asked you a question."

She spun around and marched off. He hesitated only a moment before swooping down upon her from behind. He twisted to take the brunt of the fall, then quickly rolled her beneath him. "Are you the illegitimate daughter of an earl?"

She snaked her arms up between them and pushed with a respectable amount of strength. "I wish that you did itch from head to foot and I had the scratching of thee. I would make you the loathsomest scab in all of England."

"We're in the colonies. Now answer my question."

She spit in his face. Wiping his cheek with his shoulder, he allowed more of his weight to rest upon her and bracketed her cheeks with his hands. She stilled.

"Do not *ever* do that again. Do I make myself clear?"

He saw her gathering the spittle within her mouth. He narrowed his eyes. "I dare you."

Ah. A response at last. She swallowed her spittle.

"Are you the illegitimate daughter of an earl?"

"I am not."

He hesitated. She'd answered his question. He'd won the skirmish. Now he should release her.

He stayed where he was. Of course, the leather jerkin he'd lent her may as well have been a suit of armor, for it completely disguised any curves she might possess. But a single beam of moonlight captured her face in its gentle palm. And he took his time exploring her features at such close range.

If he ignored the freckles, she was really quite comely. Her delicately shaped face was graced with a pert and dainty nose, and never in his life had he seen eyelashes so long. Long and not red, exactly, but a sort of rusty shade, like her eyes.

Oh, but her eyes were something. Big, luminous, and far too intelligent.

She moistened her generously curved lips.

He panicked at the reaction that induced. "I suppose Mary can do the cooking and cottage. You may see to the garden and my young sister."

"You're too kind."

He crooked up one corner of his mouth. Ah, victory was sweet. Rising, he turned and headed down the path—in effect, dismissing *her*.

CHAPTER | FOUR

ONSTANCE OPENED HER EYES. An exquisite child stared at her with wide-eyed innocence. The moppet's pearl-like complexion glowed with exuberance and charm. Thick jet-black curls fell past her shoulders.

Constance lifted her head.

In an immediate attempt to scramble back, the child plopped to the floor. A puff of dirt billowed around the shapeless sack that served as her dress. Drawn in at the neck and wrists with a narrow cotton ferret, the primitive gown concealed the child's build. If her heart-shaped face and delicate hands were any indication, the garment encompassed a petite frame.

Constance smiled.

Springing to her feet, the child ran out of sight.

Constance allowed her head to fall back on the pallet and sighed. How wonderful it was to wake up in unmoving quiet. No tipping deck that continuously swayed to and fro, no feet sounding on the upper decks, no stifling hold with everyone's irons rattling and banging about.

After a moment, she became cognizant of the household awakening. A whispered exchange. A muted padding from one spot to another. A crackling fire. Turning her head, she glanced toward the fire and discovered Mary hunching over its embers.

Her friend stirred the contents of a peculiar frying pan perched on three curved spiderlike legs. With a thick cloth in hand, she rearranged several wrapped objects sitting amongst the coals.

Dearest Mary. Had it not been for her, Constance never would have survived the passage over. What a pleasant surprise to find the good Lord had seen fit to keep them together. It would make everything so much easier, for both of them. Constance inhaled deeply. The savory trail of the morning's meal drifted to her.

Propping herself on her elbows, she canvassed the rustic cottage. She had seen next to nothing in the darkness of the night before. The light now seeping through a square hole in the cottage's wall provided a bit of visibility.

At one time, this sparse one-room cottage with crudely made furniture would have surely caused a wrinkling of her nose. But compared to the hard deck she had slept upon for these last two months, the complete blackness that filled the hold and the enclosed air soured by the sick, this thatch-roofed dwelling was more like a palace.

A long table with two benches made of split logs, flat side up, sat shoved against one wall. A low platform built into one corner of the room marked the only bed in evidence. Puzzled, she looked for the family's sleeping quarters, but found none. Opposite the bed sat a long wooden trunk. Clothing and utensils hung on a few pegs driven into the walls. She took it all in, her confusion mounting, until finally she noticed a split-pole ladder propped up against a small loft at the far end of the cottage.

The fire popped. Constance turned back to Mary. The fireplace took up one entire wall. Its hearth, made of flat rock, contrasted sharply with the mixture of clay and grass baked around the fireplace's wooden frame. An assortment of implements and pots hung from a beam and littered the hearth.

"You'd best rise, girl."

Yanking the covers to her chin, Constance sat up and twisted around.

A seasoned woman passed behind her carrying an armful of folded linens while the child clung to her skirts. Opening the trunk, the woman placed the makings of some pallets inside. "The men will be in shortly. We need to ready the cottage."

This must be the grandmother Drew had spoken of last night. She wasn't at all like Constance had pictured her. This woman carried herself with grace, holding her head high and proud. Her cheekbones, accentuated by the onset of old age, held an unnatural, but becoming, blush of pink. The child at her skirts hooked an index finger over her nose and thrust a thumb into her mouth.

Releasing the covers, Constance stood and stretched. Her old chemise hung limp on her frame and still smelled of unspeakable odors. After the disaster with her bodice last night, she'd had no choice but to garb herself in the only covering she possessed. With her fingertips, she plucked the chemise away from her body. "I was told I could make use of a bucket and rag this morning."

The woman nodded. "Fold up your pallet, then, and help me arrange the cottage."

Stepping onto the dirt floor, Constance leaned over and picked up the top bed sheet. "You live here?"

"For the time being." The old woman scrutinized her while tying together the two strings dangling from her cap. "I'm Elizabeth Lining, but everyone calls me Grandma."

"A good day to you, Grandma. My name is Lady Constance."

Grandma humphed. "We don't stand on formalities here in the colony. I'll be calling you Constance."

Constance handed the woman the folded spread. She allowed it to unfurl, then refolded it.

"Where are the men?" Constance asked.

"Washing at the creek."

She gave Grandma a quick peek, but the woman acted as if that was indeed an everyday affair. Moving to retrieve the bottom linen, Constance shook it out. Dirt surged upward.

Grandma grabbed the bedsheet. "Mercy, girl. You never shake the linen indoors."

Coughing, Constance rubbed her eye. "Your pardon."

While the dirt was settling, Grandma took the bedding outside.

Constance wasted no time in turning to Mary. "What do you know of our situation here?"

Darting a quick look at the open door and then the child, Mary wiped a hand on the tattered apron she wore around her waist. "The master contracted for me 'cause his married sister is due for a birthing right soon. The grandmother goes to care for her. So I am to care for the two masters, this little tyke, and the men."

"Men? What men?"

"The master bought ten indentured men—two of them brick layers. He's to pick them up from the ship this morn."

"When does Grandma leave?"

Mary shrugged. "They didn't say, but if I was to guess, it'd be right soon."

"Has anything been said about me?"

Mary shook her head. "Not a word, but I'm thinking the grandmother was pretty surprised to see you slumbering on the floor this morn, she was."

"Mr. O'Connor still hasn't told her about me?"

"I don't know, but it seems not. He was gone when I arose and the grandmother was still sleeping."

Constance caught a flash of brown from the corner of her eye, spun toward it, then relaxed. The little girl had wedged herself between the table and wall.

"And what's your name?" Constance asked softly.

The thumb stayed in her mouth. "Sallwee."

"Sally?" Constance squatted down.

Her curls bobbed up and down with affirmation.

"How do you do, Sally?"

The child's brow furrowed. "What's your name again?"

Constance thought a moment, sent Mary a mischievous smile, then looked back at the child. "My Lady."

Sally wound a lock of hair round and round her finger. "That's a lovely name."

"Thank you. Sally is a very lovely name too. How old are you?"

Releasing her hair, Sally held up two fingers. "Thwee."

Grandma reentered and placed the linen in the trunk. "Come, Constance, and help me move the benches and board to the middle of the room."

Constance stood and glanced about the room for the chamber pot. She could see the bed didn't have one beneath it, yet she couldn't imagine anyplace else to keep one. Perhaps they had a privy instead.

She hesitated, then moved to help Grandma. The roughhewn benches weighed a considerable amount. The table nearly did her in. Leaning on its knotted surface to catch her breath, she acknowledged there was no more time to spare. She must ask Grandma where the necessary house was located.

Looking up, the words stuck in her throat, for Drew's broad frame filled the doorway. With sunbeams shooting through the cracks between him and the doorframe, it was impossible to discern his expression.

"What goes here, Grandma?" he barked. "The wench looks as if she's just arisen. The day is calling."

"There were no instructions for this one, so I let her slumber."

Constance could not mistake the accusation in Grandma's tone, but Drew didn't have time to respond, for Sally had run straight to him, forcing him to swing her up into his arms as he stepped into the cottage. The little moppet grasped his face between her hands and kissed him straight on the lips.

Constance marveled at the softening of his features. After giving the child a squeeze, he set her on the ground, then fixed his attention on Constance. Derision replaced the tenderness she'd seen just moments before. "By my troth, woman. Get yourself ready. There's work to be done."

She narrowed her eyes and headed toward the door.

He stepped into her pathway. "Have you developed an affliction? There was certainly none last evening."

She stopped. "Your pardon?"

"What is wrong with your legs?"

"Nothing."

"Do not tell me a falsehood. I can see with my own eyes that you walk with a twist."

An unwelcome warmth crept into her cheeks. She should have gone to the necessary immediately upon rising. Brushing past him, she barely made it beyond the threshold in a seemly manner. Once outside, she half ran, half hobbled to the back of the cottage, then stopped short. The *master* nearly knocked her over in his effort to follow.

She scanned the clearing. Nothing here but a fenced in garden and a chicken coop. Beyond that, a legion of trees, shrubs, and vines caged in the little homestead they'd made for themselves.

"What's the matter?" he asked. "Did you not expect to see a great forest blocking your escape route?"

Maybe it was on the other side of the cottage. She hustled around to the side. He dogged her progress.

Situated a bit beyond the cottage was a crude but sturdy-looking structure. It looked much like a lean-to, but was freestanding. Its wattle-and-daub walls led to a thatched roof sloping downward in one direction. By faith, it was too big for a necessary house.

"What in the devil are you doing?" he demanded.

"It's a morning ritual I have," she answered, squeezing her legs together.

He spun her around. "Well, we have a morning ritual of breaking the fast. So I regret to inform you that my ritual takes precedence over yours. Now get back in that cottage and help with the preparations."

Oh, Lord, forgive my boldness. She took a deep breath. "Where is your house of office?"

He looked stunned. She blushed with mortification.

Throwing back his head, he let out a great howl of laughter. "Is that your affliction?"

"Yes!" she snapped. "Now where is it!"

Swiping at the water in his eyes, he spread his arms wide. "You are looking at it."

It was her turn to be stunned. "Surely you do not mean you have none!"

"That is exactly what I mean. I'll not waste good lumber on a privy when I can dig a hole just past the clearing."

Her cheeks burned again, but she wasted no more than a moment contemplating his revelation. If she found out later that he had lied, there would be the devil to pay. She plunged into the copse.

"Watch out for the poison weed," he yelled.

Poison weed?

"It is three-leafed—much in the shape of the English ivy!"

She quickly scanned the area for any three-leafed ivy.

"If it brushes up against you, you will develop a nasty itching that quickly spreads all over your person!" His chuckle from well beyond the trees riled her shattered sensibilities.

Imagine! Bellowing at her like that and—even worse—*knowing* that entire time what she was attending to. It didn't bear thinking of.

Obstinate man. She should have gone back to the ship last night. And what of last night? Wresting her to the ground in order to obtain an answer from her, then just up and leaving. Barbaric. And the ridiculous question of her legitimacy! Well, by troth, she had set him straight on that issue.

Unbidden, his face loomed over hers within her mind. It had surprised her last night by softening somehow. Much like it had this morning with Sally. And with the softening came the dimple.

She'd studiously tried to ignore it, but there was no ignoring it this morning when he greeted his little sister. Why she'd ever found dimples attractive, she couldn't imagine.

Shaking out the hem of her chemise, she cautiously made her way back toward the clearing, watching for any signs of English ivy.

The lushness of the land cushioned her bare feet. So caught up was she in the bounty beneath her feet, she almost missed a little blackbird scavenging for its morning meal.

Bless me—a blackbird with red shoulders! Slowing her steps, she shaded her eyes while it darted from the forest floor into the dense treetops. By the time she followed its path from oak to cedar to poplar, she'd returned to the clearing.

Drew was, thankfully, gone. Looking down, she took abrupt note of her appearance. She had on only her chemise. Her hair hung down her back in a braid and her bare toes peeked out with each step. She must repair herself at once.

Back inside the cottage, she stood a moment adjusting to the relative darkness. Of all the shadows merging and materializing, it was Drew's that first took shape.

He leaned against the wall, a pail dangling from his outstretched fingertips. "Since Grandma and Mary have the preparation of breakfast in order, you may go and milk the goat."

Milk the goat! She gaped at him before blushing anew at her state of disrepair.

"You'll end up having to do it for her, Drew," Grandma said. "I'll attend to it for now and you can show her some morning when you've more time."

Constance scanned the cottage. Where the devil was her clothing?

Setting down the pail, Drew walked to the wall behind her and plucked the skirt she'd worn last night off a peg. "Is this what you are in need of?"

She whirled around. Snatching it out of his hands, she held it up against her like a shield. He smiled. Sweet heavens, he had not one dimple, but two.

"Where is the bodice?" she asked.

His eyes flickered. "I fear it's not of much use to you. Wear the skirt and chemise without it."

She gasped. " 'Twould be indecent!"

He arched a brow. "Not nearly as indecent as if you tried to stuff yourself into that bodice again."

Saints above, these ill-bred colonists would say anything. Even the grandmother's presence did not temper their wagging tongues. "If you've but a length of cord, I can manage fine."

He chuckled. "It's not just a length of cord you're needing but an entire bolt of cloth."

Suppressing a groan, she dropped the issue and quickly searched for a place in which she could dress. Grandma and Mary bustled around the fire. Sally sat on the floor grinding meal with mortar and pestle. Did they do everything together in this primitive little room?

She turned back to Drew. "Be gone. I must dress."

"Miss Constance, Lady of the Realm, have you still not grasped the essence of your position here? I am the master and you are the servant. When you would like to request something of me, I suggest you couch it in the sweetest of terms."

"I am not a lady of the realm."

"That is right. You are a servant. The sooner you accept that, the more pleasant you will find your lot in life here on my farm."

"The devil's dung in thy teeth."

His smile vanished. "You will watch your language."

"I will do as I please."

"You will do as you are told or you will have no privileges."

She narrowed her eyes. "What are you saying?"

"Baths, food, and so forth are privileges awarded to those worthy of receiving them."

She didn't think so. Leaving one's servants in filth and starving them was counterproductive. "Get out. I need to dress."

He stepped forward and gently grabbed her chin. "Lesson number one: Ask with meekness and servitude."

A pox on meekness and servitude. If he were a gentleman, she wouldn't even have to ask. She kept her lips firmly sealed.

"Constance, you were bought and paid for. I have the receipt to prove it."

She jerked her chin out of his hand. "You said you would send word to my father."

"It will be at least six months until we hear back from your father."

She gasped. "Six months?!"

"Six months. Until then, you are my possession."

"Only in your own sluggish brain."

"Dear girl, it is within my rights to marry you at any time. Once that happens, you will be bound to me forever under God—father or no father."

She blanched. It had only been within the last few years that England allowed women a veto in matrimonial affairs. Had this current not penetrated the colonies? She wasn't at all sure.

"Wish you to marry me?" he asked.

"I do not!"

"Then ask me to leave in a proper manner."

In a pig's eye, I will. Hugging the dress closer to her, she opened her mouth.

He gently placed his finger over her lips. "Think, girl, before you speak."

His callused finger abraded her lips. She pushed the offending appendage away. "I wish you to go."

"Phrase it with respect."

Gritting her teeth, she impaled him with her stare. "Will you please do me the honor of leaving the cottage for a moment or two . . ." *you wretched, poisonous, bunch-backed toad?*

"Excellent." Removing a worn but clean homespun dress from a peg on the wall, he handed it to her. "Josh should be back from the creek by now. You may follow the same path as last night for your cleansing in the water. Make sure you return before the breakfast bell is rung. There's some soap on the shelf, there above the trunk."

"What of the bucket and rag?"

"Hanging there, on that peg."

Walking to the peg, she snatched up the bucket and rag. Off the shelf, she removed the soap and dropped the coarse yellowed block into the bucket. "A drying cloth?"

He retrieved a cloth from another peg.

"It's wet."

He nodded. "You have to rise early if you want first use of the drying cloth."

First use? "May I slip on my old skirt before embarking on my excursion, O Great One?"

He narrowed his eyes. "You may."

Zigzagging her gaze between him and the door, she waited. The dolt simply presented his back to her.

Setting her cloth, bucket, and fresh dress on the table, she slipped on the skirt. Drawing close, Mary silently placed a small wrapped bundle inside Constance's bucket. The sweet aroma of fresh bread surrounded the girls.

Constance glanced quickly at Drew. His back was still turned. Grandma bent over the bed tightening its ropes. Sally watched the women with unabashed curiosity, while Constance and Mary shared a smile.

Scooping up the items on the table, Constance marched out of the cottage.

———

Standing ankle deep in the creek, Constance sluiced the bucket of water over her with an invigorating rush, then lathered her hair and body for the third time. She didn't care if the crude soap stripped off her skin; she wanted no residue from that wretched ship left on her person.

She poured water down her body several more times, then stood with eyes closed, cataloging each part of herself. She felt a droplet of water slide down her neck, hit the upper swell of her breast, then plummet through the valley between. Placing her hands against her ribs, she grimaced at the ease with which she could delineate each one. Pressing her hands lower, she tested the flatness of her stomach, then stopped and circled around her hips and thighs. Yes, she'd lost a considerable amount of poundage, but she was clean. Blessedly clean.

Making her way to the bank, she retrieved her cloth from the bush, dried her face, then raised her chin. The sun wrapped its rays around her, enveloping her with warmth.

Never had she bathed in the daylight hours, much less out in the open. After the dark confinement of the ship, it was precisely the catharsis she needed. Not only did it give her an unprecedented sense of freedom, but it made her feel as if she were sharing this Eden with God Almighty himself.

She smiled. The thought of bathing every day wasn't nearly as daunting as it had been last night. With a satisfied sigh, she wrapped her hair up in the cloth and reached for the dress.

Unlike the dresses she was accustomed to, this homespun frock was all one piece. The sleeved bodice had been sewn directly onto the skirt, and there was no chemise at all, nor was there need of one. She slipped it on, and though the crude material grated against her skin, never was she more appreciative of a gown. No matter that the sleeves hung below her hands or the hem drug on the ground. The cut of its bodice covered every inch of her while its cleanliness and open-air scent intoxicated her.

She wondered whose it was, then tenderly rolled up the sleeves and made a cursory effort at drying her abundance of hair. It was a useless endeavor. She threw the cloth back over a nearby bush.

At the creek's edge, she wrung out her wash cloth, watching the leftover suds butt up against the bank before scattering and eventually dissipating.

Finding a soft patch of fragrant grasses, she lay down, fanned out her curls, and studied this wilderness called America. A duck squawked at his companion and then dove beneath the water while a bird hovered above the surface, snatching the food away just as the duck reappeared.

She frowned. He should work for his own supper instead of stealing someone else's. She quickly shied away from that thought, but not quickly enough. Not before it transformed for a fraction of a second into *When have you ever worked for your own supper?*

She hastily rolled onto one elbow and turned her attention to the land. A grand maple, shouldering back a prolific beech, craned its limbs over the creek at a gravity-defying angle. Flowers of all kinds and colors grew wild within the grove, their beauty rivaling many richly designed gardens and orchards back home.

Back home. Surely she'd be back home in less than six months. She sighed. Not so for Uncle Skelly. He would *never* make it home. Not subscribing to the king's supremacy usually meant death. But because of Papa's influence, Uncle Skelly's sentence had been reduced to deportation. In the end, it hadn't mattered.

Tears coursed unchecked down her cheeks. As a youngster in her aunt and uncle's home, she had spent many a candle-lit evening advancing her prowess for mathematics under Uncle Skelly's watchful eye. Only he had understood her insatiable zeal for numbers, for he was filled with a passion for numbers equal to her own. Or, at least, he had been. With big dreams and high hopes, he had seen to the editing of *The Ladies' Mathematical Diary* every year. Even now hundreds of submissions from mathematically talented women throughout Europe would be arriving at Skelly's home.

She'd given her uncle an oath that she would maintain the publication until his return. But he wouldn't be returning. She knew he'd never expect her to fulfill such a promise under the circumstances. Still, she *wanted* to carry out her obligation. In his honor. For his honor.

Swiping at her tears, she strengthened her resolve. As long as she had a breath in her body, she would not rest until those submissions were answered. She would use her gift for mathematics so Skelly's dream and *Diary* lived on. No matter the cost, she would survive in this land until her father came for her. She must.

A squirrel scampered across the clearing just a stone's throw from her feet, then froze. Scrutinizing her with his unblinking stare, he twitched his tail, then spun around and darted up a young oak. She turned her head, watching him leap from the oak to a larger, more mature tree.

The young oak once again drew her interest. Here was something new and strong that had survived in this land. It was about ten yards in height and had a wispy ivy plant clinging to its trunk. The plant looked nothing like English ivy but instead held dainty tear-shaped leaves.

She was fascinated with the regularity in which the twining plant encircled the column. If the oak's diameter at the top was, say, six inches and at the bottom one foot and the ivy twisted around the tree so that each twist was approximately ten inches apart, what would the length of the ivy be?

She studied the tender tree and its delicate vine. A soft breeze rustled its leaves and prompted a bird to take wing. She must set a quill to the question as soon as she returned to the cottage.

Burrowing down into her grassy mattress, she unwrapped the unusual smelling bread Mary had slipped her. Taking a bite, she marveled at its taste and texture. She had become so accustomed to the hard, chalky biscuit-bread of the ship that she nearly bit her tongue, so easily did her teeth sink into the bread. And then, by heavens, she needn't even chew, for it immediately melted.

Closing her eyes, she took great delight in the bread, in the sounds around her, and in the sweet smell of God's green earth. As had been the pattern for most of her life during moments of such exquisite pleasure, numbers danced in her head.

She pictured the young oak and its vine twisting its way to the top. If the hypotenuse line that the ivy moves around in equals z, and x equals the distance from the vertex to the top of the first turn—

The sound of the breakfast bell ringing across the countryside brought her back to the present. Finishing off the delectable bread, she stood, reached for both the drying towel and bucket, and headed back to the cottage.

———

Breakfast actually melted in his mouth. There wasn't a thing wrong with Grandma's cooking, but Mary's? Saints above, Drew had never tasted mush this good before.

"So," Grandma began, "are you going to tell me where Constance came from?"

Drew and Josh exchanged a glance. Here it comes. He'd managed to avoid Grandma thus far, but that brief respite was over. He wiped his mouth with the napkin tied around his neck. "I won her."

Grandma whipped her head around. "Won?"

He grimaced. She was so sensitive about playing cards. He pushed his mush back and forth within the confines of his trencher. Josh was going to be of no help. He and Mary, who together shared a trencher, ate with an unwarranted amount of concentration. Sally, sharing her trencher with Grandma, was oblivious. Constance had not yet returned from the creek.

"Yes," he admitted.

"Won, how?" she asked.

Focusing on his trencher, he took a bite of mush, chewed, and swallowed. "Playing one-and-thirty."

Grandma set her spoon down with meticulous care. "I hope you are jesting."

He slowly shook his head from left to right. Grandma never wasted a moment of daylight. That she would stop eating in the midst of a meal did not bode well. Even Sally began to show an interest in the conversation.

Grandma dabbed at her mouth with her cloth. "What do you plan on doing with her?"

"I know not. She claims the captain kidnapped her." He took a deep swallow of cider from his wooden noggin. "Says she's the daughter of an earl."

Grandma stilled. "What earl?"

"Greyhame or some such nonsense."

She lifted her brows. "And?"

"And, I told her I'd send a missive to her father. So I'm bound by my word to keep her for the time being."

"For the time being? England is in the midst of a civil war. Have you any notion how long it could take for a missive to catch up with the earl? He'll be moving from one confrontation to another. Why, the girl could be here for a year or more."

"What would you have me do, Grandma?"

"What skills has she?"

Slipping a finger inside the neck of his shirt, he adjusted his collar. "That remains to be seen."

"She has no skills?"

He stiffened. "She stitches."

"Every female stitches. What *skills* has she?"

Propping an elbow on the table, he rubbed his eyes. "She claims to have a talent for numbers."

After a strained moment, he felt his ears and neck burn.

Grandma nodded. "You are being punished for dallying with the devil's books."

"Grandma," he said with a sigh, "they are playing cards, not the devil's books, and simply a form of amusement for me."

She glowered at him. "Pray tell me, are you amused now?"

He looked away. Constance walked in the door.

"Good morrow, everyone," she exclaimed. "Isn't it a glorious day? Your weather here is quite quaint." She smiled as she hung her wet cloths on a peg.

Grandma untied her napkin. "I'm going to Nellie's."

Drew and Josh looked sharply at Grandma. "For a visit?" Drew asked. "You're going to Nellie's for a visit?"

"Where's a wooden plate for me?" Constance asked, searching the shelves.

Grandma scooted off the bench. "I'm going to Nellie's to stay."

Pulling off his napkin, Drew stood. "You cannot. Who will train Mary? Who will watch Constance?"

" 'The Lord is known by the judgment He executes; the wicked is snared in the work of his own hands.' "

"Card playing is not wicked!" Drew insisted.

"Psalm 9:16," she responded.

"I know which psalm it is. David was talking about battles and victories and enemies, *not* card playing."

" 'Woe unto them that are wise in their own eyes, and prudent in their own sight.' "

"By my faith, Grandma, you are testing me sorely. Now, sit down and stop this foolishness."

Grandma took two steps forward. "You will watch your tongue, young man. I agreed to train Mary, not some useless woman you acquired by wicked means."

She held up her hands, stopping his denial. "Nay. Talk no more. Nellie's babe is due any day now. She has need of me, and from the looks of this morning's fare, Mary requires no assistance. I am away."

"Grandma, please."

The tension was palpable, causing them all to jump at the pounding on the wooden door. "O'Connor? Come! We have need of your presence."

Drew scowled at the door, then looked at Josh.

Shrugging, Josh rose from the table.

Outside, four of the settlement's most influential men gathered. Drew had known them his entire life—all except for their leader, Theodore Hopkin. The governor, Sir William Berkeley, had left last month for a year's excursion to England. The Crown had sent Hopkin as his temporary replacement.

Well, at least now Drew wouldn't have to make a trip to the governor's plantation. Constance could go ahead and have her audience with him while he was here.

A fifth man stood back and to the side. It was Jonathan Emmett, the man who'd lost Constance last night in their game of one-and-thirty.

Sparing barely a glance for him, Drew looked at the others. "Is there trouble?"

Governor Hopkin furrowed his bushy gray eyebrows. "Merely a concern or two. I'm sure you can put it to rights."

Josh stepped out beside Drew. Sunlight streamed down on their secluded homestead. Oak, pine, hickory, and tulip trees towered behind the councilmen like mounted soldiers reinforcing their leaders. What Drew used to take comfort in beholding now cast a menacing shadow about them.

Hopkin cleared his throat. "Emmett, here, holds some strong accusations against you."

Drew allowed his gaze to slide past Hopkin and roam over those more familiar to him. Morden, a bear of a man, had a heart in proportion to the rest of his body—massive, generous, and malleable. Unfortunately, the preacher was nothing more than a figurehead on this council and rarely offered an opinion on anything.

Kaufman, on the other hand, held a legitimate position but reminded Drew of a thick candle with two eyes and a hook nose—fairly solid looking, but continually melting when things heated up.

Both avoided his scrutiny, while Colonel Tucker looked him square in the eye. It pleased Drew to have him here. The military man was well respected and had been particularly close to Drew's father. If mischief brewed, Tucker would bank the fire.

Hopkin pulled the waistband of his breeches up around the hill of flesh surrounding his gut. "Emmett says you succumbed to drunkenness, assaulted him, and spirited his bride away."

Drew leaned his shoulder against the doorframe. "I joined in the festivities at the meetinghouse. During the course of the day, Emmett made a wager with his bride. I won the wager and have the receipt to prove it."

"He cheated!" Emmett barked.

Drew stood straighter. "I struck Emmett for that comment yesterday. It is an untruth, and many were there to witness it."

Hopkin nodded. "May I see the receipt?"

Josh reentered the cabin to collect the voucher. Tucker's serene gaze met Drew's. Drew relaxed. Everything would be all right.

Returning, Josh handed the piece of parchment to the governor. Hopkin perused the document, then restored it to Drew. "All appears to be in order."

Emmett blustered, then quieted in the censure of the other council members.

Drew folded the document and tucked it inside his belt. "Care you to share some cider with us? We were just breaking our fast."

Hopkin again pulled up his slipping breeches. "Actually, we've a bit more business."

Drew frowned. A scattering of chickens clucked nervously about the clearing, mirroring his confusion.

Grandma stepped out of the cottage, pouch in hand. She tilted her head in acknowledgment. "Governor. Councilmen." Looking at Emmett, she simply snorted.

"Mistress Lining," Hopkin said. "What are you about this fine day?"

"It's Nellie's time," she answered. "I'm off to tend to her for as long as she has need of me."

"You are away at this moment?" he asked, looking at her bundle.

The morning's light blazed down into her eyes. She squinted over at Hopkin. "I am."

Drew stiffened. "I will escort you, Grandma, if you will but wait until our business here is concluded."

"No need. You have the indentured men servants to fetch down at the wharf. Besides, I'm of a mind for some peace and quiet." She transferred her pouch of belongings from one arm to the other. "Good day, sirs."

Hopkin tipped his hat. "Good day, Mistress. Our prayers will be with your Nellie."

Looking at Josh, Drew tilted his head toward Grandma. Josh reached for her pouch.

She swatted his hand. "Cannot an old woman get some peace when she wants it?"

Josh lifted his brows and turned back to Drew. She must be sorely vexed to scold them in front of the others. Still, he should have expected it. He knew his late grandfather had squandered away his fortune with cards, forcing Grandma and their only daughter to come to the colonies. Though neither Grandma nor his mother had ever bemoaned their life here, Grandma always lost her perspective where cards were concerned. With an almost imperceptible lifting of his shoulders, he motioned Josh to let her go.

She wasted no time in presenting them with her back. "Don't know what all the uproar's about," she muttered, setting off down the path. "I'm not in my grave and don't plan to be anytime soon. If I wish to walk to Nellie's by myself, then so be it."

Listening to her litany, Drew felt a pang of remorse. He waited until her voice drifted off on the breeze before turning his attention back to Hopkin and the council, who were busy murmuring amongst themselves. He glanced at Josh, who shrugged in a gesture of bafflement.

"O'Connor?" Hopkin cleared his throat. "Seems the situation is more serious than we realized. 'Tis a sign from God that we arrived when we did."

A sign from God, indeed. Drew crossed his arms in front of his chest and leaned back against the cottage's frame.

"How many women have you living under your roof?" Hopkin asked.

Drew adjusted himself more comfortably against the cottage. "At the moment, two."

"I see," he said through pursed lips. "And when are you and your brother planning to marry them?"

Drew stilled, as did Josh. "They're servants," Drew replied.

A babble of voices broke out amongst the council. Emmett's scrawny frame bristled. Hopkin held up his hands for silence. "These, uh, *servants*, they are of breeding age?"

Drew narrowed his eyes a margin or two. "They are."

Hopkin yanked down on his doublet. "And they are unmarried?"

Uncrossing his arms, Drew pulled slowly away from the cottage. "What are you getting at?"

Hopkin twisted his breeches up to his midriff. "And they are residing in this dwelling with you, Joshua, and your baby sister?"

Drew stiffened. "Where would you have me keep them, Hopkin? With the goat?"

The governor reddened.

Tucker quickly stepped forward. "Hopkin, I recommend the council discuss this matter at length before taking any undue action."

"Undue action?" Emmett screeched. "We dare not leave these immoral creatures with the unattended ladies fer even a moment. No tellin' what deviltry would take place in our absence."

Josh grabbed Drew's forearm, forcing him to check his inclination to knock out the few teeth left in Emmett's mouth.

"Enough!" Tucker exclaimed. "You are not a member of this council, Goodman Emmett, and have no voice here. Be silent."

Emmett narrowed his eyes.

"Hopkin," Tucker continued, "I insist we discuss this more thoroughly."

Hopkin wiped a bit of spittle from the corners of his mouth. "There is not much to discuss. These men are living in a climate that breeds corruption. Regardless of the character you insist they have, the fact remains that they find themselves in this situation through their own unsavory actions. That alone makes me question your opinion of their character."

"Unsavory?" Tucker asked. "The whole settlement was playing cards yesterday. Shall we pay them all a visit this morning as well?"

"Do not patronize me. No other man in this colony lives with unmarried females in an unsupervised fashion. Your outspokenness troubles me greatly. Perhaps I need to write our gracious king and suggest a replacement or two." Hopkin met each councilman's eyes in turn. "Any other objections?"

Drew looked to Tucker's colleagues for a show of support. None was forthcoming.

Expelling a wad of phlegm from his mouth, the governor turned back to Drew. "Under no conditions will the council of this settlement allow you to harbor these women in a licentious fashion."

Drew's breathing grew deep. "There is nothing licentious in keeping a cook and a woman to watch Sally."

"There is if you defile 'em!" Emmett shouted.

The council broke out in more murmurs. Tucker grabbed Emmett's shirtfront.

"Call them out here," Hopkin demanded over the confusion. "We would have a look at these *servants* you keep."

"And if I refuse?"

Silence fell upon the group. Tucker's grip on Emmett loosened.

"O'Connor, we would have a look at these servants or you will stand before this council on charges of misconduct and risk losing all you and your father before you have worked for."

Drew's jaw tightened. Constance and Mary stepped out of the cottage. There was no doubting they'd heard every word through the cottage's uncovered window.

Drew clinched his fists as Hopkin's gaze crawled over each woman's body with slow deliberation. The chirping chatter of the blue jays and playful antics of the squirrels mocked him and the others gathered in the clearing.

Hopkin shifted his attention back to Drew. "You and your brother will either marry these women or you will have your arms broken and your tongues bored through with an awl. Then you will be banished from Virginia, relinquishing any privileges of freedom in this country. Fornication will *not* be tolerated by this council."

CHAPTER | FIVE

UMBFOUNDED, CONSTANCE COULD ONLY stare at Hopkin.

"Morden? Have you your Bible?" he asked.

The large man with rounded cheeks and troubled blue eyes stepped forward. "I have it."

"Then let us get on with it." Hopkin turned to Drew. "Decide which woman you will wed and which your brother weds."

Drew's face cleared of all expression. "I agree to marry one, but Josh cannot. He is betrothed, with the contract negotiated and signed."

Hopkin narrowed his eyes. "Betrothed to whom?"

"Lady Hannah Eastlick of Bowden," Josh said.

Astonished, Constance snapped her attention to him.

"Why would a lady consent to marry a simple farmer?" Hopkin sneered.

"I have the contract," he replied.

"I would see it."

Josh stepped inside the cottage, then returned with contract in hand.

Hopkin briefly reviewed it. "The date set is not until next spring."

"I plan to return for her after the tobacco's been harvested and packed."

Hopkin handed the contract back. "I like it not. Even with your brother married, the situation asks for wrongdoing."

"Be that as it may," Drew interjected, "I will be eligible to chaperon once I wed. I choose Lady Morrow." He turned to face her. "Will you be my wife?"

"I cannot." She turned quickly to the governor, bobbing in a curtsy. "Governor Hopkin, I am Lady Constance Caroline Morrow, daughter to the Right Honorable the Earl of Greyhame, My Lord Randall Christian Morrow." She reveled only for a moment in the startled silence that passed before she continued. "The captain of the *Randolph* kidnapped me. I am not a felon, nor was I commissioned to come here voluntarily as a bride."

Hopkin lifted his brows. "Kidnapped? I heard nothing of a kidnapping." He turned to Drew. "What do you know of this?"

"The captain had no transport papers for her, and Lady Morrow claims he took her by force."

Emmett shoved his way to the front. "What! More likely than not, she's a lady's maid trying to better her position here."

"Perhaps," Drew said. "Perhaps not. But can we take the chance? What happens if she is indeed the Earl of Greyhame's daughter? We would have the king's displeasure for certain."

"After Marie Bernard's escapade? I think not," Emmett argued.

Hopkin frowned. "What escapade?"

"Miss Bernard was a lady's maid to one of the queen's women," Emmett said.

"What has that to do with us?"

Emmett hooked his thumbs beneath his armpits. "Miss Bernard filched a valuable jewel from one of the royal apartments and was sentenced to death fer her trouble."

"Get to the point," Hopkin urged.

"Well, due to some fancy talkin' by her former mistress, the sentence was changed to transportation. Miss Bernard was deported and sold right here in Virginia to Goodman Bushell. After a brief time, the girlie escaped and made her way up to Watertown."

"And?"

Emmett rocked back on his heels. "This is the inter'sting part. Thinking herself well and truly free, she claimed the title of Princess Jeannette Francoise Sophie, declaring herself a sister of our dear queen."

Hopkin snorted. "How could anyone mistake a runaway for a princess?"

"Miss Bernard was a wily one, she was," Emmett replied. "She'd planned to run, so she hid away a few jewels and a medallion portrait of Her Majesty. It was some impression she made. Even promised promotions to them fools up there." His matted beard quivered. "Well, her game was up when Goodman Bushell's messenger came, raising a loud hue and cry fer *her serene highness*."

Constance felt the councilmen eyeing her. Nay, judging her. If she had managed to have a private audience with the governor, she felt she could have convinced him of her situation. But she'd been around her father's friends enough to know when men and their political decisions are under the watchful eye of others, they very rarely make sound choices.

She sighed. There was naught to do but focus on Emmett and hope her exasperation over his tale was evident.

He cackled, then patted his rail-like frame. "She was hauled from her fine quarters in Watertown and back to Bushell's, where she's servin' the rest of her term."

"If you're so certain Miss Morrow is no lady," Drew asked, "then why did you pay a whole hogshead for her?"

Emmett jutted out his chin. " 'Cause a lady's maid is better'n some filthy felon."

Josh straightened. "Are you maligning Miss Robins?"

Emmett took a step back. "No, I'm just saying this talk of kidnapping is pure nonsense, and the girlie in question should be given back to me."

Back to him? Emmett thought to get her back? Absolutely not. She wouldn't allow it.

"Enough, Emmett," Hopkin said. "Let me consult with the council."

The governor and his men stepped to the edge of the clearing for a brief conference, their voices rising and falling in waves.

Constance bit her lip. They must take Drew's word on the matter. What other choice did they have? Mary glanced at her with a tight smile.

Walking back to the cottage, Hopkin hitched up his breeches. "You may keep Miss Morrow until her story can be investigated, but meanwhile, you'll have to marry this other one."

Drew's shoulders stiffened. "Miss Robins?"

"Yes."

Drew and Josh exchanged a look.

Mary paled, then took a quivering breath. "I cannot marry, good sir."

Hopkin scowled. "What's this?"

Mary visibly swallowed.

"Speak up, girl!"

She jerked, stumbling back a step. "I'm already married, I am."

"What a great bunch of tripe," Emmett exclaimed. "If I can't have back the one I originally bought, then at least let me have this wagtail. By trow, just give her to me and be done with it!"

"Married!" Hopkin roared. "To whom?"

Mary looked at her feet. " 'Tis true. My man was press-ganged into the Navy two years past. I ain't seen nor heard from him since."

"She lies!" Emmett screeched.

"He cannot marry her, Hopkin," Colonel Tucker insisted, looking to the other councilmen. They nodded their encouragement. "Even with the tiniest chance at truth, the sin of marrying one while still married to another would be too great. It is out of the question."

Hopkin whirled on Mary. "How did you get on a bridal ship if you were already wed!"

Mary cringed, falling back several more steps. Josh moved forward, partially shielding her with his body. "She's a felon, Hopkin. Her sentence was deportment. She'd no choice in the matter."

"What do *you* know of this?"

"Only that I contracted her for Drew and when we arrived at the cottage, she told my brother what she just told you."

Hopkin's face mottled. "What was your husband's name?" he barked to Mary.

Josh laid a hand against her waist, pressing her ever so slightly forward.

"Obadiah Robins," she answered.

"That could be anyone," Emmett cried. "Her brother or father or anyone."

"Occupation?" Hopkin asked.

"A street sweeper."

"Oh, fer—" Emmett murmured.

"How long were you married?"

"Four years."

"Children?"

"Two."

"Where are they?"

A discernible pause. "Dead."

This last was said barely above a whisper. Constance clasped her hands together. Poor Mary. It was clear she didn't want to talk about it.

"Why were you in Newgate Prison?"

"I was accused of committing perjury, sir."

"She was forced to testify against a lord," Josh said. "The lord's influence decided the outcome of the trial before Miss Robins ever stepped into Old Bailey."

Hopkin turned to Josh. "If I want any more of your input, I will ask for it."

Hopkin's anger was there for all to see, building as if it were a living, breathing entity. He turned to Drew, searing him with his gaze. "I am this close to banishing you, your brother, and your bawd-strutting women." He pointed his pudgy finger directly at Constance. "That one. You will either marry that one or sell her back to Emmett. And if I hear one single dispute from your lips, it will mean the end of your freedom here in the colonies, and not only yours by troth, but every member of your family's— extended or otherwise."

Tension radiated from Drew's frame.

"Morden, open your Bible," Hopkin ordered. "We've wasted enough time."

"Excuse me," Constance whispered.

Drew's head slowly pivoted toward her, along with the rest of the men present.

"Might I have a word with you?" she asked Drew.

His eyebrows lifted.

"It will only take a moment . . . sir."

He looked past her to Josh. Josh shrugged. Drew turned to Hopkin. "May I have a word with the lady?"

"It's highly unusual."

"So is this whole situation," Drew replied.

"You have two minutes."

Nodding, Drew propelled her into the cottage. Once inside, he held his finger over his lips and indicated she go to the corner of the cottage furthest from the door and window. She barely noted Sally's napping form before turning back to him. "I have a proposition for you," she whispered.

"By my faith, get on with it."

"Do you want to marry me?"

"I want to keep my tobacco farm, and I want not for my family to be banished," he answered.

"Good. Here is what I propose. You provide me with the protection of your name until my father can be notified. I, in turn, will help you around the farm. Of course, I would . . ." She averted her eyes.

He frowned. "Explain yourself."

Fingering the sleeve of her gown, she moistened her lips. "Well . . . what I mean to say is we'd be married in name, but we wouldn't, we needn't—" She took a deep breath. "What I'm trying to say is, well, we would forgo . . ." She twirled her hand in the air, indicating one corner of the room.

He turned toward the corner, espying the bed. His cheeks filled with color. "Marriage is not taken lightly here in the colonies. When a ceremony is performed, it is meant as a covenant with God until our deaths."

She reinforced the folds at her gown's waist. "Well, yes, of course. But, surely, under certain conditions, the marriage can be reputed?"

"O'Connor!" Hopkin yelled. "Your time is up!"

Drew rubbed his eyes.

She grabbed his sleeve. "Do you agree?"

His gaze found hers. There was no shielding of his expression this time. His eyes were filled with reluctance, determination, and unmistakable frustration.

"Go in after him!" Emmett screeched.

Drew turned and stalked out of the cottage. Picking up her skirts, she followed.

"Open your Bible, Morden," Drew said.

She surveyed the formidable group of men. Forsooth. It appeared that like it or not, she would be married this day. Still, exacting a promise of abstinence from Drew *before* the ceremony was much more likely than after.

She pinched his arm. "Answer my question."

He scowled.

"Give me your word, Mr. O'Connor," she whispered. "I've forced my papa to cancel five marriage contracts so far. If you wish to avoid a scene, I suggest you agree to my terms."

His shocked expression spoke volumes. Of course, five contracts was a bit of an exaggeration. She must pray for forgiveness immediately after the ceremony.

Tightening his lips, he nodded.

"Josh," Morden said gently, "go and collect your mother's wedding band. We have need of it."

Josh hesitated only a moment before doing as asked.

Morden moved his attention to Drew. "She must be married in her hair. Please loosen it."

Her mouth went dry. After a long, tense moment, Drew cupped her chin and turned her toward him. Clearly, he was distressed. Whether from the thought of loosening her hair or from placing his mother's ring on her finger or from the very act of wedding her, she knew not.

He tugged the strings of her cap and slid the covering from her head. Her braid tumbled down her back, its end brushing against her waist. She felt her heart thump loudly against her breast.

Josh returned to the glade, and Drew handed him her head cloth. Drew's eyes, however, never left hers. He stood as such for an inestimable amount of time.

"You must finish it, son," Morden prompted, his voice low and kind. "You know it is to hang completely free."

Still he made no move. He simply waited. Waited, she realized, for her permission. The heart that had near jumped from her chest before, now slowed in gratitude. He, of course, knew this marriage was not a real one. And to loosen her hair in such a manner should be the privilege of her future mate. So he waited.

She felt her face relax a bit. She had no desire to see him and his family banished simply because the preacher was going to insist her hair be worn in the manner it should for such an occasion.

She pulled her braid across her shoulder, letting her hand run the length of its tight coil before allowing it to hang free.

His gaze followed the path of her hand. His Adam's apple bobbed. Lifting the tail of her braid, he took a tentative step toward her, then began to unravel her hair. His knuckles inadvertently brushed against her. She jumped. He froze, then much more carefully continued with his task.

As he neared the top, she tucked her chin to better accommodate him. When all was in readiness, he spread his fingers wide and ran them through her tresses, draping them across her shoulders and breasts.

She raised her chin. His blue eyes had darkened by several degrees. Her breathing grew labored.

Morden cleared his throat. She and Drew centered their attention on him.

"Dearly beloved, we are gathered together here in the sight of God, and in the presence of these witnesses, to join together this man and this woman in holy matrimony. . . ."

She looked about the clearing. Even if it was temporary, she wanted to take special note of her wedding day. She almost gasped aloud when she caught sight of a doe, with a spotted fawn at her heels, well beyond the clearing. The doe, stretching her neck and perking her ears, stood transfixed.

" . . . was ordained for a remedy against sin, and to avoid fornication; that such persons as have not the gift of continency might marry, and keep themselves undefiled members of Christ's body . . ."

As the deer and her fawn loped out of sight, Constance turned back to the preacher. His words had captured her attention.

"The ring."

He held his Bible out in front of Josh. Josh placed the gold band upon the Book, and the preacher delivered it to Drew. Taking her left hand, Drew slid the warm metal onto her fourth finger, retaining hold of her hand even after the task was complete.

"Wilt thou, Andrew Joseph O'Connor, have thee . . . uh . . . oh my. Pardon me, dear, but what was your proper name again?"

She stiffened. Drew entwined his fingers with hers.

She took a deep breath. "Lady Constance Caroline Morrow, daughter to the Right Honorable the Earl of Greyhame, My Lord Randall Christian Morrow."

Morden balked for a moment, then cleared his throat. "Well, now. That's quite a name. For these proceedings, I will make use of your forename and surname."

"As you wish," she replied.

Morden pulled at the collar of his shirt. "Wilt thou, Andrew Joseph O'Connor, have thee, Constance Caroline Morrow, to thy wedded wife? To have and to hold, to love and to cherish, to comfort, honor, and keep, as long as ye both shall live?"

Drew's serious blue eyes turned to her. "I will."

She swallowed. He gave her hand a gentle squeeze.

"Wilt thou, Constance Caroline Morrow, have thee, Andrew Joseph O'Connor, to thy wedded husband? Wilt thou obey him and serve him, love, honor, and keep him, forsaking all other, keep thee only unto him, so long as ye both shall live?"

Her throat swelled. What was she doing? It had sounded so simple in the cottage. *Oh, Lord.* She looked from Drew to the preacher to the governor and back to Drew.

Easing into a smile, Drew covered their clasped hands with his free one and turned her toward him. "It's all right, Constance. The Lord says, 'Fear not, for I am with you; Be not dismayed, for I am your God. I will strengthen you, yes, I will help you, I will uphold you with my righteous right hand.' "

She stared at him in wonder. What manner of man was this Andrew Joseph O'Connor?

"I will." The words were out before she even realized she'd said them. He rubbed his thumb lightly across her knuckles.

Morden started. "Yes. Uh, very good. Uh, forasmuch as Andrew Joseph O'Connor and Constance Caroline Morrow have pledged their troth either to other, I pronounce that they be man and wife together." He closed his Bible. "Those whom God hath joined together let no man put asunder. Amen."

This was wrong. It was wrong to declare such vows when she had no intention of keeping them. It was wrong to trick these men who, in their own disillusioned minds, merely thought they were protecting her virtue.

She searched Drew's features for a clue as to what his thoughts were, but to no avail. He'd certainly surprised her with his words and gentleness. Was it genuine? Yes. She believed so. She hoped so.

Her throat ached. It was all so unfair, for both of them. And what would happen to him when the council found out about their subterfuge? Would his arms be broken? His tongue bored through with an awl? Would he lose his farm anyway? Whatever happened, it would be all her fault. Her eyes pooled.

"Our Father, who art in heaven, Hallowed be Thy name . . ."

Drew's rich baritone voice joined in with the others assembled. She moved her lips to the prayer, yet no sound came forth. Cradling one side of her face, his thumb swiped at the tears now trickling down her cheek.

" . . . And lead us not into temptation, but deliver us from evil. Amen."

A warm breeze caressed her, swirling a tendril of hair. He hooked the tendril with his finger and pulled it from her face.

"You may kiss thy bride."

She widened her eyes. That too? They must do that too? Time stood suspended, then he cupped her face with both hands and slowly lowered his lips to hers. She slid her eyes closed.

The softness of his mouth barely registered before a peculiar heat spread from their kiss, down her neck to her shoulders and throughout her body. Her lips parted in surprise.

Oh, sweet saints that be. She'd not been hugged or held for so very, very long. But this, this was so much more and so absolutely heavenly.

His hands moved to her back, pulling her closer. She brought her hands up to his arms, crinkling his sleeves within her grasp.

"Drew."

The voice came from far away.

"*Drew!*"

She clung to him as she felt him tense and pull back. He placed his hands about her arms and gently disengaged himself. When her vision cleared, it was to find him holding her at arm's length, his face bright with color.

Mortified, her gaze traveled over an entire group of flush-faced men. Stepping back, Constance felt her own face heat, then turned as Josh grazed her sleeve.

He touched his cheek to hers. "Welcome to the family, Mistress O'Connor."

"Thank you."

"What about Miss Robins?" Emmett inquired petulantly.

Hopkin took a deep breath. "Drew will clarify the particulars on her, Emmett."

"How?"

He shrugged. "He can send word with the captain."

"The captain of the *Randolph*?" Emmett cried. "He'll not bother himself with that."

"I'll pay him for his troubles," Drew said.

"I just bet you will," Emmett sneered. "If the price is right, the captain'll do anything. Including lie and report whatever you pay him to report. No, the captain is out of the question."

"Now you're willing to admit the captain is a liar?" Drew asked. "Where were these objections a few moments ago when my wife's claim of nobility was questioned?"

"I admitted the captain would lie about the lady's status," Emmett retorted. "He might know full well she's a maid yet claim she's a lady just to line his pockets."

"He might also have kidnapped her and claimed she was seized according to his orders," Drew snapped.

"Enough!" Hopkin exclaimed. "Either way, Emmett has the right of it. The captain is not trustworthy. I recommend Joshua go abroad and investigate the matter."

"Josh!" Drew exclaimed. "Absolutely not. I am about to expand my farm into a plantation. I've ten indentured men awaiting me at the wharf as we speak. The harvest is due to be cut before the month is out. I need Josh here."

Hopkin squared his shoulders. "I have wasted enough of my time and the council's time this morning. Joshua will either investigate the marital status of Miss Robins or he will marry her."

"This is outrageous!"

"Hopkin," Tucker interjected, "you are being unreasonable."

Hopkin whipped off his hat. "And I am done with your constant interference. Joshua and Miss Robins are both young, healthy persons. Confining them on this farm for the next eight months is more temptation than I am willing to afford them."

"I'll marry her," Emmett said.

"She's not for sale," Drew growled. "I need her here to cook."

"You have your *wife*," Emmett snarled.

Drew took one step forward. "If you refer to my wife in that tone again I will lay you out flat."

"I'll leave on the *Randolph*," Josh stated.

Drew whirled around. "A fie upon it, Josh, what are you saying?" He appeared at a loss for words before determination settled into his expression. "Have you forgotten there's a civil war raging in England?"

"I've not forgotten," he said. "I've also not forgotten the woman I'm pledged to."

"We can appeal this," Drew countered. "I am married and a suitable chaperon. They cannot force you to marry as well."

"Appeal to whom?" Josh asked. "The whole blasted council is standing right here.

Besides, think. While I am investigating the whereabouts of Mary's husband, I can also notify the earl about Constance's kidnapping. He's bound to be frantic."

Drew combed his fingers through his hair. "But it's already late June and the *Randolph* is empty with nothing here to load. Josh, she'll be sailing up and down the coast and maybe even to the West Indies before she's full. Add that to the months needed for locating Greyhame and Robins, and you are sure to be tardy. What then? What if you return too late to factor our tobacco harvest? With no broker for our tobacco, the whole year will be lost and our plans for a plantation with it."

"I'll be back come spring," Josh said. "In plenty of time to transport and sell our tobacco."

"But the war!"

"I'll be back."

Hopkin tapped his hat down on his head. "So be it. Councilmen, our business here is concluded. Let us away."

Drew's lips thinned with visible anger.

Colonel Tucker extended his hand to Drew's. "I'm sorry. I'm as unhappy about this as you are."

Heaving a sigh, Drew accepted Tucker's hand. "You did what you could, and I thank you for that."

Tucker nodded and turned to join the other men. Constance watched them follow Hopkin like a flock of crows. The king would hear of this as soon as she returned home.

Home. She glanced at the man who had pledged his life to hers. His brother wouldn't be back until spring? Sweet saints above, would she ever return home? Surely there was a regular schedule with ships arriving every third week or so.

She furrowed her brows. If they were all slavers, though, she had no desire to risk boarding another without protection. And she certainly had no desire to go to the West Indies.

Straightening, she pushed back the bothersome curls surrounding her face. She would return to England. She must. For Uncle Skelly. For the women of Europe. For herself.

Drew rubbed the back of his neck. His rugged muscular body shifted beneath his shirt. She swallowed. *Dear Lord, please let Josh return before spring.*

CHAPTER | SIX

"ARE YOU MY GAMMA NOW?" Sally asked.

Constance continued to slice her carrots. Ah, how to explain this? "No, dear. I'm . . . well . . . your sister, I suppose."

Sally's violet eyes widened. "I used to have sister. She got real sick. She went to heaven."

Constance paused. "I'm sorry."

"Mama and Papa live there too."

"I see." Constance laid down her knife. "What was your sister's name?"

"Sister."

Constance blinked. "Oh. I have a sister too."

"She live in heaven?"

"No, she lives in a place called England. It's not quite as wonderful as heaven, but almost."

"She call you 'Sister' or 'My Lady?' "

Constance bit her lip. "She calls me 'C.C.' "

"Sissy?" Sally's eyes lit up. "I call you Sissy too?"

Placing her hand on top of Sally's, she gave it a gentle squeeze. "That would be lovely."

An enchanting smile spread across the child's face. With it came two charming dimples.

Constance picked up the knife and glanced at Mary, who bustled around the fire. Due to the council's visit, they were late in preparing the midday meal and Mary had not stopped moving since Drew and Josh left to retrieve the indentured men.

"Knives are very dang'russ."

"Yes," Constance agreed. "Don't ever touch one."

"Or I might hurt me? Like you did?"

Constance nodded, glancing at two of her fingers, now wrapped with strips of cotton. It wasn't that cutting vegetables was so difficult; it was just that the gold band on her fourth finger kept drawing her attention away from the knife. The ring's presence not only startled her every time she noticed it, but it also reminded her of the man who had placed it there.

The knife slipped yet again, barely missing her finger.

Sally gasped. "You better let Miss Mary cut the yun-yuns."

"You mean *onions*."

"Yes. Yun-yuns."

Constance swiped a sleeve across her face, trying to shove back the curls blocking her view, and concentrated on her task. "Well, I'll strive to be more careful. Otherwise I might run out of chemise."

Sally eyed the old chemise crumpled upon the bed. "I think you'll run out of fingers."

Mary scurried over to collect the carrots, waiting while Constance scooped up her slices and dropped them into the iron pot. "I'll set these over the fire, then show you how to cut them 'yun-yuns.' " She turned and winked at Sally. "After the noon meal, we'll boil that chemise, we will. I have a feeling she'll be needing it again, and the smell of it hurts my nose."

Sally giggled as Mary struggled with the pot of carrots in one hand while pinching her nose with the other.

By the time Drew and Josh arrived with the new men, Mary had prepared a hearty vegetable soup with enough corn pone for all. The men servants were weak, filthy, and hungry. They partook of their meal in the clearing, then deposited the empty trenchers they shared in the pails by the door.

Constance watched as, by degrees, they filed in front of the cottage and faced Drew, awaiting his instructions. Josh stood at Drew's left, while she and Sally were instructed to stand behind him and to his right. Mary picked up the pails of dirty dishes and headed to the creek.

Fetid shirts and britches hung on the men like rags on a cord. None wore shoes. Their newly shorn hair stuck in odd angles from their heads, while their grim faces displayed pallid complexions beneath a night's growth of whiskers.

She recognized none of them. Her thoughts had been of Uncle Skelly on the trip over and she had taken little notice of the other men during her brief jaunts to the upper deck.

"Eight of you are to serve a seven-year term," Drew started, "two a fourteen-year term as per your contracts. For the most part, we will be harvesting tobacco. I also have plans to build a three-level house come November.

"I will clothe and feed you well and, for now, you will sleep in the tobacco barn. When the big house is built, you may have this cottage as your living quarters."

He clasped his hands behind his back, his shadow stretching beside him in the still morning light. "At the end of your terms, each of you will receive an acre of land along with corn and new clothing. I will show you your land tomorrow. If you wish to work it on your free day, you may do so. Good behavior and hard work will be the price of seeds and tools for your land."

Constance looked from one indentured man to another, noting their guarded expressions. And no wonder. Drew's manner was in sharp contrast to that of the ship captain's. They had received nothing but barking orders and immediate retribution on the ship. To now have the lure of owning land dangled before them must be a bit suspect. She tilted her head, guessing it would take a while for them to accept their master's word as truth.

"Whatever price your crop brings will be yours to keep. I will hold your monies in an account with your name. If you want to save it, you may have the whole of it come the end of your term. If you want to use it to purchase supplies or sundries, you may give me the list and I will purchase them for you."

He took to pacing in front of the men. "You will not be working in the fields alone. I will be there working beside you. Any man who works harder than I will be given a bonus at the end of the season."

He stopped. The trees whispered. The hens clucked. The men kept their focus fastened on him. "I have plans for a great plantation. You are coming in at the best possible time. If you perform your tasks well and efficiently, you will act as leaders for the next group of men I purchase. Are there any questions?"

The men were silent.

He strode back to his brother. "You have already met my brother, Master Joshua, on the *Randolph*. He is my factor and will be leaving for England with the ship."

Moving to stand behind Constance and Sally, he placed one hand on Sally's shoulder and rested his other on Constance's waist. "This is your mistress, along with my sister, Miss Sally. Members of my family and household are to be treated with the utmost respect."

Mistress. He may have agreed to an in-name-only marriage, but no one else would suspect it as such. For he had not hesitated in the introduction of her as his wife and even placed a possessive hand to her back. She kept her expression neutral.

He took several steps forward and spread his feet. "If it is escape you have in mind, let me assure you, I will track you down. The punishment for attempted escape in Virginia is thirty-nine lashes of the whip. Have no doubt that I will catch you and administer them. Personally."

The men said nothing.

He relaxed his stance. "This morning you will worm and weed the fields. This afternoon, you will help as needed around the clearing with any light work Mistress O'Connor or my servant, Miss Mary, asks of you, but you will stop before the sun sets. You are all in need of rest and good food. I will see you have it before I expect you to put in a full day's work. Any questions?"

There were none.

"Fabric with which to clothe you should be arriving in port in about two weeks. Until then, I fear you must make do with what you have." He adjusted his hat. "Let us away to the creek where you can wash, then we will head to the fields."

———

As promised, Drew worked the men throughout the rest of the morning, then had them do light chores around the cottage. Though they were hesitant to speak freely, he hoped a sense of camaraderie would soon form. After a sumptuous supper, they could barely move, so, disregarding the sun still perched in the sky, Drew allowed them to retire.

Lighting his pipe, he then helped Constance carry the dishes to the creek for their washing, early evening shadows trailing behind them as they walked. He carried the heavy pots filled with noggins, while she held a pile of trenchers.

"What's that?" she asked, indicating a flowering tree covered with creamy globular blooms in a setting of huge glossy leaves.

"A magnolia."

"Lovely. And there are so many of them." She inhaled deeply. "Umm." Setting down her load, she moved to the tree, breaking off a flower and pressing it to her nose.

The rich fragrant perfume of the magnolia drifted to him. He took a deep breath, then surveyed his land, trying to see it through her eyes. Thinking back to the two years he'd spent at Cambridge University, he recalled what few trees they'd had abroad. Here, there was enough wood to supply all of England and more.

"How did the men do?" she asked.

He hesitated a moment. "In the fields?"

"Yes."

"Surprisingly well. They seem to have reconciled themselves to their stay here and give every indication of turning into fine workers. I don't think any of them will run."

"No?"

He smiled. "Well, they thought about it when I told them we would wash every day. Still, I don't think any will try to escape. Josh has a great knack for discerning a person's character. It appears his instinct didn't fail him. The men he advised me to purchase were exactly what I needed."

"That's why he was on the transport ship?"

He studied her for a moment. "You saw him?"

She nodded. "He took pains to smuggle as much food and drink to Mary as he could."

"Um. He did the same for our men. It has made their adjustment to me and the farm much easier."

She fingered one of the creamy petals cupped in her palm. "Did he smuggle food only to those particular men?"

He frowned. What prompted that question? "There was one other man he had chosen, but who died on the passage over."

She slowly lifted her gaze. "Who?"

He shrugged. "I know not. Why?"

Taking a deep breath, she laid the flower on top of her stack of dishes, then picked them up. "My uncle was on that ship."

"Ah, yes. *The uncle.*"

She stiffened at his sarcasm, and he felt a pang of regret. Regardless of whether she had told a falsehood, he should've kept to his own counsel until he knew for certain.

Removing the pipe from his mouth, he readjusted the hat on his head. "I'm sorry."

She bit her lip. "So am I," she whispered.

They walked the rest of the way in silence.

When they reached the creek, he set the pots on the bank as a feeling of contentment flowed through him. The closing of the day was upon them, and despite the disastrous morning with the council, things were going well. It appeared his plans for a plantation would still bear fruit.

Propping himself against a birch tree, he placed the pipe in his mouth, inhaled deeply, and blew a series of smoke rings above his head. His practiced eye scanned the water's edge looking for the animals that met there to feed and hunt. The busy crossroads joining the creek and forest lay unusually still, as if sensing a human presence. Picking up a rock, he skipped it across the water. The ripples disrupted the glistening surface of the creek as the sun began its final descent in the west.

He turned to watch Constance clean the trenchers. She sat perched on the bank, her eyes rounded and focused on him.

"What?" he asked.

"Aren't you going to help me?"

"With what?"

"These dishes."

He snorted. "Have you taken leave of your senses? I've already carried the pots down here for you."

"You mean I'm ordinarily expected to carry them myself?"

"Of course. My sister Nellie did it all the time. I only got in the habit of it when Grandma took over."

"So you carried the pots for your grandmother, then sat against that tree and watched her cleanse them?"

He frowned. "This is one of my favorite times of day and your screeching is chafing my ears. Please cease."

Her lips parted. His gaze was inexplicably drawn to them. Their sweet taste, along with the incredible softness of her appalling hair, reared itself in front of him. Clamping down on his pipe, he inhaled too quickly and began coughing.

She dropped the trencher in her hands, rushed over and whacked him on the back. He jumped up and scrambled to the creek, but the trencher was already floating away. Seeing no other alternative, he splashed in after it, still coughing.

He made it back to the bank, wet, still gasping for air and, with eyes watering, fell to his knees.

"Smoking is really a nasty habit," she said, pounding him on the back several more times.

"You dropped the trencher," he wheezed.

"Yes. And I truly appreciate your heroic effort in fetching it. Thank you."

He took a deep breath. She reached out to whack him. He grabbed her wrist and held it loosely within his grasp.

"Do not hit me again."

She blinked. "I wasn't hitting you. I was assisting you in your breathing."

"Constance, I have no food caught in my throat. What are you trying to knock out? The smoke?"

She bit her lower lip. "Oh. Your pardon."

He released her wrist. "You dropped the trencher."

"You said that already, and I thanked you quite prettily for retrieving it."

"Do not *ever* drop a trencher. We've only a few as it is."

"Why do you not use porcelain or silver?"

"I'll not waste money on such as that. Trenchers do just fine."

"Oh. Well, maybe you need to make some more while I cleanse the dishes instead of slouching against that tree."

He handed her the trencher. "Clean it."

She looked down at it. "I'd say this one has already been cleaned."

"It's been rinsed. Now it needs to be cleaned."

"How?"

He frowned. "What do you mean, 'how'? You scrub it. How else?"

She looked around at the pots and other trenchers. "Scrub it with what?"

He tossed the trencher down. "With sand. Have you no power within your brain?"

She straightened. "I have never before scrubbed dishes." Back rigid, she fell to her knees on the bank, grabbed a handful of muddy sand, and scrubbed.

He located his discarded pipe and again settled back against the tree.

"I've never heard of such a thing," she began. "To clean the dishes, you rub dirt on them. It's absurd." She dunked the trencher into the water, then dunked it again.

He tightened his mouth. The tobacco in his pipe was wet. Turning it upside down, he tapped it out.

"How's this?" she asked. "Is it clean, or do I need to get it dirty again?"

He looked over at her. She had pushed up the sleeves of her gown in order to wash. Her arms were covered with freckles.

"Run your hand across it," he said. "If it's grimy, rinse it some more. But you shouldn't need to scrub it again."

She pushed the curls away from her face with her shoulder, then ran her hand across the trencher. Frowning, she dunked it back into the water.

He sighed, looked at the stack of dirty trenchers, then the sun lowering in the horizon. They were going to be here all night.

Pulling away from the tree, he grabbed a trencher and knelt beside her. When he finished, she snatched it from him and ran her fingers over it.

"It's grimy," she said and handed it back to him.

He looked at her with disbelief. "It's perfect."

Slowly, a smile crept onto her face. "Easy, now. I was merely jesting."

Jerking the trencher back, he dropped it to the side and started on another. The sloshing of the trenchers continued as they worked in companionable silence. In the distance, a woodpecker tapped out a staccato beat while a persistent dragonfly patrolled the shoreline, briefly lighting on the old raft before resuming his restless flight.

Drew had cleaned five noggins, two trenchers, and both pots before she'd finished her fourth trencher. Grabbing it from her, he proceeded to finish the last one. Rolling down her sleeves, she stood and watched.

"Well," Josh said, "isn't this a pretty picture."

Dropping the trencher in the creek, Drew jumped up and whirled around.

Constance quickly reached in and retrieved it, shook the water off, and handed it to him. "Do not *ever* drop a trencher. We've only a few as it is."

He ignored her. "What do you want, Josh?"

Josh eyed Drew's sodden breeches but said nothing of it. "I came to say good-bye."

"Good-bye?"

He nodded. "We're going to Nellie's. I need to say good-bye to her and Grandma. I'll leave from there in the morning."

"*We're* going to Nellie's? Who's *we*?" Drew asked.

"Mary, Sally, and I."

"Why are Mary and Sally going?"

Josh darted a glance at Constance. "Because."

Drew frowned. "Because, why?"

"Because it's your wedding night, you beetle-headed knave," he said, rolling his eyes. "Why do you think?"

Drew reddened. "It's not necessary."

Josh lifted an eyebrow.

Drew grabbed Josh's arm and propelled him several yards down the path, well out of Constance's hearing. Still, Drew waited to speak until she'd turned and began stacking the clean noggins inside the pots.

"We're not to have a *real* marriage, if you will."

"What are you talking about?"

Drew lifted his hat and settled it back on his head again. "I'm merely providing Constance with the protection of my name to satisfy the council. When her father returns, she plans to have the marriage terminated."

"On what grounds?" Josh asked, obviously appalled.

"On the grounds that she was forced into marriage and on the grounds that the marriage hasn't been consummated."

Slapping Drew on the back, Josh laughed. "You gorbelly. I almost believed you for a moment."

"I'm deadly serious."

Josh paused. "No. Surely you jest. Drew, look at her. She appears to be endowed with all a woman should have and more. If you but bridle her and slip her some sweets, she'll be eating from your hand long before I return."

"You overstep yourself, Josh. That is my bride you speak of."

"A bride most begrudging, it seems."

"Even so, you'll hold a civil tongue in your head when you refer to her. I've given her my word on the annulment matter and that's an end to it."

"Given her your word? To abstain until I contact her father? But I won't be back for eight extremely long months. Why would you do a fool thing like that?"

"Because she might not die before you return, and if she doesn't, I do not want to contend with the possibility of offspring, much less a wife."

"This was *your* idea?"

"Of course not. It was her condition for marrying me."

A myriad of expressions crossed Josh's face. "Sweet saints above. In the cottage . . . Is that what she wanted to discuss with you in the cottage before the ceremony?"

Drew blew a puff of air from his lungs. "Yes."

"By trow, never have I heard of anything so absurd. 'Tis folly for sure."

"Probably, but leave Mary and Sally just the same. There is no need to take them."

Josh shook his head. "Everyone in the colony knows it's your wedding night. Regardless of what the situation is, you must at least pretend to have a real marriage or no telling what Emmett will stir the council to do."

Drew drug his hand down his face. "A fie upon it."

"Mary and Sally will go to Nellie's with me tonight. I will send them back come morning."

Drew sighed and extended his hand. "Best so."

Josh grabbed his brother's hand. Leaning forward, the men embraced.

"Godspeed, Josh, and be careful. I'd appreciate your returning to factor my tobacco. If you get caught in the crossfire of that war, it will really put a cramp in my plans."

Josh chuckled and pulled away. "I'll be home come spring."

Drew nodded.

Josh strolled back down the path to Constance. "Take care of him for me, Lady Constance. I do not want to be a plantation owner. Being the second son suits me quite nicely."

Standing, Constance smiled. "He'll be fine. You have the letter I wrote for my father?"

He nodded. "I have it."

"When do you leave?"

"On tomorrow's tide."

"So soon?"

"The seaworthy old girl's anxious to go looking for cargo and has no reason to linger here."

Constance clasped her hands together. "Well, then. Have a care."

He lifted her clasped hands to his lips and kissed them. "I'll find him, Lady Constance."

She took a deep breath. "Thank you. And Josh?"

"Yes?"

"Please, call me Constance."

He crinkled his brow. "Sally gets to call you Sissy."

She smiled. "Sally is three years old."

A wicked gleam entered his eyes. "Yes, but I'm better looking."

Constance's laugh tinkled out across the clearing. "Hurry back, Josh."

He tipped his hat. "I will, sister."

Turning, he passed by Drew and bumped him to the side with his shoulder. "Try not to pick the lock before I return," he whispered, winking before sauntering up the trail.

Drew glanced toward Constance. The sunlight at her back outlined the curves hidden beneath Nellie's old dress. He swallowed. *Dear God, please let Josh return before spring.*

CHAPTER | SEVEN

THE MOON AND STARS lit up the night sky with abandon, showering some of their beams on Constance. Leaning against a girdled tree, she greeted Orion. He stood as stalwart as ever, raising his club for a kill, while his brilliant belt housed that mighty sword. She looked a bit to the left and, yes, there was Venus dazzling in the rectangle of Gemini. High above and to the right of Orion shone Jupiter.

With these old friends joining her, she could almost pretend she was in her flower garden back home. Almost. But sooner or later, she'd have to bid her friends good-night and go inside that cottage. With him.

She glanced at the cottage door. Why had he allowed Josh to take Mary and Sally with him for the night? Had he misconstrued her rather warm response to his wedding kiss? She hadn't meant to respond at all. But respond she did and with not just a little enthusiasm.

She readjusted the hem of her sleeves. Something intense had flared between them. Most likely, it was a product of the excessive tension. Still, whatever the reason, it couldn't happen again, and if he'd arranged for an empty cottage with a reckoning in mind, she would have to persuade him otherwise. Fortifying herself, she turned and entered the cottage.

Due to the heat outside, the fire in the hearth was small and gave off little light. He sat on a bench in front of the fire, smoking a churchwarden pipe, its long stem protruding a couple of feet from his mouth.

"Where are the candles?" she asked.

He slowly expelled a stream of smoke. "What need have you for a candle?"

She dabbed at the moisture around her hairline. "I'd like to work in my diary."

"The cruse is on the shelf, but it drips, smokes, and smells so bad, we never use it."

"The cruse? With grease? You've no candles?"

"No need for them. When darkness falls, the family usually retires."

"But the family isn't here."

He took a long drag from his pipe. "No, they aren't."

He'd removed his hat at some point, and the glow of the fire framed his dark curly hair with bluish highlights.

"Where's my diary?" she asked.

"In the cedar chest."

She glanced in the direction of the chest but saw nothing. The cottage was shrouded in darkness.

"Have you any parchment?"

"Why don't you just go to bed, Constance? You're bound to be worn out."

"Yes, I should be, but for some reason I'm wide awake."

He lowered his pipe. "Me, too."

She barely caught his murmured words. Stretching her arms out in front of her, she headed toward the chest. At least, she hoped she did. Her hands made contact with the wall. Moving along its rough surface, she methodically felt up and down.

"What are you doing?" he asked.

"Looking for the chest."

He sighed. "It's too dark. You'll never be able to find the booklet inside that chest without some light."

"Then where's the cruse?"

"No, you'll simply have to wait."

Tears immediately sprung to her eyes. This day had been almost more than she could bear. Too much had happened too fast. If she could just work on an algorithm, everything would fall into place for her. Swallowing, she continued her search, then jumped when she felt his hand encircle her wrist.

"Come and sit down, Constance. If you cannot sleep, then sit by the fire. Even if you found your diary, the fire would not give off the light you'd need."

"Yes it would." She pulled back her hand.

He paused. "Are you crying?"

"Don't be ridiculous. Why would I be crying?"

"No reason I can think of, but that never stopped my sisters."

"Well, I'm not one of your sisters."

A great swell of silence encompassed the cabin. "No," he whispered, "you're my wife."

She swallowed. "Why did Josh take Mary and Sally with him? Didn't you explain?"

"I explained."

"Then why?"

"Appearances. Emmett. The council."

"Who could we possibly be trying to impress with appearances? I've seen no neighbors."

"We've neighbors, Constance. They just live a good distance away. Still, word always seems to get around."

"But what does it matter? Who would care?"

"The council. Emmett. Me."

"But I'll be leaving soon. Why, I could take next month's ship. There's no need for me to wait for your brother."

He shook his head. "This isn't London, Constance. Ships are few and far between here. But even still, you'll be going nowhere until I've confirmation about your background from Josh or until your alleged father himself shows up."

She sighed. Her background again. "This is such a mess."

"Um."

They stood in the darkness. Her eyes had long since adjusted, but she still couldn't make out his expression. She could smell him, though—that now familiar mixture of male, sunshine, and tobacco. His breath tickled her face. She took a step back. "I think I will sit down."

After settling herself on the bench, she suppressed the urge to scoot to its farthest edge when he joined her.

"What's in your diary that was so important?"

"I wanted to work on an algorithm."

He stretched his long legs in front of him and propped his hand against the bench, leaning away from her. "Did you now?"

She wet her lips. "Yes."

"And which algorithm would that be?"

Placing her hands on either side of her knees, she grasped the bench seat. "I saw a fly in the cottage today."

He tapped the stem of his pipe against his lips. "Now, that's an algorithm I've never heard of."

She slid him a glance, then turned back to the fire. "I also saw a spider."

"My, what a busy day you've had."

She allowed herself to relax a bit. "Let's assume this cottage is 21 feet long, 10 feet wide, and 10 feet high. On the middle line of one of the smaller side walls and 1 foot from the ceiling is a spider. On the middle line of the opposite wall and 9 feet from the ceiling is a fly. The fly, being paralyzed by fear, remains still until the spider catches it by crawling the shortest route. How far did the spider crawl?"

He readjusted himself on the bench. "Whatever was your father thinking to indulge you in the area of academics?"

She drew a circle in the dirt floor with her toe. "He was too busy with his business interests to take much note of my activities, and by the time he realized Uncle Skelly had seen to my tutoring, it was too late."

"What of your mother?"

"She died when I was three. I've no recollection of her. But upon her death, one of my sisters and I were sent to Uncle Skelly and Aunt Katherine's country home." She tucked a loose curl at her nape back into her cap. "Since my aunt and uncle never had children of their own, they devoted much of their time and love to us."

"But what possible purpose could you have had for an education? Particularly in mathematics? 'Twas pure folly."

"Pure folly? But why?"

"Well, I would venture to guess that if your time had been spent exclusively on skills of a female sort, you'd be safe at home. Instead, you maneuver your way out of five marriage contracts and get kidnapped as well. No, it's my guess your father rues the day you learned your letters and numbers."

She flushed. "Five contracts was a bit of an exaggeration. It was only two."

"Only two? Well, then. That makes all the difference."

She stiffened. "My education encompassed what every woman is expected to know."

"Such as?"

She lifted her chin. "Piety and needlework. Catechism and the Bible. Civility, of course, was instilled by two gentlewomen and a French woman."

"And the more secular subjects?"

"Uncle Skelly hired tutors for me."

"What all were you taught?"

She shrugged. "I don't know. Several things. Latin, French, rhetoric, logic, mathematics, geometry, writing, spelling."

"Your poor father. When did he find out?"

"When I was thirteen."

He grimaced. "What did he do?"

"He fetched me home. I'd have had to go home anyway, though, since a marriage contract he'd made for me was about to mature. Having long before transferred my affection to my aunt and uncle, I went rather unwillingly."

"And now?"

She looked into the fire. "Now, I'm quite fond of Papa."

He pulled his feet back and propped his elbows on his knees. "Let us see. How far from the ceiling was the fly?"

"Nine feet."

"Nine feet. And the spider was one foot below the ceiling, correct?"

"Yes."

He took several drags from his pipe. "Have you figured a solution for your puzzle?"

She shook her head. "I do much better if I can draw pictures."

He set his pipe down. "All right." Bending toward the fire, he scooped up a handful of cold soot and spread it out. "Sketch away."

For a space of several beats, she considered him. Unable to resist, she found herself on her knees beside the pile of soot. Sketching out the cottage and insects with her fingers, she sat back. "What do you think?"

He pursed his lips. "I think I should come up with my solution and you should come up with yours. Then we can compare them."

She looked from him to the soot and back. "All right. When do we compare?"

"How long will it take you to come up with an answer?"

"How long will it take *you*?"

"I already have one."

She gasped. "You lie!"

He grinned. It was a two-dimple grin. She hastily looked down at the soot.

"How long will it take you?" he asked.

She shrugged. "Five minutes."

"Done."

She smiled. "Then go sit over there with your own soot."

Chuckling, he moved to the opposite end of the hearth. She had already started scribbling in her ashes.

Twenty minutes later, she sat back. He was still crouched over his soot.

"Your time is up," she said.

He straightened. "Humph. It's been up for some time now. I was simply giving you some extra."

She suppressed a smile. "What's your solution?"

"You first."

She narrowed her eyes. "How will I know you aren't stealing my solution?"

"How will I know you aren't stealing *my* solution?"

"I'll explain how I came about my answer."

"As will I."

"It's 30.48 feet."

He shook his head. "It's 31 feet."

She clapped her hands together. "You're wrong! I win."

"I think not. You are wrong and I win."

"The route the spider took was 30.48 feet. I'm sure of it."

"Well, then, would you care to place a wager on it?" he asked.

She nodded. "All right. If I'm wrong, I'll wash all the dishes tomorrow evening. If you're wrong, you'll wash them."

"Ha! That's no bargain for me. You're supposed to wash them anyway."

"Then what do I have that you want?"

A coal from the fire shifted. He considered her. Had she worded it any other way, that blessed kiss from this morning would never have crossed his mind. Now he was at a loss to think of anything else.

His gaze moved to her lips. He hadn't expected them to taste so good, her to feel so soft. And her response. Sweet Gemini. Had she walloped him in the stomach, he'd have been less surprised.

She cocked her head. "Is there nothing I can do as a forfeit?"

The implication set his blood pumping. "A kiss."

He heard her quick intake of breath. "I thought we had an agreement."

"A kiss does not a marriage make."

She nodded. "According to my papa, it does."

Shifting, he pulled at his pant legs. "How did you arrive at 30.48 feet, Constance?"

"I like not the conditions of the wager and withdraw from play."

He arched his eyebrows. "You concede defeat?"

"Certainly not!" She fluttered a hand about her neckline, then rested it in her lap. "Cease jesting with me, Drew."

The sound of his name flowed off her lips like the finest of wines. "I'm not jesting in the least."

"Then let us choose another prize."

"I've already chosen. I want a kiss. If you win, you may choose what you want."

A vein in her neck jumped. "A week without washing supper dishes."

"I think not."

"Then I think not about your prize." She smoothed her hands along her skirt. "I say 30.48 feet and a week without washing the supper dishes."

He pursed his lips. "I say 31 feet and a kiss, given freely."

She glanced at her drawings in the soot. "Done."

His body's reaction was swift and profound. "Done."

He closed the distance between them and knelt down on one knee beside her. She visibly swallowed before she pointed to the spider's route drawn in the ashes, along with a triangle.

"The horizontal leg of the right triangle is 21 + 1 + 1. The vertical leg is 5 + 10 + 5," she explained. "Its distance equals the square root of 23 squared plus 20 squared. That makes the hypotenuse of the right triangle—and the path the spider took—30.48 feet," she finished, running her finger along the projected path of her spider.

He studied her drawing and figures. She'd taken the cottage and unfolded it in her drawing, then connected the spider's location to the fly's in one straight line. From there, she had figured the length of the line by drawing a right triangle.

He should have thought of that. It was so simple once he saw it. He tightened his jaw. Now, not only would he have to wash the dishes for a week, but she'd know he wanted a kiss. He slid his eyes closed. *Heaven help me.*

A beat of silence. "How did you come up with 31 feet?"

He opened his eyes. "The wrong way."

She moved nary a muscle.

He made no attempt to hide his emotions. "You'd better get yourself in your pallet, wife. Right hastily."

Her gaze skittered to the bed and back. "I don't get the bed?"

By my troth, could she not see what a state he was in? "Not unless you intend to share it with me."

She scooted back. "I think I'll go make my pallet now. Good night, Drew."

There it was again. His forename. He watched the darkness of the cottage swallow her, then heard an *oomph* and a soft expletive. He knew the moment she found the cedar chest. After some muffled sounds, all was still.

"Drew?" Her address whispered across the room.

He stiffened. "Yes?"

"I'll be needing something to wear to church tomorrow."

He expelled the breath he'd been holding. "We won't be going to church until Christmas Day."

She gasped. "What?!"

"No one does. It's too far and none can afford to lose a full day in the fields every week."

"Then why in the world were they so sanctimonious about us, to the point of forcing marriage?"

He took his time in answering. "I'd like to say that just because we don't attend church regularly doesn't mean we aren't expected to live Christian lives. But the truth of the matter is, I'd two females in a settlement of men desperate for wives. I imagine they couldn't stand the thought of your being single yet out of their reach."

"But marriage only made me further out of reach!"

"Go to sleep, Constance."

He heard her mutter and flop around in her pallet, and then everything settled into silence. If anyone had told him a week ago he'd be married today, he'd have thought they were in their altitudes. If anyone had told him he'd be spending his wedding night on the opposite side of the room from his wife, he'd have thought the drunkard was addled as well.

Tapping out the contents of his pipe, he stirred the fire's embers, then looked again at her scratchings in the soot. She may not be an earl's daughter, but she wasn't common born either. So exactly what did that make her?

Your wife, whispered the inner recesses of his mind. Slamming a lid down on that thought, he made his way to the bed.

CHAPTER | EIGHT

THE SUN, AMIDST STREAKS of pink, yellow, and orange, barely peeked over the horizon. Yet Josh's attention rested not on nature's glorious display but upon Mary. Kneeling on the ground behind Nellie's cottage, her fingers moved with dexterity as she plucked chicken feathers from the hen he'd wrung earlier.

"Mary, I must away. Have you a moment?"

She paused, then carefully placed the feathers in a pouch beside her. "I do."

"When I reach England, I will inquire into the whereabouts of your man."

"Yes, Master Josh."

He frowned, then squatted down in front of her. "Your man's name is Obadiah Robins and he was a street sweeper?"

"Yes."

"When did you see him last?"

"It was the spring of '41, it was."

"And when he didn't return home, you made inquiries?"

She traced a feather with her finger. "No," she whispered.

Well, now, what was this? Settling on the ground in front of her, he rested an arm across his upright knee. "When did you discover he'd been press-ganged?"

"It was with friends, he was, when the deed took place. One of the men managed to escape. After he came out of hiding, he told his wife, who then informed me of Obadiah's mishap."

"Who did the deed?"

"I know not."

His brows drew together. "But the man who returned would surely have known."

She wet her lips. "Yes."

"Then how is it you do not?"

"I asked not." With quick jerks, she plucked the feathers again.

He tilted his head to the side. "You asked not?"

The pace of her work increased. There could be only one reason a wife wouldn't seek out her man. "Obadiah was an unsuitable husband?"

No response. Unsuitable he was, then. "I must still attempt to find him. I've given my word to both Drew and the council."

"I know," she breathed.

Fire and torment, he hated this. "The man who escaped, know you his name?"

"Arnold Parker. A peddler of oatcakes, he was."

"How many men were taken, other than Obadiah and Parker?"

"I know not."

"You were in London at the time?"

"Yes."

He watched her for a moment. It was a good thing that chicken was already dead, the way she clenched it with every pluck. Reaching out a hand, he covered hers. "It will help me in my dealings with Obadiah if I know of his unsuitable traits."

Her face tensed. She made no move to enlighten him. He released her. "I must guess then?"

She said nothing.

"Well, I would suppose he either took mistresses, was a slug-a-bed, or overindulged in drink."

She reddened. "I asked not and cared not about the women. He never missed work, and tipping the cup was not his way."

"Then what?" he asked, rubbing his eyes.

She remained silent. His hand stilled. Beatings. He knew many a man who beat his wife. His father had never once raised a hand in anger, but there were countless who did. "He mistreated you?"

Color drained from her face, yet she continued with her task. He tensed. "And the children?"

The quickening of her task was her only response. He waited. "Mary? Did Obadiah mistreat the children?"

Silent tears began to fall from her eyes. "Yes," she choked, so softly he barely heard it.

His nostrils flared. Placing his hands on either side of him, he leaned forward. "How did your children die?"

With total disregard to preserving the feathers, her pace became frenzied. He took her chin in his hand and raised it. "How did your children die?"

Her face was pale, her eyes hollow. "Obadiah had no patience for the crying. Quite mad it would drive him. I placed myself between him and the babies, but the more I did, the more vexed he became. Until one day, his anger, it turned into rage."

He slid his eyes shut. *Wretched cur, when he's found it will go the worse for him.*

Her body slumped. "I tried to stop him, I did, but . . ."

Removing the chicken from her lap, he tenderly reached for her. She came to him without resistance.

The pinks and oranges of the sky had been chased away by the sun, now shining its full glory upon them. A nearby whippoorwill repeatedly whistled the rendition of his name.

How long they embraced, knee to knee, torso to torso, he knew not. Eventually, she tensed.

He released her. "I promise you. Never again will Obadiah lay a hand on you in anger."

Her gaze flew up. "No, Josh. You mustn't confront him. It will only make it worse, it will."

"My word's been given."

She touched his arm. "Obadiah can be ruthless, and his ways are not fair."

"Thank you for the warning."

"You understand not. Where his property is concerned, it's unreasonable he is. Why, he'll kill you just for mentioning it."

"We'll see."

Her eyes welled up again. "I'll not be having another death on my hands. And if you don't have a care for my feelings, then what of your bride's? She'll not be thanking me for the demise of her man, that's for certain."

He frowned. "You wound me with such a lack of confidence. He never will lay a heavy hand on you again and that's an end to it. As for Hannah, she has nothing to do with it."

"Nothing to do with it. Nothing to do with it. What's she like, this Hannah of yours?" After a shocked pause, her face flooded with color.

He widened his eyes, hesitated, then sought to put her at ease. "Ah, how to describe Hannah?" He pursed his lips. "She reminds me of Mama's porcelain cup. Delicate, fragile, refined."

"And beautiful?"

He shrugged. "Yes. She's quite lovely."

She reached for the chicken. A breeze stirred her thick maple hair, while white feathers floated around her.

Glancing at the sun, he noted the time. He needed to go. Stalling, he gathered the runaway feathers and deposited all but one into the pouch resting at her side. "Well, I must away before the captain leaves without me."

Keeping her chin tucked, she said nothing.

He stroked the downy fringe of the single plume in his hand. "Aren't you going to say good-bye?"

"Good-bye, Master Josh."

"Josh," he corrected.

She shook her head. "Master Josh."

"You called me Josh a few moments ago."

She glanced up. "Did I? I wasn't, I mean, I didn't—"

He placed the feather against her lips, effectively stopping her words. "It's all right. I simply want you to continue with that form of address."

She sat still, her gaze riveted to his. With slow deliberation, he drew the feather to her jawline, following its sleek curve to her ear, then up to the widow's peak forming the juncture from which her heart-shaped face began. With the gentle slope of her nose beckoning, he ushered the feather to its tip. Her lashes swept down.

Ah, don't hide those lovely eyes from me, dear Mary. He skimmed the feather across her lids. They twitched, then opened. Extraordinary.

He grazed the rosy buds of pink blooming along her cheeks. What pleasure God must have taken in creating her. She held a subtle beauty, enhanced by her very nature.

Her lips parted. He guided the feather to them, tracing their enticing shape. He hesitated. Tempting as it was, he had no business kissing her, not when he had another awaiting him back in England.

He transferred the feather from her lips to his, brushing it lightly across his own. She swept her lashes down, then resumed her plucking.

Slowly, he stood. "Good-bye, Mary."

"Happy wedding, Master Josh," she whispered.

Tucking the feather safely into his cloth pouch, he noted the bittersweet taste her good tidings had caused.

———

Stirring a batter of cornmeal, salt, and water, Drew determinedly kept his back to Constance as she brushed out her hair in long, slow strokes. The color of it hurt his eyes this early in the morning.

He turned to pluck a cloth from a peg by the fireplace, then paused. She was no longer kneeling by the chest, nor was she anywhere in the cottage.

He glanced at the door, propped open with a rock. He'd given her another old dress of Nellie's this morning, and she'd been anxious to change. A movement up by the rafters caught his attention.

There she knelt, with her back to him, probably thinking the loft's shadows hid her from view. Not so. She lifted her dress up over her head. His breath caught.

He should turn around. He should leave her to do as she would. Instead, his gaze lingered, moving down to her waist where it curved in and then flared out at her hips. Those hips disappeared in the blanket she'd wrapped around her lower body.

He held himself perfectly still. He'd given his word not to bed her, but he'd never said anything about this. It was implied, though, and he knew it.

He swallowed. She'd probably never gone without underthings in all her born days. He'd never really realized until now that she wore nothing underneath the flimsy homespun dress. When the next ship came through, he'd be sure to get her some stockings, at least, and maybe some shoes.

With the help of God Almighty, he forced himself to turn back to the fire and spread some hot ashes over the hearthstone. He poured batter on top of the ashes.

Moments later, she stepped up beside him. "What are you making?"

"Ash cakes."

"But you're getting them dirty."

"When the batter cooks up, you simply lift them up and brush off the ashes."

He demonstrated how to do the first one, allowing her to do the rest while he poured more batter onto some fresh ashes. "Take that first batch out to the men," he said, "and tell them to help themselves to anything down in the orchard."

When she returned, he had another batch ready. "I'll take these out. You grab a trencher, dust those last few off, and we'll eat in here."

He returned to find two trenchers on the board. "Who's eating with us?"

She blinked from her place at the table. "No one."

"Then why are there two trenchers?"

"There are two people."

He picked one up and returned it to the shelf. "No need to wash two when we have use for only one."

Settling himself on the bench next to her, he said grace, then popped several cakes into his mouth.

She sat with her hands in her lap. "We're to eat with our fingers?"

He chewed a moment more, then swallowed. "Stabbing ash cakes with a knife might prove to be a bit futile."

She wet her lips. "I see."

Polishing off more cakes, he suppressed a smile. First no privy, then no bed, now no utensils. He'd make a colonist out of her yet. Reaching for his noggin, he downed the rest of his cider. "Mary and Sally should be back sometime this morn. In the meanwhile, please see to your chores."

She lifted her brows. "Chores? What would you have me do?"

Taking off his napkin, he stood. "You know—weed the garden, wash the utensils, gather the eggs, that sort of thing."

He stepped out of the cottage, grabbed a large iron pot, and reentered. "Here are some turtles I caught yesterday." He set the pot on the board. "We'll eat them for our midday meal. If Mary doesn't return within an hour, you'll need to chop off their heads, then drop them—shell and all—into boiling water." He plucked his hat off a peg by the door. "See you at noon."

Constance stared at the large pot beside her. After several moments, she leaned over to peek inside. The turtles were not only huge but alive. She would never make it until spring.

Thoughts of Uncle Skelly and his diary intruded. She took a deep breath. Yes, she would. She would, by heaven, make it until spring. She must. *But Lord, I'll need your help!*

Wiping moisture from her forehead, she tugged the oversized skirt from under her feet. Before this day was through, she would alter these dresses Drew had given her. Meanwhile, she would make good on her commitment to enjoy a daily bath.

The sun had gotten a jump on her by the time she returned from the creek clean, refreshed, and beaming with pride over the dishes she'd scrubbed. Wouldn't Drew be pleased?

With a tune on her lips, she carefully stacked the clean dishes in their proper places and stoked the fire. Making a wide circle around *the pot,* she scooped up a basket and headed to the chicken coop.

Situated on the southeast corner of the clearing, the chickens were imprisoned behind a rudimentary fence. The twilled wooden barricade, comprised of thin rails passing over and under sturdy posts, encircled their little house and yard. Stepping through its gate, she paused as chickens came from all quarters. Ugly creatures. "I've come for the eggs."

The hens clucked.

She backed up a step. "Yes. I don't blame you. I'd be vexed as well. Therefore, I will only take a few. Would that be acceptable?"

A large, particularly ugly gray-and-white rooster crowed loud and long.

"Ah. You must be the master. Well, I see not what you're complaining about. You're not the one that's done the laying now, are you?"

The rooster took four more steps toward her and crowed again.

She scooted down the fence line, making her way to the hen house. "Easy. I meant no offense. Pay me no mind. I'll be but a moment and then will leave you in peace."

The ornery creature charged. Shrieking, Constance swiped the basket in front of her. The other chickens in the coop yelped while the rooster fluttered its wings and tried to flog her again.

She screamed without ceasing, bandying her basket about like a sword. Before she could manage to escape, the monster caught the calf of her leg with its spurs. She knocked him to the side with her basket, allowing just enough time to put herself on the other side of the gate.

He flew against it, crowing. She screamed again as she fumbled to secure the latch. The hens raced around the coop squalling and flapping their wings.

Jerking up her skirt, she could see nothing but blood running down her calf. "Oh, you awful, awful creature! Look what you've done. Why, I'll have your head for this. Don't you doubt it for a moment!"

The rooster continued to crow and spread its wings. With a running leap, it managed to lift itself off the ground. Constance screamed and scrambled back, but despite its efforts, the cock couldn't get higher than midfence.

"It's supper you'll be tonight, you worthless clapperdudgeon," she hollered from a safe distance. "Mark my words. When the *real* master gets home, we'll just see whose side he's on. It's the mistress you've flogged and, so help me, I will savor every bite I take of your wretched hide!"

Spinning around, she limped to the cottage, back straight, head high. The eggs would have to wait.

Once inside the cottage, she jerked her chemise off a peg and ripped a goodly portion from its skirt. Plopping onto the bed, she lifted her dress for another look. What a nasty mess and oh, how it throbbed.

She bound the wound tightly, all the time visualizing that awful bird on a spit over tonight's fire. She knotted the ends of the rag together, then took a deep breath. She could have been killed. What if she hadn't been able to get out of that pen? What if the gate hadn't opened? What if it hadn't closed? Her entire body began to shake.

None of this should be happening. She should be safe at home, where she knew the rules and how to get around them. Certainly, the war had disrupted everyone's life, but this . . . this place with its barbaric ways and uncivilized people. No telling what might happen to her.

I want to go home, Lord. Home. Where the faces are familiar. Where I am loved and protected and cherished. Where we eat real food and sleep in real beds. Where I have shoes and stockings. Candles and parchment.

On the heels of that prayer, though, came not peace, but anger. Pure, unadulterated, full-blown anger. And with it a great urge to unleash it on the men who had done this to her.

She spied *the pot*. Narrowing her eyes, she rose from the bed in search of the kitchen knife, then made her way to the table with only the slightest of limps, the weapon hanging heavily from her hand.

Rolling up her sleeve, she took a fortifying breath, then plunged her free hand into the smelly water. The reptiles retreated into their shells. The turtle she grasped displayed a perfectly geometrical design on its back. Fascinating.

With the tip of the knife, she tapped what could be construed as the turtle's shoulder. "I dub thee," tap, "Sir Hopkin," tap. "Governor of the Virginia Colonies." Looking at the specimen with contempt, she lifted her chin a mite. "Because of the shirking of your duties and your treacherous behavior toward countless unsuspecting women, I sentence you to die, by beheading."

She held Sir Hopkin high for all to see while she marched him out of the cottage and into the clearing. Dusting off a place in the yard, she set him down.

He did not come out. Typical, the lily-livered fiend. "Come, Sir Hopkin. Take your due like a man, even though all know you to be a spineless, arrogant, useless knave."

Nothing. She frowned. How did one make a turtle come out of its shell? Squatting down beside the animal, she studied its design. The sun climbed higher and beads of moisture formed at her hairline before Sir Hopkin deigned to poke his uglisome head out.

She whizzed the knife down. He withdrew faster than she imagined possible. She took a deep breath. Her leg ached, her anger simmered.

After spending a good part of the morning trying to behead Sir Hopkin without success, she swiped him up off the ground, marched—well, *limped*—back into the cottage and threw him into his watery home. The turtle soup would have to wait. Cursed animals.

She rubbed her leg, then set out for the garden. It, too, was encircled by a fence woven together with shaved tree limbs. Her expertise was cutting and arranging flowers. Tilting her head, she studied the chessboard of variegated pieces. No flowers, only herbs and weeds. But which were which? She sighed. The gardening, it seemed, would have to wait as well.

Returning to the cottage, she stoked the fire, set a pot to boil and then reached for the dress she'd worn yesterday. Taking it outside, she proceeded to alter its dimensions.

———

When Drew arrived home it was to find Constance sitting prettily in the middle of the clearing wearing a dress that actually fit, while sewing on another.

The chickens in the coop squawked, the garden remained unchanged, and no smoke came from the chimney.

"Constance?"

"Drew! Oh, thank goodness. You're home." Struggling to her feet, she limped toward him.

He frowned, but only for a moment. She'd done something drastic to her gown. It looked nothing like the ones Nellie wore. It was tasteful and modest, covering every inch of her, but simultaneously accentuating all the dips and swells of her person. "What did you do to Nellie's old dress?"

Looking down, she held out the skirt of her dress with two hands. "I made a few alterations."

She slid the skirt back and forth, causing the fabric to brush from one side of her torso to the other, then lifted her attention. "I left a little room in it, though. I'm still not myself, after the voyage and all."

His gaze remained on her face, trying to banish the image of even larger proportions filling out her dress. "You are exceptionally fast with a needle."

"Yes, I am."

"Mary and Sally have been delayed."

She released her skirt. "Why?"

"Gerald sent word that Nellie's time is upon her."

"Gerald?"

"Nellie's husband."

She frowned. "Oh dear. Perhaps I should go and collect Sally?"

"No. You'd get lost. Why have you not weeded the garden?"

"I know not which are weeds and which are herbs."

"You've never gardened?"

"Only flowers."

He nodded. "And the eggs?"

Her features clouded. "Your rooster attacked me. Please wring his neck for me and we'll eat him for supper."

"What did you do to make him attack you?"

Her eyes grew wide. "What did I do? What did *I* do? That worthless cock attacked me and you want to know what *I* did? I'll tell you what I did. I screamed so loud they could hear me all the way back home. Then I smashed him with my basket. Then I told him he'd be dead before nightfall. That's what *I* did. Now what are *you* going to do about it?"

He rubbed his forehead. No one could be that inept. Even Sally could collect eggs. "Well, I'm not going to wring his neck. That's for certain."

She gasped. "Why not? I could have been killed!"

"You provoked him."

"Provoked him! I did not do one blessed thing to your precious rooster! I went into that coop, announcing my intentions to gather eggs, and he came at me full speed."

"You announced your intentions? What do you mean, you announced your intentions?"

She paused. "I walked in and told the chickens I planned to gather the eggs."

"What else did you say?"

She propped her hand on her waist. "Drew, you are testing me sorely."

"What else did you say?"

"I don't remember. I might have insulted it a time or two, but this is absurd. It didn't understand me!"

"You were crowing in his yard."

"Your pardon?"

"You were crowing in his yard. Roosters use their crow to establish territory and are very sensitive about it. If you went into the coop and started blathering about this and that, then there's no doubt he took it as a threat. You didn't let him win, did you?"

Her face registered what could only be shock. "If you are suggesting that I was to stay inside that yard and fight it out with him, then yes. I let him win. But ultimately, when his neck is wrung, the win is mine."

He lifted up his hat then resettled it on his head. "Come. I'll show you how to win."

"No. I'm not going back inside that pen with you or anyone else. Not until Mr. Meanie is on a spit."

Mr. Meanie? Suppressing a smile, he veered toward the chicken coop. She stayed where she was.

"You don't have to come in, Constance. You may watch me from the other side of the fence."

Her basket lay on its side where she must have dropped it in her scramble to freedom. Drops of blood littered the clearing. Frowning, he turned back toward her. "You are all right?"

Her lips thinned.

Body O'Caesar, he thought, I should have asked that earlier. Sighing, he entered the coop. "Hello, children, Mr. Meanie. How do you fare this day?"

The chickens squawked. The rooster ruffled his feathers.

"See you how Mr. Meanie is already becoming provoked?"

She gave no response.

"So. You've taken to attacking defenseless women, have you? Well, I've not checked the damage yet, but you'd better hope it's not too severe. It's displeased I am that you attacked my wife. You're to treat her with respect."

The cock began to dance around him.

"What? Like you not my crowing in your yard? Then come and get me, you scurvy fellow. Do your worst."

As if on cue, the rooster struck. Drew jumped to the side, making a swipe at its feet, but missed. They circled each other. Drew sang, adding a jump and a jig with each verse for good measure.

Here's to the maid with a bosom of snow;
Now to her that's as ripe as a berry;
Here's to the wife with a face full of woe,
And now to the girl that is merry:
Let the toast pass,
Drink to the lass,
I'll warrant she'll prove an excuse for the glass.

As he expected, the popular drinking ballad infuriated the rooster. Crowing with displeasure, he charged. Drew swiped again and, snagging the cock's feet, lifted him into the air, upside down. "There you have it, Constance. How to establish territory. I will hold him like this while I crow in his yard for a while longer, and when all the blood has settled in his head for a moment or two, I will release him. I, also, will have won."

"You're not going to kill him."

He paused. She had made her way to the edge to the fence and rested her arms atop it.

"No. I'm not."

"Why not?"

"We need the eggs."

"There are two other roosters in the coop."

He glanced at the other cocks, pecking at the ground in the yard. "If I kill Mr. Meanie, one of those would then establish itself as cock of the walk, and you'd have to deal with that rooster as well."

"Don't they fight amongst themselves?"

"These three roosters have grown up together, but if I introduced a new rooster into the yard, a fight would ensue."

She nodded once and turned to leave. He hated it when she dismissed him like that. He'd told her once already never to walk away from him in the midst of a conversation, and he'd meant it. Now he'd have to deal with her again on the issue. Pig-headed woman.

He waited a few more minutes before releasing the bird, then watched as Constance's Mr. Meanie wove around jiggling his head.

Letting himself out of the coop, Drew headed toward the cottage. He needed to have a look at her injury.

CHAPTER | NINE

S HE SHOULD HAVE KNOWN he wouldn't kill the rooster. Food-producing animals were too valuable in this wilderness to be terminated for the mere offense of attacking one's guests. It wasn't as if he liked the rooster more than her, it was simply a matter of practicality. So why was she harboring such hurt feelings?

Hearing Drew's approach, she allowed the hem of her skirt to fall before continuing to rub her calf.

"Why are the turtles not cooking?"

From her perch on the edge of the bed, she tried to suppress her irritation. "How do you make a turtle come out of his shell and stay out long enough to behead him?"

He took off his hat and hung it on a peg. "You hold a stick in front of the turtle and coax him to bite down on it."

She stopped her massage and looked up at him. "I'd never have thought. I did keep the embers—Oh!" Jumping from the bed, she began to work the fire. He, in turn, grabbed the pot of turtles and left.

When next she saw him, he had one pot of headless turtles and one bucket of fresh milk. She, thank goodness, had accomplished a thing or two herself—the fire was going and a pot of bubbling water hung above it, steam surging from its mouth.

"Drop the turtles into the water, and then I'll show you how to pound Indian corn into samp for the midday meal."

Had anyone asked her if she was squeamish, she'd have vehemently denied it. But always before, her meals had been set before her, cooked and seasoned to perfection. She knew, of course, she was eating animals, but she'd never given much thought to the specifics of their preparation. As she looked into the pot of bleeding headless turtles, she wondered if the pleasures of mealtime were forever lost to her.

Drew appeared to have assembled all that was necessary for the samp. She swallowed with effort, forcing her stomach back down where it belonged, then dispatched with the turtles. The *glub, glub, glub* of their descent nearly did her in. "What's samp?" she gasped.

"The most expedient meal I could think of. You simply pound corn, then pour milk on top before serving."

She tossed the last turtle in, then quickly turned to mortar and pestle, pounding corn with a vengeance.

"You're making a mess, Constance. Slow down."

She slowed. With the two of them working together, they had a goodly portion pounded in no time.

"Now, let us have a look at your injury." Standing, he offered her a hand up.

The gash was in a most improper place. "It's fine, thank you."

"I'll have a look anyway."

She wanted to refuse, but if she did, he might very well remind her that as her "husband" he had a right to look at much more than just this injury. She walked to the bed and sat, skirt down, knees and ankles together, hands locked on her lap.

"Where did he catch you?"

"Above the ankle."

A pause. "How far above the ankle?"

She willed the blush to go away. "A good two inches."

"I have a need to see it."

"I hardly even feel it anymore."

He glanced at the hem of her skirt. "What did you treat it with?"

"I wrapped it."

"No comfrey?"

"No."

He left the cottage, and she let out a sigh of relief. *Thank you, Lord.* At least she'd been spared that indignity. She started to rise, only to plop back down when he returned with a plant he'd obviously just pulled from the garden. She watched him rinse its roots, wrap them in a rag, and crush them with a rock.

"Show me." He knelt before her, focusing intently on her skirt.

Her stomach churned again, and though this sensation was entirely different from the one she'd fought down before, it was no less disturbing. She extended her injured leg and gathered a bit of her skirt at the knee, inching the hemline upward. She felt him release the knot of her bandage and unwrap it, slowing only when he came to where the cloth stuck to her abrasion.

She sat still, watching his bent head covered with that magnificent black hair, now matted down from his hat. She curled her fingers.

He immediately paused and glanced up at her. "This pains you?"

Heavens, he was a handsome man. She searched desperately for some flaw and could find nothing. The darkness of his skin and the crinkles the sun had put there actually added to his appeal. The eyes searching hers seemed bluer every time she saw them. The last time she'd seen them so clearly from this range was on their wedding day, just before he'd kissed her. She had closed her eyes against them then. She couldn't make herself do so now. "Your pardon?"

"Is the pain great, then?"

This had to stop. She could not sit here and ruminate over this temporary husband of hers. She was only here until Papa came for her, and she was less important than the rooster. "There is no pain at all."

"Your hands are fisted."

She immediately unfurled them as she felt the blood rush to her face. "I'm just a bit nervous."

"I'll be gentle."

She swallowed and gave him a slight smile. "I know."

"Then why are you nervous?"

She said nothing but knew the moment he realized the source of her unease, for his face too turned red and he quickly saw to his task. He finally managed to free the bandage. "It's bleeding again. I'm sorry. It's just that the claw mark is located such that I can't easily reach it."

"Oh, your pardon." She twisted her leg, but she could tell he was still having difficulty. After a few moments, though, he had the bleeding stopped.

"I need to put some comfrey on it."

She nodded.

He didn't move.

"What is it?" she asked. "There is a sting to it?"

"No, no. It will provide relief almost immediately."

"Then what's wrong?"

"I'm not sure how I can apply it to the back of your calf and then bandage it without loosing a great deal of the powder to the floor."

"I can do it."

He shook his head. "No, you'd have even more difficulty than I. No, what I need is for you to . . . to lie face down on the bed, please."

Neither of them moved. She allowed her skirt to fall to the floor. It was one thing to sit on the edge of the bed and have him look after one limb. It was something else entirely to lie prone on the bed and have him lift her dress and attend to her.

"I'll do without the roots," she said.

"I've already picked and crushed them. Besides, it needs the healing powers of the comfrey. That blasted rooster cut into you rather deeply, and being new to the colonies, you're more susceptible than most."

"Susceptible to what?"

"Death."

Well. That was certainly blunt. And, thankfully, made modesty seem rather trivial. Best of all, he'd just insulted the rooster. She swung her legs up onto the bed and rolled over. Her skirts were hopelessly twisted, but before she could fix them, he'd loosened them and flicked them up to her knees. She buried her face in the bedding, ignoring the outdoorsy smell of him there beneath her nose.

The comfrey roots did indeed feel wonderful. He said not a word as he worked over her, placing the powder on her injury, covering it with something soft and fuzzy, then rewrapping it with the rag. He maneuvered her leg as if it was of no import, lifting it, bending it, placing it on the bed. When the rag was knotted, she felt him glide his fingers along the edge of the bandage, smoothing it. Her stomach clenched, her heart skipped a beat, she forgot to breathe.

Was it a caress or simply a doctor seeing to his patient? She dared not move, for if it had been an innocent gesture, she certainly didn't want to overreact. And if it hadn't been? It *must* have been.

The smoothing stopped, yet she still felt his weight on the bed. She jerked when he took hold of her skirt, then called herself ten kinds of a fool, for he'd paused then in the midst of lowering it. Before releasing the hem, his fingers slowly brushed against her ankle. She spun over, landing on her back, plucking her skirt from his fingertips.

A mistake. Now she lay stretched out on his bed, facing him while he sat beside her, his eyes three times darker than they'd been before. He leapt up, grabbed his hat from the peg, and strode from the cottage.

She draped her arm across her eyes and took in great gulps of air. He *was* attracted to her. There was no denying it now. She'd seen that look on the men who'd asked for her hand in marriage and some who had not. The difference was *her* reaction. Instead of boredom or aversion, she felt every nerve in her body standing at attention—some nerves more than others.

What if he changed his mind and decided to exercise his husbandly rights? She lowered her arm to her side. She'd not be granted an annulment, that's for certain, and that would be the end of *The Ladies' Mathematical Diary*. Heaving herself up out of bed, she put the samp in bowls, hearing for the first time the indentured men in the yard.

————

The men seemed to enjoy the simple midday meal. Drew allowed them a moment's rest so he could give Constance a tour of the garden. He explained what each plant was and how it was used before rounding up his men and leaving.

The indentured men were to view the land they could claim at the end of their service. It was located on the very edges of his property and would require some time to reach. Upon his return several hours later, he found the garden weeded, the yard swept, and the smell of turtle broth floating on the air.

Removing his hat, he entered the open cottage door and came to a dead stop. A clump of lavender blossoms roosting in Mama's old porcelain cup sat in the center of the board and the movables hanging from the various pegs had been organized. All the clothing hung on one wall, the utensils on another.

Constance sat by the hearth, scribbling in the soot with a stick. She obviously hadn't heard him come in. Staying where he was, he allowed his gaze to roam over her person, his thoughts returning to when he'd dressed her leg. She had freckles there too, but lighter. And her skin. So smooth, so soft. Heaven help him, he'd tried to remain detached, had even pretended in his mind's eye doing such a thing for Gertard Jarvis. But all that had done was point out the lushness of Constance.

He'd spent much more time at the task than it required. It wasn't until he'd lowered her skirt that he realized how tense she'd been. Even still, he'd wanted one last touch. She'd near flown off the bed when he'd lingered a bit long at her ankle. All set to apologize, the words stuck in his throat when he looked into her eyes. It was not disgust he saw there. Far from it.

He took a deep breath and pushed that image, along with the one of her dressing in the loft, to the far recesses of his mind.

Lord, I cannot open myself up to her. No matter the silky skin, no matter the apparent attraction she may or may not have for him, no matter that she was his wife. It was of no consequence.

He allowed himself to remember the grief, the pain, the numbness he'd experienced as this land stripped loved one after loved one from him. Then Leah. The land had taken Leah a mere a week before they were to wed. He'd vowed never again to become involved. He'd meant it then and he meant it now.

"More spiders and flies?" he asked, his voice lower than he'd intended.

She squealed, then laid a hand against her chest. "I didn't hear you." She glanced at the window. "Where are the indentures?"

"Setting traps. What are you working on? More spiders?"

Shrugging, she set her stick down. "How did it go with the men?"

It was a wifely question. One she'd asked before, as if she had a real vested interest.

He hung his hat on a peg. "I'm glad I took them. It's the first time I've seen any animation amongst the group."

Brushing off her hands, she rose. "That's good."

"It's a start." He noticed the embers. "You kept the fire going."

She glanced at the pot hanging over the ashes. "Yes."

Yes, indeed. The pot was heating. The yard was swept. The cottage was spotless. But the eggs were still in the hen house. "You ready to gather some eggs?"

She studied him for a moment. "Do I have a choice?"

"No."

She moistened her lips. "Then I guess I'm ready."

He gave her an apron to wear, telling her to tuck it up and form a pouch for the eggs. They entered the chicken coop together, neither saying a word. The chickens rushed toward them and he could see Constance was skittish. He gathered the eggs. She, sticking close, placed them in her apron. Mr. Meanie gave them no notice.

———

At suppertime, the indentured men were not animated exactly, but certainly more relaxed. Rather than sitting stiffly alone, looking at nothing but the food they consumed, they now lounged about the clearing, some sitting, some leaning on an elbow, but all grouped in clusters of three or more, quietly visiting during their meal. Constance moved amongst them, enjoying the hum of their conversations superimposed over the drone of the forest's insects.

She'd acted as hostess to many meals, but never had she derived such pleasure from compliments and requests for seconds as she had this evening.

Although gutting the turtles was most disagreeable, she found she actually enjoyed preparing the soup. Never mind that Drew stood at her side, guiding and tutoring her through each step. No, her sense of pleasure came from a task completed from its earliest stages to its last.

"Might I 'ave another serving, Mistress?"

She turned to find an empty bowl extended to her by a set of bony arms. In between those arms were a bony face, a toothy grin, and a head of wild blond hair.

The men had reluctantly introduced themselves to her this morning when she'd given them ash cakes, but she was terrible with names and couldn't remember any of them. "Certainly, Mr. . . . ?"

"Pott. Samuel Pott, mum." He reached up to tip his hat, but of course there was no hat to tip.

She curtsied with a smile and fetched him a second serving.

"Ah, thank you, Mistress. It's a feast the king 'imself would be 'appy to 'ave."

"You're most welcome, Mr. Pott."

"Call them by their first names, Constance."

She glanced over to see Drew issuing this command while taking in more bowls for second servings. So magnanimous was she at the moment, she chose to ignore this bit of rudeness. Still, she must at some point remind him never to correct her in front of the servants. "You're most welcome, Samuel."

She looked down to see Samuel had turned as pale as death, and all the indentures stopped in midmotion. Drew might have missed the slight he'd just given her, but the men didn't and they expected her to retaliate in kind—toward Samuel.

This was only their second day away from the ship, and she knew only too well how they felt. That they were relaxed at all was indeed an impressive recommendation of Drew's ability with them.

She knelt down so as to be on Samuel's eye level. "You've nothing to fear from me or my husband. If you serve us well, you will be treated well."

Lowering his lids, Samuel nodded.

She cocked her head. "You know, I've six sisters and three brothers—all of them older than me but one. You remind me somewhat of my oldest brother. He quite enjoys his soups and chowders and has a fine set to his shoulders, very much like you. Therefore, I'll not be forgetting your name again, Samuel. Please forgive me for doing so this time."

He'd raised his gaze in the midst of this, and although she hadn't drawn a smile from him, she hoped she'd restored at least some of the casual mood from before. "Oh, no, mum. There's nothin' to forgive, there's not. But I'm much obliged, I am."

She nodded and stood. At a rustling in the brush, she turned to see Mary and Sally trudge into the clearing. "Mary! Sally!" Waving, she rushed over to them. "I'm so very glad you're back. Care you to have some turtle soup?"

Mary shook her head. "No, thank you. Grandma fed the both of us before we took leave, she did. It's sitting down for a moment I'd like to be doin' now."

"Well, let's go inside and sit, then." She looked down at Sally. "And what of you? Would you care for some soup?"

"Nellie has a baby!"

"A baby! How very wonderful. And how very wonderful it is to see you." She extended a hand to Sally, but before the child could grasp it, she caught sight of Drew and ran squealing into his arms.

Propping her on his hip, he joined them. "How's Nellie?"

"Fine," Mary answered. "It's a big lusty boy she's had."

"No problems, then?"

"No, sir."

"What did they name him?" Constance asked.

"They didn't."

"They're waiting for the baptism?"

Mary shook her head. "They're waiting until he's three."

"What?" Constance exclaimed.

"More often than not," Drew explained, "the children here never see their third birthday. So most people in the settlement distance themselves from the little ones."

"How dreadful! Surely you didn't do that to Sally?"

He tightened his lips. "I've never been able to distance myself."

"Well, I should think not."

He set Sally down. "It's not something I'm proud of, Constance." With that, he spun around and returned to the men.

"Of all the ridiculous . . ." She turned to Mary. "Come. Tell me of your visit."

CHAPTER | TEN

WITH THE CONCLUSION OF the meal, Mary oversaw Sally while Drew and Constance headed to the creek with the soiled pots, bowls, and noggins.

Once there, Constance set the bowls down on the bank. A feeling of contentment flowed through her. She'd made it through her wedding night without mishap. She had two dresses that fit her reasonably well. She'd completed several chores throughout the day. And best of all, her wager of last evening would bear its first fruit tonight. She didn't have to clean the dishes.

Propping herself against the birch tree, she regarded Drew from beneath her lashes and barely suppressed a smile. He tore into the dishes as if he wrestled the devil himself, his shoulders flexing, his arms tensing.

His mood had deteriorated by great degrees the closer and closer they'd come to supper's end. Then he'd said not a word—nor even glanced at her—during the entire walk down here. His stance had been rigid, his jaw tight.

Picking up a pebble, she fingered it for the slightest of moments before trying to skip it across the water. It fell with a dissatisfying plop, causing a chain of circular ripples to break out across the creek.

He paused for a moment before continuing with his task. Drawing up her knees, she wrapped her arms around them. "I was wondering . . . if a hen and a half laid an egg and a half in a day and a half, how many eggs would seven hens lay in six days?"

He stopped scrubbing the bowl, holding it still beneath the water. Slowly, he looked over at her, blue eyes dusted with dark thick lashes.

She smiled and propped her chin onto her knees.

He offered no smile, no dimples, no response. He simply remained crouched on the bank, staring at her.

"I have more if you'd rather try a different one."

"You have nine brothers and sisters?" he asked.

She raised her brows. "Yes. Yes, I do."

He turned back to his chore. "How many are still alive?"

"Why, all of them."

"I thought you were raised by *the uncle*."

"I was, along with Rebecca, my younger sister. But Papa fetched me home, remember?"

"Ah, yes. For the marriage contract that you refused."

"That's correct."

"And all those siblings were there waiting to take you into their bosom."

She shook her head. "No, they'd already married and left home. But Papa loved to gather them all under his roof as often as he could."

He stopped working again to look at her. "Tell me of them."

She looked at the stack of dirty bowls, then the sun lowering in the horizon. Heavens, they would be here all night at this rate.

Pushing herself up, she retrieved a bowl and knelt beside him. "My two eldest sisters were married by the ages of twelve and thirteen. Papa had contracted for my other sisters when they were even younger."

"I'm sure he thought he was acting in their best interests."

"Yes, God bless him, he did. Unfortunately, the moral integrity of the groom was immaterial, for wedding into nobility was of utmost importance."

"Women can't be choosing their own husbands, Constance. It would be a disaster."

"Financially, maybe. But I'd rather live simply and be cherished than live luxuriously and be mistreated."

"Surely it's not as bad as all that."

"You haven't met my sisters' husbands."

Their elbows brushed. "Tell me."

She set the clean bowl down next to an assortment of animal tracks stamped into the shoreline, each one unique, yet all coexisting in order to survive. She picked up another bowl. "Leoma, the eldest, wrote to me of her husband's unkindness. I saw for myself that Arietta was beaten. Kristina, the most intelligent of us girls, was bound to a drunken lout. Doreen suffered silently with her spouse's philandering, and Jocelyn, pregnant with her eighth child, was temporarily deserted by her husband."

"That's only five sisters."

"Rebecca's husband stuck her in a musty old country home and hasn't allowed her out nor any visitors in." Constance eyed his empty hands. "You're a bit sluggish with your chores this evening. If you can't visit and work at the same time, I will tell you no more."

He raised a brow. "I've already washed twice the amount you have. I was simply allowing you time to catch up."

She picked up a noggin and handed it to him. "You're too kind. Prithee, continue with your task."

He dipped the noggin in the water. "What did your brothers do to the men who abused your sisters?"

Constance harrumphed. "Norval was busy marrying one of the queen's maids-of-honor and was sent to the continent just after the wedding. Rogan fought an unsuccessful duel over another maid-of-honor, and Foley had made himself so free with the pleasures of town that, consequently, he was unable to consummate his marriage, as all of London learned the next day."

"The devil, you say."

"Yes. Not exactly the kind of men to take an undesirable brother-in-law to task. They'd be more likely to befriend him."

He took the last bowl from her. "How did you manage to make it to the age of nineteen without being forced to marry?"

Scooting away from the bank, she rolled down her sleeves. "I think Uncle Skelly must have refused to send us home, for Papa had to personally come and fetch Rebecca and me."

He stacked the bowl with the others, then picked up his pipe. "How old were you?"

"I was thirteen. Rebecca was ten."

He settled himself against a tree. "What happened?"

She wrinkled her nose. "Well, Rebecca did just as Papa told her. I, however, was not some ten-year-old child easily cowed into submission. Still, Papa moved forward, welcoming the viscount's son with open arms. The young man had barely set foot in the house before making his address to me."

Catching a movement on the far side of the creek, she gasped, then pointed at the brown furry creature sporting a black mask across its eyes and black rings on its tail. The bizarre animal dipped his dinner into the water before washing it off with his paws.

Drew watched it as well, not turning back to her until it finished and lumbered out of sight. "The savages call it an *aroughcoune*."

"I shall call it a bandit."

He humphed, then took a long pull from his pipe. "So, was this suitor's address so bad, then?"

She allowed a fleeting smile to cross her lips. "Oh, no. He was quite eloquent in his address and declared an extraordinary passion for me." She studied her nails. "Unfortunately, my aversion for him was extreme. Three weeks later he deserted the field." She looked up, and they exchanged a quiet smile.

"What happened then?"

"Well, my refusal put Papa in a rather untenable position. My rejection was embarrassing for him but not the least of his worries, for it appeared to others as if he couldn't make good on his business transactions, thus damaging his credit. Hence, he resolved I would yield . . . or else."

Drew's massive hands cradled his pipe, brushing its stem against his lips. "What did he do?"

She smoothed her skirt. "Well, you are aware, I'm sure, that women have now been granted a veto in matrimonial affairs. The woman must, of course, have weighty grounds for her refusal. Still, a veto is a veto."

His hand stilled. "Did you have weighty grounds?"

She looked at him askance. "Mr. Fenton said that no wife of his would participate in mathematical pursuits."

The beginnings of a smile touched his lips. "But surely your father exerted his wishes."

"Oh, he tried. He certainly tried. First, he cut off my allowance. That was of little consequence, though, for I simply bought whatever I wanted and had it charged to my future husband—whomever that might turn out to be. So then, he engaged the entire family, hoping they would wear down my resistance. All my brothers and sisters, along with my dearest friends, did most diligently entreat me to give in." She shrugged. "I simply told Papa that no marriage could be consummated without my consent."

A dimple appeared as one side of his smile grew. "That sounds familiar."

She gave him a quelling look. "It wasn't as desperate as Papa made it seem. I still had at least five more years before I'd be considered a full-fledged spinstress."

"So what happened?"

"Well, Papa, you see, had already passed his seventy-third year, and he felt it imperative that I find a match, even if it meant breaking this one and starting all over. So that's exactly what he did."

"Your poor father."

"Poor father! Your sympathies, kind sir, are quite misplaced. Five weeks later he had a new set of marriage articles." She stuffed bits of stray hair back into her cap. "It was not the first time Papa had tried to ally himself with Lord Milburn through a marriage contract, and I represented his last chance at securing this coveted connection."

"Did your father take out the veto clause?"

She bit her lip. "He couldn't, but he did alter his contract. This time he made sure he would not be penalized financially if I refused the suitor, and he stipulated there would be no cash down until the wedding day."

Drew stretched out his legs, crossing them at the ankles. "And what were your 'weighty grounds' this time?"

"The man was fifty years my senior."

" 'Tis not uncommon, that."

" 'Tis disgusting."

He chuckled. "That's all relative, my dear."

She shrugged. "That was about the time my brothers diverted Papa's attention. When Norval married the queen's maid-of-honor, it opened up a whole new London for the family. I quite adored his wife, Emma, but then the war broke out and it split our family as sure as an ax splits a log. Even now one brother fights another." Lowering her lashes, she swallowed. "Anyway, I was left to my own devices for a good while."

"Thus you found yourself kidnapped and forced to marry an American."

She looked out over the waters, now reflecting the deep purples and pinks of the sunset. "It's been an adventure, that's for certain."

"It could cost you your life, yet. Going on that ship without escort was foolhardy in the extreme."

"I needn't a lecture," she said, standing, "from you or anyone else."

He stood as well, his expression darkening. "Listen well, Constance. Until your father comes, I am responsible for you. Therefore, you will curb your rebellious behavior. One act of foolishness here could result in your death."

She bristled. "And what would you care? Seems it would make your life a great deal easier if I weren't around."

"It would reflect badly of my character if you did something dull-witted."

His character? She snatched up the bowls. "Well, we can't have that now, can we?"

She started to leave. He grabbed her arm. "Do not ever walk away from me in the midst of a discussion, Constance."

They stood nose to nose, cocooned in the aroma of his tobacco. She hugged the bowls to her. "And if I do?"

"Try me."

A burning devil take him. "Why are you so angry all of a sudden? Is it because you've just realized I am who I say I am?"

"You've had an entire ship's voyage to concoct whatever stories you wished."

"I couldn't possibly have made all that up and you know it. That's the whole reason you questioned me."

He stood quietly, his eyes searching hers. At long last, he spoke. "The fact of the matter is, I think I do believe you. It's the only thing that makes sense."

"Do you, Drew? Do you really believe me?"

He loosened his hold on her arm and rubbed it slightly where he'd squeezed it. "Yes, Constance, I do. If I didn't I think, God help me, I'd have already bedded you."

Her breath caught. The light caress on her arm captured her full attention. She scrambled for something to say. "And my title?"

Releasing her, he tapped her chin and picked up the other dishes. "You are Mistress Drew O'Connor until your father arrives and I can give you into his safekeeping."

Her heart surged. Heaven help her, how could she stand this until spring? "Just send me home on the next ship."

"We've already been through this. Besides, it would be too dangerous. Knowing you, you'd do something dull-witted and then I'd be held responsible."

All tender thoughts fled as exasperation surged to replace them. "*You* take me back, then."

"Don't be ridiculous. I can't leave. You'll have to wait until Josh returns." He glanced up at the dark sky. Gone was the sunset, replaced instead by the iridescence of the moon and stars. He scanned the path ahead of them. "Watch your step. The moon's shadows can be deceiving."

Lifting a corner of her skirt, she nodded, then turned. The night sounds shrouded them as they walked side-by-side to the cottage.

———

In the following week, the household fell into a comfortable pattern. Mary rose before dawn to prepare breakfast while Constance saw to Sally. After the men left for the fields, Constance and Sally did simple chores until Mary shooed them off so she could complete the tasks she deemed necessary.

"Let's go boo-ee picking!" Sally exclaimed one morning, basket in hand.

Constance frowned. "I've not seen any berries around here. Have you, Mary?"

"No, mum. There's sure to be some, though, and I'd be pleased to make you up some flummery."

"Have you been berry picking before, Sally?"

"Yes, with Gamma! I show you." Sally grasped Constance's hand, pulling her from the cottage.

Despite her concern at the twists and turns they took through the forest, they did indeed come across several shrubs covered with very small white berries. Sally picked one, rubbing its waxy coating between her fingers. Constance touched one to her tongue.

Sally seemed to find that quite amusing. "You don't eat bay boo-eez!"

The child began picking even as she spoke, her confidence such that Constance soon found herself reaching for more. She marveled at the abundance of berries, and the two of them filled the basket with a minimal amount of effort.

On their way home, they encountered a huge magnolia tree as wide around as Constance was tall. The ground surrounding it lay barren, for the mighty tree's roots drank up a great deal of the earth's nourishment and its abundance of intertwining branches and leaves kept any sunlight from filtering through.

Setting their basket down, Constance walked around the base of the tree, basking in its majesty. Sally followed, balancing herself on one root before hopping to another.

Constance tipped her head back, experiencing a moment of dizziness as she tried to see all the way to its top. "Imagine, Sally, if this were the paw of some giant creature, its head reaching as high as the heavens, its mouth holding two thousand teeth."

"Then *we'd* be ants."

She looked back at Sally. Intrigued, the two squatted down, searching for the insect in question. "Do you see any?"

Nodding, the child pointed. "Look! Maybe if we tell them we nice and they tell their ant friends, they won't sting us no more."

Constance chuckled, then froze as just a few feet behind Sally she saw a pair of very brown, very big, very bare feet. She slowly stood and placed herself between Sally and what she now saw was a very-bare-all-over boy of about ten or so years. Thank the good Lord he hadn't grown into those feet yet.

He wore not one stitch of clothing and had shaved the entire right side of his head. A crown of spiky black hair ran down the center of his scalp, and straight black hair flowed to his elbow on the left side. He had none of the paint markings on his body that she'd heard so much about, nor did he have the requisite loincloth. Ten years old or not, he was almost as tall as she and the first naked male body she'd ever seen in her life.

Her face burned as she tried to find a place for her eyes to rest. They honed in on a bow and sack of arrows slung over his shoulder. No sooner had she registered this than he laid them on the ground in front of his feet.

Well, at least it didn't appear as if he was going to shoot them, but it didn't look as if he was going to leave anytime soon either.

She heard Sally stir behind her. "Sally," she said with cool authority, "stay right where you are and do not move."

All was silent behind her. She didn't want to risk taking her eyes off of the savage to look at Sally, but a kernel of panic formed at the child's immediate acquiescence. "Sally, take hold of my skirt and give it a tug if you understand me."

She expelled a breath of relief at the answering tug. The boy stepped over his weapon, advancing slowly.

You will curb your rebellious behavior. One act of foolishness here in the colonies could result in your death. Drew's words rang again in her head. The boy was unarmed at the moment, but even so, she wouldn't have much of a chance against those young wiry muscles.

She briefly thought to send Sally racing but didn't know what the boy's reaction would be, nor did she know how many others were at this very moment hidden amidst the forestry watching. That, more than anything else, kept her immobile.

The boy's face held no expression. No signs of anger, friendship, curiosity, ill will. Nothing.

He stood before her now, a mere inch or two shorter than she. He reached up and she jumped. A flicker of disapproval ran across his face.

She had to calm down. She would wait until she had an inkling of his intentions, then go from there. Meanwhile, she'd do well to use her age to whatever advantage she could. She lifted her chin a mite and cocked an eyebrow.

He pushed in her cheek with one callused finger, then continued with his poking on her nose and chin. She decided to poke his cheek, nose, and chin. She'd gotten in no more than one poke when he jerked his head back and swatted her hand, his shock evident.

She widened her shoulders, stood to her full height, and gave him her best glare, right down her nose. He seemed amused at that but disliked it mightily when she swatted *his* hand away.

After verbalizing what she assumed was a command, he tugged loose the strings of her cap. Saints that be, she trusted poking each other's faces was not some kind of mating ritual. No, she must get a hold of herself. He was but ten years. She hoped.

"Sally, if I tell you to run, then you run as fast as your feet can carry you to . . ." Where to send her? Supposing other savages were at the cottage or were on their way? "Do you know where your brother and the men work, Sally?"

"Yes, Sissy."

Her seriousness surprised Constance, but she didn't take time to question her good fortune. "That's very good. Then, if I tell you to run, you are to fly to Drew and tell him an Indian is with me and Mary might be in trouble. Tug my skirt if you understand."

She felt the answering tug. The savage had now pulled the cap from her head. There was no masking his astonishment. He tentatively touched her hair as if it might burn him. Then he spoke to her in an unintelligible tongue while gesturing toward her hair. It was clear he wanted it down.

Drew's litany returned with vigor. *You will curb your rebellious behavior.*

Perhaps cooperation might indeed be the wisest course. She loosened the coiled braid at the back of her head, pulling the plait to rest across her shoulder. The boy sucked in his breath, lifted the end of her braid, and led her like an animal to his sack of arrows.

Tales the English traders recounted of scalps that hung on lines stretching between two trees assailed her. When the Indian removed one of his arrows, Constance filled her lungs. "Run, Sally, run! *Now!*"

She heard the child scrambling away. The boy jerked Constance's braid, a string of gibberish coming from his mouth. The language might have been foreign to her, but the tone and scowl on his face were universal. Tears sprung to her eyes at the force of his jerk. His gaze shot to Sally before returning to her and voicing his displeasure again.

When he took to shaking his arrow in her face much like a mother scolding a child, a surge of anger spurted through her. With Sally gone, it was between the savage and herself. If he thought for one minute she'd meekly let some naked whelp have her scalp or anything else, he was in for a surprise. With a strength borne from fear and backed up with prayer, she shoved the young warrior right off his feet. Unfortunately, he still had hold of her braid. She went right down with him, gasping from the pain.

He quickly rolled atop her, pinning her arms beneath his knees. She bucked and kicked and squirmed. "Get off me, you poor, base, rascally, cheating, lack-linen toad! You'll not get one lock of hair without a fight, the likes of which you've never seen before. *Now, get thy brown nakedness off me!*"

When she reduced her struggles to catch her breath, she saw that the boy had a huge smile across his face. He said something to her, nodded his head in agreement with himself, and said it again. He then, without a by your leave, lifted her braid, chopped off a good six inches with his arrow, and jumped to his feet.

The shock of it held her immobile for no more than ten seconds before she was on her feet, running after him. He'd already grabbed his bow and arrows and was darting off into the forest.

"Come back here, you cutpurse! Come back here so I can hack off a length of your hair and see how you like it!" The boy was as swift as a rushing river and out of sight before she'd even finished her outburst.

Grabbing the sudden stitch in her side, she stopped and sucked in gulps of air. Thank heavens she'd sent Sally away. Her rich dark hair would have been much more of a prize for him. As her heartbeat slowed, she rubbed her sore head, then lifted her newly shorn braid.

How dare that heathen do such a thing. Never had she taken a pair of scissors to her hair. She might not care for it too terribly much, but it had been with her for nineteen years and she'd not planned on giving it up anytime soon.

Sally is alone in the woods.

The thought whipped through Constance, sending her heartbeat back up to a horrendous speed. Worse yet, Constance had no idea where the tobacco fields were and therefore, no idea which way Sally had headed. Whirling around, she raced toward home. Drew and several of the men met her before she'd even made it a quarter of the way.

"Sally?" she cried.

Scanning the forest around her, Drew slid to a stop. "Sally's fine. They have left?"

Relief poured over Constance before being replaced by fury, the likes of which she didn't even try to suppress. "How should I know? One minute we were relaxing under a magnolia, the next minute some knotty-pated youth was waving an arrow in my face."

Drew had the men fan out to check the area while keeping a few to watch his back.

She lifted up her shortened braid. "Look what that impudent goat did! He whacked off my hair!"

Drew fingered her hair, but held fast her gaze.

"And I thought those savages wore clothes! He had not one stitch on. Why, I understood that even the less important ones wore grass and the like, but this one must have been in the lowest of the classes, for he wore not one single blessed thing. He was naked, Drew. *Naked*. And with Sally right there and he not the least bit concerned about it. What's the matter with these Indians? Haven't they heard they're supposed to cover themselves? Just how backward are these heathens?"

The men returned with no sign of any Indians. Drew sent them back to the fields, all the while fingering her braid. "He was a youth, then?"

"Yes, thank God, but he was a sturdy one. When I shoved him down, you'd have thought that little chest of his was made of armor."

"You shoved him down?!"

"Of course! You think I'd let some runny-nosed youngster scalp me without a fight?"

Cursing under his breath, he quickly surveyed the area again, grabbed her hand, and started jogging home. "We needs must go."

She threw a glance behind her. "Are they after us?"

"I hope not."

She put a hand to her head but didn't slow. "My cap. In the confusion I left it and the basket of berries behind."

"Where?"

"By a big magnolia tree."

"We can't go back now. I'll fetch them later when I can better ascertain the situation. Now hush and concentrate on the path. I want you not to stumble."

They made it home without further incident, but she could plainly see Drew was worried. Mary put a pot of cider on to warm then sifted dirt from some floured corn.

Sighing, Constance lowered herself onto the edge of the bed, allowed Sally to climb into her lap, then watched Drew pace the cottage floor, musket in hand.

His face was creased, his mind far away. She tried to catch his attention, but he was having none of it. If he didn't stop soon, though, she'd become dizzy just from watching.

Pulling her braid across her shoulder, she unraveled it, wincing at the tenderness in her scalp. Sally placed a thumb in her mouth and snuggled against Constance's shoulder. Thank goodness the child was safe. Shaken, maybe, but safe.

Constance combed her fingers through her own hair, swallowing back her tears as she looked at its jagged edges. She could have been killed, so what were a few inches of hair? The tears, however, continued to threaten.

Drew stopped his pacing and stood, watching her closely.

She rubbed a lock between two fingers. "The boy had no hair on one side of his head. Is that some sort of punishment they use to control ill-behaved boys?"

"No. The Powhatan men shave the right side of their heads to keep it from becoming entangled with the bowstring when they're preparing to shoot."

"What of the women?"

"The unmarried girls have the front and sides of their heads shaven but allow the back to grow long. The married women allow all their hair to grow."

"Are they pretty?"

"Beautiful. Of an exquisite and delicate shape. Had they fair skin . . . well."

Constance shifted uneasily on the bed. "Sally wanted to pick bayberries."

He took to pacing again. "You should have found plenty. They're everywhere right now."

"What do you use them for?"

"Candles, soap, that sort of thing."

"Oh. Well, Sally handled herself rather remarkably for a moppet of her age."

He looked at the child, a suggestion of a smile crossing his lips. "You've Grandma to thank for that. She prepared all of us for danger from the moment we learned to talk."

"How? How do you teach a three-year-old such a thing?"

"You'll have to ask Grandma."

He moved to the square hole cut into the cottage's wall, surveying the area outside. "Constance?"

"What is it?" She ceased to breathe. "Do you see something?"

He shook his head. "No, not right now. But I want you to know that having lived here all my life, I speak some of the native tongue. Still, there are various signs the Indians use for those who don't speak." The long barrel of his musket rested against his leg. "When an Indian lays down his weapon, it is an indication of peaceful intentions."

She stiffened. "Whacking off someone's hair is not what I consider peaceful."

He glanced at her, then returned his attention to the clearing. "Compared to losing your life, it is. They don't as a habit, though, chop off braids. I can only hope it's because he'd never seen red hair before."

"It's auburn."

"It's red, and I'm surprised he didn't kill you for shoving him down. The only explanation I can think of was that he was alone and no one witnessed his dishonor.

"We've had 'friendly' relations with the Powhatans for twenty years now, but there are several in our settlement, including me, who lost family members in the Massacre of '22. It will take many more peaceful years before the trust between the savages and the colonists is fully restored."

She stilled. He'd lost someone in the massacre? She pulled Sally closer. Now was most probably not the time to ask. "Are you saying I could have started a war because I didn't willingly give him my hair?"

"If he had killed you, yes."

She sat in shock, thinking of all the lives that could have been affected if the boy had brought another with him or if she'd provoked him beyond what was acceptable. A wave of vulnerability swept through her. "I want to go home. Better I do something dull-witted on a ship than here. That way, I've only my own life to answer for."

Withdrawing from the window, he moved to retrieve his hat from a peg. "You'll not be going anywhere, Constance. Now you know relations are supposed to be friendly . . . unless, of course, they come painted for war or they neglect to lay down their weapons."

"What does it mean when they poke your nose, chin, and cheeks?"

He paused for several moments before a smile tugged at his lips. "I imagine it means he had never seen freckles before."

Freckles. A pox on those wretched things. Then a smile hovered on her lips. No wonder the boy was so appalled when she poked his face. "Where are you going?"

"To get your cap and berries."

"All is well, then?"

From the shelf, he took a small charger filled with gunpowder that was secured to a circle of rope. Slipping it over his head, he opened the door. "I'll soon find out. Bar the door and window and stay inside until I return."

All hints of amusement fell from her face. Swiftly, she moved Sally from her lap and barred the door while Mary barred the window.

CHAPTER | ELEVEN

THE NOON SUN WINKED off the sea of tobacco, reminding Drew of his boyhood. Back then, he'd shared this task with his father while the tobacco plants towered above his and Josh's heads. Now, he stood surrounded by servants and the tobacco barely reached his shoulder.

A gentle breeze ruffled the crop set not in straight neat rows, but planted in what appeared a haphazard fashion, each plant in its own little mound of dirt a few paces apart from the others. The sturdy green plants had been snapped off at the top, allowing the strength of the plant to flow into its long broad leaves.

There was never enough time to weed the entire field, but Drew had gotten a pretty good jump on weeding the little area around each mound, having his men help him finish up last week.

Now, they were searching the massive plants for great horned worms about the size of Drew's little finger. Many a time had he walked these fields pulling grass-green worms off the leaves, snapping them in half, then dropping them onto the ground.

The task required a sharp eye but not a great deal of thought. And therein was the trouble, for his mind kept wandering, recalling Constance as she looked yesterday with her fear masked as indignation. With her arms about his baby sister. With her hair rippling over her shoulders. By Pharaoh, if the color of it wasn't starting to look downright . . . pleasing.

Still, when she actually ran her fingers through that thick, curly mane of hers, he'd been in complete control. Not a single carnal thought had crossed his mind. He nodded. Yes. That was what was important.

Now he needed to focus on suppressing the panic he'd experienced, for he'd been filled with an inordinate amount of it when Sally had half run, half stumbled into the fields out of breath, wide-eyed and crying that Constance was "scare-ed."

He rubbed the back of his neck. It was clear something would happen to Constance. It was only a matter of time. *Bolster my defenses, Lord, so when the worst occurs, I won't be affected.*

He sighed. Affected very much, that is. For the truth of it was, he would indeed be affected. Perhaps it was because he felt it his responsibility to keep her safe for her father. So maybe panic wasn't bad.

Yes. That was it. Panic was acceptable, for her father's sake. Desire was not. And if yesterday was any indication, he'd just about gotten the desire under control.

He'd found no trace of the Indians when he'd gone to find her basket nor had they been to visit—yet. They would, though. And when they did, Lord willing, it would be of a peaceful nature.

"You missed one, Isaac." Drew picked the worm off the tobacco leaf, snapped it in two, and tossed it aside. "The next one you miss, you eat."

"Yes, sir."

Drew smiled as Isaac searched the next plant more carefully. He would eat one before the day was through, just as Drew had eaten more than he could count when his father followed behind him during the worming of the fields.

None of those occasions was pleasant, but swallowing that first one was always the worst. Still, one worm could wipe out a whole section of tobacco within a day. The men must be made to understand the importance of killing every last worm.

The sun beat relentlessly upon them, the moisture in the air encasing them. Drew thrived on it. This was his legacy, and he could always find solace here, where he'd spent the largest amounts of time with those he now missed.

He wiped his brow. To his way of thinking, nothing could compare to laboring over his crop, tending to it with meticulous attention and vigilance while sweat sluiced down his body and the sun burnt into his skin. He inhaled deeply, his chest expanding with pleasure over all that was his. "Isaac?"

Isaac stilled, then turned back to the plant he'd just deemed worm free. Drew lifted a leaf, revealing a green worm about two inches in length clinging to the underside. "You missed one."

Isaac swallowed. "I'll be more careful, sir. Much more careful. Won't happen again."

Drew raised an eyebrow.

Isaac straightened. "Sir, I . . ." He looked at the worm and then back at Drew.

"In the past, I most often swallowed them whole. They're a bit on the crunchy side if you chew them."

Isaac wiped his hand across his mouth. The other men stopped to watch. "You, sir?"

Drew nodded. "My father used to follow me when I wormed the fields."

"They didn't hurt you none?"

"No, it's just a little worm."

Normally, you were a youngster when you ate your first worm. Being the eldest, Drew had had the pleasure of watching Josh eat his first worm. But never had he seen a grown man have to eat one.

Wiping his hand against his leg, Isaac peeled the worm from beneath the broad leaf. His Adam's apple bobbed several times, then he looked again at Drew. "Swallow it whole, you say?"

He shrugged. "I did. Of course, the risk is it might get stuck in your throat. Whichever way you prefer, it makes no difference to me."

"Would you be willing to let me have another chance, sir?"

"That worm could've wiped out a good portion of the field by this time tomorrow. There are no second chances when it comes to worms."

Isaac looked to the others. A couple appeared sympathetic, most displayed fascination. He again looked at the worm lying rather dormant between his fingers.

Drew lifted his hat and repositioned it on his head. He saw no reason to treat a grown man more delicately than he would a little tyke. One's first worm should be a memorable occasion. "I might ought to mention, the first worm I ate didn't stay long in my stomach. Of course, I was but a lad, barely out of wet pants. You, I'm sure, will have no such trouble."

What color there had been in Isaac's face left him. Drew chuckled. "Come, it's just a little worm. Eat it and be done so we can continue our work."

Squeezing his eyes shut, Isaac took a fortifying breath, popped the worm into his mouth, chewed two, maybe three times, and swallowed. A cheer rose up from the men. Drew whacked him on the shoulder. "Well done, man!"

Isaac turned as green as the tobacco.

Drew's smile widened. "Sweet saints, Isaac, don't cast up your accounts in the field. Run yonder if you must."

A great many chuckles followed Isaac as he clapped his hand over his mouth and sprinted to the edge of the field, heaving the moment he reached its edge. Upon his return there was much back slapping and congratulations all the way around.

The worming proceeded, but an air of festivity had taken over, and poor Isaac was the brunt of much ribbing for the rest of the afternoon. Drew smiled, thinking farming was indeed a wonderful occupation.

―――――

The sky rumbled and the air smelled of rain. Mary noted, however, that the men hardly seemed aware of it, so much fun were they having at Isaac's expense. As she served them their evening meal, she peeked over at Isaac, having by now heard in great detail of his initiation into farming. The men had been ruthless in the telling, each having his own slant.

She knew the poor man had never farmed in his life. Indeed, he had been the night watchman back home, shouting, "Past four o'clock of a fine spring morning. Past four o'clock, and all's well," as he made his way through London aside lifeless shuttered houses.

She'd felt a kinship to him, though, for one of the few signs of life displayed at such a time would be on Bread Street, where she and the other bakers of London worked. Their ovens glowing, they would withdraw piping hot loaves, the aroma filling their little bakeries and escaping out into the street. Isaac's cry would always be a bit more buoyant as he neared the end of Bread Street, knowing his duty for the night was almost over.

She'd heard his cry every morning for years, yet they had never met, nor even seen each other.

As fate would have it, though, it was Bread Street that caused Isaac's fall. One of the bakers down a ways from Mary's shop had started to make a habit of slipping a pinch of fresh bread to Isaac as he passed by. On one such morning, the store's owner caught them and had them both arrested. Isaac's sentence was deportment; the other man lost his life.

Such were not the ways here, not with Master Drew. Here, she was able to make an extra bit of bread for Isaac, glad to see he never went wanting again. It was a small thing, really, but it made them both feel they'd somehow cheated the hangman.

"Miss Mary, what's this green stuff in our carrot pudding?"

Chuckles reverberated along with the thunder. Isaac's spoon paused on its way to his mouth, his face still looking a bit sickly.

The infectious mood tugged at her. "I'm not right sure, Thomas. Master Drew brought them to me this noon, he did. Said they would make better farmers of any man who ate them and would I please mix them into the evening meal."

Isaac made a show of digging through his pudding before taking a big mouthful. "It's the best carrot pudding I've ever 'ad in me whole life, Miss Mary. Course, it's the only carrot pudding I've 'ad in me whole life."

More chuckles. "Ho, that'd be the truth of it," Thomas teased. "He'd been spendin' all 'is time eatin' bread, he 'ad!"

Mary shook her head at their nonsense, while the men murmured in agreement.

Constance came out to the yard to check on things, immediately sensing a mood shift, caused by her presence, no doubt. Still, she could do nothing about it. Such was the way of master and servant. She'd never much thought about it before, but never before had she longed to be included. It wasn't to be, though. There were strict rules governing the relationship between master and servant. There always had been and there always would be.

The rain held off throughout the rest of the meal and into the evening's chores. She and Drew didn't linger over their time at the creek, though. The air was heavy and mosquitoes swarmed about. Constance spent almost as much time swatting them off of her as she did cleaning the dishes.

After that first night of Drew's forfeit, never again did she recline against the birch tree. She sat side-by-side with him as his helpmate, and to her surprise, when the week was up, he did not revert back to his old ways. Only after he had helped finish the dishes would he pick up his pipe and relax. It wasn't too long before she looked forward to the quiet walks with him where they shared this task, as well as time alone together.

Ever since her Indian encounter, he had carried his musket with him, and tonight was no exception. She smiled, remembering his blatant efforts last night to calm her lingering unease. He'd managed quite nicely by throwing her an unexpected mathematical challenge.

"Twenty-eight," he had said.

Muddy sand filtered through her fingers as she paused in her scrubbing. "Pardon?"

"Twenty-eight eggs. Seven hens would lay twenty-eight eggs in six days—at the rate you suggested, anyway."

She sat back on her heels. "Yes. You are quite right."

He quirked an eyebrow. "I know."

Suppressing a smile, she returned her attention to her chore.

"I've one for you now," he said.

She glanced at him. "Oh?"

Running his hand across his trencher, he laid it down and picked up another. "Sally and Sissy, four feet apart, walk side-by-side around a circular pond. How far does each walk if the sum of their distances is one mile?"

She bit the inside of her cheek. "Have you a solution already?"

He shook his head. "No. It occurred to me the other day when Sally regaled me with tales of daisy-chain crowns and meals by the pond, but I haven't given it much thought since."

She reached for a noggin. "I'll need to work in some soot. That's an algebraic problem."

"Humph. You need to work in the soot for all your problems."

She smiled. "We'll compare solutions tomorrow."

He winked. "Prepared I will be."

Droplets of rain found their way through the tree's covering, and the wind picked up speed, putting her recollections to a close. There would be no comparing of solutions this eve, not when the skies might open up at any moment. She sighed. She'd come up with an answer to his puzzle and had looked rather forward to lingering here with him.

A huge clap of thunder shook the very ground beneath them. Gathering up the dishes, the two hurried down the path toward the sanctuary of home.

Constance awakened at Drew's prodding. The cottage was still shrouded in darkness. "What is it? Has something happened?" she whispered.

"No. It's simply time for you to learn to milk the goat. I'm tired of doing it for you every morning. Come."

Wonderful. She rubbed her eyes. "I'm not dressed."

"See to it then. I'll meet you outside."

Rising from her pallet, she slipped on a dress and twisted her hair up into a cap. Maybe she would have time to go back to sleep after the milking.

Last night's rain had cooled things off but left a muddy mess to walk in. The mud oozed through her toes as she headed for the goat barn. Rubbing her arms against the chill, she saw Drew had already brought out the animal and stood conversing with it.

One hand held the stool and pail while the other scratched the goat's chin. She watched as he bent his head to its ear, whispering, nuzzling, chuckling. The animal bumped its nose against Drew's face in response.

Ruffling the area between its ears, Drew straightened and turned to find her watching him. Their gazes collided and her heart did something peculiar.

The animal nudged him. Without releasing her from his intense look, he slid his knuckles up and down the goat's jawline, yet it was her own body that did the reacting.

Had he done it a'purpose? No. She didn't think so.

Finally he set down stool and pail, then patted the ugly gray creature. "This is Snowflake."

Constance moved a little closer. She'd seen the goat many a time wandering about the area rummaging for food, but she'd kept well away from it. "Shouldn't we tie her up or something?"

"No. She doesn't mind the milking. Come and sit."

Rubbing her arms again, Constance took her place on the stool. Drew squatted and reached around her, grabbing one of Snowflake's teats. He squeezed and milk squirted into the bucket.

Fascinated, she watched the flexing and giving of the muscles along his arm, the sweep of short dark hairs decorating its surface. She closed her eyes, inhaling the morning's dew and dampness combined with a blend of man and beast.

Dawn touched the sky and, like some mighty conductor, cued a solitary songbird for the morning's prelude. First a tentative chirrup from far away, and then another before it received a lonely trill in response. Next came a warble, and in the moments that followed a melody burst forth, grounded by the steady *pang, pang, pang* of milk hitting the bucket.

The panging stopped. "Now you try."

Constance opened her eyes, allowing her gaze to journey from his rolled-up sleeve to his muscular forearm. Her perusal leisurely progressed to his powerful hand coddling the goat's pink teat. He released it, resting his elbow on his updrawn knee.

Her leg muscles contracted, then she reached out and touched a teat, quickly withdrawing her fingers.

He chuckled. "It won't hurt you."

Wiping her hand on her skirt, she reached forward again, grasped one, and pulled. Snowflake jumped. Constance squealed and the forest quieted for a moment.

"No, no. You roll your fingers down her teat. Like this."

He reached around, magically making the milk flow out. She tried again. Snowflake turned her head and baahed.

"Baah, yourself." She looked to Drew. "This isn't working."

"Watch." He placed an open palm on the teat. "Roll your fingers down. First this finger, then this one and so on. You must set a faster pace, of course, but yanking is not what milks her."

She attempted to copy his actions, but still no milk.

He placed his arm alongside hers, cupping her hand in his, then guided her movements. Her skin leapt to life at every point he touched. It was most unnerving.

The milk hit the pail. "After you squeeze, cup her udder so more milk will flow in."

His chest now lay against her shoulder, his muscled arm still flexed against hers. And in a rush, the thought tumbled upon her. Sweet heaven above, she was falling in love.

CHAPTER | TWELVE

*I*N LOVE? BUT HOW? How could that be? She paused while her breathing grew rapid and her heart pulsed. Then she made herself be completely honest, realizing it wasn't all that hard to believe.

He was, after all, a God-fearing man. He had agreed to her marriage terms, comforted her when she'd needed it, shown her how to survive in a new land, and at long last, he had believed her. He'd accepted she was Lady Constance Caroline Morrow, daughter to the Right Honorable the Earl of Greyhame. He'd accepted it because she had told him so. He also dallied in mathematical challenges.

Add that to a beautifully made body and a breathtaking face, and you have one lost battle before it ever began. She swallowed. The question now was what to do.

"Constance? Go ahead, you try."

She took a deep breath, throwing back her head. "Look at the sunrise, Drew. It's exquisite."

He glanced up at the sky. "It's exquisite every morning. If you'd like to watch the sunrise, I'll wake you early tomorrow. Right now, we need to milk the goat."

She gave him a sweet smile and turned back to Snowflake. Cupping the udder, she rolled her fingers down the teat, ejecting a squirt of milk. She caught her breath and turned to him with delight. "I did it!"

He gave the slightest of nods. "Very good. Now continue with that over and over until the pail is filled."

Turning back to the milking, she tried again. Her expression fell. None was forthcoming. She tried several more times.

"You're squeezing too hard. Remember to let the milk flow in after you squeeze."

She tried again.

"No, like this." He placed his hand over hers, his whiskers grazing her cheek. Her insides fluttered.

"Relax your hand, Constance."

She relaxed. He repositioned her fingers.

"Cup the udder. Like this."

The pit of her stomach felt queasy. In truth, she needed to decide what to do about this and right quickly. She cupped the udder.

"Good. Now try to milk her."

He guided her hands. The concert playing through her veins drowned out all other sounds. Did he know? Could he tell? She angled her face to look at him. He was so close. He turned toward her then, which brought their lips near touching. What would he do if she tilted her head and pressed her lips against his?

The goat was forgotten, but their hands remained joined.

"Drew?" she breathed.

He jumped up and back like a sprung spring. The morning song within her slowed. Breathing became a challenge. An emotion just short of horror raced across his face.

He cleared his throat. "If you milk with two hands, it will go more quickly."

She waited a moment, letting him see her desire, before turning her attention back to Snowflake. She covered one hand with the other.

He tunneled his fingers through his hair. "No, Constance. I meant to milk two teats at once."

She moved to another teat. With very slow progress, she managed to extract some milk.

"We usually get a full pail from her each morning."

She nodded and continued with the task at hand.

He hesitated. "Constance, I . . ."

Stilling, she swept up her lashes.

"Nothing." He clamped his mouth shut and strode away.

Snowflake followed him, knocking the pail over on her way. Constance squealed and tried to save what little milk she had. There was only enough to cover the bottom of the pail.

———

The friendly elm held its shady arms over the teacher and her pupil in the yard. Constance leaned against the trunk and smoothed her skirts around her. "You are to keep *both* eyes closed during the prayer."

Sally's brow furrowed. "I just seeing if you eyes closed."

Constance quirked a brow. "Do you remember yesterday's verse?"

She nodded vigorously. " 'J was a Jay, that pwattles and toys. K was a Key, that lock'd up bad boys.' "

Sally's bright eyes shone with pride, and Constance suppressed the urge to gather the child up and laugh with delight. "Your *Bible* verse."

"Oh!" she said, her eyes wide. " 'Listen to me, my child-wen, for blessed are those who keep My way.' Boberb eight, thirty-two."

"Perfect. And the abecedarius?"

Sally jumped to her knees, causing a billow of dirt to rise around her. Squeezing her eyes shut, she chanted the alphabet.

"Oh, Sally, that was excellent. It's pleased I am with you." Picking up the gingerbread slate, she dusted it off and handed it to her. "Remember you what two and two added together make?"

"Foe!"

"Exactly." She leaned over Sally's shoulder as the moppet painstakingly wrote out the numeral with a piece of weathered oyster shell. It took up almost the entire slate. "What are one and two?"

"Thwee!"

Constance smoothed a hand down Sally's back. "My, someone I know will be eating a lot of this gingerbread slate if she continues in such an excellent manner."

Beaming, Sally continued with her work.

"What is the meaning of this?" Drew barked from the edge of the clearing.

Constance gasped. Sally hopped to her feet and ran to him. "Sissy learn me! Look!" Holding up her slate, she presented it to him.

He looked at Constance, his eyes conveying his fury. "What on God's green earth do you think you are doing?"

Although the words were not meant for Sally, she could see the child's anguish at his disapproval. "Sally, your verse for tomorrow is Proverb 14:17, 'He who is quick-tempered acts foolishly.' "

Tears welled up in the girl's eyes. "I do my numbers wrong?"

Constance opened her arms. "You did them perfectly. But enough for today. Let us close in prayer."

Sally crawled into Constance's lap, folded her hands, and bowed her head.

"Govern us with Thy grace, O eternal Wisdom, and direct our steps in Thy way. Amen."

"I keep my eyes shut, Sissy."

She brushed Sally's tears. "That's a good girl. Now run along inside and see if Mary is in need of any help." As soon as Sally made it through the door, Constance rounded on Drew. "How dare you! She's been working and working on her lessons, and you've no right to crush her that way."

"I will do much more than that if I ever catch you filling her head with such things again. She is to attend to tasks as belong to women, not meddle in things that are proper for men, whose minds are stronger."

"Stronger, ha! All your brains buttered would not fill two spoonfuls."

He straightened his spine. "You will heed me on this, Constance."

"How can you ask this? She's a bright child, her memory has no bounds, and already she's learned her tables. Her potential is incredible."

He took a step toward her. "I am the master, she is my sister, and I said *no*. That is the end of it."

"She is my sister too."

"Not for long."

She blinked. He was, of course, right. But more and more she'd been toying with the idea of staying. Certainly, life wasn't as easy here as it was in England, but when she was with Drew, easy didn't matter. For every color was deeper, every taste richer, every sacrifice sharper. He might be acting like a woodcock at the moment, yet, still, here with him, she was alive. Really alive. Even her home in England, her uncle, her math didn't compare to what she felt for Drew. She nodded her head. She wasn't toying with the idea at all. She had, in fact, made up her mind. She wanted to stay.

CHAPTER | THIRTEEN

OF COURSE, SHE NEED not give up her math. She could edit the journal from here almost as easily as she could back home.

She didn't think Drew would have any objection either, for he'd originally planned to accept their marriage. She was, after all, the one who'd insisted on the annulment. And if that weren't enough, he desired her. Hadn't he demonstrated such many a time throughout the last several weeks?

Yes. Yes, he had. And for the first time ever, she reciprocated the feeling. She took a deep breath. "No, Sally's not my sister. Not really. But I've been meaning to talk to you about that."

He waited, posture stiff, eyebrows drawn. Perhaps this wasn't the best of times.

Still, she wanted the matter settled. She moistened her lips. "It's obvious you want to take me to wife, Drew. And since I'm already here, we're already wed, and there are no better prospects waiting for me in England, I agree to be your wife in all things. I will, of course, still need to edit *The Ladies' Mathematical Diary*, since Uncle Skelly no longer can."

He said absolutely nothing. Doubts assailed her. Surely he wouldn't refuse her. He wouldn't dare.

"Do you see how schooling has ruined you? Listen to yourself. Think you I will fall at your feet the moment you crook your finger?"

She blinked, momentarily baffled. "What is it? You wish a financial settlement? It's a bit late for that, but I'm sure Papa would concede, and truly, I should have thought of it earlier." She pursed her lips. "You could probably get eight thousand pounds out of him, but I definitely wouldn't settle for less than seven thousand."

"That is as much vain bibble-babble as I've ever heard, and thank you, but no. I've no wish to be yoked to a woman of learning."

She sucked in her breath. Had she imagined those quiet moments that had passed between them? Imagined the desire she'd seen flare in his eyes? Placed more on them than was meant to be simply because she'd wanted to? Oh, sweet heaven above, she hoped not. That would be too humiliating by half. "What are you saying, Drew?"

"I'm saying I want you not as a wife. And even if I did, I certainly wouldn't allow you to participate in mathematical pursuits nor teach Sally anything improper."

Her heart pounding, she clasped her hands together, tried to swallow but couldn't. "I see. Please forgive me. I foolishly thought it was *my* idea to keep the marriage chaste. I was under the impression marriage was not taken lightly in the colonies and when a ceremony is performed, it is meant as a covenant with God until the couple's death." She lifted her chin. "Perhaps you are right. Perhaps I have been thinking entirely too much, for I'd even begun to worry about how our annulment would affect you after my departure, particularly in regard to the council. I had thought perhaps they might still banish you, or at least break an arm or two."

He opened his mouth then slowly closed it.

She took a step back. "No, no. Prithee, say no more. You've made yourself abundantly clear, and I should have known it without us having to undergo such an awkward scene." She blinked her eyes rapidly. "My apologies. I'll not bother you with it again, nor will I teach Sally anything other than religion and womanly type skills." She whirled and rushed into the cottage.

Heaven help him, he'd handled that badly. But what was he to do? He had no idea she'd ever consent to stay. Besides, he'd never had anyone propose to him before. It didn't help any that she'd all but said she would *settle* for him since the only clumberton waiting in the wings was fifty years her senior.

He rubbed his eyes with the palms of his hands. He was stunned she remembered so much of what he'd said to her when they'd frantically negotiated the terms of their marriage. But remember she did, and she had no trouble throwing it back at him.

Then all that diary business. How could she possibly think he'd let his wife involve herself in academics? He'd certainly been in the right there and didn't regret putting a stop to those tutoring sessions either. He sighed. He should never have encouraged her in that area to begin with. Should have, in fact, thrown out that diary back when she first got here. Words his father had taught him echoed within.

> Be to her virtues very kind;
> Be to her faults a little blind;
> Let all her ways be unconfin'd;
> And clap your padlock—on her mind.

Yes. He'd done the right thing by refusing her. But how was he going to walk inside that cottage as if nothing had happened?

He'd taken no more than two steps when he saw them. All were boys, all were naked, and one wore a bit of red braid around his neck. Drew took a deep breath. *"Comoneetop."*

The boys nodded and laid down their weapons. A good sign. That and the fact that they'd come without any fully grown men. Still . . .

"Constance," Drew called. "Bring the mats from inside the cedar chest."

She took forever. When finally she appeared with them, she went no further than the door, looking quickly to Drew, concern etched on her face.

"It's all right. Give me those, and we'll also need my pipe."

She glanced between him and the Indians, worrying her lip. "Where are your men?"

"In the fields. I came back early because a ship has come with cloth and other goods. Now go on. As of yet, there's nothing to fear, and I'm still in need of my pipe. Get the churchwarden."

Laying out the mats, he motioned for the boys to join him. They had just settled in a circle when Constance, her eyes trained on Drew, returned with his churchwarden pipe.

He sighed. "It might help if it was lit."

She blinked. "I've never done such a thing in my life. I know not how."

He pierced her with his gaze. This gathering was of extreme importance, and the last thing he needed to deal with in front of these visitors was an unsubmissive female. "I'm sure you can figure it out since you are so very brilliant. Do it and do it now."

Nodding, she whirled around, then froze. *"My hair!"*

Drew jumped to his feet, unsure of her intentions. The boys responded in kind.

"He's wearing my hair."

"Ignore it and go light the pipe. Quickly."

She narrowed her eyes, pinning the youth with her displeasure. "I like it not."

The boy grinned and made a short statement to his friends. They all nodded in agreement, repeating what he said, as if to try it out on their tongues.

"What did he say?" she asked, tension radiating from her stance.

"He's given you a name."

"What is it?"

"I'll not tell you."

How she managed to make her back any straighter he couldn't imagine, but she did and the boys noticed it as well.

"What did he call me?"

Drew hesitated. "He said you will from this day forth be known as Red Spotted Wildcat."

He barely wrapped a restraining arm around her waist before she lunged. With a look of apology to his guests, he wrested the pipe from her hand, shifted her in his hold, slung her over his shoulder and took her into the cottage.

———

She was going to kill them both. First she'd do away with Drew, and then she'd deal with the Indian. She continued to struggle, but Drew held fast. There apparently would be no relief from this ignominious position until he was good and ready. And it appeared he wouldn't be ready until he carried her like so much baggage up to the loft and out of Mary and Sally's sight. That was just as well. What she had in store for him would not be appropriate for Sally's tender ears.

They were nearing the top of the ladder now, yet she continued with her struggle. He cursed and she gasped when his ascent faltered, but he managed to stay on.

At the top, he none too gently flung her onto the ticking. The force of the landing knocked the very breath from her and a wave of dizziness assailed her.

"In truth, Constance, you are pushing me beyond what any man should be expected to endure. Those may be youth out there, but do not fool yourself into thinking they are harmless. Their skills as warriors are not honed to perfection as of yet, but it's warriors they are, if a bit rough around the edges. Before you come racing back outside waving a broomstick above your head, you might, for once, consider the consequences. Is a useless lock of hair or a title you consider unacceptable worth your life, my life, Sally's life, and the lives of countless others?"

She raised a hand to her spinning head, keeping her eyes closed.

"Did you hear anything I said?"

"Every word."

"And?"

She considered his words. "I will not attack your *friends*, but neither will I play hostess to them. Go light your own pipe."

There was a moment of silence. The dizziness passed and she risked opening her eyes. He knelt on one knee, hovering above her. Close above her. She clamped her jaw against the direction of her thoughts. Had he not humiliated her, rejected her, tormented her? Oh, she wanted not to deal with this. She just wanted to roll over and escape in sleep. "Go away."

"You will stay in the cottage until they are gone?"

"I will stay right here in this tick."

His breath fanned her cheeks. "Very well. I will come tell you when they've left."

He stood. Rolling to her side, she closed her eyes and curled up into a ball, listening for his retreat. He took a few steps before returning. She felt a coverlet feather across her body and snuggled beneath it. Then he was gone.

———

"She still asleep?" he whispered.

Mary nodded. "Not heard so much as a peep from her."

Propping the bolts of cloth against the wall, he looked up toward the loft. Mary had already seen to the men's supper and had even cleansed the dishes. Constance should have wakened long ago.

Had her seasoning begun, then, so soon? Most of the servants went through a period of sickness where their bodies tried to adjust to this new world, a good percentage of them never making it past their first season here. It was so common, he and his fellow colonists had begun to call it "seasoning." But usually it happened within their first few months, not their first few weeks.

He swallowed. Would she be dead by morning, or would it be a long drawn out process? Thank God they hadn't consummated the marriage. At least there was no babe to worry about.

Placing one foot in front of the other, he forced himself to go up and check on her. The loft was warm and she'd flung off her covers. Her cap lay carelessly to the side of the tick, her mussed hair full about her head. He cleared his throat.

No response.

"Constance?"

Nothing. He frowned and knelt down to touch her forehead. Relief swept through him. No fever. Could it be fatigue and nothing more? He hoped to God that was the case . . . for her father's sake, anyway.

He brushed the hair from her eyes. "Constance? Wake up. You've missed supper."

Slowly, she twisted onto her back, stretching her arms and legs in a feline gesture. He didn't know where to look, or where *not* to look.

Open your eyes, Constance. Open your eyes and remember your anger with me before I forget myself.

Her eyes fluttered open. She smiled at him with an intimate I'm-glad-to-see-you, sleep-induced smile. His breathing became labored.

"God ye good den." The timbre of her voice could have melted butter.

He nodded.

She looked to the open side of the loft. "They've left, then?"

He cleared his throat. "Yes. Long since."

"What did they want?"

"To make peace."

"Just like that? He apologized, then?"

No. "Yes. You're feeling well?"

She propped herself up on her elbows. By trow, he would not look at the tension that caused in the fabric of her bodice.

"You say they've long since left? Why didn't you wake me?"

He shrugged. "I thought you might could use a bit of rest. How are you feeling?"

She sat up, noticed her twisted skirt, and turned a lovely shade of pink while quickly righting it. "I . . . oh, I'm fine. Thank you. You're sure it went all right?"

"With the Indians? Yes. Better than I'd hoped. Seems you made quite an impression. Or your hair did, anyway."

At its mention, she gathered her tresses up and shoved them into her cap.

He stood. "Come and share a trencher with me. It seems we've both missed supper."

Supper? She'd missed supper? Suddenly ravenous, she followed Drew down the ladder. Sally sat in a corner as Mary plaited her hair for the night. Smiling, Constance winked at her. Sally tilted her head and tried desperately to wink back, scrunching up her face in various contortions.

And so it was with a smile that Constance began her meal with Drew. As he made inroads into their food, though, she glanced at the fire and felt a pang of concern. There was no extra. When she looked back down, Drew's spoon was upon the last scoop of carrots.

She slammed her spoon down, stole the carrots from him, and stuffed them into her mouth.

He looked at her in surprise. "Those were mine."

She shook her head and swallowed them. "I had not even had one taste. Those were mine."

He frowned a bit but said no more, turning his attention to the meat. Again, he inhaled it, giving her little chance to do more than chew and swallow one bite to his four.

Looking to the window, she pointed and gasped. As soon as he turned his head, she snatched up the remainder of the meat, stuffing the whole of it into her mouth. He turned back to her, his eyes widening. "Constance! That was the last of the meat."

"I know," she managed around her mouthful.

He reached for the bread. She got to it first, tore it in two, and handed him half. After what could only be called a warning glare, he dipped his bread into the gravy, slopping up a goodly portion of it. She chewed faster but could only watch as the gravy and the greens began to disappear.

Shouldering him back some, she blocked his way and swallowed what was in her mouth so as to partake of some greens.

"Constance, what has gotten into you?"

She ate three spoonfuls before answering. "You do this every single meal. You eat twice as much as I do, leaving me next to nothing."

"I'm twice your size. It's only right I have the most. Now, scoot over and share the greens."

She hovered over the plate. "I'm fair to starving tonight. I'll only eat my share. You may have your half when I'm done. And no more gravy for you either."

"Constance, this is ridiculous. I'm still hungry and I want some greens."

"You'll have some greens, just as soon as I'm finished."

"I'll have some greens *now*."

She hugged the trencher to her, shoveling her share into her mouth. Placing his hands on her waist, he moved her to the opposite end of the bench, wrenched the trencher from her, and placed his back to her while eating what was left of the greens.

A good deal of her hunger had been appeased now, but the gravy was quite tasty and she only wanted her half of it.

She came up behind him and reached over his shoulder to dip her bread into the gravy. He snatched away her bread. She gasped. "Give that back!"

"Not likely. You ate all the meat, most of the greens, and the last bite of carrots. Your meal is over."

"I didn't eat all the meat. I ate only my share and that's *my* half of the bread. Now give over."

Slopping it in the gravy, he took a huge bite. Hunger had nothing to do with it now. She'd been a fairly good sport about her whole predicament. She'd tried her hand at cooking, she'd done her share of cleaning, she'd milked that wretched goat, and she'd even planned to face down Mr. Meanie alone. To top it off, she'd offered to stay and had that offer thrown back in her face. The very least he could do was let her have her portion of the meals.

She yanked at his arm with no success and then reevaluated her position. In order to eat that bread, he'd have to bring it to his mouth. And when he did, she'd grab it. She ceased to interfere yet stayed behind him, waiting to strike. And strike she did, but he anticipated her and blocked her move with his shoulders.

In desperation, she grabbed his elbows and jerked back, keeping the bread from reaching his mouth.

How they ended up wrestling on the floor, she wasn't quite sure. But there was really no contest. He not only had her pinned, but he still held the roll out far beyond her reach.

He didn't even attempt to hide his amusement. "No more naps for you. I think I prefer to share my trencher with you when you're a bit more tired."

She squirmed and writhed beneath him in an effort to get away. Then, wonder of wonders, that smug expression on his face transformed into what could only be tagged desire.

So she hadn't imagined it, after all? No, if the quickening of his breath and the tensing of his body were any indication, the man definitely desired her, but that yearning would go unrequited because she was educated and therefore unacceptable. Well, since he'd been so absolute in the making of his bed, she'd ensure the lying in it would be uncomfortable in the extreme for him.

Ever so slowly, she skimmed her nails up the length of his torso until her palms rested against his chest. "I'm still hungry, Drew," she whispered.

His gaze fell to her lips. She moistened them. He jumped to his feet, tossed her the bread, and made a hasty retreat from the cottage.

She closed her eyes, praying for God to grant her wisdom. It was then Sally jumped on her.

"Sissy, you're lots more fun than Gamma!"

Good heavens. She'd forgotten all about Sally and Mary. Opening her eyes, she sat up and put a calming arm around the child. Mary had made herself right busy at the fireplace.

Sighing, she kissed Sally's head. "To bed with you, my girl. I'll be up in a moment to tuck you in."

Constance watched her make her way up the ladder before standing. That entire episode had done much for her self-esteem, and she now had no need to cover her head in shame at her attempt to set their marriage aright. Certainly she was annoyed with him, but at least she hadn't imagined an attraction that wasn't there.

Moving to the table, she mopped up the last of the gravy, slowly chewed her bread, and hoped to heaven her *own* bed wouldn't be too uncomfortable.

CHAPTER | FOURTEEN

DREW HURLED THE BROKEN treenail across the yard. He should have finished making this cursed chair hours ago and yet here he sat, still trying to drive wooden pins through the last two joints. Now he only had one treenail left. If he broke this one, he'd be making *two* more.

He picked up the gimlet and checked the hole he'd bored through the joints. It was all her fault. Thanks to her, he needed a chair, for he would not share one more trencher with that shrew. Not after last night.

He sighed. He'd been doing so well, had almost conquered his traitorous thoughts. Setting down the gimlet, he worked the treenail into the hole.

If he didn't know better, he'd think she was doing it a'purpose. *I'm still hungry, Drew.*

Hungry? What folly. She was foxing him, trying to lead him astray. Well, no more. No more would he leave this to chance. He was going to remove every last opportunity she might have for such mischief, beginning with the sharing of trenchers.

Picking up the hammer, he gently drove the treenail the rest of the way through. Many a master in the colony had a chair, and now he would as well. He would sit at the head of his board in his own chair, eating out of his own trencher. If it meant she had more to wash, then so be it.

And that was another thing. No more would he carry her dishes to the creek and help her clean them like some smitten half-wit. No, the tobacco looked ready to chop and cure. He'd have plenty to keep him busy there, and he'd also have Thomas and Samuel begin the brickmaking. It was time to get started on the house.

The treenail went through, thank God. Picking up a small block of timber, he began the arduous procedure of carving one more wooden pin. At least he hoped it was just one more.

———

She chewed. The fish held no taste for her, and swallowing became more and more difficult. There was plenty of it, though. Her trencher was fair to brimming with food. She sighed, forced another swallow, and took another bite.

When he'd brought in his chair she'd been quite impressed. He'd made the thing within a day's time, and it was beautiful. It might not have all the spindles, cushions, and elaborate carvings as those back home, but it was handsome just the same. He'd come in without a word, set his thronelike chair against the wall, and turned and left. Sally had been mesmerized, touching it, crawling beneath it, and finally asking if she might sit in it "real quick."

Constance hadn't been much better. She'd stroked it too, surprised to find it so smooth. A simple carving of several large broad leaves fanned across the upper back and along the arms. She traced the leaves with her fingers, knowing his had been there first.

Never did it occur to her he'd made it so he would no longer have to sit by her. Imagine. Going through all that. The fish threatened to stick in her throat. She took a swallow of cider.

Breaking off another bite, she thought back to how she used to scoff at her friends, thinking them silly and feeble-minded to snivel and cry over what they claimed was a broken heart. She'd never dreamed of expending such emotions on a man.

Yet here she sat, barely able to eat, wishing she had the luxury of succumbing to such sentimentality. She stole a peek at Drew. He didn't seem to have any problem eating his supper. In fact, he seemed to be enjoying his meal with great relish.

It made no sense. She *knew* he desired her as a man desires a woman. She might not have been so sure if she hadn't endured that longing herself. But having experienced the feeling, she could certainly recognize it in him.

Yet he'd refused her. And all because she was educated. She frowned. Then why had he not only encouraged her mathematical games but actually participated in them? She shook her head. Something just wasn't right. She glanced at him again. Perhaps she'd confront him tonight at the creek.

The next bite was a bit easier to swallow. Yes, they were due to compare solutions to his puzzle tonight. Kneeling at the creek side-by-side would be the perfect opportunity to bring the subject up. Perhaps, just perhaps, she ought to tell him of her feelings then as well. What did she have to lose? He'd already rejected her. The worst he could do would be to reject her again, and that was no different from what he was doing now. And there was, of course, the possibility he would change his mind. Hadn't Uncle Skelly always said there was nothing more attractive to a man than a woman in love?

With a sigh of relief, she finished the meal, if not enjoying it exactly, at least no longer choking on it.

Anxious to be alone with him, she wasted no time in dumping the trenchers and cooking utensils into the pots for carrying to the creek. Drew went to the fireplace, as usual, to light his pipe, then walked to his chair. But instead of setting it back against the wall, he placed it in front of the hearth and sat down.

She frowned. "Drew? Are we not going to the creek?"

Stretching his legs in front of him, he blew a stream of smoke into the air. "I think you've grasped the way of it now and no longer need my assistance. You may proceed without me."

A deep gripping pain seized her chest. He couldn't mean that. "I'll be happy to clean them, Drew, but won't you please help carry them for me?"

He stayed silent so long, she feared he might not answer. Surely he wouldn't make her voice the request again. Finally, he folded his hands against his chest and looked down at them. "I think not, Constance."

So soft were his words, she barely heard them. But the effect they had on her could not have been any stronger had he shouted them. Her throat closed, and she barely had time to pick up the pots and exit the cottage before all saw the tears quickly filling her eyes.

Stumbling down the path, she allowed her tears to fall freely. How naïve she'd been to think a second rejection would be no worse than the first. Thankfully she hadn't proclaimed her feelings for him like some pitiful peagoose.

At the edge of the creek, she dropped the pots to the ground, her arms stinging. Sinking to her knees, she blindly reached for the dishes, scrubbing them with vigor one after the other until finally she doubled over and allowed the deep sobs to come forth, racking her body.

———

The embers in the fireplace had dwindled down to a dull glow, and his now cold pipe lay drying against the hearth. Mary and Sally had long since retired, and still she was not back. Anchoring his elbows on his knees, he propped his chin against fisted hands. Where *was* she? Surely it didn't take her this long in the mornings and the afternoons to cleanse the dishes.

Might she be trying to do mathematics in the dirt by the creek? Nay, it was much too dark, yet it was plain she'd been upset and he knew the math somehow soothed her.

He glanced at the chest. The diary was in there. She referred to it often, but he wasn't exactly sure what it was. Certainly, he'd flipped through it that first night she'd arrived, but he hadn't given it much thought since. Of a sudden, he could think of nothing else. Well, almost nothing else.

He leaned his head into his hands. She'd said she wanted to edit it because her uncle couldn't. It needed editing? He looked again at the chest. Oh, fie for shame. Standing, he strode to it and threw it open. There the pamphlet lay. Right on top. If it hadn't been so easily accessible, he might have talked himself out of digging through the chest in the dark. As it was, he saw its outline, clearly delineated in the shadows.

Picking it up, he returned to the fireplace, stoked the fire a bit, and sat down on the hearth. The compact volume of some twenty leaves lay squarely in his palm, just the size to tuck away in a lady's reticule. *The Ladies' Mathematical Diary* blazed across the cover in fancy gold letters beneath which was written *A Woman's Almanac Adapted for the Use and Diversion of the Fair-Sex*. Opening it, he took a much longer look at the booklet.

It appeared to be an annual publication, initially giving solutions to last year's puzzles, each answer accredited to a woman. He rolled his eyes as he noted one answer set to verse.

> When EIGHT fair shepherdesses to your view,
> Were altogether met beholding you,
> Who came to see their harmless flocks of sheep,
> Which daily they did on the common keep;
> The number just ONE HUNDRED, TWENTY-EIGHT,
> On which they did so diligently wait.
> Which numbers both do very well agree:
> The question's solved as you may plainly see.

The second half of the journal had about fifteen questions, all equally absurd. Still, he found himself wondering which was greater—three solid inches or three inches solid.

The last leaf posted the residence of one Skelly Torrence Morrow, to whom subscribers could send their solutions. The first women to submit correct answers would have their names published in next year's almanac.

He looked through it one more time and almost passed over the preface again before Morrow's signature at the bottom caught his attention. It was a lengthy address stating the English lady mathematician was of high distinction both at home and abroad. Further down, he encouraged the fair sex to attempt mathematics and philosophical knowledge once they saw here that their sex had "as clear judgments, as sprightly quick wit, as penetrating genius and as discerning and sagacious facilities as their male counterparts."

What a great bunch of tripe. Nevertheless, Drew found himself finishing Morrow's discourse, wherein the man admitted to having seen women cipher and was fully convinced the works in the diary were solved by members of the fair sex. He concluded by relating "all should glory in this as the learned men of his nation and foreign nations would be amazed were he to show them no less than four or five hundred letters from so many several women with solutions geometrical, arithmetical, algebraical, astronomical and philosophical."

Four or five hundred? The man was daft. Drew drug a hand down his face. *This* was Constance's uncle? The man she held in such high esteem? The man whose footsteps she wanted to follow? No wonder her head was so cluttered.

A distant clank of a pot signaled her approach. He bolted to the chest, tossed the book inside, and made it to the bed just before she entered.

He watched her from beneath half-closed lids, then held himself still when she stopped mere feet away, staring at him. He couldn't see her face, but when she finally moved to put the dishes away, her steps were heavy, her shoulders slumped. He closed his eyes against her, convincing himself she was tired. After she settled onto her pallet on the other side of the room, a great deal of his tension eased. He was glad she'd made it home, tired or otherwise.

CHAPTER | FIFTEEN

THE DAYS GREW SHORTER, the nights grew cooler, and Constance grew lonelier. The magnificent reds, oranges, and yellows of October had come and gone, yet she hadn't reveled in their glory, nor did she take any particular notice to the suggestion of winter just around the corner. She merely went about her duties, performing no more and no less than what was expected of her. Even Mr. Meanie ceased to draw her out.

The morning after *the rejection*, as she secretly referred to it, she had marched into the chicken coop, strode directly to Mr. Meanie, and said, "Do your worst."

The contemptible creature did nothing, so she sang, adding a jump and a jig to each verse for good measure.

Here's to the man with a heart made of coal;
Now to him who refuses to marry;
Here's to the husband who hasn't a soul,
And now to the man that is hairy:

Let the toast pass,
Break the long fast
I'll warrant he'll prove an excuse for the glass.

Mr. Meanie charged. With a swipe of her hand, she snagged his legs and held him upside down, giving him the biggest dressing-down of his life. Since then, Mr. Meanie had kept his distance.

Drew had kept his distance as well. In the past four months, he and the men had cut all the tobacco, impaling their stalks onto slender sticks that they hung head down across beams in the ventilated tobacco barns to wilt and cure.

Her shoulders slumped. Those months had certainly taken their toll on the indentured men. Seven had been struck infirm; two did not survive. Still, time marched forward, and the surviving servants carried on.

The curing would last through winter, allowing most Virginia farmers to have a few months' rest. Not so on the O'Connor farm. The men worked from dawn to dusk on the big house, Drew at their side. He would leave before Constance awoke, only to return well after she'd retired.

In the beginning, she had visited the construction sight. Still not wanting to believe *the rejection* was final, she'd bounded up the mighty hill that overlooked the shimmering bay Fiddler's Creek fed into. The men had labored with shovels, carving out a massive cellar near the peak of the slope, their silhouettes sharp against a cloudless blue heaven.

But the higher she'd climbed and the closer she'd gotten, it was Drew her focus had honed in on as he stuck the blade into the ground, stomping on it with his boot. Shoulders, arms, and legs bulged and rippled while he loosened the dirt, bent over, grasped the shovel low, and slung the dirt to the side before repeating the ritual in its entirety.

How differently men moved than women. Smooth, fluid, and graceful, yet one hundred percent male. She'd come to a dead stop simply to feast on the sight before she'd realized what she'd done and pressed forward.

At first, she had offered suggestions concerning the length, breadth, and area of the house, the distance between its posts, and even the location of the house so one could walk the shortest distance possible from the house to the creek to the barn.

But Drew managed to find fault with every suggestion she'd made, openly hostile with his rebukes. Stung, she'd eventually not only quit making them, but quit going to the hill altogether.

If he didn't want to know where the hand stick must be placed so that the end of the wooden beam and the men at the ends of the stick carried equal weights, then so be it. If he didn't want to know what angle the ridge and what height the side walls must be so that the wind blowing from either of those quarters would have the least effect on the building, then so be it. It was of no matter to her.

Knotting her thread, she bit the end off and shook out the final pair of winter breeches she was fashioning for the men.

"Can we go now?" Sally asked.

Before responding, Constance placed the sewing implements in a small mahogany box, then hung the breeches on a peg. Her headache had returned this morn and what she'd really like was to rest here in the cottage. But she'd been promising Sally this outdoor meal for some time now, and the little thing's expression was too much to resist. "I suppose so."

Clapping, Sally skipped to the covered lunch basket while Constance fetched a cloth. "We won't be long, Mary."

Sally swept out the door, then turned to look at Constance while walking backward. "Let's go to the meadow and do chain daisies!"

"Oh, dearling, the daisies are all gone now. They only like warm weather."

"But it is warm!"

Constance caught up to her and took the basket. "I know, but it hasn't been. I fear the daisies wouldn't be there."

"Can we go see?"

A suggestion of pain stirred in Constance's lower stomach. Touching it, she sighed. It had been at least three weeks since she'd had these nagging head and stomach irritants. She'd thought she was over them. Well, maybe they would pass quickly this time.

"Can we?"

"What? Oh, no, Sally. It's simply too far. There's a nice spot a little ways up, though."

Sally's expression turned sullen, and she hoped the child wouldn't be in one of her tempers. She just didn't feel like coaxing her into a better mood.

They walked the rest of the way in silence, Sally kicking the dirt, Constance ignoring her spurt of assertiveness. Once there, she spread out the cloth under a big oak tree and made a concerted effort to be more cheerful and entertaining throughout the meal. Sally was having none of it.

"Can we go to the meadow after sweets?"

"No, Sally. We cannot. Oh, look! Mary's packed us some apple butter biscuits. Here."

Sally crossed her arms and furrowed her brows. "I don't want any."

Constance replaced the biscuit in the basket. "Let us away, then. I fear my head is spinning and you seem to be finished."

Sally huffed. "Oh, I'll eat one."

This last spell of dizziness sent a wave of nausea through her. "No, you may have it when we arrive home, but truly, I needs must return."

The child jumped to her feet, her eyes filling with tears. "That's untruth. You just not want to. You never go where I want. Never do what I want. Only we sew, sew, sew. Why don't you like me!"

Oh, dear Lord, please help. "Sally, come. I adore you and I'm sorry. I'm simply not feeling well."

She was sobbing now. "I only want go to the meadow."

Constance opened her arms and Sally crawled into them. The child had become restless and moody with the onset of winter. She had an active mind that needed to be engaged.

Constance sighed, then tightened her lips. A pox on Drew for refusing Sally her academic pursuits. She would have to confront him again, even if she had to go to the big house to do it.

Leaning back against the oak, she cradled Sally and closed her eyes. Sweet, sweet Sally. She must pay more attention to her, do more. Share more.

When she next opened her eyes, it took her a moment to place where she was. A brisk wind carrying the smell of rain whistled through her skirts, emphasizing the sudden drop in temperature. Tucking several stray tendrils under her cap, she glanced around. "Sally?"

No answer. Surveying the sky, she frowned. Dark clouds had moved in, and she could make no sense of the time. How long had she slept? "Sally?"

Quickly throwing the leftovers into the basket, she stood and shook out the linen, allowing the cloth to whip in the wind's flurry. "Come, Sally. We need to head back."

Still no response. An inkling of concern flittered through her. Securing the folded spread with the basket, she searched the area.

Sally answered none of her beckonings. Might she still be angry, even now hiding somewhere close but refusing to come forth? "Sally, come here this instant."

Nothing. Constance's frustration climbed. "Sally! There is danger for you unless you are with me. Now stop this silly game and come."

Light seared the sky just before a deafening crash of thunder reverberated through the forest. That should have brought the child scurrying. It did not. She frowned. Sally must have walked all the way home by herself. Still, Constance cupped her mouth with both hands and called again.

Her eyes narrowed. She had no doubt Sally knew her way home. The child could navigate the forest much as Constance could find her way about London. Well, she would not do so again. It would be to bed without supper for Sally this night.

Snatching up the basket and cloth, she hurried home, her irritation growing with each step. The first few drops of rain fell as she entered the cottage.

Mary, hands dusted in flour, looked up from pounding her dough. "Well, I was a'wondering about you."

Constance shook her head. "We drowsed a bit, me longer than Sally, though. Where is she?"

Mary paused. "What mean you?"

Constance set the basket down and glanced up at the loft. "Sally. Where is she?"

"She's not with you?"

Constance floundered. "She's not come back?"

"No, mum." Straightening, Mary wiped her hands on her apron. "I've not seen her since you left this morn."

Her throat tightened. "What time is it?"

"Why, the close of day will not be too long in coming now."

Constance shinnied up the ladder. "You're sure? You've not seen her at all? She's not in the tick?"

"No, mum. Should I check outside?"

Constance nodded, and the two of them searched the goat barn, the elm tree Sally liked to climb, the perimeter of the clearing, and then the cottage one more time. The ever-increasing shower tattooed the thatch roof, each rap heightening her anxiety. "Where's the bell?"

"The master took it a few days ago, he did. The clacker fell off."

Constance grabbed her shawl. "Stay here in case she comes, Mary. I'm going for Drew."

———

"Thomas! Get those braces up here, else all our hard work will be laying at our feet come storm's end!"

"We're here, sir!"

Drew motioned him and two of the others through the house's skeleton as they barreled down the hall with all the spare lumber they could find. They'd just finished sheathing the second story but as yet had no roof nor chimney. Without the proper braces, a forceful wind could blow the whole house down. As it was, this sudden wind caused the exterior to whine and skirl.

With a rhythm established from months of working together, Drew and Thomas secured a length of timber at forty-five degrees across one wall while the other two men did the same to a second wall. Not for the first time did Drew feel frustrated with his father's sketch, which called for a huge house shaped like a cross. Now, instead of a mere four walls to brace, he had twelve.

Rain slid in rivulets from his hat's brim as he quickly checked the sturdiness of the brace, satisfied with its placement. "I'm going to see what's taking the men outside so long."

Thomas nodded before moving to help the others.

Hurtling down the stairs, Drew rushed out the front door's frame, then jumped out of the way as another crew forged inside with more bracing lumber.

A sheet of wind and rain struck him, knocking him a bit askew before he hunched over against its force. Body O'Caesar, but it was cold. He hurried around the house's perimeter, his boots sinking into the soggy ground as the water covered a good two inches of shoe with each footfall. They'd gotten more rain than usual throughout the season, so the ground had little use for this dousing and wasn't absorbing like it should.

No sooner had he spurred the remaining men on than he noticed the rain rapidly draining into the trench around the basement walls. He hurried toward it, surprised at the amount of water already accumulating. A fie upon it. Although the trench was needed to do all the exterior work on that lower level, if it filled up with water and sloughed in, the mud avalanche could collapse the bricked-in cellar and, subsequently, everything built on top of it.

Hastening back inside, he bounded down to the basement, chilled and suddenly fatigued. No water had seeped in yet, but if the rain continued with this kind of ferocity, it wouldn't be long before it did. Standing in the middle of the cool, clammy, soon-to-be kitchen, he pinched the bridge of his nose. There was not enough time to pack full the entire trench, but he had to do something. *Help me, Lord.*

The syncopated drumming of hammers above-stairs provided a bass for the monotonous roar of rain teeming outside the narrow barred windows that lined the top of the room. Moving swiftly from one to the next, Drew put up the shutters. By the time the last was secured, he'd formulated a plan, flimsy though it was.

Taking the stairs two at a time, he nearly collided with Thomas as he reached the first floor. "Collect half the men and help me embank the dig-out and divert the flow of the storm's runoff. Have the others continue to brace the interior."

Barely had they begun their labors when, for a moment, he thought he heard Constance call forth. Jerking his head up, he peered through the deluge but saw nothing. The perpetual downpour had not slackened but continued with its merciless assault, punctuated by ripple after ripple of distant thunder.

He waited a moment more, then wiped his face against his shoulder and returned to his task. Pouring a load of excavated dirt from the wheelbarrow, he began to develop a dike around the trench, then paused. There it was again.

Squinting his eyes, he just made out her advancing silhouette, then jumped to his feet and jogged toward her. What the devil was she doing out in this mess? Well, by trow, whatever it was, she'd have to handle it herself, for he could not leave the house.

It took him but a moment to take in her drenched clothing and the sodden shawl weighing her down. It wasn't until she was within reach, though, that he saw the dismay in her eyes. "What?"

"Sally," she gasped.

He could see her struggle to breathe, pulling vast amounts of air into her lungs. Saints above, had she *run* the entire way? "What? What of Sally?"

"She's gone."

Gone? *Oh, dear God.* Grabbing her arm, he jerked her erect. "What do you mean, gone?"

"I mean *gone.* We were having our midday meal out-of-doors, and I must have fallen into a light slumber. When I awoke, she was gone. I assumed she went home without me, but when I arrived home, she wasn't there. She wasn't there, Drew! Have you seen her?"

All too quickly, the flash of alarm he'd experienced turned to anger. He shook her hard. "By my life, Constance. *Gone* means *dead*. Never say to me she's gone. Do you hear me? Never!"

Tears filled her eyes. "Drew, you're hurting me. Stop."

He immediately released her, only to then catch her elbow, steadying her. Panic once again took hold as her words made their full impact. "You're sure she's not at the cottage? Never before has she run off."

Constance swiped at her eyes. "I know. I know. We had a disagreement. She wanted to go to the meadow. She was tired of—"

"I'll be right back."

Tearing back to the trench, he quickly found Thomas. "Sally's lost. Stay here and have the men do what they can to protect the house. Isaac, Samuel! With me!"

The flight back to the cottage with the two men following and Constance sludging along beside him was but a blur. All he could think was, *not Sally*. God wouldn't be so cruel as to take Sally from him too.

So many little ones. His sister Margaret, only a few months old when their cottage burned during the Massacre of '22. Drew had just turned seven, Josh was six, and Mama had left them in charge while she collected berries. Since Margaret was asleep, they decided to climb the big elm tree and carve their names into its branches with their new knives. It was from that vantage point they saw the Indians suddenly appear, invade their cottage, then set a torch to it. Flames clothed their thatched roof with a fiery cape in a matter of moments.

Josh mimed his desire to take on the Indians and save Margaret, pointing to his new knife. Drew, however, shook his head, some greater power alerting him to the folly of such an action.

The fire raged, its heat suffocating. Thick, swarthy smoke inundated them, parching their throats, stinging their eyes, and making the act of breathing near impossible. The Indians fled, and Drew wasted no time in shinnying down the tree.

The crackling and roaring of the fire blistered his ears, its scorching breath propelling him back, back, back. Josh grasped his hand and Drew turned, his utter helplessness and horror mirrored in Josh's eyes.

Mama told him afterward they were living on land the Indians claimed and the natives had only been trying to take back what was theirs. She also said he'd saved both his and Josh's life, which would have been lost along with the baby's, but never did his guilt lessen. Margaret had burned to death, and she'd been under his care. He should have left Josh up in that tree and gone after Margaret alone.

His mother never blamed him, never scolded him. Still, he'd heard her cry herself to sleep more times than he could count, and he'd watched as Grandma carried much of the load for the months following the massacre.

Five years later, Nellie was born, followed by Alice. Never would he leave their side when he was placed in charge. As a result, he and Josh taught them to fish, shoot, and swim. The girls taught them to prepare a midday meal, chase butterflies, and pick wild flowers.

When Josh was eighteen and the girls were still in pigtails, they all exchanged poignant embraces before Drew boarded a ship bound for Cambridge University.

By trow, but he missed them. The newness of England and the novelty of university life never quite extinguished the dull ache his longing for home evoked. Then he met Leah.

Everything changed. The landscape came alive, the days passed more quickly, and his desire to lay the world at her feet overwhelmed him. By the time his two-year stint was completed, he'd talked her into going to Virginia to be his wife. She agreed only when he promised to give her a few months to adjust to the colony before they spoke their vows.

Upon their arrival, he discovered little Alice had died some six months earlier. He'd never received Father's letter nor the news that he had twin siblings, Sally and Sister.

Still, he'd yet to hear the worst. The week before his ship docked in Jamestown, his beloved mother had been bitten by a snake, right there in the clearing. She'd died in a matter of days.

Leah nursed him through his grief, only to have pneumonia strip her of life three months later, a mere week before they were to wed. That left Grandma, Father, Josh, Nellie, and the twins.

Ah, the twins. So rambunctious were they, the family hadn't been given but a moment to consider their losses. Sally babbled nonstop, while Sister followed her like a shadow, never uttering a sound. Then the inevitable occurred. He lost Father and Sister to burning fevers, and now, Grandma and Nellie to his brother-in-law.

A crack of thunder pealed through the heavens. They'd just made it to the cottage, but with no sign of Sally.

CHAPTER | SIXTEEN

SLIPPING A COILED ROPE over his head and shoulder, Drew perused her sodden clothes, drenched hair, and shivering body. "You're not going."

Constance straightened. "I am going—with or without you. So make up your mind. Do we leave separately to search for Sally or together?"

He sighed. If he let her go, she'd surely catch her death. If he didn't, she'd most likely do precisely what she claimed, and then he'd have two lost females to find.

Whirling around, she grabbed one of his jerkins from the peg. "Enough! I am away. Do as you will."

With that, she slipped the jerkin on and stomped out the door. He slammed his eyes shut, prayed for patience, then nodded to his men. "Let us away."

The wind, rain, and cold blasted him, immediately causing him to withdraw into his deerskin jacket. He hesitated only a moment before following Constance. His jerkin looked ridiculous on her, riding clear down to the backs of her knees, causing her skirt to bunch and billow out at the bottom. The sleeves of the jerkin weren't attached to it, but its heavy leather should at least keep her torso somewhat warm and dry. It was clear she was heading in the direction of the meadow.

He jogged to her, the men close behind. "Are you going this way a'purpose or are you just storming off for the sake of storming?"

She gave him no glance. "Sally wanted to make daisy chains, so I'm checking the meadow first."

"There are no daisies this time of year!"

That earned him a glance, searing though it was.

They trekked through the dark, wet forest, tripping on roots, loose stones, and slippery rocks while the crash and reverberation of thunder brawled above their heads. The trees protected them somewhat from the downpour, but not from the lashing of wet branches writhing in fury. Try as he would, he couldn't shield her from their vicious bombardment. There was nothing to do but forge ahead.

Somehow, he should have made her stay home. He'd just about decided to send her back anyway when they arrived. The meadow stretched before them, its dead browned blades flattened by the torrent hurtling ever downward while surrounded by trees whose tops twisted and whipped in the howling wind. He stopped and scanned the meadow, squinting against the darkness in hopes of finding a trace of Sally huddled in its barren expanse.

Constance did not stop, but waded right into its midst. Cupping her mouth, she called for Sally, the wind swallowing her cries. Her silhouette took on a desperate edge, her attempts to run to every corner of the patch thwarted by the greedy mud sucking her feet into its sticky muck.

Lightning seared the sky. He watched, his chest squeezing his lungs, as she turned 360 degrees, searching, searching, before covering her face and sinking slowly to her knees.

The oppressive rain exploded in his ears and onto his body before he even realized he was plunging toward her, desperate to pull her out of the mire. He grasped her arms, but she shrunk from him, shaking a vehement denial with her head. Falling to his knees before her, he tried again. "Come, Constance! We needs must get beneath shelter, for surely we are testing the fates to boldly sit here just daring the lightning to strike us!"

She raised her head. The desolation and despair he saw in her eyes frightened him with more intensity than he'd ever imagined.

"You were right! You were right, Drew! I never should have been educated. If I hadn't defied convention and Father and everyone else, I'd be home now, safely married. And you would be warm and dry and content in your home. Josh wouldn't be chasing all over a war-infested country, you wouldn't have a wife you never wanted, and Sally—" She choked, closing her eyes, and then forced them back open. "And Sally wouldn't be lost in this godforsaken forest. It's all my fault and I'm . . . so . . . so . . . soooooorry!"

He gathered her against him, not trusting the feelings rioting through his person. *Dear God, let Sally be safe. Let this woman in my arms not be forced to endure any misplaced guilt.*

Then, there in the midst of the storm, the cold, the blistering wind and the turbid muck sloshing against their legs, he experienced a quiet, calming, overwhelming peace. As sure as he knew that rain fell from the sky, he knew that, for now, Sally was all right.

Resting his lips against Constance's sodden hair, he closed his eyes, knowing, yet still not quite able to believe, what else had just been revealed to him. Raising his face to the heavens, he allowed the rain to beat against him. *Surely I can't be . . . in love with Constance? Can I?*

No confirmation nor denial from the omnipotent tranquillity flowing through him, only a suggestion of immense satisfaction.

Drew shook his head. *But she has red hair!*

The thought came to him, *And who do you think* made *that red hair?*

Well, fie. There was no arguing that. Pursing his lips, Drew nodded once. *Your pardon.* A pause. *And Sally? Where is she? Where?*

Nothing. No response. The sound of the rain returned, the cold seeped into his limbs once again.

He opened his eyes, not to find some parting of the heavens or the miraculous cessation of the storm, but to find something even better—Constance's warrior friend, standing not ten feet away and gesturing to him. Drew smiled.

Bracketing Constance's head with his hands, he tipped her face up toward him. "Ah, little Lady of the Realm, don't lose all your pluck now, just when I'm needing it the most. Come. I think I might know how to find Sally." Hooking her hair behind her ears, he lowered his mouth to hers, kissing her with the urgency of a man who loves his woman but has not the time to express it.

Clearly, Drew had gone mad. There was no other explanation. Why else would he be kissing her without so much as a by-your-leave in the middle of a rain-drenched field while Sally's very life was in danger?

She shoved him hard. He fell with a very satisfying splat onto his backside in the filthy water. She started to rise, only to have Isaac and Samuel appear at her side to offer her a hand. Accepting their help, she hauled herself out of the muck, whirled around and then she saw him. That awful, lily-livered Indian boy. He was clothed this time, in deference to the weather, she assumed. Still, she refused to look at the lock of auburn hair dangling from his neck, but it was there in her peripheral vision and it incensed her. "Sorry to disappoint you, Little Chief, but I'm rather busy right now and don't have time for any hair-cutting ceremonies at the moment. Perhaps another time?"

Picking her sodden skirts out of the mud and with every intention of walking in the other direction, a hand at her waist stopped her. "He knows where Sally is."

She spun around to look into Drew's eyes. "Where?"

"He didn't say where, only that she was all right."

The warrior turned and disappeared into the thicket. Drew grabbed her hand, and the group scrambled to follow. The young Indian made no concessions for her graceless and less than proficient attempts to keep up. She glanced at Drew, but he didn't seem annoyed. Neither, though, did he attempt to slow his pace as he dragged her in his wake. Stubbing her toe again, her cry escaped before she was able to stop it, a wave of dizziness sweeping over her.

"Here, Isaac. Take Constance and follow as best you can. If you can't keep up, return home. Know you the way?"

"Yes, sir."

She felt Drew's release of her hand and Isaac's subsequent support beneath her elbow. "Wish you to return, Mistress?"

Shaking off the vestiges of her dizziness by sheer force of will, she tightened her resolve. "Not until we find her. Make haste! We're losing sight of them."

They continued on for what seemed hours when the sound of the rain changed. No longer was it pelting only the earth, but a source of water as well. A river? An extension of Fiddler's Creek? The ocean?

She inhaled but could smell no salt, and then they were upon it. A roaring, rocky, muddy stream tumbling toward some distant goal in a swell of rapids.

She could see where an assortment of large rocks provided a stepping-stone bridge of sorts when the stream was not high. And there, crouched in the middle of it, on a rock surrounded by a surging and billowing maelstrom, was Sally.

"I thought that wretched Indian said she was all right!" Constance screamed. "What's the matter with him, leaving her in the middle of all this? She might have fallen in and drowned before we ever got here!"

But the Indian was nowhere to be seen, and Drew was hurriedly wrapping his rope around a tree. The other end was already tied in a noose-like fashion.

"Hold on, Sally! We're coming!" she cried.

Sally looked up and her rock wavered. Squeezing her eyes shut, Sally groped for the edge of the rock just as a wave broke against it, cascading over her. She began to slip, and Constance threw a frantic look at Drew, noting he was now securing the knot.

Sally regained her balance, but the stream was vicious and if Drew's large body disturbed the precarious hold the soil had on Sally's rock, they might lose her still.

Constance eyed the location of Sally's rock, guessed at the velocity of the river, took into consideration her own weight and quickly calculated at what approximate point she needs must enter the water. Throwing off the jerkin, she grabbed the free end of the rope, slipped it around her waist, and plunged in several yards upriver.

"No, Connie! No! Oh, God, no!"

The icy water stole the very breath from her. She kicked, gasping while the current wrapped around her skirts, tangling her legs and sweeping her at a frightening pace toward the jagged stepping-stones. Regaining her breath, she kicked again with all her strength, paddling her arms toward Sally.

Help us, Lord. Help us.

Her feet skimmed the bottom and, though the pull of the water remained strong, Constance managed to forge bit by bit toward Sally, but the angle was wrong.

She hadn't counted on that initial depth of the water. She'd assumed she'd be able to retain a standing position throughout her flight. If she didn't correct her course, she'd miss Sally altogether.

The rock tipped once again. Sally held tight to the rock's edge, but her body had lost its traction. She now lay stretched out against the rock, hanging on only by her fingertips.

She was three. She was cold. She was exhausted. There was no way she could hold up her own weight.

From the corner of her eye, Constance saw Drew splash in downstream, probably in hopes of catching Sally if she tumbled into the water.

Whether it was strength borne from horror or God's own hand pushing her to their goal, Constance didn't question, but the next moment she was at Sally's side, wrapping her arms around the child's waist and digging her feet into the tumultuous soil. "Let go, sweet. Put your arms around my neck."

Sally whimpered, still holding fast to the rock.

Constance reached up to disengage her little hands just as another wave sluiced onto them. The rock gave way and they both went under.

Constance retained her hold on Sally, but the frightened moppet kicked and fought and squirmed for freedom. Their surge to the surface abruptly halted. Constance swirled toward the source of their constraint to find her skirt trapped under the rock.

Resisting panic's temptation, she tugged, but with no result. Should she let Sally go? Would Drew see the child? Catch her?

Poor Sally was frantic now in her bid for air. The rope around Constance's waist dug into her. Someone must be trying to pull her out.

She kicked. They pulled. Sally squirmed. How long had they been under? How much longer could Sally last?

Constance was about to release the child when she felt her bodice begin to separate from her skirt. Strong fingers dug into the hole, renting the skirt off and they were free.

She surfaced, coughing, sputtering, and hugging a limp Sally to her. Drew took the child, then hesitated. "Connie?"

"Go on," she gasped. "I'm right behind you."

He stood in what must have been indecision for a moment before swimming with Sally to the water's edge. The current carried them well downstream before they reached land.

Isaac and Thomas began to reel Constance in. The nausea, the blackness, the shakes all descended at once.

Keep going. Keep going. Just a little farther. It was her last thought before water once again engulfed her.

CHAPTER | SEVENTEEN

THE FIRE POPPED AND hissed, its heat cocooning the cottage with warmth. Brushing back her curls, Drew placed his palm against Constance's forehead. Was she a bit hotter now, or was it his imagination? Sighing, he rubbed his face.

"Her fever is rising again?"

"No. She's fine."

Mary touched Constance's forehead. "Mayhap it's more cool cloths I should be getting."

He whirled toward her. "It's not Constance. It's the cottage. This infernal room is like a tin foot stove."

Clasping her hands together, Mary started to move away.

"Wait. I'm sorry. I . . . it's just . . ." He gulped in a breath. "Did she feel warmer to you?"

Mary hesitated. "Yes, sir. Same as yesterday. Feels fine in the morn, but as soon as noontime arrives, up goes her fever, it does. I just hope it goes back down again this eve."

"Drew?"

He turned, the sight of his baby sister causing his heart to swell. "Sally Elizabeth. Come sit upon my knee and tell me a story."

Once in his arms, he withdrew a kerchief from his cloth pouch and held it to her nose. "Blow."

She did as instructed, not once, but several times. As he tucked away the kerchief, she wiped her nose on her sleeve. "Sissy gone to heaven?"

He tensed. "No. She's merely sleeping."

"But, I wake. Sissy need wake. Why Sissy not wake?"

"Sissy's taken ill—not from being in the water. Sissy's having her seasoning. That's all."

"Does she fever?"

"Sometimes she has a fever."

"Papa and Sister have the fever." Sticking her thumb in her mouth, she pinched his shirt between the thumb and finger of her other hand, rubbing the fabric back and forth. "Papa and Sister go to heaven."

Swallowing, he pulled her head against his chest. Back at the river, he had thought he'd lost this child. But she'd been spared, coming through the trauma with amazing resilience. She had lain limp on the tree-gnarled bank for agonizing moments before all the water she'd taken in had finally poured from her mouth.

At first she'd been cold, wet, and disoriented, but once home and bundled up in her tick, she'd slept the whole night through. Upon waking late yesterday morn, she complained only of "hurt fingers" and hunger—nothing else.

He'd laid those tiny little hands in his palm, carefully examining them. There was a cut or two, but mostly just bruising, probably from gripping the rock. She'd evidently made her way halfway across the stream, became frightened, and simply sat down on the rock. The longer she sat, the higher and more turbulent the stream became.

Thank God she was all right. Her appetite had returned full force, though swallowing caused some discomfort. No doubt the exposure had taken its toll in the form of a tender throat and blocked nose. But he'd had her inhale the vapors of steamed sage and thyme and then drink hot tea. No one would ever guess she'd nearly drowned just two days ago. "I thought you were going to tell me a story."

"Know not how."

"Um. Then maybe I'd better tell you a story. Which one would you like to hear?"

"Talk about the dog tree."

"The dogwood tree?"

She nodded, snuggling in for the well-known legend.

Mary approached with a bucket of water and a rag. Scooting his chair out of the way, Drew oversaw while Mary sat on the bed, wrung out the rag, and bathed his wife's face.

"I ready now, Drew."

He kept his eyes on Constance. "In days of old, it was said the dogwood tree grew large in size and as strong as an oak. Because of its strength—"

Sally pulled back. "You forgot the largest-tree-of-the-forest part."

Pausing, he looked at her. "It was among one of the largest trees of the forest." She settled back against him, and he looped his arms around her. "Because of its strength, it was chosen to make the cross from which Jesus was crucified. This so grieved the dogwood tree that Christ, even amidst His great suffering, sensed it and made a pledge. Never again would the tree grow large enough or strong enough to be used for such a purpose."

Mary rinsed her cloth, then began on Constance's neck and chest.

"That not the end."

Drew stirred himself. " 'Henceforth,' said He, 'the dogwood tree shall grow tall and slender, with its blossoms of white symbolizing the cross and their centers representing the crown of thorns. The outer edge of each petal shall be touched with brown, as with the rust of nails. And all who look upon the tree will remember the cross.' "

"Why it has no flowers now?"

"It's winter."

"Then how we know which one is the 'pecial one?"

"From its size."

Mary replaced the covers around Constance and started wiping down her face again.

"There no daisies too."

Drew slid his eyes closed. "No. There are not."

"Cuz it winner?"

"Yes. Because it's winter."

Sally slid off his lap and moved toward the bed. "Can she hear me?"

Mary paused and looked at Drew. He cleared his throat. "I know not."

"Sissy?" Sally said, her head tilted. "When you go to heaven, tell Jesus He should keep flowers all time. Even in winner."

Drew shot to his feet. *"She's not going to die."*

Sally turned to him, her eyes large and luminous. "Yes. She is."

Fisting his hands, he grabbed his jacket and stormed from the cottage.

————

Constance stirred and swept open her eyes. "Sally?"

Grandma looked at her feverishly drawn face and smoothed the edges of the coverlet. "She's fine. Only a scratch or two to show for her troubles."

"Thank the Lord." Her voice came from within. She closed her eyes. "What are you doing here?"

"I came as soon as the weather allowed."

"But, how did you . . . ?" she rasped.

"Drew sent one of his men the day it happened."

"Nellie—"

Grandma moved closer, wiping Constance's brow. "Is fine. Her baby's fine. Sally's fine. We're all fine."

"Drew?"

"He's running us all mad."

Constance strained to open her eyes. "Mad?"

Grandma tsked. "I was merely jesting. Here, take a sip of this."

Grandma cupped Constance's head and brought the broth to her lips.

She groaned but swallowed once. "I must arise. Just . . . give me . . . a . . ."

She sunk back into the sweet oblivion of sleep.

————

Fists clenched, Drew towered over his grandmother. "Why did you not send for me?"

She handed him a cup of stew. "Raise not your voice to me, young man. She was only awake for a moment."

"She asked for me?"

"She asked for Sally."

He glanced across the room. Mayhap she'd wake again.

————

"Fetch more blankets, Grandma," he snapped. "The shivering's getting worse."

Grandma went to do his bidding while he sat on the bed, tucking the covers tightly around her body. It was nearing noon.

"So ccccccold." Her eyes never even opened.

He jumped to his feet. "I know, love. I know. I've more blankets coming." He swiveled around. "Make haste! She's cold!" Grandma handed him a pile of blankets, and he layered them atop Constance. "Is that better? Constance? Can you hear me?"

Nothing.

"The fire," he said over his shoulder. "Stoke the fire! She's cold!"

Grandma didn't move.

"Make haste! Do you not ken she's cold?"

Grandma's lined face softened. "Her fever's coming back, Drew. In a moment she'll be burning up again. The blankets we can peel off. The fire is not so easy. We'll leave it as it is."

"A fie upon you, Grandma! She's going to shake right out of this bed! Now stoke the blasted fire!"

"When did you fall in love with her?"

He stopped, the last blanket hanging from his hands, then returned to his task. "Will you *please* stoke the fire?"

"No."

He placed the blanket over Constance with meticulous care, sank onto the edge of the bed, and covered his face with his hands. "I thought you came to help me tend to her. Why are you not helping?"

Grandma gathered his unbound hair and smoothed it behind his shoulders. "I didn't come to *help*. I came to *tend* to her. I assumed you would be out working on the new house with your men. I never dreamed you'd leave that project for them to do unsupervised, yet you've ventured out only a handful of times and didn't stay gone for long at that. Why did you even bother sending for me?"

He turned his face, resting it on his fists while looking at Constance. "The shivering's stopped."

Grandma sat down beside him, rubbing her gnarled hand back and forth across his back. They stayed as such for several long moments.

Drew sighed. "I beg your pardon for cursing and raising my voice. I . . . I have no excuse to offer."

"The woman you love is seasoning. No need to ask my pardon."

"Will she die, do you think?" he asked, pinching the bridge of his nose.

Moving her hand to his waist, she gave him a brief squeeze. "It's too early to tell. Until these spikes of fever start to decline, we won't know."

"But there was next to no fever yesterday. And she's awakened several times. Long enough to drink a bit of broth, anyway."

"You know how the ague and fever are. One day good. One day bad. The bad days getting worse and worse until either the fevers peak and begin to decline or the fevers peak and . . ."

He lowered his forehead into his hands. "She wasn't to go in after Sally. When I heard that splash, I know not which I felt more strongly—anger or terror. But I didn't have time to reel her back in, plus go after Sally." He took a deep breath. "Then they both went under. By my life, it reminded me of . . . of Margaret. Of a sudden, I was seven again staring at that burning cottage, knowing Margaret was in there, knowing it should have been me instead."

Grandma stroked his hair. "Margaret's death wasn't your fault."

"She was under my care."

"You were a child."

"It makes no matter."

She paused. "I was there too."

He looked sharply at her. "What mean you?"

"I came upon the savages directly after they'd set the torch to the roof," she said, tears filling her eyes. "I thought all three of you were in there. Instead of confronting them, I ran for your father." She shook her head. "No, I should have been the one to save Margaret."

"They'd have killed you."

She nodded. "As they would have you."

He wrapped his arm about her. "Father never would have expected a woman to stand up to them."

"Constance would have." She swiped her cheeks.

"Constance has no power within her brain."

Grandma leaned back to look at him. "Constance is smarter than most men I know."

He allowed his arm to slide from Grandma's shoulder. Resting his elbows on his knees, he clasped his hands together. "Why say you I love her?"

"Because of your actions."

He stood and strode to the fire. Propping his hand against its frame, he studied into its leaping flames. It was true and he knew it. Not only because he'd like to have her between the sheets, though heaven knew he certainly craved that, but because of her very being. Her spunk. Her determination. Her devotion to her uncle. Her devotion to Sally. Her devotion to her Lord.

But, God help him, he didn't want to succumb to those feelings. For he knew only too well the pain it would lead to. Why, even now her life hung in a fragile balance.

"I've tried to keep her at a distance," he said. "I have."

"Ah, Drew. Have you not figured it out yet?"

He said nothing.

Grandma rocked a bit. Back and forth. Back and forth. "I know not why you thought to distance yourself from her. You've never even been able to distance yourself from the little ones. You were drawn to your baby brothers and sisters from the moment you laid eyes on them. So was Nellie. You should see her with that baby of hers. Why, you'd think that child was the king's heir.

"Yet Nellie's husband has given their little one no more than a second glance. Not even has he held that sweet boy. If, God forbid, they do lose the baby to this unsympathetic land, who do you suppose is the richer? Nellie, for having shared what precious moments God granted her with the babe, or Gerald, who would have lost the opportunity to know, hold, and love his firstborn?"

"Gerald."

Grandma hooted. "Oh, Drew, you're missing the point on purpose." Slowly, she sobered. "But make no mistake. You've a wife here that you love, whether you like it or not. You might lose her and you might not. If you don't, I suggest you spend what additional time you have with her sharing that love to its fullest. Otherwise, you will die a very lonely man."

"Lonely men don't get hurt."

"Lonely men are the most bitter creatures of all." She rose and pulled a blanket off Constance, refolding it.

"What are you doing?"

"Her fever's back."

Drew reached for the bucket. "I'll fetch more water."

———

"You're sure you won't stay?"

Grandma shook her head. "There's no purpose. You've Mary here to cook for the men and for you. You have the men to labor on the big house. And since you refuse to leave Constance's side, there is really nothing for me to do. Besides, I miss my great-grandson."

"But what of Sally? You're sure she's fit for travel?"

"Travel!" Grandma snorted. "I'd hardly call a trek to Nellie's *travel*."

"Still, only a week has passed since her ordeal."

Grandma glanced down at Sally, her little face shining beneath the layers of clothing wrapped around her head and body. "She's fine, Drew."

"I see Nellie!"

Drew sighed. "Very well. Isaac will escort you." He gave Grandma a hug. "Is there nothing special I should do for Constance?"

Grandma patted his cheek. "Pray. 'For everyone who asks receives, and he who seeks finds, and to him who knocks it will be opened.' "

He nodded and lifted Sally into his arms. "You tell Nellie that if she doesn't give that nephew of ours a name, we'll be calling him . . . oh, what say you? Jael?"

Sally crinkled her nose. "I never heard that name."

Drew smiled. "It means 'mountain goat.' "

———

She barely suppressed a groan. Her head hurt. Her stomach hurt. Her whole blessed body hurt. Opening her eyes, she oriented herself, noting she lay in Drew's bed and he slumbered in that chair of his.

His hair was unbound, his face unshaved, his clothes wrinkled. He looked almost as bad as she felt. She turned her head a bit. Mary bustled around the fire as usual, but nowhere was Sally. Looking back at Drew, she discovered his gaze fastened upon her. She tried to smile but couldn't quite manage it.

"How do you feel?"

"Thirsty."

He rose then returned with some broth. She tried to lift her head, but he slipped his hand beneath her in assistance. The broth flowed down her throat but didn't set well within her stomach. "No more."

Setting the broth aside, he perched on the bed. "Are you cold? hot?"

She gave a slight shake of her head. *Fine,* she mouthed.

He touched her forehead. "No fever right now. It was bad yesterday, though."

"How many days?" she whispered.

"About eight. You should start getting better, though. I'm thinking the worst is over."

"Sally?"

"She's fine. Gone with Grandma to visit Nellie and the new baby."

"Grandma. I thought I'd dreamed it."

He brushed her hair back from her face. "Is there anything you want? Anything I can get you?"

"It hurts."

He rubbed her arms. "What hurts?"

"Everything."

He leaned down and placed a light kiss on her head. "I'm sorry."

She smiled slightly, then closed her eyes. It was too much effort to keep them open.

———

The fever didn't drop as it usually did in the evening. Instead, it continued to climb higher and higher. He bathed her with cool cloths when she burned. Wiped her with dry ones when she sweat. Still, it did not cease.

Her limbs swelled and her pallor dimmed, causing even her freckles to lose their luster. She tossed her head, she moaned, she looked near death. It would happen tonight. She'd either survive or she wouldn't.

He'd never prayed so hard in his life. He barely noticed Mary refilling the bucket, replenishing the rags, subduing the fire.

If you let her survive, I'll allow her to educate Sally.

Her fever continued to rise. He threw the covers from the bed, bathing her arms and legs as well as her face and neck. Moments later, her nightdress was saturated with her sweat as was the bedding.

He stripped her nightdress from her, frantic to mop the perspiration from her body. Mary moved to his side with fresh linens. He lifted Constance into his arms, hugging her to him while Mary tightened the bed ropes and changed the linens.

If you let her survive, I'll never have another lustful thought about her.

He and Mary slipped a dry nightdress onto her. She was ablaze again, her skin now a deep bright red. He quickly laid her down and set to swabbing her with cool water.

Please. Please. Don't let her die.

The water all but sizzled against her skin. Her temperature couldn't go any higher. It couldn't. Yet it did. He slipped his hand into hers. She squeezed it in response.

Yes, Constance. I'm here. I'm here. And then he realized. She wasn't responding to him. Her whole body was tightening up. She was going into a convulsion.

Oh, God! Oh, God!

Her face tensed. Her body became rigid. He wrenched his hand from hers, quickly turning her head to the side.

Breathe, Constance! Breathe! Her body remained rigid, her chest still. He prayed and prayed and prayed.

All right! All right! If you let her survive, I'll honor my marriage vows and keep her to wife for the rest of my entire wretched life. Just let her live! I love her, Lord! I love her!

Her chest caught. Her body slowly relaxed. She began to breathe again. Jerking a cloth from the bucket, he proceeded to bathe her, prepared to continue doing so for as long as it took. He never noticed the tears coursing down his face.

CHAPTER | EIGHTEEN

I LIED, LORD. ABOUT THE *lustful thoughts part.*

His eyes traced the curves beneath her covered sleeping form. She was resting peacefully, the fever, for now, subdued. It had come and gone in spikes for the last several days, each spike lower than the last. In another couple of days, it should leave her completely.

Then what? How, in all that was holy, would he tell her he wanted her for wife after giving her such a blistering rejection when she'd first offered to stay?

He sighed. He'd not had much time to think about his promises to God. Heretofore, he'd continued to care for her during her feverish bouts, trying to catch a bit of sleep in between.

He was wide-awake now, though, and thinking of all he'd said and done. That's when the lustful thoughts began. So worried had he been before, he'd barely even been cognizant of her as a . . . well, as a woman. But his subconscious had evidently been paying very strict attention. And now that the danger was over, it was reminding him with remarkable accuracy and frequency of her slim graceful arms. Her dainty curved feet. Her long willowy legs. Among other things.

He closed his eyes, trying to slow his errant thoughts. Instead, he recalled the moments he'd held her while Mary had changed the bedding. Her skin had been creamy and smooth, burning not only where he'd touched, but burning his very soul.

He took a deep breath. Yes, he'd definitely been lying about the lustful thoughts part. Still, she was his wife and now that he intended to make an honest go of it, surely it was permissible to have such thoughts about one's own mate. He frowned. He couldn't seem to call up one Scripture that said as such. Surely it said that somewhere. He grabbed his Bible and lowered himself into his chair.

"So husbands ought to love their own wives as their own bodies; he who loves his wife loves himself. For no one ever hated his own flesh, but nourishes and cherishes it."

Well, he certainly loved her body, but no matter how he manipulated the passage, he knew it had nothing to do with that. He continued to flip through the pages.

"Wives, submit to your own husbands."

An excellent verse, but not what he was looking for at the moment. He turned back toward the front.

Aha! *"Rejoice with the wife of your youth. As a loving deer and a graceful doe, let her breasts satisfy you at all times; and always be enraptured with her love."*

He slammed the Good Book closed. God would not hold him to the lustful thoughts part of his promise. As for the rest, he intended to keep to the letter his pledge.

He cringed at the thought of educating Sally, but perhaps that would work to his advantage. Constance would be very pleased at the prospect of tutoring her again.

After storing his Bible beneath his chair, he looked toward the bed. She was staring at him. Feeling color flood his face, he shifted in his chair.

"God ye good den."

He nodded. "Good afternoon."

She lay still for a few more moments. "I'm hungry."

He lifted the corners of his mouth a fraction. "That's wonderful."

"Might I have something to eat?"

"Certainly." He stayed where he was.

She frowned slightly. "Drew? Is everything all right?"

He cleared his throat. "Fine, fine. Everything's fine." He turned his head slightly but kept his eyes on Constance. "Mary? Might you bring Constance a bit of broth?"

Constance looked to the fire and then different spots in the cottage. "Mary isn't in here."

He twisted around. "Oh. So she isn't. Well, I'll get you something in a moment or two."

She moistened her lips.

His breath caught. "Or three."

Touching her hand to her forehead, she frowned again. "I also need to, well, your pardon, but I need to make use of the chamber pot. Um, *now*."

He shot to his feet and made his way hastily to the door. "I'll find Mary."

"Drew! Your coat!"

But he was already out the door.

———

Constance drank in the sight of his ruddy cheeks and nose, along with his wind-tossed hair. Peeling off his jacket, he shook the snowflakes from its folds and hooked it on a peg. "You look wonderful," he said, easing into a smile.

He was dressed for winter. He'd attached the sleeves to his leather jerkin with cording and donned thick woolen breeches. Stockings and shoes had been exchanged for boots. "Compared to what?" she asked.

He moved to the foot of the bed. "Compared to this morning, compared to yesterday, compared to last week, I don't know. You simply look wonderful."

It was a bald-faced lie, but she wouldn't argue with him. "Were you at the big house?"

He nodded.

"Did it suffer any from the storm?"

"What storm?"

She hesitated. "The *rain*storm, Drew. You remember the one? I believe Sally got lost in it?"

He raised a brow. "The house is fine."

She smoothed the coverlet's wrinkles. "Is the roof on yet?"

"Hardly. We only started on the chimney this morn."

Frowning, she looked up. "I thought you said I'd been ill for almost three weeks."

"You have."

"Then what in the world have you been doing?"

He stiffened. "The siding is on. The windows and doors are in. And the cornice boards have been completed. Is that all right with you?"

She shrugged. "I was simply worried about the snow. What with no roof, won't the snow cause problems?"

"No." He strode to the fire, rubbing his hands together in its warmth.

She sighed. "When will Sally be home?"

"I'll bring her home after the Christmas service."

Christmas. Sweet heaven, she'd forgotten all about it. "What is today?"

"The first day of December." Scooping some stew into a bowl, he brought it and a spoon to her. "Here."

She set them on her lap. "I'm tired."

"Just a few bites, then you can rest."

It took such effort to eat, and their conversation was already draining her. She stared at the steaming bowl.

The bed tilted from Drew's weight, then he took the bowl and spoon in hand. "Open up."

She wrinkled her nose. He grinned boyishly. "I promise not to miss, *if* you open up like a good girl."

She opened her mouth, the warm concoction pleasantly appeasing. He said nothing as she chewed, just watched her mouth until she swallowed. Before presenting her with the next bite, his gaze briefly touched hers. She skittered hers away.

She opened her mouth and again closed it around the spoon. He withdrew it much more slowly this time, then returned it to the bowl. Chancing another glance at him, she ceased to chew. His stare was bold and unabashedly direct. Something stirred deep within her.

He brushed her cheek with his finger. "Eat."

She finished the bite in record time.

His gaze, soft as a caress, touched her lips. "Open."

She hesitated, then opened her mouth. He fed her another bite. Broth trickled from the corner of her mouth. Before she could wipe it, he was there with the spoon, scooping it up. His eyes then locked with hers as he drank from the spoon, cleaning it thoroughly within his mouth.

Her pulse pounding, she forced herself to swallow. "I'm all done. Thank you." She slid under the covers, turned to face the wall, then closed her eyes. But her heartbeat slowed not and her desire for him swelled.

She'd make certain he never saw it, though. Never again. Many tense moments of silence passed before he finally stood and moved away.

———

Upon awaking, she first looked to his chair. He wasn't in it, but neither was it empty. Rising up onto her elbows, she scanned the cottage. Mary was grinding with mortar and pestle, but Drew was nowhere in sight.

The chair had been pushed next to the bed, well within her reach. In its seat lay a gingerbread slate with a huge heart-shaped leaf resting atop it. On the leaf was inscribed a message.

A cylindrical bucket is 6 inches in circumference and 4 inches high. On the inside of the vessel 1 inch from the top is a drop of honey. On the outside of the vessel on the opposite side, 1 inch from the bottom, is a fly. How far will the fly have to go to reach the honey?

She studied the dry leaf, tracing its shape with her fingertip. What beautiful foliage this land produced. She'd never dreamed.

She reread the geometrical exercise, then sighed. He'd finally acknowledged her interest in mathematics again. He must be feeling awfully sorry for her to have instigated such a thing. Still, she was pleased. Closing her eyes, she pictured the bucket, the honey, and the fly.

————

"You're home early today."

Drew shrugged out of his jacket. "We can only do about eight feet of bricking per day without squashing the mortar. So I'm having the men sheath the roof for now, then in the morn we'll do more bricking. How do you feel?"

"Better and better. I'm even beginning to miss my baths."

He tsked, waving his finger to and fro. "What would your father say?"

"He'd be scandalized."

Chuckling, he glanced to the fire. "Has she been eating, Mary?"

"It's lucky you are that you came home early, Master, for I fear there's a wolf in her stomach, I do."

Constance watched them exchange a smile, then looked at her hands. Things were different between Drew and Mary now. No longer was Mary meek and subservient around him. She looked him in the eye. She grumbled if he interfered with her chores. She laughed frequently and easily with him.

He was different as well. The barrier he'd always placed between him and others outside his immediate family was no longer there. He teased her. He whispered with her. He shared his laughter with her.

Constance refused to acknowledge the knot beneath her chest. She adored them both, and if they had found something special to share, she'd not sit here and moon over it. Lifting her chin, she blanched to find Drew standing behind his chair, staring at her.

"Have you decided how far the fly will have to go to reach the honey?"

Her gaze ricocheted from him to the untouched gingerbread slate and back up to him. "I've been toying with the idea in my head. Do *you* know the distance he must go?"

He took a deep breath. "I have no idea."

"I see." She bit her lip. "Well, I . . . it was . . . thank you. I really appreciate your giving me the puzzle. I've just been too tired as of yet to give it my full attention."

He picked up the slate and leaf, then lowered himself into the chair. "You must not be as well as you appear, then."

She gave him a tentative smile. "No, I do feel much better. Truly, I do. I simply tire very easily."

He nodded. "That will pass."

They sat in awkward silence—nothing like the easy silence that passed between him and Mary. This was tense and uncomfortable. She groped for something to say but could think of nothing.

He shifted. "The snow has ceased."

"Has it? Oh, Drew, I'm so glad. I did worry you and the men wouldn't be warm enough. Are you . . . uh . . . they warm enough?"

"Fine. Just fine. Everyone's plenty warm."

Another stretch of silence, this one worse than the last. She contemplated her toes, wiggling them underneath the coverlet. He studied his nails. Then they both looked at each other.

"Why don't you eat something, Drew? Mary made some wonderful—rack-coon, was it, Mary?"

Holding her arm above the fire to test its warmth, Mary shrugged her shoulders. "You needs must ask the master. My tongue has a time with those savage words, it does."

"Aroughcoune."

"Yes. That. Mary baked some today."

"Is there any left or did your wolf eat it all?"

"Mary exaggerates. There's plenty."

He continued to sit there. Saying nothing, just staring at her. *Say something, Constance. Quickly.*

She fingered the string that gathered her nightdress together at the neck. "Um, I think I can sleep on my tick again. You needn't give up your bed any longer. I'll—"

"No."

She stilled. "But, your bed."

"You need to stay quiet for many more days. I'll not risk your having a relapse."

"But—"

He leaned forward, close to her ear. "I like having you in my bed, Connie. Please."

Her eyes widened. His face turned a dull red. He shot to his feet. "I believe I'll have some dinner now after all."

Tossing the slate and leaf to the foot of the bed, he strode to the shelves and retrieved a trencher. She followed him with her gaze, dumbstruck. Her insides jangled, her heart pounded. He couldn't possibly mean what she thought he did. No, that's why he was so embarrassed. It had come out sounding different from what he'd intended.

Still, Connie? *Connie?* Where had that come from?

He had his aroughcoune now but did not return to his chair. He, instead, sat on the hearth, legs extended, feet crossed, eyes glued to the food he was devouring.

She allowed her attention to roam back to the slate and leaf. The *heart-shaped* leaf. Could it be? Might he actually be—no. Impossible. He was merely feeling sorry for her. Responsible for her. It was Mary who received all the soft looks. Mary with whom he was at ease. Mary who was uneducated.

The thudding of her heart slowly settled back to its natural rhythm. She must be very, very careful not to allow herself to misconstrue his actions to fit what she wanted them to fit.

Closing her eyes, she pictured the bucket, the honey, and the fly.

What a clodpate. Drew pounded another nail into the roof's sheathing, thinking of a thousand things he *should* have said but didn't. No, he'd just blurted out whatever thought happened to be in his worthless head. By trow, but his tongue did twang as readily as any buzzer's.

Holding two nails in his mouth, he withdrew a third and continued with his hammering. Treating the woman you were trying to court like some heifer at rut time was disastrous at best and irrevocable at worst. She'd barely gained the strength to feed herself. He should be coddling her, not pressing her with clumsy advances.

Pausing, he took a moment to look out over his land. At the bottom of the hill and several acres beyond lay the James River, where soon he'd build a huge wharf so the tobacco ships could sail right to his front door. This spring would be the last time he'd need to roll hogshead after hogshead to the public warehouses.

He felt a surge of satisfaction. Mayhap he'd build Nellie a barge so she and Gerald could row over for a visit. And Sally, wouldn't she love to run down and welcome Josh home from his factoring fresh off the ship? By trow, but it was going to be grand.

His elbow rested on his knee, the hammer hanging from his hand. Would Josh have little ones of his own racing down this slope? Most probably. He rolled the nails from one side of his mouth to the other. Would he and Constance have little ones racing down it as well? Did he even *want* babes of his own?

He looked to the half-finished barn. If they were to have children, he should probably go ahead and make a necessary. And a smokehouse. He sighed. And if Constance was to be the mother, he might as well construct a schoolhouse. She would surely want to educate not only the O'Connor offspring but every woman in the colony. Forsooth, his father must surely be spinning in his grave.

His grave. How many more would Drew be digging before he was laid in his own? More than he'd want. Some small and from his own seed, no doubt. Would it be worth it?

A cool breeze wafted from the river as he squinted against the sun's descent. What if just one of the babes survived? What if the child grew to adulthood? What would his dreams be? His pursuits?

He gripped the hammer. Yes. *Yes.* He wanted children. Lots and lots of them. But first, he must convince Constance to stay. And that was going to take some doing.

He thought for a moment, then straightened, slowly removing the nails from his mouth. He knew just the thing to get back in her good graces.

What in heaven's name was he up to? He'd been acting near giddy from the moment he'd arrived home. They'd eaten and visited, same as every night, but he was much like a young boy awaiting his birthday surprise.

Moments ago, he'd whispered furiously with Mary while she stoked up the fire and set several pots to boil. Now he stood on his chair, hanging a large sheet from several old ceiling hooks. When he was finished, the cloth completely enclosed a small portion of the room just in front of the fireplace.

She blushed with mortification. They wanted some privacy. How could she have been so addlepated? She would *not* lie here in his bed and force them to hide behind a curtain for . . . for whatever it was they were going to do. She would sleep in her tick tonight and she'd brook no argument.

Drew appeared from behind the curtain, his glance dashing away from her the same moment it found her. Saints above, how awful. She was about to tell him her intent when he whisked himself out the door.

"Mary, quickly. Get over here and help me up to my tick before he returns."

Mary peeked around the curtain. "Up to your tick? Whatever for?"

Constance threw back the covers. "Let's not make this any more embarrassing than it already is. Just help me up there and with haste."

"Mistress! Get back under those coverlets. You'll catch a chill for certain."

Mary bustled over, and Constance, her feet already on the dirt floor, held out her hand for help. "Come. I can't make it clear up there by myself. Now, make haste. He might return any moment."

"Of course he'll return, and he'll be plenty furious if I assist you with such a thing. I'd just as soon not have to deal with his wrath, I wouldn't. It's hard he is working to try and please. I'll not be spoiling it, I won't."

Constance stilled. Oh, dear. She was probably right. He'd be angered and then their little tête-à-tête would be ruined. Blast. She'd simply have to feign sleep. Immediately. "Perhaps you're right. Already I'm feeling weary. I think I'll go on to bed now. Dig you den, Mary." With that, she dove under the covers, turned her back to the curtain, and closed her eyes.

"Merciful me. What a pair the two of you are."

The door slammed open, a cold rush of air swooshing into the room. Constance peered beneath her lids just long enough to see him haul in a huge half-barrel of some sort.

She squeezed her eyes shut, willing herself to ignore their whispered giggles and the sound of splashing. He came and went from the cottage several times, chilling the room even more. *What in the world?*

Finally all was still. "Connie?"

She took the deep, even breaths of a slumbering person.

He touched her shoulder. "Are you awake?"

"She's awake," Mary said from across the room.

Constance felt a rush of heat suffuse her cheeks. Thank the heavens it was dark. What could Mary be thinking?

"I've a surprise for you, Connie. Would you like to see?"

She stilled. A surprise? *For me?* She slowly lay back on the pillows. The darkness was even more pronounced than usual, for the curtain shrouded the fire and its light.

"Come. I've something for you."

"Right now?"

"Right now." He peeled back the covers and helped her sit before scooping her up into his arms.

"Drew! Sweet heavens, I can walk."

He said nothing but carried her to the curtain, then stepped inside it. Immediately, light and heat embraced them. And there, in the midst of it was a barrel of water, with a scent rising from its depths, the likes of which she'd never smelt before.

Setting her gingerly on the hearth, he allowed his hand to travel the length of her arm to the tips of her fingers, where his lips touched them. "For you, my lady. Enjoy."

Then he was gone, the closing of the cottage door loud in the subsequent silence, the gooseflesh on her arm still tingling.

Mary stepped forward. "Come. Let's get you into the bath so the master doesn't have to linger overlong in the cold."

A bath? *A bath?* She looked up. Mary smiled. "Come. It's just right."

As if in a dream, she allowed Mary to undress her and assist her into the barrel. The warm water swirled around her, encircling her as she lowered herself into it. The water came up to the slopes of her shoulders, teasing them as it lapped up over her.

Dipping hands and soap into the tub, Mary quickly worked up a lather from which the most delicate fragrance arose. Constance sat as if disassociated with her own body.

Closing her eyes, she felt Mary lather her arms, her back, and her hair, before pausing. "Wish me to continue?"

Constance stirred. "I've never before submerged myself in water. Have you?"

"No, mum. Is it as heavenly as it looks?"

"Even more. Do you suppose I'll be going to hell now?"

"No, mum. If it was to hell you'd be sent for such a thing, the master wouldn't have allowed it to happen to you. Wish me to continue?"

Constance opened her palm. "No thank you. I can finish."

Mary nodded. "I'm going to go check on Snowflake. It's time for her evening milking."

"Surely Drew has seen to it for you?"

"It's best I go check. You will be all right?"

"Yes. I'll be fine. Thank you. And Mary?"

"Yes, mum?"

"I'm sorry you're having to do my chores as well as your own."

A small shy smile touched Mary's features. "I'm happy to do them for you, Mistress. It's glad I am you're feeling so much better."

She turned and left, a soft whoosh and a click the only signs of her departure.

When he saw Mary leave the cottage, he'd assumed Constance had finished. Not so. He could see clearly her silhouette through the curtain with her head hung back over the edge of the barrel.

Mary should never have left her. Didn't she realize how dangerous it was for Constance to fall asleep in a tub full of water? He stepped inside the curtain and froze.

Constance's hair, still full of lather, was piled atop her head, her eyes closed, her face relaxed. The graceful curve of her neck gave way to delicate shoulders peeking above the water's edge.

"This is absolutely divine, Mary. You must try it next. But first, I needs must rinse my hair. Will you help me?"

He should turn around and walk out. He picked up the empty bucket. Dipping it beneath the surface, he filled it with water. Constance, eyes still closed, covered her face with her hands and bent forward. "I'm ready." Her voice was muffled and husky.

He poured the water over her hair. It took several more dousings before all the soap had washed out.

"A rag. Is there a rag I can use to dry my eyes with?"

He knelt beside her and placed a dry rag in her hand. She pushed her hair back, drug the rag down her face, peeped over the top, then squealed and sunk deep into the water.

"Will you be my wife, Connie?"

The fire crackled. She said nothing. Only stared at him through those long lashes spiked with water.

"I mean, my *real* wife. Till death do us part?"

The rag came further down her face, revealing her nose, mouth, and chin. "Why?"

Because I love you. Because I want my children to be your children also. He remained silent.

"What about Mary?"

He frowned. "I wouldn't sell Mary. She could stay."

"Oh, Drew, please. I like it not that you can buy and sell Mary, or me, or anyone else at your whim. And that's not what I meant. I thought, well, things between the two of you are . . . different."

He relaxed some. "We worked long and hard to care for you while you were ill. I'll always be grateful to her. But I've never had any feelings for her. Besides, I'm married to you. Even if I had interest elsewhere, I would never pursue it while married to another."

"And do you have interests elsewhere?"

"No."

"And do you have . . . feelings for me?"

"Yes."

"What kind of feelings?"

He should have known she'd demand it all. He took a deep breath. "Love feelings." Reaching for her hand, he flattened it against his chest. "Deep inside here."

Her expression softened, and she moved her hand up to comb a piece of hair back from his face. The tip of one shoulder rose above the water's surface. He kept his eyes on hers, but there was nothing amiss with his peripheral vision.

"Five inches," she said as she continued to comb her fingers through his hair.

He frowned. "Your pardon?"

"The fly," she whispered. "He has only to go five inches to reach the honey."

He was silent for a moment. "He'd have gone much, much further if he'd had to."

A mere hint of a smile touched her lips. "What think you if the honey meets him halfway?"

He lowered his eyes to half-mast. "Is that a yes, Connie?"

She nodded once. "I would be very honored to be your wife, Andrew Joseph O'Connor, until death do us part."

Cupping her face with his hands, he leaned forward and brushed his lips against hers.

CHAPTER | NINETEEN

HIS KISS WAS GENTLE and achingly sweet. Her own calm, however, had long since shattered.

Love feelings. Until death do us part. He didn't want Mary! He wanted *her*. And she, most definitely, wanted him. Burrowing her fingers into the thick hair at his nape, she returned his kiss.

He'd asked her to stay. Forever. She would be the real Mistress O'Connor. She would live in his big house. In his chamber. With him.

His caress moved down her arms, his callused thumbs brushing her inner wrists. The pit of her stomach whirled. Every nerve stood on end.

He raised his mouth, his breathing ragged. "We needs must stop."

She shook her head. "Why?"

"It's too soon. You're not well."

"Oh, but I am. I am!"

Resting his forehead against hers, he closed his eyes. "Ah, Connie-girl. I'll not indulge in a piece of stair-work here aside the tub when Mary could walk in at any moment."

Her water-slicked skin cooled as air engulfed the chasm between them. She settled back against the barrel. He was right, of course. But when? When would Mary not be here? She didn't have the fortitude to ask.

Rising to his feet, his gaze roved leisurely over the swell of her breasts peeking just above the surface. With a delayed sense of modesty, she sunk a bit deeper into the water. Eyes dark with desire, he turned and disappeared behind the curtain.

———

A maiden is 27 steps ahead of her sweetheart and takes 8 steps while her sweetheart takes 5; but 2 of his steps are equal to 5 of her own. How many steps will he have to take before he can capture the maiden within his arms?

Smiling, Constance laid the leaf back upon the chair, then swept her hair to the side. It was a gnarled mess, for she'd fallen asleep without braiding it.

Dragging her fingers through tangle after tangle, she recalled last night's events, relishing each exchange, each revelation, each touch. After he'd left, Mary had bustled into the cottage, helping her from the barrel and into a clean nightdress. Then he'd returned, removed the curtain, stoked the fire, and settled her onto a pallet while he brushed her hair. When next she stirred, it was to wake up in his bed with another heart-shaped leaf at her side.

She paused, closing her eyes. *Mistress O'Connor. Mistress Constance Caroline O'Connor.* She still couldn't quite believe it. She must concentrate on regaining her health so that very soon she could wake up next to the man instead of his love letters.

———

It was a length of fine green wool that lay at her bedside this time. Fingering it, she chided herself for being disappointed. Not with the fabric, of course, but with his absence. It had been three days since his address and she'd not seen him once.

Picking up the material, she drew it into her lap, almost missing the heart-shaped leaf wedged within its folds.

You may make yourself a new Christmas Day gown, and though I look forward to seeing you in a lovely confection, I shall be jealous of it and wishing it were me that hugged those luscious curves. Make haste, my love, in your pursuit to good health.

Heat stole into her face and she darted a quick glance at Mary. But Mary paid her no mind, just continued to knead and punch the lump of dough beneath her fists. Constance reread the missive, his words provoking a scandalous reaction in her.

"Mistress?"

Constance jerked guiltily, her face burning. Stuffing the leaf under the coverlet, she attempted a casual smile. "Good morrow."

"How feel you this day?"

She took a fortifying breath. "I'm tired of laying abed, Mary. I wish to break the fast at the table."

Wiping her hands on her apron, Mary reached for a trencher. "You're sure you feel up to it? It's early yet, it is. The master left word you were to stay abed for another fortnight."

"You've seen him?"

"I see him every morn."

"Did he say what has kept him away from the cottage?"

"It's anxious, he is, to finish the roof. Seems it's time to be putting the tobaccy leaves in those great barrels."

Constance bit her lip. "And he thinks to keep me abed for another fortnight?"

"Those were his words, they were."

Fluffing up her pillow, Constance leaned back against it. Was that truly what needed to be done? She didn't want to take ill again, but still, she couldn't possibly lie abed the entire two weeks. "Very well, Mary. I'll break my fast in bed, but if I continue to feel fit, I might sit in his chair for a short while this afternoon."

———

And so the week went. Constance worked in her diary, she sewed on her gown, she sat for spells in his chair, and she slept quite a bit. She'd just woken up from one such nap when Drew burst into the cottage.

"We're dried in!" His tall, raw-boned body exuded triumph edged with self-satisfaction as he swaggered to the bed, planting his feet on the dirt floor like some captain at the helm of his ship. An open, honest smile spread across his face, wreathed in dimples.

She couldn't help but respond with a smile of her own. "The roof is on, then?"

"The roof, the chimney, the siding—everything! All that's left is the interior."

She held up both hands. "Congratulations."

He strode forward, grasped them in his, and brought them to his lips. "Thank you."

They stayed as such, absorbing the first sight they'd had of each other since making their pledges. My, but he was handsome. Massive shoulders beneath his coat, cheeks and nose red from the chafing wind, and his eyes. Eyes the color of a robin's egg—frank, admiring, and deliriously pleased.

"What's next?" she asked.

Releasing her hands, he removed his jacket, his movements hardy and robust. "The tobacco. I should have been well into the packing of the hogsheads by now, but I'm behind."

"Because of the house?"

He gave her a crooked grin. "Among other things."

She flushed. "But I thought you didn't send the tobacco back until spring."

"It depends on when a ship comes through. One year we had a ship come just after Christmas and half the colony wasn't ready. Those that were, reaped the bigger profit."

"And those that weren't?"

"Waited for the next ship, which didn't arrive until March."

She frowned. "But what about Josh? Isn't he supposed to factor the tobacco for you?"

"Hopefully he'll be on whichever ship comes through first." He eased down onto the bed, taking her hand into his lap. "How do you fare?"

"Very nicely. Mary won't let me do a thing, so I've no choice but to be a slug-a-bed all the day long."

He hooked a stray tendril behind her ear. "Good for Mary."

She lowered her lashes. "Thank you for the wool. It's beautiful."

"Is there enough for a proper gown?"

"Oh, yes. Plenty." She smoothed the blanket over her legs. "But, Drew, I'm unsure of the styles here. Are they the same as in London? Precisely what is a proper gown?"

"Whatever you make will be perfect."

"And you'll let me attend the Christmas service?"

He nodded. "As long as you continue to improve, I think it will be all right."

"There will be other women there?"

"Every woman from this part of the colony will be there."

"Grandma too?"

"Grandma too."

She leaned against the wall, and he reached behind her to adjust the pillow. "Did you get my note?"

She smiled. "Yes. The sweetheart didn't have to take any steps to capture the maiden within his arms."

His eyes widened. "How did you figure that?"

Leaning forward, she glanced at Mary tending the fire, then whispered, "The maiden turned 'round and ran straight to him!"

Chuckling, he hooked her chin with his finger. "Such shocking behavior from a maiden? I think not. You'd better check your work again. It was thirty steps he took."

"Yes. You're quite right. But I still think if the maiden had any sense at all, she'd have never run away."

He, too, shot a glance at Mary before leaning forward and briefly touching his lips to hers. "What about my other note? Did you find it?"

Liquid honey poured through her. "I most certainly did," she whispered. "What were you thinking to write down such things? Why, anyone could have seen it."

He grazed her lips with his thumb. "I didn't write down the half of it. Besides, Mary can't read."

Her pulse skittered. "Oh, Drew. I'm feeling ever so much better."

His eyes darkened. "Are you?"

She nodded.

After a slight hesitation, he picked his jacket up from the chair and pulled it on. "Where are you going?"

"I've hogsheads to pack, my sweet. I won't be back until well after nightfall."

"For how long?"

"Until they're done."

"The whole crop?"

"Pretty much."

Her shoulders drooped.

Drawing the strings on his jacket tight, he gave her a tender smile. "I'll try to check in when I can."

"Can't you take your meals here? The tobacco barn's not as far away as the big house."

He shook his head. "It uses up precious daylight to come back here for meals. We've little enough light in the day as it is." His gaze lingered on her lips. "I'll be thinking of you, though, Connie-girl. Rest assured, I'll be thinking of you."

———

And think of her he did, for every day something new greeted her when she awoke. A length of fine silk ribbon the color of oyster shells, a real wax candle to read by after dark, several more mathematical puzzles, and yesterday, a pair of soft homemade leather shoes—one shaped for the right foot, one shaped for the left. Ah, such luxury.

When she opened her eyes this morning, a large blackened cooking pot sat in his chair. Frowning, she peered over its edge, then squealed. Covering her mouth with her hand, she looked to Mary. "What . . . ?"

"It's Mr. Meanie, it is. The master said he'd be home for supper this night and he says to me, 'Mary, it's something special I'm wanting to give my wife for supper.' A few minutes later, he comes back with Mr. Meanie hanging limp in his hand. He was going to put the cock right in the chair, but I stops him, I did. Thought he best set it in a pot first."

Sliding her hand to her neck, Constance peeked into the pot once again. The gray and white rooster lay at an awkward angle, a sad reflection of his once proud demeanor. Mr. Meanie. *Mr. Meanie.* Drew had killed his precious rooster. For her.

Tears welled within her eyes. The ribbon, the candle, the shoes, as sweet and special as they were, all paled in comparison, for this, without a doubt, was an act of genuine love.

Swiping at her eyes, she flung the covers back and slid her feet to the floor. "I want to cook it, Mary. Can you tell me what to do?"

"Oh, Mistress. You needn't do that. I'll be happy to cook that old rooster for you."

Shaking her head, Constance moved to Mary's side. "You don't understand. I *want* to cook it. Please? Will you teach me?"

Mary blinked. "Why, of course I will. Just don't tax yourself. If you start feeling woozy, promise to tell me?"

Smiling, Constance threw her arms about Mary. "Oh, thank you! I will, I will."

She pulled back. "And don't worry. You've seen how I'm more out of bed than in these days and getting stronger by the minute."

Mary didn't look convinced but argued no further. "You'd best put on an old dress, then, for you've some plucking to do."

————

Drew knew she'd be pleased, but he wasn't prepared for the sight greeting him now. Constance stood beside the board dressed in Nellie's remade frock, with all that glorious hair tucked beneath her cap. Her cheeks were flushed, her smile captivating and her eyes brimmed with life, pleasure, and unmistakable warmth.

Sweet heaven, but she was beautiful. She glided around the board toward him. "Welcome home, Master Drew."

Her low, silvery murmur so distracted him, he almost missed the significance of her words. *Master* Drew? He searched her eyes, then felt his chest expand a good two or three inches. She was pleased with him. Very pleased.

Pressing her skirt against her thighs, she poked out the toe of one shoe. "Look, they're perfect. Much better than Nellie's discards."

His gaze moved down the length of her. "I can't see much of it. Perhaps you could lift the hem of your skirt a bit more?"

Withdrawing her foot, she tsked. "Such suggestions, good sir."

Their eyes met.

"Thank you," she whispered. "I'm saving the ribbon for Christmas, I haven't had to make use of the candle yet, and as you can see, the shoes serve me well. Where did you get all these things?"

"That'd be telling."

Her features softened. "Did you make the shoes?"

He nodded once.

"There's a left one and a right one. You'll spoil me." Leaning toward him, she placed a hand against his chest. "Thank you."

His blood pounded. He covered her hand with his. "I should have done it long ago."

She twined her fingers within his. "You killed Mr. Meanie."

He swallowed. "Yes."

Taking another step forward, she stood on tiptoes and touched her lips to his. "I love you."

He froze for a mere instant before propelling her to the door, slinging his jacket around her shoulders, and pushing her outside. The door hadn't thumped to a close before he'd crushed her against him, his mouth claiming hers.

Running his hands up and down her spine, his mouth strayed to her ears, her neck, her shoulders. She threw her head back, her cap floating to the ground as mountains of hair spilled atop his arms.

It was then he saw the coat no longer covered her but lay crumpled at her feet. "Your jacket."

"Leave it."

Snagging the coat, he again settled it about her shoulders, scooping her hair from beneath its confines.

Her lids fluttered open, eyes smoldering with desire. "When?"

His heart slammed against his ribs. "I will arrange it."

She fisted her hands, wrinkling his shirt within them. "When?" she whispered.

"Tomorrow."

———

She couldn't eat a thing. Her body hummed, her nerves stood on end, her skin prickled.

Drew ate like a starved man. "This is wonderful, Mary. Absolute perfection."

"The mistress made it, she did."

He paused, drumstick halfway to his mouth. His attention swerved to her. "Wanted to roast the little roister yourself, did you?"

Constance pulled her focus away from his lips, suppressing a smile. "Such wit. I wanted to learn to cook. For you. I thought it was a good place to start."

Tearing a piece of meat from the bone with his teeth, he held her gaze and chewed. "Very tasty."

A quiver surged through her, pooling at the pit of her stomach. "Thank you."

"Aren't you going to try it?" He wiped his sleeve across his mouth.

She studied the wing and thigh on her trencher. She hated Mr. Meanie. But she'd gotten to know him and they'd reached an understanding of sorts. Now she was to have him for supper.

"Don't tell me you're feeling guilty?"

Breaking off a piece of the wing, she brought it to her lips and took a bite. It did taste good. Very good. "I wonder if all grouchy males are this palatable."

Drew choked.

She looked up, tilting her head. "Are you all right?"

He turned a dull red. "Eat your supper, Connie."

CHAPTER | TWENTY

S HE COULDN'T DO ANYTHING right. She'd been clumsy in the milking of Snowflake—which resulted in a near miss from the goat's hoof, she'd knocked her shin against the bench, she'd sewn a sleeve on inside out, and now, she'd kicked over the sand bucket they kept for extinguishing cooking fires.

Falling to her knees, she scooped handful after handful of sand back into the bucket. The more she scooped, the bigger the mess. In a few short hours it would be nightfall, and she'd be Drew's wife in every way.

Her face heated. How ever did one make it through their own wedding party? She'd never much thought about it before, but every guest *knew* what was going to happen between the couple come sunset. She paused, looking at the sand. How awful!

Mary knelt down beside her. With expert hands she corralled the scattered sediment and returned it to the bucket. "Mistress, I'll do this, I will."

"No! *I'll* do this. I made the mess; I'll clean it up."

Mary slowly withdrew her hands, then stood. Constance sat down on her heels. "Your pardon, Mary. I didn't mean to snap at you."

"What ails you, Mistress?"

The door opened. Constance jumped to her feet.

"What happened?" Drew asked.

Constance stood mute. Mary resumed scooping the sand.

Surely it wasn't time yet! It was still light outside. Drew closed the door. "Connie?"

She started. "Oh! I, uh, I kicked over the sand bucket."

"Are you all right?"

"Fine! Fine. Just fine. How are you?"

A slow smile spread across his face. "Very, very fine."

She blinked.

Mary paused and slowly stood. "I think I'm going to see if there are any eggs in the hen house, I am. I'll be back in a . . . while." Grabbing her shawl, she slipped out the door.

Drew raised an eyebrow. "What was that all about?"

Constance clasped her hands together. "I think she must need some eggs."

"She's going to have a hard time finding any in the middle of December."

"Will she?"

He hesitated, then slowly stalked toward her. "I haven't been able to get a thing done. I forgot to attach the bottom head to a barrel before filling it with tobacco, I mislabeled two hogsheads, I strode straight into the tobacco press, and I let go of the packing lever before it was time."

She moved backward. "Oh, Drew, you peagoose. Are you nervous? You've nothing to fear."

A charming grin split across his face. "Well, that's certainly a relief."

Her back connected with the wall. "You're laughing at me."

He narrowed the distance between them. "Never."

"It's still daylight!"

He propped his hands on either side of her, bracketing her in. "I couldn't wait another minute."

She ducked underneath his arms, flitting to the other side of the cottage. "Drew! You can't possibly be serious."

Pushing away from the wall, he headed toward her again. "No, but a kiss would be rather nice. Just to hold me over."

Her pulse leapt. She glanced at the door. "Well, maybe a quick one."

He shook his head from left to right, coming closer, closer.

Her heart beat painfully against her breast. "Drew, maybe we'd best . . ."

He laid his hands upon her shoulders, running his palms up and down her arms. "You're so unbelievably beautiful."

He kissed her forehead, his hands moving, moving, never staying still. Her eyes drifted shut. Up her arms, across her shoulders, down her back and up to her shoulders again.

Slipping an arm about her waist, he traced her lips with tiny kisses. "Ah, Connie-girl."

She slid her hands inside his coat, cataloging the strength of his waist and back. His mouth covered hers, weakening her resolve.

The door flew open.

They jumped apart, Drew spinning to face the intruder, Constance hiding behind him.

"Josh!" Drew surged forward, leaving Constance where she stood. "Well. This is certainly a surprise."

She was too mortified to move. Surely the earth would be merciful and swallow her whole. It didn't. She had mere seconds to compose herself while Josh dropped his cloth bag and the brothers embraced.

"You're back! How did you get here so quickly? I'm not even finished packing the hogsheads!"

"I came over with a group of settlers who were heading to that new colony, Maryland." He pulled back from Drew's hug. "You say you've not finished with the hogsheads? Why not?"

Drew reddened. "I've been busy."

Josh lifted a brow. "I'll just bet you have." He moved to her. "Lady Constance. You're looking lovelier than ever."

Disregarding the high color she felt in her cheeks, she strode for a sense of normalcy. "Welcome home, Josh."

He bowed low and deep, drawing her hand to his lips. "I must say what an honor it is to have a *real* lady as my sister-in-law."

Her gaze flew to Drew. Lifting a corner of his mouth, he winked. She slowly exhaled. So he really had believed her.

Josh straightened, then stared at the locket hanging about her neck. "What's this?" he asked, gathering the locket into his palm.

It had completely escaped her mind. Drew had left it for her this morning, and in all the confusion she'd forgotten to thank him. "Drew gave it to me."

Josh's eyebrows raised. "Did he? And when did that happy event occur?"

"This morning," she said, blinking in confusion.

Josh froze, swerving his attention to Drew. *"This morning!"*

Drew reddened again, saying nothing. Josh turned back to her. "Do you know what this is?"

"It's a locket."

Josh released his hold on it, watching it settle against her throat. "It was my mother's locket. Father gave it to her on their wedding night."

She felt the color in her face intensify, and she searched Drew's face. He stood stiffly, saying nothing. She clasped the gold ornament within her hand. "Oh, Drew." Sidestepping Josh, she moved to him. "Thank you."

He nodded his head once, the silence crackling. She took a deep breath. "I think I'll go check on Mary. I'll be right back."

The door clicked softly behind her.

"Body O'Caesar, Drew! I've been gone since June and you're just now getting around to bedding her?"

"Watch your tongue."

Josh rolled his eyes. "Your pardon, Drew, but I'm, well, just . . . amazed."

"Well, you're testing my temper."

"Your temper must be at the very breaking point. Six months!"

"You overstep yourself, Josh," he growled.

"But am I reading this situation correctly? Tonight is to be your wedding night?"

"Not anymore."

Josh threw back his head and laughed. "By trow, but it's good to be home, big brother."

The women reentered the cottage. Constance looked between the two of them— Drew was obviously agitated, Josh delighted. *Same old Josh,* she thought, then watched him refocus on Mary and come forward with another courtly bow.

Capturing Mary's fingers, he brought them to his lips. "Ah, my sweet, gentle doe, what pleasure to again behold your wondrous charms. Did you miss me, for you did lie upon *my* heart with a most alarming frequency."

Constance frowned. His words lacked the light tones she was used to hearing from him.

Astonishment touched Mary's face. She snatched her hand out of Josh's. "Where's your bride?"

Josh took on a wounded expression as he pressed a fist to his heart. "Though Hannah once declared her undying love for me, it seems another had the greater part of her fickle heart, and all her fair words to me were but lies."

"She cast you out, did she?" Drew asked.

Josh looked back at him. "With brutal haste."

Had she not been studying Josh so intently, she would have missed the pain that flashed within his eyes. She quickly glanced at Drew, but he didn't seem to have noticed.

Pasting a grin upon his face, Josh slapped his stomach. "Ah, Mary, 'tis starving, I am. Have you anything for me to eat?"

Mary bustled to the fire. Josh waited, then gravitated to Drew's chair. "What's this, big brother? Have you a sudden need to establish yourself at the head of the table?"

Constance watched Drew's expression turn stony. Josh looked at the two of them and grinned before, bold as you please, settling into the chair. He ran his hands along its arms and pushed himself against its back. "Well done, *Master*. It seems it should serve the purpose it was made for. Does it?"

Constance held her breath. The edge to Josh's voice was unmistakable.

Drew arched a brow. "Kindly remove yourself from *my* chair and come with me. I wish to show you the big house."

"Your pardon, Master." Springing from the chair, Josh brushed nonexistent dust from its seat. Mary handed him a hunk of bread.

Tearing off a bite, he chewed and slowly scanned the cottage. Constance watched him swallow, sober, and take a deep breath. "Where's Sally?" All pretense had vanished from his expression.

Drew offered him a small smile. "She's fine. She's with Grandma at Nellie's."

Josh's shoulders visibly relaxed, and he stuffed the rest of the bread into his mouth. She blinked as his charm reappeared and he bowed once again to Mary. "Thank you, my lovely creature. I shall count the moments until I may return to the cottage and partake of your delicious meals."

Drew grabbed him by his coat sleeve and shoved him toward the door. "Out." He looked at Constance, shrugged, then followed Josh out the door.

———

Drew's chest swelled with pride when they rounded the bend and the house came into view. Josh stopped short, a slow whistle coming from his mouth. Magnificent and impressive, its newly whitewashed exterior gleamed against the artistic sky lines. Its enclosed porch and stair towers gave it the shape of a cross, curving Flemish gables springing from its eaves. Triple chimneys protruded from both the east and west ends, unique in their very nature.

Patches of snow surrounded the house, lying like miniature lakes in every direction. Neither spoke as they climbed the slope, ice crunching beneath their boots. On the front steps, Drew threw open the doors, allowing Josh to enter first.

The interior had yet to be completed, of course, but the window casements with lead glass panes were in place, minus the trim work. Josh moved from the enclosed porch to the great room, looking out one of the windows facing the James. "I'm overwhelmed. What will you call it?"

Closing the paneled front doors, Drew shrugged. "I haven't decided yet. Any suggestions?"

"I'll have to think on it." Josh peered at the fireplace. "The tile backing turned out well."

"Yes. I'm very pleased with it."

Josh walked into the huge barren opening, testing the sturdiness of the expensive Dutch tiles with his hands. "I'd forgotten about bringing them over for Father, it's been so long."

"Come, I'll show you the rest."

Drew took him through the parlor and up a flight to the two chambers, one directly above the parlor, the other above the great room. "This will be my and Constance's bedchamber. Yours is there across from us."

Josh walked over to his chamber, a mirror image of Drew's. The fireplace, though a bit smaller than the ones downstairs, still dominated the vacant room. "I was not expecting so much."

"Why ever not?"

Josh shrugged. "I'm hardly ever here. It seems a waste of space."

"It's not as if I've *bestowed* something upon you. We are partners, and there would be no new house if it were not for your factoring skills. You may be gone a good bit of the time, but this is your home, and this chamber is no less than what you should have. Besides, when you marry, your wife will not be with you on your trips, but here with us."

There. He'd given Josh an opening to speak of the broken betrothal.

"What of children?" Josh asked. "Constance will be wanting a nursery close at hand."

Drew allowed the opportunity to pass. "True. But I would imagine she'd want to keep the little ones in the chamber with us until they are older. Then when she's ready to move them, we've plenty of room up in the garret. Come, I'll show you."

Along the way, he pointed out the beamed ceiling supporting the next story's planked floor and the staircase's newel-posts with a half baluster set into it.

"With what will you finish the walls?"

"I'm going to panel the great room and parlor, then plaster everything else. Did you check on the furniture I ordered?"

Josh nodded. "A ship should come through in March with your beds, chairs, tables, chests, and all."

Drew took a deep breath of satisfaction. "Excellent. Now, come down to the cellar and see the kitchen."

The thumps of their footfalls echoed in the stairwell. Josh slapped Drew on the back. "Her father really is the Earl of Greyhame, you know."

"You tracked him down, then?"

"There was no need, for he was still at his manor. He's an old gaffer, Drew, well into his seventies, I'd say, and too old to take part in the fighting. So he furthers the cause by giving his silver and other valuables to the king, as well as sending his sons into service—those that weren't for parliament, that is."

"How was your reception?"

"Very good until his relief was replaced with anger. The Lady Constance has evidently been a bit of a trial for him. And when he found you'd married her, I feared he would expire on the spot. I sought to pacify him by giving him her missive, which evidently contained her plans for an annulment. That, however, only caused him more anxiety. He claimed her reputation would be in tatters if word got out, especially since he'd recently found a suitable match for her."

"A suitable match?"

"Um. Some young, handsome aristocrat he felt would appeal to her."

"And wouldn't do him any harm either, I'd wager."

"Quite so."

"So what conclusion did you reach?"

"The earl can't leave his home right now, but he's making plans to fetch her this spring."

Drew raised his eyebrows. "I thought you said he was seventy-something."

"Oh, he's old, all right, and substantial in both paunch and pouch"—Josh hinted at a smile—"but mark you, he'll be here come spring. You can count on it."

Drew raked his fingers through his hair. *Lord help us all.*

They reached the bottom of the stairs. Sleeping ticks littered the cellar's brick floor, and a pile of lifeless ashes lay heaped in the huge fireplace. Josh turned a questioning glance to Drew.

"The indentured men. I saw no need to make them stay in the tobacco barn once we'd dried in the house."

Josh nodded then moved through the room. "Not only brick walls but a brick floor? Was that in Father's plan?"

"Not the floor. I thought it might make for a happier cook, though, if she had a brick floor rather than a dirt one."

Josh lifted one corner of his mouth. "Might provide your bottomless belly with a few more succulent dishes as well, eh?"

"Couldn't hurt." Sucking in his stomach, Drew made a concave area. "I'm always in need of a hearty meal." The brothers shared a smile. "Come. The milk closet is over here."

They examined the dairy and another room filled with empty wooden kegs for storing fruits and vegetables. Finally, they stood at a door with a bulkhead entrance while Drew expounded on how easy it would be to transport food from the garden and such without having to traipse through the main house.

Josh leaned against the brick wall, crossing his ankles, and looked the room over before returning his attention to his brother. "It's a fine plantation home you have here, Drew. Father would be very proud."

Drew pulled the door shut, latching it with a rope. "The men you recommended have worked out better than I'd dared to hope. I couldn't have done it without them."

"They survived the seasoning, then?"

Drew shook his head. "Not all of them. Seven suffered at one time or another and we lost Browne and Payne. Still, I never expected to have eight men come winter. So I'm grateful."

"What about the women?"

Drew moved toward the stairwell, heading up to the front door, Josh at his side. "Mary never had so much as a sniffle. Constance nearly died."

Josh stopped. "My sword, Drew. What did she get?"

"The ague and fever."

"When?"

"In November."

Josh blew a stream of air from his lungs. "Yet Mary had nothing?"

Drew shook his head.

"Do you think Mary's still likely to take ill?"

"I don't think so, but one never knows." They continued on to the front door, where Drew paused, his hand on the knob. "I'll not have you trifling with her, Josh."

"Her husband's dead."

"Is he?" He expelled a breath of air. "I guess I'll have to tell her this eve."

"No!"

Drew lifted his brows.

"I'd like to tell her."

"As you wish. But that changes nothing. Widow or not, she's under my care and she's an indentured servant, which means she can't marry until her service to me is over."

Josh stiffened. "She could marry if someone bought out her contract."

"She was transported by the court's command, Josh. If I were to release her before her sentence is up, it would mean her death."

"Only if she went back to England."

"Do you wish to wed her, then?"

Josh blanched. "Mary? Well, no."

Drew opened the door. "Then I'll not swap arguments with you. She's under my care, and if you or any other man trifles with her, it will be my temper they face."

"Do you credit me with so little scruples, then, that you think I'd force myself upon our own servants?"

"I've no concern whatsoever that you would even consider force. I said I'd not have you *trifling* with her."

"And if she's willing?"

"You're her master, Josh. She won't say nay to you whether she wishes to or not. If you want her, you'll wed her first."

Josh's lips thinned. "Hear me well, Drew. Because you are the firstborn, I am willing to cooperate with you—up to a certain point. But I'll not let you nor anyone else tell me who I can *trifle* with and who I can't."

Drew narrowed his eyes. "She's under my care and as long as she is, that means you are a protector of her also. I will not have her put into a position where she must fend off the very person who's supposed to be protecting her."

"Thus, any man can trifle with her but me?"

"*No* man can trifle with her, *especially* you, and that's an end to it. Have I made myself clear?"

Josh held himself erect. "Rest assured, you've made yourself perfectly clear." Spinning around, he stormed down the front steps. Drew hesitated, then pulled the door shut behind him.

————

He disliked being in a chair at the head of the board when Josh was home, particularly after the exchange they'd had at the big house. Their father had certainly never seen the need to establish himself in such a way. But there'd really been nothing left for Drew to do. So he'd just pulled the chair up and taken his place.

He glanced over at Josh. His brother, never one to stay angry long, was back to his old self, entertaining the ladies and telling them of the news from London. He gave them updates on the skirmish and answered Constance's endless questions about her family and friends.

Drew ate his last bite of rabbit, its tender, juicy texture setting well within his stomach but not improving his disposition. He'd planned for this to be his wedding feast, not Josh's homecoming.

Mary rose to collect the trenchers and take them to the hearth, Constance following her lead. He and Josh shoved the board against the wall, then moved his chair and one bench to the fire.

Picking up his pipe, Drew leaned back and took great pleasure in observing his wife as she scrubbed a trencher with sand from the sand bucket.

He sighed. He, of course, was pleased to have Josh safely home, but for the first time in his life, he resented Josh's presence and the lack of privacy the cottage provided. Still, he was loath to send him packing off to Nellie's on the very day of his return.

The women made short work of the trenchers, then stacked them on the shelves.

"Come join us, ladies," Drew said. "I've a need to look at something other than this ill-mannered brother of mine." He watched them return, Connie taking a place on the end of the bench farthest from his chair. Stifling his disappointment, he focused on the fire.

"Well, Lady Constance, you've asked after everyone in your family, you've asked after several of your female companions, but you've yet to ask me of your father's reaction to your nuptials."

Drew stilled.

Constance laid her hands upon her lap. "Only because I'm quite certain of what his reaction was once he read my letter."

"Are you?"

She nodded. "Anger. A great deal of it."

"I didn't give him the letter right away, but once I did, you're quite right. His anger was something to behold."

She bit her lip. "And?"

Josh stretched out his legs, crossing them at the ankles. "We had a bit of a discussion, and then he said he'd come and fetch you back this spring."

Constance's back straightened. *"Spring!"*

"Yes. Is that too long to wait, my lady? I'll take you back on the next boat if you wish it."

Drew furrowed his brows as her face filled with color and her jaw tightened. Quickly thinking back to the summer night he'd brought her home from the ship, he remembered with clarity her confidence that once her father received word, he would immediately come for her. That bounder. That she wanted to stay now was not at issue here. Her father's indolent attitude was a slap in her face. "Enough, Josh. We'll discuss this later."

Josh sent him a hard look, full of resentment. "I'll have it from her own lips that she desires to wait. Otherwise, I'll take her back. We wouldn't want her to feel obligated to you simply because you're her *protector.*"

Drew lurched to his feet. "Outside."

Josh immediately stood.

Constance jumped between them. "Sit down, the both of you. Sit down. And of course I want to wait—I mean, stay. I've already made that perfectly clear to your brother, Josh, but I appreciate your giving me the opportunity to return home right away if I'd wished. Now *sit down.*"

Drew slowly sunk back into his chair, his temper barely in check. Josh walked to the shelf, slipping the courting stick out from where it had been wedged. He thrust the stick toward Drew. Drew straightened himself in the chair. What was the matter with Josh? He was acting like a princox. Drew looked at Connie. She gave him a slight shrug of her shoulders. Clearly, she was baffled as well. He made no move to take the stick.

"Do you not wish to woo your lady? You remember how it's done. Just think back. Gerald certainly had no problem wielding it."

Drew narrowed his eyes. Josh was intentionally trying to provoke him. He knew the subject of Gerald was a sensitive one. He knew Drew felt responsible for Nellie's indiscretion, for Drew had had no previous experience with courting rituals.

But it didn't take much intelligence to figure bundling a young woman, bundling up her beau, and then allowing them to lie abed and whisper love words to each other was anything other than a recipe for disaster.

Leah had refused to bundle with him, and Josh had never taken advantage of the custom, so Nellie had been the family's first.

He'd held serious doubts about the wisdom of it, but Josh had made little of those concerns, Nellie had badgered him and everyone else in the colony did it. Even Grandma hadn't objected to the practice. So he'd given in.

When Nellie finally admitted to her condition, he'd been furious—with Gerald, Nellie, Josh, Grandma. Everyone. But most especially with himself. And it had all started with that blasted courting stick.

His lips thinned with irritation. It was pure folly Josh was up to.

Drew watched Josh present one end of the stick to Mary. "Sweet maid, be so kind as to hold this against your ear."

She glanced at Contance and hesitated before lifting the stick's end to her ear. Josh placed his lips at the other end of the hollowed out log and whispered something into it.

Color flooded Mary's face as her gaze collided with Josh's, and she quickly lowered the stick to her lap.

Drew surged forward, wrenching it from him.

Josh bowed to Drew. "No need to grab it from me. I had planned on letting you use it." He sat on the bench. "Go ahead. Mary and I will chaperone."

Drew clasped the stick with both hands, then slammed it against his thigh, slinging the broken halves into the fire. "You've overstepped yourself. Be gone from my sight."

Josh rose, the muscle in his jaw pulsing. "Certainly."

He watched Josh climb up the ladder to the loft and descend with two cumbersome ticks slung over his shoulder. "Come, Mary. It is time."

Mary scrambled to her feet, heading to the door.

Drew curled his fists. It was nothing short of an open challenge. He'd made it clear where he stood on the matter of Mary, yet Josh was flaunting that directive. Not only flaunting, but from the way Mary had responded to his call, Josh had obviously made some kind of arrangement with her.

Josh opened the door.

"A moment, you two!"

Mary froze, and Josh impaled him with his glare.

"Where go you?"

"From your sight, I believe the instructions were."

"Those *instructions* were for you, not Mary."

"She's going with me. We will spend the whole of this night in the big house. But do not worry. I will see to her *protection*."

"She goes nowhere."

"On the contrary, Drew. It is your wedding night, if you will, and I, for one, fear that if you don't have total privacy you might never manage it."

By my troth! He pierced Josh with his gaze. "Mary, get yourself up to the loft."

Mary quickly tried to acquiesce, but Josh encircled her arm. "Nay. She goes with me."

"She will not."

Keeping a loose hold on Mary, Josh dropped the ticks and squared his shoulders. "She will."

Lord help me! It would serve no purpose whatsoever to come to blows with him, other than to possibly relieve him of whatever devil was in his craw. With supreme effort, Drew reined in his temper and calmed his voice. "I'll have your word about the concerns I shared with you earlier."

They stood in silence for several moments before Josh lifted his chin a notch. "I give you my word, none of the concerns you have will come to pass this night. Get your shawl, Mary."

Mary looked up at Drew. He nodded once. She grabbed her shawl and flew out the door, Josh right behind her with their ticks once again slung over his shoulder.

CHAPTER | TWENTY-ONE

THE DOOR SWUNG BACK open, unable to latch itself after Josh had slammed it. Constance moved nary a muscle. Drew, with a heavy tread, pushed the door shut. "This isn't exactly the way I had the evening planned."

She clasped her hands together.

He turned around and leaned against the door, resting his head back as well. He surveyed the beam work supporting the thatched roof. "He's changed. I haven't seen him act this way since he was ten and three. He said not a word to me about his broken betrothal, but whatever happened has obviously affected him greatly."

"Hannah Eastlick is a vicious woman."

His gaze snapped to hers. "You know the lady Hannah Eastlick of Bowden?"

She nodded. "Quite well. Her father and mine dealt together often, and I must confess those business dealings were not as forthright as they should have been. Regardless, Hannah often accompanied her father to our home and I was responsible for her entertainment."

"How did you know she was betrothed to Josh?"

"The day of our marriage, he spoke of it to Governor Hopkin."

"Why say you she's vicious?"

She took a deep breath. "I've both witnessed it and been the recipient of it. She's deceitful, manipulative, self-centered, and cruel."

His eyebrows shot up. "All that?"

"Well, according to my brother Foley, she also plays the part of the maiden quite well but is, in fact, without discretion."

"He told you that!"

"Certainly not. He told my other brother and I was . . . I uh . . . overheard it."

He shook his head. "Josh is usually very good at discerning a person's character."

"She's a master at deception. It was quite some time before I realized her true nature as well."

"Then it's glad I am he's rid of her." After a moment, he rubbed his hand across his mouth. "About your father, Connie. Josh didn't tell you everything. The earl not only wants you home, but he has—"

She held up her palm, stopping his flow of words. "I want to stay, Drew. It will be wonderful to see him this spring, but he'll return home without me."

"But, he—"

"Not another word. My mind's made up."

He appeared to think that over, then pulled away from the door. "Are you cold?"

She rubbed her arms. "Um. A little."

He moved to stoke the fire, then indicated the bench with his hand.

"It will be a cold walk for them this night," she said, settling her skirt about her.

Drew nodded but clearly his mind was elsewhere.

She tried again. "I wish I could see the new house. Now everyone but me will have seen it."

He sat down beside her, took her hand in his, and rested them atop his thigh. "Not just yet. Though you're well, I want you to stay that way so you can attend the Christmas service with me next week. The meetinghouse is quite a trek from here. I would that you were rested for it."

"How far away is the meetinghouse?"

He pursed his lips. "If we walk at the rate of 3 miles an hour, we shall be 10 minutes late, but if we walk 4 miles an hour, we shall be 20 minutes too-soon. Know you now how far it is from here?"

She arched a brow. "You thought that up ahead of time."

"Maybe."

Suppressing a smile, she cleared her throat. "I've a question for you too."

He nodded once.

"I ask you, sir, to plant a grove, to show that I'm your lady love. This grove though small must be composed of 25 trees in 12 straight rows. In each row 5 trees you must place, or you shall never see my face."

His eyes flickered. "How long will it take you to solve my puzzle?"

"How long will it take you to solve mine?"

"I already have."

She choked back a laugh. "You lie."

"How long will it take you?" he asked.

"Fifteen minutes."

His gaze caught and held hers. "Care to place a wager on it?" He skimmed a callused thumb across her knuckles. "And this time, there will be no bargaining over dishwashing."

Her heart fluttered. "Then what will we wager upon?"

"A kiss. A kiss freely given."

"And if I win?" she said, swallowing tightly.

His eyes darkened. "I'll forfeit much, much more than just a kiss."

She fingered the locket about her neck. "I'll need my slate."

He bent toward the fire, scooping up a handful of cold soot and spreading it out on the hearth. "Sketch away."

For a space of several beats, she considered him, then found herself on her knees beside the pile of soot. She quickly scratched several numbers into it before glancing back over her shoulder. "Clock's ticking. You'd better get over there with your own soot."

Chuckling, he moved to the opposite end of the hearth. Twenty-five minutes later, she sat back. He was leaning against the hearth, one leg extended, one bent, his face propped atop his palm. He removed the pipe from his mouth. "About time."

She narrowed her eyes. "You're awfully sure of yourself."

A slow smile stretched across his face.

"What's your solution?" she asked.

"Come see."

She rose to her knees, shuffling over to his drawing. He had indeed laid out a grove in which 25 finger indentions were placed in such a way that each row held 5 indentions for a total of 12 rows.

"What's the answer to my puzzle?" he asked.

She sat back on her heels. "Church is a five-mile walk from here."

He smiled. It was a two-dimple smile. "Wrong. You lose."

Her eyes widened. "How so?"

He smoothed the soot beside him, effectively erasing his grove, then scribbled numbers into the ashes. "If d is the time it takes to walk to church at 3 miles per hour and 4 miles per hour respectively and the difference is half an hour, then d over 3 minus d over 4 equals one-half. Multiply both sides by twelve to eliminate the fractions and you have $4d$ minus $3d$ equaling 6. Church is a *six*-mile walk from here."

She studied his figures. Oh no. How could she have miscalculated something so elementary?

"What formula did you use to come up with five miles?" he asked.

Her eyes drifted closed. "The wrong one."

He brought his hands together with a clap, a tiny cloud of soot tickling her nose.

She opened her eyes, but he'd already moved to resettle himself upon the bench. Spreading his knees, he rubbed his thighs. "I'm ready for my forfeit."

Heat stole into her face. Looking one more time at his figures, she pulled her trapped skirt from beneath her knees, then slowly stood.

His gaze roved boldly over her. A flash of self-consciousness threatened her resolve before she reined it in. Gliding toward him, she moved between his knees, stopping just short of touching him. His Adam's apple bobbed.

"Close your eyes," she whispered.

He immediately acquiesced. She pecked him on the nose, then whirled, darting back to the fireplace, but not before he snagged a portion of her skirt.

"I don't think so." His voice had dropped two octaves.

She looked behind her, watching as he wrapped her skirt about his fist, effectively reeling her in. "I gave you the forfeit! One kiss. Freely given."

"That was not a kiss and well you know it."

"It most certainly was. That you neglected to specify where and how the kiss was to be administered is no fault of mine."

He had her between his knees now and gave a quick jerk, causing her to drop onto one of his legs. He touched a finger to his lips. "Right here, Connie. I'll have one right here."

She bit the insides of her cheeks. "Really? Or else . . ."

A glint of mischief entered his eyes. "I dare not threaten to make you sit here all night until you do so, or you might very well take me up on it."

A giggle worked its way up, then she sighed with an exaggerated sense of resignation, wrapped her arms about his neck, and pressed her lips to his. That was the last bit of control she exerted over the kiss, for he immediately took charge. All thoughts of forfeits and challenges fled from her mind. She parted her lips, he deepened the kiss.

Shifting, she sought to slow the pace a bit. He pulled her closer, but the bench made his movements awkward, threatening to unseat them at every turn.

Tearing his mouth from hers, their eyes met, a flurry of butterflies brandishing their wings within her tummy.

"Are you frightened?" he asked.

She swallowed. "I didn't think I would be. I thought I'd be . . . oh, I know not. The only word I can think of is, well, anxious."

He became very still. "*Anxious* as in *impatient*?"

Heat flooded her face.

He squeezed her waist. "It's not a shameful thing to be feeling, not for your husband."

"How do you know?"

"I looked it up in the Bible."

She covered her mouth with her hand. "You didn't!"

"I did. And it's very biblical to be wanting your mate. As a matter of fact, it says to rejoice in the sharing of your flesh—to relish it, even."

She smiled behind her hand. "It does not."

"It does too. Proverbs 5:18."

Laughter bubbled up from her throat. She knew perfectly well it said no such thing, but she'd never expected him to soothe her in such an outrageous way.

He frowned. "I'll show you."

She tightened her grip on his shoulder, stopping him. "Where are you going?"

"To get my Bible."

"Right now? You can't get your Bible out right now! I'm, I'm, we're just about to, to . . ." She'd never be able to go through with this if he got out his Bible. She wiped all humor from her face. "I believe you. Proverbs 5:18. 'Rejoice, relish, and romp with your husband.'"

He chuckled. "I'm serious, Connie, and I won't have you feeling ashamed or unclean over anything we do in that bed, tonight or any other night."

"I won't. I feel unashamed and very clean. I promise. But please don't get out that Bible."

"What? Think you God can't see us right now?"

Groaning, she slid off his lap and covered her face with her hands. He sunk to his knees in front of her, drawing her hands down. "I love you. You love me. We are man and wife. God is watching, Connie, and He is very, very pleased."

I love you. It was the first time he'd ever said it to her. She'd known it, of course. Known it since he'd killed Mr. Meanie, but she hadn't realized how much she wanted to hear the words. A warm glow flowed through her.

And, truth was, she *didn't* feel ashamed. And she *had* in the very back of her mind worried over it. Smiling, she tilted her head to the side. "Shall we rejoice?"

He grinned. "By all means."

Lifting her into his arms, he carried her to their marriage bed.

CHAPTER | TWENTY-TWO

A CACOPHONY OF VOICES FILTERED up from the cellar, punctuated by short barks of laughter. Josh dropped the ticks, quietly closing the front doors behind him. "Wait here."

The clamor grew louder as he made his way down the stairs. Standing on the bottom step, he watched as one-by-one the men noticed him, stopped speaking, and jumped to their feet.

He advanced into the room. "Dig you den."

Thomas stepped forward and they clasped hands. "Welcome home, Master Josh."

"Thank you, Thomas. It's good to be back. I can see the lot of you have been enjoying Mary's meals. You men were but a big bag of bones when we first arrived."

A few chuckles and murmurs of agreement answered him. He made a point of greeting each man with a handshake, a slap on the shoulder, and a comment or two. He mentioned his sorrow over the loss of Browne and Payne, as well as his pleasure that everyone else was in such good health. They relaxed some, but none resumed their seats on the floor.

"I decided to try out my new chambers and thought I'd best come down and warn you of my presence. I had no wish to confront any of you in the midst of the night thinking I was a cutpurse of some kind."

More chuckles and murmurs. He scanned the bricked-in room. "You've been busy. The house is spectacular, and Drew says the tobacco crop is one of the best we've ever had. It's pleased I am to come back to such news."

All but Thomas lowered their chins and shuffled their feet. "Thank you, sir."

" 'Tis I who should be doing the thanking." Josh slapped Thomas again on the shoulder. "Well, I'm going to borrow some of the split wood I saw outside and then retire. Good night, men. I'll see you in the morning."

———

Flames cavorted among the logs, devouring the pine kindling before taking the slow-burning oak into its embrace. Josh poked at the fire, trying to maximize the amount of heat it put forth, for the barren chamber was cold, as well as quiet and very still.

Nary a sound reached them from belowstairs. Josh glanced at Mary's form hovering just inside his doorway. He hadn't wanted the men to know she was here, aware of what the implications would be if they had. He'd planned to have her sleep here in his chamber while he slept in Drew's with no one the wiser. But the more he thought of it, the more impractical that became.

What if one of the men did come abovestairs? How could he even begin to protect her when he lay in a completely different room? There weren't even any doors yet. And those men had been without women for a very long time. She'd be lying alone here much like a lamb waiting for the slaughter.

Besides, it was deuced hard to warm these huge chambers, and he had no desire to lug up another stack of lumber. No, it would be best if they both slept in here together, where he could keep his eye on her. "Come, Mary. Warm yourself."

She did as he instructed, but with obvious hesitation. He gave his full attention back to the fire, thinking it might put her more at ease if he were to be engrossed with its care.

When the fire became too hot to tend, he retrieved the ticks from across the room and threw them in front of the hearth. "Sit down, Mary. Please."

She wrung her hands, then did as he asked, looking much like a newly placed fence post—stiff, sturdy, and rigid. He settled onto the other tick, propping his elbow on his bent knee while fingering the toothpick in his mouth. Silence permeated the room while each watched the flames paw at the thick pile of logs.

It was highly improper what they were doing. And both knew it. The emptiness of the house and room only added to the feeling of isolation and seclusion. A room even as bare as the cottage at least had a bed, a board, benches, and chests. This room had absolutely nothing except two ticks, a man, a woman, and a very large wooden floor. To pretend the atmosphere wasn't wrought with tension was ludicrous.

He glanced at her, feeling sure she was cognizant of it. She still held herself perfectly erect in the midst of her tick, arms wrapped around knees that hugged her chest beneath her skirt. He rolled the toothpick to the other side of his mouth.

Adding to the impropriety of it all was the risk of being caught by one of the eight men only two stories below them. If they were to be discovered, the men might think Mary was free game from then on. He sighed. He should have left her at the cottage and come here alone. "Do you wish to go back?"

If possible, her body stiffened even more. "Needs I?"

He slowly removed the toothpick from his mouth. "I'll not be making any advances on you, if that's what you mean."

The grip she had on her hands relaxed some. "I see no need to return until morning, I don't. Not unless *you* wish it."

"No. No, I don't."

She looked at him then, but didn't ask. Didn't ask why he'd baited Drew. Didn't ask why he'd whispered inappropriate words through the courting stick. Didn't ask why he'd been making such an idiot of himself. But she didn't need to. Those huge eyes of hers said it all.

He clamped down on the toothpick. "I found your husband."

She pulled her attention away from him.

"He was already six feet under, though, so I couldn't tear him apart for you. Seems somebody else beat me to it."

Laying her forehead against her updrawn knees, she made no comment.

"Wish you to hear the details?"

"You are sure it was Obadiah?" Her voice was muffled but very distinguishable in the vacant room.

"I'm sure."

She shook her head. "I care not for the details, I don't."

Look up, Mary. Are you crying? Or are you simply relieved? Look up and let me see. She remained as she was, hiding within the folds of her skirt.

"I saw where you lived. Where you worked. Met your neighbors."

The burning logs shifted, spitting out tiny flickers of fire before settling into a new position. His gaze moved over the nape of her neck, exposed by her position and tickled by a few fine dark hairs slipping from beneath her cap. "Ruth Parker sends her greetings."

She turned her face toward him while keeping her head against her knees.

"She's expecting her eighth. Might well have had it by now."

He watched in fascination as she slowly blinked her eyes, a leisurely down sweep of lashes, tarrying for a moment before swinging open again. She asked nothing and, indeed, he had nothing more to tell. Her neighbors had been very reluctant to talk to him at all. If it had not been for this Ruth woman, he might never have found Obadiah—or his remains, as the case may be.

"Why didn't you marry her?"

So jolting was her question that it took him a moment to realize she wasn't talking of Ruth but of Hannah. He took a deep breath. He hadn't spoken about it to anyone. Not in England, not here, not anywhere. He'd simply posted the announcement and left.

Yet with Mary, he didn't have to be the successful tobacco factor from the colonies. He didn't have to be the I'm-okay-even-though-I've-been-jilted younger brother. He didn't even have to be the *master*, as Drew implied. With Mary, he need only be Josh. He snapped his toothpick in two. "I found her between the sheets with my best friend."

He heard her quick intake of breath and chuckled humorlessly. "Know you what the saddest part is? I regret the loss of my friend more than I do the loss of Hannah."

"I'm so sorry, Josh, but it's glad I am that you found out before the wedding day."

"I'm still incensed about it, Mary. The humiliation was beyond words."

He tightened his lips. "I had intended to remain in England once I married and simply receive Drew's shipments and fill his orders from there. I'm the only factor I know of who travels back and forth and have only done so to help Drew with the harvest. But he has men to help him with that now. So even though the marriage is off, I'm leaving when the next ship comes through."

She slowly lifted her head up off her knees. "He'll be heartbroken, he will. He cares for you very much and speaks of you often."

"He has a new wife, a new home, and a new life. He'll get over it."

She said nothing for a long, long time. "Know you how to read your Bible, Josh?"

He humphed. "Between my mother, my father, and my grandmother, they made sure I read the thing frontward, backward, and upside-down. Alas, I've memorized half of it, I think."

"Lucky, you are. I know not how to read and have only heard what the Father offered on an occasional Sunday morn."

"I would be happy to read to you, Mary. Any time you'd like."

She offered a hint of a smile. "Do you believe what it says?"

He squinted into the fire. "Yes, I suppose I do."

"Hmm."

He slanted her a glance. "What does that mean?"

"Oh, I know not," she said, lifting her shoulders. "Just thinking of how I believed as you did, yet still Obadiah robbed my happiness."

Frowning, he shook his head. "What are you talking about? One has nothing to do with the other."

Unraveling her hands, she turned her face toward him. "That's what I thought. I thought if I was clever or careful I could save my babies. But in the end, I couldn't. I realized I had no power at all. So I gave God complete control over my life, I did."

"When was that?"

"When Obadiah killed the babies."

He was silent a moment. "I mean no disrespect, Mary, but since that time your husband was press-ganged and murdered and you have been tried for perjury, deported, indentured, and sold. If that's what you can expect by giving God 'control,' then I think you'd be better off handling things on your own."

She turned back to the fire. "Just be careful that you don't let Lady Hannah rob you of your home, your family, or your very soul."

He shifted, seeking a more comfortable position. "I had decided to leave Virginia long before I discovered Hannah was a bedswerver."

"I speak not of your leaving, I don't. I speak of your easy and caring nature."

"You refer to a glass-gazing, knotty-pated, naïve Josh. He exists no more."

Silence. "Then I will mourn the loss of him."

She stretched out on her tick, and after a moment's pause, he followed suit. They now lay feet-to-feet along the front of the fireplace. After a long while, her deep, even breathing reached his ears.

He, however, didn't sleep but for snatches at a time, finally rising in the predawn hours to stoke the fire.

He had wanted Drew to have the pleasure of waking with his bride in total privacy. With that in mind, he'd brought corn pone over yesterday and left it in the storage room belowstairs, and he intended to have the men fed and packing hogsheads by the time the sun touched the horizon.

For Mary, it would mean a morning off from her ever-present task of feeding the multitudes. Opening the cloth pouch on his belt, he removed a battered chicken feather and ran his fingers along it for quite some time before brushing it across his lips, laying it beside her, then moving downstairs to wake the men.

———

Christmas Day dawned bright and sunny. Constance smoothed her hand down the waist of her new dress, anxious for Drew's reaction. He'd been quite busy the past week, and she'd not seen much of him after that first day.

She hadn't seen much of Josh either, for that matter. He'd continued to sleep in the big house, though Mary returned to the loft, and he only took the evening meals with them, opting to stay in the fields the rest of the time.

She wondered how Sally and Grandma were. They would see them at the service today. Grandma planned to stay on with Nellie, but Sally was to come home with them afterward. Constance couldn't wait. She'd missed the little moppet terribly. Her only regret was she hadn't been able to personally give her the green dress she'd made from her leftover fabric.

But Josh had insisted on taking it to her yesterday. He'd wanted to see Grandma and Nellie and then stay the night with them, meeting Drew and Constance at church on the morrow.

Well, the morrow was here, and she couldn't wait to embark on her first outing as Mistress O'Connor. The walk to church would totally wet the bottom of her skirt and soil her shoes, but it mattered not. It was Christmas Day, she'd meet new friends and Drew would be at her side the whole day through.

A great deal of noisy crunching heralded the approach of Drew and his men on the icy ground outside the cottage. She tightened the bow at her chin, ran a hand down her stomach, then glanced at Mary. "Are you ready?"

Mary nodded, her only concession to Christmas being a beautiful lavender ribbon tied about her waist. Constance had oohed and aahed over it before Mary finally confessed that Josh had given it to her.

The door opened, and Constance's heart stopped beating. Drew had dressed for the occasion as well. She'd grown so used to seeing him in the same type of garments day in and day out she'd never imagined him wearing anything else. But, oh, what a sight he was in his burgundy doublet slashed along the sleeves to accommodate the full white shirt bulging from its slits. Fine linen had been sewn to the cuffs and front opening, shown to fine effect against his camel-colored jerkin. His loose maroon breeches matched his doublet and were fastened below his knees. He reached up and removed a stiff beaver hat. He looked from Constance to Mary, then indicated with a nod of his head for Mary to leave. Mary scurried out of the cottage, grabbing her shawl before closing the door behind her.

"You said you had enough material for your gown."

Constance blinked, glancing down at her dress. "I did."

"Then what happened to the bodice?"

"Nothing happened to it. Why? What's wrong?"

His face filled with color. "What's wrong? What's *wrong*? The upper swell of your breasts are exposed!"

She laid a hand across her chest. "Is it lower than what the women here wear?"

"By trow, Connie, look at it!"

She jerked her hand down to her side. "I *asked* you what the fashions here were, and you said anything I made would be fine! Scooped bodices are all the rage in London and usually cut much, much deeper. But this one is perfectly decent. Am I to believe *no one* here wears scooped bodices?"

"Of course not!"

She swallowed hard, holding her tears in check. "I see. Well, I'll just wear one of my everydays, then." She turned her back, moving to retrieve one from a peg.

Softening his voice, he took a couple of steps forward. "Haven't you a neckpiece or something?"

She shook her head, silent tears now pouring down her face.

"Are you crying?"

She shook her head again, but he'd moved behind her, turning her to face him.

"Oh, Connie. Maybe the other women do wear scooped bodices. I honestly know not. All I know is, when you try and pack yourself into a bodice of that sort, well, it worries me. What if you had to sneeze or something? You'd be in jeopardy of . . ."

Her shoulders wilted. "That is the most addlepated thing I've ever heard. This neckline barely dips below my throat. I'm not in jeopardy of anything."

He looked unconvinced. "I suppose you could leave it on. The meetinghouse doesn't have a fireplace, so we'll all be in overcoats. No one will ever know."

"What about afterward?"

He rubbed his palms up and down her arms. "The men's military exercises are all out-of-doors, and any indoor activities will be in the frigid meetinghouse. You can simply claim you're not used to these Virginia winters and wish to keep your overcoat on. The bottom of your skirt will still be visible."

Bitter disappointment pushed more tears from her eyes.

"Now what's wrong? I said you could wear it."

She drew in a shaky breath. "I w-wanted you to l-like my dreeessssss."

He moved his gaze over her. "The gown makes my mouth water, love."

She swiped at her tears. "Drew, will the other women take off their overcoats?"

He nodded. "Yes."

"Then I want to take mine off. I can't possibly keep it on all the day long."

He glanced at her neckline. "Oh yes you can. Now wait here and I'll be right back."

Moments later, he returned with a beautiful fur draped across his arm. Constance stroked the soft orangish-red fur, cool to the touch from being outside. "Fox?"

"Yes."

"When did we eat fox?"

"We didn't. I made the Indian boy who chopped off your braid give me something in return. He decided fur the color of your hair would be a fair exchange."

She buried her fingers in it, running them against the grain. "It's stunning."

"So is your hair."

Looking up at him, she smiled. "Oh, Drew, you're such a peagoose."

He opened up the fur, placing it across her shoulders.

"It's a cape! And calf length! I thought it was a lap robe."

He smiled, pulling the hood up over her head and tying the front closed.

She preened, looking down at the lovely contrast it made against the green of her skirt. "Perhaps I won't need to take it off after all."

He pulled her against him and gave her a swift, hard kiss. "Merry Christmas, love. Now, we needs must go. The others wait upon us."

Outside, the eastern sun delved through the barren forest, scattering a profusion of tiny rainbows from the ice-covered branches to the earth's crystal floor. A handsome young bird wearing a leaf-brown jacket and a white bib at the throat fluttered to a branch, emitting a lovely series of descending halftones in a clear, loud voice.

Cool air bathed Constance's face, bringing the crisp, clean scent of winter with it. None of it, however, had the effect on her that the chair sled did.

Constructed of wide oak boards, the sled itself was nothing more than a chair on runners with a handle attached to the back for someone to push. But strewn across its sides and back were a series of yellow wild flowers woven together to form a garland of sorts. The daisylike flowers were no more than an inch in diameter but grew in clusters and were very numerous.

She fingered one, a delicate petal breaking off into her hand. "They're beautiful. Wherever did you find them?"

"Josh spotted them on his walk home from the wharf. He only mentioned them because they don't usually bloom this late in the season."

She brought the petal to her nose. "What are they called?"

When he failed to reply, she looked up at him, noting the mixture of humor and consternation in his expression.

"What?" she asked.

"They're called *sneezeweed*."

A smile tugged at her lips. "You're jesting."

"I wish I were."

She bit the insides of her cheeks. "Do they make people sneeze?"

He hung his head, but suppressed laughter caused his shoulders to bounce. "For some."

Laughter rippled from her lips, his low and throaty chuckle harmonizing with hers.

In that moment, when his crystal blue eyes held hers, when his straight white teeth contrasted pleasingly with his tanned face, when those deep dimples framed his smile, she knew once again. Knew there was no other place she'd rather be on Christmas Day or any other day than right here with Andrew Joseph O'Connor.

He extended a hand to her.

"I would have been happy to walk."

"I don't want you to take ill again."

"Where did you get the sled?"

"I made it."

"For me?" she asked, running her hands along its smooth surface.

He nodded.

"When?"

"Over the last month or so. Come. We needs must go."

She put her hand in his and allowed him to settle her into the seat. He handed her a small pile of blankets, which she secured on her lap, then he placed a tin foot stove with fired charcoal at her feet. Removing one of the blankets from her lap, he draped it over her and the stove, effectively creating a cocoon of warmth.

Had she been in London, it would have been less than what she was accustomed to. But here, in this wilderness, with Drew the one attending to her, she felt much like the queen herself.

"Warm enough?" he asked.

"It's wonderful, Drew. Thank you."

He seemed to remember their audience then, and handing a musket to Thomas, positioned himself behind the sled. With him pushing, they, as well as Mary and the men, began their six-mile trek to church.

CHAPTER | TWENTY-THREE

S O MUCH HAD CHANGED since she took ill six weeks ago. Winter had well and truly set in with remnants of snow here and there, icicles dangling overhead, and a frigid temperature numbing her cheeks. She saw no wildlife other than a few birds, but was once again humbled by the profusion of trees this land offered. Around every bend, there were more, reaching for the heavens with bare, knobby, ice-covered limbs.

And the sky. Lord have mercy, she'd never seen such a bright, rich blue stretching for miles with nary a cloud in sight. The absence of leaves on the trees stripped away all obstruction, allowing the blue wash overhead to envelop her within its magnificence.

The men all offered to help push her sled, but Drew wouldn't hear of it, so they instead centered their attention on Mary, an air of festivity injected into their tones.

Constance smiled. So effectively had the men encircled her friend, each trying to outdo the other with clever remarks, that she was completely hidden from Constance's view. At one point, Isaac walked backward in order to better catch her attention, only to stumble on a root and fall down with a resounding splat.

The other men made much of this display until Mary rushed forward to assist and ask after him. Through that one stunt alone, he had out-maneuvered every man there, and Constance delighted in watching their exasperated expressions, obviously wondering if Isaac had done it a'purpose.

They'd covered much ground now, and she expected to come upon the meeting-house and perhaps other churchgoers at any time. She was laying her head back to question Drew when she realized he had slowed their progress to not much more than a crawl, falling well behind Mary and the others.

"What?" she asked.

He looked down, wiping the unease from his expression. "What?"

She twisted around in her seat. "What worries you?"

"Nothing!"

She smiled. "Do not pretend with me, Drew. Something is amiss. What is it?"

He allowed what little momentum they had to fizzle out.

She waited, but he shrugged and then set to the path again. "It was nothing. Really."

Placing a hand on his, she gave it a gentle squeeze, and he stopped.

"Of what were you thinking?"

He swallowed, avoiding her gaze. "Everyone will be there."

"And . . . ?"

"And, everyone will see the chair sled."

"And . . . ?"

He looked down at her. "And I can't ever in all my days remember anyone arriving at church in a chair sled covered with sneezeweed."

She bit her lip. "Would you like to take it off? I mind not." She hesitated, then furrowed her brow. "I was, however, looking forward to Sally's expression when she saw the flowers. Perhaps if we leave the garland here, we could retrieve it on our way back? She could see them then. What think you of that?"

It was clear he was still vacillating.

"I truly do not mind, Drew."

He lifted his hat up, then resettled it upon his head. "Well, actually, I've . . . uh . . . never seen anyone under the age of eighty arrive in a chair sled."

She widened her eyes. "Oh, my. Perhaps I'd best walk the rest of the way."

He scowled and began pushing the sled again. "No. It matters not."

She heard the others backtracking, most likely to see what was keeping them. "Drew, this is my first time to meet the community. I really have no desire to arrive in the same fashion as a grandmother. Pray, let us leave the sled here and I'll walk."

"Ho, there!" Thomas called. "All is well?"

Drew paused and Constance threw off her covers, scrambling out of the sled. "Actually, Thomas, I'd very much like to walk the rest of the way. Would you be so kind as to carry the foot stove? And perhaps some of you others could assist with these blankets?"

She had the blankets dispersed and all in readiness before Drew had a chance to object, then watched him glance at the abandoned chair sled and Thomas. "Perhaps we should push this up behind the brush here so it won't be in anyone else's way if they happen along."

Thomas lifted his brows but said not a word as he helped Drew hide the chair sled. Constance made sure she not so much as batted an eye. When they were on their way again, Drew slipped his hand into hers.

She looked up at him. "Thank you. I would have been most disconcerted to arrive in such a manner if it was inappropriate. I very much want to make a good impression."

He pulled her against his side. "You could have arrived atop a wildcat and no one would have said a word. They will adore you."

That was a gross untruth, but it mattered not. Only a man in love would say such a thing, and it warmed her through and through. She leaned against him, and he gently squeezed her waist.

———

The steady beating of a drum reached Constance's ears well before her first sight of the meetinghouse. About six times the size of their cottage, the long wooden structure commanded attention, mighty oaks and locust trees flanking its sides. From its yard came the mingled sounds of children shouting, loved ones greeting, the church drummer summoning, and that hum of life that denotes civilization.

Constance took stock of the assembly of people, immediately noting the scarcity of women. Two she recognized from the boat, while a smattering of children ran betwixt and between those gathered. Her gaze ground to a halt on one particular man, the likes of which she'd never seen before.

He stood within a group, laughing and conversing together with them, dressed much in the same fashion as Drew, with doublet, jerkin, and matching breeches. What held her attention, though, was not his attire but the beautiful deep ebony color of his skin.

Having been cursed with freckles, she remained ever fascinated with people whose skin was smooth and flawless. This man's was not only smooth and flawless but rich and glowing.

"Who's that?" she whispered to Drew.

"Where?"

"The man with the black skin."

" 'Tis Adam Lucas. He came to Virginia as an indentured servant some years ago. He has since completed his service and owns a good piece of property north of here." He glanced at her. "I suppose you've never seen a person with black skin. Most of the blacks haven't been here as long as Lucas. In fact, he's waiting for one particular woman to finish her indenture so he can marry her. He offered to buy out her contract, but her master wouldn't sell it to him, much like I wouldn't sell Mary's if someone were to ask."

"But he's the only black-skinned person I see. Where are the others?"

"There aren't that many, actually. The Royal African Company usually takes them to the West Indies or Brazil, where they bring in more money as slaves. We've not much use for slaves here. It's less risky to buy an indentured servant's labor for a few years than to gamble a lifetime investment in a slave who might die a few months after purchase."

"Oh, Drew. I like not the idea of anyone being purchased, whether it's cost effective or not."

"Well, with indentured servants, we're not really purchasing the person but their labor. Though, probably, you're right about the other." He moved her hand to the crook of his arm. "Lucas is a good man, a good farmer. Honest and well respected amongst us. It would have been terrible for him had he been sold into slavery."

"Drew!" Sally suddenly burst from the crowd, projecting herself straight toward them. Constance could see the green of her new outfit, soiled and wet beneath her overcoat.

Drew caught her up into his arms and swung her about. "Ah, pumpkin! How I've missed you."

She locked her arms and legs about him, and the two remained tight within their embrace while a young woman approached, a babe nestled in her arms. "Happy Christmas."

"Happy Christmas, Nellie. How do you fare?"

Constance watched Drew bend to plant a kiss upon her cheek. Her eyes were the same clear blue as Drew's but framed with light brown eyebrows and lashes. Her hair lay neatly tucked up inside her cap. Nellie immediately made an opening in her bundle, exposing the babe's face, which scrunched up the moment the crisp air struck it. "Look. Isn't he beautiful?"

Drew's expression softened. "Ah, Nellie. He's bald, pink, and has no teeth. What's so beautiful about that?"

Nellie's laugh tinkled out like musical chimes while she covered the babe back up and turned to face Constance. "Hello. I've heard much about you. Your cape is exquisite."

"Thank you. Drew surprised me with it this morn." She clasped her hands together. "Your son is, indeed, quite handsome."

Sally lifted her head from Drew's shoulder. "You woke up. I thought you go to heaven, but Gramma said no."

Constance touched Sally's leg. "And Grandma was right. I'm planning to stay here for a very long time. And look at you! I think you've grown a whole inch, and I see you're wearing your new dress."

"Can I pet your coat?"

Constance reached out, and Sally went straight into her arms, rubbing her face and hands against the fur. The child's weight felt so good, so right. Constance hugged her a little more tightly, then smiled to see Grandma emerge from the peripherals.

"Well, it looks as if this will, indeed, be a very happy Christmas," the old woman greeted. "How do you fare, Constance?"

She answered positively while Grandma linked her arm around Drew's waist. "Thought you didn't like red hair."

One of Drew's dimples kicked in as he draped an arm about Grandma's shoulder.

"Must have me confused with someone else, but I'm not surprised. Seems to happen to most of the older set at some point or other."

That was the last exchange made before they were sucked into the crowd. Drew took Sally from her arms, all the while introducing her to farmer, after farmer, after farmer. Nellie eventually commandeered her away from Drew's side and introduced her to some of the women.

All nodded politely and allowed her to stand in their circle, but she found she had not much to say as they discussed cooking and babies and the tobacco seedlings they evidently nursed within their cottages. She wondered where Drew's were and if she was supposed to be nurturing them.

She scanned the crowd for him and found him staring at her. My, oh my, but he was easy on the eyes. She gave him an intimate smile. With Sally no longer in his arms, he excused himself and headed her way.

He'd made it almost halfway when behind her the word *sneezeweed* caught her attention. She turned an ear to the group of men.

"You jest! Why would Apperson put sneezeweed on their chair sled?"

"Perhaps it doesn't affect Apperson's granny and she wished to have her chair bedecked."

"But Apperson hates the stuff. Can't get near it without sneezing his head off," a new voice interjected.

"No, it wasn't Apperson's sled. It looked brand new."

"Who else would need one?"

"What about you, Josh? You've got a granny."

"Wasn't us," she heard Josh reply. "You know how Grandma loves to hike through these woods. Besides, she'd never do such a fool thing. Sneezeweed on a chair sled. What rubbish."

"Then who else would need one?"

"Maybe it wasn't for a granny," someone suggested.

Silence fell amongst them. "What mean you?"

"Well, it was hidden, I tell you. Would've missed the thing if it hadn't been for little Henry stumbling upon it by accident."

"But why?"

"I'm thinkin' one of the men with a new tobacco bride sought to impress his maid and wanted not to be discovered."

Murmurs rippled. "Impress his maid? With sneezeweed?!"

Many guffaws. "Who do you suppose it was?"

Constance stiffened, recognizing that Josh had voiced the question.

"Perhaps it was your brother, O'Connor. He has a new bride."

"Sensible Drew? Unflappable Drew?" Josh responded. "I hardly think so."

Constance threw a look at Drew, words of warning on her lips. But it was too late. The men had waylaid him, greeting him and pulling him into their midst.

"You'll never guess what we discovered, O'Connor. A chair sled."

"My, what an exciting morning you've had, Caskie."

A few chuckles reverberated before the Caskie fellow continued. "No, no. Not just any chair sled. But a newly constructed one . . . covered with *sneezeweed*. Now, you wouldn't be knowing anything about that, would you?"

"Caskie, it's addled you are. Why would anyone put a garland of sneezeweed on a chair sled?"

"A garland?" piped in another voice. "Who said anything about a garland?"

Constance slid her eyes shut, mortified as the men closed in on their prey, all speaking at once. "Was it a garland, Caskie?" "Look, O'Connor's turning red, he is." "By Pharoah, Drew, did *you* do that?" "What's amiss, O'Connor? Yer lady love need a'sweetening?" "She must, for 'tis a new fur cape she's a'wearing today as well." "Fur and sneezeweed. You sure know the way to a lady's heart, O'Connor."

And on it went, the laughter and jesting growing louder by the moment. Constance shifted her feet. The women within her circle, she noticed, had at some point begun to listen as well and now all looked at her, their expressions fraught with curiosity.

Nellie cocked her head. "Well, Constance. It's pleased I am. Grandma told me he fancied you, but I believed her not. I've been feeling quite guilty, for it was because of me that Grandma left, forcing him to purchase a bride. I see all those hours of worry were for naught. Did he push you in that chair sled all the way here?"

Constance nodded, noting some of the women's expressions softened, while others were tinged with a bit of good-natured humor. The men behind them teased Drew mercilessly, all of which he seemed to take in good sport, turning their jests about until he'd managed to move the focus to someone else.

In the next moment, he stood by her side, placing his hand against her waist. His face was still rather flushed, and Nellie didn't let it go by. "Sneezeweed, Drew?"

He grinned. "Jealous?"

"Surprised."

"Remind me, and I'll have a talk with Gerald. Give him a few tips."

"Promise?"

"Absolutely."

"Then tell him I want a real crane in my fireplace instead of just a lug pole, I'd like a pudding pan and . . . a fur cape."

He chuckled. "Done. And what of you Goody Trible? Need I speak with Seward?"

And so the conversation went, each woman telling Drew what she wished her husband would provide for her—all of whom included within their list a desire for a fur cape—and Constance realized he was not merely being polite, but very cleverly arming himself with ammunition for the time when those gentlemen teased him about the sneezeweed. After a moment he turned to the woman next to Constance. "Now, who might this be?"

Nellie introduced the woman, Kendra Woodrum, explaining some Francis Woodrum had purchased her as a bride at the same time Drew had purchased Constance.

"I see. You know my wife, then?"

"I remember her very well. She came to the ship not with the rest of us, but just before we sailed wearing a green gown the likes of which took my breath away."

Surprised, Constance looked at the girl more closely, for she had no recollection of her. Thick brown brows stretched above her doelike eyes, while a mouthful of teeth dominated her kind face.

Then she remembered. This girl had been ill the entire voyage, miserably seasick. At the time, Constance had thought only of herself, of rebuking the captain, and of returning home. She'd not concerned herself with the other women in that hold nor with what had become of them—other than Mary, of course. Now she wished she'd not been so apathetic.

Kendra offered up no complaints concerning her husband.

"Come now, Mistress Woodrum," Drew implored. "I've known Francis my entire life. Am I to believe he's a model husband?"

" "Course I am, O'Connor. Wouldn't catch me giving my wife sneezeweed." A young round-bellied man with a full black mustache and beard slipped his hand beneath Kendra's elbow. It was the same man who'd kept Emmett from pawing Constance during the auction.

"I see you've not given her a fur either," Drew said.

"So I haven't. Where the devil did you get it?"

Drew straightened his spine. "Why, I caught the first fox with my bare hands. Wrestled him to the ground, only to have more pounce on me. But when the dust settled, it was only I who remained standing."

The other women tittered, Nellie rolled her eyes, Francis hollered. "Ho! Wise men say, 'He who hath not a good and ready memory should never meddle with telling lies.' "

Drew smiled. "I have a good and ready memory."

The steady drumbeat changed in tempo to a *rat-a-tat-tat*. The crowd silenced and turned to the door of the church, where the preacher, Morden, who'd performed their wedding ceremony, stood. "Come, my children. Receive God's Word and blessing."

CHAPTER | TWENTY-FOUR

SHE HADN'T BROUGHT ANY food. As soon as the service was over, every other woman had hurried to retrieve their precooked contributions while some of the men laid boards on the backless benches and others built a huge bonfire outside. Drew had left almost immediately to help, the others of the family doing the same.

She stood alone and unmoving in the sea of activity as it took on an almost abstract quality. People swarming in different directions, but each with a sense of purpose in their steps. The room transformed from a church with its uniform rows of benches into a social whirl complete with food, ale, and suppressed excitement.

She jumped to the side to avoid being rammed with a bench, moved back a step or two to make room for three women carrying earthen pots, and circled around a tub of ale, until finally she had been driven into a corner, an island of self doubt.

Why hadn't Drew told her she was to bring something? She'd had no idea. Christmas was so different at home.

Of course, with the war and all they wouldn't have observed the full rites of Christmas with mummings and dancing about Maypoles and processions. Still, a Yule log would have been lit, carols sung, a service attended, and Christmas boxes exchanged, culminating with a feast of Christmas pies, plum pottage, oranges, spices, figs, wine, and more, all displayed around a mighty boar's head sporting a lemon within its ferocious mouth.

Why, just last Christmas she'd organized the celebration for her father. Yet she'd never prepared the actual food, brought in the Yule log, nor hunted down the boar. She'd simply orchestrated the events.

The torrent of movement had ebbed somewhat, now replaced with a hum of conversation, the women and girls around the table, the men and boys outside. Constance glanced out the arched doorway, trying to catch sight of Drew but without success.

She watched the hub of women chattering and communing amongst themselves. She hadn't realized how artificial and coy the ladies in London were, herself included, until she watched these colonials. They were sincere, unaffected, and freely touched one another—something unheard of at home.

Two women shared a hug. Another squeezed the arm of a friend with affection. A couple of younger women pressed shoulder-to-shoulder, heads together, whispering animatedly before breaking apart in laughter.

No guile. No wielding of fans. No subtle insults. Just open, honest expressions of friendship. Her heart filled with longing. Her stomach twisted into knots. How was she ever going to fit in? For she was only now beginning to realize much more than an expanse of dirt flooring separated her from these women.

The longer she cowered in this corner, though, the harder it would be. She tried to summon up the confidence that allowed her to move with poise and certainty in elite ballrooms throughout London. Yet poise and certainty were not what she needed here.

Here, she was expected to drop all pretenses and expose herself as she was. She'd never done such a thing in her life, at least not with anyone other than her immediate family and Drew, of course.

As it ended up, Sally took the matter into her own little hands, breaking away from Nellie and running to Constance, commanding everyone's attention at the same time. "Sissy!" she hollered. "Come see what I bring!"

She allowed Sally to pull her to the table, the other women opening their ranks to make room for her. Sally pointed to a basket of shelled pecans. "Look! I made myself!"

Constance oohed and ahhed, praising the child for her efforts.

"What did you make, Sissy?"

She surveyed the oysters, fish, wild fowl, corn puddings, pumpkin fritters, dried apricots, and spoon bread displayed around several dressed turkeys. Heat rushed up her neck and face. "I . . . I didn't realize." She looked at the others. "Drew didn't tell me. That is, I—"

An older woman tsked and shook her head. "Now, isn't that just like a man? Doesn't tell his new wife Christmas dinner was to be eaten here. Why, you've probably a whole spread waiting to be put on the coals at home."

The other women mumbled in understanding. Constance didn't correct their misconception and glanced at Mary. Obviously Drew hadn't told her either.

"Worry not about the food, Mistress O'Connor," one of the women offered.

"It's Constance."

The older woman nodded. "Yes, we know. Not a female over the age of twelve that wasn't wishing she could have Drew O'Connor to spouse."

Good heavens. Her cheeks blazed with embarrassment.

The old woman moved forward, grabbing Constance's hand within her shaky grasp. "I'm Granny Apperson. You go on and take that fancy cape off and sit with us a while."

The men had started filing in, complaining for food. The women ignored them.

Nellie transferred her babe into another woman's arms. "Oh, yes, Constance. I've been wanting to try your cape on all morning. May I?"

Constance paled. The day had warmed up considerably and most had discarded their overcoats. All were attired in simple homespun dresses. They weren't faded or well worn, but freshly dyed and very carefully ironed. Obviously their best.

They weren't anywhere near as fine as the wool Drew had given her, and their styles were homogeneous. Not a scooped neck in sight.

The room had quickly filled, the men looking over the food, but now in a rather subdued manner, as if curious to what the women were puttering about. Constance scanned the faces for Drew. No luck.

She bit her lip. There was nothing for it. No matter what she did, disaster would be the result. If she didn't remove her cape, she'd appear selfish and self-centered. If she did remove her cape, she'd not only upset Drew but alienate every woman there. Her gown was one of nobility, and these women would know it the moment they saw it.

Still, if she was going to offend the women, it would probably be best to do so with her apparel rather than with a condescending attitude. Besides, she wouldn't dream of disappointing Nellie by refusing her request. She slowly released the loops on her cape and slipped it from her shoulders.

An overwhelming silence descended. All movement suspended and every eye—male, female, and child alike—was fixed on her.

After a lifetime of agony, it was Nellie who responded with a near swoon. "Oh, Constance! Is this what they're wearing in London now?"

Bless her sweet soul, Nellie had, in her unaffected way, shown awe and genuine feminine appreciation for a lovely piece of frippery, totally disregarding the out-of-place design and neckline. Constance would not dare to explain that she'd have been laughed right out of church had she worn something so simple and unadorned back home. "Yes, but I'd much rather have a gown like yours."

Nellie's gaze, marked with amusement, flew to hers. "If I thought I had a prayer of filling yours out, I'd trade with you right here and now."

Constance felt color rush to her cheeks again. Honestly, these colonists said anything, anywhere, anytime.

She barely suppressed her urge to jump back when Granny Apperson stuck her hand into the side of her neckline, fingering its border. "Did you make this, girl?"

She nodded.

"Look here at this fancy needlework, Nellie. She's embroidered green tobaccy leaves all the way around. Would have missed it if I hadn't been standin' so close."

Nellie, as well as a good dozen others, leaned forward to examine her work.

Releasing her hold on the gown, Granny clucked. "I sure would be likin' a dress like this 'un." She again eyed the dress up and down. "Think you could show me how to make one?"

"Me too!" Nellie exclaimed, echoed by several of the others.

Overwhelmed, Constance could only nod. That they showed no censor nor ridicule for the gown, but instead embraced it, humbled her. How different they were from those she associated with at home. Never would they have allowed an opportunity like this to pass without using it to make themselves seem superior. Even she had caught herself doing so to others. She didn't deserve such consideration—was unworthy of it, in fact. She didn't belong.

"It's done, then," Granny announced. "Before we leave today, we'll decide on a time to gather at the O'Connor's for sewing lessons. It'll have to be after we've all had time to order some fabric, though."

"Best we not act too hastily." All eyes shifted to Jonathon Emmett. "Never would *my* wife garb herself in such a manner."

Constance stiffened.

Granny narrowed her eyes. "Well, Goodman Emmett, no need to get your breeches in a twist. I'd be worryin' about gettin' a wife before I worried about what she would or wouldn't wear." She clapped her hands together. "Say grace, Morden, and be quick about it so we can eat!"

Morden gave a brief blessing, and then pandemonium broke out. There were no plates. People just picked up what they wanted and ate it. Communal spoons were left in the puddings and other foodstuffs that required utensils. The turkeys, torn apart piece by piece, were eaten with fingers. The oysters dropped down people's throats.

Constance stood in mute fascination.

"Ale, Connie?"

She turned to find Drew at her elbow, a noggin of ale in his hand.

She shook her head. "Your thanks, but I drink not spirits. I'll just have what the children are having."

"They're having ale."

"You jest."

He nodded his head toward the cask where a young boy of no more than five stuck his face underneath the spigot to catch a mouthful of the brewed liquid.

She took the noggin from Drew, sipped from its contents, then shuddered, pressing it back into his hands. "I'm really not thirsty." Their fingers brushed and she glanced up. "I'm sorry about the gown, Drew. I wanted to leave the cape on, but—"

"We'll discuss it another time." His eyes flashed, and then he turned. A heaviness centered in her chest as she watched him stride from the meetinghouse.

Moments later, Josh touched her sleeve. "Worry not, sister. He's fighting his own demons right now, and there's naught you can do. Meanwhile, partake of some supper, else your actions might be misconstrued into something they are not."

She quickly blinked back her threatening tears, giving Josh a hesitant smile.

He gently squeezed her elbow. "Easy, now."

"I didn't know," she whispered, frantically searching his eyes for understanding.

"About the demons?"

"About the gown. When he gave me the fabric, I asked him what the women here wore, but he said naught. I didn't even make an evening gown, but a very average day gown, thinking that would be most appropriate. You know the fashions in London. Can you see I wasn't trying to—"

He increased the pressure on her elbow. "Hush. You look exquisite."

"I look like a freak."

He bussed the top of her head, turned her toward the table, and nudged her forward. "Go fetch something to eat. I'll be right back."

———

"What's the matter with you? Can you not see she's scared to death?"

Drew thought this would be a remote enough spot for some privacy. Evidently not. "What do you want, Josh?"

"I want you to go to your wife. Can you not see she's entirely out of her league?"

"Oh, I can see that, all right. I was a fool to think otherwise. She's not only out of our league, she's from a different world altogether." He threw a pebble into the surrounding forest. "She's no colonist, and I've known it all along. I simply chose to ignore it." He rubbed the back of his neck. "No, she belongs in a blasted palace made of gold and platinum with jewels around her neck and servants at her beck and call."

"What a great bunch of tripe. She's not the queen. She's your wife and she needs you."

"It's of no use, Josh. These women have essentially asked her to be a seamstress. Can you imagine? An earl's daughter as a seamstress. And did you see her face when everyone started eating? Did you see how shocked she was? She's used to eating at tables with cloths and porcelain and silver candelabras. Not some pine board with a bunch of dirty farmers shoving food into their mouths. She doesn't belong here any more than Her Royal Majesty would."

"Is that what she told you?"

"She didn't have to. I have eyes."

"You have a pickled brain is what you have. I'll allow she might have been taken aback for a moment, but she's not so shallow that she would judge people simply because of their eating habits."

"You've blinders on where she's concerned, Josh. But, pray, step back for a moment and reflect. Her father has some wealthy young aristocrat waiting at this very moment to give her everything she wants and deserves. And she does want those things, whether she realizes it or not. Take her gown, for instance. You saw it. She couldn't have better illustrated to others she was a member of the privileged class had she screamed it from the rooftops."

Josh lifted his shoulders in a gesture of confusion. "So, her attire's a bit fancy. What has that to do with anything when it's so obvious it's you she adores?"

"For how long? How long will that last, do you suppose? I might be amusing now, but am I worth giving up the entertainments of London, the sprawling manor she's used to living in, the family she'll never see again? For what? For some paltry house with a parlor and a great room? For a life where she socializes with others on Christmas, Whitsunweek, and court days, isolated on a farm the other forty-eight weeks of the year? I hardly think so."

"She told me, rather emphatically as I recall, the first night I returned, that she wanted to stay."

"That was before."

"Before what?"

Drew pulled his hat from his head, spinning it to the ground with a flick of his wrist. "She was lonely, Josh. I had just helped her recover from a life-threatening illness. She probably imagined me as some romantic knight of old that saved fair damsels." He blew out a puff a breath. "And I took shameless advantage of it."

"And now it's too late."

Drew peered into the thicket. "I know not. What think you would happen if she went back? I could secure a divorce for her here, and she could tell those in England that I'd died. God knows, it happens all the time out here. No one would doubt her." Drew turned to Josh when he did not respond, surprised to see his brother's face red with anger.

"You worthless piece of horse dung. Does she mean so little to you that you would discard her like some worn out boot?"

Drew took no offense, but instead slumped his shoulders in defeat. "Nay, Josh. God help me, I love her. I love her enough to see I've no right to ask her to stay."

Josh's rigid stance relaxed. "Does she love you?"

"Oh, she thinks she does."

Josh retrieved Drew's hat, wiped some condensation from it, and handed it back to him. "Then why borrow trouble? As long as she isn't asking to leave, and she *thinks* she loves you, why not wait and see what happens?"

Drew thumped his hat's rim, the impending sense of loss so acute it was that of a physical pain. He sighed heavily. "Because I'd rather her leave now. The longer she stays, the harder it will be to let her go."

"Be not false with yourself, Drew. It would tear you apart no matter when she left, now or later. Might as well ride it out for as long as you can. Who knows? Maybe she'll think you're worth staying for." He slapped Drew on the shoulder. "In any case, you're her husband now and she's foundering. Why not show up on a white steed to save her? Might buy you a few more days—and nights."

Drew raked his fingers through his hair. He couldn't believe this was happening. Couldn't believe he'd done this to himself again. Anger rippled down his spine and he clinched his jaw. But done it, he had, for he'd allowed himself to be vulnerable, and this time, this time was by far the worst. Assailed by an overwhelming fear over his impending loss, he settled his hat upon his head.

———

She wasn't good enough for him. How could she have been so naïve? Drew needed a woman like . . . well, like any of these dear ones around her. After listening to them talk, she realized they not only cooked but they made their own soap, their own candles, their own baskets, their own preserves, their own home remedies, their own spirits, their own . . . everything.

Back home, her father either purchased those items, or she had the servants make them. She had a rudimentary idea of what was required, but never had she been involved in the actual process.

She sighed. The only thing the women talked of that she had any skill at was sewing and quilting.

What a shallow existence she'd held. Even her lofty goals for her mathematical pursuits were frivolous compared to what these women did. Why, some trapped and dressed their own wildlife, while others went into the tobacco fields and worked side-by-side with their husbands.

She could hardly tend the garden, much less harvest tobacco. It had taken weeks before she'd even collected the eggs by herself. And she'd made a muck of her most important job, Sally, nearly costing both of them their lives and endangering Drew's.

He was bound to be having second thoughts. And who could blame him? So she could read Latin, speak French, write in a lovely script, and spell like a master. What good was it?

No wonder Drew had scoffed at her education. She truly hadn't needed it. She certainly hadn't used it—not here nor even in England.

It was a waste. She was a waste. How long would it be before he tired of her and her inadequacies? How long before he lamented being forced into marrying her? Already he showed signs of displeasure, storming off earlier because she'd disobeyed him and removed the cape, thus exposing her ignorance for all to see.

And, as she now realized, her shortcomings were a reflection on him. Were the other men at this very moment making jests about poor Drew being saddled with an ignorant wife?

Would these women be forbidden by their husbands to associate with her? Would she be seen as a bad influence? Would Drew lose his place in their society, for there were places, as she'd begun to realize. Nothing as elaborate as England's hierarchy, but a hierarchy nonetheless.

There were slaves and indentured servants. Then, the small farmer, known as *Goodman*. The larger land owners became *Master*, often taking a place of office in the community.

There was no professional army but rather a local militia. The captain accepted his rank as entry into the gentry, and everyone addressed him by his title. There was also the crown-appointed governor, of course, and his council.

The women cleared away the remains of dinner, replacing it with a dessert course of Indian meal pudding, syllabubs, seedcake, and small tarts.

"I wonder who will win first rights to the mistletoe this year," someone said from near her elbow.

Now there was something familiar. Constance always enjoyed the scrambling and confusion that ensued as soon as Papa suspended a huge branch of mistletoe from the center of the ceiling. She smiled as she recalled herself and other young ladies running into corners screaming and struggling, threatening and remonstrating. In short, they did everything but leave the room until such a time as they found it useless to resist any longer and submitted to being dragged to the center of the room for a kiss from some charming gallant.

Of course, Papa would merely stand directly under the berried bough, arms open wide, until he was surrounded by the whole body of young ladies and kissed by every one of them!

"First rights?" asked the woman with all the teeth—Kendra, she believed.

She voiced the question of many who were attending this celebration for the first time. Of the fifty or so brides who'd shared the voyage with her, about a score were present. Of those not in attendance, some lived too far away to come, while many others had died. Still, the veterans seemed to enjoy the task of introducing their colonial customs to all the newcomers.

"We've a shooting contest between the unmarried men," Nellie explained. "A keen shot can sever the mistletoe right off the tree outside. The one who retrieves a cluster from the loftiest point on the tree gets first rights. The losers save their clusters, then try to make use of them on the sly."

"The women," another girl chimed in, "gather together as the winner walks amongst our ranks. He then holds the cluster above the lady of his choice, who must forfeit a kiss."

"After the kiss, she picks off one berry," Nellie added. "Once the berries are gone, so ends the kissing."

"Granny Apperson made up rules after the year Jordie Bacon kept claiming kisses from the same girl over and over—each kiss a bit longer than the last—and she already married to another!"

The women tittered, and Granny Apperson took a long pull on her pipe before blowing out a slow stream of smoke, content for now, it seemed, to let the younger set do the telling.

A woman with skin browned from the sun nodded her head. "At first she wasn't going to allow any of the married women to participate, but that only left two girls. So then she set down that the men could claim no more than three kisses from any one girl."

A matronly woman took a sip from her noggin. "It went on like that for several years until the O'Connor boys came of age."

A collective sigh rippled through the group. Nellie turned to Constance. "Jonathon Emmett had won three years in a row when Drew first came of age. They're both crack shots, and it was neck-and-neck there for a while as the two of them knocked cluster after cluster off the tree. Drew finally tired of the game, aimed a good ten feet above Goodman Emmett's last shot, and picked one clean off, proving to all he'd only been toying with his competitor. Emmett couldn't match him."

Another woman several years older than Constance smiled in what appeared to be fond remembrance. "I'll never forget standing with the other girls that day as young Drew looked us all over, each of us hoping to be chosen." She chuckled. "He didn't disappoint a one of us, did he, Granny?"

Granny Apperson smiled. "No, he didn't. Of course, the next year Josh came of age and after that either one or the other of those two won. Call it the O'Connor era, we do."

"Who finally beat them?" Constance asked.

The group stilled, no one answering. Granny Apperson stirred, smiling sadly. "Leah."

The hairs at the nape of Constance's neck prickled. "Who's Leah?"

Again, no one answered. Granny sighed. "Drew's betrothed."

Blood drained from her face. Nellie reached over, patting her hand. "It was a long time ago."

"Tell me."

Nellie turned her attention back to her sleeping baby. Constance looked at Granny Apperson.

The old woman removed the pipe from her mouth. "Drew had never before shot like he did that day, nor has he since. It was something to see. The contest had just begun when he walked up, aimed, and felled a cluster from the very top of the boughs. No one else came close."

"I thought Leah won."

"No, child, that's not what I meant. Certainly, Drew teased not the women as he usually did. When they had assembled, he walked straight to Leah and claimed three kisses. Then slipping his knife from his scabbard, he sliced the end of her cap string off, tied it onto the remaining cluster, and hung it above the meetinghouse archway, announcing to all that he was through and any female caught under the mistletoe was free game."

Another woman sighed. "It was the most romantic thing I'd ever seen."

Constance furrowed her brows. "Then why did you say Leah beat him?"

"I meant Leah beat down his youthful exuberance, for she died a few weeks later," Granny said, melancholy touching her features. "Every Christmas since, Drew has still won the contest, but he never again titillated the girls to whom he would award his favor. He's simply claimed one kiss from his grandmother, then hung the mistletoe above the archway."

Constance swallowed. "How tragic."

Granny Apperson lifted her brows. "He seems to be doing mighty fine this year."

Constance kept her face free from expression, not wishing to disillusion the old woman with what she had begun to suspect was the real truth.

CHAPTER | TWENTY-FIVE

CONSTANCE WATCHED COLONEL TUCKER lead the men in musket drills. By the time they were through, instead of taking a minute and a half to load their muskets, it took only three-quarters. They practiced many of the rank speeds the men back home did, but Nellie explained it was only so the men could load without thinking, for the Indians didn't come straight at you the way Englishmen did. Instead, they took advantage of cover, often surprising their quarry.

"I thought relations were friendly."

"Oh, they are," Nellie assured her. "But it's still important to practice. One never knows."

Constance turned back to the assembly of men who were now breaking up in preparation for the mistletoe ceremony. She'd enjoyed watching Drew go through the choreographed movements with the others as the Colonel called out commands, "Shoulder your musket!—Poise your musket!—Cast about your musket!—Draw forth your scouring stick!—Ram down your charger!" and so on until finally giving fire.

Even in a crowd, his presence commanded attention. He'd discarded jerkin and doublet, bringing the muscles of his arms and back into prominence as they rippled beneath his white shirt.

She'd seen him shoot the musket before, for several times he'd brought it with them to the creek for target practice after cleansing the dishes. And she'd enjoyed watching him then as well.

Leaning his musket against a tree, he shrugged on his doublet and jerkin, then moved to her, sweat lining his brow. "How fare you?"

She pushed back the hood of her cape. "Well."

"Are you tiring? Need we leave?"

"I'm growing a little weary, but I'd like to stay and watch the mistletoe ceremony. May we?"

He nodded. "Very well, but we'll leave as soon as it's over. You've had a long day."

He placed a hand beneath her elbow, catching up to the others as they moved down a path toward a rather sturdy oak. In the midst of its leafless branches, mistletoe shot from the trunk with boughs of brilliant green, decorated in an abundance of white berries, its richness a precious gem in the otherwise barren surroundings.

Granny Apperson grouped the women together and then the unmarried men. Constance and Mary gravitated toward each other to stand side-by-side for the ceremony.

Shots echoed throughout the forest as men applied their musket drills to loading and aiming for the mistletoe in record time. Within minutes the competition had narrowed to three—Josh, Goodman Emmett, and the man they called Caskie.

Young Caskie wiped a palm against his breeches.

Emmett cackled, his scrawny beard quivering. "Just imagine you're having yer sights on one of them red-skinned savages, Caskie. That'll make yer aim true."

Constance frowned. Caskie raised his musket, fired, and missed.

Emmett pounded him on the back. "Well, son, step back now and take a good look at how it's done." Emmett prepared his weapon with exaggerated slowness, drawing attention to each of the forty or so steps it took to prime. "Now, where you fell short, boy, weren't in your aim but in the picture you held inside yer head. You got to actually *see* them beggarly devils, naked but for a covering acrost their loins and heathen paintings of all kinds profaning their bodies."

With what few teeth he had, Emmett uncorked one of the apostles around his neck, pouring powder down the barrel of his gun before replacing the cork onto the little bottle. "Of courst, it's important to remember those whoresons fight not with honor. Oh, no. They slither like vile snakes behind tall grasses and trees just waiting fer a chance to strike at us God-fearing Christians. And all because they think we're the fulfillment of some heathen prophesy about whites coming to take their lands." Snorting, he opened the gun's cap. "Why, everybody knows God meant for us to have this land so we could Christianize them barbarians. Ain't that right, Preacher?" Shouldering his musket, he took aim and fired at a particularly lofty cluster, bringing it to the ground.

Disgust for his uncharitable words and attitude was soon replaced with a flicker of anxiety as Constance realized his shot was well above the ones Caskie and Josh had felled before. If Emmett won, she could be subjected to his kiss—possibly even three.

Josh took less than a minute to prepare his piece, aim, and fire. He said nary a word. Relief swept through her as a clump of mistletoe bounced from branch to lower branch before finally making its way to the ground.

Emmett rocked back on his heels. "That's it! That's what I'm talking about." Joining his musket to his wrist, he loaded with remarkable speed. "Did you see that, Caskie? Why, O'Connor here was prob'ly thinking about the time them bloodthirsty savages came in '22 and set a torch to his family's cottage, even while his baby sister lay inside, helpless in her cradle. Story has it ol' Josh here watched the whole thing from up in a tree, his knees a'knocking and doing nary a thing to save her."

A black silence descended over the crowd. Constance's gaze flew to Drew, her breath momentarily cut off. Every muscle in his body exuded tension, his face cold with fury.

Josh took a menacing step forward. Emmett quickly shouldered his musket and fired. A cluster of berries tumbled to the ground.

Panic took hold of Constance. What was the range of these muskets? What if Josh couldn't reach a higher point due to the limitations of his firing piece? Josh loaded his musket with carefully controlled movements, then held the gun loosely within his grip, his attention pinned on Emmett.

Emmett's smug expression slowly slipped as he looked between Josh and the primed musket. "Meant no offense, O'Connor. Just giving Caskie a few pointers."

"It's Christmas day, Emmett, and need I remind you that without the Indians we wouldn't be here, for our grandfathers would never have survived?"

Emmett's lips thinned. "Oh, those lily-livered curs *saved* our grandfathers all right, but only to fatten 'em up for the kill in '22."

"All was fine until your father murdered their leader."

Emmett's face reddened. "He was openly wearing Morgan's cap! And after Morgan had been missing for days!"

"Morgan went with Nemattanew on a friendly trading expedition. Nobody knows what *really* happened. Morgan could have been attacked by a wild animal for all we know, but Nemattanew the Immortal was never given a chance to explain, was he? He was simply killed out of turn by a lowly Englishman whose 'patience had been tried' because he didn't like Nemattanew's hat."

Josh's grip on his gun tightened. "The result was a massacre, famine, and epidemic that killed hundreds upon hundreds, then a ruthless counterattack by us where even more perished." He leaned into Emmett's face. "I'd just as soon avoid having my loved ones put through that again. Wouldn't you?"

Emmett took a step back, his eyes taking on a fanatical light. "Seems we've an Indian lover in our midst."

Constance gasped.

Governor Hopkin stepped forward, placing himself between the two men. "Enough, Emmett. We are at peace with the Indians and, God willing, will remain that way. O'Connor, it's your shot."

Constance looked back to Drew only to discover he had moved up to the front, very close to his brother's back. She started at the explosive report of Josh's musket, then swung her gaze back to the tree, but saw no mistletoe descending. She scanned the tree's boughs. Maybe it had gotten caught in another branch. The crowd murmured and her pulse beat erratically. Had he missed?

Anxiety spurted throughout her body. She knew, in the deepest core of her being, that Jonathon Emmett would come to her, not once, but all three times. Bile rose in her throat. With extreme effort, she swallowed.

Josh's face looked grave as he stepped back, and Emmett reloaded his piece, silent now. So Josh hadn't missed after all. She folded her arms against her waist. *Thank you, God.*

Emmett once again took aim. Constance held her breath, tension tightening every muscle. A loud discharge. A miss. A roar from the crowd. Josh had won.

Her limbs went buttery with relief. She shook, she gasped for air, she barely managed to remain standing. Mary grabbed her elbow. "Mistress! Are you all right?"

Drew strode through the crowd, then encircled her waist with his arm. Josh rushed to them.

"Your pardon, Josh. She's overdone today, I fear."

Josh nodded. "Best take her home, then."

The brothers exchanged intense looks, communicating on a level she couldn't begin to broach. Josh tipped his head once, turned to Mary, and paused for a moment before approaching Granny Apperson. He suspended his mistletoe above her head, and the startled old woman looked up as he hooked a thumb beneath her chin, awarding her a gentle kiss right on the lips.

Straightening, he winked at her as she plucked a berry from the cluster. "I hereby start a new tradition, Granny," he proclaimed in a voice that reached every person present. "I say the winner claims one kiss and one kiss alone, then hangs the mistletoe above the meetinghouse entry, giving all a sporting chance."

The single and married men alike roared their approval, and Granny Apperson held up her hands for silence before announcing, "Let it be so!"

Drew held Constance still, allowing the revelers to swarm past them as they followed Josh back to church.

Emmett sauntered by, his gun resting against his bony shoulder. "Too bad yer not feeling well, Mistress, or you might have been able to catch me under the mistletoe and seen just what could've been yers had yer *husband* not cheated me out of yer hand in matrimony."

She felt Drew tense, but before he could respond, his grandmother approached. "Run along, Emmett," she said, "for 'he who envies admits his inferiority.' "

Drew quirked a brow. "You'll have to speak more plainly, Grandma. *Inferiority* is too long a word for Emmett here to grasp."

"You hush up too, Drew, and get your woman home." Grandma gave Emmett a push, prompting him to proceed forward. When he and Grandma moved around the bend, Drew nuzzled the top of Constance's head. "Are you all right?"

She rested her cheek against his chest. "I am fordone. I want to go home."

———

I want to go home.

How prophetic had that statement been? Drew thought. Had she meant England? No, of course not. She'd meant the cottage, but still, that wasn't her *real* home.

He hammered a head onto the barrel of tobacco, effectively sealing it. Home for her was something he couldn't begin to reproduce. Even if he built some huge manor house, it would be for naught. The manors in London were made for entertaining, and no one "entertained" here. There were no dances, no balls, no teas. There wasn't even a city.

Lifting one shoulder, he wiped his brow against it, then continued hammering. If only he hadn't gambled that long ago summer night. But then, Emmett would have her.

If only he hadn't married her. But he'd had no choice.

If only he hadn't loved her, bedded her. But he did and had.

The only thing to be done now was to send her back, for she was as misplaced here as a rainbow trout in a school of gasper goo. Jamestown was nothing more than a harbor for their tobacco trade. They had no theater, no roads. They didn't even have horses.

He shoved the hogshead onto its side, then rolled it to the barn. She didn't belong here. It had all become so clear on Christmas. And ever since, nothing had been the same.

She'd slept almost solid for those first few days after the celebration, and he'd begun to grow concerned. But she'd evidently just been taxed. Once she caught up on her rest, she'd immersed herself in the running of the cottage like never before, starting with that ludicrous sneezeweed she and Sally had draped across the bedposts.

What worried him, though, was how she insisted on cooking the meals. It had caused some tension heretofore absent from the cottage, for Mary, of course, resisted relinquishing her duties to her mistress, but Connie insisted. And once Connie dug in her heels, Mary hadn't a prayer.

With assistance from Isaac, Drew heaved the barrel up on its end, wedging it next to other hogsheads lining the outside of the barn. Only a few more to go, and his shipment would be ready to roll down to the public warehouse near the wharf.

He watched Isaac move back to the tobacco press. It wasn't just the cooking either. For some reason, Connie had decided to launch into all kinds of domestic projects. She'd tried to make candles out of the old bayberries she and Sally had picked last fall, but not only were there not enough berries, but neither could she get the temperature of the fire quite right. At first, the candles came out lumpy, so she added fuel to the fire. Then the paraffin became so hot it melted the already deposited wax right off the candles she was re-dipping. She ended up with a huge mess, a bunch of wasted wicks, and about four questionable-looking candles instead of thirty. The yard sure smelled good, though.

Drew returned his attention to the task at hand. Pulling the knife from his scabbard, he carved the O'Connor identity mark and the grade of tobacco into the barrel's side. Connie's attempt at soap-making hadn't gone much better. She'd managed to drip the lye all right, but when it came time to mix it with lard, she'd used the leftover candle wax instead, got the proportions wrong, and could never get it to harden. The yard sure smelled good, though.

He moved to the next hogshead and reached inside to break off a piece from the top leaf, testing for quality. The thing to do was to let her go back to England. Right now she was young, and this domestic role of hers was new. But she'd grow older and wiser, and the newness would wear off. And that was the crux of the whole problem.

When that happened, she'd compare the life she could have had in London to the life she had in the colonies. It wouldn't measure up. *He* wouldn't measure up. He needed to send her back.

He could never marry again, of course, but what was that compared to this torture of knowing his wife was miserable?

Satisfied that the grade and quality were good, he picked up a new head for sealing the barrel. Yes. He'd send her back as soon as the next ship came through. It was the decent thing to do. The responsible thing to do. Weariness engulfed his body in tides. It was the only thing to do.

He hammered the head's rim. Meanwhile, he'd have to address her endless questions about the tobacco seedlings. He'd planted his close to Halfway Creek in a patch of sunny new ground with a southeastern exposure. He'd covered his seedbed with oak leaves and straw, then laid oak boughs on top for protection. Now that the weather was mellowing and the frosts appeared to be gone, he'd planned to remove the debris and expose his tender plants so they could grow strong and large enough to be transplanted come May.

He couldn't possibly tell Connie of his precious seedbed. She'd insist on helping and ruin it for sure. And if anything happened to those plants, there would be no crop and he'd be in great trouble.

He lifted up his hat, then resettled it on his head. He still had some seeds left, though. Every planter worth his salt saved many more seeds than he needed in case some were lost or mildewed or didn't sprout. Mayhap he could collect some of those extras and make a flatbed for her to keep in the house. If she killed those, no harm would be done. If she didn't, he'd take her out to the fields come May and show her how to plant them in little mounds.

He stopped, disgusted with himself. What rubbish. He would have no earl's daughter working in his fields. She wouldn't even be here come May. The ship with his furniture was due in a few more weeks, and he'd see that she sailed back to England aboard it.

He again swung the hammer down onto the barrel, catching the tip of his finger. Cursing, he yanked back his hand, then hurled the hammer across the yard. Josh and the men paused, then continued with their packing.

With his finger throbbing, his teeth grinding, and his heart breaking, he pulled his hat low and strode after the hammer.

———

Constance aroused herself from the melancholy that weighed her down. Drew had insisted she tutor Sally, even though she now knew how ridiculous that pursuit was. The child would be much better off hanging on to Mary's skirts and learning of what *really* mattered. Drew had been adamant, though, so here she and Sally sat at the table.

The child was, as usual, quick and eager to please. They'd concluded their reading lesson and now practiced rules for behavior at the table.

With a spoon, Sally scooped some imaginary food from her empty trencher ever so slowly. "Eat not with greedy bee-haver." She sipped from the very tip of the spoon.

Constance gave a slight shake of her head. "Make not a noise with your tongue, mouth, lips, or breath in your eating."

Sally scooped up more invisible victuals, stretching her mouth wide in order to poke the spoon inside without making any noise.

"Very good. Now watch me." Constance demonstrated with her spoon, stretching her lips like Sally had. Sally clapped a hand over her mouth, giggling.

"What do you find amusing?"

"You open too much."

Constance smiled. "Do I? Please show me how to correct it."

Sally demonstrated, this time placing the spoon in her mouth with decorum and without noise. And so the morning went as they practiced breaking imaginary bread instead of biting it, sloping the knife instead of holding it upright, and drinking to the health of Sally's elders.

As she watched the child's efforts, tears threatened at the back of Constance's eyes, and a nauseating sinking despair overcame her. She'd decided she must go back to England, just as soon as the next ship arrived. It wasn't what she wanted to do but what she had to do. Drew had all but told her outright he no longer wanted her for wife. Why, he'd completely withdrawn his affection after Christmas.

What a disaster that day had turned out to be. She'd left the cottage with hopes high and outlook bright, only to have her expectations dashed time after time throughout that fateful celebration.

Her many inadequacies had become glaringly apparent, but exactly which of those had caused Drew to retreat from her so completely she did not know. Up to then, he'd loved her. He had.

Was it that pox-smitten dress? Her ignorance of their customs? Her physical weakness—which prompted the whole chair-sled mess?

Whatever it was, it was major.

At first, she'd thought to soothe his fears by showing him she could be a good colonial wife. Yet the harder she tried, the more obvious it became that she didn't belong.

And worse, he didn't even want her to perform those wifely duties for him. He wanted Mary to. Mary, who should have been his wife in the first place. Or Leah. Now there was an appalling discovery.

She swallowed. All this time and never had he mentioned his long lost love. He wouldn't even speak of her now. When Constance had questioned him, he'd only said, *"It's done and no longer an issue."*

No longer an issue! Why, Leah was not some tobacco bride he'd bought on a whim. Oh no. Leah was a young woman he had met, fallen in love with, and *brought* home—clear from England. Nellie had told her so.

What a fool she'd been. She should have accepted the first marriage contract her father had ever presented her with. Only now, after it was too late, did she finally realize why brides were left out of such negotiations. Because they had no idea what was best for them.

Constance reached over, tucking a stray curl into Sally's cap. What a pair she and Sally made, both wanting to make daisy chains from a field that no longer produced them. Her daisy chains, though, were of becoming the perfect colonial wife for Drew while editing *The Ladies' Mathematical Diary* for Europe.

What ignorance. What arrogance. And not only the "perfect colonial wife" part. What made her think she could edit the *Ladies' Diary*, especially from here? And what made her think the world would stop spinning simply because the *Diary* quit publication? Why, for all she knew, Aunt Katherine had already returned this year's submissions, disclosing to all that the *Diary* was no more. And even if she had not, Drew would most likely have forbidden it.

"Look not earn-ist-lee at any other that is eating."

Constance blinked.

Sally looked at her expectantly.

"Your pardon." Kissing the top of the child's head, cap and all, she gathered up the trencher, noggin, and spoons. "All done for today. Let us pray."

As soon as the prayer was over, Sally shot out the door to enjoy the springtime sun finally beginning to warm the land. Soon, new life would burst all around them.

Constance stacked the utensils on the shelf. Spring wouldn't bring new life to her, though. The new life she sought here in the colonies was not to be had. At least not for her.

———

She watched him cradle the handkerchief as if it held hundreds of precious gems instead of tiny seeds. "Would you like to help me start a seedbed for my next tobacco crop?" he asked.

She pulled her gaze away from his hands—callused yet gentle, loving, wonderful. "I thought you were supposed to have started one already."

"You don't have to help. I merely thought . . ."

They were alone in the cabin. He had come home in the midst of the day, an unusual occurrence. Mary had wasted no time in taking Sally outside to feed the chickens.

"No, I want to help. What do I do?"

"Hold out your hands."

She cupped her hands as he gingerly transferred the cloth. Their fingers connected, and a shiver of longing spread through her. The seeds blurred.

God help her, she would not cry. Not again. She'd done enough of that to last her a lifetime. She rapidly blinked back her tears.

Placing one hand beneath hers, he removed some seeds from the cloth she held. She allowed her eyes to flutter closed, relishing the feel of his touch.

"Before sowing, you test the seeds by throwing a few into the fire. If they sparkle like gunpowder, they're good and should produce."

She gave him a curt nod, keeping her head carefully bent. He removed his hand, then tossed his seeds into the fire. They immediately popped, shooting sparks outward.

She looked up, surprised to find his attention not on the fire but on her, an odd heaviness and a twinge of pain lurking in their depths.

She closed her fingers over the handkerchief, nestling its contents within her grasp and pressing it against her waist. "The seeds are good."

"Yes. Mix a fair amount of them with some ashes and we'll sow them."

"Show me."

He retrieved an earthen jar and filled it with soot. "Put some in here," he said, holding it out for her.

She carefully siphoned a number of seeds into the jar, then laid the handkerchief on the table.

"Good. Now stir it."

Allowing him to retain hold of the jar, she sunk her finger into the mixture and slowly whirled it around. And around. And around.

She needed to go ahead and tell him. Tell him of her decision to spare him from any more of her bumbling ways. Tell him of her decision to release him from any misplaced responsibility he might have for her. Tell him of her decision to leave.

"Why are you crying, Connie?" he whispered.

She jumped back, wiping her finger against her apron. "I'm not."

It was a foolish statement, of course, for even now, she felt fresh tears fall from her eyes.

"You don't have to help me with the tobacco. I thought you wanted to. I mean, you had asked, and . . ."

She swallowed. "I very much want to care for your seedlings. I know not what's wrong with me. I've never been such a watering pot in all my life."

"Are you in pain?"

Not like you mean, but yes. Oh, yes. My heart is rending in two. "No."

"Then what is it?"

Tell him. A frenzied desperation infiltrated her body. *No.* She didn't want to leave. What she really wanted was to stay. Stay and be his wife. And maybe an editor on the side?

What would he do if she voiced such a thing? What would he say? She searched his eyes. What if he said yes? She felt her throat closing up.

But he wouldn't. He'd say no. "Why have you not taken me to the big house, Drew?"

After a moment, he averted his gaze, the tension within him palpable. Then, as clearly as if someone had lifted blinders from her, she saw. Saw what she'd been oblivious to all along.

Her decision to leave or not to leave was inconsequential, for clearly Drew had already made up his mind. *He* was going to send her back, and she had no say in the matter whatsoever.

Her cheeks burned. And here she thought she was being so noble, so sacrificial. Yet all the while, he'd intended to send her back regardless.

An internal roaring resounded in her ears. "Don't answer that." She turned and found a shallow wooden crate. "Is this what we plant the seeds in?"

He hadn't moved, but his attention had now honed in on her.

She took a deep breath. "I'm sorry, Drew. Forget I spoke. Is this for the tobacco?"

After another long pause, he set the jar down on the hearth. "We need to talk."

Her composure slipped a notch. "No we don't. Everything's fine, truly. Come. Let's plant the tobacco. You get the crate, I'll get the seeds."

She hustled forward and reached for the jar, only to be halted by a gentle grip on her wrist. "We tried, Connie, we did. But we both know . . . it just isn't going to work."

No. Not yet. She wasn't ready. She needed more time! She broke free from his grasp, picked up the jar, and plopped down onto the hearth. Swishing the ashes inside with her finger, she dug a small hole. "How much dirt is there in a hole the dimensions of which are an inch, do you suppose?"

He squatted down beside her, his knees cracking. "I haven't taken you to the big house because, all things considered, I thought it best not to."

She jumped to her feet. "Let's go plant the tobacco."

He stood and closed his hands over her shoulders. "Connie."

Tears surged to her eyes, tumbling down her cheeks. "Please, Drew, please. Can we please just plant the tobacco?"

Maybe if she did a good job with the seedlings he wouldn't send her back. If he would give her a chance, he'd see. She would water them, nurture them, set them in the sun. Whatever it took. And it would be the best blessed crop he'd ever had in all his days.

A tiny niggling voice reminded her he'd be better off without her. She drove it from her mind, convincing herself that if she could just do this one thing, it would be a start. Her heart thumped madly as she waited for his answer.

Backing up a step, he let his hands fall. "Very well. We'll plant the tobacco, for now."

CHAPTER | TWENTY-SIX

IT WAS HER FAVORITE time of day, and for a short while it managed to chase her oppressive sadness away. During this early morning hour, the world belonged to her, for though she was up, hundreds more throughout this primitive land still snuggled in their ticks, resisting the moment they must arise.

Not Constance. She and her dear companion, Snowflake, took in nature's concert every morning. They had standing reservations, with the best seats in the house. She rested her cheek against Snowflake's coarse hide, working milk from the goat's teats by rote as they waited for the concert to begin.

Sweet heaven, this country had taken her by surprise. It was lovely in the summer, a virtual painter's palette in the fall, a marvel in the winter, and an absolute Eden in the spring. She wished she'd paid more attention to her art lessons. How glorious it would be to capture this place and keep a piece of it with you always.

She breathed in the freshness of dawn, picturing in her mind the multicolored spectacle spring made of itself here. Many of the unfamiliar trees and shrubs she'd learned of last summer now clad themselves in blooms that took the very breath from her body.

Dogwoods crowned with thick, lush clusters of white looked as if snow covered their boughs. Spicebushes filled her senses with fragrance while simultaneously awarding a charming yellow floral display. Wild trumpet creepers in blossom festooned the trees. And trimming these exquisite ensembles were iris, lilies, poppies, peonies, larkspurs, hollyhock, and more.

The concert was in full swing now, bursting with twitters, whistles, cackles, and fluting. Some short and staccato, some with crescendo, some with irregular haphazard rhythms.

The milking was done, her hands lax against her knees. Yet Snowflake stood still, cushioning Constance's upper body as she rested against the gentle beast. She opened her eyes. A hare, no bigger than the coneys back home, sprang across the clearing. She smiled as she followed its progress until it disappeared into the thicket.

A movement captured her attention, and finding its source along the perimeter of the yard, her eyes widened. *What in the world is that?* A slow-moving, furry black creature with a wide white stripe from its head to its tail lumbered into the yard. Constance slowly lifted her head from Snowflake's side. The goat fidgeted, backing up a step or two.

Constance quickly grabbed the pail and pulled it out of harm's way. Snowflake turned and headed toward the front of the cottage. Constance stayed on the stool and looked again at the fascinating animal moving toward her.

"Good morrow. And what might you be?"

"*Eeeeth, eeeeth, eeeeth, eeeeth.*"

"I see. And might you be hungry? I can give you not the milk, but I might be able to round up some chicken feed. Would you like that?"

The animal paused and, nose twitching, examined Constance with its marblelike eyes. Reaching into her pocket, she tossed some feed to the animal. It froze, erecting its white-plumed tail into the air.

Constance sat very still, sensing she'd frightened it. After several long moments, it lowered its tail and ambled forward, snatching up the feed before scurrying back into the safety of the forest.

She sighed. Oh, how she loved this country. Thoughts of smelly, crowded, confining London crept into her musings. She didn't care to ever see it again. She missed it not. Not at all.

She did miss her family, though. Still, Uncle Skelly, God rest his soul, and Aunt Katherine had been her real family, and she'd been taken from them years ago. Her siblings were busy with their own lives and, of course, the war. And Father, too, for that matter.

But here, here she felt . . . well, free. Free in that she had no tedious social obligations to fulfill. Free in that she could venture forth alone without putting her person or reputation in jeopardy. Free in that everyone was quite expected to be unconventional. Even now she wore no shoes.

She burrowed her toes into the grass. Why, she'd never realized how cumbersome the numerous garments and undergarments she wore at home had been until she'd come here and discarded all for one simple gown. And now that the weather had warmed, everyone put away their shoes, not wanting to use them when there was no need.

She dipped her finger into the milk, then brought its creamy taste to her mouth. Yet while she felt free, she also felt so vulnerable. She always seemed to be sabotaging something, her relationship with her husband included.

But today was a new day. Maybe this would be the day the tobacco seedlings would nose their way to the surface. Maybe this would be the day Drew took her to the big house. Maybe this would be the day he decided to keep her.

Please, Lord. Let this be the day.

———

The seedlings didn't come forth that day, nor did Drew. But a week or so later, a tiny suggestion of green grazed the surface of the soil, and now her plants had reached about an inch in height. Drew had been pleased. She had been ecstatic.

Still, he hadn't shown her the new house. She could have gone and seen it for herself. She certainly had the time and the desire. But she'd fantasized so often about going there with Drew, being carried over its threshold in his arms, wandering through its corridors together, that to go there now without him would be the same as admitting defeat.

And she was far from admitting defeat. Her cooking was improving. Her seedlings were thriving. And she had a new pet she called Blackberry. He visited her most every morning during the milking and many an evening at the creek while she washed dishes. If the animals here accepted her, then surely it was a sign from God that Drew would too.

Please Lord, let it be a sign.

———

The sun had gone down, so Constance brought her treasures inside. They now stood two inches tall, and a new one had just sprung up this morn.

Placing the flat carefully on the shelf, she picked up her diary and recorded a puzzle that had come to her when she'd watered her flat this afternoon.

A seed is planted. At the end of two years it produces a seed, and one each year thereafter. Each of these, when two years old, produces a seed yearly. All the seeds produced do likewise. How many seeds will be produced in twenty years?

———

The salty air whipped Drew's hair against the side of his face. He stood on the shore before the weather-beaten *Myrtilla*, sitting low in the water, anchored some one hundred yards out on the Chesapeake Bay. In its hatch rode, among other things, enough furniture to fill his house. Soon, that furniture would be replaced with tobacco. He should be pleased. Drew was anything but.

Crewmen crowded the deck, continually coming and going, their step quick, their ribald laughter carrying across the water. A lusty tune of a milkmaid and her lover cut through their den of exchanges. A sturdy sailor came into the bows, dumping a bucket of refuse overboard. Screeching, the seagulls swooped down, their squawks drowning out all other sounds.

Maybe he could keep the ship's presence from her. It wasn't out of the realm of possibilities. Only men came to shore for the unloading and loading of ships, none of whom would have any reason to make a social stop at his cottage.

So, if he could ensure that Josh and the indentured men remained quiet, he might could secret the furniture off and the tobacco on, then allow the *Myrtilla* to sail again before Connie was ever the wiser. But, no, Josh would be on board with the tobacco, and he'd not leave without saying good-bye.

Drew wasn't sure how much longer he could stay away from her anyway. He helped not with the washing of dishes, he came home for only one meal a day, and he'd created a handful of extra projects to keep him busy until she fell asleep each night.

He'd repaired the old raft that they never used at the creek and even now had begun to whittle a new hickory handle for an ax whose handle still had plenty of wear left.

He'd considered relinquishing their bed to her completely but could never quite bring himself to do so. He'd be sleeping in an empty one soon enough. Still, he mustn't join with her, for the risk of pregnancy was too great. They were lucky she wasn't already breeding. Sending her home a "widow" was one thing; sending her home a "widow" with child was something else entirely. Something he wouldn't do.

———

Constance stared at Mary, then sunk down into Drew's chair. "You cannot be serious."

Mary continued to stir the pudding. "You know it to be true, you do."

Constance placed a palm against her stomach. She'd kindled? Surely not. She would have known. Wouldn't she? "But I've not been ill."

"Consider yourself lucky."

She took a deep breath. "Now, Mary. I've been through quite a lot these past several months, what with the kidnapping, the marriage, the seasoning. It could simply be my poor body is a bit abused and confused."

"Your body knows exactly what it's doing."

"But how can you be certain?"

"You're tired all the time, you are."

"Of course I'm tired. I did not but collect eggs before. Now I do much, much more."

"You cry all the time."

Constance lifted a brow. "I've never been married before."

"You cannot eat large meals, yet you're continually nibbling on everything in sight."

"That's part of learning how to cook. I must taste so as to see what the concoction needs. Then, when the meal's finally ready, I've tasted so much, I'm too full to eat."

"Your breasts are tender?"

Constance said nothing.

Mary turned, amusement touching her eyes. "You're with child, all right. And soon, me thinks you'll be feeling the wee one squirming around in there, you will."

A warm glow flowed through her. Tears rushed to her eyes. She was going to have a baby! Drew's baby! She hugged her stomach. *Oh, thank you, thank you, thank you. A baby. Imagine that.*

She couldn't wait to tell Drew. She stilled. Drew. What would he think? Would he be happy?

Of course he'd be happy. But . . . but what about their marriage? She knew in the deepest core of her being that once she told him, he wouldn't send her back.

Would he be bitter? Resigned? Would he feel trapped? But what could she do? Go on to England and never tell him he had a child? Of course not. That would be unthinkable.

"How far along do you suppose I am, Mary?"

"How long has it been since your last monthly?"

Constance blushed. "Since December."

"I'd say you're close to four months, then."

"How long before I show?"

"Within the next few weeks, I'm thinking."

Constance bit her lip. "Mary, I'm not going to tell Drew right away."

Mary stopped stirring midmotion, looking sharply at her.

"Please. Don't say anything."

After a moment, Mary nodded. "Yes, Mistress."

A sure sign of her displeasure, the use of *mistress* was. But it couldn't be helped. The babe changed everything.

Constance would have to stay now, but it would be ever so much better if Drew thought it was his own idea. Men were so very testy when they felt pushed into something.

She clasped her hands together. Yes, she must make certain he insisted upon her permanence here—before he found out about the babe. And she had very little time.

She pursed her lips. Winning his adoration by performing wifely duties around the cottage had reaped nothing. She must think of something else.

A slow smile crept upon her face. There was one thing he'd never been able to distance himself from, even in the beginning. She smoothed her apron down. And of that, she had plenty. Plenty with which to use in the seduction of her husband.

———

"Drew! Drew! We bring you lunch!"

Drew gave one last push against the lever, wedging an opening in the large crate, then looked to the west. Sally bobbed across the grass with cap, caught by its strings around her neck, flopping against her shoulders, her long black curls fluttering free. Constance followed a few paces behind.

She carried a large cloth-covered basket in one hand and reached high above her head to wave with the other. His senses leapt to life. Propping his lever against the crate, he moved to the edge of the shipment.

Sally reached him first. "What's in the boxes?"

"Furniture."

Sally darted off to investigate before Constance even reached them.

Drew wiped his forehead with a handkerchief as he watched Connie's progress. The sun splashed onto her shoulders, and his gaze traveled to the gentle sway of her hips.

He stayed as such until she stopped mere inches in front of him. She raised a delicate freckled hand to her chest, marking the swells of her labored breathing. "My, it's been a while since I've walked out here."

A while? It had been a blasted century. As far as he knew, she'd not been here since Sally's mishap. So what was she doing here now?

He stood rigid as she scrutinized the house.

Her eyes filled with an indefinable emotion. "Oh, Drew. It's magnificent. I had no idea." She turned to him. "Will you show it to me? I've so wanted to see it."

He waved his hand toward the structure. "Help yourself."

A small intimate smile crept onto her lovely sunburned face. "I'd prefer a guided tour. From you. Please?"

"I'm rather busy."

She peeked around his shoulder, exposing a nice portion of freckled slender neck. "So I see. What have you in the crates?"

"Furniture."

Her eyes widened. "Furniture! You told me not the house was finished. When did you complete it?"

"A fortnight ago."

Her face lit with pleasure. "Why, that's wonderful! Congratulations! We must have a celebration."

He had to put some space between himself and her. His blood was pumping, his heart was hammering, and his senses were reeling. "What are you doing here?"

She hesitated, then held up her basket. "I decided to bring you something special for your midday meal."

He frowned. Had her voice taken on a husky quality, or had he imagined it?

She raised the basket higher, pressing its handle against her chest. "Go ahead, take a peek."

He quickly lifted a corner of the cloth.

"Trout," she whispered. "I caught it and made it myself."

"Caught it?"

Her entire face spread into a smile, dazzling him. "With a frying pan! You've never seen such a thing, Drew. The trout are so plentiful, I needed only to scoop my pan into the water and up came enough fish for dinner and supper too!"

He couldn't help but smile at her enthusiasm. "I know. So you fried it up too?"

She hugged the basket closer to her, nodding her head proudly.

There may have been trout in the basket, but it was the scent of Constance that filled his senses. Lilacs and woman. A lethal combination.

He gave himself a mental shake. Her ticket home was floating right down by the wharf, and he'd not stand here billing and cooing in the meanwhile. He glared at her. "I already have a meal."

Turning, he moved back to the crate he had been working on. He'd meant to hurt her feelings, but he'd not done a very good job of it, evidently, for she followed him to the crate and rested her shoulders and back against it, flinging her chin up toward the sky. Long cinnamon-colored lashes lay against her cheeks as he moved his gaze along the enchanting profile she displayed.

Grabbing the crate's side, he wrenched it off, jostling her from her position. It mattered not. She settled right back against it.

"I'm not leaving, you know."

His heart stopped beating. *Did she know about the ship?*

"At least not until you've eaten my trout."

Lips thinning, he grabbed the basket from her. "Then by all means, let me eat."

She jumped from the side of the crate, laying a hand against his. "No, not here. Not like this. Take me inside, Drew. Take me inside, show me the house, and we'll sit down and eat in there."

He jerked his hand free. "Why?"

"Because it's important to me. I want to see what you've worked for, what you've sweated for, what you've forsaken your family for."

He whipped himself up to his full height. "Forsaken my family for? Just what is that supposed to mean?"

"Sally and I never see you anymore. You leave before dawn and return well after nightfall. You've even quit taking meals with us. She misses you." She fingered the laces at her neck. "We both do."

He scoffed. "It's a lonely life, the life of a farmer's wife."

"Only if that wife is a widow. Which I'm not. What keeps you out so long?"

"Somebody's got to work around here."

She took a deep breath. "And that somebody's got to eat." She lifted a brow. "I went to a lot of trouble to fry that fish for you. So you'd best just resign yourself to taking me inside, showing me my new home, and eating your midday meal."

He spun on his heel, heading toward the house. "Well, don't do me any more favors."

He didn't want her in the house. It held no memories of her within its walls, and he'd wanted to keep it that way. But she was going to ruin that for him too.

Well, so be it. He would take her inside. He'd show it to her. He'd eat her pox-smitten trout. Then he'd kick her fancy backside out.

He slammed open the front door, moved into the great room, dropped the basket of trout onto his new hardwood floor, and plopped down to eat. He'd taken no more than two bites when her voice reached him from the front steps. He looked up to find her hovering in the doorway.

"Will Sally be all right out there?"

"Of course," he replied. "The men will look after her."

She hesitated. "I've never been in before."

He ripped off another bite of fish with his teeth. "Well come on, then. Otherwise, go away and leave me be."

Her shoulders straightened and she stepped across the threshold, pausing there before entering the great room. Removing the bones from his mouth, he said not a word as she circled the room, touching this, running her fingers along that.

He found some spoon bread in the basket and shoved it into his mouth. "You obviously made the bread too. Mary sure didn't."

She sighed. "No, she didn't."

"Well, I wish you'd let her. That's what she is, Connie. My cook. And I like the way she does it." He tunneled around in the basket. "Is there anything to drink?"

"Yes. There's some cider in the wine skin there on the left."

He dug through the contents, purposely abusing the other prepared foods, then yanked out the wine skin, squirting a stream of cider into his mouth.

She settled across from him, her skirts billowing out around her. "The workmanship is exquisite, Drew. I had no idea the house would be so fine."

He wiped his hand across his mouth, then burped. "Even we colonists have some skills."

"That's not what I meant," she said, loosening the top of her bodice. "I meant—"

"What are you doing?!"

She froze, eyes wide. "What?"

He jumped to his feet. "Don't *what* me! You know exactly what I'm talking about."

She looked down at the basket. "Is something amiss?"

He ground his teeth together. "Your bodice, Constance."

She snatched her hand away from her laces. "I was merely warm."

"Well, it's spring and Virginia gets much, much hotter come summer. So if you're hot now, you'll be miserable in the summer."

Tears filled her eyes. "I don't mind."

He fisted his hands. "Well, I do! Now lace your bodice and get out of here."

She fumbled with her lacings. "But I haven't seen the house."

"Out!"

She stumbled to her feet. "Why are you shouting, Drew? Why are you angry?"

"I'm not shouting! I'm not angry! I'm just ready for you to be gone from here, and as soon as the ship in port is loaded with tobacco, I will put you on it and be done with all this!"

Her gaze flew to the window facing the water, but of course, she wouldn't be able to see the ship from here. "Right now? There's a ship out in the harbor right now?"

Bitter cold swept through him. Was that eagerness tingeing her voice? He couldn't quite tell. "Yes."

"And . . . and you want me on it?"

He felt his chest heave in order to take in enough air. "Yes."

She moved toward the window, her back to him. "Why?"

Because I love you and I want you to be happy, not miserable. "You don't belong here, Connie. And you know it."

She bent her head down. "Because of my math?"

"Among other things."

"But we're married, Drew. We said a handfast, to Morden, to God, and to each other."

"Consider yourself a widow."

She spun around. "But you're not dead!"

"No one will know."

"I will know! God will know! Surely you do not think I would return home and take another husband when I already have one?"

His temper began to climb. He said nothing.

"Well, I'll not do it, Drew. I'll never take another. Not ever." She bit her lip. "I want not to go. I want to stay."

By my troth, must she rip his heart from his very chest, leaving nothing in its wake? "So you think, but years from now you'll be thanking me."

She wrung her hands. "You're attracted to me, Drew. I know you are."

His heart slammed against his ribs. "It matters not."

Tears spilled over and onto her cheeks. "How can you say so? It matters. It does."

"It doesn't. Not in the long run."

"When did you decide to send me back?"

Forsooth, why couldn't women have been given the foresight of men? Why couldn't they see what was best for them? Why must they always fight it? "You know when."

"Christmas Day."

"Yes."

"Yet you're still attracted to me."

He clinched his teeth together. "Yes."

"Then take me to wife, Drew. Just one last time before you send me away. Please."

Heat shot straight through him. "Absolutely not."

A new flood of tears. "Why? *Why?*"

Because it would kill me, it would. His mind scrambled for another answer, then zeroed in on one equally as important. "Because my seed might take root, and I do not want you to have my child."

CHAPTER | TWENTY-SEVEN

"COME *ON,* SALLY!" SHE snapped, turning around for the umpteenth time.

Sally pumped her pint-size legs but gained little ground. For the first time, resentment reared its ugly head. If it hadn't been for Sally, Constance could have made if not a dignified, then at least a swift, exit from the big house, then given herself over to the vanquishing weight bearing down upon her heart.

Instead, she'd had to go out to where Josh and the men were eating their meal and exchange pleasantries before collecting Sally and heading toward the cottage as if her very life hadn't just been wrenched from her body. But it had. And if she succumbed now, Sally would no doubt report it all to Drew in vivid detail.

Compressing her lips, Constance marched back toward the child.

Sally's steps faltered, her eyes widening. "I hurry!" she implored.

She hauled Sally up and off her feet, propping the child against her waist as they moved toward home. Sally wrapped her legs and arms around Constance, whimpering.

Constance hardened her heart, offering no comforting word or gesture, for she had nothing within her but anguish. Nothing. By the time they reached the clearing, Sally had exchanged whimpers for actual sobs. They were minor compared to the sound Constance made upon the sight that greeted her. Screeching in horror, she barely kept herself from dropping the child. *"Noooooo!"*

Letting Sally down with a thud, Constance ran toward her seedbed, waving her arms. "Shoo! Shoo!"

The goat looked up inquiringly, a tobacco stem still in its mouth.

"No! Oh, no! How could you! *How could you?!"*

The goat shied away, then bolted when Constance struck its flank with every bit of force she could muster. Pain shot through her hand, surging up her arm. She paid it no heed but spun to face the damage, then fell to her knees, covering her mouth.

The flat of tobacco seedlings was no more. Snowflake had nipped the buds off all but two plants. Short stubby stems no more than a quarter inch tall stuck up above the imprisoned earth. An agonizing wail slowly escaped from her as she grabbed her stomach and rocked back and forth.

Mary rushed outside. Looking at the scene, she quickly captured Sally in her arms, carried her into the cottage, and left Constance to grieve alone over the ruined seedbed.

Constance plunged her fingers into the fertile soil, tangling them in the roots beneath the surface. Curling her fists, she yanked the fibers out, crushing them within her hands.

She squeezed harder, harder, her arm muscles quivering, her fingernails drawing blood. The desolation within her strained against the boundaries of her being until like a great serpent of the deep, she roared to her feet, hurtling the roots at the seedbed.

They hit with a very soft, dissatisfying thump. She booted the flatbed with her foot, jamming her bare toe and moving the flatbed not one mite.

Fury clawed through her. *Blast these infernal seeds. Blast Drew. And blast him for making me care!* With quicksilver movements, she grasped the flat's edges, pulling it up and over. Dirt spilled out into a huge jumble, and she let the crate fly.

You want me not to bear your child? Well, you're too late, you three-suited knave! You're too late! She kicked the dirt, stomped the roots, and cursed with renewed vigor.

"Sissy? Your di'ry make you feel better?"

Constance jerked her head around to see Sally tentatively holding out the diary, her tiny chubby hands extended.

It wasn't until she tried to focus that she realized tears obstructed her view. Mopping her eyes with a hard swipe, she lost sight of Sally and beheld only the diary.

The pamphlet took on a life of its own, growing larger and larger in Constance's eye, until she perceived it as a laughing, mocking, heinous creature.

She snatched it from Sally's hands. The child gasped and stumbled backward, her lower lip quivering. But Constance merely spun and raced away. Away from the cottage. Away from the seedbed. Away from Drew.

For nothing would she slow. Not for the sharp stitch in her side, not for the tearing flesh on the bottoms of her feet, not for the nausea swimming in her stomach. She noticed not the blooming dogwoods, the colorful phlox sprinkled alongside the path, nor the stillness of the forest. She simply plunged forward, eyes straight ahead.

She heard the creek before she smelled it, smelled it before she saw it, and then she was there, racing toward it. With legs whizzing over the ground beneath her, she cranked her hand back, squeezed the diary tight, then launched it through the air.

The momentum of her action slammed her to her knees. With nothing short of sheer determination, she caught herself on her hands, never losing eye contact with her journal as it arched above the water then somersaulted into it with a splash.

Sunning turtles slipped from their logs. Unsuspecting ducks squawked and flapped their wings, painting ribbons of water in their wake. *The Ladies' Mathematical Diary: A Woman's Almanac Adapted for the Use and Diversion of the Fair-Sex* bobbed to the surface before swirling downstream.

Constance stayed on her hands and knees watching until it turned from a booklet, to a speck in the distance, to nothing. Then she curled up into a ball and wept.

———

Drew worked like a man possessed, driving his brother and the other men with excessive pressure. They tore open crates, unloaded furniture, and hauled it into the house. But the satisfaction, the fulfillment, the exultation he had expected to accompany this moment were sorely lacking.

In their place was mirthless, pathetic dejection. He cared not about the superior craftsmanship of the pieces they unloaded. He cared not if any had been damaged during their shipment. He cared not if he even had furniture.

Sunlight poured through the huge diamond-paned windows, exposing a jumble of chairs, tables, and assorted pieces crowding the great room. The men jostled about, lugging bits of a bed abovestairs, stacking chests against the walls, fitting drawers into an elaborate secretary, none of them talking, none of them exhibiting the relaxed air that usually permeated the atmosphere.

Drew gave Josh a nod, then moved back outside to the few unopened crates remaining. The physical demands of tearing open wooden boxes suited his mood. Picking up the pry bar, he wedged it into a seam.

Connie's reaction to his words had surprised him. Shock, acute anguish, then blazing anger had played across her features in a matter of seconds. He'd realized immediately she'd misinterpreted his words. Typical of a woman.

He didn't mean he thought her *unworthy* of bearing his children, only that it was *unwise*. Yet he chose not to clarify his statement. Let her think what she would.

As strong-willed as she was, any crack he revealed in his defenses would soon be a huge crevice if she discovered it. No, it was best to let her think the worst.

The crate resisted his efforts to open it. Cursing, he moved the bar down to another point in the seam. The rest of the furniture should be in the house well before sunset. As soon as the job was done, he'd walk over to the public warehouse and see how the loading of tobacco progressed.

They'd spent the last week rolling their many hogsheads there and collecting the crates of furniture. With no animals for pulling, the transfer of crates over the pock-ridden terrain had been long and arduous, with Drew, Josh, and the men all dragging borrowed flatbed wagons back and forth more times than he cared to remember.

He'd decided that would be the last time he did any dragging of that magnitude. He would have a couple of extra weeks before planting commenced, and he'd use those weeks to build himself a dock right at the bottom of the slope here.

A tight bubble formed in his stomach, growing larger and larger while he tried to dismiss the fact that Connie would be gone and would never see his new dock, nor anything else, for that matter.

He glanced up, the Indian boy's rapid approach giving him pause. The boy had filled out since he last saw him, his arms and chest taking on a more refined edge. But that wasn't what held his attention.

It was the manner in which the boy approached. Ordinarily, he stood at the perimeter of the yard and waited until he was noticed.

Of their own volition, Drew's feet moved toward the Indian, each step quicker than the next until he matched the boy's hurried lope. They met halfway. "What is it?" Drew asked in the native tongue.

The young warrior hadn't yet learned to guise his emotions as well as his adult counterparts. Still, it was hard to decipher other than the fact that the boy was troubled, maybe even torn.

"What?" Drew repeated.

The boy's nostrils flared with each rapid intake of breath. His lips thinned. "My leader, Opechancanough, grows old. And with age, so grows his bitterness. He speaks with great hatred for the white planters as they turn ancestral land into sot weed. Again and again Powhatans die from white man's disease and from white man's anger."

A shadow of alarm touched Drew as he translated the words within his mind. "White man's anger? Someone has died from white man's anger?"

A steely light entered the boy's eyes. "One of my brothers take ground nuts and tuckahoe from land once ours but now claimed by your John Emmett."

Unease swept through Drew. "And did Emmett detain the next available Indian for the paying of compensation as agreed upon between your chief and mine?"

The young warrior's jaw tensed. "John Emmett killed the next Powhatan he see."

Needlelike pricks spread from Drew's scalp to his toes. "Sweet, merciful God."

"Opechancanough set forth big plan. My brothers fan out through our overtaken land and approach the white planter with no weapons or war paint. Upon entry into the homes, they attack with whatever implement at hand, slaying all, then burning their dwellings with the dead and wounded inside."

Drew's heart slammed within his ribcage, then accelerated in tempo, each beat faster and harder than the next. "When?"

"Now."

No! Panic surged through him, gnawing at his throat. He grasped the boy's forearm, squeezing. *"My wife?"*

"You must go to her. Quickly. My brothers move toward there even now."

Drew whirled around, barreling up the hill toward the big house.

"White Coon?" the youth called after him.

Drew spun back to the boy, his chest heaving.

"We are enemies," the young warrior said in his guttural language. "If we meet again, it will mean death for one of us."

Drew nodded. "So be it. And thank you." Turning his back again, he sprinted to the house.

———

"Josh! *Joooosh!*"

His brother and the other men poured out the front door.

"*Indian attack!* Quickly, to Grandma and Nellie!"

Without another word, Josh grabbed a pry bar and raced toward his sister's home.

"Thomas! Take two men and get to the public warehouses! Hurry!" He tossed the remaining men pry bars, hammers, and anything else he'd happened to grab on his flight up the slope. "Isaac, sound a warning to the east!"

Isaac caught a hammer and headed out with a companion.

"You two, to the west! And make haste! There's not a moment to spare!"

No one asked him how he knew, no one asked him for details—they simply took the orders and executed them.

Denouncing himself a fool for having no guns in the new house, he clutched the remaining pry bar in his hand and outstripped the wind in an effort to reach Connie and Sally. He leapt over tree roots, plowed through overgrown brush that whipped against his legs, arms and face and focused on reaching the cottage rather than on what might take place if he were too late.

Please, God, please. Let me not be too late!

The distance between the big house and the cottage had never seemed so far. He pushed himself even harder, unaware of the protests his body made.

He was closer now and neither saw nor smelled smoke. A good sign. *Please, God, please. Let me not be too late!*

Pebbles sprayed from beneath his boots, sweat plastered his shirt to his chest, his hair fell loose from its leather binding. *Almost there, God. Almost there. Hold on, Connie!* He accelerated, thoughts of Connie and brutal Indians consuming his mind.

Just one more bend. He made no effort to disguise his approach but exploded into the clearing, a bloodcurdling scream on his lips as he sighted the Powhatan ready to torch his cottage.

He rushed the Indian, driving the pry bar against the warrior's wrist, sending the torch flying. Drew followed the lever's momentum, whirling around with it full circle before slamming it into the Indian's head. The pry bar swung from Drew's grasp upon contact, shooting white heat up his arm.

The Powhatan careened and then fell to the ground. Drew checked his temptation to run into the cottage, forcing himself to first make sure the Powhatan would not rise again. He reached down for the Indian's neck. The warrior's arm flashed up, grabbing Drew, kicking him, and tossing him backward before he had a chance to react.

Then the Indian was there, on top of him, encircling his throat with a vengeance. Drew butted the Powhatan's arms. The pressure against his throat increased.

He clawed at the Powhatan's face, flesh collecting beneath his nails. The pressure increased.

The warrior's tight-lipped grimace hovering above him faded in and out of view. Drew gasped for breath. His ears began to ring.

He was going to die. *Connie! Sally!* No. Not yet. He couldn't die yet. He had to breathe. *God, help me! Help me!*

The crackling of the fiery torch penetrated the fog within his brain. The torch. The torch. The fire from the torch. He could hear it. Feel it. Almost taste it upon his lips.

Drew flailed his legs. Bucked his hips. And with supreme effort, rolled to the left, reversing positions with the Indian while plunging his enemy into the spreading fire.

The viselike grip around his neck loosened only slightly, and Drew sucked in a trickle of air while driving his knee into the Indian's chest and yanking against the warrior's wrists. The acrid smell of singed flesh teased his impoverished lungs. The sizzling of human skin resounded in his ears.

The Powhatan acknowledged none of it. Drew sucked in another paltry breath. He couldn't begin to imagine the torment the Indian must be undergoing. Even Drew's own body smoldered from the searing heat.

The warrior held firm to Drew's neck, though, glaring at him and squeezing, tighter, tighter. Apprehension twisted within him. What manner of man was this? *Let go, you fiend!*

The Indian dug his nails into Drew's neck, then shoved him back and off. They broke apart, bounding to their feet, channeling their focus onto each other instead of the torturous pain racking their bodies.

Drew circled to the left. The Powhatan mirrored his moves, a slow, satisfied smile creeping onto his face. If it came down to a bare-handed struggle, Drew would die. And they both knew it.

Drew's gaze swept the area where the pry bar had fallen, then quickly returned to track the Powhatan. The pry bar would be of no use. It now lay in the midst of the spreading fire, flames engulfing it. A trail of flames tickled the base of the cottage. He must kill the Indian before the fire reached the thatch roof or all would be lost.

The Powhatan lunged, making a swipe at him. Drew jumped back and free. He glanced at the ax buried in the tree stump. The Indian saw it as well. The Indian was closer—just barely.

They both broke and ran for it, but Drew detoured, snatching up the new hickory handle he'd been whittling, which was still a good six feet long and stood propped against the mulberry tree.

The Powhatan whirled to face Drew with the ax. Drew rested on the balls of his feet, bending his knees and facing the Indian with a hickory handle turned quarterstaff. The Indian smiled, swirling the ax above his head, then tossing it from hand to hand.

Drew cocked a brow, spinning the quarterstaff within his grasp. An earsplitting shriek pierced the air as the Indian rushed Drew with an overhead swing of the ax.

Drew swept his quarterstaff up with both hands, blocking the half-moon slash toward his head. The moment the ax handle connected with his dense pole, he jerked the staff backward, whipping the ax out of the warrior's hands to fly harmlessly behind his own back.

In less than a heartbeat, Drew snapped his right hand forward, slamming the right butt of the staff into the Powhatan's left temple, stunning him. Capitalizing on his advantage, Drew dropped to his left knee, sweeping the quarterstaff behind the warrior's knees, knocking him off his feet and hard onto his raw back.

He heard the Powhatan's breath rush from his body and followed up with a sharp jab, thrusting the end of his staff into the Indian's throat, crushing his voice box.

Drew jumped back. The Indian's eyes bugged. He clawed frantically at his throat, rolling onto hands and knees while he choked. Drew dropped his weapon and grabbed the warrior by his hair, jerking him to his knees. The Indian grasped Drew's arms, but the pressure behind his grip faded even as he made contact.

With the same detached passion he used to destroy wild game, Drew placed the Indian in a headlock and snapped his neck, dropping the Powhatan's lifeless body onto his face in the settling dirt.

He knew he'd wrestle with it later, but there was no time to think of what he'd just done. Flames now licked two sides of the cottage. He had to get in there. Now.

He didn't allow himself to hesitate. But he knew. Before the end of his struggle with the Indian, he knew. Knew what he would find once he set foot inside that cottage. For if anyone had still been alive, they would have come outside to assist him in destroying the enemy. But maybe, just maybe in the Indian's rush to move on to his next prey, he had merely knocked them unconscious.

Drawing the neck of his shirt up over his mouth and nose, he plunged into the cottage. Scorching heat and dense smoke blasted him in the face. He dropped to his knees. A layer of murky but navigable air hovered about three feet deep over the cottage floor.

He found Mary and Sally immediately. Both lay prone on the dirt floor. Both were dead.

CHAPTER | TWENTY-EIGHT

DREW WATCHED HIMSELF AS if from afar as he placed Sally atop Mary, then gathered them both in his arms and staggered back out of the cottage in a crouched position. The anguish, the grief, the misery had to be moved someplace else. There was no time for it now. He needed to find Connie.

Settling the girls well beyond both the cottage and the Indian, he whipped out his handkerchief, tying it about his face as he pitched himself back into his beloved home, now filled with billowing clouds of black, uncompromising smoke.

Narrowed into slits, his eyes burned, while his throat, raw and chapped, sucked in air. She wasn't on the floor, or he'd have seen her when he first came in and found the others. Dropping to his hands and knees, he scrambled toward the bed.

The thickened smoke and shortage of air made his head spin. Was he still moving in the right direction or was he going in circles? He couldn't see a blessed thing.

He cracked his temple against the bed frame, blinding himself for a moment. At least he'd found the bed.

Rising up on his knees to check the mattress, thick, heavy smoke strangled him. He ran his arms along the tick. Nothing. He sunk again to the floor. Where *was* she? The board. Maybe she lay on the board.

The roof had caught now, and bits of fire rained from above. Whipping the tick off the ropes, he covered his back with it as he slithered on his belly, so impermeable was the smoke. His lungs ceased to function. He was losing awareness. He had to find Connie.

Then he heard it. A soft, mourning, heart-wrenching wail from far, far away. Had he imagined it? No, there it was again and she was calling him. Calling his name.

Hold tight, Connie! I'm coming! I'm coming! Keeping his face close to the dirt, he pulled his knees up beneath him and moved toward the sound. The roaring of the fire blistered his ears, but her high-pitched plea cut through it all. He shuffled toward it, praying desperately as he went.

———

Her throat was dry, her eyes parched from crying when she finally pushed herself to her knees and wiped her face with her apron. Thick, moist clouds had moved in front of the sun, threatening rain.

What held her attention, though, was Blackberry. The striped animal stood a stone's throw away, facing her, his body tensed, his ears flattened, his tail erect. The hairs on Constance's nape tingled.

Blackberry drummed his front paws on the ground with an astonishingly loud *thump . . . thump, thump.* He repeated the long, short, short rhythm two more times.

After a taut moment, he lowered his tail, then turned toward the forest. Constance scanned the thicket as well but could see nothing. The forest lay eerily quiet. Blackberry sniffed several times, his nose prodding the air around him, before finally dismissing whatever had concerned him and ambling toward her.

She ran a hand over his downy coat and long, fluffy tail. "What's the matter, young fellow?"

She perused the forest again but could see nothing amiss. Blackberry climbed up her torso with his front paws, nudging her chin with his cold nose. She sniffled and lay back down, the animal flopping over onto his back as she did so.

She massaged Blackberry's tight tummy and forced herself to confront the weighty slab of desolation inside her. She might not have a congruous marriage anymore. Her interest in scientific pursuits might have lost its allure, but she had a God. And He'd given her a baby. Drew's baby. And for that reason, she must prepare herself for the long journey back to England. She cuddled the black and white animal, fresh tears filling her eyes. "Oh, Blackberry. I don't want to go."

Pearls from her time here strung together in her mind. The graceful deer poised outside the clearing on her wedding day. The smell of Drew's pipe when they washed dishes at the creek. Surprised delight after submerging herself in a tub of deliciously warm water. Learning to milk Snowflake. Taming Mr. Meanie. Berry-picking with Sally.

Sally. Regret, spiced with sadness, sprinkled through her. Oh, but she was going to miss the little moppet. Her actions toward that sweet, precious child this afternoon had been inexcusable. She must apologize to her, with not only words, but with a great display of affection.

Blackberry rolled onto his feet, burrowed closer, then turned in circles until finally settling in the crook between Constance's stomach and legs.

"And you. I'm going to miss you too." She scratched behind his ears. He tucked his head underneath and wrapped his tail around himself.

I've been a fool, Lord. A fool. I've placed myself, my marriage, and my mathematics above you. I've made them my gods, and as you can see, I've made a huge muck of things.

She ran her hand down Blackberry's coat. *Still, you've blessed me. You knit a babe together with your own hands and placed it to nest inside of me. Thank you, thank you, thank you.*

Because I know you will tolerate no other gods before you, I give you my marriage, my mathematics, myself, and this sweet, precious babe inside of me.

Her eyes drifted closed.

How long she slept, Constance was unsure, but when she awoke, Blackberry was gone and something was . . . burning?

Frowning, she sat up, wincing at the stiffness of her limbs. What was burning?

Then she saw it. Black, ominous smoke curling in great gusts toward the heavens.

"Fire!" she screamed, scrambling to stand up. A biting pain tormented the soles of her feet. She ignored it as thoughts of a fire took hold.

Hiking up her skirt, she ran pell-mell for the cottage. Her foot caught on a root, and she sprawled to the ground, the impact knocking her senseless. Shaking her head clear, she hoisted herself up, barely giving her body a chance to fully rise before her feet dug into the ground again as she ran and ran and ran.

Blood drained from her head. Her mind swam. *No! I will not swoon! I cannot swoon! Sally! Mary! Oh, sweet Lord! I cannot swoon!* Nausea churned in her stomach. Breathing became an exercise in futility. The smell of fire spurred her on.

The crackling and roaring of flames reached her ears, the cottage's demise, her eyes. *Oh, Lord!*

She saw the Indian first, then Sally slumped atop Mary. A wrenching pressure ripped throughout her body, starting deep in the pit of her being. It spiraled up into her chest, suffocating her. Her knees buckled. "No!" she screamed. "Noooooooo!"

Falling to the ground, she tried to crawl to them but got tangled in her skirt. She wrested it from beneath her knees, finally reaching the woman and child. "Oh no. Oh no. Oh no," she sobbed.

Scooping Sally into her arms, she drew the limp body to her own, rocking it, patting it, murmuring to it. "Wake up, Sally, wake up. Don't go. Please, pumpkin, don't go!"

Sally's head toppled like a rag doll from one side to the other as Constance rocked. She burrowed her fingers into the child's hair, bracing her little head and feeling a huge sticky lump at the base of it.

Nausea rushed up Constance's throat, and she bit her tongue to keep it at bay. She couldn't succumb to it yet. She had to wake up Sally first. She had to apologize to the dear little thing.

She reached out and grabbed Mary's arm. "Mary, Mary. Fetch me a cool cloth. I can't get Sally to wake up." But Mary only lay there.

Constance shook her. *"Mary!"* She'd injected her most severe tone, one she'd used back home when dealing with recalcitrant servants but had never before used on Mary. "Get *up*, I say. I need help. I hurt Sally's feelings, and I need to tell her that I'm s-sorry. That I d-didn't mean it. That I l-l-love her!"

But Mary would not get up and Sally would not wake. Constance squeezed her own eyes shut, then squeezed Sally to her heart. "Drew!" she screamed. "Drew! Sally w-won't w-wake uuuuuuup! Dreeeeeew!"

How many times she screamed his name, she didn't know, but suddenly he was there, wrapping his arms around her, Sally trapped between them. He ran his hands up and down Constance's back, neck, and hair, kissing her forehead, her eyes, her cheeks, her mouth with quick, frantic pecks.

The stifling smell of charred wood engulfed his shirt, smothering her. She pushed at him. "Stop it! I can breathe not! You're going to hurt Sally!"

But he didn't stop and anger twisted inside her. She released Sally long enough to shove him away. But when he fell back, so did Sally, her body contorting in an unnatural way.

"Now look what you did!" She gathered Sally to her again, this time cradling her like an infant. "I'm trying to wake her up, not squash her to death." She looked up at Drew through tear-streaked eyes. "She won't wake up!"

Tears were pouring from Drew's eyes as well, and he looked like death itself. Dried blood lay in streaks down the left side of his head and matted his long hair. His face was plastered with black soot. Blue and purple imprints crisscrossed his neck. "What happened t-to you?"

He licked his parched lips, then moved them, but no sound came out. He tried again but only croaked. Impatience flickered in his eyes, and he jerked his head toward the cottage.

Constance looked at it dispassionately as flames consumed all four sides and the roof. She became vaguely aware of an immense heat pressing against her body. "It's on fire," she stated.

His expression changed. He stood, plucking her to her feet. Holding fast to Sally, Constance crumbled back to the ground. "Stop it, Drew. I need to stay with Sally."

His hands bit into her arms, and he hauled her to her feet again, his mouth working, guttural sounds emitting from it. He pointed to the cottage, to Sally, and then to the forest.

"You want me to take Sally away from the fire?" she asked.

He nodded and pointed to the path.

"Take her to the creek?"

He nodded again and spun her toward the path, giving her a push. She started to fall, but he grabbed hold of her skirt, propping her up again. When he let loose, her feet wavered but she stayed upright. She turned back to him once more and said, "Please tell Mary to come too."

He leaned down and swung Mary into his arms.

———

He knew not what to do first. Tend to the burning cottage or to Connie. He decided on Connie, for by himself there was not much he could do about the spreading of the fire, and Connie was in no shape to fend for herself.

He would get her to the creek and follow it to the James River and on to the ocean. For if the forest were to catch fire, he wanted to be far, far away.

He hoisted Mary to his shoulder and trotted to catch up with Connie. She was still talking to Sally. Talking about showing her some friendly blackberries. Forsooth, he hoped she wouldn't catch the mind sickness.

He remembered some who'd lost everything in '22 and how mind sickness took over their bodies. And this surprise attack was exactly like the other one. The last had killed near four hundred. He wondered how many this one would claim.

His thoughts gravitated to Josh. Had he reached Grandma and Nellie in time? What about his new baby nephew? Would he be orphaned . . . or worse? He blacked the thoughts out, refusing to consider the possibility of losing them too. As far as Sally and Mary went, he would not, could not, dwell on it now.

Connie was alive and he had to keep her that way. To think of anything else would undermine his ability to do so. He tuned out her sentimental blabbering and started planning for what he would do if they encountered more Indians. Or what he would do if the wind picked up and the fire spread so rapidly they became cut off from an escape route.

His throat ached, his lungs burned, his heart remained resolutely numb. Connie's progress was slowing with each step, her hold on Sally more and more precarious. When she snagged a toe and lurched to the ground, she refused to release Sally. Both fell with a thud.

Quickly lowering Mary, Drew dropped to his knees. Connie lay face down in the dirt, her shoulders shaking.

"Get up, Connie." His throat barely croaked out the words. "We need to keep moving." He placed a hand on her arm. "Come."

She reacted like a wild animal, jerking herself up with teeth snarling and claws barred. "Touch me not! Just leave me be! I see not what the hurry is anyway. In case you haven't noticed, Drew, she's dead. Did you hear what I said? Sally's dead! *They're both dead!* Don't you even care?"

Tears spilled down her cheeks, and he watched her crawl to Sally's side, straightening the child's dress into neat folds.

A raw and primitive anguish seeped into his soul. He had tried to tell her. One should never, ever allow himself to get too close to the children. The odds were too high against you.

But Connie had scoffed at such advice and now look at her. So torn up with grief she didn't even recognize the peril her own life was in this very moment.

This was why she must go back. This was why she couldn't stay. He would not have her go through this again with her own children. And she would. As sure as the sun, she would.

And it would rip her sweet, tender heart from side to side, top to bottom, corner to corner. He knew it for a fact, for his at this very moment lay in tatters. Again, curse it all. *Again.*

"*Drew,*" Connie screamed, grasping Sally's face and rapidly patting her cheek. "Oh, sweet saints above! Did you hear that?" She snapped her head up to look at him. "Did you? I think she moaned!"

But, of course, she hadn't. Connie was delusional. Still, it would be more expedient to recheck Sally than to try to convince Connie otherwise.

He moved closer and held Sally's wrist with one hand while placing his other hand against the lifeline located in her neck.

Connie stilled, waiting for his reaction. Sitting back on his heels, he slowly shook his head. "I'm sorry, love. I feel no heartbeat. Now, we really needs go. The wind is blowing this way, and we need to keep moving."

He looked down again at Sally, then ceased to breathe. Had her little chest risen and fallen, or had it been a trick of the wind?

"But I *heard* her, Drew. I know I did!"

He grasped Sally's wrist again and leaned over her inert body, lifting one eyelid and then the next. He could neither feel nor see any sign of life whatsoever, yet he heard it too. As soft as a butterfly's wings, it was. The slightest of whimpers.

Oh, my Lord! Have you spared her? Have you?

Eyes wide, he looked up at Constance. "Yes! Yes! I heard it!"

"Mary! Check Mary!"

He rushed over to Mary, checking her and checking her again. "No. We've lost her, Connie. I'm sure of it. But we must move now, quickly. We must get Sally to the creek."

He scooped up Sally and laid her in Connie's waiting arms.

"You're sure you can manage her?" he asked.

"Yes, yes. Get Mary. Make haste! Make haste! Oh, hang on, Moppet. Hang on."

By the time he picked Mary up and laid her over his shoulder, Connie had already started scurrying to the creek, Sally held tightly across her breast.

The fire was gaining ground. He could hear it. Smell it. Feel it. He knew Constance's pace was awkward and slow not only from fatigue, but also to keep from jarring Sally too much.

The wind whipped, picking up momentum. Fiery sparks floated all around. Thick smoke chased their heels. The braying of the fire sounded menacingly close. They had to reach the water. And quickly.

He hastened his steps, prodding Connie from behind. She increased her speed.

The wind surged, flattening their clothes against their backs. Flames leapt ever toward them, gaining so fast the smoke and heat soon became overpowering.

He opened his mouth to tell Connie to run. Smoke swirled into his lungs. He swallowed and tried again. "Run, Connie."

She didn't respond. He moved past her and turned around, jogging backward. "Run."

Mary's body jostled against his shoulder while Connie's eyes conveyed a message of heartbreak and commiseration. She couldn't run. Her skirts would trip her for certain. He opened his free arm.

She grasped Sally's waist and lifted her up to him. Folding the child into his embrace, he tried to bore a message of urgency into Connie. "Run."

She glanced back, then lifted her skirt, picking up speed.

He increased his backward lope. *"Run!"*

She ran. He whirled around, keeping pace beside her. The wind rose yet again. A swelling of fire crashed at their heels. They weren't going to make it.

At that moment, when the heat became unbearable, when he realized they were going to perish in nature's furnace, when he thought of all he still had to live for, an indomitable desire to survive burst upon him. Mary was gone, and maybe even Josh, Grandma, and Nellie too. And Sally's life still hung in the balance. But Connie was alive, and he wasn't ready to give her up.

God forgive me. Without ever breaking stride, he released Mary to Him, allowing her to tumble to the ground. His heart lurched, his breath caught, then he repositioned Sally and called out to Constance.

She turned to him. He swooped down, flung her over his shoulder, and sprinted. Sprinted toward the creek. Toward life. Toward salvation.

CHAPTER | TWENTY-NINE

THE WIND CHANGED. AND with it, the fire's direction. One minute it nipped at their heels, the next it receded into the distance. Drew kept running.

They reached the water. He plopped Connie down onto her feet, handed Sally to her, and splashed into the creek, swimming toward the raft.

He swiftly untied it, swam back, and pulled it up onto the shore. "Quick!" The two of them laid Sally onto the raft. Connie flopped down next to her.

He pulled the raft back into the water, wrapped the tie cord around his hand, and scissor-kicked his legs, pulling them downstream. His leg muscles prickled, his lungs labored, his head throbbed. He concentrated solely on moving them farther and farther from the fire. When it became too much, he veered to the water's bank.

His feet finally touched bottom, the mud suctioning each step. Constance jumped off the raft, went completely under, then popped back up, holding tightly to the bound logs until her feet touched and she could help pull the craft in.

The water shallowed, and they fell to their knees, tugging the raft behind them. Flopping back over onto the grass, arms flung above his head, he closed his eyes and sucked in air.

"She's alive, Drew," Connie said between breaths. "She twitched once and moaned twice."

When he could summon enough energy, he lifted one lid. By trow, Connie was a mess. Her cap had long since fallen off, leaving her hair plastered to her head in a wet tangle. Her face was pale, her clothes sodden, her posture dejected. But she was alive. Alive. Never had a sight been so sweet.

He reached for her hand, gathering it into his, their water-shriveled skin finding solace together. He gave a slight tug and she tumbled over, half on top of him, half on the grass.

"I love you." It was all he could manage at the moment, though he wanted to tell her more. Much more. But he needed to save his strength, for it was a good distance yet to the bay.

"Did you hear what I said about Sally?"

"Yes." But he was afraid to dwell on it, for at any moment her life could be snuffed out.

More minutes passed, and he knew they'd tarried as long as they dared. Forcing himself up, he rose. "We need to keep going. The fire's still spreading."

She shook her head. "You and Sally go ahead. I think I'll stay right here."

He bent down on one knee, combing a swath of hair from her eyes and hooking it behind her ear. "We needs must go, Connie."

Her weary gaze traveled over the water. Heavy clouds billowed overhead, darkening the sky.

He rose again, helping her to her feet. "Come."

She crawled back onto the raft, collapsing onto her stomach next to Sally instead of sitting. Connie groped around with one hand until she found the child's, then clasped it within her own. He swallowed, then pushed the crude vessel into the water. Kick, pull, breathe. Kick, pull, breathe. They were making progress, but it seemed so slow. So very, very slow.

Images of leaving Mary behind hammered against the periphery of his mind. Her hair uncovered and matted, her body contorted. He shoved the images away, forcing himself to concentrate on moving downstream.

He lasted longer this time before having to move to the water's edge. He was no less exhausted, though.

Not so Connie, for she found her voice as soon as he pulled the raft to shore. "What are you going to do?" she asked, sitting next to him on the bank.

About what, he wondered. Sally? Mary? The fire? Her? Their lives together? He slid his eyes closed. "Sally and I are going back to England with you. You can be the king's accountant for all I care, but if you go, I go."

When he'd made that decision, he didn't know. Somewhere between the fire and this creek bank, he supposed.

Surprise lit her voice. "But you're a tobacco farmer. We grow not tobacco in England."

He rubbed the muscles in his legs. She pushed his hands aside and took over the massage. Sweet saints, how could something feel so good and hurt like the dickens all at the same time? "I'll be a factor, like Josh. The O'Connor Tobacco Agency. And you can just forget about that 'young, wealthy aristocrat' who's waiting for you. I'm not sharing."

"What young, wealthy aristocrat?"

"The one your father's contracted for you."

"Oh. Well, that's good, for I want him not anyway, whoever he is." She paused in her labors. "Drew, do you really want to go to England?"

"I want to stay with you."

"Forever?"

"Forever."

She started to work on his other leg. "I want to stay with you too."

Such simple words, yet they sluiced through his system, restoring energy where moments before he'd been flagging. He peered at her from beneath his lashes, but she was concentrating on her task, her tongue captured between those pretty white teeth.

Her brow furrowed. "If we stay here, would you have to fight in a war against the Indians?"

He winced, and she lessened the intensity of her massage. "No. Usually the second and third sons, or those who lost everything, do the fighting. The rest will stay and continue to cultivate tobacco, thus ensuring permanence in the colony."

She moved her attention to one of his arms, kneading it like a roll of dough. "I want to stay here."

He fully opened his eyes. "Stay here? Why would you want to do that?"

She pressed her thumbs into his palm, then worked the joints in each of his fingers. "I like it here. No, I *love* it here."

He closed his fingers over hers, halting her administrations. "We just went through a massacre and you *love* it here?"

She looked at him, crystals of the creek's water still dancing on her lashes. "I want to stay."

His heart pounded. "What about that editing work of your uncle's?"

She swallowed, tears springing to her eyes. "It's a bit insignificant when you consider what's taken place these last few hours, think you not?"

A seed of hope buried within struggled to burst forth. He suppressed it. "Connie, it could happen again, along with any number of other things. Have you considered the well-being of our children?" His eyes darkened. "For there *will* be children."

"And?"

"And their chances of survival would be much better in England."

"Horse dung."

He blinked.

She moved to his other side, setting to work on his right arm. "There are hard times in England. Disease. Why, even a war." She shook her head. "I want to stay here."

He pulled himself up to a sitting position and scanned the band of forest around them. "Connie, look at it from a mathematical point of view. I come from a family of nine, and Sally and I just might be the only ones left today. You come from a family of twelve. Eleven of you are left."

"Uncle Skelly died."

"That doesn't count."

She cocked a brow.

He ran his fingers through his hair, rivulets of water collecting between them. "Okay. So he counts. Still, the odds are better in England."

Her expression drooped, disappointment evident within her eyes. "Oh, Drew. You are not God. Think you if the Almighty has need of one of our offspring, He will not be able to find them in England?"

He rested his forehead in his hands. He didn't want to think about God right now. What kind of God allowed a child to be savagely attacked? He stood. "It's time to go."

Without resistance, she returned to the raft, checked on Sally, and lay down, once again entrusting her life to him. He splashed into the water.

The skies rumbled, and a hint of smoke drifted across the water. The fire had not spread this far as yet, but its smell still clung. He hated to think of the damage the fire would do, for in spite of his words to Connie, he loved it here too.

Still, to raise a family in this primitive land was another matter. Foolhardy at best, a death wish at most.

"Drew?"

He grunted, pulling them through the water.

"I'm with child."

All motion stopped. Had she grown wings he'd have been less appalled. With child? *With child?!* He spun the raft so that she lay next to him instead of behind him. Only when she glanced down, frowning, did he realize he was paddling neither his legs nor his arms but was standing upright. They'd hit a shallow.

She rolled onto her side, propping her head in her hand. "Surprise."

He looked at her stomach. *With child! God help him.* "When?"

"I think it will arrive in about five months. Maybe sooner. I'm not really sure."

Stark, vivid fear hit him full force.

She must have seen it, for she placed a hand against his cheek and gave him an affectionate smile. " 'Fear not, for I am with you; Be not dismayed, for I am your God. I will strengthen you, yes, I will help you, I will uphold you with My righteous right hand.' "

It was Isaiah 41:10. The very same verse he'd recited to her during their wedding ceremony. Why did it fail to bring him comfort?

She smoothed his hair back from his face. "You must not worry, Drew. You must simply let God and nature run their course."

That terrified him even more. "I don't like the way God and nature run their course."

Tenderness touched her face. "There is naught you can do. Why, think of Sally. It is God who has spared her life and who still holds that life in the palm of His mighty hand."

Oh, Lord. Up to now, he'd managed to avoid those thoughts. But before he could stop it, pain crashed into his heart as his gaze drifted to Sally. So still she lay, each breath a miracle. And he could do nothing to wake her. To heal her. To ensure that she survived. Not one blessed thing.

Unbidden, long sable curls framing sparkling eyes and a mischievous smile filled his vision. He recalled with clarity the powerful, instantaneous feelings he'd experienced the first time he'd held her. She in one arm, her twin sister in the other, identical in appearance. And now, there was a very real chance that he could lose her. Even still. Just like that. He wasn't ready to give her up, was never ready. He felt so infernally helpless.

Moisture rushed to his eyes while tears swelled in Connie's. He tried to swallow but couldn't. Like a trembling volcano, the pain, the grief, and the horror erupted without warning. A cry of agony burst from his lips, his groan echoing across the water even as Connie rolled from the raft into the creek and wrapped her arms around his neck. He cinched her to him and cried. For Sally. For his family. For himself.

Only after some time did he realize Connie was crying too. Eventually, their sobs turned to silence, a silence of nothing. Still, they remained in the middle of the shallow, clasped to each other, waiting for the emptiness to cease and for the healing to begin.

But it already had. For somewhere in the furthest corner of his heart was a little worm, wiggling with excitement about the overdue realization that Connie really did desire to stay. About the tremendous mercy God had shown by sparing Sally, so far. And about the news of a baby. *His and Connie's baby.*

I give up, God. You made me. You know how I am. I cannot keep my distance. Nor can I keep those I love alive. Only you can do that. Only you are God.

I give over. I fall prostrate before you. What you see fit to bless me with I will rejoice over. When you takest away, I will turn to you for solace. For you are the One and Only God.

He lifted his head. The smoke had begun to thicken again. The fire was still spreading. "We need to keep going." Slipping a hand between them, he rested it against her stomach. "How do you feel?"

"Like I've run the length of this country and back, then swallowed the entire river."

His eyes widened in alarm.

She lifted a corner of her mouth. "I'm fine, Drew. Truly, I'm fine."

He believed her not, but there was nothing he could do. So he lifted her back onto the raft, and they once again headed toward the bay. They'd traveled no more than a few feet when a ball of light zinged the air above them, followed immediately by a deafening peal of thunder. He quickly propelled them to the bank, grabbed Sally, and hurtled both Connie and himself out of the water.

The crack continued to resound, each clamor a tiny bit less in volume than the last. No sooner had it stopped than the heavens opened up. It was as if God had sent a legion of angels to scoop the contents of the ocean into buckets and dump them onto Virginia.

In mere moments, the ground was afloat and the great fire was surely no more than a smoldering mist. They scrambled to the forest's interior for protection from the pelting shards until, finally, the rain began to slacken into a steady drizzle.

He scanned the area around them, untouched by fire, and got his bearings. Though they'd traveled what seemed like miles in the winding creek, if he wasn't mistaken, they were just a short walk from the big house.

"Hold out your arms."

Connie cupped her arms, and he gently placed Sally in them, then scooped the both of them into his.

"What are you doing?!"

He took a fortifying breath. "I'm taking you, Sally, and our baby . . . home."

CHAPTER | THIRTY

I T LOOKED AS IF Drew would carry her over the threshold after all, and Sally as well. Enormous relief and thankfulness had swept through Constance when the big house came into view as fresh and untouched as a young maid. And now, Drew took the front steps two at a time, pushed open those great double doors, and carried her across the threshold before climbing up the stairs to the master chamber.

A chill from being wet and suddenly indoors took hold of her. She must get Sally and herself out of these sodden clothes haste, posthaste.

The child was still breathing but lay heavy against Constance and had not yet made any signs of awakening. Constance had seen nothing of the house but the great room the last time she was here but didn't have the luxury of savoring her new surroundings. Her attention was centered on Sally.

Still, when they entered the master chamber, there was no avoiding the bed. Large enough for an entire family, the high post mahogany bed stood on four stately legs and was closed in at the head and foot by ornately decorated wooden panels. Though it had poles for bed curtains on the two open sides, none had been hung yet and no tick lay on the ropes.

She tightened her hold on Sally as Drew set them down in a chair.

"There's some dry wood belowstairs in the kitchen," he said, "and as soon as I get a fire going up here, I'll tighten the ropes and put the tick on the bed. You will be all right for a moment?"

"Yes, yes. Go ahead."

He looked around the room and snatched a wool coverlet off a stack of folded linens on a nearby dressing table. He shook it out and draped it around Connie's shoulders like a cloak, arranging its folds so that Sally would be covered as well. "I'll be right back," he said and hurried out the door.

She could barely see the top of Sally's head peeping through a gap in the coverlet. The sweet body heat they shared warmed Constance. Swaying from side to side, she hummed a lullaby while allowing her attention to wander across the chamber.

It was huge. The cottage could have fit into it two times. Furniture was planted haphazardly throughout. Two drop-leaf tables, several chairs, trunks, and a dressing table as fine as any back home took up much of the space.

A sapling broom stood propped in one corner, and a chest of drawers with butterfly pulls received an elaborate walnut Bible box complete with lock and key.

The beautifully plastered walls held three window casements with diamond-shaped lead glass panes, along with two additional windows in the attached alcove that would serve nicely as a nursery.

A brief movement below her feet caught her attention, and she could just barely discern Drew through the minute cracks in the plank flooring that set upon beams and served as a ceiling for the great room underneath.

Footfalls on the stairs reached her ears seconds before he strode into the room, dumping his load of wood into the fireplace that took up two-thirds of the west wall. "I've some heart of the pine to mix in with the regular pine and oak, so the room should heat up quickly. Are you all right?"

"Yes. As soon as you're done, though, I need to get Sally out of these wet things."

He nodded, igniting the wood with some flint, then quickly pressed fingers and thumbs to his lips, blowing a steady stream of air through the tiny hole he'd formed. The fire responded immediately, devouring the kindling and enfolding the dry logs.

He stood. "Let me tighten the bed ropes and throw the tick on first, so you'll have someplace to put her when she's dry." He grabbed the bed key, and starting at one end, wedged the large wooden peg between the rope and bed frame, twisting, then releasing. From section to section, his movements were quick and sure until he'd made it all the way around.

The tick lay beneath the bed, and she knew it must weigh a tremendous amount. How he had any strength left with which to wrestle it onto the ropes amazed her.

"There," he said, blowing a puff of air from his lungs. "She'll be able to sleep tight now, and the tick is feather instead of straw, so there'll be no bed bugs to bother her."

A feather bed. Oh my.

Together they worked silently, she disrobing and drying Sally, he covering the tick with linen and fetching water from the kitchen. When all was ready, she carefully laid Sally on the mattress, covered her with wool, then finger-combed her hair away from the swollen bump at the base of her scalp. Dipping a rag into the bucket of water, she began to wash the blood from the wound.

"I've no garden here yet, nor any comfrey," Drew said. Leaning forward, he tenderly touched the gash. Sally moaned. He sent Constance a look filled with hope and relief. "A good sign. Perhaps she'll waken soon."

When they'd done all they could, Constance wrung the rag out into the red-tinted water, a shiver going through her.

"You next," he said. "Out of those clothes and into bed."

She nodded but didn't move from Sally's side. The thought of undressing exhausted her. Where would she find the strength such a task would require? "I'm filthy. I'll ruin the new bed."

"I'll bring you some fresh water."

"I've no clothes to change into."

His grin was downright wicked. "I know."

A short laugh escaped her, yet still she made no move. He leaned down to place a light kiss on her forehead before grabbing the water bucket and leaving the room.

He returned to find her exactly where he'd left her, sitting on the edge of the bed, shoulders slumped, eyes closed. Surely she hadn't fallen asleep like that.

As he drew nearer, though, he saw tears pouring from her eyes and streaming down her cheeks, jaw, and neck, then trickling into the folds of her neckline. Yet she made no sound nor any move to wipe them from her face.

He set the bucket down. "Connie? What's wrong? Are you all right?"

She raised her gaze to him, her eyes swollen, red. "Mary."

She'd barely whispered it, yet that one short name held immense anguish and misery within it.

"Oh, Connie." He reached down and pulled her up into his embrace. "I know. I know."

"She had such a hard life." Her voice was muffled and broken against his shirt.

He cupped her head, holding it against him.

"And yet she was so giving and unselfish. She showed me how to survive on that ship, you know, when she could have easily left me to flounder or perish, even." She hiccupped. "She comforted me when Uncle Skelly died. She offered encouragement here when I was having such trouble adjusting. She taught me so much. Listened. Shared. Even prayed with me. Oh, Drew," she wailed, "how am I ever going to manage without her?"

Sobs racked her body. Tightening his hold, he stroked her hair, kissed her head, rubbed her shoulders. Mary had come to mean much to him as well. He'd not thought of her as a servant. Hadn't for quite some time. He'd thought of her as a friend. A sister. An angel.

Oh, Lord. Why? Why would you take sweet, sweet Mary from Connie? From Sally? From me? Have you really such an urgent need for her to be with you? I don't understand. Will never understand.

Connie trembled, and he knew he must get her warm and safely tucked into bed.

Tilting her head back, he kissed the tears from her cheeks and placed a soft, tender kiss on her lips. Then scooping her hair off her face and shoulders, he began loosening her skirt and bodice. She stood mute and dejected as he peeled the sodden clothing from her frame and washed the mud, sand, and debris from her person, all the while supporting her lest she crumble to the floor.

Thank you for giving me this woman.

He patted her dry, careful not to hurt her bruised and battered body, then wrapped her in soft linen.

Please protect her and the baby. Please, Lord. It is my heart's deepest desire.

He lifted her into his arms and laid her next to Sally. Connie rolled to her side, curled her knees up, and sucked in a choppy breath.

She was asleep before he'd finished tucking the wool coverlet beneath her chin. After spreading her clothes in front of the fire, he shucked his garments off and splashed water over himself. He paused to stoke the fire and then crawled onto the tick beside his beloved family.

———

The dowdy, scrubbed, heavily laden ship rested peacefully on the blue water. It carried the usual three masts, the fore and main square-rigged, the mizzenmast lateen, while her poop deck graduated into three different levels up over the stern.

Drew had seen many a ship just like it over the course of his life, but this one, this one he would never forget. "You won't change your mind?"

Josh shook his head. "I've been wanting to do this for a long time. I was waiting only for you to acquire enough help so as to run the farm without me."

Drew looked from the *Myrtilla* to his brother. "If I'd known, I never would have bought the indentured men."

Josh's mouth tipped up. "That's why I told you not of my intentions."

"But why must it be so final?" Drew removed his hat, tapping it against his thigh. "What was so bad about coming back and forth with each shipment?"

"Nothing. It's just not what I *want* to do. I've never liked or excelled at farming the way you have. It's the factoring I enjoy. If I live in England, I can factor not only our tobacco, but many others'. I can factor full time, Drew. I . . . I'll be my own man." He pursed his lips. "The best part, of course, is I won't have to answer to Grandma anymore."

Drew attempted a smile but could not muster one forth. "You'll get dragged into the war. You know you will."

"I'm the second son here, Drew. If I return to help you farm this summer, the colony will have by then organized a counter force against the Indians in which I would be expected to participate." He shrugged. "It seems no matter where I go, I'll be fighting a war of one kind or another."

Drew studied his brother. Something wasn't quite right. Everything he said made sense. But, still. Drew narrowed his eyes. "Mary. Is that what this is all about?"

A mask descended over Josh's face. "Not to worry, Drew. I'll send you a *replacement*." His inflection made the word sound heinous.

Drew angled his head. "Mary could never be replaced, and that's not what I meant. Nor am I worried about a cook. Connie learned more than I realized about food preparation, and when her time approaches, Grandma will come and see to the cooking for her." A salty breeze disturbed the hair against his shoulder. "No, I wasn't speaking of cooking at all. I was speaking of *Mary*. Did you perhaps have deeper feelings for her than you let on?"

His brother's jaw tightened. "I'm going to stay in England because I like it there. I want to live there. I can be a successful factor there." He picked up his bag. "I needs must go."

Drew's throat thickened. "Your pardon. I spoke out of turn."

After a tense moment, Josh's shoulders wilted. "No, it's your pardon I must ask for. My-my feelings for Mary are jumbled within me and I—" the telltale tick in his jaw pulsed—"I'm not yet ready to think much less speak of them."

Pain congealed within Drew. "I'm sorry I was too late for her. I-I'm sorry we couldn't give her a proper burial. And if it makes you feel any better, I loved her too."

Josh took a deep breath. "It wasn't your fault." He scanned the shoreline. "I'm just glad Sally is mending and showing no signs of head weaknesses." He turned back to Drew. "And, of course, I'm vastly relieved that Nellie and the rest are all right."

Drew nodded, a spurt of anger replacing the hurt of just moments before. "I'd give anything to get my hands on Emmett."

"So would the Powhatans."

"You don't think the Indians kidnapped him and took him back to their camp for . . . retribution?"

"I don't. It's not their style. I think if he'd been home they'd have been very deliberate in killing him and careful to leave what remains there would have been for all of us to see."

"Then where is he? Every man in this settlement wants a piece of him."

"I know not, Drew. I know not. But his life here is over—one way or another."

"Still, I—"

Laying a hand on Drew's shoulder, Josh squeezed. "Our losses were great, but it could have been worse. We could have lost additional family members and we could have lost the big house." He compressed his lips, the tick in his jaw pounding. "Is it callous to be relieved the house was untouched?"

Drew took his time answering. "If it is, then I am calloused as well, for I was not only thankful the house still stood, but also that the seedlings were unharmed and the cured tobacco was safely intact within the ship's hull."

His brother nodded.

"I want not to anger you, Josh, but Grandma had some parting words she wished me to give you."

Josh gave him a sideways look. "That sounds ominous. Why didn't she say them to me herself?"

"She's distraught." He shook his head. "This massacre was so much like the last one, I'm sure she's reliving it some. In any case, she asked that I place a Bible in your bundle."

Josh glanced at his bundle. "I thought it burned in the fire."

"It did. Morden gave her two more—one for each of us."

"Why, Drew? She knows I've read it already."

"Yes. I'm aware of that. We both have read it." He sighed. "Still, I'm glad she insisted on it, for I confess I have turned to it and the One who inspired it often of late and have discovered this . . . this freedom—from guilt, from failure, from the responsibility of keeping everyone alive."

Josh rubbed the back of his neck. "I know not what to say. You've caught me a bit off guard."

"I know and I'm sorry. I wish we had more time. I wish I were better with my words. But will you read it over again? With a perspective of freedom instead of as a book full of rules? Mayhap starting with the New Testament this time?"

Josh took a deep breath. "I could try, I suppose."

"Thank you."

Josh extended his hand. "Take care, brother."

Drew grasped his hand and pulled him into an embrace. "I'll continue to refer to the second bedchamber as yours. So if you ever have a need or desire to return, know that it waits in ready for you."

They held tight, then broke apart, neither bothering to hide the sheen in his eyes. Turning, Josh walked out to the end of the pier and jumped down into the dinghy. Drew placed his hat on his head and watched the sailor row his brother to the *Myrtilla*.

The dinghy pulled alongside the great boat, and Josh climbed its wooden steps along the sloping side of the flat, holding his bundle over one shoulder. He swung up onto the deck, then leaned against the port bulwarks looking out to his brother and home.

Drew inhaled. The salty air smelled good. Fresh. Not like the acrid air of decay permeating the desecrated land over so much of the area. Too soon the bosun's voice traveled across the water. "Let fall your main! Bring your cable to the capstan! Break out anchor!"

Young sailors with shirts open to the waist scurried to and fro across the deck. Josh remained a still figure in the midst of the chaos.

The fore and main topsails flew up, as did the square and lateen sails on the poop. With a creak and a moan, the weather-beaten girl moved slowly out of the harbor.

Drew watched the seagulls dip and swell in her wake until the squawking birds were mere dots, the ship but a toy boat, and his brother a poignant memory.

CHAPTER | THIRTY-ONE

Five months later

ANSWERING THE KNOCK, DREW yanked open the front doors just as an earsplitting scream from abovestairs rocked the house. In an effort to remain upright, he squeezed the door handles with an iron grip, though he felt all circulation drop to his toes.

The haggard, overdressed old gaffer in front of him straightened his spine and turned as red as his doublet. "By my life, what goes here!"

Drew scowled. "Who are you?"

The portly travel-worn man narrowed his eyes. "I am the Right Honorable the Earl of Greyhame, Lord Randall Christian Morrow, and if that was my daughter, *you* are a dead man."

Another scream from abovestairs descended into the hall, but this screech was nothing like the one before. This one was the unmistakable bawl of a newborn baby.

The blood rushed back up from Drew's toes to his head in a whirling mass, causing Connie's father to appear in triple. *It's here. The baby is finally here.*

Fighting the urge to run up the stairs and into their bedchamber, he blinked. Only two fathers stood before him now. Drew felt a slow smile spread across his face as he took a wobbly step back. "That first scream, my lord, was indeed your daughter, my wife, and if you kill me, your grandchild will be quite without a father. Won't you come in?"

Lord Randall barreled inside, brandishing his cane in Drew's face. "You beggarly knave, I was told this marriage was in name only! Who gave you permission to consummate the vows?"

"Theodore Hopkin, governor of this colony, representative of the king, and it's going to cost you plenty, for that daughter of yours is nothing but trouble. What in the blazes were you thinking to allow her an education?"

Drew bit back his smile at the man's shocked expression. Nothing like landing the first punch.

Lord Randall furrowed his bushy gray brows. "I knew not about her education until it was too late."

Drew straightened the cuffs of his shirt. "Well, be prepared to pay dearly for it. No man should have to suffer through what I do with the constant spouting of the most addlepated word puzzles you could imagine." He took the man's bag, then extended a hand toward the great room. "Please, have a seat."

The poor man's bluster dissolved, a look of resignation on his face. "Blasted chit." He shuffled into the room, settling his substantial girth into Drew's chair.

The game had begun. Drew poured them each a noggin of ale and took the chair across from him. "I require fifteen thousand pounds."

Lord Randall spewed ale across the floor. "What! Surely drink has tickled your poor brain. You're a *farmer*, you impudent rascal. I'll give you five thousand."

Drew plopped his drink onto the table at his side, its contents sloshing over the rim. A satisfied smile broke across his face. "Excellent." He stood. "When will you take her back to England with you? Today? Tomorrow?"

The old man's red-rimmed eyes widened. "I cannot take her back. Why, she's already birthed a child!"

Drew shrugged. "Fifteen thousand or I send her *and* the babe back, with or without you."

Lord Randall opened and closed his mouth several times, then shifted uncomfortably in the chair. "Well, is she . . . is she happy?"

Drew arched his brows. "What, in the name of the sword, has that to do with anything?"

His father-in-law scowled. "It has everything to do with it, you impudent knave."

He slanted Lord Randall a glance. "My price is still fifteen thousand."

Her father surged to his feet, the blood vessels in his face fair to bursting. "You'll see not a blessed shilling until I've spoken with my daughter."

Drew moved to the secretary, withdrawing a fully written and prepared marriage contract. "Feel free to peruse this in the meanwhile."

Lord Randall whipped the document from Drew's fingertips, then bent his way to his bag, pulling out a bundle of correspondence. He shoved it against Drew's chest. "And *you* feel free to peruse these."

Drew took the bundle, loosening the bow secured about the numerous packets. All were addressed to one Skelly Torrence Morrow, all were from women. Drew slowly lifted his gaze to his father-in-law's smug one.

"They were willed to her." The old gaffer patted his round stomach. "Enjoy."

Hurried footfalls from the stairwell interrupted any response Drew might have had. He spun around. Sally, now four years old, bounded through the door.

"Drew! We have a baby!"

He scooped Sally up into his arms, his heart accelerating as he barely retained hold of the correspondence in his hand. Grandma entered at a more sedate pace, then came to an abrupt halt. "Well, by heaven, if this isn't a surprise. God ye good den, Randall." She turned to Drew. "It's a girl and Constance is fine."

A girl. Connie was fine. Oh, thank God. *Thank God.*

Excitement, jubilation, and triumph exploded within him. He wanted to shout from the rooftops. He wanted to bang on his chest. He wanted to rush abovestairs and see for himself.

Instead, he turned to his father-in-law, but before he could say a word, Lord Randall whipped himself to attention, adding a good two inches to his height. "Lady Elizabeth!"

Drew blinked. *Lady* Elizabeth? He studied his grandmother with narrowed eyes. "You *know* him?"

She smiled. "Why, of course. I broke Randall's heart once many a year ago."

Drew regarded Lord Randall. Broke his heart? The old man looked as if he'd been poleaxed.

Drew's focus snapped back to the issue at hand. "Connie's fine, you say?"

"Oh, yes. Just fine. Go on. You can go see her now."

He hesitated, glancing at the stairs.

Grandma smiled. "Go on. Randall and I have things to discuss, and she's asking for you."

He looked at Sally, gave her a huge smile, and spun her around until they reached the stairwell. Her delighted squeal filled the hall. After setting her on the floor, he ruffled her hair, took a deep breath, and raced up the steps two at a time.

———

Constance pivoted her head toward the door in time to see her husband hovering about its threshold. "Hello."

He moved into the room, his well-muscled body hesitant, his thick onyx hair mussed, his face showing signs of fatigue. He surveyed the disarray within their chamber, then focused his attention back on her. "Are you all right?"

She patted the tick beside her. "I'm wonderful."

He inched closer, stopping just short of the polished mahogany bed. His attention was fastened to the squirming mass swaddled in her arms. "Grandma said it's a girl."

"Yes." Constance moved the blanket away from the babe's face so he could better see her.

His eyes widened, his Adam's apple bobbed, his face paled. "Oh, Lord."

Constance suppressed a smile. "What are you hiding behind your back?"

He looked startled, then nodded toward the babe. "I want a closer look first."

Constance laid the bundle against her shoulder. "And I want to see what's behind your back."

He glanced between her and the babe, then pulled his hands in front of him. "These are for you."

He handed her a stack of correspondence, tattered and worn along its edges. The moment she read Uncle Skelly's name inscribed across the first one, she knew what it was. Her gaze snapped to his. "Where did you get these?"

"They were willed to you. It appears you are now the official editor of *The Ladies' Mathematical Diary*."

Confused, afraid to allow even the possibility to cross her mind, she flipped through the many packets. "But . . . how?"

Drew answered not and she looked up at him again.

"Would you like to be the editor of *The Ladies' Mathematical Diary*?" he asked.

She held her breath. "You wouldn't mind?"

His expression softened. "No. No, I wouldn't."

A kernel of excitement stirred within her. "But what will everyone say? What if they disapprove and take you to task for my presumptuousness?"

He waved his hand in a dismissive gesture. "Oh, they'll never believe a woman could solve such puzzles. They'll just assume I'm humoring you by editing it myself and allowing you to put your name to it."

She raised her eyebrows. "But you wouldn't be."

He humphed. "They'll never hear me admit it."

"I will," she said, a smile curving her lips.

He shrugged. "They'll believe me, not you. Now let me see our baby."

She allowed a soft chuckle to escape.

"Daughter?"

Constance turned toward the voice in the doorway, and the world came to a halt. "Papa?"

He nodded his head once.

She handed the babe up to Drew, then opened her arms wide. "Papa!" He entered, bending over to return her embrace.

"Oh, Papa! Whatever are you doing here?"

He straightened, pulling at his doublet. "I received a rather frantic message from my daughter some time back. This message contained tales of kidnappings and forced marriages"—he quirked a brow—"and annulments."

She slanted a glance at Drew, but he was paying them no mind, his attention totally captured by the infant cradled in the crook of his arm. She took a moment to relish the picture they made before turning back to her father. "I changed my mind."

"You were kidnapped not?"

"I was kidnapped."

"You were forced not into marriage?"

"I was forced into marriage."

"You want not an annulment?"

"I want not an annulment."

"Why?"

She now had Drew's full regard. She smiled tenderly at him. "Because I love my husband. I love the colonies. And there is nowhere on God's green earth I'd rather be."

"He wants a fifteen thousand pound settlement."

"Fifteen thousand!"

"He says you're a great deal of trouble."

She hesitated for one startled moment before choking back a laugh. "I am."

"I thought so." He leveled Drew a look. "If I pay you the fifteen thousand, do you swear to keep her?"

Drew reared back his head. "Forever?"

Her father scowled. "Forever."

"Oh, I suppose." He gave a long-suffering sigh. "If I must."

She bit the insides of her cheeks to keep from laughing outright.

Her father turned to her. "You will sign the papers this time?"

With an effort, she sobered her expression. "I will sign."

Seemingly satisfied, he indicated the babe in Drew's arms with a tilt of his head. "I advise against educating her. Will cause you nothing but grief if you do."

Drew nodded gravely. "I quite agree." He followed her father to the chamber door, closing it behind the man. When Drew turned back around, his shoulders shook and a smile wreathed his face.

She returned his smile. "That was really quite awful of you."

He moved forward, blithely unrepentant. "He deserved it. He shouldn't have been near so lax with your well-being."

"He did the best he could."

"I disagree. But I don't really want the money. I say we settle it on our children."

Her breath caught. "Oh, Drew, that would be lovely." She patted the tick. He settled down next to her, laying their daughter in her lap, then peeled back the layers of swathing. He examined her tiny toes, rubbed her little tummy, and smoothed her eyebrow with his fingertip. "She's beautiful."

Love swelled within her, filling every corner of her being. "She has red hair."

He ruffled her startlingly bright downy hair, then cupped her head, placing a kiss on her nose. "It's auburn."

"It's red."

Their daughter scrunched up her hands and legs, waving them wildly in the air. He opened his palm, allowing the babe to kick his hand. "Is she like a puppy?"

Constance choked. "What!"

He looked up. "Will she get her spots later?"

Laughter bubbled up from within her as she playfully whacked him on the shoulder. "Yes. Yes, I'm afraid she will. As soon as the sun touches her skin, the freckles will appear."

A delicious two-dimple grin spread across his face. "Good. I find I'm rather partial to freckled redheads." The babe squalled, and he shushed her while rubbing her tummy. "I want to give her a name now. I want not to wait until she's three."

Her heart full, she fingered the bluish-black curls covering his bent head. "Then let's name her Mary Elizabeth O'Connor, after Mary and Grandma."

His gaze collided with hers and, after a beat, he smiled. "And so it shall be."

Leaning over, he captured her lips with his, and she encircled his neck, rejoicing in the love God had bestowed upon them.

She was a woman who had it all. A bit of her past through Uncle Skelly's diary, an anointed present through her fine marriage, and a promise of future blessings through the fruit of their love, even now wiggling within the shelter of their embrace.

And sending up a heartfelt prayer, she thanked Him, for behold, it was very good.

Many Virginia colonists truly did secure themselves a bride for a payment of 120 pounds of tobacco. The purpose of this practice was to induce the men of the colony to remain, build homes, and raise families—thus ensuring England's presence in the colony. At first, "young and uncorrupt maidens" (usually spinsters and widows) volunteered for this unique duty. But the Crown was only able to round up a hundred or so volunteers, while the demand was for significantly more. So they eventually resorted to transporting female prisoners. Every so often, an unethical ship captain would kidnap an innocent woman of high moral fiber, transport her, and sell her. Thus the premise for *A Bride Most Begrudging*.

The first edition of *The Ladies' Diary* was compiled by Englishman John Tipper, a schoolmaster who taught science and mathematics. Inexpensive and compact, it was the first almanac on the market expressly targeting a female-only audience and wildly popular. Though I have Constance using it in our story, the real *Diary* did not make an appearance until 1704. Many of the puzzles and solutions used in our novel were taken verbatim from the *Diary*, as was the *Diary's* preface—which was written by Tipper's successor, Mr. Henry Beighton. Other puzzles were taken from *Mathematical Wrinkles*, by S.I. Jones.

As so often is the case in the history of our nation, battles over the land upon which we encroached took many lives. In 1622 and again in 1644, the Powhatans rose up to protect their sacred home. And the colonists fought back. I very carefully researched these particular events and portrayed them as accurately as possible in the fabric of my novel. The massacre of 1622 cost the lives of almost 350 settlers and contributed to a famine and epidemic that killed another five or six hundred. It also brought on a counterattack against the Indians, in which scores of settlers and hundreds of Indians perished. The massacre of 1644 was almost as destructive as the first. These confrontations might have lasted for many years if Sir William Berkley had not captured Opechancanough. Berkley planned to take the Indian chief to England as an exhibit of the healthiness and long life of the American natives, but one of the soldiers shot him in the back. In 1646, Opechancanough's successor made a bid for peace and renounced title to the land between the James and York rivers below the falls.

And lastly, I have a confession to make. It would have been much more historically accurate to have used the King James version of the Bible when quoting Scriptures throughout the novel. However, I personally have a bit of a time understanding that translation and chose, instead, to use the New King James version because I understand it better and am more familiar with it. Forgive me?

In Him,
Deeanne Gist

COURTING
TROUBLE

Corsicana, Texas
July 1874

THE COWBOY, GOLDEN-SKINNED, BLOND and blue-eyed, plunked down a wad of bills on the auctioneer's table. "I believe I'll take that lunch basket." He turned and picked Esther Spreckelmeyer out of the crowd with his intense gaze. "That is, if it's okay with Miss—"

"Es-sie!" her mother called.

The ten-year-old girl glanced at her bedroom door, then back at her "cowboy."

"I'd love to share my basket with you, sir," she whispered, "but if you would excuse me for just one minute? I'll be right back. Promise."

Flinging open the door, Essie left behind her make-believe Fourth of July celebration populated with figurines, baby dolls, and imaginary friends. "Coming, Mother!"

She vaulted onto the banister, slid all the way down, flew off the end and executed a perfect landing—feet together, back arched, hands in the air. Just the way those pretty ladies in the circus had landed when they jumped off the trapeze.

"*Essie.* How many times have I told you not to slide down the railing?"

She whirled around. "Papa! I didn't know you were home."

"Obviously." Her father shook his head. "When you are finished with your mother, you are to write a one-hundred-word essay on the reasons females should not slide down banisters. It is to be on my desk before supper."

"Yes, Papa."

He tugged on her braid. "Go on now, squirt. I'll see you at dinner."

She flung herself into his arms. "I'll try to do better, I will. It's just so much fun. And I'm very good at it. I never fall off anymore. And if I'm going to be in the circus when I grow up, then I must practice."

He patted her on the back. "I thought you wanted to be a wife and mother when you grow up."

She offered her father a huge smile. "Oh, I do, Papa. I do. Didn't I tell you? I am going to marry either a cowboy or the ringmaster of a circus. But whoever he is, he's going to buy my box supper at the Fourth of July picnic."

Sullivan Spreckelmeyer blinked in confusion, but Essie had no time to explain. Mother didn't like it when she tarried.

Twenty Years Later

ESTHER SPRECKELMEYER HATED THE Fourth of July. This day above all others reminded her that everyone in the world went two by two. Everyone but her. She would have stayed home if she could have gotten away with it, but her father, the judge for the 35th Judicial District, expected his family to attend all social events.

Standing in the quiet of her family's kitchen, she determined that this year was going to be different. She had turned thirty last week and she needed a husband. Now.

She straightened the red-and-white gingham bow wrapped around her basket handle, then checked the contents one more time. Fried chicken, sweet potatoes, hominy, dill carrots, black-eyed pea wheels, deviled eggs, cow tongue, and blackberry tarts.

Cooking was of utmost importance to a man in search of a wife. Whoever bought her box supper today at the auction would need to know that with Essie, he'd be well taken care of.

Her father entered the kitchen, pulling on his light summer jacket. "What do you have in your basket this year, dear?"

She took a deep breath. "I don't want you bidding on it, Papa. Nor the sheriff, either."

Papa came up short. "Why not? What's wrong with your father or uncle winning it?"

"If the two of you bid, no one else will even try."

His gray eyebrows furrowed. "But no one has tried for years, other than that youngster, Ewing."

Essie cringed. Ewing Wortham was seven years her junior and used to dog her every step. At the ripe old age of ten, he offered two measly pennies for her basket. No one, evidently, had the heart to bid against him, and every year after he proudly bid his two cents. She could have cheerfully strangled him.

She'd received her height early and her curves late. Between that, her penchant for the outdoors, and her propensity for attracting the admiration of incorrigible little boys, her basket had been passed over more times than naught. Especially since Ewing had gone away to school.

Swallowing, she lifted her chin. "Nevertheless, Papa, I don't want either of you bidding on it."

"I don't understand."

"If neither of you bid, someone will step up to the task."

"Don't be ridiculous," her mother said, entering the kitchen and tucking a loose curl up under her hat. "No one's going to bid on your basket, Essie. Now let's go. We're going to be late."

Papa opened the door. Mama stepped through, the taffeta beneath her silk moiré skirt rustling. Essie gripped the edge of the table and stayed where she was.

"Are you coming?" Papa asked.

"Only if you promise not to bid."

He stood quiet for a long minute. It wasn't hard to understand why the people of Corsicana elected him term after term. Everything in his bearing exuded confidence and invited trust. His robust physique, his commanding stature, his sharp eyes, his ready smile.

"Come along, Sullivan," her mother called. "Whatever are you doing?"

He stayed where he was. "I'll have to leave during the auction, then, Essie. I would not be able to stand it if Ralph held up your supper and no one bid."

"That's not going to happen."

He tugged on his ear. "All right, then. Your uncle and I will slip away before your box comes up for auction—if you're sure."

"I'm sure."

But she wasn't. And between their arrival at the park and the start of the auction, Essie's self-assurance flagged. What if someone older than Papa bid? What if someone much younger than her bid? What if no one bid?

She glanced up at the blue heavens stretching across their small east Texas town and sent a quick prayer that direction. After all, she only wanted a husband, a house, and some offspring. Was that so much to ask? The Lord commanded His children to be fruitful, to multiply, and to populate the earth, and Essie intended to do her part.

Mr. Roland stepped onto the red-white-and-blue-festooned podium, stuck two fingers in his mouth and whistled. The piercing sound cut across the hum of the crowd, quieting the townsfolk as they gathered round. Essie placed a hand against her stomach to calm the turmoil within.

Boxes and baskets of every size, shape, and color covered the tables beside the podium. And though no supper had the owner's name tacked to it, everyone knew whose basket was whose, for the ribbons or doodads on a girl's box revealed her identity as surely as a stamped beehive identified Dunn Bennett china.

She adjusted her bon ton hat with its silk netting, handsome plume, and two bunches of roses all trimmed in red-and-white gingham. She had ordered it from the Montgomery Ward catalog specifically for this event, knowing it would set off her pale blond hair, which she had twisted tightly against her head.

Skimming the crowd, she swallowed. Papa and Uncle Melvin were nowhere in sight. Lillie Sue's box came up first and the bidding began in earnest, the young bucks all vying for the privilege of sharing a meal with the doctor's daughter.

Essie studied the unmarried men and widowers close to her age. There were not too many of them. Mr. Fouty, a cotton farmer from south of town. Mr. Wedick, a widower who'd outlived three wives so far. Mr. Crook, owner of the new mercantile. Mr. Klocker, Mr. Snider, and Mr. Peeples.

She cataloged every man in attendance, discounting the ones who were too old, too young, or too unsuitable in temperament or occupation. A silence descended and Essie turned to the podium.

Mr. Roland held her basket high. "Come on now, fellers, bid her up. If this basket belongs to who I think it does, you'll find something guaranteed to delight yer fancy."

No one offered a bid. Essie's stomach tightened. Her head became weightless. Blinking, she tried to see through the sunspots marring her vision.

"Now, boys. A basket like this is worth more than a pat straight flush. So, who'll start us off?"

Still no one bid.

Pretty little Shirley Bunting leaned over and whispered to her friend, "I cannot imagine why some old biddy would keep bringing her basket year after year when she knows nobody wants it. How embarrassing for her father."

Her friend nudged her and indicated Essie with her head.

Shirley turned, eyes wide. "Oh! Hello, Miss Spreckelmeyer. A lovely afternoon we're having, isn't it?"

Essie inclined her head. The girls hooked elbows and, giggling, disappeared farther into the crowd.

Someone yelled, "Where's Spreckelmeyer? Why ain't he speaking up? We're ready to bid on Betty Lou's."

Essie focused on the auctioneer, refusing to look anywhere else.

Mr. Roland scanned the crowd and stopped when he came to her. "Where's yer daddy, Miss Spreckelmeyer?"

She took a trembling breath. "He stepped away for a moment."

"Well, then, why didn't ya say so? I'll just put this here basket to the side, and when he gets back, you have him come on up and get it. I know he's good fer it."

She attempted a smile but wasn't sure it ever formed. The bidding on Betty Lou's basket commenced, followed by Beatrice's, Flossie's, Liza's, and the rest. By the time the auction finished and everyone dispersed, Essie's basket stood alone on the podium.

Slowly moving forward, she picked it up and walked home, never once looking back.

———

Fredrick Fouty
Points of Merit:

- *Still has hair*
- *Has two young children, so our own offspring would not be too far apart in age*
- *Hardworking*
- *Loved his wife, God rest her soul*

Drawbacks:

- *Tight with his money*
- *Smokes*
- *Drinks spirits*
- *Only attends church on Sundays, but not Wednesdays*
- *Lets the children run wild*
- *Doesn't like pets*
- *Doesn't enjoy the outdoors*

Essie closed her eyes and tapped the top of her bronze Ladies' Falcon pen against her lips, trying to envision the men who had attended the picnic. Opening her eyes, she wrote Mr. Klocker's name down and proceeded to cover the ruled octavo notepaper with a list of his attributes and shortcomings.

Within the hour she had a comprehensive list of the eligible—and attainable— bachelors in Corsicana. She blew on the wet ink and stamped the pages with her blotter. There was something a little frightening about seeing the words in black and white.

Was this what men did when they considered whom they wanted to court? If so, what would a man list under the positive and negative columns concerning her? Whatever it was, she'd obviously come up short.

Placing her pen in its holder, she leaned back in her chair and studied the papers spread out on her desk. *Father, guide me,* she prayed. *Show me which one.*

But no answer was forthcoming.

Closing her eyes, she whirled her finger above the papers as if stirring some giant cauldron, then spontaneously landed her finger on the table. She opened her eyes.

Mr. Peeples. Leaving her finger in place, she leaned to the right so she could read what item she'd pointed to.

- *Bits of chest hair poke up out of his collar*

She snatched her hand away. Maybe she should sleep on it. Pray more about it. And in the morning, she would choose a man and launch her campaign.

———

Essie rapped on the back door of the Slap Out. It was a ridiculous name for a mercantile, but Hamilton Crook refused to call it Crook's Mercantile. Said it would be bad for business.

So everyone in town had offered their suggestions until some farmer came through exclaiming he was "slap out o' rum." Followed by another fellow who was "slap out o' salt pork and powder shot."

One of the regulars had chuckled and said, "You oughta call this place 'Slap Out'!"— never dreaming, she was sure, that the name would stick.

Essie pulled her shawl tight about her shoulders. The sun had risen, but it was too early for the store to be open. She had wanted to arrive in plenty of time to explain her idea without the risk of customers interrupting.

She knocked again and sighed. She had always hoped her married name would be something elegant, even regal. Anything was better than Spreckelmeyer, or so she'd thought.

Now she was beginning to wonder. Going from Essie Spreckelmeyer to Essie Crook had been the biggest drawback to choosing Mr. Crook as her future husband. Hard to say which name was worse.

The door swung open. Mr. Crook stood in his stocking feet, shirttail out, black hair completely mussed. "Miss Spreckelmeyer? What is it? What has happened?"

Goodness. He looked even younger than she had guessed he was. His youth was the other negative in his column, but she'd thought the gap between them was small. Now, inspecting him up close, she wasn't so sure.

A baby cried in a distant room. Mr. Crook stuck his head out the door, looking to see, no doubt, what disaster had brought the town's old maid to his back doorstep.

His gaze fixed on her bicycle propped against the building. "Has your riding machine blown a part?"

"No, no. I just need a short word with you, if you don't mind."

The baby's complaints turned from belligerent to downright frantic.

"Might I come in?" she asked.

He glanced toward the sound of the baby. "This is a rather awkward time for me. The store will be open in another hour. Perhaps you could stop by then?"

Her immediate instinct was to nod and scuttle away. But she needed a husband and she'd decided Mr. Crook would do quite nicely.

She pulled the screen door open and stepped inside, forcing him back. "No, I'm not sure that's a good idea. You go ahead and tend to yourself and the baby, though. I shall wait right here for you."

"Really, Miss Spreckelmeyer." He frowned, and already she found herself wanting to smooth down the patch of hair sticking straight out from his head. Perhaps it was a sign.

"I'm afraid I will be busy right up to store opening," he said.

"I understand. Run along now. I'll be here when you get back."

He hesitated.

She removed her shawl and hooked it on a hall tree. "Go on with you. I'll be fine."

She had to raise her voice to be heard over the baby's screeches. After another second or two, he turned his back and disappeared up the stairs that led to his personal quarters.

The closing of a door abruptly cut off the baby's cries. A baby who desperately needed a mother. She squelched that thought for now. First things first.

She glanced around the narrow storage area. She'd never been in the back of the store before. It smelled of lumber, leather, soap, and grain. Empty gunnysacks lay piled in a corner. Shelves lined two walls and held a hodgepodge of tools and gadgets, dishes and jars, cloth and brooms. Harnesses, straps, and whips hung from ceiling hooks.

A couple of crates sat shoved against a wall with sacks of grain leaning against them. A wooden bar bolted the large barn-like door where barrels were delivered. The unvarnished plank floor beneath her feet had turned gray from exposure.

Mr. Crook's store was only two years old, the first competition the old Flour, Feed and Liquor Store had seen since opening in 1858. With the Texas Central Railroad now coming through town, businesses were popping up everywhere.

Essie moved through the curtained barrier between the storage room and the store, stepping onto the stained, varnished, and newly shined floor of the Slap Out. Sunshine seeped in around the edges of the drawn window coverings, filling the store with muted light.

She took a deep breath. This was her first taste of what her role as Mrs. Crook would be like. The large, still room invoked a sense of peace, tranquility, and rightness.

She belonged here. She just knew it. Mr. Crook might not have bid on her basket yesterday, but he needed a woman and helpmate. That baby needed a mother. And Essie was the perfect candidate for the job.

She just wished she could remember whose basket Mr. Crook *had* bought, but that entire auction was nothing but a muddle in her mind, as fragmented as an unfinished puzzle.

She strolled behind the counter, her bootheels clicking against the solid floor as she ran her fingers along bolts of wool, dimity, gingham, percale, linen, and lawn cloth. She skimmed her hand across balls of yarn in every color of the rainbow, then tapped one side of a scale, setting it to swinging and causing its brass pans to jangle.

She picked up a bottle of Warner's Safe Nervine—reading the label's claim of healing, curing, and relieving of pain—then set it back down and scanned the vast assortment of tonics, pills, and powders. She'd have her work cut out for her learning which medicine was best for what.

Beside these items, drawers and bins stretched from floor to ceiling across the middle section of the wall, each carefully labeled compartment filled with spices, coffee, tobacco, candy, buttons, peas, and most anything else imaginable.

And if she had her way, she would soon be proprietress over it all. But first, she must slip behind the lines, learn the lay of the land, and then take over to the point where Mr. Crook would become almost dependent upon her. Where he couldn't imagine life in the store without her. Once there, advancing from helper in the store to helper in the home was just a staircase away.

She smoothed her hand up the nape of her neck. She mustn't waver from her goal. She must stay strong in her purpose no matter how nervous she felt.

Still, subtlety would be the order of the day. She didn't want to scare him off by pushing too hard, too fast. Heading to the ready-made clothes section, she removed an apron from one of the shelves. Shaking it out, she tied it around her waist and mentally cataloged the boots, shoes, long johns, hats, bonnets, and handkerchiefs that lined the tables and shelves in this little nook.

She returned to the back room, picked up a broom and began to sweep the store, starting in the farthermost corner where the stove, chairs, and checkers had been set up. She was nearly finished with the entire floor when Mr. Crook came through the curtain.

His short black hair had been slicked down and parted in the middle, while square spectacles perched upon his nose. Rosy cheeks graced his oval face, making her wonder if she had been the one to put that color there.

He grasped the opening of his cassimere coat and tugged, drawing her eyes to the snappy plaid vest he wore along with a four-in-hand tie.

"Miss Spreckelmeyer? What are you doing?"

She looked down at the broom in her hand. "Oh. I just thought I'd make myself useful while I waited."

He strode forward and snatched the broom away. "That is quite unnecessary. Now, what emergency has brought you to the Slap Out at this early hour?"

She clasped her hands together. "No emergency, sir. I didn't mean to worry you."

"Then what is it?"

Stay strong. "I know things have been a bit difficult for you since Mrs. Crook's passing, and I thought I might ease your burden a bit."

He smiled warily. "Well, that is quite thoughtful of you, but Mrs. Peterson watches the baby and takes care of my meals."

"Oh no. I didn't mean that. I meant with the store. The other evening I saw you sitting at your desk burning the midnight oil, so to speak, and realized you must do nothing but work and sleep and work and sleep. I thought maybe if you had an extra hand, perhaps you could do some of that bookkeeping during the day."

He rocked back on his heels. "Are you, uh, asking for employment, Miss Spreckelmeyer?"

She gasped. "Good heavens, no. I had no intention of charging you for my assistance. I merely meant to give you a helping hand."

"I see. Well, I don't know what to say. That's very kind of you, but—"

"No need to say anything a'tall." Smiling, she patted his arm. "I'll just finish up with this sweeping here, then start dusting the shelves."

She took the broom back and put it to work on the last section of flooring, praying he'd be too polite to refuse her offer.

He removed a handkerchief from his pocket and dabbed his forehead. "Miss Spreckelmeyer, I really don't quite know how to say this, but—"

"Oh, now, Mr. Crook, no need to thank me. It's my pleasure."

"No, you misunderstand. What I was going to say was—"

Five succinct hammers sounded on the door. "Hamilton? You in there?"

Mr. Crook withdrew a pocket watch from his vest and popped it open. "Please, miss. I appreciate your concern and your very generous offer—"

She rushed to the door and gave the shade a good yank. It flew up, wrapping itself around a cylinder at the top, flapping as it rotated several more turns than was necessary.

"Oh, look," she said. "It's Mr. Vandervoort come for his coffee, and the beans are not even ground yet." She waved to the man outside, whose bushy gray brows rose in reply. "You go ahead and let him in," she said. "I'll do the coffee." She scurried to the bins, scooped out some beans and poured them into the mill.

Mr. Crook had not so much as budged.

She shooed him with her hand. "Go on."

Vandervoort jiggled the door. Mr. Crook glanced at him, then her, then moved to unbolt the latch.

"Wall, what's all the holdup about?" Vandervoort asked, pushing his way into the store. "Miss Spreckelmeyer," he said, touching his hat.

"Howdy, Mr. Vandervoort," she said. "We're off to a slow start this morning, but I'll have a fine pot brewing in no time."

"What're ya doin' here, woman?" he asked.

"I'm just temporarily helping out Mr. Crook. Seeing as he hardly has any time whatsoever to spend with his precious little baby girl and all."

Vandervoort harrumphed, then headed to his usual chair in the back.

Mr. Crook approached her. "Really, Miss Spreckelmeyer," he whispered. "I must ask you to stop this foolishness. I do not need any assistance."

Refusing to concede defeat, she girded herself with bravado, grabbed the grinder's handle and began to rotate the wheel. Little by little, coffee granules dropped into the hopper. "Well, it looks to me, sir, like you do need some help. Misters Richie, Jenkins, and Owen will be here any moment, and you haven't even started up the stove yet."

"That's because you threw off my entire morning."

"Pishposh. I did no such thing."

"Miss Spreckelmeyer, release that coffee mill at once."

She hesitantly let go and stepped back. "Well, all right, then."

"Thank you." He took a deep breath.

"You're welcome. I didn't know grinding up the beans was so important to you. But don't worry. I'm a quick study. I'll know your peculiarities in no time."

Without giving him a chance to respond, she bounced over to the stove and began to lay out the wood.

"Need any help with that, Miss Spreckelmeyer?"

"No, no, Mr. Vandervoort." She paused and looked up at him. "There is something you *can* do for me, though."

"Why, sure, ma'am. What is it?"

"You can do a better job of aiming your tobacco. That spittoon has a nice large mouth on it. Missing it smacks of sheer laziness, and I don't relish the thought of mopping up all that nastiness day in and day out."

He straightened. "Why, yes, ma'am. I'll do right better. Just see if I don't."

She reached over and gave his arm a squeeze. "You are such a dear. Thank you."

Hamilton Crook stared at the woman reprimanding his customer. She'd rolled up the sleeves of her olive-colored shirtwaist and wrapped a white apron around her grosgrain skirt. He knew his clothing, and hers were fine pieces. The shirtwaist sported the newest puff sleeves and choker collar while her skirt held tone-on-tone scrolling designs.

Her pinchback straw hat, however, was another matter entirely. With a wavy-edged top from which tulle poufs protruded, white flowers, fern and willow leaves surrounded vertically wired ribbon loops. Most impractical for store clerking.

He shook his head, peeking into the grinder to see how many beans were left. Why in the blue blazes was the spinster daughter of the district judge doing charity work in his store? What was wrong with working in an orphanage? Or sharing a meal with old Mrs. Yarbrough? Or helping out with the church bazaar?

He looked around. To compensate for the name this town had *slapped* on his store, he made sure he not only kept it in tip-top shape with all the goods organized and grouped, but he also kept it clean and well stocked. Had there been complaints? Or was this do-gooder just a frustrated busybody who had singled him out as her next "project"?

Whatever the case, he needed to politely but firmly inform her that if he wanted help, he could well afford to hire someone. And that someone would not be an old maid who was notorious for wearing outrageous hats and who scandalized the town matrons by riding on a bicycle with her skirts hiked up to her knees.

CHAPTER | TWO

THE MORNING BROUGHT FEW customers, giving Essie plenty of time to dust the shelves, polish the scales, wash the windows, and grind the sugar. Mr. Crook sequestered himself in the back corner, nose buried in his papers. Essie hoped the smell of a clean store and a fresh pot of coffee brought a token of pleasure to his tedious task.

As she worked, Misters Vandervoort, Richie, Jenkins, and Owen took turns sliding checkers back and forth across a grimy board. Sometimes they pondered each move and sometimes they pushed the little discs without any apparent thought, but all the while they debated everything from the destiny of man to the finest bait for catching fish. No matter where the conversation strayed, though, it always came back to the topic on everyone's mind, the question of Corsicana's economic future.

"Wall, we gotta do somethin'," Jenkins was saying. "With cotton prices droppin' ever' day and Mr. Neblett's seed house shut down, this town's gonna shrivel up and die."

"What about putting up some brick buildings in the square?" Owen suggested. "That would attract businesses to town."

Vandervoort harrumphed. "Who's gonna want to build shops in a town with such a pathetic water supply?"

The bell on the door tinkled and the Gillespies' oldest boy ventured inside with a roll of hides under his arm. He wore a tattered corduroy coat with pockets vast enough to hold small game and oversized trousers folded up to reveal worn-out boots with so many holes it was a wonder they offered any protection at all.

"Good afternoon, Jeremy," Essie said, making her way to the counter. "What brings you into town today?"

The scrawny teener nodded slightly and doffed his old felt hat from his head. "Miss Spreckelmeyer. I come to ask Mr. Crook fer some oatmeal, rice, and cod liver oil, please, ma'am."

She smiled and patted the flat surface in front of her. "Well, Mr. Crook is working with his ledgers. Why don't you show me what you have."

Jeremy exchanged nods with the old-timers, then laid his hat on the counter. The checker game resumed and Essie caught a whiff of the young man, coughed a little, then tactfully breathed through her mouth.

One by one he unrolled his hides the way a fortune hunter might unfurl a treasure map. He smoothed out two raccoon skins, one rabbit, and one possum.

It was the possum that did it. Wrung out her chest like a tightly twisted mop. For she'd never known anyone to bother with skinning a possum. Most folks scalded them in boiling water, then scraped them hairless. And yet, the Gillespies had sent their eldest to town with an actual possum hide, of all things.

She fingered the raccoon, careful not to show signs of anything but admiration. She needn't look at the boy to recall how big his brown eyes looked within his hollowed-out face.

"Why, these are mighty nice, Jeremy," she said. "Did you do the skinning?"

"Yes, miss."

"Well, you're quite talented with a knife. I do believe these ear holes are some of the best I've ever seen. Should raise the value of these skins by a good twenty cents each." Her fingers moved to the animal's snout. "And would you look at that nose button? Still attached and everything."

He straightened slightly. "It all starts with how you insert the gamblin' sticks, miss. You gotta grip right firm-like and the tail will slide off the bone slicker 'n calf slobbers."

She stacked the hides carefully. "You don't fool me, Jeremy Gillespie. It takes more than tightly clamped sticks to skin an animal this cleanly. Now, how much oatmeal were you needing?"

She measured out the exact amount he asked for, not questioning for a moment whether or not Mr. Crook wanted the hides. When she started on the rice, Jeremy wandered over to the gun cabinet, keeping his hands clasped tightly behind his back.

Mr. Crook joined Essie. "What do you think you are doing, Miss Spreckelmeyer?"

"Lower your voice, Mr. Crook. I'm filling Jeremy's order. What does it look like I'm doing?"

"It looks like you are giving away the store."

"He brought in a trade."

Mr. Crook flipped through the hides. "These hides are worthless. I'll not trade good merchandise for—Great Scott!" He flung back the top three and stared aghast at the fourth. "What is that?"

"It's a possum."

"A *possum*?"

"Hush," she whispered, tying a knot around the top of a small burlap sack filled with rice. "Can't you see his family is starving? Just look at the boy."

Mr. Crook began to roll up the hides. "No. Absolutely not. I will not trade for these ridiculous skins. Go return those items to their appropriate bins. I will handle this."

She grabbed his arm. "Don't. Please, Hamilton."

His jaw slackened and it took her a moment to realize she'd used his given name. She'd been thinking of him in her imaginings as Hamilton, and it had accidentally slipped out.

Her face burned, but she remained firm. "Surely this one time will not hurt."

"The Gillespies have been charging all their purchases against this year's crop, and cotton is now at five cents on the Exchange and dropping. I cannot afford to extend any more credit to anyone. Especially not the Gillespies."

"How much for this rice and oatmeal, along with a vial of cod liver oil?" she asked.

"He wants liver oil, too? Ridiculous."

"How much?"

He picked up the two small sacks of oatmeal and rice, judging their weight in his hands. "Two seventy-five for these, plus twenty-five cents for the liver oil."

She quelled her reaction to the extravagant quote. Her family bought their grains by the barrel. She had no idea small portions cost so much.

"And the hides?" she asked. "How much credit for the hides?"

He held her gaze. "None."

He made to move past her, but she tightened her grip on his arm. "I'll replace your rice and oatmeal tomorrow from my own personal stock and pay for the liver oil with cash."

"Absolutely not."

"Why? What possible difference could it make?"

He leaned close. Whiffs of his shaving soap teased her nose. "I do not know what you think you are doing here, Miss Spreckelmeyer, but you are coming perilously close to overstaying your welcome."

She lessened the pressure on his arm, changing it to more of a caress, then softened her tone. "I'd like to purchase those hides you have for three dollars even, please, sir."

He studied her over the rim of his glasses. "You will have to buy them from Jeremy, then. I would not lower myself to carrying possum hides."

"It would wound his pride and embarrass me. Please. Just this once?"

He hesitated in indecision, then slowly straightened. "All right, Miss Spreckelmeyer. I will award the Gillespies three dollars credit for the hides . . . just this once."

"I'll pay you back."

"No. No you won't. But leave me out of the negotiations and make sure Jeremy understands not to set foot in here again with any more hides. Is that clear?"

For a moment she imagined what it would be like once they were a couple. She would fling her arms about him and thank him effusively for his consent. For now, she simply let the warm feelings flow freely through her eyes and smile.

She rubbed her thumb against his stiffly ironed sleeve. "Thank you. I'll always remember your kindness."

He jerked his arm away. She scooped up the sacks and called for Jeremy, asking him to bring her the liver oil. While she poured some into a small vial, she explained that he was fortunate to have brought those skins in when he did, for after today they wouldn't be taking any more hides for trade. Seemed Mr. Crook would no longer be stocking them.

———

Essie ruined three hats that first week at the Slap Out. This morning a wall-mounted bracket lamp snagged the chiffon ribbon on her latest hat, bringing her up short like a dog on a leash.

"My stars and garters," she murmured, unhooking herself from the bronze sconce, then stuffing the trim back up into her Evangeline hat. "Here they are, Mrs. Quigley."

Essie laid ribbed hose, wool hose, leather stockings, and plain stockings on the counter. "This is our selection of boys' hosiery, the leather being the best, of course, giving fifty percent more wear than any of the others."

Mrs. Quigley picked up the plain cotton stockings.

"Those are some of the most satisfactory, ma'am. See the wide elastic hem at the top? That will help keep them from sliding down."

Mrs. Quigley squinted for a closer examination.

"They have double-spliced heels and toes, as well," Essie continued, "and are thirty-five cents each."

The Quigleys lived on the south side of town in a neatly kept house with a wide front porch. Mr. Quigley worked in the gristmill and had fathered a whole passel of youngsters. Three of them stood solemnly beside their mother, but Essie knew full well their behavior at school was less than pristine.

"And who is to be the recipient of these fine stockings?" Essie asked the boys.

"Grundy," the older one said. "He's always runnin' around without his boots on, tearing up his hose."

"Am not."

"Are too."

Mrs. Quigley silenced the boys with a look.

Essie smiled. "Well, I suppose we've all made a muck of our hosiery a time or two." She turned her attention to Mrs. Quigley. "Have you seen our new magic darner?"

She retrieved the little loom-like machine that would mend hosiery, silk, wool, or cotton. "It's small enough to fit inside your sewing basket and so easy to use, even the children could operate it."

By the time Essie was done, she had sold them three pairs of stockings, the magic darner, a pattern for a five-gored skirt, and several remnants of cloth.

After the Quigleys left, Hamilton joined her behind the counter and held up a satin rosette. "Did you lose this, by any chance?"

Her hand flew to the right side of her hat and discovered a gap. "Oh my. I seem to catch my trim on something every time I turn around." She took the rosette and tried to return it to its proper place but could not make it stay.

He chuckled. "Here. Let me."

She held herself perfectly still while he secured the flower back onto her hat. Her nose was mere inches from the buttons on his double-breasted fancy wash vest and the knot on his silk necktie. She breathed in the scent of his shaving soap, along with a hint of mustiness.

Her gaze veered to his raised arm and the damp stain on his shirt. The intimacy of seeing such a personal thing did queer things to her stomach. Blindly, she grabbed the counter to steady herself.

"There," he said. "That should hold, for a while, anyway."

She lifted her chin, the brim of her hat revealing his jaw, cheeks, and nose one linear inch at a time. She moistened her lips. The brown eyes behind his square spectacles were as warm as hot cocoa and at very close range.

"You have quite a knack for sales, Miss Spreckelmeyer."

"It's nothing, really," she whispered. "I just know everybody and what kinds of things they need, is all."

His mouth hinted at a smile. "That may be true, but there is a difference in knowing a thing and actually making the sale."

He stepped back and began to roll up the selection of hosiery Mrs. Quigley had decided against. "I have to admit," he said, "having you here this past week has been wonderful."

Her lips parted. "For me, too."

"Well, perhaps we should make the situation a bit more permanent?"

She sucked in her breath. "Yes. Oh yes."

He glanced at her and smiled. "Well, then. I shall pay you two dollars and fifty cents a week, starting now."

She blinked. "No. I mean, that's not necessary."

"Of course it is." He handed her the leather stockings and started on the wool. "You have a ribbon hanging down the left side of your hat."

She stuffed it back up. "Thank you."

"You're welcome." He handed her the rest of the hosiery and headed to his desk in the corner.

———

July gave way to August, and the hot summer sun broiled Collin Street. Hamilton forced himself to smile and nod from the Slap Out's front porch as horses, wagons, and townsfolk scurried to his competitor's establishment, causing dirt to surge upward in constant turmoil.

Word had spread early this morning that Charlie Gillespie and his boys had brought in a big black bear hide and traded it to the Flour, Feed and Liquor Store. Hamilton struggled to hide his chagrin.

The Slap Out faced east at the corner of Eleventh and Collin, offering him a clear view of the Pickens' place one hundred yards down on the opposite side of the road.

He squinted into the sunlight. Jeremy Gillespie bounded out of the Feed Store and headed down the street, straight toward him.

"Miss Spreckelmeyer!" the boy hollered, waving his hand high in the air. Essie had busied herself all morning dragging various goods outside in hopes of luring a few customers in, but even Vandervoort and his cronies had failed to make an appearance.

She turned at the sound of her name, then leaned far out over the railing, waving back. The unladylike position hoisted up her hems, exposing her petticoats and a pair of well-worn boots. Her backside poked out in an ill-mannered fashion.

"Hullo!" she yelled back.

The Widow Yarbrough, passing by, jerked her gaze toward the spectacle, then raised a disapproving eyebrow at Hamilton. He cringed with embarrassment.

Miss Spreckelmeyer's toes left the plank flooring, and for one horrid moment he thought she might tumble right over the side, but she managed to keep her balance and land safely on the porch, showing no distress over her near mishap.

"We caught us a bear," Jeremy exclaimed.

"I heard!" she answered. "You must tell me all about it."

"Oh, you gotta see her to believe her. I'd have brought her to the Slap Out first, but last month you done said Mr. Crook's got more hides than he needs."

"And so he does," she said.

"Not bear hides," Hamilton growled. "One can never have too many bear hides."

She glanced up at him, a confused expression crossing her face. "Well, we have no one but ourselves to blame, Mr. Crook. 'The miser is as much in want of what he has as of what he has not.' "

He stiffened. "There is no 'we,' Miss Spreckelmeyer. Furthermore, I am not a miser. And that black bear would have been mine if not for you."

Jeremy whipped off his hat. "Beggin' yer pardon, Mr. Crook. It weren't Miss Spreckelmeyer's fault Pa took the bear to old Mr. Pickens."

She smiled. "Oh, but I'm afraid it is, Jeremy. I didn't specify earlier that we are quite interested in large-game hides. It's only the small ones that we no longer stock."

Jeremy glanced between the two of them, then began to back up. "Wall, I'll be sure to tell Pa to bring the next one straight to you."

Like there will be a next one, Hamilton thought.

"Thank you," she said.

The Gillespie boy replaced his hat, then turned and hustled back to the Feed Store.

"I'm so happy for them," she said. "They'll have food a-plenty now."

Hamilton pushed his glasses up his nose. "Do you have any idea how much money you have cost me?"

She blinked. "Nonsense. No one is going to actually purchase that bearskin. Why, it would cost a fortune."

"That may be so, but folks far and wide will go to the Feed Store to have a look at it, now, won't they? And while they are there, they will make other purchases and then have no reason to come to the Slap Out."

"Hmmm. I see what you mean." She thrummed her fingers against her skirt. "Well, we will simply have to come up with something better."

"Better than a black bear hide?"

"Yes." She hooked her hands behind her, throwing her shoulders back and calling attention to the pale blue dimity shirtwaist she wore. It was a ready-made that he kept in stock and he'd easily sold three times the number he normally did. He felt certain it was because the style suited Miss Spreckelmeyer, and other women thought it might flatter them, as well.

She took a few lazy steps toward him, her head cocked to the side, a blond wisp escaping her coif. "Any ideas?" she asked.

He frowned. She stood close, so close that he could see each and every nuance of color in her blue eyes and smell the hint of clove she used for fragrance. He could even hear her breath coming and going in regular intervals.

"Perhaps we should have a contest," she murmured.

His frown deepened. "There is no 'we.' "

"Or a tournament."

Hamilton studied her. He knew full well she was after a husband and he had no interest whatsoever. He hadn't meant to encourage her. Had not, in fact, realized until it was too late that when he praised her for her performance, she took it in a much more personal manner.

But in the month since Essie had forced herself on him and the Slap Out, his sales had soared—at least until she'd sent his business across the street to gawk at a bearskin.

Never had he seen such a salesclerk, though. She sold leather preserver to the carriage and harness dealer. Sold books on midwifery to the doctor. Sold fancy goods to the ladies.

And even though she freely squandered inventory on those in need, his profits had soared.

As a shopkeeper she would do, but as a wife? Never. Hamilton knew he could do much better than the town spinster. Still, he had to tread carefully.

He was an outsider to Corsicana, and though the townsfolk tutted behind their hands over Miss Spreckelmeyer's unorthodox tomboyish ways and her ridiculous hats, she was a local and they were quite fond of her. Treated her much like they did Cat, the town stray.

If the tabby showed up on their porch, they'd give her warm milk. If a storm was brewing, they'd give her shelter for the night. If mischievous boys were mistreating her, they'd interfere on her behalf. But their sympathies did not extend to the point of actually taking her home and calling her their own.

No. Miss Spreckelmeyer was the town spinster and he, for one, deserved better.

She noticed his scrutiny and her eyes brightened. "A checkers competition. What do you think about that?"

"I think, Miss Spreckelmeyer, that you and I need to have a talk."

Her face softened. She took another step forward. He took one back.

"All right, Hamilton. When would be a good time for our . . . talk?"

That was another thing. Calling him by his given name when he'd not given her leave to do so. No wonder the men of this town had shied away when she came calling. Never had he met a more forward, unpredictable and impulsive woman. And from such a good family, too. For their sake and for the sake of his good standing in the community, he would be sure to let her down gently.

"Tomorrow evening," he said. "After store closing. Would that suit?"

A soft sigh escaped her lips. "Yes. Yes, it most certainly would."

———

Essie could not believe her good fortune. Had she known how easy it was to bring a man to heel, she'd have done so years ago. But then, perhaps it had nothing to do with "fortune" and everything to do with God's plan for her life. Finally—*finally*—His plan was bearing fruit.

She laid her new summer skirt and shirtwaist across the back of her bedroom window chair, careful not to crease or wrinkle the freshly ironed garments.

She knew how much Hamilton liked it when she wore ready-mades from their store, and she wanted to be sure to please him tomorrow. For tomorrow, after store closing, he was going to declare his intentions.

Oh, how she wished she could wear one of her lovely hats, but she'd given up on trying to wear them in the store. If she were to don one now, it might spook him.

She laid a white linen detachable collar and matching cuffs on her toilet table, the only concession to extravagance in the ensemble she was preparing. Glancing in the mirror, she caught her reflection. The reflection of the soon-to-be Mrs. Hamilton Crook.

C H A P T E R | T H R E E

ESSIE GROANED, CLUTCHING HER stomach and curling up tightly on the bed. Mother dipped a cloth in cool water, then wrung it out. Essie eyed the array of clothing hanging limp on the chair so far away.

Mother draped the cloth across Essie's forehead.

"I have to get up. Mr. Crook is expecting me."

"You cannot. You're too sick. Besides, you've no business forcing yourself on that poor man. I cannot imagine what you have been thinking to make such a spectacle of yourself. It's downright embarrassing."

"Please, Mother. You've made your opinion on this crystal clear, but I haven't changed my mind. I'm going to continue working at the Slap Out for as long as Mr. Crook will have me."

Her insides gurgled and she slapped a hand over her mouth. Mother pulled the chamber pot from under the bed, uncovered it and held it while Essie emptied her stomach again.

There was nothing for it. She'd have to send word to Hamilton that she would not be in to the store today. Nor to their little tête-à-tête afterward.

———

"I'm telling you it *is* here. Miss Spreckelmeyer said so. She knows how I have been waiting and waiting for that book. You must locate it straightaway, sir. I insist."

Mrs. Lockhart punctuated her demand with a thump of her cane, sending a ripple up her arm, across her shoulders, and through her sagging middle.

Hamilton forced a polite smile. "I will look yet again, ma'am. Do you happen to remember the title of the work?"

"Certainly. Don't you think I'd remember what volume I ordered?" The elderly woman pinched her lips together revealing a spider web of creases and folds around her mouth. "Honestly. I detest dealing with such simplemindedness. When is Miss Spreckelmeyer to return?"

"As I said earlier, she's taken ill today. I expect her to return as soon as she is able."

"Well, it can't be soon enough. Now hurry it up, young man. Miss Spreckelmeyer would have had the book all wrapped up and tied with string by now."

"The title, Mrs. Lockhart. It would be helpful to know the title."

"I told you that already. Will you *please* pay attention. It is a work by Mrs. Bertha Clay entitled *Clarabel's Love Story*."

"Yes, ma'am. If you will excuse me, I'll check once more in the back."

He allowed a scowl to cross his face the moment he stepped through the curtained partition. *Clarabel's Love Story*. What in heaven's name did that old boiler want with a love story and where in the blazes would Essie have put it?

He'd already checked all the lower shelves and he couldn't imagine it being on any of the high ones. Still, he upended an empty fruit crate and climbed on top to better see the upper shelves. He shoved aside lantern holders, trunk locks, and carving tools, awakening dust motes long in hibernation, then picked through sulphur candles, butter molds, and nursery-bottle fittings.

As he searched, his hand brushed against a familiar eight-inch rod attached to the bottom of a black suctioning device shaped like a bowl. Much to his surprise, it had arrived in the post mere days after his wife's passing. The order had been of such a delicate nature, his wife had not even told him of it.

When he'd first unpacked the contraption, he'd researched it in his catalog. The advertisement claimed that this "bust developer" would build up and fill out shrunken and undeveloped tissue and form a rounded, plump, and perfectly shaped bust. In the weeks following its arrival, he'd eyed most every woman in town, speculating about which mystery lady in Corsicana, Texas, had decided to compensate for her lack of that greatest charm, a bosom. But the owner of the enhancer had never come forward to claim her purchase, and it had been sitting on this shelf ever since. He smirked at the memory, then returned it to its place on the shelf and continued his search for Mrs. Lockhart's novel.

The bell on the door jingled and voices in the store increased in volume. Saturday was his busiest day of the week. He couldn't waste any more time on the book. He returned to the front and told Mrs. Lockhart she would have to come back Monday.

"Well," she said. "I had planned to fill an order today, but perhaps I should go to the Feed Store instead. Mr. Pickens always knows where *his* inventory is."

"My sincerest apologies. From now on I will be sure to coordinate the location of all my stock so that both Miss Spreckelmeyer and I can find it at a moment's notice."

Through round spectacles, she scrutinized him from the part in his hair to the tips of his boots. "See that you do. I shall be back first thing Monday morning."

The rest of the afternoon went much the same. Miss Lizzie wanted a woman's opinion on what color would suit her best. She went down the street for Mrs. Pickens' advice—and cloth.

At just past three, Preacher Bogart arrived wanting Miss Spreckelmeyer to describe to his wife the new baptismal pants Essie had mentioned. They evidently had boots sewn right onto them, like wading pants except nicer. Hamilton looked them up in the special-orders catalog but could find no such thing. The Bogarts went to the Feed Store to see if Mrs. Pickens had ever heard of them.

An hour later, Mr. Bunting wanted Miss Spreckelmeyer's advice on whether to buy his wife a brooch pin or a hair charm for their twenty-fifth wedding anniversary. Hamilton gave his opinion, but Mr. Bunting decided to ask Mrs. Pickens.

Even Vandervoort and his cronies were out of sorts. Miss Spreckelmeyer had promised to play the winner of their checkers match, for none of them had yet beat her. They grumbled over their game until closing, then left without saying good-bye.

By the time Hamilton locked the door, he'd made fewer sales for the day than he had in months. Especially for a Saturday. He pulled down the shade on his front door. Perhaps he should consider what Miss Spreckelmeyer was offering him. She was a bit on the muscular side, a bit on the bossy side, and a bit on the eccentric side, but she certainly knew how to close a sale.

———

Essie arrived at the store Monday morning at her normal time. Her ailment had lasted only a day, leaving Sunday for her to regain her strength and her anticipation. She'd taken great care with her toilet this morning, donning the clothes, collar, and cuffs she'd planned to wear Saturday and taking extra care with her hair.

Hamilton opened the back door. "Essie," he said. "I'm so glad to see you."

She stood as still as a hunter who had his prize quarry in range. Hamilton had used her given name. And in the very next breath, all but said he'd missed her.

He stepped back, widening the door. "How are you feeling?"

"Much better. Thank you." She crossed the threshold and plucked her apron from the wall hook. "I'm so sorry about Saturday. How did it go?"

But he didn't answer and she looked up. Her hands hesitated. She had been blindly tying the bow of her apron behind her, causing her shirtwaist to temporarily tighten across her chest.

His gaze rested at the very place her buttons strained. She drew a breath, startled. Never before had he made his interest so clear.

She quickly finished her bow and fluffed her apron, reveling in the rapid tempo of her pulse.

"Everything was all wrong without you," he said, his voice sinking into an intimate register. "The customers were disconcerted. The coffee came out too strong. The fancy-goods department was in shambles before noon. And," he took a deep breath, "sales were down."

In the windowless storage room the shadows were deep and the corners dark. If she were imagining this moment, it would be the perfect time for him to take her into his arms. But she wasn't imagining it and she wasn't quite sure how to encourage him.

"It's all right," she said. "I hardly ever get sick and I'll have everything fixed up quicker than a hen on a hot griddle."

Yet she didn't move, knowing that the moment she did, the mood would be broken.

He took a thorough survey of her person. "You're a passable-looking woman, Miss Spreckelmeyer."

"Essie," she said, barely above a whisper. "Please, call me Essie."

———

Essie's mother had always told her not to stare at a man. *"How can he get a good look at you if you're always staring at him?"* she would say. Remembering this advice, she was careful to keep her gaze on anything but Hamilton.

Yet she'd felt his regard all day, whether she was helping customers, weighing items, or wrapping purchases. When he asked her to clean out and organize the storage room, she put it off as long as possible, not wanting to be out of sight or out of mind.

Instead, she settled down for a match of checkers with Mr. Owen, while Misters Vandervoort, Jenkins, and Richie gathered round to offer advice to their friend. They were playing the best of five games. Owen was down by two.

"You be red this time," he said.

She began placing her pieces on the dark squares closest to her.

"What'd the judge think of last month's meeting, Miss Spreckelmeyer?" Mr. Richie asked.

"Of Corsicana Commercial Club?" she asked, putting the last checker in place. "He was pleased the members voted in favor of tapping some shallow artesian wells. Otherwise, we would continue to be a one-staple community with no hopes of bringing in new businesses."

"Anything happen so far?"

Essie moved between her own pieces, edging closer to Mr. Owen's with each turn. "They put together a water-development company and took bids from various contractors."

"What'd they say?"

"That three wells will give us a flow of 750 thousand gallons of water a day."

Mr. Jenkins whistled.

"Better not do that, Lafoon," Mr. Vandervoort warned.

Mr. Owen froze, his big, pudgy fingers resting on a black disk.

"She wants you to jump that, 'cause soon as you do you'll be in a worse spot than you are now."

"Well, if I don't, I'll lose three pieces."

Vandervoort shrugged. "Do what ya want, then."

Owen jumped Essie's piece, opening the lane to his king row. She moved that direction.

"How they gonna get that much water to flow up through them wells?" Mr. Richie asked.

"Papa said they wouldn't need any pumping installations at all. Said there is enough natural pressure to fill standpipes and storage tanks. Crown, please, Mr. Owen."

Scowling, he crowned her checker. "What about the seed house? Any word on what the town's supposed to do with that vacant monstrosity now that Mr. Neblett's gone belly up?"

"No," she sighed. "I'm afraid there was no news on that front."

A few minutes later, she won the match.

"That's it," Owen said. "I'm goin' out front to whittle awhile. Y'all comin'?"

The men shuffled outside. She put away the checkers, wiped off the board, then glanced up to find Hamilton staring at her from his desk chair.

"You ought to let them win once in a while," he said.

"I've tried, but then we get to talking and I forget to make bad moves."

He raised his hands above his head, arching his back.

"Tired?" she asked.

"A little."

"Can I get you some coffee?"

"That sounds good."

She chose a black enamel cup from those hanging beside the stove, knowing it was Hamilton's favorite. She handed it to him, basking in her intimate familiarity with his likes and dislikes.

"Thank you," he said, taking a sip.

"You're welcome."

The hum of conversation from the front porch filtered through the walls. His foot dislodged a burlap bag leaning against his desk, causing the beans inside to shift and resettle.

Rolling back his chair, he slowly pushed himself to his feet. "Why haven't you ever married, Essie?"

Blood rushed to her cheeks. *No one ever asked me.* But she couldn't say that. "The right fellow never did come along, I guess."

Every impulse she had urged her to close the gap between them. She stayed where she was.

"You look nice today," he said. "Tidy. Did you do something different?"

Yes. Yes, I did. "No. Just the same ol' me, I guess."

The town cat's meow made them both jump.

Hamilton frowned. Essie smiled.

"Cat!" she said. "What are you doing in here?"

She scooped up the short-haired, scrawny animal and rubbed her nose against its neck. "You looking for some attention?"

Hamilton stared at Cat, the color draining from his face.

"What is it?" she asked.

He took a hasty step back and plopped down in his chair. "Nothing. Nothing at all. Did you finish up in the back room?"

"No. I haven't even started. I'll go do that now."

"Thank you. And take that . . . that stray with you."

———

Essie started with the top shelves, dusting, organizing, wiping down and cataloging while humming "I Just Started Living." Hamilton had almost made a declaration. Right in the store in the middle of the day when anyone might have walked in.

He hadn't said anything about talking with her after closing, but she hoped he would. If he didn't lose his nerve. She smiled. He always seemed so appreciative when she accomplished some task around the store. So she was determined to get as much of the back room done as she possibly could.

Her fingers strayed to a black rubber bowl. Pulling it off the shelf, she discovered it had a long, straight rod attached to its bottom. *What in the world?*

Was it a stand of some sort? A rain catcher? A candy dish? Whatever the thing was, she wiped it clean, then made a note to herself to ask Hamilton. He'd certainly know.

———

Hamilton locked the door, pulled down the shade and took a deep breath. He'd studied Essie all day long. She had a strong, symmetrical face, with high cheekbones and bold lines—nothing delicate about it. Her cheeks dimpled when she smiled, her lower lip was fuller than the upper, her blue eyes were a bit too large, and her nose was a bit too thin.

What he couldn't determine, however, was what kind of shape she had hiding under that skirt. He knew her legs would be long. He just didn't know how much meat they'd have on them.

He'd seen her calves when she rode her bicycle—shoot, the whole town had seen them and there wasn't an ounce of extra padding on them.

A woman ought to be soft. Voluptuous. Something a man could cozy up to. Not wiry and hard and muscular.

Oh, she had curves up top. Nothing overflowing, but nothing that would require an enhancer, either. Her stomach, however, was as flat as an iron. Would it be as hard?

He'd almost reached out and touched her today. Just to see.

But the woman already had wedding bells clanging in her head. He'd best not make any advances at all until he was sure. Absolutely sure that he could live the rest of his life with a woman he truly just did not find attractive. He'd managed to tolerate her bossy nature during working hours, but could he do the same every day and every night for the rest of his livelong days?

The thought gave him pause. He knew all about bossy women. His mother had ruled the roost while he was growing up, henpecking her husband and sons until Hamilton could hardly stand it anymore. He'd promised himself he would never, ever marry a mouthy woman.

Essie wasn't mouthy, exactly, just stubborn. And old. And set in her ways. A man liked to have a young, fresh gal on his arm. One he could shape and mold. One who would make the days go by quick and the nights go by slow. Not a woman who'd be turning gray a few short years after the nuptials.

If his conscience would let him, he'd write a list of all she offered and all she didn't. But that would be too cold. Too mercenary. Too unforgiving, by half.

He could hear Essie in the back throwing out a bucket of cleaning water. Humming to herself off key. He had perfect pitch and tuned the church organ by ear every Sunday before services. He could not abide an instrument that was so much as an eighth of a step off. Essie was a full half step off.

Maybe he should make a trip up to the wholesalers in Dallas. Get away for a few days. Think through exactly what he wanted to do.

"Hamilton?"

He turned. She might have been tidy earlier, but she was a mess now. Her blond hair stuck out in tufts, her hands were red from scrubbing, her apron was filthy, her face was smudged.

"Guess it's time we call it a day," he said.

She clasped her hands in front of her. Waiting. For something. He racked his mind. It wasn't payday. Wasn't . . . anything.

"Did you want something?" he asked.

She licked her lips. "Did you?"

"No. Not that I can think of."

"Oh." She shifted her weight. "I cleaned up all the top shelves and half of the middle ones."

"Excellent."

"I guess I'll finish the rest of them tomorrow."

"That'll be fine."

Still she stood there.

He adjusted his glasses. "Well. Good night, then."

She sighed. "Good night, Hamilton. I'll see you in the morning."

———

Back home in front of the mirror, she pulled the pins from her disheveled hair. The candle on her vanity guttered in the breeze from the open window.

She was losing him. She could feel his hesitation. His doubt. His second-guessing. She had to do something. Fast.

She said her prayers, then climbed into bed. Was it because she got sick? Because she beat Mr. Owen at checkers? Was Hamilton still sore about that bearskin?

Whatever it was, she knew the quickest way to his heart was through his store. She must do something drastic. Something that would bring the town to his store in droves.

CHAPTER | FOUR

MORNING DEW DECORATED THE lawns of Essie's neighborhood. Dappled sunlight from the eastern sky splashed onto the shimmering blades butted together like an endless green carpet.

She kept to the road, her strides long and brisk as she headed to the Slap Out, beseeching the Lord to give her a revelation. Some idea, some inspiration that would cultivate customers as numerous as the grass in these yards.

The screams of a child jerked her out of her reverie. Scanning the area, she spotted a young boy and girl in the vacant lot toward the end of the street.

The boy, who couldn't be more than six or seven, had placed himself between the girl and whatever was frightening them. Arms spread in a protective gesture, he stumbled back. The girl continued to scream and peer around his shoulder.

Lifting her skirts, Essie sprinted to them. As she approached, she recognized Emily Wedick, one of the many Wedick girls, and Harley North, an orphan who lived in the state's facility just outside of town.

"What is it?" Essie gasped. "What has happened?"

Harley, brown eyes wide with terror, pointed to a large, flat rock surrounded by weeds. Napping on top of its smooth surface was one of the most gorgeous prairie king snakes she had ever seen.

"Hush!" she whispered, laying a hand on Emily's shoulder. "You must hush at once."

The screams subsided into whimpers.

"Quickly, run next door and ask Mrs. Pennington for a gunnysack. Hurry."

The freckled girl darted away to do Essie's bidding, her long red braids flapping behind her.

"Is it poisonous?" Harley asked, his bare feet sticking out of trousers a good three inches too short.

"No, no. On the contrary, it is one of the finest snakes you'll ever see."

During her snake-collecting days, she and Papa had invented a rating system. The yellow-bellied water snake ranked higher than the ribbon snake. The hognose above the water. The rat above the hognose. The speckled king above the rat. And the prairie king above them all.

This snake was an exceptional specimen, with the smooth, dry scales of a recently shed skin. As it glistened in the morning light, she noted spots of chocolate brown speckling its beautiful tan hide, and its small head wore brown lightning bolts.

The girl finally returned and handed an empty flour sack to Essie.

Holding a finger to her lips, she silenced the children. With slow, quiet steps, she advanced, loosening her hold on the flour sack until it gaped open, then, with her free hand, snatched the three-and-a-half-foot reptile from the rock.

Emily screamed. The snake writhed and twisted in Essie's hand, spraying her with musk, but never attempted to bite her.

She lowered the king into the flour sack, knotted the opening, then spoke to it in a soothing voice. "Hush, now. It's going to be all right."

"Golly, Miss Essie," Harley said, his eyes wide. "What are you gonna do with it now?"

The snake hissed and wove around.

"I'm not sure. Are y'all okay?"

"Yes, ma'am," he said, though the girl still hovered behind him.

"Why don't you walk Emily home, Harley? Think you could do that for me?"

"I reckon."

"Go on, then. I'll take care of the snake." She waved them off, then headed back home. She'd have to bathe after being sprayed, which would make her late for work. But she wasn't worried. It was no coincidence the Lord had dropped this piece of manna from heaven. She'd prayed for something better than a black bear hide, and she'd gotten reptile royalty.

Everything was going to be fine now. Just fine.

————

Essie set the flour sack, snake and all, just outside the back door of the Slap Out.

"Sorry I'm late," she said, entering the storage room.

Hamilton hoisted a bag of grain onto his shoulder, then turned. "Is everything all right? You're not sick again, are you?"

"Good heavens, no. I hardly ever get sick." She tied her apron on. "I figured I'd go ahead and start on the rest of these shelves. You think you could mind the store without me for a while?"

He nodded. "So long as Miss Lizzie doesn't want any more fabric, I can. But if it gets busy, then come on out front with me."

"Will do."

The entry door jingled and he strode through the partition. As soon as he cleared the curtain, she grabbed a peach crate, wiped it down and laid a bed of newspaper in the bottom. Rummaging through the shelves, she found a small bowl, an empty cracker box, and a piece of poultry netting.

Outside, she scoured around for a limb, cleaned it and returned to organize the king's crate. Once all was in readiness, she opened the bag and poured the lightly floured snake into the crate.

He coiled immediately, lifting his head high and furiously buzzing his tail.

Essie smiled. "You don't fool me. I've known the difference between a rattler and a prairie king since I was knee-high to a grasshopper."

The reptile whirred in reverse, darting inside the open-ended cracker box, buzzing away. The front door jingled again.

Essie placed the mesh screen across the opening, weighing it down with a couple of rocks.

"You hungry? Well, you better stop your fussing, then. I have no intention of feeding you anything until you settle down. You hear?"

The quivering tail rat-a-tat-tatted against the wall of the box.

———

Essie's stomach growled and she glanced at the clock behind the counter. Almost noon. They'd been unusually busy for a Tuesday. Neither she nor Hamilton had had time to do anything other than wait on customers and it still hadn't slowed. A couple of women were perusing Hamilton's selection of garden teas, and old Mr. Mapey was just walking in.

"Hmmm," Mrs. Lockhart said, spinning the catalog toward Essie. "What about this one?"

Essie looked at the title Mrs. Lockhart pointed to with her crooked, wrinkled finger. She'd finished reading *Clarabel's Love Story* in one day and wanted another of Mrs. Clay's novels.

"*Beyond Pardon*," Essie read. "I'm not so sure. Sounds a bit, um, questionable, don't you think?"

The woman's face wilted in disappointment.

Essie absorbed her surprise at Mrs. Lockhart's tendency toward such silly books. She should undertake a more improved course of reading. "What about *Ivanhoe* by Sir Walter Scott?"

Mrs. Lockhart crinkled her nose and squinted at the catalog through her spectacles. "What about *Only One Sin*?"

Good heavens. "Well. I suppose everyone's sinned at least once."

The elderly woman straightened, a triumphant look upon her face. "Perhaps even twice!"

Essie nodded. "Shall I order—"

A crash, a scream, and a shocking curse from the back room brought everyone to a standstill. The curtained door swished open. Hamilton stood at its entrance, face flushed, eyes snapping with violent anger.

His gaze found Essie at once. "Get back here."

She stood frozen to the spot.

"*Now!*"

She jumped. "Would you excuse me for a moment, Mrs. Lockhart?"

The woman's regard bounced between Essie and Hamilton, her eyebrows going up. "Of course, dear. I'll just look over the book list a little while longer. You'd best go on, though."

Hamilton's shoulders rose and fell like a bellows breathing a flame to life. He clenched the curtain open with a balled fist, then released it as she slipped by him, cutting them off from curious stares.

Grabbing her arm none too gently, he propelled her around some fallen buckets and toward the peach crate. "Just what the blazes is that?" he hissed.

"A snake?"

He swore. "I know what it is, Essie. I meant what is it doing here?"

She touched her stomach. "Hamilton! You mustn't curse."

His eyes narrowed. "Essie Spreckelmeyer, I will commit a much more grievous sin than that if you do not explain yourself immediately."

She knelt beside the crate and lifted the top just a crack so he could glimpse the speckled treasure within. "That's our bearskin."

"What are you talking about?"

"When everyone hears what we have, they'll come from all over to see it."

"You expect me to put that thing out there where my customers are? Woman, are you demented or just plain stupid?"

She sucked in her breath. "There is no need to get testy, Hamilton. This is an excellent plan." She snapped the crate lid shut. "Why, it's even an answer to prayer."

"An answer to prayer? *Satan* uses snakes, Essie, not God."

She rose to her full height and brushed the dust from her skirts. "Don't be ridiculous. God made it and He gave it to me."

"Then you can jolly well take it back home with you. I'll not risk injuring one of my customers."

"No, no," she said, clasping her hands in an effort to remain patient. "It's not a rattlesnake. It's not poisonous at all. It's a prairie king snake. They're quite harmless and not nearly as irritable as other kinds of snakes."

They stood facing each other, the only sound that of the snake's tail buzzing inside the cracker box.

"Then why is it rattling?" he asked.

"It's only shaking its tail, trying to scare off its enemies. You would, too, if you'd been living in the wild all this time and suddenly found yourself confined to a cracker box. It will settle down."

"And what if it doesn't?" he said, his voice rising.

"Hush," she whispered. "Someone will hear you."

"I want that snake out of here."

She grabbed his shirt-sleeve. "Don't you see? It's perfect. Most snakes have scars from encounters with their enemies. But this one—this one has no bobbed tail, puckered wound, healed sore or anything. It's as if God had been protecting it all this time just for us. Why, never have I caught such an exquisite specimen."

"*You* caught that thing?"

She cocked her head. "Well, of course. Where do you think I got it? The Flour, Feed and Liquor Store?"

He yanked his arm free. "It will scare more customers away than it will bring in."

"I don't think so. Especially if we have a snake-naming contest."

He crossed his arms.

"Everyone can submit names for the snake," she explained, "and then we can put it to a vote and whoever wins can receive a prize from the store." She tapped her fingernail against her apron. "But it must be a big prize. Something that will generate excitement . . . and sales, of course."

"A prize? Like what?"

"Oh, I don't know. A pocket watch or a brooch or a . . . a camera! That would be perfect. It would appeal to men, women, and children alike."

"A camera? That's way too much money. I'm not giving away a camera."

"I'm not talking about a new order. I'm talking about overstock. Why, you have a Hawkeye Junior up on the shelf right there. Never been opened. I found it when I cleaned up yesterday."

He scanned the shelves, then grabbed a large rectangular box. "This thing costs seven dollars and twenty cents."

"Well, yes, but to keep using it, the customer will have to buy glass plates, which cost ninety cents each, or a roll of film, which is fifty-five. Besides, you have two Hawkeyes out in the store going nowhere."

He glanced down at the peach crate and scratched the back of his head. "I don't know, Essie."

"I do. We'll get the whole community involved. We can take nominations for names this week, give everyone the following week to cast their vote, and announce the winner of the prize the Saturday after that. Townsfolk will talk about the contest in their parlors, at their dinner tables, and at their social club meetings. And if for no other reason than curiosity, they'll come in to see the snake."

She held her breath. She knew it would work. She'd make sure of it.

Handing her the camera, he sighed. "All right, but you're in charge of that serpent. I'm not cleaning its cage or feeding it or running this contest. You'll have to do it all. And if it upsets my customers, it goes. Is that understood?"

She grabbed his lapel, gave him a quick peck on the cheek and then released him before he could blink. "Oh, thank you, Hamilton. You'll not be sorry, I promise."

Scurrying out of the storage room, she returned to the counter and placed the camera underneath. "Now, Mrs. Lockhart, I believe you were wanting to order *Only One Sin* by Mrs. Bertha Clay, is that correct?"

But Mrs. Lockhart ignored the catalog. "Is everything, um, all right, dear?"

"Why, yes." Essie glanced at the other customers eyeing her curiously. "Oh, you mean *back there*?"

Mrs. Lockhart gave her a nod.

"Yes, ma'am. We have everything all settled now."

"Do you, indeed?"

"Yes, ma'am."

"Splendid, splendid!" She patted Essie's hand. "Now, I should like to order *Only One Sin, Beyond Pardon,* and *A Mad Love,* please."

———

The following morning, Essie arrived at the store before Hamilton came downstairs. She slipped in the back door, lit a candle and set it down beside the king's crate.

After the initial shock of his capture had worn off yesterday, the snake had settled down and not rattled his tail at all. He'd even begun to nose around his new home of wood, tree limb, and newsprint. The final test would be whether or not he would eat. She'd had snakes before that had been so shocked by captivity, they'd refused to feed.

Opening her drawstring coin pouch, she lifted out a live white mouse by its tail and placed it in the crate.

Soon as it hit the newspaper, the mouse scurried to the corner, quivering. The snake poked its head out of the cracker box, forked tongue searching the scented air. Essie nodded, willing him to strike. The king stiffened, then shot forward and grabbed its prey, swallowing it whole.

Praise the Lord, Essie thought. *All will be well.*

C H A P T E R | F I V E

HAMILTON WRAPPED UP TWO dozen finishing nails. "That'll be ten cents, George."

The young carpenter reached into a deep pocket of his brown duck overalls and pulled out a handful of change, all the while keeping his gaze on Essie.

Boys of every size and shape stood shoulder to shoulder, surrounding her like staves in the side of a barrel. She held the snake in her hands, letting it coil around her wrist and slither up her arm and onto her shoulder.

The boys watched wide-eyed as she took the snake by the neck and held it out for them to touch. A couple of the braver ones ran their fingers along the smooth, dry scales.

"That's one strange woman," George said. "Ain't natural the way she's so brash."

Hamilton agreed but refrained from saying so. The snake had definitely created an uproar, which had been good for business, but not so good for Essie. He wondered how a girl with so much smarts could have no sense of propriety. Her mother was well-known for being socially correct in every way. The poor woman must succumb to vapors on a regular basis over the behavior of her daughter.

Still, the snake brought in crowds of children and with them came their mothers, milling around, gossiping and shopping. So as long as customers came to watch, he'd ignore the unseemly side of the spectacle.

He glanced back at George, surprised to see the man's face bright red.

"Meant no offense," George said.

"None taken."

The man quickly paid for his purchase and hurried out the door just as a stranger entered. A tall cowboy. He stood inside, taking a quick survey of the store. The snake caught his eye immediately, but he soon pulled his gaze to Mrs. Tyner and her maiden daughter, Miss Sadie. Approaching them, he doffed his hat, laying it across his chest, and bowed slightly.

Both women simpered. The cowboy winked at the older woman, then looked the younger up and down.

"How-deeeeee-do," he said, slow and lazy.

Miss Sadie's cheeks filled with color and Mrs. Tyner hustled her back to the dry goods section, where Mrs. Lockhart examined a bolt of cotton.

The man strolled through the store, bowing, smiling, and "howdy-do"ing every woman regardless of age, shape, or size. His spurs jangled with each step and scraped Hamilton's carefully polished floor.

The cowboy paused at the stove and introduced himself to Vandervoort and his cronies. The whole shop grew quiet, the patrons craning to overhear the conversation. The ladies pretended to fiddle with various sundries as they marked every move the cowboy made and whispered furiously to one another.

He set his hat down and unhooked a tin cup from the wall, then poured himself a cup of coffee. After taking a sip, he wandered over to where Essie was holding court. Hamilton drew satisfaction in advance for what he knew Essie's reaction would be to the philanderer. She was not one to have her head turned by a pretty face and charming manners. No, she'd set him in his place, all right.

The cowboy stood like a captain on the quarterdeck, his feet spread wide. He took another sip of coffee. Essie glanced up, her lips parting as she gaped at the wrangler.

The snake, forgotten in her hands, slithered up her arm, across her shoulder, behind her neck, and back around, draping itself across her like a winter scarf. It glided down her chest, calling attention to her womanly features as it lifted its head into the air.

The man tracked the reptile's progress, and the corners of his mouth crooked up. "My name's Adam. Adam Currington. And if your name's Eve, I do believe I'm in a whole passel of trouble."

"Her name ain't Eve, mister," young Harley North said. "It's Miss Essie."

His smile widened, forming large brackets on both sides of his face. "Eve. Essie. That's mighty close, if I do say so myself."

"You cain't call her that lessen she gives ya permission. 'Til then, you'd best be calling her Miss Spreckelmeyer."

His eyebrows lifted. "Spreckelmeyer? The judge's daughter?"

She nodded, still in a daze.

He set his coffee on a barrel and stepped through the circle of boys. Lifting his palm like a beggar, he let the snake pass from her chest to his hand, then up the length of his arm where it crinkled his blue shirt and coiled around muscles that were clearly accustomed to heavy work.

"I do believe this is the prettiest catch I've seen in a long, long while," he drawled.

Hamilton scowled. The cowboy wasn't looking at the snake. He was looking at Essie. What the blazes was wrong with her? Couldn't she see he was all talk? A man with looks like that could want only one thing from a spinster woman.

Hamilton came out from around the counter, but Mrs. Lockhart intercepted him.

"I've been suffering from a most troublesome headache, Mr. Crook. Might you have something for me?" she asked.

He hesitated, glanced at Essie in frustration, then changed directions and headed to the medicinals.

The cowboy from Essie's childhood dreams had materialized before her very eyes. And, oh my, but he was even more beautiful in the flesh.

The prairie king ventured from the man's arm on up to his neck. Its head disappeared momentarily while it circled around only to return again to the front.

The tail end of the three-and-a-half-foot snake still clung to her neck, effectively tying her to Mr. Adam Currington. The king lifted its head, testing the air with its forked tongue. She reached out and the pet glided across to her hand. Currington moved closer, letting the snake encircle them.

"What's its name?" he whispered.

"He doesn't have one yet. We're in the middle of a naming contest, actually. Would you like to enter?"

"You gonna be the judge?"

"One of them."

"Is there a prize, too?"

She nodded.

He stroked his finger along the snake's back where it crossed her shoulder. "Yes, ma'am. I surely would like to play, then."

His hat had left an indention in his blond hair, bringing out a few streaks of brown that matched the brows framing his blue-green eyes. When he smiled, the coppery skin crinkled around their corners.

"I'm afraid you'll be well on your way by the time the winner is announced," Hamilton said, startling Essie into taking a step back.

She gathered up the snake, which Mr. Currington released reluctantly, then squeezed through her audience of children to place it back in its crate.

The stranger stuck his hand out toward Hamilton. "I'm Adam Currington, one of the crew that's been hired by the Commercial Club to dig a few water wells for y'all."

Disappointment surged through Essie. "You're not a cowboy?" she asked, placing two rocks on top of the mesh lid.

He retrieved his coffee and rested his weight on one leg. "Well, I reckon I am, ma'am. But it gets mighty hot and lonely on the trail, so I decided a change might be nice."

"You're a drifter, then," Hamilton said.

Essie frowned. "Mr. Currington, this is Hamilton Crook, proprietor of the Slap Out."

"Howd—"

"Lookit here, Miss Spreckelmeyer," Jeremy Gillespie hollered, charging into the store with six of his twelve siblings behind him, chattering in excitement. Withdrawing his hands from the large pockets of his jacket, he held two live mice suspended by their tails in one hand, three in the other.

Sadie Tyner screamed, startling everyone including Jeremy, who loosened his hold on the mice. Three of the five fell with a thump to the floor and scattered in all directions.

One of the furry critters scampered between Adam's legs and he jumped back, sloshing coffee onto his sleeve. The judge's daughter dove for the mouse, stretching out full length on the floor and knocking Adam's feet right out from under him.

He pitched sideways to keep from landing on her, spraying coffee in the general direction of heaven. His shoulder clipped a barrel as he hit the floor, knocking over a box of ball bearings. The metal balls scattered onto the wooden floor, pinging with each bounce.

As he rolled out of their way, he found himself pressed cheek-by-jowl against Miss Essie. The gal had managed to trap one of the escapees in her outstretched hands, then, quicker than a flea, she hopped up and ran with it to the back, giving Adam no nevermind at all.

The youngsters had taken up the chase like hounds after a fox, barking and squealing and shouting. The scrawny little miss who'd started the ruckus with her scream hadn't let up. She'd vaulted onto a table of ready-mades, knocking shoes, hats, long johns, and bonnets onto the floor. One of the old beans pushed the girl's mother behind him, shielding her with his body—as if that was going to accomplish anything.

Adam sprang to his feet and raced through the store, grasping women by their waists and lifting them onto any available surface, whether it be table, counter, barrel, or chair. The one with a cane he was particularly gentle with, excusing himself even as he placed her on a countertop.

He heard her sigh like a schoolgirl just before he saw Essie storm out of the back room with a small cage and a black bowl that had a rod attached to it. She set the cage down in front of the teener who'd brought in the mice—and still had two dangling from his fingertips—then thrust the bowl contraption into the hands of a bowlegged old John standing wide-eyed by the checkerboard.

"Here," she shouted over the commotion. "Use this."

"I see one!" one of the youngsters hollered. Essie pushed the man in that direction, then scanned the floor looking for the third mouse. Her gaze halted abruptly and she flew across the room to a small gap between some shelves and a wall of bins.

The fancy-pants proprietor stood dazed, motionless, and as worthless as a milk bucket under a bull. Adam hurried over to catch the mouse Essie had spotted, but before he could reach her, she knelt down on all fours and squeezed her arm into the crack between the shelves.

The space was too dark and narrow to look into, so she pressed her ear against it and blindly felt inside.

"Need some help?" he asked, squatting down beside her.

"I have it, sort of."

"Sort of?"

"The very tip of its tail is underneath my finger. I'm just trying to . . ." She clamped her tongue between her teeth, then gasped. "Botheration!"

She leapt up, searching the floor around them. A lump beneath her skirt caught his attention. The pesky thing was climbing her petticoats like a ladder.

"Hold still!" he hissed. She froze and he flicked up her skirt, sliding his hand between the dark serge and white petticoat underneath before latching on to the varmint.

When it dawned on him where his hand lay, he glanced up at her face, trying to gauge her reaction. He might have long been floundering in the mire of sin, but she looked like somebody'd shown her a fifth ace in a poker deck.

A thunder of boots on the wooden floor at the other end of the store drew his attention. The old cuss with the newfangled mouse catcher spun around like a button on a privy door, trying to capture the wily rodent.

The children shouted. One of the women swooned. A quick survey of the room assured him no one was taking notice of him and Essie.

Keeping a tight hold on his own mouse, he rotated his hand so his knuckles rested against her leg, layers of soft, ruffled petticoats shielding her skin from his touch. He was in no hurry as he drug his hand down her long, long leg.

For a moment, her expression turned soft and dreamy. She was a ripe one, all right. But she was the judge's daughter and possibly Mr. Prissy Pants' betrothed. She must have remembered this herself, for she suddenly jerked away from his touch.

He pulled his hand out and dropped her hem, taking in the dips and swells of her landscape as he stood.

"Did you . . . did you get it?" she whispered.

"Right in the palm of my hand, sweetheart."

A cheer rose up from the other faction. "He caught it! He caught it! Mr. Vandervoort caught it!"

Adam gave her the mouse and gently squeezed her waist. "They're calling for you, Miss Essie. You'd best go see to them."

Essie helped Mr. Vandervoort put the last mouse into the cage while the children all spoke at once. The cowboy lifted the women by their waists and set them back on solid ground. The sound of his pandering voice, full of false solicitude, turned Hamilton's stomach.

The last time he'd experienced this kind of anger was when his older brothers had bent the tip of a willow tree to the ground and told him to grab on with both hands and feet. They let go and left him clinging upside down for what had seemed like hours.

He still remembered how helpless he'd been, stuck atop that tree with no way of getting down. If anything, this was worse.

The front door wrenched open and Sheriff Dunn stomped in. "What in tarnation is going on?" His hollering brought silence as quickly as a gavel in a noisy courtroom.

Dunn was a solid man. Not tall, not short. Not fat, not thin. Just solid. His gray, bushy moustache hid his mouth and made Hamilton want to sell him a moustache comb and scissors every time he saw him.

Gripping his rifle, Dunn scanned the room, taking in the Gillespie boy and then halting altogether on the cowboy.

"Uncle Melvin," Essie exclaimed, hurrying toward him. "There's no need for distress. Just a little game of cat-and-mouse."

Vandervoort let out an amused bark.

"Crook?" the sheriff asked, still keeping his attention on Currington.

"Everything's fine," Hamilton answered.

The tension in the room dissipated with his words, only to be replaced with a resurgence of excitement as Essie, Vandervoort, and the children all started explaining what had happened. The cowboy helped the last two women from their perches without a word, then picked up his hat and slipped out the door.

Hamilton noted the sheriff missed none of it, though he appeared to be listening to Essie's explanation.

"So you see, it was really my fault," she continued. "I had told the children that anyone who brought in a mouse for our snake would receive a chance to actually feed it."

With Currington gone, the sheriff relaxed and rubbed his neck. "Looks like a twister went through here. You catch 'em all?"

"Yes, we did. And I'll have this mess cleaned up in no time."

He smiled. "I know you will."

Sheriff Dunn was Mrs. Spreckelmeyer's brother and a lifelong friend to Mr. Spreckelmeyer. As Essie's uncle, he held particular affection for her. Hamilton suppressed the urge to roll his eyes, irritated over the sheriff's partiality to Essie almost as much as he had been over the cowboy's easy banter.

"Want to see the mice?" she asked.

"I'd rather see the king."

She grabbed his hand and pulled him toward the snake's crate.

After a long look, the sheriff whistled his appreciation. "That's a beauty, sugar. You catch that all by yourself?"

"She shore did," little Harley said. "This thing here had me and Emily Wedick scared something awful. But Miss Essie snatched it up with her bare hands and stuffed it in a gunnysack. She didn't scream or nothin'. And she caught two of them mouses, too."

Dunn chuckled. "Well, if she keeps this up, I just might have to deputize her."

Some of the women snickered and Mrs. Tyner, who a few moments earlier had been perched on the counter, put her hands on her hips and snorted.

"Of all the ridiculous things," she said. "A woman deputy, indeed."

Sheriff Dunn straightened his spine, having no tolerance for disparaging remarks concerning his niece.

Old Vandervoort jumped in, waving the bust enhancer in the air triumphantly. "Well, I'll tell you something. I ain't never seen a mouse catcher that works so good as this one. Where'd you get this, Miss Essie?"

Miss Sadie Tyner took one look at the thing and gasped, clapping a hand over her mouth. Hamilton appraised the girl, comprehension dawning, only to blush profusely when Miss Sadie caught his speculative perusal. Blood drained from her face.

"Why, I found it gathering dust in the back," Essie answered. "Would you like to purchase it?"

"I surely would," Vandervoort replied, tucking it under his arm like a fancy gentleman's riding crop.

"Me too," Mr. Owen said. Followed by seconds from Jenkins and Richie.

"Wonderful. Hamilton?" Essie turned to him, flushed with pleasure. "If you'll write their orders, I'll start cleaning up this mess."

He snatched the bust enhancer out of Vandervoort's grasp. "This isn't for sale."

"Oh," Essie replied. "Well, all right, then. We'll just order Mr. Vandervoort one, too."

"No," Hamilton said, beads of sweat forming on his brow. If these ladies figured out what this was he'd be ruined.

Essie frowned at him.

Shaking, he wanted nothing more than to toss her out on her backside. He cleared his throat. "I'm afraid . . . that is, I'm sorry, but the firm that made them has . . . has failed."

Miss Sadie pressed a handkerchief to her brow, looking faint, but apart from Hamilton, no one took notice.

"Oh no!" Essie said. "Are you sure?"

"Quite sure." Turning his back, he stomped to the storage room and shoved the enhancer back up on the top shelf.

———

Settling herself onto the piano stool in the parlor, Essie allowed her fingers to move across the keys, playing Beethoven's "Für Elise" by heart. Since childhood, Essie had whiled away the hours sitting at the keyboard. And this was the piece she always played when she wanted to indulge a particular fantasy—an idyllic afternoon being romanced by her imaginary beau.

During the prelude, they picnicked beside Two Bit Creek and fed each other bites of egg salad sandwiches. His lips grazed her finger accidentally. She blushed and pulled her hand away.

As the interlude began, they swung up onto their horses and raced neck-and-neck around Waller's Bend, their mounts stretching and straining forward. At the last moment, she bent down, urging the horse forward, and pulled ahead of her cavalier. She hadn't realized, of course, that he had held his horse back, allowing hers to win.

The piece moved into a crescendo, and she pulled her mount to a stop. He drew his horse next to hers and brought her hand up to his lips for a kiss.

A knock at the front door interrupted her musings, but not her music. She softened the notes while her mother answered the door.

"Hello, Melvin. Sullivan's back in his office."

"Actually, Doreen," he said, "I was thinking to enjoy this mild weather we're havin'. Would you mind telling him I'm waiting for him on the porch?"

"Not at all."

Essie moved into the final lines. Her mother and Uncle Melvin had talked during the part of the music where she married the man of her dreams. Now she and her "husband" sat at a dinner table with a horde of their offspring gathered round. He said a prayer of thanksgiving. For their meal. For their children. And for their everlasting love.

She left her finger on the final key until all sound faded. This past month, Hamilton had played the part of the gallant in her dreams, but tonight he'd been replaced by Mr. Adam Currington.

The cowboy embodied the very thing dreams were made of. Exceptional looks. Exceptional charm. Exceptional . . . everything. A man like him would love the out-of-doors. Animals. Riding. Fishing. She closed her eyes, reliving their shared intimacy, feeling once more the tingles that had run down her leg this morning.

Dusk settled in, but she didn't light a lantern. Instead, she sat still on the piano stool, unmoving in the growing dark. A breeze fanned the curtains along the front wall, bringing with it Papa and Uncle Melvin's voices from the porch as they discussed the prophecies of Isaiah. The conversation eventually drifted from Scriptures to town happenings. When Adam's name was mentioned, though, Essie's senses came to attention.

"You know much about him?" the sheriff asked.

"He told the Club he'd lived in the desert so long he knew all the lizards by their front names and was ready for a change."

Essie smiled. Sounded like something Adam would say.

"Well, he sure had all the ladies at the Slap Out in a twitter."

"I can just imagine," Papa said with a laugh.

"Speaking of ladies in a twitter," the sheriff continued, "how's things between Crook and our girl?"

"Strangest thing," Papa said. "Doreen was so sure Essie was making a fool of herself chasing after him up at his store and all—"

"I wouldn't say she was chasing him, exactly."

"—but I'll have you know he approached me after church last Sunday and asked to come speak with me this week."

The creaking of Uncle Melvin's rocker came to a stop. "Is he going to make a declaration, do you think?"

"What else could it be?"

Essie's heart galloped.

"Think he's good enough for her?" Uncle Melvin asked.

"If Essie thinks so, then I don't see I'll have much choice."

The rocker started creaking again. "I reckon so. He was good to his first wife. Runs a clean place." He sighed. "I hope the young'uns take after Essie, though."

Papa chuckled. Essie slipped from the parlor and up to her room, savoring this momentous news. She pushed all thoughts of Adam Currington firmly from her mind.

Mrs. Hamilton Crook. Mrs. Esther Crook. Mrs. Crook.

O Lord. Thank you, thank you, thank you.

C H A P T E R | S I X

HAMILTON LOCKED THE SLAP Out's door and let out a sigh, savoring the stillness that came at the end of a busy day. After a pause, he turned to where Essie was tallying votes. The snake-naming contest had brought more trade than any tactic he'd ever tried in the past.

She sorted the final votes into neat stacks on the barrel that normally held a checkerboard. Banjo, Willie Waddle, Laddie, Colonel, and Butcher were the names still in contention.

"Doesn't look like the Willie Waddle stack is doing too well," she said.

"Thank goodness. I can't imagine how such an undignified name made it into the top five."

She smiled. "There's no accounting for taste."

He refrained from commenting.

She wore a navy-and-white shirtwaist with novelty buttons and puff sleeves. Her blond hair had begun to loosen from its pins, but ever since the catastrophe with the escaped mice, she'd curbed her behavior some and, for the most part, conducted herself with total propriety.

The woman might be unconventional. She might be too outdoorsy. She might be plain looking. But she sure could bring in the customers.

The stairs creaked and a moment later Mrs. Peterson peeked in. Alarm flashed through him. She'd been looking after baby Mae since his wife's death and never disturbed him unless it was urgent.

"Mrs. Peterson?" he said. "Is everything all right?"

The frumpy woman entered from the storage room, carrying Mae in her arms. "I'm sorry, sir, but I cannot stay late tonight. My grandson turns two today and my daughter's having me over for the celebration. Had you forgotten?"

Relief poured through him. "Well, yes, I'm afraid I did. But you go ahead, of course." He took Mae and saw Mrs. Peterson out the door.

The baby kicked her legs and waved her plump arms up and down. At some point in the last seven months, Hamilton had gone from being angry at the child for Eleanor's death to treasuring her for the link she provided to his late wife.

"Oh, Hamilton," Essie said, staring at the baby. "Look how big she's gotten."

"Has she? It's hard to tell when you see her every day."

Shifting in her chair, Essie opened her arms. "May I?"

"Certainly." He handed her the baby.

Essie smiled and stroked Mae's cheek. The baby turned her head and took Essie's little finger into her mouth. "Oh, my goodness. I can see you're a hearty eater."

Watching Essie coo and cuddle Mae brought an unexpected tightness to Hamilton's chest. Mrs. Peterson was an old woman. Fifty, at least, maybe older. She looked nothing like Essie when she held the baby.

Essie looked soft and womanly and, for the first time ever, downright attractive. The tightness in Hamilton shifted slightly into something he'd not felt in quite a while.

Mae grabbed a piece of Essie's hair and yanked, freeing it from the pins. Essie laughed and bent over, rubbing noses with his baby.

"Ummmmm," she said. "There's nothing quite so yummy as a baby's neck." She nibbled on Mae's neck, eliciting a squeal of delight from the baby.

Hamilton swallowed.

"She smells like oatmeal," Essie said, then looked up when he didn't respond.

Mae pounded and pushed against Essie's chest, molding the fabric of the shirtwaist to her curves. Tendrils of hair fell across her shoulder and down her back. Her blue eyes, framed with what he now realized were exceedingly long lashes, shone with joy. Dimples framed her mouth.

Bending down, he placed one hand on the back of her chair and the other on top of the barrel, and kissed her while she clutched his baby in her arms.

It was a fleeting kiss, the barest of touches, really. But when he pulled back, he pulled back only an inch. Just enough to see her lips, smell her scent, feel her breath.

He acknowledged his desire, then cupped Essie's chin and kissed her again. This time with the intention of finding out just exactly what the town spinster was made of.

Mae began to protest and Essie pulled back. "Hamilton," she whispered, "I'm not at all sure this is proper."

He felt a quick pang of guilt. Whether it was due to feeling desire for a woman he didn't love or for feeling desire at all, he didn't know.

"You're right," he said, straightening and pushing his glasses up his nose. "My apologies."

A look of confusion crossed her face. "Oh, please don't apologize. Never tell me you're sorry, Hamilton. Are you?"

He lifted Mae into his arms. "I'm afraid I won't be able to help you tally these votes tonight, Essie. Perhaps we could do it in the morning?"

She rose, concern etched onto her face. "Are you angry with me?"

"Not at all."

"You're acting angry."

"No, I'm not. You know what I'm like when I'm angry and this is not it."

She tucked her hair back up into her pins. "I see. Well, then, I'll just, um, let myself out. Good night, Hamilton. Good night, Mae."

———

Essie reread the paragraph for the umpteenth time, but still her thoughts wandered. She glanced at her mother, envying her ability to sit calmly in her parlor chair stitching an ornate *S* on the corner of her handkerchief, as if she hadn't a care in the world. As if it were only another ordinary Sunday afternoon.

"Is the book not to your liking, dear?" she asked.

"Where is he, Mother?" Essie asked.

"I have been thinking," she said. "I don't believe I shall plant morning glories along the front verandah next year. Have you noticed how many bees they attract?"

Essie looked out the parlor windows, accepting her mother's none-too-subtle change of topic. "I like the sound of their humming. It's soothing."

"It's distressing. And a constant reminder you could be stung at any moment. No, I shan't plant them so close to the house again. Have you any suggestions for their replacements?"

Essie sighed. "No, Mother. I haven't the slightest idea."

She and Hamilton had announced the snake's name and the winner of the camera yesterday amidst much fanfare and excitement. By day's closing they'd had record sales. But Hamilton had been distant and distracted.

Essie had been beside herself with excitement. He'd kissed her. All that was left was for him to make his declaration to Papa. He'd said nothing of their kiss all day yesterday, nor should he. But she'd relived it a thousand times in her mind.

This morning she'd taken great care in preparing for church. He'd treated her the same as he always did, greeting her and her family with the friendly politeness he greeted everyone else with. But the entire time, she knew he would be coming to the house today to make his declaration, for he'd told Papa he'd be by before the day was up.

Turning the page, she surreptitiously smoothed out the pieces of paper she'd inserted into the book. *Fredrick Fouty, Charlie Wedick, Winston Peeples, Hamilton Crook.*

She paused, reviewing the assets and drawbacks she'd assigned to Hamilton. If she redid the list today, she'd have so much more to put in his "asset" column.

"Did you hear the news at church?" Mother asked.

"I'm sorry?" Essie said, looking up from her musings. "Did you say news?"

"Yes. I heard that Ewing's coming home."

"Ewing? Ewing Wortham?"

"Mm-hmm. He's to graduate from that fancy Bible college in Nashville in another few months, and our church is considering him as a replacement for Preacher Bogart once he retires."

"That would be awfully strange, wouldn't it?" Essie shook her head. "Seems like yesterday he was running around in short pants and pulling the girls' pigtails. I can't quite picture him at the pulpit, can you?"

The knock was abrupt, causing Essie to jump. In a slow and unruffled manner, her mother set aside her stitching and answered the door.

"Good evening, Mr. Crook. Won't you please come in?"

"Thank you, Mrs. Spreckelmeyer. I was, uh, wondering if I could visit with the judge for a few moments?"

The sound of his voice filled Essie. She closed her eyes, wanting to commit to memory every detail of this life-changing occasion.

"Yes, he's been expecting you. If you would like, Essie is in the parlor and I'm sure she'd be glad to keep you company while I tell him you are here."

Essie stood as he entered.

He still wore his Sunday clothes, his hat grasped tightly in his hands. "Miss Spreckelmeyer."

"Mr. Crook," Essie said. "Please, sit down."

They both sat while her mother went to get Papa.

"Yesterday's winner was quite the topic at church this morning, I noticed," she said.

He nodded. "I'm so glad Willie Waddle was not the winning name. Having a pet snake is bad enough. But having one named Willie Waddle would have been more than I could bear, I'm afraid."

"Well, Colonel is a grand name, I think."

"Yes. Yes, I agree." His gaze caught, then narrowed on her book. "Is that one of Mrs. Lockhart's novels?"

Essie sighed and placed the closed book on the table beside her. "I'm afraid it is. She's foisted it on me, insisting I read it. I have been trying for an hour to get past the first few pages but haven't had much luck."

"I should hope not."

Silence.

"How is Mae today?"

He smiled. "Fine. Just fine. She's such a good baby, you know."

Essie returned his smile. "She's lovely, Hamilton. Very much like you."

His eyes widened and Essie could have ripped her tongue out. Oh, where was Mother? "May I get you something to drink? Some lemonade, perhaps?"

"Yes, please. If it's no trouble."

She hurried from the room and with fumbling fingers poured the lemonade. Upon her return, she found Hamilton studying Mrs. Lockhart's novel. She froze, tray in hand.

Hamilton snapped the book shut, the edges of her personal papers peeking out. "I must admit, it has been very interesting reading after all."

"Hamilton," she said, placing the tray on a nearby cart. "Let me explain."

"Mr. Crook?"

They both started at Mother's beckoning.

"Judge Spreckelmeyer will see you now. Won't you come this way?"

Essie placed a hand on his arm. "Wait—"

He shook off her hand, his eyes frosty and distant. Mother glanced between the two of them before escorting him out, their footsteps echoing down the hall.

Moments later her mother returned to her chair and gave Essie a brief, questioning look before plying her needle.

Essie picked up the book. Her hands shook so badly, she immediately sat and rested the novel upon her lap. The clock chimed the quarter hour, then the half hour.

Her father's door opened.

"Thank you so much for seeing me, Judge."

"Anytime, Crook. Anytime. Good day, now."

"Good day to you, too, sir. And thank you."

The front door opened and closed. The sound of Hamilton bouncing down the porch steps reached the ears of those in the parlor. When all was silent, Papa stepped into the room.

Mother lowered her stitching. Essie clutched her book.

He looked first at Mother, then at her. "He asked if the Slap Out could be granted a license to act as a post office."

Essie waited, but he said nothing more. "Is that all he asked for, Papa?"

His entire face showed his distress. "I'm sorry."

"A post office," Essie repeated. "Well. Will you give it to him?"

"It's not my decision, ultimately, but I agreed to initiate the paper work and to give him a recommendation to the state."

She nodded. "Good. That's . . . why, it's wonderful news. I know he's thrilled. Thank you, Papa."

"Squirt," he whispered.

But she'd already left the room.

———

"I'm going up to market in Dallas for a few days," Hamilton said. "Do you think you can handle things while I'm gone?"

Essie paused before slipping a bolt of fabric onto the shelf. "Of course. When were you thinking of leaving?"

"Right now."

"Right now! But . . . but what about Mae?"

"Mrs. Peterson has agreed to stay with her while I'm gone. I've already sent my trunk to the station."

"Oh." Essie looked around the store, trying to get her bearings. Since their incident in the parlor, she hadn't known quite what to do or say. He'd been completely unapproachable, either barking at her or ignoring her.

"Hamilton, about yesterday—"

"I won't be away for more than two or three days and will be back before Saturday, in any event."

"I see." She straightened a stack of handkerchiefs on the table.

"Well, good-bye, then." He pushed his glasses up.

"Good-bye, Hamilton. Godspeed."

———

ES: DELAYED STOP BE BACK MONDAY STOP
HAVE BIG SURPRISE STOP HC

Essie pressed the telegram against her heart. Absence really did make the heart grow fonder. She slipped the telegram back into the envelope and placed it in her apron pocket.

She'd never been sent a telegram before. It was heady, receiving such a thing. And he wasn't mad anymore. Was even going to bring her a surprise to make up for their little misunderstanding.

She raised the shade and propped open the door to the Slap Out.

———

Essie held the mouse catcher high over her head, gently twirling it in a circular motion. Each boy crowding around her had placed his name in the black bowl at the end of the rod.

"Mr. Vandervoort?" Essie asked. "Would you like to do the honors?"

He looked up from the checkerboard. "Why, shore, Miss Essie." Standing, he hitched up his trousers and looked the group over. "All these fellas brought in a mouse?"

"That's right. You pick a name from the bowl, and that's who gets to feed Colonel."

Vandervoort raised his hand and fished inside the bowl.

"*Essie!* What in the blue blazes are you doing?"

Essie jumped. Vandervoort jumped. The children jumped.

"Hamilton! You're home!"

He strode to her, his hair mussed, his complexion windburned, his eyes furious. He snatched the mouse catcher out of her hand, spilling a couple of names from its bowl.

She had no idea what he was angry about and she didn't care. She was so very glad to see him. "Mr. Vandervoort?" she said, never taking her eyes off Hamilton. "Whose name did you draw?"

"Lawrence's."

She turned her attention to Lawrence. He was about six years of age and from one of the better families in town. "Congratulations, Lawrence. You won! Would you like me to show you how to feed Colonel?"

"He will have to wait," Hamilton said. "I must see you in the back."

She smiled. It was so good to have him home. "Of course." She glanced at Lawrence. "I'll return in just a moment."

Hamilton grasped her arm and propelled her to the storage room. As soon as they made it through the curtain, he spun her around.

"What's the matter?" she asked.

He shoved the mouse catcher toward her. "Hold this."

She took it.

"Don't move."

He disappeared into the store and then returned with the catalog in hand. He slammed it onto a barrel. "Page two hundred thirty-one," he said, then swept back into the store.

Frowning, she put down the mouse catcher and turned to page 231 in the catalog. Strewn across the top of the page in large, bold letters were the words: THE PRINCESS BUST DEVELOPER AND BUST CREAM.

She touched her hand to her lips, quickly skimming the advertisement. A drawing of the mouse catcher accompanied a lengthy explanation of the product. *A new scientific help to nature . . . will produce desired result . . . comes in two sizes . . .*

She moved her attention to the second half of the page. *BUST CREAM . . . delightful cream preparation . . . forms just the right formula for wasted tissues . . . greatest toilet requisite ever offered . . .*

She closed her eyes. Mortified. It could not be. Oh, how would she ever face him again? Any of them. But, no, the others didn't know what it was, either. Why, they had even wanted to order some.

What a scandal that would have been if those old-timers had bought bust developers and started chasing mice all over town with them. Choking, she opened her eyes and picked up the developer, examining it. She placed it over herself, then jerked it away, embarrassed. Horrified. Fascinated.

Did it actually work? Who had ordered it? And why had the customer never picked it up? She quickly did a mental count of the women in town, but she couldn't imagine anyone ordering such a ridiculous thing. She slipped it back up on the top shelf.

Nothing in all her born days had prepared her for how to handle a situation such as this. But Hamilton was home, and he had a surprise for her. And nothing was going to keep her from that surprise—not even his understandable anger about her innocent mistake.

She stepped out from behind the curtain. Hamilton was waiting on a petite woman Essie had never seen before. He glanced up and turned a startling shade of red. She felt her own skin flush.

He excused himself and headed toward her. A surge of excitement shot through her. She'd seen married couples share moments such as this. Communicating with each other across a room and at a level that no one else could match.

As embarrassed as she was, she could not help but enjoy the thrill of sharing this intimate moment with him. He stopped in front of her, shielding her from the view of others.

"I don't know what to say, Hamilton. I'm horrified."

"You didn't know."

"I certainly did not. But whose is it?"

Red stained his cheeks again. "The order was placed without my knowledge. It arrived after Eleanor passed, and I had no way of discovering whose it was."

"Did you see how much it cost?"

"I know. I can't throw it out because someone in this town has paid for it. So I'll just have to keep it up on that shelf until it is claimed. But in the meanwhile, I don't think we should be using it to trap mice and have drawings."

Essie could not stop a tiny chuckle from escaping. "Of course not."

He frowned. "This is not the least bit amusing, Essie."

"Miss Spreckelmeyer?"

Essie peeked around Hamilton to see Lawrence, mouse already in hand. She crooked a finger at him and took his free hand. "Would you excuse us a moment, please, Hamilton?"

"Yes, yes. Hurry it up before he drops it."

She smiled and led Lawrence to Colonel's cage.

"First," she said, "you must remove the mesh top from the crate."

The other boys gathered around. Lawrence handed her the mouse, then placed the two rocks on the floor and lifted off the mesh top. Colonel tested the air with his forked tongue, but otherwise didn't stir himself.

Lawrence retrieved the mouse, holding it by its tail.

"Drop it in," she said.

"Will it hurt the mouse?" he asked.

"How animals obtain their food is designed by God," she said. "He made the mouse and He made the snake. We must trust that He knew what He was doing."

"Will the mouse go to heaven?"

She hesitated only a moment. "I pray it is so."

He dropped the mouse into the crate. Colonel clamped his mouth around it, then proceeded to swallow it whole. The boys made noises of approval.

A sound behind them caused Essie to turn. The new customer Hamilton had been helping swooned. Jeremy Gillespie caught the woman. Her alabaster skin was as smooth and white as a china doll's, her rich black hair startling in its contrast.

Hamilton rushed to her side. "Darling? Darling? Are you all right?" He took her from Jeremy and patted her cheeks. "Katherine? Can you hear me?"

Cold swept through Essie's innards, spreading to her limbs. She stood.

Hamilton found Essie with his gaze. "Can you do something? She's fainted."

Essie moved by rote to the medicinal section and took some smelling salts from the middle shelf, then poured cold water into a tin cup. A cousin. An in-law. A sister. *Please, Lord. Let it be a sister.*

A crowd of people had gathered. She excused herself and they made a path for her. Hamilton took the salts and waved them under Katherine's nose.

She was a shapely woman. Soft and lush, where Essie was hard and firm. Small and petite, where Essie was tall and long. Pale and fragile, where Essie was sunburned and tough.

Her eyes fluttered open. "Hamilton?"

"I'm here, my dear. I'm here."

She smiled at him. This was no cousin or in-law or sister.

Trembling, Essie knelt opposite Hamilton. She dipped her apron into the cup of water and swabbed the woman's face.

A tiny bit of color returned to her cheeks. "Thank you."

"Of course," Essie said. "Are you better, ma'am?"

"Yes. But I think I'll just rest a moment. Such a shock, you know. That poor little mouse."

Essie lifted her gaze to Hamilton.

He swallowed and looked down at the woman. "Katherine? I'd like you to meet my store clerk, Essie Spreckelmeyer. Essie? This is my new wife, Katherine Crook."

CHAPTER | SEVEN

ESSIE'S HEARTBEAT ROSE. HER breathing grew labored. The blood drained from her head down to her stomach, leaving her dizzy and slightly ill.

But she would not faint. She refused to succumb. Her mind gave her body strict orders to settle down, but it would not listen. She wiped her face with the corner of the apron she'd just used to wipe Katherine Crook's. Mrs. Katherine Crook.

How could he? she thought. He'd kissed her only last week. Surely he'd not been engaged this entire time?

"My goodness," she managed, hoping her voice did not betray the upheaval within her. "This is a surprise."

Mrs. Crook had closed her eyes again, oblivious to the introduction and the undercurrents it provoked.

Hamilton's glasses had slid to the end of his nose, giving Essie an unobstructed view of his eyes. He looked so different without his glasses. So young.

His hands were full, so Essie reached over and pushed his glasses up where they belonged. "Congratulations," she whispered.

"Essie," he said, but she lightly touched her finger to his mouth, shushing him.

"I believe your wife has fainted again. Perhaps you should take her upstairs and when she awakens introduce her to your . . . your baby."

To her horror, a sheen of tears glazed her eyes. She dare not blink or they'd fall and her humiliation would be complete.

"Katherine and I have known each other since childhood," Hamilton said. "We ran into each other in Dallas. It was as if we hadn't been apart for more than a day or two, so quickly did our rapport return. I had no idea she'd been married, much less widowed. And, well, one thing led to another and—"

"Hamilton," Essie said, nodding toward the crowd gathered around them.

He glanced up and scowled, then slid his hands beneath his wife, lifting her as he rose to his feet. "Essie, will you follow me, please?"

No, Hamilton, no. You cannot ask me to follow you while you carry your bride up those stairs and across the threshold.

But she rose and went with him through the curtain, as far as the stairs.

"Hamilton," she said.

He paused, his wife limp in his arms. The gold band encircling his fourth finger jumped out at Essie. She looked at Katherine's hands, but they were still hidden inside her gloves.

"I think it best if I stay with the store," Essie said. "Mrs. Peterson will know what to do. If you need a doctor, have Mrs. Peterson come and tell me. I will see to it."

His Adam's apple bobbed. "Essie, I don't know what to say."

"Go on. We'll be fine down here."

"Are you sure?"

"Absolutely."

"You're a marvelous woman. Any man would be lucky to have you." He hesitated, as if weighing his words. "I also know you to be rather competitive and if you'd allow me, from one friend to the other, I think you should know: The man likes to do the chasing, Essie."

He turned his back, walked up the stairs and disappeared across their threshold.

———

Essie sat in her window seat, a place of succor since childhood. A tiny alcove carved out of her bedroom wall with a soft cushion to sit on and fluffy pillows to lean against. It was her cleft in the rock, a place where she could hide within the shelter of His wings.

Moving aside some papers, she tucked a crocheted blanket about her feet and looked out the window on the flower gardens below. Gardens she and her mother had planted, with buds arranged by color so they would make a pretty picture when they bloomed. But summer and the hot Texas sun had overbaked the blossoms, leaving brown, shriveled patches in place of once-vibrant colors.

She touched the glass that separated her from the out-of-doors, and nature's display blurred as she refocused on her hand. Her ringless hand.

He had married a childhood friend. A widow.

Why, Lord? Why does she get two husbands when all I want is one?

It didn't make sense. She'd be such a good wife and mother. Why was God keeping her from doing the very thing He made her for? Surely it couldn't be because she'd made some silly little list.

She laid her forehead on her upraised knees. What was she going to do now? She couldn't just up and quit working in the store. That would be too obvious. Too humiliating.

But Essie had thought of it as her store for so long that she wouldn't take kindly to changing things around simply to suit the new mistress.

Yet Hamilton's wife would want to do things her way. And like it or not, Essie would have to oblige her. Perhaps she could get herself fired. But, no, she didn't want to sabotage the store or Hamilton.

So she'd stay. And she'd work. And she'd quit, just as soon as she gracefully could.

Cranking open the window, she took a deep breath. The breeze lifted the papers littered at her feet. She slapped them down with her hands before they flew away, then gathered them up.

Hamilton Crook
Points of Merit:

- *Has an infant who needs a mother*
- *Has a new store and needs a helpmate*
- *Cared for his wife, God rest her soul*
- *Attends church*
- *Would profit from having a hometown girl in his store*

Drawbacks:

- *Horrid last name*
- *Younger than me*
- *Never see him outdoors*
- *Works past the supper hour (but that would change once he married me and had some help)*
- *Doesn't have any pets*

She folded the pages in half, then ripped them down the middle without even looking at the other men on her list.

————

It would have been so much easier if Essie could have hated the new Mrs. Crook. But no one in their right mind could hate Katherine Crook. The petite woman epitomized kindness and sincerity. She spoke softly. Listened intently. Laughed easily.

Essie was completely intimidated. Hamilton was completely captivated.

Only a week had passed, but Katherine had easily won over the old cronies. Her only fault was her opinion of Colonel.

In Katherine's mind snakes were synonymous with Satan. She could not distinguish one from the other. And Colonel must have sensed it somehow, for he'd quit eating.

The snake had grown an inch, he'd remained calm and tolerant—never striking in anger—then for no apparent reason he'd stopped feeding. Essie had tempted him with several different mice at several different times of day. No luck.

Perhaps the crate had become too confining. She didn't know, but she had to free him. And she'd need to do it now while the fall weather was still mild.

The boys in town were crushed. They'd grown very attached to Colonel. Particularly the little orphan, Harley North. He'd come so far since she'd seen him screaming in fear that long-ago morning. Now he couldn't get enough of the prairie king.

He, Lawrence, and Jeremy entered the Slap Out as solemn as if someone had died.

"Hello, boys," Essie said.

They congregated around Colonel's crate.

"Can we hold him one last time?" Harley asked.

"Of course," Essie said, removing the mesh top. While the boys took turns holding and petting the snake, she moved his crate to the back and cleaned it.

"Are you all right?" Hamilton asked, closing the large barn-like door that had been flung wide during a delivery of pork barrels.

Essie picked up an empty gunnysack. "A little sad, I suppose. He's a wonderful snake."

"I'm sorry."

Sorry for what? she thought. *For having me underfoot all the time? For the awkwardness between us? For ever hiring me in the first place?*

"I've been thinking, Hamilton," she said, playing with the string at the top of the burlap bag. "Since Colonel's leaving and all, I thought maybe it would be a good time for me to move on, as well."

"What do you mean, 'move on'?"

"Quit," she whispered.

He said nothing. She looked up and felt a pang of guilt. He looked so torn. He had to know she couldn't stay, no matter how successful she was at selling his goods.

"You don't have to go," he said.

"You know I do. But I thank you. I haven't had such a grand time in forever and a day."

"When do you have to . . . leave?"

"I'll stay through Saturday."

"So soon?"

"I think it best. But if you ever need anything, if Katherine gets sick or something, just send word."

He surveyed the storage room as if its shelves would offer him a compromise of some sort.

"Well," she said, lifting up the gunnysack, "I'd best get this over with."

The boys placed Colonel in the sack, and Essie knotted the top.

"Maybe we ought to bring the mice, too," Jeremy said. "We could let 'em out close to where we free Colonel. Then he won't have to go so far to find some dinner."

They walked through town with Jeremy carrying the snake and Lawrence carrying a sack of mice. They passed the men drilling the community's new water wells. Adam Currington took off his hat, swiped his brow with the back of his hand and waved.

He stood tall and lean, silhouetted against the blue sky. His shirt-sleeves were rolled up, his hip cocked. He placed his hat back on his head, adjusting it until he had its brim at just the right angle.

The boys waved back, hollering out a greeting. Essie tucked her chin. They continued walking for a good half mile until they reached the banks of Two Bit Creek.

The sounds of town had faded, replaced by the gurgling of the creek, a woodpecker searching for bugs, two squirrels playing chase. Birds of vivid blues, yellows, and reds flitted from tree branch to tree branch, each chirping over the other.

"What do you think about this spot?" she asked.

The boys looked around. "It's a right nice place, Miss Essie," Jeremy said.

Lawrence poured the mice on the ground like a schoolboy releasing his marbles from a pouch. They scurried in all directions. Jeremy untied his gunnysack, lifted Colonel out and placed him on the ground. The snake froze, tongue darting, then slithered through the weeds toward the stream and disappeared beneath some brush.

Essie envied Colonel's freedom to go where he wanted. To do whatever he fancied. Accountable to no one.

Harley buried his face in her skirt.

She stroked his hair. "Maybe I'll take you boys snake hunting one day soon. Would you like that?"

Lawrence sighed. "My ma probably won't let me. She makes me do girly things, like play the piano."

Jeremy nudged his shoulder.

His eyes widened. "Oh. I didn't mean nothing by that, Miss Essie. You aren't like other girls."

I know, Lawrence. I know. "Come along, we'd best be heading back."

They had just made it to the dirt road outside of town when the sound of a wagon made Essie shade her eyes.

"Lookit, Miss Essie!" Harley yelled. "It's the peddler man!"

The boys took off running, Essie right behind them. Levi Baumgartner pulled his horse to a stop, causing the pots and pans in his wagon to clang. "Whoa, Clara. Whoa."

A black-and-white dog put two paws up on the wagon's sideboard, barking and wagging his tail.

"Howdy, Mr. Bum!"

"Well, it is Lawrence, a clever *shaygets*, to be sure. What are you and your friends doing way out here?"

"We were lettin' our snake go on account of he quit eatin'," Harley said, trying to catch his breath.

Mr. Baumgartner chuckled, then tipped his hat. "Miss Spreckelmeyer. A delightful surprise." He was not an old man, but he looked like one and spoke like one. He had lines on his brown face and a thick black beard covering his chin.

"Hello, Mr. Baumgartner," she said. "Welcome to town."

"Thank you. How is Pegasus?" he asked, eyes twinkling.

"Wonderful. She's in excellent health."

Jeremy looked up from petting the horse's nose. "Who's Pega Siss?"

"That, my boy," the peddler replied, "is the name of Miss Spreckelmeyer's bicycle."

"Your ridin' machine has a name?" Harley asked.

"Of course," she said. "My horse has one. Why shouldn't my bike?"

The dog barked, distracting the children.

"Can we play with Shadrach?" Lawrence asked.

Mr. Baumgartner set the brake lever and gave a command in Yiddish. The border collie sailed off the wagon and into the circle of boys. They chased the dog, then laughed as the dog chased them. After a while, Shadrach collapsed at his master's feet, panting, back legs extended, tongue hanging out like a bell pull.

"Whatcha got in yer wagon this time?" Jeremy asked.

Mr. Baumgartner opened up the back of his wagon, pushing aside brooms and tinware and a whole tub of shoes. "I have a hunting knife with a seven-inch clip blade," he said, handing the knife to Jeremy.

The teener held it reverently, touching his thumb to its tip, and a drop of blood instantly appeared. "She's a beauty."

He gave it back to the peddler without even asking the price, for whatever it was would be too much.

"What about me?" Harley asked.

Mr. Baumgartner handed him a china dog no bigger than his little finger.

"It's Shadrach!" Harley exclaimed, showing the treasure to the rest of them. "You ought to get your pa to buy this, Lawrence. He could buy you whatever you want."

Lawrence frowned. "He don't like buying from the peddler man."

Jeremy nudged him.

"What?" Lawrence asked. "What'd I do?"

"Nothing, boy," Mr. Baumgartner said, ruffling his hair. "You've not done a thing. But you've also not asked about Miss Spreckelmeyer. Don't you think she might like to see what I have in this wagon?"

Harley wrinkled his nose. "Oh, don't start showing your ribbons and stuff or we'll be here all day."

"Ah, but Miss Spreckelmeyer is special. It's not the ribbons that catch her eye. Only the goods that promise excitement or adventure will intrigue our fine German *shiksa.*"

The boys peered into the covered wagon, and Essie felt herself respond to his teasing. "Did you bring me some excitement and adventure, Mr. Baumgartner?"

He bowed. "For you, I bring the world."

Harley snorted. "That won't fit in yer wagon!"

Mr. Baumgartner's black eyes lit with mischief before he disappeared inside the canvas bonnet. They heard him shifting trunks and goods, murmuring to himself in a language they didn't understand but loved to hear.

Finally he jumped down from the bed. "I have something especial for you."

Essie took the bulky offering and examined it. The block of wood looked to be eight inches in length and five inches wide. It had leather straps with buckles across the top and a long rope on each side. Also attached to the sides were four wheels made of boxwood—two on each side.

"What is it?" she asked.

"Wheeled feet," he answered.

"What?"

He drew out another block of wood exactly like the one she held. "You strap them onto your shoes. Like a bicycle, except for the feet."

Essie stifled a giggle. "Truly? That's truly what they are for?"

"Try them."

"But how do you pedal?"

"You don't. You just . . . go."

She looked between him and the wheeled contraption, tempted beyond belief. They were still outside of town and no one but these boys would see her.

"You must all swear to secrecy," she said.

Jeremy grinned. Lawrence made an *X* over his lips. Harley saluted.

She looked at Mr. Baumgartner. "I'm going to break my neck."

"That's what you said about the bicycle." He patted the wagon bed. "Here. I'll help you put them on."

Jeremy made a stirrup with his hands and boosted her up onto the wagon. Mr. Baumgartner placed one of the blocks of wood against his thigh, guided her booted foot on the block, then strapped her in.

When all was ready, Mr. Baumgartner handed her the ropes that were attached to each block. "Hold on to these."

He and Jeremy set her on the ground and held on to her elbows.

She lifted up the ropes of one block like a marionette. "That can't be right," she said.

Mr. Baumgartner scratched his beard. "Perhaps we use the ropes to pull you."

"You've never seen them used?" she squealed.

"Who needs to see them used? They have wheels. You strap them on and go."

She arched a brow. "How?"

"Give me the ropes. I'll be the horse. You be the cart."

"Absolutely not. You'll pull my feet right out from under me."

"Then bend your knees and lean forward. Jeremy? You get behind her and push. Give me the ropes, shiksa."

She handed him the ropes. Jeremy grabbed her waist.

"You ready?" Baumgartner asked.

Essie bit her lower lip. "Giddy-up!"

Jeremy pushed, the peddler man pulled and Essie screamed, landing with a *thunk* on her backside, skirts tangled.

Baumgartner let out a string of Yiddish, clearly chastising Jeremy for dropping her.

She raised her hands in the air. "I'm fine, I'm fine. Help me up."

They helped her up.

"You pull, Jeremy," Baumgartner said, grabbing her waist tightly. "Hold on to me, Miss Spreckelmeyer."

Essie locked on to his wrists. "Go!"

Jeremy pulled, Mr. Baumgartner steadied, and they rolled about a foot before her skirts became tangled in the wheels and both she and the peddler ended up in the dirt.

"Botheration!" Essie said. "I need my bicycle skirt. Here, help me up."

They did. She wadded up one side of her skirts and handed them to Harley. The other side she handed to Lawrence, instructing the boys to keep her hem away from the wheels.

They tried again but as soon as Jeremy increased his speed, he jerked her feet forward and they all went tumbling.

Mr. Baumgartner whistled for his dog and positioned him in front of Essie. "Here, Jeremy. Give Miss Spreckelmeyer the ropes and take my place behind her. Shiksa, hold on to Shadrach's tail. He will pull you more smoothly, I think."

"Won't that hurt him?"

"No, no. Won't hurt him at all. Boys, grab on to her skirts."

When all was in readiness, Mr. Baumgartner gave Shadrach the command to go and off they went. This time they made it almost six yards before falling.

"Yes! Yes!" Mr. Baumgartner said. "You have it. Now, again without me. I am going after my wagon."

By the time they reached the edge of town, Essie could travel almost twenty yards without falling.

"We're going to have to stop now, boys, or our secret will be out," she said, breathing heavily.

"Oh, one more time, Miss Essie!" Jeremy said. "Nobody can see us from here. Please?"

"All right. But after this, we really must stop."

It was their best run yet. Shadrach got to going so fast, Essie let go of his tail, Jeremy let go of her waist, and the boys let go of her skirt. Freedom. Blessed freedom. Just before reality struck.

"I don't know how to stop!" she said, rounding a bend in the road. "Look out!" she screamed.

But it was too late. She'd barreled right into Adam Currington, knocking him clear to kingdom come.

CHAPTER | EIGHT

ESSIE LAY FACEDOWN IN the dirt—her scraped chin throbbing, her palms embedded with gravel, a tear in the elbow of her shirtwaist. But her pride suffered a worse blow than all those put together.

Shadrach reached her first, sniffing and whining. Jeremy, Lawrence, and Harley arrived fast on the dog's heels.

"Are you all right, Miss Essie?"

"Bee's knees, you were goin' fast!"

"Do you think Mr. Bum will let me give 'em a try?"

Essie planted her hands beside her shoulders and pushed up. She hadn't risen very far when strong hands clasped her waist and lifted her to her feet.

Her legs wobbled and Adam drew her up against his side. "Woman, what the fiery furnace are you doin'?"

She pushed a hunk of hair out of her eyes. "I'm so terribly sorry, Mr. Currington. Are you all right?"

Chuckling, he smoothed the rest of the hair away from her face. "Well, Miss Essie, I must admit, you shore know how to sweep a man clean off his feet."

The sparkle in his blue-green eyes conveyed genuine teasing rather than the patronizing tolerance townsfolk usually showed her.

She felt herself smiling in response. "I assure you, that was not my intention."

He touched a finger to her chin. "You look like you been fightin' a bobcat in a briar patch."

"I'm fine, thank you. You can let go now."

He continued to hold her. "What are those things you're wearin'?"

"Wheeled feet, I'm afraid."

"You shoulda seen her, mister," Harley said. "Shadrach was pullin' her and—"

Jeremy shoved him. "Hush up. Yer sworn to secrecy."

Harley slapped a hand over his mouth and gave Essie an apologetic glance.

Adam quirked an eyebrow, a slow smile creating deep grooves on either side of his mouth. "Well, now, I like a woman with a few secrets." Leaning over to better see her shoes, he grabbed a handful of skirts and started to lift.

She swatted him.

"Now, Miss Essie," he said, snatching his hand back. "You threw me so high I could've said my prayers before I hit. Surely yer not gonna keep me from seeing these wheeled feet, are ya?"

"I'm not entirely sure it would be proper, Mr. Currington."

He pulled her more tightly against him. "Call me Adam," he whispered in her ear, then placed his arm beneath her knees, scooped her up and sat her on the ground. "Now, show me."

But there was no need to, for the large blocks of wood protruded from beneath her skirts.

Adam pushed aside her hems and turned her foot this way and that. "Woman, has the heat addled your think box? It'd be safer to walk in quicksand than to wear these things."

He began to unbuckle them.

Mr. Baumgartner came around the bend, pulling his wagon to a stop. "Take your hands off her," he said, jumping to the ground.

Adam stilled and rose slowly to his feet. Shadrach growled.

"It's all right, Mr. Baumgartner," Essie said. "Mr. Currington was simply helping me with the buckles."

"Jeremy will help you," the peddler said.

Jeremy immediately loosened the straps and handed the wheeled feet to Essie.

She scrambled up, ignoring the soreness in her muscles. "I plowed over Mr. Currington by accident."

"What are you doing way out here?" Mr. Baumgartner asked him.

"I was lookin' for the judge, actually." Adam turned his attention to her. "I saw you pass by earlier and thought you might know where he is."

"He's not in his office?"

"No, ma'am."

"What's the matter?"

"We were drilling and when we got about a thousand feet down, oil started fillin' the water hole. We tried to seal it off, but it's runnin' uphill, and it'll be deep enough to wash a horse's withers if we don't do somethin' quick."

"Good heavens." She handed the wheeled feet to the peddler. "Can you give us a ride to town?"

"*Ye.*"

"Come on, Mr. Currington." She headed to the back of the wagon, Adam right behind her. "Jeremy, go tell my mother that Mr. Baumgartner is in town and to set an extra plate for supper," she shouted over her shoulder.

Adam tossed her in the wagon, closed the hatch, then leaped over it, knees and feet together. Never had Essie seen such a graceful vault. It took her a moment before she registered his boots were covered in oil.

She quickly grabbed a dripping pan hanging nearby and set it under his feet to keep him from ruining the wagon. The merchandise stacked around them formed a turreted and private alcove. The wheels of the wagon groaned in protest to the pace the peddler set, dirt forming a cloud in their wake.

Adam braced his hand on the floorboards behind her, his shoulder bumping hers with each sway of the cart. He stared at her, but she looked at her lap, out the back of the wagon, and at the various trunks beside her before finally turning to him.

"I must look a fright," she said.

"I do believe you have the longest eyelashes I've ever seen in my whole entire life."

"I do?"

"Yes, ma'am. You surely do."

The wagon continued to rock, her skirts inching toward him with each bump of their bodies. There was no room to scoot away, so she corralled her encroaching hem and tucked it tightly beneath her legs to keep it from touching his trousers.

"Who's the peddler man to you?" he asked.

"Excuse me?"

"Why does he get to sit at your supper table tonight?"

"Oh, I don't know," she said. "Papa has a great deal of respect for God's chosen people. Mr. Baumgartner always stays with us when he comes through town."

"Stays with you? He gets to stay with you, too?"

"Why, yes."

Adam surveyed the interior of the wagon. "Well, I think I might seriously consider becomin' a peddlin' man if it means I would get to sit by you at supper and sleep near you at night."

Essie straightened. "Mr. Currington. You mustn't say such things."

"Now, don't go gettin' all stiff with me, Essie. I'm just a mite jealous, is all."

Jealous? Of what? But the wagon pulled to a stop before she could voice the question.

Adam stuck his head out the back. "I gotta go, sugar."

They'd stopped at the field bordering Twelfth Street where the water well was being drilled. Her father, along with several other town leaders, had crowded around it.

Adam started jogging toward them. "Much obliged for the ride, mister," he said over his shoulder.

Essie began to climb out of the wagon, but Mr. Baumgartner came around back, stopping her. "You'd best stay put, shiksa. Out there is no place for a woman."

"Papa won't mind."

"No, but some of those other *goyim* might."

She hesitated, wanting to see for herself what was happening. But perhaps the peddler was right. She'd been the focus of much speculation after Hamilton had come home with his new bride. And her current disheveled state would definitely raise eyebrows. She didn't savor bringing down any more unfavorable talk.

She'd just have to wait until Papa came home to find out what exactly was going on.

———

Mother took great pains to look after Mr. Baumgartner's dietary restrictions. She prepared the biscuits without lard and kept the milk well away from the meat.

Essie swallowed her bite, then dabbed each corner of her mouth with a cloth. "How much oil is coming out of the well?"

"It's all over the place," Papa answered. "The ground is so saturated it caught fire twice already."

"How?" she asked.

"Umphrey dropped his match on the ground after lighting his cheroot. We'd barely extinguished that blaze when a spark from the forge started up another one."

"Mercy me," Mother said.

"The boys are digging a massive sump a few yards away from the well so they'll have someplace to drain the oil. Hopefully that will help."

Mother began to collect platters from the table. Essie stood to help.

"Is the water well ruined?" the peddler asked.

"No, we just need to keep drilling. Once we get past this oil-bearing stratum, we should find water. It'll slow things down, though."

"Are you finished, Mr. Baumgartner?" Essie asked.

He leaned back and patted his stomach. "Yes, shiksa. It was excellent, as always. *Dank.*"

She removed his plate while Mother stepped to the sideboard and spooned peach cobbler into some bowls.

"Everyone's up in arms over the delay," Papa continued, "but I'm going to send a sample of our crude to Pennsylvania for evaluation."

Mr. Baumgartner twirled his finger in his beard. "Are you thinking to drill for oil instead of water?"

"I think it's worth investigating."

"And if the oil is good, what will you do?"

Papa shared a smile with the peddler.

"Isn't it election year?" Mr. Baumgartner asked.

"It is."

"Are you thinking to hang up your robe and become an oil tycoon?"

Mother paused in serving dessert.

"Oh, that might be a bit premature at this point," Papa answered.

But Essie wasn't fooled. The men dipped their spoons into the warm peach cobbler, its sweet fragrance filling the dining room.

"You're going to drill for oil, aren't you, Papa?"

He didn't answer and she wasn't sure if it was because his mouth was full or because Mother was in the room. But his eyes shone when he looked up at Essie.

She served herself a bowl and sat down.

"What happened to your chin?" Papa asked.

"I took a bit of a tumble this afternoon."

"In the store?"

"No."

"Off your bicycle?"

"No."

"Then where?"

She glanced at Mr. Baumgartner. He paid particular attention to his dessert.

"Out by the creek," she said. "We were freeing Colonel and I, um, stumbled."

Mother tsked. "For heaven's sake, Essie."

"You never could get the snake to eat?" Papa asked.

"I'm afraid not."

"A shame. He was a beauty."

————

Essie hunched over the massive mahogany desk, adding the column of figures one more time. Papa was knee deep in campaigning for another term, which left her with the task of gathering information on oil production.

The "water" well was producing 150 gallons of oil a day, and the analysis from Pennsylvania came back pronouncing the crude as having "definite commercial value." So Papa had organized the Sullivan Oil Company and made extensive leases for mineral rights near the water well. Essie had tried to persuade him to call the company Spreckelmeyer Oil, but he thought his first name sounded better.

He entered the office, loosened his four-in-hand tie and collapsed into a chair opposite Essie. His jovial face showed signs of fatigue and his blue eyes had lost a bit of their sparkle.

"Long day?" she asked.

"My mouth hurts from smiling so much," he answered. "What about you?"

"I finally got those estimates you were waiting for." She slid the papers she was working on toward him. "Excavating the oil would be fairly simple. You could drill a well with two men. It's what to do with the crude afterward that's the problem."

He studied her figures. "This says we could complete a well for about five hundred dollars."

"That's my best guess, anyway, but that doesn't include storage tanks, pipelines, a refinery, and the manpower that goes along with it."

He handed the papers back to her. "All we need to do is hit a gusher or two. Once that happens, word will get out and the oilmen will come running."

"And what will you do with the oil in the meantime?"

"Put it in whatever we can find or dig some more sumps. Too bad we can't find some way to store it in Neblett's old seed house."

"Papa, there's no guarantee you'll find more oil."

"True. But let's assume we do. Think of what it would mean for our town—our entire state."

Essie leaned back in the huge leather chair. "Oil is useless unless it can be turned into kerosene. All the refineries are up north."

"I know." He wound the tie around his hand. "The whole thing appeals to me, is all. Working outside. Getting my hands dirty. Striking that big one."

She propped her arms on the desk. "But you're going to be sixty soon. You can't be taking on something like this at your age."

"Says who? Noah was five hundred before he went into shipbuilding." He shrugged. "Besides, I think the discovery on Twelfth Street bears looking into."

They were kindred spirits, the two of them. She understood his desire to take a risk, to challenge the odds, to try something new.

"This is a bit more serious than betting a little pocket money on Mr. Mitton's horses," she said.

"A bit."

"How are you going to do all this and still fulfill your civic duties?"

"Maybe God has something else in mind for us both."

He said nothing further, just held her stare.

She began to shake her head. "Oh no. I'm a woman. Working in a mercantile is one thing. Running an oil company is something else altogether. Mother would have a fit."

"You're the best man for the job. I'll handle Mother."

"And the men in town?"

"I'll handle them, too." He nodded toward her chin. "You want to tell me what really happened while you were releasing Colonel?"

She touched the scab that had started to form. "I tried out some wheeled feet that Mr. Baumgartner had in his wagon."

He absorbed that bit of information, and the twinkle that had been absent when he'd entered the office was back in full force. "You trading in your bicycle?"

"No. Just supplementing."

He chuckled. "You better not let your mother catch you."

She raised a brow. "I thought you could handle Mother?"

"I can . . . up to a point." He stood and walked to the door. "I've arranged for a man by the name of Davidson to come down and look the oil field over."

"Where's he from?"

"Pennsylvania. He'll be here within the week."

———

If Mr. John Davidson was surprised to see Essie accompanying him and Papa to the fields, he didn't say so. Nor did he include her in any of the conversation.

But Essie preferred it that way. Being invisible had its uses. It allowed her to size him up as they walked the one block from the railway station to Twelfth Street, and Papa always appreciated the unguarded impressions she collected due to being ignored.

The oil scout wore no suit, coat or tie, but simply a cotton shirt and belted trousers. Mud frosted his boots and hat, while a neatly trimmed moustache made him look older than she suspected he truly was.

"Will you be doing sample digs or running tests in the ground?" Papa asked.

"Neither. I'll just be looking."

"For what?"

"Well, there's no real science to it. I personally use a little geology, a little doodlebugology, and a little common sense."

"Doodlebugology?"

"That's a method oil scouts employ by using wiggle sticks, forked limbs, doodlebugs, that sort of thing." He smiled. "There's one man by the name of Griffith who puts this platelike thing in his mouth that has coiled springs protruding from it. I can't tell you much about its workings, but when he stands over oil, there's a little lever that turns around. And that's where he recommends his customers drill."

Essie and Papa exchanged a glance.

"I mostly look at the surface of the field and the vegetation in the area. You go to any oil field and you'll see it differs a little bit from the surrounding territory."

A strong, unpleasant odor coming from the oil began to pervade the air about the time they reached the intersection of Dallas and Twelfth. Turning south on Twelfth, they continued down the plank sidewalk, past the Poker Palace and Rosenburg's Saloon.

Men wove around them, horses waited patiently at hitching rails, and someone on a piano played "Do, Do, My Huckleberry, Do." Mr. Riddles came out of a domino parlor, gave her a sidelong glance and tipped his hat. Most decent women wouldn't be seen east of Beaton Street, but she was with Papa, and folks were used to her coming and going as she pleased.

The sidewalk ended, and several yards later the field began. Mr. Davidson tramped right across the oil-covered ground. A giant earthen pit on the east side of the field held thousands of gallons of oil, with more trickling in.

Mr. Davidson walked the perimeter of the field, then picked up a piece of wood the size of a broom handle. He peeled off the bark and started jabbing it into the ground, working it down as far as he could before moving to the next spot.

The water well at this location had been finished, finally breaking through the oil-bearing strata and into water at around 2,500 feet. Adam and the rest of the crew had moved on to drill the second and third wells on the other side of town.

Mr. Davidson tossed down his stick and headed toward Essie and Papa.

"What do you think?" Papa asked.

The oilman looked out on the field like a mother hen preening over her chicks. "Well, Judge, if it were mine, I'd be drilling on it before the week was out."

C H A P T E R | N I N E

ESSIE BUMPED DOWN BEATON Street, pedaling Pegasus—Peg, for short—over the old bois d'arc blocks paving the street. The wooden surface alleviated one problem—dust—and created another—discomfort for every vehicle traveling down the jarring road.

Turning east onto Jefferson Avenue, she waved at Mr. Mitton as she passed his wagon yard. She longed to pull over and admire the thoroughbreds he boarded in stables so fine the locals referred to them as "Mitton's Hotel," but she needed to speak with the artesian well drillers. She continued on past the icehouse, the county jail, and the Anheuser-Busch Beer Depot, the smell of horses from the wagon yard still lingering in the air.

At the edge of town she spotted two men kicking down a well while Adam watched, wiping the back of his neck with a bandanna. Sweat rolled off the cable-tool boys as they each placed a foot in the stirrups hanging from a fifteen-foot log.

The rig sat underneath a high tripod of poles and looked like a child's seesaw made with a tree trunk instead of a flat piece of wood. She noted the fulcrum was way off-center, and one end of the log was fastened to the ground.

The other end of the log—where the men in the stirrups were—projected up into the air at about a thirty-degree angle and was so far away from the fulcrum that it held a surprising amount of spring. The men grabbed on to the tree and threw their weight into the stirrups, forcing a heavy iron bit, which dangled from a cable between them, into the ground to break up a little of the earth.

They quickly repeated this motion over and over until one man took a break and Adam replaced him. Moisture stained Adam's blue shirt beneath his arms and between his shoulder blades. Essie stopped Peg and laid her on the ground. Brushing dust from her calf-length split skirt, she advanced on the men. "Good afternoon," she called.

The drilling stopped, and Adam jumped from the stirrup to approach her. "Miss Essie. Aren't you as purty as a little red wagon?"

She smiled. "I don't believe I've ever been compared to a wagon before, Mr. Currington."

He made no effort to hide his perusal of her, from her red-trimmed Benwood hat all the way down to her bicycle boots. "You ever seen a little red wagon?" he asked.

"Of course."

"Then you know there ain't nothin' purtier."

"I know no such thing," she said, shaking her head and passing him by without pause.

He hastened his stride to keep up with her. "You ride that thing all the way from your house?" he asked, glancing over his shoulder at her riding machine.

"I most certainly did." She stopped a few feet away from the rig. "How do you do?"

The other two men doffed their hats.

"Miss Essie, this is Mr. Pugh and Mr. Upchurch. Fellas, this is Miss Spreckelmeyer, the judge's daughter."

Mr. Upchurch's whip-thin body surprised Essie. She would have thought drilling required more muscle. Perhaps his legs, hidden in the folds of his waist-overalls, were thicker than the rest of him. The removal of his hat revealed a head shaped like an egg and just as smooth. What hair he lacked on top he made up for with his moustache.

Mr. Pugh, a stocky and solid man, scowled, bringing his black eyebrows together in such a way that she couldn't tell where one brow ended and the other began.

"Gentlemen," she said, "I'm sorry to interrupt, but I wanted to contract you for another job when you are finished with this one."

They glanced at one another.

"I would like you to drill a well about two hundred yards south of the one on Twelfth Street. This one would not be for water, however, but for oil."

A beat of silence. Mr. Pugh recovered first. "We have us another job already scheduled. Over in Waco. Besides, we drill water wells, not oil wells." He crammed his hat back on and began bailing loose rock and dirt out of the boring hole.

"How long will you be in Waco?" she asked.

"Longer than you wanna wait," Pugh answered.

Mr. Upchurch remained motionless, hat in hand.

Essie turned to Adam. "I need two drillers. Do you know where I might find some?"

"Who's providing the grubstake?"

She hesitated. "The payroll, you mean? My father, but I'll be running the project."

He rubbed his jaw. "Don't you think your pa's saddle is slippin' a bit? This is cotton and cattle country. The judge has as much chance of a future in crude as a one-legged man in a kickin' contest. If it's oil he's interested in, he'd be better off in cottonseed oil."

"We're not looking for a business partner, Mr. Currington. We're looking for drillers."

The men exchanged glances.

"Never mind," she sighed. "I'm sorry to have disturbed you."

Adam grabbed her wrist. "Whoa there, filly. Not so fast. Rufus?" he asked, still holding on to her. "What if you and Arnold went to Waco without me? Then I could see about rustling up somebody else to help me with Miss Spreckelmeyer's well. What do you think?"

Upchurch rubbed his egg-shaped head with a handkerchief and looked at Pugh.

"You saying you'll work for a *woman*?" Pugh asked.

Adam scrutinized her again. She tugged her hand free.

"Now, Rufus. I wouldn't be workin' for just any woman. I'd be workin' for this here woman. And I have to tell ya, the thought don't bother me none a'tall."

Mr. Pugh gave a sound of disgust. "Just what are me and Arnold supposed to do, then?"

"You'll find somebody. Same as me."

"What are you gonna drill with?"

Adam thought a minute. "He's got a point there, Miss Essie. They'll be taking this rig with 'em. I'd have to build you one of your own."

"That would be fine, Mr. Currington. Can you come by the house tomorrow to settle on the details?"

"It'd be my pleasure."

———

Adam arrived late in the day, standing on Essie's porch, spit and polished in a crisp white shirt, red neckerchief, and blue denim trousers with brass rivets at the pocket corners.

He removed his cowboy hat. "Afternoon, Miss Essie."

"Mr. Currington. Please, won't you come in?"

She led him to Papa's office and poured them each a glass of lemonade. "Thank you for coming."

He guzzled the beverage in one prolonged swig. Head back, eyes closed, Adam's apple bobbing. Swiping his mouth with his sleeve, he sighed. "Ah, darlin', my throat was drier than a tobacco box. Thank ya."

She accepted his glass. "Would you like some more?"

"Not right now."

"Well." She took a sip of hers, then set it on the tray. "I've put together a list of materials I'm assuming we'll need to construct a rig, but I thought you should take a look at it and see if I left anything off."

He set his hat in a chair and perused the list she gave him.

"The lumber I'll purchase from Mr. Whiteselle," she said. "The cable and drill bit can be made down at Central Blacksmith Shop."

"And the stirrups?"

"The carriage and harness shop."

He handed the paper back to her. "You're gonna need the smithy to make a few more down-hole tools," he said.

"Like what?" She picked up Papa's pen and dipped it in an inkwell.

"Metal connectors, rope sockets, a sinker bar, jars, and an auger stem."

Still standing, Essie leaned over the massive desk, scribbling furiously on the parchment, forgoing the precise lettering she'd learned at the Corsicana Female College.

Adam hovered over her shoulder, watching. "Make sure the lumberyard gives you hemlock, ash, or hickory for the spring pole and something sturdy, like oak, for the fulcrum."

After several moments, she replaced Papa's pen and blew on the paper. When she straightened, Adam stayed put, his eyes a translucent mosaic of blue and green.

"Why do you do that?" she asked, baffled.

"What?"

"Crowd me."

"Am I crowdin' you?"

"You know you are."

"I don't mean to. It's just that when I stand right close I can smell them cloves you use in your toilet."

She caught her breath and glanced at the door, open only a crack. "You're not supposed to notice that kind of thing," she whispered.

A smile lifted one side of his mouth. "I notice everything about you, Miss Essie."

"Why?"

Shaking his head, he took a step back, putting a proper distance between them. "The fellas in this town are either blind or fools. Maybe both."

She frowned, searching his expression. "Your pardon?"

He pointed to the list on the desk. "We're gonna need a weight to anchor the butt end of the spring pole. If you don't want to pay the smithy to make you one, I can see about finding a heavy boulder or somethin'."

"Do you think you could come with me when I place these orders?" she asked, glancing at the parchment. "That way we'll be sure to get exactly what we need."

"You tell me when and I'll be there."

———

The clink of iron reached Essie and Adam well before they arrived at Mr. Fowler's Central Blacksmith Shop. They paused just inside the dark, cavernous building, allowing their eyes to adjust. A blanket of heat and hazy smoke swaddled them, along with the smell of burning coals.

With his back to them, Mr. Fowler worked the bellows while the tip of his poker turned from red to white and flames danced. A dirty, once-white apron string wrapped Fowler's waist like Cleopatra's asp, dividing his blue shirt from his waist-overalls. Releasing the bellows, he removed the iron from the flame and hammered on the hot metal, sending sparks in all directions. He'd barely managed half a dozen strikes before having to return the poker to the fire.

"Howdy, Miss Spreckelmeyer," he said, looking up and moving toward them. He gave Adam the once-over. "And you're one of them water-well drillers, ain't ya?"

"Good morning, Mr. Fowler," Essie said. "And yes, this is Mr. Currington. He's going to stay on and build another rig, but this one will be for Papa."

When the men leaned in to shake hands, Essie was surprised at how much taller Adam was. She'd always thought of Mr. Fowler as a huge man. But she realized now the bulk on him was more from tickling the anvil than from height.

"Your pa has a hankerin' for a water well out in his own backyard, then?"

"Not exactly," she said, glancing at Adam. "He's going to drill for oil."

Mr. Fowler stared at her a second, then doubled over with laughter. She schooled her face, knowing full well his reaction would have been vastly different had Papa been the one stating their purpose.

"Now, Mr. Fowler," she began.

He silenced her with a raised hand, sobering, his mirth replaced by a mask of professional gravity. She motioned to Adam, who held their lists and diagrams, when out of the corner of her eye she caught Mr. Fowler cracking another smile.

She arched an eyebrow.

"Sorry," he said.

There were other smithies in town, but J. T. Fowler was among the most capable and enterprising. And once he realized she was serious, he would not only fill her order but he'd do it quickly, expertly, and with respect.

"Here's what we're gonna need," Adam said. He spread the piece of parchment on a rough wooden counter and began to explain everything. Mr. Fowler nodded and asked a few questions, his amusement vanishing as he became absorbed in the details. When they had finished, he gave Essie a conciliatory smile.

"I'll get started on this right away," he said.

Outside, the sun was so bright Essie shaded her eyes. Adam glanced back over his shoulder at the blacksmith's shop, shaking his head.

"Thank you, Mr. Currington."

"Call me Adam. And it was my pleasure," he said, winking as they headed down Eleventh Street.

"Shall we go see about the stirrups?" she asked.

"We can do that, but Mr. Weidmann's kitchen is one block over on Collin Street. How 'bout we take a detour and have us some o' that fruitcake he makes? I can smell it clear from here."

As he said the words, her nose registered the delectable aroma of fresh bread and something indefinably sweet.

"It's still morning. Won't you spoil your dinner?"

"No, ma'am. I've found there's never a bad time for a visit to Mr. Weidmann's bakery."

Town activity had picked up with the advancing morning. Wagons trundled up and down the street, stirring up dust, horses cutting between them. The stray tabby, Cat, darted past Essie and Adam. Men conversed about everything from the price of cotton to the November election to the abandoned seed house.

Being the judge's daughter, Essie knew most everyone, so they were forced to stop and chat a few times along the way. She introduced Adam as one of the artesian well drillers, explaining he'd decided to stay in town awhile longer.

The townspeople looked at him askance, displaying forced politeness.

"I don't believe the folks of your town like me very much," he whispered after they broke away from a conversation with the school superintendent and the wainwright.

"It's not that. They would simply prefer it if you had been born here."

"How long you reckon it'll take before they forgive me for that slight?"

"Oh, I would think twenty years should do the trick."

He shook his head. "More like forty, you mean."

They shared a smile, and he opened the bakery door.

"Ach, look at this fine German *mädchen* who comes to see me." Mr. Weidmann circled around his table to take hold of Essie's shoulders and kiss both her cheeks. "*Wie geht es Ihnen,* Fräulein Spreckelmeyer?"

"I'm fine, Mr. Weidmann. And you?"

"I am good. Very, very good." He turned, grabbing Adam, and gave him the same greeting he'd given Essie, bringing a shade of red to the cowboy's cheeks. "You watch out for this one, Fräulein. Eternally hungry for my fruitcake, he is. Pesters me night and day."

"Is that so, Mr. Currington?"

"I'm afraid it is, ma'am," Adam said, patting his stomach.

"*Ja,*" said Mr. Weidmann. "I will get you some."

The bakery was more of a kitchen than anything else, but it had a small table pushed into one corner. Adam pulled out her chair and she sat, relishing the smells of vanilla, apricots, dates and pineapple.

Mr. Weidmann brought them each a large slice of cake resting on brown paper. "I am sorry, but I have no plates or forks."

"It's all right. This will be fine." Essie broke off a portion with her fingers, while Adam lifted his entire piece and took a large bite.

"So tell me, Mr. Currington, how does a cowboy end up drilling water wells?"

"Just decided to do somethin' different, I guess."

"But why?"

He took another big bite, slowly chewing the confection, his carefree manner diminishing. "It happened a while back."

Mr. Weidmann washed and chopped cherries on the other side of the room, paying them no mind. So for now, the two of them had the place to themselves.

"What happened?" she asked.

"I grew up on a ranch. My pa was a cowboy and my grandpa before him. So I been steer ropin' since I was ankle-high to a June bug."

She took another nibble, waiting.

"A couple of years ago, a big ranchman in Gonzales County asked me to be the trail boss for his yearly drive from San Antonio to Abilene, Kansas. It was my job to plan the route, to decide when to stop, where to bed down, where to cross creeks, that kinda thing."

"I've heard that only the top cowhands make those kinds of trips."

"I reckon that's so." He picked at a splintered piece of wood on the rough table. "We had two point men ridin' up front directing the lead steer, then the swing and flank boys along the sides, with the tail riders bringin' up the drag."

"How many were in the herd?"

"Eighteen hundred. Everythin' went fine 'til we reached Waco. Then a gully washer came. It rained 'nough to have everybody wishin' they'd grown fins instead of feet."

"What did you do?"

"All that rain made it too dangerous to cross the Brazos. We had no choice but to wait 'til the river went down. We lost so much time, I decided we'd go east to Shreveport instead o' Kansas. Last thing I wanted was to get stuck in the middle o' winter. Some o' the other fellas disagreed, so I told 'em I'd get the herd there in good shape or I'd take off my spurs and never make another roundup."

She rested her hands in her lap, no longer interested in the fruitcake before her.

He scratched the top of his head, causing his blond hair to stand up a little on the right. "We got across the Brazos okay, but then Spanish Tick Fever took hold of the herd and the farther we went, the more we left behind. Dead."

"Oh no."

"By the time we hit the Trinity River, we only had five hundred left." He swallowed. "And when we reached Shreveport, we had fewer than a hundred."

"But that wasn't your fault."

"I was the trail boss, and I'd given my word. So I sold my horse and saddle."

She gripped her hands, hiding them in the folds of her skirt. A cowboy's horse was more than a source of transportation. It was his constant companion. A friend he could talk to and confide in.

More than his mount, though, the cowboy prized his saddle—and quite often it cost more than the horse itself. It was undeniably the very last thing he parted with.

"I'm so sorry, Adam."

He pushed the crumbs of his fruitcake around with his fingers. "You gonna eat that?" he asked, indicating her abandoned piece.

She slid it toward him. "Is that when you started drilling?"

"No. I got a job on a wagon train carryin' goods to Memphis, Tennessee. Then

I started loadin' and unloadin' merchandise for the riverboats. Did that 'til about six months ago."

"What happened then?"

"A showboat pulled in and I met up with Pugh and Upchurch."

The last of the cake was gone. She folded her paper in half, then in half again, trapping the crumbs inside. She did the same for his, wondering what his father's and grandfather's reactions had been.

If they had taught him everything they knew, how could they have let him give up something he so clearly loved? But to ask would be intrusive.

A woman came in to place an order with Mr. Weidmann. Adam dropped a coin on the table, then he and Essie slipped out. This time Essie didn't reprimand him when he took her elbow and stayed close enough to smell the cloves she used in her bath and for her to smell the Yankee shaving soap they sold at the Slap Out.

CHAPTER | TEN

WATCHING ADAM CONSTRUCT THE rig these last few weeks reminded Essie of her embroidering. Just as every stitch she took revealed more of the final picture, each piece of lumber Adam added gave more definition to the rig.

She suggested they hire Jeremy as helper. If scrawny Mr. Upchurch could manage it, then Jeremy certainly could. Adam protested, though, saying the teener was nothing but a farm boy.

Her crossed arms betrayed her determination. "You'll have to train him, then."

Jeremy was eager and hardworking, as she knew he would be, and so proud of earning ten whole cents a day. For all his previous bluster, Adam set about training the boy as if he hoped to make a top hand out of him, never hazing or harassing, always answering his questions patiently and offering plenty of encouragement.

Adam tightened the second stirrup they'd hung on the spring pole. "You ready to give it a whirl, Boll Weevil?"

Jeremy grabbed on to the pole. "You say when."

"Go!"

They jumped into the stirrups, and the pole bowed down and up, responding to their lead. The shade of a bois d'arc tree in the corner of the field didn't quite reach the workers. Some of its bright yellow leaves fell to the ground—many blowing into a freshly dug oil sump next to their new rig.

Essie watched the man and boy bounce a few more times, then clapped. "It's working! All we need now are the cable tools."

They stepped out of the stirrups.

"How long before Mr. Fowler's got 'em ready?" Jeremy asked. He looked as if he'd grown four inches over the summer, but only in a vertical direction. He'd not added any meat or muscle to his spindly frame, and his loose clothing made him look even thinner.

"He said he'd have the tools by first o' next week," Adam answered.

The three of them admired their handiwork before Essie finally stirred herself. "Well, Jeremy, I guess you'll have yourself a few days off before the real work begins." She handed him his first wages.

"That's right," Adam said. "And come Monday, you be ready to sweat like a hog butcher in frost time."

"I'll be here and ya won't hear me complainin' none." Jeremy palmed the bag of coins, testing its weight. "Fer now, though, I'm gonna go over to the Slap Out and get the young'uns a sassperilly candy. Boy, won't they be surprised!"

He took off running, shirttail flapping, skinny legs pumping. They watched him disappear across the open field, down the dirt road and on into town.

"You sure were right about him, Essie. He works hard as any I seen and was all swoll up like a carbuncle just now, wasn't he?"

"He did seem pleased. I wish I could see the expression on those children's faces when he comes home with candy. I imagine it'll be their first."

"First? They ain't never had candy?"

"I wouldn't think so."

Adam loosened the bandanna from around his neck, wiped his face, then looked at the now-empty road. "Yes, sir, that boll weevil 'uld do to ride the river with."

She smiled. "Well, would you like to follow me to the house and I'll give you your wages, as well?"

Mischief transformed his face. "Actually, ya know what I really wanna do?"

She found herself shaking her head.

"I wanna ride your wheeler. Would ya mind?"

Glancing at Peg, she worried her lip. "It's not as easy as it looks. You can't just swing into the saddle and say 'giddy-up.' "

"So teach me."

"What?"

"Teach me."

"Here?" she squeaked.

He scanned the area. "No, we probably ought to go out there where you practice on your wheeled feet when you think nobody's lookin'."

She took a short breath. "How do you know about that?"

With a shrewd smile, he took her elbow and steered her toward her bike. "I already done told you, I notice everything about you."

———

"The knack of balancing is really all that needs to be *learned*," Essie said, holding Peg by her handlebars. "The rest comes with patience, perseverance, and practice."

Adam stood with one hip cocked, his arms crossed in front of his chest and an indulgent smirk on his face. The breeze stirred up a few fallen leaves and shook more from the branches above them.

"You're not taking this with the proper amount of seriousness," she said. "I don't want you to fall and hurt yourself."

"Just show me how it works, Essie."

He rolled up the sleeves of his blue cotton shirt, then made sure it was securely tucked in to the denim trousers hugging his hips. Dust dulled the shine of his big silver belt buckle, but it still managed to capture a glint from the setting sun. She could tell how proud he was of it by the way he hooked his thumb behind the belt.

She wondered if he ever wore suspenders like the other men. If he had, she'd never seen him.

"Well, first," she said, "I'm going to have you coast down this gentle slope. When you take your seat and proceed, don't grasp the handles too tightly, and *never* lean on them."

The sun blazed onto the grass-covered incline, but the ground was still a bit moist from recent rains.

Adam straddled the vehicle, grabbing the handles as if they were horns he had to wrestle with.

"It's not a bull, Adam. Relax your grip."

He complied.

"Now, if you lose your balance and start to fall, touch the ground with your toe on whichever side the machine is falling to right yourself again."

He nodded.

"Remember, don't use the pedals. The incline will give you plenty of speed for balancing and steering."

"Relax my hands and no usin' the stirrups."

"Exactly. Are you ready?"

An excited smile spread across his face. "My heart's beatin' faster 'n a grasshopper in a chicken yard."

"You don't have to try it, Adam."

"Step aside, ma'am. I got some dust to churn up."

Releasing the handlebars, she backed away. In one fluid motion, he spread his legs wide and rolled down the hill in perfect balance, as if he'd been riding for months.

It had never occurred to her that he would manage to stay balanced so long. But he had, and in another couple of yards the slope would turn into a full-fledged hill.

"Whoooo-wee!" he hollered, his momentum picking up. He stayed aright even as he accelerated before finally hitting a rut and flying through the air, bicycle and all.

He tightened his grip and tried to hug the machine with his body the way a person would when jumping a horse.

"Don't lean!" Essie cried. "Angle your legs out! Keep the wheels straight!"

But he curled into the bicycle as if man and machine were one, then crashed to the ground. The crunch of metal blended with his gasp as the jarring contact of wheels and ground knocked the wind out of him.

He swerved out of control, fell in a tangled mess and slid down the hill before slowing to a stop just feet before he'd have collided into a tree stump.

Essie hiked up her skirts and raced to him, slipping on the grass. "Oh my goodness!"

He lay motionless on his back, his silver buckle winking in the sun.

"Adam, Adam!" She skidded to a stop and fell to her knees. Moisture seeped from the damp ground through the fabric of her brown skirt and petticoats where she knelt. "Can you hear me? Are you all right?" She touched his forehead, brushing hair out of his eyes.

Groaning, he tried to spit a leaf out of his mouth. She snatched it away.

"That saddle o' yours hit me in the caboose and sent me fer a flight to Mars."

"Don't move," she sighed in relief. "Just tell me what hurts."

He opened one eye. "I'm achin' in a lot o' new places."

She swept a quick glance down the length of him but saw no obvious injuries. "Anyplace in particular?"

Both eyes opened. The sun reduced his pupils to mere pinpoints. The rays of his blue-green irises were like the spreading of peacock feathers.

"You gonna kiss it and make it better?" he asked.

Her hand stilled, but her heart thar-rumped. "I'm serious, Adam."

"You think I'm not?" He turned his head and gently nipped the inside of her wrist, prompting a reaction in places far removed from her hand.

She snatched it away. "You mustn't say—or do—things like that."

"Why? Because I'm the hired hand and you're the boss's daughter?"

"Because I'm a woman, you're a man, and only engaged couples do such things."

"That ain't so, Essie. Lots o' couples do it, and not 'cause they're engaged, but because they like each other. And it feels real nice. And it chases away the loneliness. You ever get lonely, Essie?"

Yes.

He recaptured her hand, nuzzling it like a horse searching for a sweet, the stubble on his cheek abrading her palm.

"Them married folks," he said, "they never think about us. What it's like to go without bein' touched. Without bein' loved." He raised himself up into a sitting position. "You ever been kissed?"

Once.

"I'd shore like to kiss you, girl."

And try as she might, she could not deny her interest in kissing him, too. How could she not? She'd never seen a more beautiful man. And never had one made her insides jump the way he did. Certainly Hamilton hadn't. Not even once.

And Adam was right. She did grow tired of relying on stray animals and the occasional child for a scrap of affection. She longed for more. Much more. But no matter what he said, contact of a personal nature was not done unless the man had spoken to the woman's father first.

But she'd let Hamilton kiss her and he'd not spoken to Papa . . . or to her. So perhaps couples did share such intimacies without parental permission.

She reviewed in her mind some of the young courting couples in town. Shirley Bunting and Charlie Ballew. Flossie Shaw and Dewey Taylor. Lillie Sue Gulick and Hugh Grimmet. Every single one of those girls had been looked at the way Adam now looked at her.

He placed a hand at the base of her head, tunneled his fingers into her hair twist, and pulled her toward him. She did not resist.

"Close your eyes," he whispered before covering her lips with his.

This was *nothing* like the kiss Hamilton had given her. It was all movement and coaxing and lushness. She rested her hands against his shoulders to keep from falling.

He grasped her waist and slid her close. It happened so quickly, she had no time to protest.

Wrapping his arms fully around her, he released her lips only as long as it took for him to angle his head in the opposite direction and swoop in to kiss her again.

She completely gave herself over to the experience, relishing the warmth and pleasure it induced.

"Open your mouth," he murmured.

"Wha—?" She never finished the question, shocked into stillness. He gave her no quarter, no time to assimilate, no time to react. Only took and gave. Gave and took. And, oh my, but it was heady.

Breaking the bond between their lips, he buried his face in her neck. He smelled of salt and sweat and man. She hugged his head against her, registering the texture of his thick, beautiful hair, the feel of his day-old beard scratching her skin.

"I'll be hanged, but you're sweet," he said, finally releasing her.

And when he did, her sanity returned. She scurried back like a crab, plopped down, then touched her hair, appalled to find it tumbling about her shoulders.

"It's all right, darlin'," he said, scooting himself next to her again. "Easy, easy. I'm not going to hurt you."

He reached for her.

She grabbed his wrist. "No," she breathed. "We must stop."

He froze, his arm caught between the two of them by her hand. "Nothin' will happen, Essie. I just wanna kiss you a little longer."

"Nothing will happen?" She released him and pressed a hand to her chest. "Something is already happening."

Groaning, he pulled her back within his embrace. "Don't say no, girl, please." He showered quick kisses along her hairline and tugged on her ear with his lips.

She slid her eyes closed, longing to give in. He latched on to her neck with his mouth. The delicious reaction that provoked was frightening and unexpected.

She shoved him away and jumped to her feet, stumbling backwards.

He stayed on the ground watching her, propping himself up with one hand, his eyes simmering with sensual promises. She turned and raced up the hill, leaving him, the bicycle, and a temptation so strong that surely she'd burn in hell for even contemplating surrender.

———

Essie had to force herself not to run down the deserted dirt road on the outskirts of town. She slipped behind a tree to straighten her loose hair—but it was her loose behavior that made her hands shake.

Her mother would expire on the spot if she were to ever find out. Essie could not even imagine what kind of retribution such a tawdry deed would provoke.

Once, when she was a girl, she had overheard one of the men in town say Widow Edmundson had an itch, and all his friends had laughed in response.

Later that week, she'd seen their parrot, Joe, scratching himself with his beak. So she'd taught it to say, "Joe has an itch."

Joe started saying it all the time. And when he did, Mother would turn redder than blazes and Papa would muffle his amusement. Essie had to break a switch off a tree, then bring it to her mother for a whipping.

Essie never understood what she'd done wrong. She'd taught Joe to say lots of things and had never gotten in trouble. But now, with the aftereffects of that kiss still humming through her body, she had a very good idea what exactly an itch was.

Mortification seeped into her being. What if Adam told the men in town that *she*, the town's old maid, had an itch? Tears sprang to her eyes. Surely he wouldn't.

Dear Lord, please, please, don't let him tell anyone. I promise not to ever, ever do that again. Just don't let anyone find out. Especially not Mother.

She'd almost reached the bend in the road that would take her into Corsicana. She slowed her step, knowing she couldn't just brazenly walk through town. Someone would see her and they'd know. Know what she'd been doing.

She brushed the dirt from her skirt but could do nothing about the two spots of moisture covering her knees. Nor could she wipe away the shame of her wanton response to Adam's kisses.

Stopping, she looked back over her shoulder, but Adam was nowhere to be seen. She'd half expected him to ride up on her bicycle and poke fun at her.

Because clearly he'd kissed before. Probably more than once or twice. And clearly, she had not. So why did that make her feel embarrassed when she'd been taught such virtue was a badge of honor?

But she knew why. By her very nature she wanted to be the best. At everything. Including kissing. And she would never know how she measured up, because she would never ask. And she would never do it again.

CHAPTER | ELEVEN

C UTTING BACK AND FORTH through the woods around town had made Essie's route home three times as long, but she didn't begrudge one single step, thankful for the protection the trees and brush had offered. She stood within their shelter, gauging the final leg of her journey. It was a good hundred yards to her house, and wide open.

She removed what few pins she had left in her hair, stuck them in her mouth, then finger-combed her hair once again, pulling it together at the back.

When she had all within her grasp, she twisted until it coiled up like a snake against her head and then transferred the pins into strategic spots. The style was severe and sloppily done. Anyone who knew her well would know she never wore it this way, but it would have to do.

She stepped into the open just as Mrs. Lockhart rounded the bend. Would the woman see something different? Something she oughtn't? Essie forced herself to walk in a sedate manner.

"My dear, dear girl," Mrs. Lockhart said, "how have you been?"

"Very well, thank you. And you?"

The elderly woman touched Essie's arm. "Such a surprise how Mr. Crook married up so fast to that woman from Dallas. I haven't had a moment alone with you since. How are you managing without him?"

"My work in the Slap Out was temporary from the start. I was just helping out until he could find someone permanent."

Mrs. Lockhart tsked. "You needn't feed me that twiddle-twaddle. I know a budding romance when I see one." She shook her head. "Why, look at you, so stiff and stern." She patted Essie's hand. "I always have preferred the stories where the woman wounds the man, not the other way around."

Essie glanced at her home. So close, yet so far. "Yes, well, perhaps the new Mrs. Crook will be able to recommend one from the catalog for you."

"Very commendable of you to say so. Commendable, indeed." She tilted her head. "Have you read the book I loaned you?"

"No, ma'am. Not yet."

The woman brightened. "Well, you must do so right away. Might teach you a thing or two about how to hold on to a man once you have him."

A spurt of defensiveness surfaced, giving Essie an overwhelming urge to explain exactly who had left whom this very afternoon, but she didn't dare.

"Don't give up, dear. However, you must desist from that ridiculous hairstyle.

Much too off-putting for attracting a man." She glanced up and down Essie's frame. "And these tomboyish ways of yours have gone on long enough. Why, just look at your skirt. A mess, to be sure. I insist you read Mrs. Clay's novel. She's all-knowing about these things." Mrs. Lockhart punctuated her pronouncement with a tap of her cane, then continued on her way.

Essie made no pretense about moving sedately any longer. She all but ran the rest of the way home, flew through the front door and right into her mother.

"What on earth?"

"Oh, I'm sorry, Mother. I wasn't watching where I was going."

Her mother took Essie in with a glance, and her eyes filled with misgiving. "What has happened?"

"Nothing. Nothing at all."

"What happened to your hair?"

Essie touched the back of her bun. Still intact. "It came loose when I was out riding and I lost some of my pins. This was the best I could do under the circumstances."

Her mouth tightened. "You fell off your machine, didn't you?"

Essie said nothing.

"Where? In town?"

"No."

"Well, thank heaven for that, anyway." She continued to examine Essie, disappointment evident in her expression. "I have prayed and prayed about the way you cavort about town on that thing. Have you no shame whatsoever? Do you ever wonder why you are an old maid?"

Essie sucked in her breath.

"I'm sorry to be so blunt, but it is time to face the facts. Look at you. Thirty years old and not a prospect in sight. A confirmed spinster. And it's no wonder when you drag in with mud on your skirt and your hair in shambles."

Essie swallowed back the hurt. "My hair is not in shambles."

"It is! And do you even care? Is that bicycle so important you'd rather have it than a man? Than babies of your own?"

Essie flinched. She would, of course, rather have a man and a family, but must she really choose between that and her love of the outdoors? Surely it wasn't an either/or decision.

"Is it something I've done to make you act this way?" Mother asked.

"Of course not. It's nothing to do with you."

"It's everything to do with me. You're my daughter. A reflection of me and all I stand for. And what about your father? If you haven't a care for what people think of you or me, what about him? He holds a very important position in this town. Have you no appreciation for how hard he works? For the constant insinuations he puts up with on your behalf?"

Try as she might, Essie could not ignore the sting her mother's words inflicted.

She knew from long experience that keeping silent was the quickest way to end these "discussions." But they never ceased to hurt. Deeply.

Mother sighed. "Your father wants to see you right away in his office, but do not even think about going in there until you have at the very least put your hair to rights."

"Yes, Mother." She hurried up the stairs.

———

Essie sat in one of the upholstered armchairs opposite Papa's desk, catching him up on their progress.

Mother stuck her head in the office. "Mr. Currington's here." She stepped back and allowed him entrance before Essie had a chance to compose herself.

He'd cleaned up, shaved, and combed back his hair, though it was still wet. How many pairs of those riveted, double-seamed denim trousers did he own?

She brushed a dried piece of dirt from her sleeve, wishing she'd had time to do more than re-pin her hair and change her skirt. But Papa had called for her before she'd had a chance to wash. As a result, she felt like a goose to Adam's swan.

His cowboy boots thumped against the hardwood floors as he crossed the room to shake Papa's hand. "Sir."

"Essie tells me you've made quite the progress."

"Yes, sir." He pinned her with his gaze. "I'm glad she's pleased with me."

Feeling a slow blush move up her neck, she glanced at Papa. He, fortunately, did not notice the double entendre, nor even look her way.

"She's been singing your praises all afternoon," he said.

"Has she now? Well, I'm mighty glad to hear that."

She scrutinized the papers she was holding, praying that she could make it through this meeting without exposing her feelings.

"Have a seat, son."

"Thank ya, sir." He sat in the chair beside her, boots together, knees wide apart. "I stopped by the smithy's on my way over."

Adam went on to explain to Papa how the down-hole tools worked, when Mr. Fowler would have them ready, and when they should break ground.

"Will Jeremy slow you down, do you think?" Papa asked.

"Oh, he may be slim as a bed slat, but he's a hard worker. And I'd rather have that than somebody that's always sittin' on his endgate. We'll get along fine, I reckon."

"Excellent. Essie? Do you have anything else?"

"I think that about covers it." She stood and circled around the desk, withdrawing Adam's wages from one of the drawers.

Both men stood.

"Here you are, Mr. Currington," she said. "Thank you for all your hard work."

He took the pouch. "It's been my pleasure, Miss Spreckelmeyer."

"Yes. Well. I'll walk you to the door."

"No need, ma'am."

"I insist." She led him down the hall and stepped out onto the front porch with him, closing the door behind them. She touched a finger to her mouth, indicating the open windows.

They walked to the white picket fence outlining the yard. Only when they reached the gate did she dare to speak, and even then in a whisper. "Where's my bicycle?"

"It was purty bent up, girl. I toted it down to Fowler's."

"Why? What was wrong with it?"

"The frame was kinked some. He'll have it fixed in no time."

Touching her waist, she looked in the general direction of the blacksmith's shop. "What did you tell him?"

"The truth."

She snapped to attention. "You *what?*"

"I told him the truth, Essie. I've learned it's best not to make my stories wider than they are tall."

"But . . . but—oh dear. We'd better go back inside and talk to Papa. He'll know what to do."

She turned around, but he grabbed her wrist. "Hold on, there, girl. I told him I tried your machine out and that it threw me forked-end up."

"Oh. That's all?"

"That's all."

"Nothing else?"

"Nothin' else."

It was a moment before she realized he still held her wrist. She pulled loose and examined her fingernails.

"I can't court ya proper-like, not with you being the judge's daughter and all."

She looked up. "What has that to do with anything?"

"I'm a drifter, Essie. Nobody wants a drifter comin' to call."

She hesitated only a moment. "I do."

His expression softened. "Yer pa would squirt enough lead in me to make it a payin' job to melt me down."

"You don't even know him."

"I know he's up for reelection. I know he's mighty powerful in these parts. I know him and the sheriff use the same toothpick. I know it'd only take a nod from either o' them and I'd be doing a midair ballet from a cottonwood."

Disappointment wilted her shoulders. She didn't think it would be as bad as all that. Truly, Mother would be more of a problem than Papa. Even though she acted it, she wasn't so desperate to see her daughter married off that she'd settle for just anybody. And a drifter would definitely fall into the "just anybody" category.

Essie also knew Papa's tolerance level dipped awfully low before an election. If Adam were to ask permission now and Mother put up a fuss, Papa would capitulate simply because it was easier.

"It don't mean we can't see each other," Adam said.

"I thought you said—"

"I said we can't court. I never said nothin' about spoonin.'"

"You mean, secreting away behind my parents' backs? So that no one knows?"

"Now, I don't know as I'd say that, exactly. Let's just say we'd be keepin' things private fer a while."

"You mean until after the election?"

"That'd be better, I think."

"I don't know, Adam. Perhaps if I spoke with Papa first."

"No! No, don't do that. It ain't right. The man's supposed to do the talkin.' When it comes time, I'll go to him. Promise you won't say nothin.'"

The front door opened and Papa came down the steps, settling his hat on his head. "You still here, Currington?"

"Just finishin' up a few particulars with Miss Spreckelmeyer, sir."

They stepped apart and Papa passed between them. "Good day, then."

"Same to you, sir."

"Bye, Papa."

They waited until he'd walked several houses down, then Adam turned back to her. "Promise me, Essie. I mean it."

"No, Adam. I'm sorry. Either you speak to my father and court me properly or we don't court at all."

He stepped through the gate. "Suit yourself, then."

He started down the sidewalk, his lazy gait capturing her attention and her imagination. Panic took hold. She knew without a doubt he wasn't just walking out of her yard, he was walking out of her life.

He was handsome. He was charming. He was an outdoorsman. And if she didn't take him up on his offer, there might never be another one—from anyone.

"Adam?" she called.

He hesitated, then waited while she hurried to him.

"Perhaps I was a bit hasty," she said.

Tipping the brim of his hat back, he shifted his weight onto one foot but offered her no encouragement.

"If I agree to this, um, private courtship, you'll speak to my father after the election?"

He gave a slow nod. "Yes, ma'am. I surely will."

She glanced up and down the street. Papa had long since turned the corner. There were no carriages, no horses, no people to witness her surrender.

Election Day was almost seven weeks away. What possible harm could come from keeping their courtship a secret for those few weeks?

"Very well, then. But I want to be the one to pick up my bicycle when it's ready."

"If that's what you want. Maybe when we pick everything else up Monday morning, Fowler will have that for us, too."

She nodded.

He rubbed his neck. "I'm sorry I messed it up."

The tension that had gripped her only moments before eased. "It wasn't your fault. I didn't expect you to go so far down the hill."

"I did purty good, then?"

"You did outstanding."

"Why, thank you, ma'am." Winking, he pinched her chin, then continued down the sidewalk. "I'll swing by here first thing on Monday, then," he called over his shoulder.

———

An unexpected lethargy fell over Essie. She thought about her mother's diatribe. It had a sharper edge to it than usual. She had actually verbalized what had heretofore been unspoken in their house: the word *spinster. Old maid. No prospects in sight.*

But she did have a prospect. And she thought of him constantly, reliving their first meeting at the Slap Out. His unexpected interest. His disillusionment over that cattle drive. His devotion to building her a rig. His bicycle ride down the hill. His kisses afterward.

Essie straightened her cuffs. Mother had certainly been wrong about the bicycle in this instance, for it was that very vehicle that had brought her and Adam together.

She wondered where he was. What he was doing. What he'd spent his wages on. Was he thinking of her as much as she was thinking of him?

The weekend dragged as she waited for Monday to arrive. On Saturday, she finished all her washing and ironing, helped Mother put up some pumpkins, and baked some bread.

She wondered what denomination Adam was, for she'd never seen him at church, and this morning was no exception. Something else for Mother to complain about once he expressed his intentions.

Without her bicycle, Essie grew listless. She could practice her wheeled feet, but she wasn't in the mood. She could take little Harley snake hunting, but she didn't much feel like that, either. She'd invited Papa to go fishing, but he and Mother were going to the Dunns' for their weekly Bible study.

The house was quiet with them gone. No breeze stirred the curtains. She sat on the front porch for a while, waving to her neighbors as two by two they went here and there.

She went inside and played the piano, but even that didn't hold her interest for long. Spying Mrs. Lockhart's novel on the table, she thumbed through it, wondering what secrets it held—if any.

Taking it upstairs to her bedroom, she fluffed her pillow, curled up in bed and began to read *Clarabel's Love Story.*

Clarabel was a tough, passionate woman jilted by a lover who was too poor to marry her. Distraught, she married the first "acceptable" man to ask her—a stodgy

Oxford graduate. The match was so distasteful, the couple moved to separate homes only three days into the marriage.

Clarabel exhibited strength in supporting herself but never forgot her original suitor. Later, he returned a wealthy man and they engaged in an illicit affair. Love triumphed when the Oxford man died.

Essie closed the book, her mind in a whirl. The sentiments expressed in the novel were completely unacceptable in life as she knew it. But Mrs. Lockhart was a respectable, churchgoing matron. And she had knowingly given the book to Essie, suggesting, even, that Essie emulate Clarabel.

But didn't Mrs. Lockhart find it shocking? The point of the entire novel was to raise her romantic standards by lowering her moral ones.

Perhaps Adam was right. Perhaps there really were couples who did such things. Even right here in Corsicana.

Was that why she had never married? Had her decency scared men away? She thought of the numerous weddings that had been performed this summer. Had those brides given themselves to their men before the vows were spoken?

She placed the book on the bedside table and lay back on her bed, watching the light and shadows of twilight fight for dominance on her ceiling.

The darkness eventually won.

CHAPTER | TWELVE

ONCE ADAM AND JEREMY started drilling, Essie's presence at the field was superfluous. She could take lunch out to them each day, but she didn't want Adam to think she was "chasing" him. So she only took lunches out on Fridays.

This Friday was no exception. She dressed casually, but carefully, in a new bicycle dress she'd made. The dark Turkish trousers fell below her knees and were so full that when standing they appeared to be a skirt.

She buttoned a matching double-breasted jacket over her vest, collar, and tie to accommodate the cooler weather that had begun to settle in. Holding her tongue between her teeth, she pinned on a modest, fur-trimmed hat with two shortened peacock feathers the color of Adam's eyes, then checked herself in the mirror.

Fashionable but not overly done. The quintessential modern woman.

She skipped down the stairs, running her finger along the banister and bumping it against a series of old nails sticking out every few inches. As a youth she'd slid down the banister more times than she could count. One time she fell off halfway down and sliced open her chin.

Mother made Papa drive nails into the railing, leaving about an inch of each nail sticking up. The family had become so accustomed to them, they didn't even notice them anymore. She really ought to have Papa remove them.

In the kitchen, Essie took some boiled eggs from the icebox, along with three jars of tea, and nestled them in a basket with frog legs, cheese, potato croquettes, pickled okra, and fig tarts—all made by her own hand.

After securing the basket to her bicycle, she headed to Twelfth Street. It had been two weeks since Peg's repair. Plenty of time for Essie to get used to the new clicking noise Peg made with each rotation of the wheels.

But she simply couldn't keep the sound from registering. Instead of causing concern, however, the noise reminded her of Adam and the passionate kisses they'd shared. Neither she nor Peg would ever be the same again.

She glanced up at the sky. Clouds bunched together like suds in a washtub, obliterating the sun's rays and graying the town. On main thoroughfares, she had some protection from the wind. But once she left the shelter of the buildings, the blustery weather threatened to tip her and Peg over.

She tucked her chin and squeezed the handlebars, fighting the wind at every turn. It battered her hat, whipping against the brim and straining her hair where it was pinned, but she didn't dare let loose of the bike. Fat raindrops began to plop from the sky as she reached the field.

Adam saw her coming, left the rig and jogged to her. "Better slide off yer saddle, girl, before them clouds open up."

She relinquished the bicycle to him and they ran for cover, slipping beneath the thickly clustered, arching branches of an old magnolia that formed a leafy cupola clear to the ground.

He hastily propped Peg against the tree's trunk, grabbed Essie around the waist and pulled her flush against him. "Quick, before the boy comes."

He captured her lips with his and gave her a hurried but thorough kiss. "By gum, I've missed you," he said, then released her as Jeremy approached.

"Hey, there, Miss Essie," Jeremy said, bending down into their shadowed haven. Earthy smells rose from the dormant soil they'd disrupted with their presence. A gentle tapping of rain began to sprinkle the leaves sheltering them.

Still trying to recover her composure, the best she could do was nod a greeting.

Jeremy zeroed in on the basket secured to her bike. "You bring us some lunch?"

She stared back at him, totally devoid of words.

A slow, delicious smile crept over Adam's face. "Don't be teasin' us, now, Miss Essie. That boy there's a mite narrow around the equator and I'm so hungry I could eat a sow and nine pigs."

She blinked. "What? Oh. Of course. Help yourself."

Jeremy began to loosen the rope binding the basket to her bike, his back to them. Adam took a leisurely surveillance of her, from her skewed hat to her bicycle boots and back up again, not bothering to disguise his interest.

She flushed hot, then cold, trying to think what Clarabel would do. And in the next moment found herself examining him with the same boldness he'd used with her.

He'd been still before, but she detected a subtle tensing of his muscles as she pored over him. Cowboy hat. Lifted brows. Wide lips. Shadowed jaw. Extensive shoulders. Molded chest. Silver buckle. Cocked hip. Massive thighs. Cowboy boots.

From the corner of her eye, she saw Jeremy releasing the final knot on the basket, so she swept her gaze up to Adam's and forgot to breathe. She'd never seen such heat, such desire, such impatience in a man's eyes.

It filled her with a surge of power. And the upper hand shifted from him to her. She knew it. He knew it. And it released in her something she hadn't known she possessed.

Wickedness? she thought. Perhaps.

"I have something sweet for you today," she said.

Adam's lips parted.

Jeremy turned around. "You always bring somethin' sweet, Miss Essie."

She held Adam's gaze. "So I do. So I do."

Adam swallowed.

Essie took the basket from Jeremy. "Shall we sit?"

Jeremy plopped down.

Adam jumped forward and grabbed her elbow. "You'll get your skirt dirty."

"It's all right," she said.

"If I had a jacket, I'd lay it out for ya."

She breathed in the smell of him, part sweat, part salt, part shaving tonic. "I know."

He increased the pressure on her elbow for a mere second before helping her settle on the ground. Gone was the teasing banter that came so easily to him, replaced with an intensity that she knew she'd caused.

Her mother was wrong. She wasn't undesirable. She may be thirty and she may ride a bike, but she'd caught the attention of not just a man, but a gorgeous man. A man who could have his pick of any woman he wanted.

"Oh, lookit this," Jeremy said. "Frog legs. My favorite."

Essie spread a small, square cloth over her skirt. "I didn't realize you favored them. You should have told me sooner."

Jeremy took a big bite. "Hmmmm. Where'd you catch 'em?"

"Not far from where we let Colonel loose."

Adam paused. "*You* caught the frogs?"

"Of course," she said, unscrewing the jar of pickled okra and popping a piece into her mouth. "I'm not as good at catching them as Jeremy is, though."

"You do all right, Miss Essie," Jeremy responded.

A gust of wind broke through their barrier, lifting the cloth on Essie's lap. Adam clapped a hand on her leg to keep the napkin from blowing away.

He surreptitiously caressed her through her skirts. "Careful, girl. You're fixin' to lose somethin'."

She glanced at Jeremy, then lifted her cloth, dabbing the corners of her mouth. "I'll be careful."

Adam smiled. "Where'd you learn to catch frogs?"

"At my grandpa's farm. He has a place out near Quitman. I used to go there every summer."

"By yourself?"

"Well, Mother would take me, but she never stayed the way I did. First day of summer, she'd wake me up early in the morning and we'd take the train. Then Grandpa would pick us up in a carriage pulled by two palomino horses."

"I never rode in a train," Jeremy said.

"Where would you go if you could?" Essie asked.

He put a chunk of cheese in his mouth. "Don't really know," he said around his mouthful.

"What did you do up there all summer?" Adam asked her.

"Lots of things. Grandpa's syrup mill was my favorite, though. The horse would walk in circles all day turning the mill, pressing sweet juice out of the sugarcane. Sometimes I'd help pour the juice into big vats where they slowly cooked it, and this wonderful aroma bubbled up from it."

"You ever get to have any o' that syrup?" Jeremy asked.

"Yes. They'd pour it into jugs or tin buckets, and at the house I'd get to eat ribbon cane syrup on Grandma's hot, buttered biscuits."

Rain started to leak into their haven, causing the three of them to scoot closer to the trunk of the tree.

"My grandpa ain't nothin' like that. He don't do nothin' but drink the day away."

Essie had known Jeremy since he was a tiny baby, and this was the first time she'd ever heard him so much as mention his grandfather—Corsicana's town drunk.

"You have a grandpa, Adam?" he asked.

"Shore do."

"He drink?"

"Shore does."

Jeremy took a gulp of tea from his glass jar. "Is he a drunk?"

Adam dug around in the basket for a boiled egg as if Jeremy had asked him nothing more than if the sky was blue. "Nope. He likes to look at the moon through the neck of a bottle, but he knows his limits. Best cowboy that's ever lived."

"He the one what taught you ropin'?"

"Him and my pa."

"You ever seen Adam rope?" Jeremy asked Essie.

"No, I haven't."

"You gotta show her, Adam. Miss Essie'd be impressed. 'Course, she'd want you to teach her how, though."

Adam glanced over at her. "I'll teach her. I got a whole passel o' tricks I could show her."

He took a bite out of his egg, and Essie looked down. The advantage had somehow shifted back to him.

The rain stopped, but a few gusts of wind rustled the big, glossy leaves around them, loosing random droplets of water. They finished their meal, leaving not so much as a crumb behind.

"That sure was good, Miss Essie," Jeremy said.

"Thank you."

She took a sip of tea, then reached for the lid, but Adam snagged the jar from her, turned it to the exact spot she'd touched with her lips and drank deeply, finishing all that was left.

"That was mighty sweet," he said, handing the jar back to her and scraping his mouth with his sleeve.

A crack of thunder reverberated above them.

"You may as well head on out, Jeremy," Adam said. "As long as the Old Man up there is stompin' on his campfire and sending sparks a-flyin', we ain't got no business under that tripod o' poles."

Jeremy's eyes lit up. "You sure?"

"I'm shore, but when the lightning stops, you come on back."

"I will." He hesitated. "What about Miss Essie?"

"I'll stay here with her until everything settles down."

"That okay with you, Miss Essie?"

She schooled her expression to show none of the commotion going on inside her. "Of course. I'll be fine."

Jeremy stood and brushed the backside of his waist-overalls. "Well, thanks again, Miss Essie, and I'll see ya later today, Adam."

He ducked out into the field, and she listened to his rapid footfalls splashing through the puddles until they were no more.

Adam said nothing, just looked at her. The tension inside her built. She thought of how bold she'd been earlier and felt herself blush. What in the world had she been thinking?

He picked up a corner of her skirt and gave it a gentle tug. "Come here."

And so she had her choice. She could take her bicycle and leave or she could scoot over next to Adam and learn some new and unsearchable things. Things she might never have another chance to experience if she didn't seize this opportunity.

Stiff. Stern. Old maid. Spinster.

That's what she was and what she would continue to be unless she secured this man's interest. And if that meant allowing him to steal a kiss or two, so be it. In fact, she found the idea more than a little thrilling.

She shuffled over on her knees. As soon as she was within reach, he caught her to him and brought them both to the ground.

"I was so afraid you were gonna say no," he said, then covered her lips with his.

Her hat forced her head into an uncomfortable angle. His belt buckle dug into her. Her shoulder landed in a small puddle. None of it mattered.

She wrapped her arms around his neck and kissed him back with everything she had. He held her tight, one hand between her shoulder blades, the other at the small of her back.

An explosion of thunder from far away slowly faded like a music box that winds down. A moment of silence as the earth stilled in anticipation of once again being quenched of its thirst. A gradual tapping of water on the leaves above and the ground outside increased in sound and speed, culminating in a waterfall from heaven. So much. So fast. The soil could not absorb it all at once.

"Your hair," he said. "Can I see your hair?"

Wrenching the pin from her hat, she flung them both to the side and sat up. She tugged at her pins until her hair fell down her back, then ran her fingers through it, savoring the freedom of having it loose.

He sat up and cradled her face with his hands, his eyes smoldering. "You are beautiful."

He kissed her again with an exquisite gentleness that undid her more than the earlier impatience. He tasted every inch of bare skin he could. And when he'd finished with her face and neck and hands and fingers, when he'd finished smelling and stroking and worshiping her hair, he placed her hand over the buttons of her double-breasted jacket and left it there.

If she removed it, her modesty would still be intact, with her vest and shirtwaist remaining. She slowly undid the buttons. He pushed the jacket off her shoulders and down her arms. Then waited.

She unhooked her vest.

He freed her of it, then unfurled her tie and slipped it from her collar. Nothing they'd removed allowed him access to more than he'd had before. But the act of disrobing made her feel vulnerable. Wanton.

He kissed her again. His hands took liberties and she allowed it. Relished it. Wanted more of it. And that's when she heard Papa's voice.

"He and Jeremy must have run for shelter," Papa said, "but if I know Adam, they'll be back. He doesn't waste a moment of daylight."

Essie gasped. Adam touched a finger to her lips, then held her still against him. When had it quit raining?

"Well, I have to confess, you were right and I was wrong. Currington looks to be on the up-and-up."

It was Uncle Melvin. She felt Adam tense. Panic filled her. If they were caught, Papa could be reasoned with. But Uncle Melvin always swung first and asked questions later.

The two men discussed the progress of the well and what they'd do if they hit a gusher. What they'd do if they didn't. How far they were in the drilling. How much farther they had to go still.

Adam's thumb made a circular motion on her waist. His breath tickled her hair. After what seemed a lifetime, Papa and Uncle Melvin left the field, passing right by the tree.

She and Adam stayed still and huddled together for several minutes. When they were sure all was safe, Adam pulled back but did not release her.

"You all right?" he asked.

"I think I'm going to cast up my accounts."

He smiled. "Me too." He pecked her lips. "Come on, I'll help you with your things."

He did not allow her to do anything for herself. He hooked all the hooks, buttoned all the buttons, and tied all the ties. By the time he had finished, they were both as worked up as they'd been before.

He threaded his hands through her hair, cupped her head and kissed her. Thoroughly.

"By jingo, but you are sweeter than a honeybee tree." He kissed the end of her nose. "I'm afraid you're gonna have to put your hair back up. That's one thing I can't do for ya."

"My mother is going to know."

He searched for her scattered hairpins and plucked them from the ground. "No, she won't. I'll make sure ya look as prim as a preacher's wife before ya leave."

She took more care with her hair this time, tucking it into a French twist. Adam watched unabashedly, handing her pins as she needed them. She picked up her hat.

"Wait," he said, pulling her to her feet. He drew her against him and kissed her again. "Come to the show with me."

"What?"

"There's a ten-cent show at the Opera House tonight."

She sucked in her breath. "A ten-cent show? But those are the low-comedy shows. I've never been to one in all my life. Besides, I thought you said we couldn't openly court."

"We can't, but we could meet there. Like it was an accident or somethin'." He rubbed his thumb along her jaw. "Please?"

She vacillated, afraid of what would happen if she went. Afraid of what would happen if she didn't. She might very well lose him if she refused. And to lose him now would be unbearable.

Her mother's words once again droned through her mind. *"No one's going to bid on your basket . . . not a prospect in sight . . . spinster . . . old maid."*

"I'll be there," she whispered.

He kissed her again, helped her get her hat on straight and sent her on her way.

CHAPTER | THIRTEEN

ESSIE HAD NO IDEA what to wear to a ten-cent show. When Papa took them to the Opera House to hear a concert or soloist, she and Mother always dressed in their finest. Surely that would not be the case for the low-comedy shows.

By the same token, she wanted to look nice for Adam. It was their first official outing, clandestine though it was. She threw yet another dress on her bed and reached for a pale blue crepe de Chine. It was made in princess effect and covered with black chenille polka dots. The waist was tight-fitting and the vest would show white lace at the neck, which would be duplicated at the edge of the sleeves and in a flounce at the bottom of her skirt.

She put it on, turning around and looking over her shoulder into the mirror. She could wear her hat of blue tulle with black chenille dots and a black bird-of-paradise. She'd had it specially made to match the gown.

"Essie?" Her mother tapped on the door.

"Come in."

Mother opened the door, glancing at the clothing heaped on the bed, draped over the chair, and slung over the footboard. "What are you doing?"

"I'm going to play piano with the orchestra at the Opera House before tonight's performance and then again between acts."

"Play at the Opera House? But why? What happened to Mr. Graham?"

"He's playing the cornet between acts, and reverting to piano during the actual program."

"I don't understand. You've not played for them in years."

"No, but you know how Mr. Creiz has been trying to persuade me to become a permanent member of the staff orchestra ever since Mrs. Graham has taken ill and Mr. Graham has been hinting at retiring."

"Well, yes, but you're not actually considering it, are you?"

"No, no. I'm just helping him out tonight." Essie picked up a brown velveteen and slipped it on a hanger.

"I thought you were going to the card party in Pinkston with us tonight."

"I'm afraid that will no longer be practical," Essie said. "I'd have to go on horse now since you'll have the carriage and by the time I arrived, there would only be an hour or so before it was time to turn around and head home."

"Well, for heaven's sake. I wish you'd checked with me first. Your father is campaigning. It's important the entire family attend these socials."

Essie placed a ribbon collarette in her drawer and slid it closed. "I'm thirty years old. An old maid. Remember? Perhaps I should start acting like one."

Mother stiffened. "Just what is that supposed to mean?"

A breeze from the window sent a starched linen cuff flitting to the floor. "Old maids don't check in with their mothers. They make their own plans. Live their own lives. You know. Like Aunt Zelda."

"Don't be ridiculous." Mother picked up the cuff and slapped it back onto the toilet table. "Zelda's eccentricities shamed the entire family. She was a constant source of embarrassment."

"Was she? I always remember her as being a great deal of fun."

"You are still living in my home, young lady," Mother said, stepping to the window and yanking the gossamer curtains together.

"I'm not a *young* lady anymore."

Mother frowned. "Nevertheless, you will do me the courtesy of checking with me before you make any plans."

Essie folded a corset cover. "I will do you the courtesy of *telling* you my plans when I've decided what they are."

"I don't like your tone, Esther."

Essie straightened. "Don't you? Well, please forgive me."

Mother narrowed her eyes. "What is the matter with you?"

"Nothing. I guess your little lecture a couple of weeks ago has me considering exactly what my role is now. And my responsibilities."

"Nothing has changed, dear."

Essie smoothed a piece of fur trimming one of her cloaks. "You're mistaken, Mother. Everything has changed."

———

Essie guided Cocoa to the left when she reached Tenth Street and headed to Molloy's Livery. Remembering what Adam had said about not making his stories wider than they were tall, she had gone straight to the Opera House after leaving the oil field that afternoon. She'd asked Mr. Creiz, the leader of the orchestra, if she could play with them this evening.

He'd immediately agreed. She'd explained she didn't want to play during the actual performance, since she'd not rehearsed with them, but instead just at the beginning and during the interludes. He had been delighted.

She pulled Cocoa to a stop just inside the livery's gate. A lad of twelve or thirteen rushed out to help her dismount.

"I'm not sure how late I'll be," Essie said.

"Don't matter none, miss," he said. "She'll be here when you get back, no matter what time it is. What's her name?"

"Cocoa."

"I'll take good care o' her."

Essie slipped him a coin, then went around to Hunt Avenue and approached the front entrance of the Opera House just as the orchestra, in full regalia, came out, all talking at once. The swarm of men wore deep blue suits and hats with light blue braid and a red sash tied about their waists.

She stopped the trombone player, a large man always ready with a smile. "Mr. Collier?"

"Oh, howdy, Miss Spreckelmeyer. Tony says you're gonna play with us tonight."

"Just during the in-betweens. What are you doing out here?"

"We're fixin' to parade up and down Beaton Street."

"You are? Why, I didn't know you did that."

He leaned in and whispered, "We always do that before the girlie or minstrel shows. Helps get the attention o' folks on the street and brings in a bigger crowd."

Essie flushed. "I had no idea. I . . . I'm afraid I was unprepared for that."

He laughed. "Oh, we don't expect our guest players to do that. Just us regulars."

When they reached Beaton Street, Mr. Creiz signaled for attention, raised his baton and gave a count. They started in on "Sweet Rosie O'Grady" and set off down the street. Essie stood back, unsure of what to do.

Mr. Crocket's drum kept the rhythm, while the piercing notes of the brass carried above all the other instruments. They passed the barbershop, the jewelers, and the hardware store. Men poured out of the Bismarck Saloon, yelling encouragement to the orchestra and hooking up behind them.

Her social circle was so small, she often forgot about this side of town. The side where churchgoing women rarely went. And never without escort. She didn't recognize one single person, other than the orchestra members. And they had always been just this side of respectable.

She began to question the wisdom of her plans. Perhaps she needed to go back to the livery and ride Cocoa out to Pinkston after all. Instead of meeting Adam tonight, she could play cards with men and women her parents' age. A few were her age, too—but they all had spouses and children and homes of their own.

"A penny for your thoughts."

She turned. Adam stood close behind her, freshly pressed and smelling of Yankee soap. His crisp white shirt contrasted sharply with the deep golden hue of his skin. His cowboy hat could not shade the brightness of his clear blue-green eyes.

She still couldn't quite believe that just hours ago she'd been wrapped in his arms and he in hers. How she looked forward to the time when they could openly court. When she could walk into church on the arm of the handsomest man in town. Her. Essie Old-Maid Spreckelmeyer.

"Hello," she said, a bit of shyness creeping over her.

He removed his hat. "You look mighty nice."

"Thank you." *So do you.*

He stood silent. Serious. "I've been thinkin' about ya all day."

She warmed at his words.

"Wonderin' if you were gonna come. Wonderin' if you didn't, how I'd not even wanna stay for the show. Wonderin' if you did, how I'd keep my hands to myself."

Her pulse picked up.

"I didn't expect you to get here before me. Have ya been waitin' long?"

She shook her head. "I arranged to play piano for the orchestra tonight, so I had to come early."

His face fell. "The whole time?"

"No, no. Just between acts."

They stood on the steps, adjusting to the newness of what was happening between them.

"Did ya tell your folks where you were goin'?"

"I did. They're playing cards with some friends out in Pinkston tonight. They don't suspect a thing."

"When will they be back?"

"Late."

The words settled around them like the last brush of sunset before night falls.

"I wanna kiss ya right here. Right now."

She surprised herself by answering, "Me too."

He slipped his hand into hers. "Come on, Miss Spreckelmeyer. We'd best be joinin' the fun, else we might miss the show altogether."

"What if someone sees us?"

He cocked his head. "Would you join the fun if you were with Jeremy?"

"Yes, I'm sure I would."

"Then we've nothin' to worry about."

He pulled her by the hand, down the steps and into the street. She savored the intimacy of it. Never, ever, had a man led her around in such a way. Always, they took her elbow. Occasionally touched her waist. But this—this was so much more personal.

She lifted her skirt to keep up with his long strides. The orchestra now played "Daddy Wouldn't Buy Me a Bow Wow," and the crowd of revelers had grown larger and noisier. Adam took the two of them into the thick of it. Folks bumped and jostled her from all directions.

Adam kept his hand in hers, hiding them within the folds of her jacket. She checked the men and women crowded around them and caught the attention of George Bunert, the harness maker, staring at her from a few feet away.

She shook her hand free. "Hello! How are you?" she shouted above the noise, waving.

He wove around a few people to reach her, then removed his hat. "I didn't expect ta see ya, Miss Spreckelmeyer."

They had to shout to be heard. "My father had to be in Pinkston this evening, so I am here on his behalf to visit and greet his in-town constituents."

"By yerself?"

"No, no. Mr. Currington, my father's driller, is here with me."

She tried to introduce the two men, but the noise level made it nearly impossible, and the crowd ended up separating Mr. Bunert from them. She lost sight of him as Adam tugged at her jacket and bent his head to her ear.

"You wearing all this stuff to protect you from me or the weather?"

She smiled. She'd chosen to wear her three-quarter-length coat, knowing it would be dark when the show was over and the ride home on Cocoa would be cold.

Instead of answering, she indicated his shirt-sleeves. "Aren't you cold?"

He reclaimed her hand. "No, ma'am. Not when I'm with you, sugar. Not when I'm with you."

His thumb drew a circle on her palm. She darted a quick look around, but no one gave them any notice. And they wouldn't see anything untoward if they did. His hidden caress continued and though it was no more than a simple gesture, its very secretiveness in such a public place was in many ways more potent than what they'd shared underneath the tree.

He winked and began to sing with the crowd.

> "I'll be so glad when I get old,
> To do just as I likes,
> I'll keep a parrot and at least,
> A half a dozen tykes;
> And when I've got a tiny pet,
> I'll kiss the little thing;
> Then put it in its little cot,
> And on to it I'll sing:
> Daddy wouldn't buy me a bow wow! bow wow!"

He raised her hand above her head and simultaneously spun her at the waist. When she completed her turn, he positioned her directly in front of him, face forward. The crowd had grown and become more packed together. Adam placed his hands at her waist, his thighs bumping against the back of her legs as they walked in unison to the music.

The orchestra began to make a horseshoe turn and head back to the Opera House. She reveled in the festiveness of the men. The excitement of having this cowboy with her. The anticipation of what the evening would bring.

When they reached the steps, the orchestra stayed out front, continuing to draw more folks in. She turned her face toward Adam. "I have to go. Where will I meet you?"

"*What?*" he said.

She saw his mouth form the word but could not hear him over the noise.

He leaned down and put his ear next to her lips, his cowboy hat concealing her from view. Instead of repeating her words, she took his earlobe in her mouth and tugged. His hold on her loosened and she slipped from his grip, running up the stairs and glancing back just before entering the Opera House.

She smiled to herself. Judging from his expression, no meeting place would be necessary. He'd find her.

CHAPTER | FOURTEEN

MR. MIRUS TOOK ESSIE'S coat and waved her up the steps of the wide stairway that led from the street level to the mezzanine. Several offices and club rooms opened off this second floor and were divided by portable walls that could be taken down to form a large dancing area for the annual Fireman's Ball. She expected she'd be attending the next one with Adam.

She continued on up the steps to the third level and entered the theater. All light and gold leaf, it rivaled anything in Dallas or Houston. A carpet covered the entire main floor, giving it an air of splendor. Recessed in the center of the ceiling was what everyone referred to as "the sun"—a large cluster of mirrored electric and gas lights.

Essie made her way down the east aisle, enjoying the stillness of the auditorium. There were no benches, only wicker seats with backs. She glanced up at the box her father owned. This would be the first time she'd view a show with someone other than him and from some other vantage point.

Just as she reached the bald-headed rows and descended into the orchestra pit, the crowd began to enter. The men were noisy, rowdy, and not at all like the patrons she was accustomed to. She didn't see one single woman.

Feeling awkward and a bit conspicuous, she picked up the sheet music on the upright piano and focused on the pieces she'd be sight-reading. A few minutes later the rest of the orchestra joined her but did not take the time to tune up. Instead, the lights dimmed and Mr. Creiz conducted them in the prelude.

The music moved quickly and robustly. Essie's fingers flew across the keys, and by the time they hit the crescendo she was out of breath. The men whistled and stomped. The lights went out. The curtain rose.

Essie slipped through a side door in the pit, skirting the auditorium and entering the deserted lobby, where statues and friezes of nymphs, cherubs, and winged figures decorated the hall. The gold carpet cushioned the sound of her heels.

She found Adam by the balcony steps. He beckoned her over and she hurried to his side.

"Come on," he said, ducking under the rope that cut off the balcony entrance.

"It's closed," she said. "No one else is up there, are they?"

"No, ma'am." He lifted the rope. "It's reserved. For the two of us. Now, hurry before someone sees us."

She dipped under the rope and followed him up the steps. At the top, the sudden darkness disoriented her. He grasped her hand and tugged. Instead of leading her to the first, or even second, row of seats, he settled them into the buzzard roost at the very back of the deserted balcony.

The stage had been transformed into a fancy ballroom, complete with flamboyant wall sconces, chandeliers, grand paintings, and gigantic windows. A lovely woman in a lavish gown sat center stage, earnestly visiting with an imaginary gentleman.

Her voice was high, affected, and gushingly southern. "Ah, so kind of you to find me this charming nook, Mistah Rushah. I feel *some* bettah now, thank you. And I believe I *would* like a cup of chocolate." She waved her handkerchief and called after the imaginary man, "Vewah *light* refreshments, Mr. Rushah, *vewah* light!"

Adam rested his arm on the back of Essie's chair, running a finger along her shoulder. She pretended not to notice. But behind her schooled features, she was paying very strict attention.

When the imaginary gentleman left the stage, the southern belle's manner changed entirely. She leaned back on the settee, sighed, and spoke to the audience in a natural voice. "Thank goodness that insipid specimen is gone. That ponderous old Smith came down full weight on my foot!"

She thrust her foot before her. "These slippers are several sizes too small but so Parisian, you know." Sitting up, she took a furtive look around. "I don't believe anyone is looking. I'm going to slip this one off—just *got* to stretch my poor toes a little!"

The woman crossed her legs and began to slowly lift the hem of her skirt. The men in the audience shouted and whistled. When she'd exposed one stocking-clad leg up to her knee, she bent forward.

The neck of her bodice gaped, causing another roar of approval from the men. She ran her hands down her calf and made quite a show of removing her shoe.

Essie watched with horror and fascination, her heart hammering in her chest. Adam's hand made its way to the back of her neck. He slipped a finger inside the top edge of her collar and moved it back and forth like a pendulum.

"Gracious!" the belle exclaimed. "I've danced a hole as big as a dollar in my stocking." She leaned back and lifted her foot in the air, exposing her toes and rotating her ankle round and round. A profusion of petticoats teased the men, offering them brief glimpses of her legs.

"My, what a relief to have that shoe off," she sighed.

Adam leaned closer, placing a kiss on Essie's neck. She caught her breath, then closed her eyes as he continued his foray, only to reopen one eye when the actress continued with her monologue.

"Here comes an English lord," the actress said, "strutting with importance, like the peacock he is."

Adam touched her chin, turning it toward him and gaining her full attention. He lowered his lips to hers.

"I'm going to shock him," the actress said. "Shatter his delicate English nerves. I'll play the wild, woolly Western girl."

Their kiss deepened and he slipped his arms about her. She touched his face, exploring it as if she were blind. Learning the texture of his skin, the angle of his jaw, the softness of his eyebrows.

"We believe in women's rights out West, Lord Catchum." The actress's voice had turned loud and nasal. "Disgusting? Not a bit. Did you ever see any Western women? Didn't? Missed the experience of a lifetime. They're awful smart. I'm a specimen."

The armrest bit into Essie's side. Adam took her hands and placed them behind his neck, then he began to explore *her* face, but with his lips.

"Why, they know as much about business as the men do. Yes, sir, they doctor, practice law, and extract teeth without pain. Then they make things red-hot for the saloon people—especially in Texas."

The men in the main gallery below them hooted and bellowed.

Adam's hands roamed, igniting an intense, deep desire. She didn't scold him for his boldness but instead wondered what he'd do if she were just as bold with him.

"How do they look? Purty well, as a whole. Most of them got rather big waists, but then, there's lots o' air out there in Texas that's got to be breathed, and they couldn't do it harnessed in an eighteen-inch belt."

Adam groaned and rested his forehead against hers. "I don't know how much more o' this I can take, sugar," he whispered.

"You want to stop?" she asked. "Why?"

He grasped her head between his hands and kissed her hard on the lips. "Let's get outta here."

"The orchestra."

"Leave it. You shouldn't be playin' for this kinda show anyway."

He picked his hat up off the seat next to him, put it on, and ushered her to the exit. Pausing, he pulled her against him and kissed her soundly one last time while cloaked within the theater's darkness.

"I'll overlook your breach of propriety in not proposing to me," the actress scolded. "You look startled, Mr. Catchum."

Adam released her. "Come on," he whispered.

They'd almost made it down the stairs when Adam stopped short.

Uncle Melvin stood in the lobby, his widened gaze tracking their descent, his sheriff's badge twinkling in the gaslight. For a moment he was frozen like one of the statues, but he quickly came to life.

"Just what do you two think you're doing?" he hissed, striding toward them, displeasure evident in his expression.

Essie caught her breath, her pulse shooting up to an alarming level, and she quickly touched the back of her hair to make sure all was in place.

Adam held up the rope.

Forcing down her panic, she slipped under it. "Good evening, Uncle."

"Don't 'good evening' me. What's going on?"

"Why, nothing. I'm playing incidental music with the orchestra, but Adam came to tell me he didn't think it a good idea for me to stay."

"What were you doing in the balcony?"

"I couldn't very well sit in the auditorium with the men."

Uncle Melvin glanced between the two of them. "Why didn't you stay in the pit?"

"I tried, but when the woman on stage began to remove her slippers, I became uncomfortable and retreated to the balcony."

He absorbed this bit of information and she hoped the barrage of questions was over and that he wouldn't catch her in her lies. She wasn't sure how much longer she could create answers without tripping herself up.

"What about you?" he asked Adam.

"I saw her outside during the before-show parade. When she left the pit, I followed to make sure she was all right."

Mr. Garitty, president of the Opera House, joined them. White hair encircled the sides of his head, leaving the top shiny. "Is there a problem, Sheriff?"

Uncle Melvin turned. "Did you know Essie was playing in the pit tonight?"

He shook his head. "Not until I saw her during the overture and asked Mirus about it."

"She has no business being here."

"I agree. If I'd known earlier, I would have warned her."

Essie touched Uncle Melvin's sleeve. "I'm sorry. I'll be sure to ascertain what show is playing next time. But no harm done. Adam has said he wouldn't mind seeing me home."

The sheriff scrutinized her. After a moment, he moved his attention to Adam. "I'll take her home, Currington. You can return to the show."

"It's no trouble for me, sir," Adam said.

"Nor me."

Adam looked at her. "Well, then. Good evening to you, Miss Spreckelmeyer." He touched the rim of his hat and pushed through the main entrance of the theater, the door clicking shut behind him.

———

Essie guided Cocoa out of the livery to where Uncle Melvin waited. So far, she'd managed to keep her irritation in check. But she was not at all pleased at having her evening cut short.

They rode together in silence. When they turned onto her street, the anticipated lecture began.

"That was a fool thing you were doing back there, girl."

She said nothing.

"What possessed you?"

"I've never been to a ten-cent show. How was I to know what it was like?"

He tipped his hat back and scanned the sky. "You're not talking to your pa. You're talking to me. So quit stretching the blanket. You know good and well there's a reason you ain't never been to a ten-cent show. Now, what were you doing there?"

"I went there for a clandestine meeting with an unsavory man," she snapped. "What do you think I went there for?"

He yanked his horse to a stop. She kept going.

"You better stop that thing right this minute or I'll hobble your ears."

She stopped.

He pulled up next to her. "Your mother's been tellin' my Verdie that you've been acting something awful lately. I'd never have believed it if I hadn't seen it with my own eyes. What's gotten into you?"

"Oh, I'm sorry," she sighed. "I didn't mean to bite your head off."

He touched his ankles to his horse's side. She did the same.

"Wanna talk about it?" he asked.

"Not particularly."

"Well, I don't know if I'm gonna give you a choice this time."

She looked down at the reins in her hands. "I'm just tired, is all."

"Tired? Of what?"

"Of being pestered for riding a bike. Of being scolded for acting like a man when I'm helping Papa with the business. Of having my every move criticized. Mother called me an old maid, you know."

He sucked in his breath. "That ain't true."

"Oh, but it is." A rush of renewed anger swept through her. "And that's when I decided that if I was going to live the rest of my life in that house, then I was going to make a few changes. And it was going to start with Mother."

They rode into her yard and he watched her dismount. "Just what is it you plan on doin'?"

"I'm not a child, Melvin. I'm thirty years old. It's time to cut the apron strings. Live my own life. And if that means playing the piano at the ten-cent show, then I will do so. And I don't care what Mother or anybody else says."

She walked Cocoa to the barn, suppressing the urge to say even more. Melvin dismounted and followed, holding Cocoa while Essie shoved the bar up and pulled the massive barn door open.

"Thank you," she said, reaching for Cocoa's reins.

He didn't release them. "Go on inside, girl. I'll put her up for you."

"No. I know you have things to do. I can do it."

He touched her elbow. "You'll ruin your gown. Now, go on."

She hesitated. "You sure?"

He nodded. When she reached the back door, she looked at her uncle. He stood by the barn, watching her.

"Are you gonna tell Mother where I was?"

"I thought you didn't care about her opinion anymore."

She fingered the buttons on her coat. "I don't. But that's no reason to borrow trouble."

He took his time answering. "Those ten-cent shows can get purty rough, Essie. Tonight's was not so bad. But most of the gals up on that stage—or worse, the ones in the audience—aren't even fit for a drinkin' man to hole up with. If you start playin' piano for them, the fellas are gonna think you're something that you're not."

She dropped her gaze.

"Is that what you want? You want your name to come up right alongside the names of those saloon gals who bare more hide than an Indian?"

"Of course not," she whispered.

"Then you better tell Creiz you ain't playing for any more of them ten-cent shows."

"Yes, sir," she replied, then slipped inside and gently closed the door behind her.

———

Melvin put Cocoa to bed, then returned to the Opera House. As town sheriff, he tried not to stray too far from the ten-cent show, in case of trouble. But he'd never expected to find his niece in attendance.

Moving into the lobby, he headed to the west wall, trying to reconcile in his mind what all she'd said to him, none of which bode well.

He wished he'd not revealed his presence to her. That way, he could have followed and seen for himself what was going on, if anything. With Currington involved, though, their actions were immediately suspect.

Essie might be thirty years old. She might think she was all grown up. But she always saw the good in people. Never the bad. And if Currington had designs on her, she'd be a sitting duck.

Melvin positioned himself against a column in the theater's lobby and waited. When the show ended, the men poured out. Adam was easy to find, being taller than most.

Melvin pushed his way through the crush and grabbed Adam's arm. "You got a minute?"

They stepped to the side, letting the others swarm past.

"Sheriff," Adam said.

According to the judge, this boy was hardworking, responsible, and good with Jeremy. So what was it that just didn't sit right?

"I wasn't happy to see my girl here tonight," Melvin said.

"No, sir. I felt the same way when I saw her." Adam shook his head. "She's awful smart about some things, but I'm thinkin' she wouldn't be able to tell the skunks from the house cats."

Melvin pulled a toothpick out of his inside pocket and worked it in between his teeth. "And which are you, Currington? A skunk or a house cat?"

Adam took a hard look at the sheriff. "I'm not gonna take offense at that 'cause I

know yer just concerned about Miss Spreckelmeyer. But if anybody else had asked, I'd
o' kicked 'im so far it would take a bloodhound six weeks just to find his smell."

"You threatenin' me, son?"

"Just statin' a fact, sir."

"Well, then, let me state a fact for you," he said, pointing the toothpick at Adam.
"I put a lot of stock in my girl. I find out somebody's been playin' her, and he'll end up
shaking hands with St. Peter. I can promise you that."

"I'll be sure to pass that along, sir." Adam touched his hat and headed down the
stairs to the street.

CHAPTER | FIFTEEN

ESSIE THOUGHT OF ADAM constantly, yet she still forced herself to stay
away from the fields until Friday. She knew Jeremy wouldn't have given her
presence a second's notice, but she didn't want to risk being discovered, nor
risk losing Adam by being too forward.

Hamilton had said men liked to do the chasing. So she'd decided if Adam wanted
to see her, he'd figure out a way. Only, he hadn't.

Maybe he had decided to lay low for a while after their close call at the Opera
House. Whatever the reason, she'd not seen hide nor hair of him.

But no matter, for today was Friday and today she'd take the boys some lunch. She
wanted to wear a skirt instead of her bicycle costume, so she left in plenty of time to
walk out to the Twelfth Street fields.

The sun warmed her skin, counteracting the briskness of October's air. The few
trees sprinkling town offered bouquets of red, yellow, and orange foliage.

She hoped she hadn't overdone it with her toilet. The grayish green gown she wore
had a short Louis Seize coat with a cutaway that opened widely onto a double-breasted
white vest with two rows of buttons. A large cravat of white chiffon draped her bust,
and a green straw hat trimmed with ribbon and black plumes perched smartly atop
her head.

Adam didn't even try to conceal his pleasure at seeing her. He stepped back from
the rig, wiped his neck and forehead with his large red handkerchief and tracked her
progress as she approached.

He took in her attire and her hat. She felt a spurt of pride. Hats were her one weakness. The wider, the taller, the more ornate, the more she liked them.

And wearing a fabulous hat would be rather pointless if the rest of her ensemble
was lacking. So, she found herself indulging in the very latest of fashions.

"Miss Essie," he said, "you are the purtiest thing I ever did see."

"Hello, Adam. And thank you."

"What'd ya bring us?" Jeremy asked.

She handed him the basket. "Why don't you go pick us out a spot of shade. We'll be right there."

Jeremy grabbed the basket and hustled toward the big bois d'arc tree.

"Where ya been?" Adam asked. "How come you haven't been out here all week?"

"I didn't want to be in the way."

He flicked a quick glance at Jeremy. "I'm thinkin' it's the boy that's in the way right now."

Me too, she thought.

He looked her over again. "You have any idea how bad I wanna kiss you?"

Yes.

"We're gonna have to do somethin' about that. I can't keep going days and days without seein' ya, and then havin' to mind my manners when I do."

"Hey!" Jeremy yelled. "Y'all comin'?"

Adam removed his hat and made a low, courtly bow. "Miss Spreckelmeyer? Will ya do me the honors?"

He held out his arm, and she hooked her hand inside his elbow. Tucking his arm in, he covered her hand with his and walked her toward the tree. Instead of keeping the requisite distance between them, she leaned into him. With each step her body brushed his upper arm. He ran his thumb over her knuckles.

Jeremy had found the cloth she'd brought and had spread it out for them to sit on. "She brought us some sandwiches."

"What kind?" Adam asked, helping her settle.

"Fish, looks like."

She smoothed her skirts. "One moment, Jeremy. I'm sure Adam will want to say grace first."

Jeremy retracted his hand.

Adam looked a bit startled, then bowed his head. "God bless the grub. Amen."

"Amen."

Essie frowned at his abbreviated, awkward prayer. Even hungry, he should have taken time to properly thank the Lord.

The boys didn't seem concerned, though, and dove into the food, drinking deeply of the tea and wasting no time in finishing off all that she had brought. For the most part, they restricted their conversation to expressions of appreciation. But that was just fine with her.

A married woman might receive such compliments often enough to take them for granted, but for Essie it was a rare occasion. Even when she did receive a kind word on her cooking, she usually had to share the credit with her mother. But these Friday lunches were all her own making, and watching Adam devour them was a special pleasure.

"You goin' to the Harvest Festival, Miss Essie?" Jeremy asked, slowing down. Once dessert was the only thing left, he usually tried to delay the return to work as long as he could.

"Of course. I wouldn't miss it."

"I heard they're gonna have a tightrope walker this year. Is that what you heard?"

"Papa told me he was a peg-legged man and that he's going to walk the rope with a cookstove strapped to his back."

"No foolin'? Did ya hear that, Adam?"

"Shore did." He had finished and lay on his side, propped up on his elbow. He made no secret of studying her.

"The Commercial Club's done asked Adam if he'll do some ropin'. He's gonna be part o' the show, too."

"Is that so?" She shot Adam a questioning look. "Well, I hadn't heard that."

"Yep. He's been practicin' ever' day now." Jeremy sank his teeth into a molasses cookie. "Why don't ya show Miss Essie some o' yer tricks?"

A slow smile crept onto Adam's face. "Would you like that, Essie? Would you like to see some o' my tricks?"

"Say yes, Miss Essie," Jeremy said. "You'll take a shine to it. I know ya will."

A warmth spread inside her. "I believe you're right, Jeremy. I believe I'd like it very, very much. Please, Adam. Will you show me?"

"It'd be my pleasure, ma'am." But he didn't move. "Why don't ya go get my rope, Jeremy."

The boy jumped up and headed over to the rig.

"How much longer 'til Election Day?" Adam asked her, lowering his voice.

"Not until after the festival."

"I can't keep this up for another month. I wanna see ya tonight. And tomorrow night. And the night after that."

Her pulse began to race. What was he saying? That he wanted to speak to Papa before the election or that he wanted to meet secretly with her on a more frequent basis?

Jeremy returned with what looked to be a twenty-foot rope. Adam coiled it loosely and stepped out from beneath the tree. The moment he cast the rope, it began to whirl, never once touching the ground.

He didn't look at what he was doing but kept his attention on her. The rope responded to the merest flick of his wrist. He kept his loop low and parallel to the ground, spinning it around the outer perimeter of his body—round the front, the side, the back. Then he switched hands and spun the rope to the other side and back to the front, where his right hand once again took over.

Keeping the spinning loop low and in front of him, he jumped in and out with both feet. At one point he stayed inside the loop and brought it up over his body until he had it twirling high above him. He did figure eights to the side. He made the loop larger and larger and even larger before bringing it back to a more normal circumference. He rolled it over his left leg just above the knee and then under.

He spun it high above his head and held it there for so long that she lowered her gaze from the rope to him. With a start, she realized he was still looking at her.

"Come here," he said.

She could no more resist than if he were the Pied Piper himself. She rose and stood before him.

"Closer," he said.

She took a step forward.

"Closer," he whispered.

She moved into his space.

The rope came down, encircling the two of them and trapping them inside its magic.

"I want to see you," he whispered.

"When?"

"Tonight."

"How?"

"The Opery House?"

She gave a slight shake of her head. "Too risky."

"The creek?" he said, keeping his voice low.

"Jeremy and some of the other boys fish out there at night."

He paused. "The magnolia tree?"

Her heart began to hammer. "What time?"

"Eight o'clock." He whipped the rope back up above them, and she returned to the blanket.

———

She sat in corset and drawers, staring at herself in the toilet table's mirror. This was not like going to the show. At the Opera House, she could pretend they'd gone with the intention of watching the performance.

But there was only one thing to do beneath the shelter of that magnolia tree. And heaven help her, she wanted to . . . and she didn't.

Perhaps it was more a question of *how much* she wanted to do. She loved the kissing. The feel of his arms wrapped tightly around her. The smell of his soap. The texture of his hair. The exclamations of marvel he made when they were sharing intimacies.

Yet each time, his hands had become more bold. And instinctively she knew that this time, if she went, he might not be satisfied with touching her through her gown.

She smoothed her hands down her figure. Clarabel may have allowed it. Other girls in Corsicana may have allowed it. But could she allow it? And if she didn't, would she lose him, along with her chances for marriage?

But he'd not spoken of marriage. Nor of what he would do to support them. Nor had he spoken of love.

Perhaps they should discuss those things tonight. First. And then what? What if he spoke of marriage and commitment and love? What then?

She ran a brush through her hair. Then he should be willing to wait.

So why was she trying to decide whether or not to wear the corset cover in her hope chest? The one she'd made herself all those years ago and put away for her wedding night?

Setting the brush down, she removed her everyday corset cover from a drawer in her wardrobe and determinedly buttoned it on.

––––––

Slipping away from the house had been no trouble. Mother and Papa had invited the mayor and his wife over for a game of dominoes.

She'd told Papa she was going to do some night fishing at the creek, and she fully intended to do so. After she met with Adam.

Wearing an old, worn skirt and shirtwaist, appropriate for fishing, soothed her conscience. She'd not taken any pains with her hair or her toilet. She wore no hat.

And she wore her ugliest and most threadbare underclothes. She'd die before she let anyone see them. That ought to keep her honest.

The oil field was abandoned and dark. The crickets clattered so loud they almost drowned out the other trilling insects. But the frogs gave them some serious competition, and a thrush that had yet to go to bed played its flutelike song.

Essie's boots crunched across the brown grass, her fishing rod and tackle box gripped firmly in her hand. Taking a deep breath, she bent beneath the magnolia's branches and pulled up short.

Adam stood leaning against the trunk of the tree, but it was the blanket and pillows he'd spread out on the ground that drew her attention.

"How did you get those here without someone seeing?" she whispered.

He stepped forward and took her rod and box. "Are we going fishing?"

"I am. A little later, that is."

He set the items on the ground and led her to the blanket. "I didn't want ya to have to make explanations if your gown got dirty, so I brought us a blanket."

"And the pillows?"

He gave a rakish smile and shrugged.

She swallowed. "Adam, I—"

"Shhhh. Sit down and tell me about yer week. I want to know what ya did ever' minute you were away from me."

They sat on the middle of the blanket, facing each other, Indian style.

"But our voices will travel," she whispered. "Someone might hear and come investigate."

"We'd hear them long before they'd hear us. But we can whisper if it'd make you feel better," he said, taking both her hands in his.

"Yes, please."

"So, what'd ya do last week?" he whispered. "Start with what happened when the sheriff hauled you home."

She lowered her chin. "He was very concerned."

" 'Bout what?"

"About me attending the ten-cent show."

"He's only tryin' to protect ya."

"I know. I just wish they'd all leave me alone."

"Did he say anythin' about me?"

"No. I'm sure it never crossed his mind that we had gone to the balcony to, um, be alone together."

He smoothed a tendril of hair from her face. "I've relived our time in the Opery House a hundred times in my mind."

"You have?"

"Well, shore. Haven't you?"

She slowly nodded her head.

He raised their clasped hands to his lips, kissing her knuckles. "I remember the honeyed taste of yer lips." He bit the tip of her finger. "The smell o' cloves in yer hair." Next finger. "The feel of yer hands on my shoulders." Third finger. "The feel of my hands on yer—"

She flung herself free, grabbed his cheeks and pulled his lips to hers.

He moved her to his lap. "Ah, just as sweet as I remembered," he mumbled.

There was no him. No her. Only them. It lasted forever. It didn't last long enough.

"Oh, Essie. You're killing me, darlin'," he breathed.

She tried to see his eyes in the dark, but couldn't. "What?"

"I'm wantin' you something fierce, girl." He cupped her chin. "Do ya know what that means?"

"I think so."

"Lemme show you."

She said nothing.

"Please."

"We're not married."

They were still whispering. The sounds of the night creatures paled in comparison to the roaring inside her as right and wrong waged war.

"But we will be," he said.

"We will?"

He grasped her shoulders and leaned back where he could see her. "Well, o' course. What'd you think?"

Euphoria bubbled over inside her. "You never said anything."

"Maybe not with words, but I've sure as shootin' shown ya."

She wrapped her arms around his neck. "Oh, Adam. I love you."

He clamped his mouth to hers and they tumbled to the ground, stretching out on the blanket. It was much, much later before she realized he'd never said he loved her, too.

CHAPTER | SIXTEEN

MELVIN HEADED TO TWELFTH Street, an unlit lantern in one hand, a rifle in the other. He'd meant to get out there much sooner, but he'd been held up by two bar fights and a runaway horse.

He pulled his hat low. He was gettin' too old for this.

The night was unseasonably warm for October but still cool enough to be comfortable. He'd seen Currington earlier this evening with a pouch slung over his shoulder and thought the drifter had decided to move on without tellin' the judge. So Melvin followed him.

And what he'd discovered was much worse than if the cowboy had skipped town. What he'd discovered was that no-account preparing himself a little love nest.

Melvin wondered who the poor, gullible thing was this time. He'd seen girls fall a hundred times before and would probably see a hundred more before he was through. But it never ceased to rile him.

He pictured the young gals in town who had been flirting with disaster lately—Ruth Smothers, Carrie Quigley, Lorna Wedick. There were plenty right now for Currington to choose from. Girls whose parents were blind to what their "little angels" were up to.

And it always fell to him to be the bearer of bad news. Blast Currington for putting him in this position. He'd planned on being inside their hidey-hole before the couple had shown up.

That way, he'd avert the disaster; he'd make sure the gal knew she'd be better off standing in a nest of rattlers than giving herself to a no-good drifter; and he'd run Currington right outta this town.

It'd be too late for that now. Instead, he'd be taking Currington and his girly home to her mama and papa. He hoped it wasn't the Smothers girl. Her mama had enough vipers in her brood already with those boys of hers without having to deal with one of the girls.

He slowed his pace and approached quietly, but he needn't have bothered. The two of them were making enough noise to wake the dead. He paused right outside the tree, disgusted at the sounds coming from inside.

"Currington?" he barked, readying his rifle.

A gasp and a scramble.

"Get out here."

No response.

Melvin set the lantern on the ground, struck a match and lit the wick.

"I'm comin'," Currington answered.

He stepped out from beneath the tree, shirttail hanging and an unfastened silver belt buckle peeking from between the shirt's opening.

Melvin's insides started to churn. "Who you got in there?"

"How'd ya know we were here?" the boy snarled. He was blazing mad.

Well, good. That made two of them.

"Who you got in there?" Melvin repeated.

Currington eyed the rifle and clamped his mouth shut. Melvin could hear frantic movements coming from inside the shelter. Whoever it was evidently had some repairing to do.

"Come on outta there," Melvin said, none too gently.

More scrambling.

"Who is it, Currington?"

The boy refused to speak.

"Either you come out here on your own, girl, or I'll come in there and drag you out."

She whimpered.

"Give her a minute, Sheriff," Adam said, his tone more threatening than respectful.

Melvin checked his impatience, then after another moment decided he'd waited as long as he was gonna. "That's it." He pulled back the branches.

Squealing, the girl curled her knees up under her skirts, wrapped her arms around them, and bent her head. Long blond hair flowed loose down the back of her worn shirtwaist. She rocked herself.

Squinting his eyes, he studied her. The girl was familiar, but with her face hidden, he couldn't quite place who it was. Grabbing the lantern, he held it high. Evidence of lost innocence spotted the blanket.

Blast.

"Come on," Melvin said, more gently this time. "Come on out."

She raised her head. Air rushed out of his lungs. No. No! Not *Essie.*

Distress, humiliation, and stark terror played in rapid succession across her face.

He plunked down the lantern, then dropped the branches and rifle. "You son of a—"

Currington took a step back, bringing his fists up, but not fast enough. Melvin threw a punch, sinking it hard into the boy's jaw.

"No!" Essie screamed.

Adam started to fall back, but Melvin grabbed his shirt, hauled him upright and hammered him another one. This one had a satisfying crack accompanying the blow and sent the cowboy flying.

"Stop it! Stop it right now!" Essie screeched. "I mean it!"

She threw herself at Melvin and tried to hold him back.

He grabbed her shoulders. "Did he force you?"

Her eyes widened. "No, no. Of course not."

"You can't mean that, Essie."

"It's true." She hung her head, avoiding his eyes.

He glanced behind her. Adam knelt on the ground, holding his face, blood leaking from his nose.

Melvin hauled her against him, hugging her tight. "What the blazes were you thinkin'? Sneaking off to meet some good-for-nothin' drifter? He's not worth two hairs on your head. What possessed you to do such a thing?"

She was crying. Hard. He was nearly crying himself.

"I love him," she said. "We're going to be married."

"You better believe you're gonna be married! If I don't kill the snake first."

Melvin slammed his eyes shut. In his mind's eye he saw Essie's dishevelment. Unbound hair. Wrinkled skirt. Shirtwaist buttoned unevenly. How in all that was holy did this happen? How was he gonna tell his sister? Or his best friend?

Anger roiled inside him. He glared at Currington, but the cowpoke must have known better than to make eye contact. Essie sniffled and took choppy breaths.

Melvin petted her head. "Go on back under the tree and make yourself presentable. You look a mess."

She pulled away from him, keeping her chin tucked.

"Take the lantern," he said.

She turned, saw Currington's blood, and rushed to his side. "Are you all right?"

He didn't answer her.

"Let me see." She pulled his hand away from his nose and sucked in her breath. "Oh, Adam. Oh, darling. Is it broken?"

He shrugged, then grimaced.

She lifted her skirt and ripped off a portion of petticoat. "Here. Try to apply some pressure."

Taking the fabric, he tenderly pressed it to his nose.

She whirled on Melvin, fury coming off her in waves. "How could you? How *could* you?"

"You're lucky he's still breathin'."

She narrowed her eyes. "*You're* lucky he's still breathing." Whipping up the lantern, she disappeared beneath the tree.

Her betrayal hit him square between the eyes. He'd known her, loved her, protected her for thirty years. And in the blink of an eye she switched her loyalties. To this slag. And now, they'd be married. He'd have to put up with this fly-by-night for the rest of his days. At church. At parties. At dinner tables. He snarled.

Currington lifted his pain-coated gaze, then rose to his feet. He buttoned his shirt, tucked it in, and fastened his belt.

Melvin should have killed him. Hung him. Beat him to death. Something more than a couple of well-placed punches.

Essie stepped out from the tree. Her hair was all pinned up, her shirtwaist back in order, her fishing pole and tackle box in her hand.

A defiant light came from her eyes. Not a tear to be seen.

"Let's go," Melvin barked.

Adam's bleeding had, for the most part, stopped. She tore off a fresh piece of petticoat. He accepted it and touched it to his nose, then took the fishing pole and tackle box for her.

———

The walk home had never seemed so long. She vacillated from being shamed to furious to scared out of her wits. Surprisingly, it wasn't facing her mother that scared her the most. It was facing Papa. Because she knew he'd be crushed. Disappointed with the daughter that had never—in his eyes—done any wrong.

The things that Mother always nagged her about were often the very things Papa was most proud of. But not this time. This time they'd both be shocked. Horrified. Enraged.

She didn't want to face them. How could she, knowing they'd find out what she had been doing?

She was so worried about the confrontation, she hadn't even had time to assimilate everything that had happened between her and Adam. The mysteries that had been revealed. The mysteries that had not.

Would they be married tonight? By her father? Would Adam be joining her in her very own bedroom? And have breakfast with the family in the morning? How awkward.

She glanced up at him. He looked neither left nor right but straight ahead, his expression hard, his nose swollen. She slipped her hand into his.

He looked down. A slight softening touched his eyes and he squeezed her hand.

She loved him. He loved her. Whatever happened, they'd face it together.

When they approached the house, Uncle Melvin cursed.

"The mayor's still here," he said, then scowled at their clasped hands. "Let go of her and let me do the talking."

Adam released her hand and put some distance between them. They entered the house and the two couples in the parlor looked up from their game of dominoes.

Mayor Whiteselle owned the brick and lumberyard south of town. He was one of those rare persons who liked everybody while still being genuine. Of medium build, he had ears that stuck out from the side of his head, a rapidly receding hairline and a thick brown moustache. He and Papa stood.

"Well," Mother said, "hello. Come on—" She looked at Adam's nose and the blood splattered on his shirt front. She jumped to her feet. "What happened?"

"He ran into somebody's fist," the sheriff said.

"Oh dear."

"Essie said she'd get him fixed up," Uncle Melvin continued.

All offered words of concern, except Papa. He knew Uncle Melvin too well to be fooled.

"Essie, why don't you take Adam to the kitchen," Papa said. "Maybe the rest of us ought to call it a night."

They began to put their game away, and Adam followed Essie from the room.

As soon as they were in the kitchen and out of earshot, he grabbed her hand. "I'm sorry about this, girl. I have no idea how the sheriff found out."

She suppressed the panic she felt and put on a brave face. "Well, no sense in worrying about it now. Things will be bad at first, I'm sure, but my parents love me. They'll settle down once the shock has passed. We'll just have to weather the storm together."

She realized with a start that his nose was crooked. It hadn't been crooked before.

"You all right?" he asked. "I mean, did I hurt you . . . very much?"

She looked down, embarrassed. "I'll be fine," she whispered.

He squeezed her hand. "I'm sorry."

She bit her lower lip. "How's your nose?"

"That sheriff may be a man-eater, but he'll find me a tough piece o' gristle to chew."

"You sit on down, then," she said, dropping his hand. "I'll break up some ice."

She'd just finished wrapping ice chips in a cloth when she heard the mayor and his wife leave. Her parents and the sheriff immediately joined them.

"Is it broken?" Mother asked.

"I haven't examined it yet," Essie answered, not wanting to alarm Adam.

"Sit down, Doreen."

Mother hesitated at Uncle Melvin's command. She looked between the four of them. "What? What is it?"

Papa pulled out the chair across from Adam, keeping his hands on its back even after Mother sat in it. Essie handed the compress to Adam and stood behind him as he placed it on his nose.

"I'm sorry to have to bring you this news, Doreen, but I found Currington and Essie in a compromising position this evening."

Mother frowned. "Essie is constantly compromising herself with the townspeople."

"Yes, well." Uncle Melvin cleared his throat. "Fortunately, no one from town saw this one. Only me."

"Then what's wrong?"

Papa slowly straightened, his eyes widening.

Uncle Melvin nodded his head. "She's been ruined, Sullivan. I'm sorry."

The knuckles on Papa's hands turned white from clenching the chair. His face tightened and he skewered Adam with his gaze before returning it to Uncle Melvin. "By force?"

Melvin shook his head in the negative. Papa's lips parted in shock.

Twisting around in her chair, Mother looked up at Papa. "What is happening, Sullivan? I don't understand."

"Is this true, Essie?" Papa asked.

She swallowed as her father stared at her in disbelief. "Yes," she whispered, unable to deny the truth.

His expression transformed into something fierce and frightening. He moved his steely gaze to Adam. "I trusted you. Stood up for you when others were quick to judge. And you repay me by taking advantage of my most treasured possession?"

His tone rose higher and higher with each accusation. Adam met Papa's gaze without flinching but offered no rebuttal.

Realization dawned on Mother. "No. No. You can't mean . . ." She gaped at Essie. "You haven't . . . you didn't let him . . . oh, Essie. No. Surely even you wouldn't be so foolish?"

Straightening her backbone, Essie took a deep breath. "I love him and he loves me."

"Mercy me. What are we going to do, Sullivan?"

"Yours was the fist he ran into?" Papa asked Melvin.

"It was."

"I wish it had been mine."

Essie pressed her fingers to her mouth. *Oh, Papa.*

Mother stood. "They must get married. At once."

But Papa was shaking his head. "No. She'd be bound to him for the rest of her life."

"She's already bound to him! In God's eyes they are one."

Warmth flooded Essie's face. She glanced at Adam. He'd not moved nor said a word. Just held the ice compress to his nose and watched.

Papa slammed his fist on the table. "No, Doreen. Marrying him because they had relations is a senseless reason to wed. We would be shackling her to a philanderer. I won't do it. We will run him out of town."

"No!" Essie said.

"And what if she is with child?" Mother cried at the same time.

A swell of silence followed her question, its implications echoing in all their minds. Mother turned solid red, as did Papa and Melvin. Essie parted her lips, stunned. So much had happened so fast, she'd not seriously considered the possibility.

She glanced at Adam. He was watching her, gauging her reaction. She touched her stomach and smiled tremulously.

"Tell him, Melvin," Mother said. "Tell Sullivan they must wed."

But Uncle Melvin said not a word.

Papa stormed out of the room and slammed into his study. Mother quickly followed. Essie stood frozen, listening to their shouts, though she could not tell what they were saying. Never in her entire life had she heard her parents yell at each other.

Adam reached for the chair beside him and pulled it out for her. She plopped down.

Uncle Melvin strode to the window above the washbasin and looked out. The glass reflected back his hard expression.

In a few moments, Mother and Papa returned.

Papa's face was flushed, his eyes murderous. He slapped the Bible in his hand onto the table. "Stand up, you two, and prepare yourselves to speak your vows."

CHAPTER | SEVENTEEN

ADAM LOWERED THE COMPRESS from his nose and rose to his feet. "May I say somethin'?"

Papa did not respond. He didn't need to. If he'd been a dragon, he'd have been breathing fire.

"With all due respect, sir," Adam continued, "I think it's a mistake to be sayin' the vows tonight."

Roaring, Papa lunged at him, but the table stood between them. Uncle Melvin grabbed Papa.

Essie jumped to her feet.

"Don't get me wrong, sir," Adam said, taking a step back. "I wanna marry her. But I don't wanna shame her."

"Well, it's a little late for that, isn't it?" Papa shouted.

"Papa, please," Essie said.

"Shut your mouth!" Papa yelled, jerking free from Melvin's hold.

She sucked in her breath, unable to control the moisture springing to her eyes. Never had Papa said such a thing to her or raised his voice, for that matter.

"What I'm tryin' to say, sir, is that if we marry hurry-up like, it'll create talk. And there's no reason to. The only people that know about me and Essie having our weddin' night two jumps ahead o' the ceremony are here in this room."

Papa ground his teeth.

"If we marry tonight, like this, the whole town'll know. And I just don't see why we should put Essie through that."

Mother touched Papa's arm. "He has a point, Sullivan."

"What are you suggesting?" Uncle Melvin asked Adam.

"That we announce our intentions. That I court Essie all proper-like. And that we marry at the end o' the month or somethin'."

Essie's heart swelled. He was willing to wait for her to be his bride in order to protect her from any vile gossip.

"Perhaps that would be best," Mother said.

Papa looked ready to explode. He glared at Adam. "You will conduct yourself with complete propriety. You will not so much as kiss her until the vows have been spoken."

"Papa," Essie exclaimed.

"I told you to *be quiet!*" he bellowed.

Adam stiffened. Essie stumbled back.

"Sullivan," Mother hissed under her breath. "Be reasonable."

"Be reasonable? Be reasonable!" He jabbed a finger in Adam's direction. "He has tumbled our daughter and you want me to be *reasonable*?"

Mother gasped. "That is quite enough!"

"It doesn't even come close to being enough. Enough would be stringing him up by his personals on the nearest cottonwood tree!"

Mother pressed a hand to her throat.

"Sullivan," Uncle Melvin said, his voice low.

The two friends exchanged looks. Essie dashed away a tear, only to have another fall.

"I mean it, Melvin." Papa took a deep breath. "If they have to marry, I *will not* have him touching her until after the vows have been spoken."

"I'll honor yer wishes, sir," Adam said. "All courtin' will be done in full view of chaperones."

Papa stood breathing like a horse who'd run a lengthy race.

"There," Mother said, tugging her cuffs. "That's settled. Now let's pick a date. I think it needs to be sooner than later in case Essie is in a family way."

Everything was happening so fast. No one was asking her what she wanted. It was to be her wedding, after all.

"How 'bout during the Harvest Festival?" Uncle Melvin suggested. "Everybody will be there and it wouldn't be the only attraction, so to speak, which will give folks things to talk about other than the wedding."

Essie frowned. She *wanted* her wedding to be talked about. She wanted it to be a grand affair, not some peripheral event that would take second fiddle to the fair.

"The Harvest Festival," Papa agreed. "Now get out of my house."

"Papa!"

Adam gave her arm a quick squeeze. "Yes, sir." He turned toward her.

She forced herself to relax. The details of the wedding could be worked out later. For now, she wanted to set Adam's mind at rest.

She'd always heard that eyes were the windows to the soul, so she let down her guard, exposing her heart, and allowed him to see into the very core of her being. *I love you.*

His expression softened. "I'll see you tomorrow, girl," he whispered and winked.

Uncle Melvin followed Adam down the hall, their footsteps ringing on the wooden floor. When both men had left, Papa turned to her.

"Get to your room," he ground out. "This minute. Before I say something I regret."

Grabbing her skirts, she ran up the stairs, then slammed her bedroom door shut.

———

Essie crawled beneath her covers, pulling them clear to her neck and drawing comfort from their shelter. Neither Mother nor Papa had come upstairs yet. She wondered what they were saying to each other. About Adam. About her. About what had happened.

She thought back to all the times her father had been in volatile situations. As a judge, there had been plenty of them. And never, ever, had she seen him lose control—though in several instances it would have been warranted.

So to witness it now, and know she had been the cause, filled her with remorse. She'd not really thought about how her decision to give herself to Adam would affect others. She had naïvely assumed it would only affect her and Adam.

And now it was too late. For the rest of their lives, Adam and Papa would remember this night. And so would she.

Now that she was alone, she allowed the tears that had been pressing against her all night to flood her eyes. She wanted Adam and Papa to get along. To like each other. Respect each other. Befriend each other.

How long would the rift between them last? A lifetime? Surely not. But Papa was a judge by occupation. It's what he did. And when he made his decisions, he did so with firmness and finality.

Would this bitterness extend to his grandchildren? She couldn't imagine that it would. But then, she couldn't have imagined Papa's actions tonight, either.

She thought of the reassuring smile and wink Adam had given her before he left. Would the very things that she found charming be things Papa would resent most? Oh, she hoped not. Because if Adam tried to suppress those things, he'd be suppressing his very self.

The stairs creaked and she tensed.

"Oh, Sullivan," came Mother's muffled sob as she and Papa reached the top of the stairs and walked past Essie's door. "What will we do if—?"

"Shh," he soothed, though his voice cracked as he whispered, "We'll trust God, that's what we'll do. And we'll pray. . . ." Their door clicked quietly closed and she heard no more.

Rolling to her side, Essie bunched her pillow beneath her head and closed her eyes against a new wave of tears. A cricket outside her window called loud and longingly for its mate.

For the first time in her life, she heard its distress. Its edge of desperation. And she, too, realized that after tonight no one could comfort her the way Adam could. No one. She'd so much like to be held in his arms right now.

She allowed herself to review in her mind the consummation of their relationship. Because of the darkness beneath the magnolia, she had no images to recall, only sounds. Touches. Feelings.

At first it had been marvelous. Yet as things had progressed, she'd found some of the intimacies not to her liking. And some downright painful. But she'd not wanted to disappoint Adam. So she'd allowed him free rein. But in truth, she'd felt more like a martyr than a partner.

Perhaps that's why the marriage act was referred to as a duty. She sighed. What a shame, for it had started out so wonderfully.

She touched her flat stomach through her nightdress. Could it be . . . might she really be with child? Would the intimacy they'd shared result in the miracle of a baby? Part her? Part him?

She wondered what their child would look like. She pictured the three of them going to church together.

Drifting off to sleep, she realized she'd never asked Adam what denomination he was. She'd need to do that first thing.

———

Essie could not believe she'd slept so late. Trying to decide what to wear the day the town would find out about her betrothal—while simultaneously knowing it was also the day after her parents had caught her with her lover—was extremely difficult.

She wanted to choose something light and carefree and flattering. But she didn't dare. So she chose a taupe cashmere house gown perfectly suitable for home wear, yet also very becoming. It had a small, snug-fitting yoke of black velvet at the waist and a modest high collar of the same velvet. The sleeves were tight-fitting with pointed cuffs at the wrist.

All was quiet except for subdued voices coming from the partially open door of Papa's study. Taking a deep breath, she walked past it without looking in, making a beeline for the kitchen.

"Essie?" Papa called.

She stopped, turned around, and pushed open his door. Mother and the sheriff sat opposite Papa's large desk. Mother's eyes were red and when she looked at Essie, a fountain of tears tumbled from her eyes. Pressing a hanky to them, she jumped up and hurried from the room.

Uncle Melvin slowly stood. "Mornin."

A spurt of anger she didn't even realize she'd been harboring for him jumped to the surface. She did not answer his greeting.

He glanced at Papa. "I'll see you later," he said, then hesitated in front of her. "Essie, I . . ."

She lifted her chin but focused her eyes on some distant spot over his shoulder.

"I had to do what I did," he said. "Surely you see that."

What she saw, though, was the image of her beloved uncle breaking Adam's nose. "Shall I walk you to the door?" she asked, her tone perfectly modulated.

Sighing, he placed his hat on his head. "No, thank you. I'll see myself out."

She stepped out of his way, then met her father's gaze.

He looked as if he'd aged ten years in one night. She noted for the first time that he had almost as many white hairs as gray. His jowls were loose. His eyes dull.

"Come in, please," he said. "And shut the door behind you."

Her stomach did a somersault. She closed the door.

"Have a seat."

So formal. She smoothed her skirt beneath her and sat in the upholstered chair across from him.

"I'll cut right to the chase." He took a deep breath. "Currington has skipped town."

She frowned. "What?"

"He's gone, Essie. Pulled up his stakes. Flew the coop. Squirreled off."

She shook her head. "You're mistaken."

"I'm afraid not."

She thought of the smile and wink Adam had bestowed upon her last night. "I don't believe you."

"Jeremy came by this morning when he didn't show up for work. So I had Melvin go to the boardinghouse. Mrs. Williams said Currington packed up late last night, paid up the rest of the month's board, and left. We've scoured the town for him. He's gone."

"There's some other explanation. I'm sure of it." But all of a sudden, she wasn't sure of anything.

Papa leaned back in his chair, steepling his fingers, and waited. Waited for her to accept the truth.

But she couldn't. Adam loved her. She knew he did. She raced through her memory, trying to recall when he'd told her that very thing. And her stomach began to feel queasy. For though she had expressed her love for him, he had never actually said those words to her. Had only implied it. By his actions.

She took a fortifying breath. "He said he'd come see me today and he meant it. I've no doubt he'll be here any moment."

"The word of a man who takes advantage of women is worthless."

She shot to her feet. "You've done something," she cried. "After I went to bed last night. You threatened him, didn't you? Or offered him a bribe. Tell me."

Papa's face cleared of all expression. "Upon my honor, I did nothing of the kind. Nor did your mother. Nor did your uncle. That scallywag tucked his tail and ran. Leaving you at the altar without caring for one moment whether or not you are carrying his child."

She wrapped her arms about her stomach, wondering who had moaned. Then she realized it had been her.

Papa remained seated, not a shred of sympathy or compassion on his face. "You are relieved of your duties with Sullivan Oil."

Falling back into the chair, she shook her head. "What?"

"Your mother was right. It's my fault all this has happened. I've given you entirely too much freedom and have encouraged you to disregard the dictates of society. That stops now."

"No, Papa."

He leaned forward, resting his arms on the desk. "I am handing you over to your mother. Your actions will be dictated by her. And I will endorse and support every decision she makes."

Essie grabbed the arms of the chair. "Please, Papa, please. Don't do this. I . . . I know I've hurt you. I know I've shamed you. But please. Mother will squash me. She'll stomp out every bit of pleasure I have in life."

His mouth tightened. "I'd say you've had more than enough *pleasure* lately to last you a lifetime."

She sucked in her breath. Had he slapped her across the face, she couldn't have been more hurt. But instead of the tears that she expected, an all-encompassing anger swept through her.

"How dare you," she said.

He slowly rose, squaring his shoulders and letting her see the formidability that she'd always known was there. Never before, though, had it been directed toward her.

"No," he said. "How dare *you*."

———

She waited all day, but Adam never came.

Skipping breakfast the following morning, she rummaged through her father's box of tools, little caring for the recklessness with which she handled his things. Finding a hammer, she grasped it, retrieved a tiny block of wood from the woodpile, and stormed into the house.

She slammed the door. Kicked over a chair in her path. Stomped up to the top stair and began to remove the nails in the banister.

She could hardly see what she was doing, so blurred were her eyes by desperate, angry tears. But no matter what, those nails were coming out. Today. Now. This very minute.

One by one she jerked them free, sending them flying. Disappointed at the puny tinkle they made when landing.

Mother came rushing from the back of the house and stopped short.

Essie paused and seared her mother with a look that caused the matronly woman to take a step back.

"Let me make myself perfectly clear, Mother," Essie said, not even trying to staunch the flow of her tears. "If I want to slide down the banister, then I will slide down the banister. If I want to teach a parrot to curse, then I will teach a parrot to curse. If I want to give myself to every man in the county, then I will give myself to every man in the county. And I dare you—no, I *beg* you to come up here and try to stop me."

Sorrow and tenderness consumed Mother's features. Papa jerked open his study door, his face livid.

"No," Mother said to him.

He stopped short, his chest pumping like the cable tool on Adam's rig. "I will not—"

Mother narrowed her eyes, bringing Papa's words to a sudden stop. He whirled around and slammed his door shut behind him. Mother left the way she had come. Essie returned to her task, albeit with a little less oomph.

Moments later Mother came back and strode directly to the bottom stair. With a hammer and wedge of wood, she began to remove the nails on the lower part of the banister.

Essie swallowed, then proceeded with her task. Each nail brought them closer and closer to completion and closer to each other. It was Mother who removed the last one.

They stood face-to-face on the middle steps. The white, smooth skin that her mother took such pride in was splotchy and swollen.

She offered the nail in her hand, palm up. Essie took it and defiantly flung it across the entry hall. It ricocheted from wall to wall to floor, finally rolling to a stop.

"Oh, Essie," Mother said. "I'm so, so sorry, baby."

For what? Essie wondered. For the nails? The restrictions? The critical things she'd said to Essie over the years? Or was she sorry that her daughter's dreams and future hopes had been shattered by a man who had used her and left her for greener and younger pastures?

"For what?" Essie choked.

"For everything," Mother said. And then she opened her arms.

Essie hesitated only a moment before falling into them, sobbing, wailing, expending the anguish that consumed her.

Mother held her. Rocked her. Patted her head.

She heard Papa's door open. And she knew that the two of them were staring at each other over her shoulder, grieving simply because their daughter was.

CHAPTER | EIGHTEEN

ESSIE'S LEGS BEGAN TO fall asleep. Still, she stayed on her knees. Bargaining, for the most part.

If you bring Adam back, I promise to spend more time in your Word. I'll read it more, memorize it more, dwell on it more.

She racked her brain for the sorts of things that would please God.

I'll do more service for the church. I'll clean the sanctuary, bring plants for its beautification, teach Sunday school. If only you'll bring Adam back.

She rested her forehead on the edge of the bed.

I'll spend several days a week at the State Orphan's Home. I'll care for the children, teach them some skills, shower them with affection. Please, Lord. Bring Adam back.

She wondered if she was carrying his babe. On the one hand, she wanted a baby so badly she could hardly credit it. And at the moment, she couldn't care less what the townsfolk thought of her bearing one out of wedlock. But she knew she would care one day.

She didn't want the child to grow up with the stigma of being a bastard. She'd never known one personally, but she'd heard they were treated like outcasts. She couldn't imagine her friends and neighbors doing so. Or maybe she could.

Yet she could not bring herself to pray that there was no babe. Instead, she continued to implore God to bring Adam back.

She considered confessing her sin of fornication, but she wasn't sure she was truly sorry for it. She knew she should be. But she wasn't, entirely.

Oh, she was sorry for the pain it caused her parents. She'd be sorry for the pain it might cause her unborn child—if there was one—and the shame it would bring to her parents. But she couldn't be completely sorry she'd learned what happened between a man and a woman.

She'd always wondered and now she knew.

"I'm sorry that I'm not sorry," she whispered. "But please, please, won't you still bring Adam back to me?"

Her bargaining turned into begging.

A knock sounded on her bedroom door. "Essie?"

Essie stayed where she was. The door squeaked open.

Her mother entered and sat on the edge of her mattress. "Come sit by me for a moment."

Icy prickles of pain bombarded her legs and feet when she joined her mother on the bed. A penance, perhaps.

"You need to come downstairs and eat."

"I'm not hungry."

"Just the same, you've not eaten all day."

Essie wondered if she'd be bound to her mother's schedule for the rest of her life. If she would be living in this house, this room, until her parents' deaths and then her own.

It wasn't a bad place, but she didn't want to live in her father's house. She wanted to be like other women. She wanted to "leave and cleave." But there was only one way to achieve that. And her ticket to freedom had abandoned her.

Please, God. Please.

"The ladies at church are going to sell some baked goods at the Harvest Festival," Mother said. "They need someone to work the table for them. I told them you would help."

Yesterday Essie would have agreed without a moment's hesitation. Today she resented her mother making arrangements on her behalf.

"I'm not sure I'm attending the Harvest Festival."

"Of course you are."

"In the future, I do not want you offering my services to anyone without my permission."

Mother sighed. "If you mope about on the heels of Mr. Currington's sudden departure, people will put two and two together. You must pretend nothing has happened."

"I cannot."

"You must."

"I will not."

Mother rose. "Yes, you will, Esther. Yes, you will."

———

Essie refused to eat.

"I'm fasting," she told her mother, then she wedged a chair underneath her door-knob and read her Bible.

She read Ecclesiastes.

" *'Vanity of vanities, all is vanity.'* . . . *Whatever my eyes desired I did not keep from them. I did not withhold my heart from any pleasure. . . . I said of laughter—'Madness!'; and of mirth, 'What does it accomplish?' "*

She memorized verses, then chapters. She ignored her mother's pleas to come out. Her father's commands to unbar the door.

Hours turned into a day, then into two days. Still she read. Memorized. Fasted. Christ had gone without food for forty days. Surely she could share in His sacrifice.

She wasn't worried about her baby—if there even was one. She had complete faith that God would take care of it. She was, after all, fasting. An endeavor that God would honor by protecting any babe He'd created.

Papa kicked the door open, his face red. Whether from anger or exertion, she wasn't sure. She stared at him, unmoved and unrepentant. Mother led her to the kitchen and fed her.

The food did not settle well and left her stomach shortly after reaching it. She had no energy. No interest in bicycling. No will to do anything other than sleep and read her Bible.

For the first time, she realized what a burden she must be to her parents. All she'd ever done was make mistakes, and that was probably all she'd ever do. She should have long ago left the nest. Yet here she was, still in their home. Eating their food. Encroaching on their privacy. Spending their money on fine clothes.

In the weeks that followed, she restricted herself to the simplest of attire. Dark skirts, white shirtwaists, no hats. She tried not to eat too much, so as not to be a burden. She worked harder than ever before around the house and garden.

She gathered all her hats and put them in burlap bags.

"What are you doing?" her mother asked.

"I'm going to give my hats to the poor," she said, descending the stairs with three bulky sacks.

Mother pointed to a corner of the hall. "Set them there. I have some things to give away, as well. I'll put yours with mine."

The next day the bags were gone. Essie wondered what it would be like to see someone else in town wearing one of her hats. She wondered if she'd care.

She took a basket of bedding out to the clothesline. Her mother joined her.

"There is no babe," Essie said, pinning one corner of a sheet onto the taut wire before securing its other corner.

Mother paused, a pillow slip in her hand. She offered no response, good or otherwise.

———

Essie chose another pecan from the bucket, cracked it open, then began to pick out its fruit. The sun had risen more than an hour ago, and she had been on the porch shelling pecans long before the first glimmer of light had touched the sky.

In an effort to ward off the cool breeze, she adjusted a blanket thrown about her shoulders.

Her mother pushed open the screen door and stepped out onto the back porch. "The Harvest Festival is today."

The day Essie was supposed to have married Adam. She placed a shelled nut into a bowl at her side.

"Have you decided what you are to wear?" Mother asked.

"I'm not going." She cracked another nut.

"You'll miss the tightrope walker."

"I'm no longer interested in such frivolities."

Mother eased into a rocking chair. "Essie, dear. I think it is time we had a talk."

Essie raised a brow. "I believe it's a little late to be discussing the birds and the bees, don't you?"

Mother blushed but remained steady. "Actually, I would venture to guess there is quite a bit you don't yet know, but that is not what I wanted to talk about."

The sun touched a corner of the porch but offered no relief from the chill in the air. Essie's fingers ached from the cold. She ignored it and harvested another pecan.

Mother moistened her lips. "Young women are taught that losing their virtue is synonymous with losing their right to marry." She paused. "I want you to know, your father and I do not agree with that line of thinking."

The pecan Essie was picking splintered. She popped the ruined fruit into her mouth, its dry texture rough and hard to swallow.

"What I'm trying to say is, if you think you can no longer marry because of what happened between you and that young man, then I think you will find that is not the case."

"Oh, Mother," Essie said. "What you and Papa believe about such things means nothing. It is what the man in question believes that is at issue. And I would venture to guess, no man wants used goods. Besides, I cannot credit any man wanting me, chaste or no."

"I have complete faith that God has someone for you."

Essie rolled her eyes. "Are you quite through?"

"You do not have to give up your zest for life," Mother said, leaning forward. "You needn't give up your hats, either, simply because you made a mistake."

"Perhaps I want to give those things up. Perhaps I am tired of adventure and extravagant hats and wild living. It has brought me nothing but ridicule and scorn. I cannot believe that you, of all people, are trying to discourage me from living decorously."

"Oh, Essie. I am merely pointing out that to try and mold yourself into some image the town has of a 'proper woman' is no way to experience God's grace. You have made a mistake. Well, it wasn't the first and it certainly won't be the last."

"That's not the way you raised me. Why the sudden change of heart?"

"Maybe I've come to realize that, under the circumstances, riding bicycles and sliding down banisters are not really worth worrying over."

"Well, it doesn't matter anyway," Essie said. "My new life of works and quiet living will please God. No more mistakes for me."

The sun edged closer, teasing the hem of Essie's gown.

"You cannot make yourself righteous by simply changing your behavior," Mother replied.

Essie stiffened. "I'm sure I don't know what you mean."

"What I mean is that when Christ died on that cross, He took your sin upon himself. The very one you committed with Mr. Currington. As well as all the ones you have committed in the past and will commit in the future."

Cracking another pecan, Essie stuffed down the lump rising in her throat.

"Have you so little appreciation for His sacrifice that you would fling it back in His face by trying to earn your way to heaven?" Mother rose.

Essie's fingers stilled.

"Tell me this, dear. What good is God's mercy if we never have need of it?"

She reentered the house, leaving Essie alone. Her hands lay still. A half-shelled pecan rolled from her fingertips and clattered onto the porch. The sun slowly climbed up her skirt and onto her lap, blessing her with warmth for the first time in a long, long while.

———

Buggies filled the roads. Single buggies, double rigs, and even some "Hug-Me-Tight" carriages with barely enough room for two. Horses of all kinds pranced through the streets, kicking up dust as they clip-clopped amongst the throng.

A giant tent had been staked out on Ninth Street. Beneath its shelter were rows of tables and booths selling every kind of goods imaginable. Children pulled taffy. Women circled around quilts. Men bet on the horse race that was to be run later in the day.

Mr. Lyman had parked his old wagon next to the tent, the perfume from his spicy chili pervading the air. He stirred his concoction in a large iron cauldron over charcoal coals. Bowls of chili were five cents each with an added bonus of all the crackers you could eat for free. His dog, Wolf, lay at his master's feet, never leaving his side.

A rope high up in the air stretched taut, spanning the street between the balconies of Keber & Cobb's Confectionery and Castle's Drug Store. A mule-drawn street car gave its "last call" warning for potential riders.

The excitement of the atmosphere began to draw Essie in. She wore a dark wool skirt and white shirtwaist beneath her simple cloth cape and velvet collar. Her hat was dark and modest.

When she'd returned to her room this morning, two of the sacks she'd discarded earlier leaned against her bed. Inside were the hats she'd told Mother to give away. She assumed Mother had given the missing third sack to charity.

Essie wove through the aisles underneath the tent, looking for the table where she was to work. The ladies from her church had set up a baked-goods booth, and Essie was to help man it for a few hours. Just like she'd told God she would. Only, He hadn't delivered His end of the bargain.

She passed Mr. Weidmann's booth where people lined up to buy fruitcake. She waved to him, but he was so mobbed with customers, he didn't see her.

At long last, she found her table. Sitting behind it was Katherine Crook. Hamilton's beloved wife. She wore an exquisite gown of broadtail fur and moiré combined in an intricate design. A high collar of chinchilla was surrounded by a lower collar of Russian sable, both framing her delicate face.

Her hat, however, did not live up to the gown's requirements. Instead, the flat design with very little ornamentation appeared incongruous with the rest of her costume. Still, Essie's ready-mades were pauper's fare next to hers.

"Well, hello," Essie said.

"Miss Spreckelmeyer." Her tone was polite but cool.

"I'm supposed to help sell at this booth. Are you coming or going?" Essie asked, circling behind the table.

"I just arrived. I didn't know you were to be working with me. I'd heard you were, um, indisposed."

"Had you? How very strange." Essie looked over the goods on the table and began to rearrange them.

"What are you doing?"

"I'm grouping the goods so that they will be more pleasing to the eye and so they will make more sense to the customer." She put the meringue pies on one end and the frosted cakes on the other.

"You'd best take note, my dear," Hamilton said, stepping up to the table. "Essie has quite a knack for sales. I've no doubt the hours she works will be the most profitable for the booth."

Katherine clicked her tongue. "Honestly. You say the most ridiculous things sometimes."

Essie looked up in surprise. "Hamilton. My goodness. How are you?"

A healthy color tinged his round cheeks, no doubt from the brisk weather. There was nothing cool about his gaze, though. It conveyed warmth and kindness. She smiled in response.

His square spectacles had slid down his nose so that their upper rims divided his irises in half. She longed to push them back up so she could see his brown eyes without interference.

He tipped the brim of his derby. "You haven't stopped by the Slap Out in ages. Haven't you missed me, Essie? I've certainly missed you."

Out of the corner of her eye she saw Katherine stiffen. Flustered, Essie didn't know how to respond. For the truth was, she hadn't missed him at all.

CHAPTER | NINETEEN

HAMILTON DRANK IN THE sight of Essie. There was something different about her. She was more reserved. More circumspect. More . . . refined.

He'd have expected her to wear her most outrageous hat to a festival such as this. Yet she wore a very understated hat and a somber costume.

She had greeted him with eloquence instead of exuberance. She rearranged the items on the table in a slow, deliberate manner. He liked this new Essie. He liked her very much.

"What has kept you away?" he asked.

"I've been . . . busy."

"Drilling oil wells?"

"Not anymore. Papa decided it wasn't proper and has banned me from them."

"Really?" Katherine said. "That's not quite how I heard it."

Essie glanced at her, but Katherine busied herself placing oatmeal cookies in a tin container.

She'd been a model wife, his Katherine, and he loved her to distraction. But he discovered she'd developed a penchant for gossiping. She had an uncanny ability to pluck out two completely unrelated events and connect them together in the most absurd fashion.

Take Essie, for example. Her father's endorsement of her role in his new oil venture had Katherine's tongue twanging. Then Jeremy would come to the store and inadvertently mention something that intimated a relationship brewed between Essie and the cowboy who worked for Sullivan Oil—which was ridiculous, of course. Hamilton had seen for himself the type of women Currington had favored, though he couldn't very well tell Katherine that.

When the drifter left town unexpectedly and the judge reversed his decision to let Essie work in the oil field, Katherine decided it was because Essie and Currington had been involved in a licentious relationship.

Hamilton had never heard of anything so preposterous. And the more he tried to defend Essie's honor, the more adamantly his wife justified her theory. It had progressed to the point where he wasn't sure if Katherine was able to separate the truth from whatever fantasy she had concocted within her mind.

"Mrs. Lockhart misses you," he said.

"I miss her, too."

"Well," Katherine said, "I can't imagine what you were thinking, Miss Spreckelmeyer, to perpetuate the decline of a churchgoing woman. Were it up to me, I'd refuse to order those scandalous books she's so attached to."

Hamilton frowned. "But it isn't up to you, is it, my dear? It's up to me."

Essie looked between the two of them. "You must admit, Hamilton, they are shameful. Mrs. Crook is right about that."

Katherine pulled back, causing her chin to collapse into folds against her collar. "And just how would you know that?"

A hint of a smile touched Essie's lips. "She insisted I read one. *Clarabel's Love Story*, I believe it was. Quite shocking."

Gasping, Katherine sent him an *I-told-you-so* look.

He suppressed a groan and did what he could to repair the damage. "That was very businesslike of you, Essie. I can't seem to impress upon Katherine the value of familiarizing herself with the items we carry. Yet you were always so good at that."

"Oh, nonsense," Essie said. "I read that book long after I quit working at the Slap Out. And I'm sure the customers just love Mrs. Crook." She stayed Katherine's hand.

"You might want to put those pralines next to the divinities. Don't you think it would be more attractive that way?"

Katherine slammed the pralines back down where she'd had them, breaking one in half. Essie gave her a confused look.

"Well," Hamilton said, "it was good to see you again." He turned to Katherine. "I'll come back for you after a while." He held her gaze for a moment, telegraphing his thoughts: *And be nice.*

She huffed and turned her back.

———

Essie had forgotten how much she enjoyed selling things. Didn't matter if it was a bag of nails or a piece of cake. She loved the challenge. And the people. And the competition.

"Mr. Vandervoort!" she exclaimed. "How in the world are you?"

The old nester sauntered up to the table, then coughed up and swallowed an accumulation of phlegm. "Well, Miss Essie, things are pretty dull in the Slap Out without ya. No snakes, no mice—" he leaned forward with a teasing light in his eyes and whispered, "—and no 'mouse catchers.' "

Essie caught her breath.

He winked, then said more loudly, "Yep. I surely did want me one o' them mouse catchers. But Hamilton wouldn't sell me one to save his life."

She bit her lip, but not before a giggle escaped.

"What?" Mrs. Crook said. "You're in need of a mouse catcher, Mr. Vandervoort?"

Patting his chest, he chuckled. "Oh, I don't know that I'm in need o' one, exactly. But I shore would like another gander at it. That Hamilton won't let me have so much as a peek."

"You mean, we have what you want and he won't sell it to you?"

"He has his reasons," Mr. Vandervoort said, rocking back and forth on his feet.

"Well, perhaps I could help you the next—"

"Can I interest you in some tutti-frutti?" Essie interrupted, picking up a square and offering it to him. "Or perhaps some penuche? Mrs. Whiteselle made it, you know."

"Excuse me, Miss Spreckelmeyer," Katherine said. "I believe Mr. Vandervoort and I were in the middle of a transaction." She smiled at him.

"It don't matter none," he said. "I think it already sold, actually."

"No," Essie said under her breath.

He nodded. "You didn't know? Well, shoot. I was hopin' you could tell me who the lucky owner was. I'd surely like to know."

Covering her mouth with her hand, she couldn't suppress her amusement. "That is too bad of you, Mr. Vandervoort. For shame."

He guffawed. "Ah, Miss Essie. You gotta come have a cup o' coffee with me and the boys. We still talk about the day that cowboy came into town and wound you up so tight with the snake that you ended up dropping all those mice."

Mirth fell from her as quickly as if she'd been doused with a bucket of cold water. "I didn't drop the mice."

"Well, maybe you didn't. But that feller shore did tangle you up." He picked up a square of tutti-frutti and handed her two pennies. "We'll see ya later."

She watched him walk away, images of that day flashing through her mind.

"They do talk about it quite often," Mrs. Crook said. "Seems it was the first time they ever saw the cat capture your tongue."

Essie dropped the pennies into a cigar box. She had no idea anyone else had been watching the two of them. But of course it made sense that they would have been the center of attention. Adam had not only been a stranger, but he'd been a gorgeous stranger. Every man and woman in the place would have tracked his every move.

He wasn't so perfect now, though. He had a crooked nose. She wished they all could have seen that.

"It was the same man who worked on your father's oil rig. A Mr. Currington, I believe?"

Nodding politely, Essie scanned the crowd for a potential customer.

"I do declare, he turned every girl's head in town. But it was evidently young Shirley Bunting who claimed to have captured his heart."

Essie whipped her head around. "What makes you think that?"

A knowing smile touched Katherine's face. "Hadn't you heard? He was to escort her to this festival. She purchased fabric to make an autumn jacket in honor of the occasion. That's how I know."

Essie didn't believe it. She would have heard something. But she'd been so absorbed in her own little dreamworld that she hadn't noticed much of anything since Adam began his seduction of her.

"You're a bit pale, dear. Are you all right?" A look of realization came over Katherine. "Oh no. You didn't have . . . *feelings* for him, did you?"

Essie forced herself to take slow, deep breaths. "No, no. Of course not. Whatever gave you such an impression?"

Katherine cocked her head. "Well, it only makes sense, him being so handsome and all. And the two of you working so close together right after Hamilton jilted you."

Essie stiffened. "I don't know what you're talking about."

"No need to get defensive, dear. Hamilton told me all about how you chased after him, no matter how many times he tried to discourage you."

Mortified, she couldn't believe he had shared such a thing with Katherine. A spurt of anger shot through her.

She imagined them sharing other intimacies, then talking about her, laughing as they discussed what a pathetic old maid she was. The fragile palisade she'd erected around her heart began to crumble.

"Mr. Currington left town rather quickly, as you well know." Katherine looked left and right, then leaned close. "The night he left, he came knocking on our back door to settle up his accounts. There had been some trouble. Woman trouble. And the sheriff was running him out of town."

Essie felt like an exposed possum caught in the open while a hunter took aim with his shotgun. Too bad she couldn't "play dead."

"Unbeknownst to Hamilton, I had come down the stairs in my stocking feet to make sure all was well. I stopped when I heard the men's voices." She licked her lips, warming up to her story. "I could tell Hamilton was angry. He'd never much liked Mr. Currington, you know."

"No," Essie said. "I hadn't realized that."

"Yes, well. He asked who the woman was, but all Mr. Currington said was that she wasn't the kind you pay for. Nor was she the kind you'd want to marry. Too old, he said."

Breathing grew difficult. The tent, the crowd, the tables began to close in on her. She needed to get out. She needed air.

"At first I thought it was Shirley, but she's just a young little thing. I wonder who it could be?" Katherine gave Essie a penetrating stare. "Whoever it was, he was clearly using her to slake his thirst for pleasure. Why else would a man like that toy with an older woman?"

She knew. This woman knew Essie's secret. Or at the very least, she strongly suspected. If Essie were to run, all would be confirmed.

"Poor Shirley," Essie managed. "She must be devastated."

Katherine chuckled. "Hardly." She indicated someone with a nod of her head.

Essie turned. Shirley Bunting, in a form-fitting jacket of satin merveilleux shot in copper shades, walked by with an entourage of men trying to gain her favor. The young woman laughed and teased and flirted.

"Well," Essie said, hearing her voice tremble and hoping Katherine didn't notice. "I'm so relieved. It would have been tragic for her to have found out Mr. Currington was stringing her along while pursuing interests elsewhere."

Katherine raised a brow. "I do believe, Miss Spreckelmeyer, it wasn't Shirley he was stringing along. But someone else. Someone older." She smirked. "But clearly, not wiser."

———

Essie strode from beneath the tent and headed to Mr. Lyman's wagon for some chili. Anything to occupy her hands and her mind. Had Katherine Crook known Essie well, the game would have been up. But she didn't. And hopefully, Essie had bluffed her way through these last three hours without giving herself away.

The animosity Katherine held toward Essie was as clear as the sky above. What she couldn't fathom was the reason for it. Why would Katherine dislike her so completely?

It was Katherine, after all, who got the man. Not Essie. It was Katherine who'd had two husbands, while Essie hadn't had so much as one. It was Katherine who ran the store with Hamilton, while Essie had no purpose in life whatsoever.

It didn't make any sense. Nevertheless, she'd have to be very, very careful. One little slip and all would discover her shameful secret. She'd told herself it didn't matter what the townspeople thought, but it did.

It mattered a lot. And not just for her sake, but for her parents' sakes. It would ruin Papa's chances for reelection, just a few days away. And it would reflect badly on Mother. The women of her circle would somehow think it was Mother's fault.

"One bowl, please," she said, handing Mr. Lyman a nickel and patting Wolf on the head. The dog lifted his nose and slapped his tail against the ground in appreciation.

"Here ya are, Miss Spreckelmeyer," he said. "You better go on now. The peg-legged man's fixin' to walk that rope."

She glanced over at the crowd that had begun to form and headed toward them. The thick, hearty fare tasted like no other chili she'd ever had before. She welcomed the warmth it provided as the sun began its descent.

Up on the balcony, she could see several men strapping a cumbersome cookstove to a man's back. The crowd around her chattered with excitement.

"Miss Essie," someone called.

She turned. "Jeremy!"

He wove his way through the crowd until he reached her side. "It's mighty good to see ya," he said. "I shore do miss those lunches you used to bring us."

"I miss them, too," she answered, smiling sadly as she thought of the picnics she'd shared with Adam and how much she'd enjoyed them.

She looked Jeremy over. All that cable drilling had added breadth and form to his once-skinny body.

"What happened with you and Adam?" he asked.

She stiffened. "What do you mean?"

"Well, golly, Miss Essie. Anybody could see y'all were sweet on each other."

She forced a laugh. "Oh, don't be silly. We were just friends."

"I don't know," Jeremy said, looking at her askance. "I seen the way you two would get yer heads together and whisper-like. And his eyes would light up like firecrackers when he'd see ya comin'."

Did they? she wondered. It made her feel a little better that Jeremy had seen something, too. At least she hadn't been the only one to imagine an interest that clearly wasn't there.

"I'm afraid you're mistaken, Jeremy. We were just friends."

"Well, if ya say so, but you shore never looked at me the way ya looked at him. And you and me is friends."

She cleared her throat. "Yes, well."

"He was gonna rope fer everybody today. Remember?"

Yes. He was also going to marry me today. She tried to put the thought from her mind.

"I could o' watched him do them ropin' tricks all the day long. That new feller that works with me now? He ain't near so easy to get along with."

"Oh? I'm sorry to hear that."

"Maybe if ya bring him some lunches, too, it'll improve his disposition some."

She smiled, then froze as she caught sight of Katherine and Hamilton standing a few feet away. Hamilton's attention was focused on the tightrope walker. Katherine's was focused on Essie.

Her heart started to pound, wondering how much the woman had heard, if anything.

"Lookit!" Jeremy said, pointing. "He's fixin' to go."

Essie turned and shaded her eyes. The man began to slide across the rope one foot at a time, his wooden leg stiff, his other leg bending for balance.

The crowd hushed, not daring to breathe as he inched his way across the rope. The stove was obviously heavy and awkward. It looked to Essie as if it was not evenly distributed across his back, but a bit heavier on the left.

He teetered. The audience gasped, then held their breath until he regained his balance. His clothes were as black as the stove, making the rope slashed across his body more pronounced.

The farther he came to the halfway mark, the more the rope sagged, giving in to the tremendous weight. The man wavered again, far to the left.

Essie sucked in her breath. He windmilled his arms, but the stove interfered with his motions. He leaned to the right but overcompensated, and the stove shifted.

Before anyone could so much as react, the man fell with a crash to the ground.

CHAPTER | TWENTY

WOMEN SCREAMED. CHILDREN BURIED their eyes in their mothers' skirts. Men rushed forward.

"Let me by," Essie said, shoving aside those in her way.

When she finally broke through, she saw that the stove had landed on top of the man, trapping him beneath. He was still alive, but just barely. Blood pooled beneath his mop of dark hair, accentuating the clammy whiteness of his face.

Her father and Dr. Gulick bent over him. Uncle Melvin shooed the crowd back.

"Do you want a preacher?" the doctor asked.

No answer.

"Can you tell me where you're from?" Papa said.

Still no answer.

The crowd parted, making way for Preacher Bogart. He knelt beside the dying man. "Do you know Jesus Christ, son?"

The man's eyes fluttered open. "Please," he gasped. "A rabbi. I am a Jew."

A fleeting look passed between the men.

Papa caught sight of Essie. "Get me a rabbi."

They exchanged the briefest of glances, knowing full well there was no rabbi in Corsicana, Texas. But there was a Jew.

She whirled around and fought her way through the press, heading to the north side of the tent where she'd seen the peddler's wagon.

"Mr. Baumgartner! Mr. Baumgartner! Come quick," she screamed.

He jumped from his wagon seat where he'd been trying to see over the crowd and raced toward her. Grabbing his hand, she pulled him behind her.

"The rope walker," she said over her shoulder. "He's asking for a rabbi."

Mr. Baumgartner increased his speed so that by the time they arrived he was pulling Essie behind him.

Papa and the preacher stepped back. Mr. Baumgartner touched the man's forehead and spoke over him in Yiddish.

The man visibly relaxed, said a prayer in Hebrew, and died.

Mr. Baumgartner closed the man's eyes and then looked at Papa. "His Hebrew. It was perfect."

Papa placed a consoling hand on Mr. Baumgartner's shoulder.

"I wonder if he had any kids," little Harley North said, startling Essie. She'd not even noticed him standing next to her. He looked up. "If he did and there's no mama, then they'll be orphans. Like me."

She lifted him into her arms and hugged him close. He encircled her with his arms and legs, pressing his face into her neck. The boy was too young to have witnessed something so horrible. Still holding him, she walked away so the men could do what needed to be done.

———

For the first time in its history, the festival closed down early and the horse races were postponed. Essie set Harley in a chair at her mother's kitchen table, placing a plate of cookies and a glass of milk before him.

"Is this where you eat with yer ma and pa ever' meal?" he asked, his gaze touching the gingham curtains framing a window, the indoor water pump Papa had installed for Mother, and the fancy Sunshine cooking range in the corner.

"Yes, it is."

"Golly. I wish I had somethin' like this. We all eat in that big ol' ugly room with nothin' but tables and chairs."

She smoothed back the black hair covering his eyes. He needed a haircut. "You snack on these cookies while I go put on my bicycle costume," she said. "Then I'll give you a ride home on my handlebars. How does that sound?"

"You're leavin'?" His eyes widened and he grabbed her skirt. "What if the judge comes home? Or yer ma? And they see me eatin' their food?"

"It'll be all right, Harley. You just tell them Miss Essie gave them to you. They won't mind."

"Ever'body minds. Nobody wants a orphan in their kitchen. Nobody."

She frowned. "That's ridiculous and not the least bit true. Why, I want you in our kitchen and I'm somebody."

His eyes darted to the back door.

"Hush now, and eat up. I'll hurry. I promise." She pried his hand from her garment and quickly made her way upstairs.

Removing her skirt and petticoats, she began pulling on a short skirt, bloomers, and leggings. The wonder in Harley's voice as he'd examined their kitchen provoked feelings of compassion and not a little guilt. She'd just this morning resented their home, thinking of it more as a prison than anything else. Yet little Harley would give his eyeteeth to live here.

She fastened the final button of her boot. She had already taken so much time, she didn't want to delay any longer. Not bothering to change her shirtwaist or hat, she came out of her room, heard voices, and quickened her pace.

Harley stood on a chair before a table with an apron wrapped twice around his little body. He pounded a lump of dough with one fist and then the other as if he were trying to annihilate it.

"I'm makin' some biscuits, Miss Essie," he exclaimed, his eyes bright.

Smiling, Mother cracked an egg into a bowl. "Watch what you're doing, Harley, or else you might miss the dough and deliver a fatal blow to the table."

Realizing the trip to the orphanage would wait, Essie removed her hat, picked up the empty plate and glass Harley had snacked from earlier and carried them to the washbasin. Then the three of them continued with dinner preparations, Mother and Essie doing most of the work and Harley doing most of the talking.

"What do ya think they'll put on the peg-legged man's grave? 'Here lies a man with one leg. If ya knows where he's from, please make his mark here.' "

Essie and Mother exchanged glances.

"You think he has family?" Harley continued. "Do Jews have families, Miss Essie?"

"Yes, of course they do," Essie answered.

"How do ya know? He only had one leg. Ladies are awful picky. I'd bet they'd want their fella to have both his legs."

"You can't judge a man by the way he looks," Essie said. "A good man without legs would be a far better friend than a bad man with both his legs intact. It's not what's on the outside that counts, but what's on the inside."

"Unless you're a orphan. Nobody wants a orphan no matter what he looks like on the inside."

She started to contradict him, then held her tongue. What he said had some truth to it. Folks put a lot of stock in family backgrounds. If someone from a good family were to marry an orphan, there would be a scandal of huge proportions.

Still, she had come from a good family, and nobody'd wanted her. They'd especially not want her now. Now that she was a full-fledged spinster. And a ruined woman.

But Harley was different, she told herself. He had his whole life ahead of him. And who could resist him, orphan or not?

"That's not true," she said.

"Is too."

"Is not."

Harley studied her for a moment, then opened his mouth as wide as he could, showing her every single tooth and his tonsils to boot.

She blinked.

"Well?" he asked. "What do you think? Am I purty on the inside?"

She smiled. "The best I've ever seen. And that's the truth."

"Really?"

"Really. Now, use this pin and roll out that dough." She positioned the roller in his hands. "Start in the middle and work your way to the edges."

He couldn't manage it, so Essie placed her hands over his and guided him. With Mother puttering around behind them, Essie could almost pretend Harley was her son. Almost.

She thought of Adam and once again tried to imagine what their child would have looked like. Or what a child of hers with Hamilton would have looked like. What would it be like to have her stomach swell as it held a life that God had knitted together with His own hands?

She inhaled, then stopped herself midstream. Harley needed a bath.

"Maybe the peg-legged man was a orphan," the boy said, "and that's why he was by hisself."

"Possibly." She moved the roller to a thick section of dough. "Here, try to spread it out evenly. Like this."

The dough started sticking to the pin. Essie sprinkled it with flour.

"You sure are good at this, Miss Essie. How come you ain't married?"

She heard Mother pause in the middle of chopping some carrots.

"I don't know," Essie answered softly.

"Ain't ya purty on the inside?"

Mother resumed her task with sudden vigor.

No, Essie thought. *I'm not.*

He twisted around when she didn't answer. "Lemme see."

She shook her head.

"Come on. Open up. I'll tell ya the truth."

She glanced at Mother, but the woman acted as if chopping vegetables required every bit of her attention.

Essie slowly opened her mouth.

Harley studied her for so long that she became embarrassed and closed her mouth. *See, I told you so.*

"Well," Harley said, "I ain't never peered inside o' anybody before. Only horses. And I can tell ya this, yer insides is a whole lot purtier than Mr. Mitton's horses. And he boasts somethin' awful about them beasties."

"Thank you," she whispered.

"Miss Essie, do ya think ya might could wait 'til I get a little taller? Then you and me could marry up, seein' as how we both think the other 'un is purty on the inside."

A rush of affection for the boy filled her. "Well, Harley. Those are some mighty strong words to say to a lady. So, I'll tell you what. When you get a little, um, taller, if you find that you are still interested, why don't you ask me again?"

"You're just sayin' that 'cause you don't wanna marry no orphan." His shoulders drooped.

"No, no, that's not true. It's just that you are supposed to speak with my father first. But I think you probably ought to wait a few years before you do that. All right?"

"All right. And as soon as they let me, I'll start votin' fer him, too."

She smiled. "He'd like that very much. Now, put the rolling pin aside. It's time for the biscuit cutter."

———

They ended up riding Cocoa to the State Orphan's Home. After the excitement of the festival and the big dinner they'd fed Harley, the boy could barely keep his eyes open. He'd have fallen asleep and tumbled off the bicycle's handlebars, so they'd taken the horse instead.

"Listen, Harley," she whispered. "Do you hear that cricket with evenly spaced chirrups?"

"Uh-huh."

"That's a temperature cricket. If you count the number of chirps within a fifteen-second span, then add forty, you can calculate the temperature outside. Let's try it. Ready? Go."

She silently counted. "I counted sixteen. That would mean it's fifty-six degrees outside. How many did you count?"

A soft snore escaped Harley as he relaxed against her. She wrapped her cloak more tightly around them, trapping their warmth inside. The stench of his dried sweat breached the covering. The boy reeked, but she'd not had time to give him the promised bath. She planned to return to the orphanage tomorrow to see he received both that and a haircut.

A nighthawk darted by, startling Essie with its sudden, erratic advance. Its nasal *peent* cut through the drone of insects. Essie couldn't see it anymore or the female it was trying to impress, but she could hear the explosive ruffle of its wings as it dove toward the ground, swooping upward at the last possible moment.

She suppressed her irritation. Wasn't there anywhere she could go without being constantly reminded of males and females and their courtship rituals?

The entire world goes two by two, Lord. All except for me. Why? Why did you cut me out of my inheritance?

And now it was too late. She was ruined. Even if the Lord sent a man her way, she'd not be able to marry him without confessing she'd given herself to another.

And that would be the end of that. So why even bother? She would have to resign herself to life as a spinster.

But she didn't want to. She couldn't quite let loose of that elusive dream. She wanted it so badly. Was Mother right? Would a man be willing to accept a woman who'd been used by another? She didn't think so.

What if she didn't tell him? What if she pretended he was the first?

She discarded the thought immediately. Even if he never found out, she would know. And God would know. Deceit simply wasn't an option.

She sighed. It was a waste of time to contemplate such things anyway. Her chances for catching a man were over. Over. The sooner she accepted it and moved on, the better.

They crested a hill, and Cocoa blew a gust of air from her lungs, shaking her mane. Essie steadied her.

The full moon backlit a conglomeration of buildings nestled at the bottom of the hill. She could just make out the superintendent's residence and the children's dwellings behind it. Barns and sheds sat tucked toward the back edge of the property, a picket fence encompassing all.

Cocoa's hooves crunched the gravel path. A clapper rail called out in evenly spaced clicks. As Essie neared the gate, she realized it wasn't a bird she heard, but the rhythmic creak of a rocking chair on the superintendent's front porch.

And whoever was rocking had stopped and headed toward the fence. "Who goes there?"

She pulled her mount up. "Essie Spreckelmeyer. I have Harley North with me."

"Miss Essie?" he asked.

She squinted, trying to see who it was. "Yes. Who's asking?"

"Ewing Wortham."

"Good heavens. You're back from Bible school in Tennessee?"

"That's right." He moved next to her, then lifted his arms.

She relinquished Harley to him. The boy stirred, then settled against Ewing's shoulder.

"Are you a preacher, then?" she asked.

"Only if someone hires me as one."

Slipping off Cocoa, she tied the horse to a fence post. "How long have you been home?"

"Only a few hours."

They stepped through the gate and headed to the boys' dormitory.

"Oh my. Were your parents even here? Most folks were still at the festival."

"It was pretty quiet," he said, boosting Harley up.

"Is he heavy?"

"No, he's fine. Ma said there were a few stragglers that hadn't made it back. Which one is this?"

"Harley North. We don't know much about him. A farmer from Blooming Grove brought him into town a couple of years ago saying his parents had died of smallpox."

They reached the cabin where the boys slept.

"I'll get him settled, Miss Essie."

She stroked Harley's head. "Thank you. I'll be back tomorrow to check on him. The accident today upset him."

"I heard it was pretty bad."

"It was awful. It happened so fast, Ewing. And right in front of all those youngsters. Once the shock of it wore off, the menfolk formed a tight ring around the man, shielding him from view, but by that time the image of that poor soul resting in a pool of blood, all crushed and broken, was indelibly stamped in my mind." She shook her head. "I'm sure it will be a long time before any of us sleep soundly through the night."

"Did he have anyone with him?"

"Unfortunately, no. Ends up the name he went by was one he'd adopted as a performer. They're still trying to find out who he was and where he was from. But no matter what, this town will see to it that he has a proper mourning and burial. Mr. Baumgartner is instructing us in the Jewish traditions for such things."

A pig frog grunted several times in rapid succession. A gnat buzzed in her ear.

"Well, I suppose I ought to head on home," she said. "Good night and thank you for helping me with Harley."

"If you'll wait a minute, I'll walk you back to the gate."

"That's all right."

"I insist." Before she could respond, Ewing hurried into the dormitory.

It was so dark, she hadn't been able to have a good look at him, but she remembered him well. He was six or seven years younger than she was, and they'd both attended the one-room schoolhouse together as children.

He'd been a pest, always wanting to come with her when she went fishing or hunting. It used to drive her to distraction. He'd been noisy and easily sidetracked, while she'd been very serious about her pursuits. And she still hadn't quite forgiven him for bidding his measly two cents on her box suppers all those times.

The door creaked open and he crept out. "Sorry it took so long. I didn't know which bed was his."

"Did he wake up?"

"Only for a moment. He's fallen back asleep now, though."

She turned toward the front gate, but he stopped her. "No, Miss Essie, come this way."

"Why?"

"I'm going to saddle Rosebud and escort you home."

"Oh no, Ewing. That's not at all necessary. I wander these hills alone all the time."

"Not when I'm around, you don't."

She smiled. "Really. I'll be fine."

"Miss Essie, I don't mean any disrespect, but I'm saddling up Rosebud. If you leave ahead of me, I'll have to push that ol' girl in order to catch up. You wouldn't want to distress her like that, now, would you?"

She placed her hands on her hips. "You haven't changed one single bit, Ewing Wortham. Still blackmailing me into letting you tag along. Didn't that Nashville Bible school teach you anything?"

"Yes, ma'am. Taught me to take care of our women. Now, come on and help me with Rosebud. She always liked you better anyway."

All Essie wanted was to go home and crawl into bed. Instead, she resigned herself to doing the polite thing and followed the "preacher."

CHAPTER | TWENTY-ONE

MOISTURE COLLECTED AGAINST THE walls of the barn. Essie tugged her cloak together to ward off the chill, yet it did no good. The smell of leather, hay, and muck filled her senses. Ewing lit a lantern.

Oh my, but he's grown up, she thought. Gone was the chubby, freckled kid who'd dogged her every move, and in his place was a young man. Still light-haired, still quick to smile, still on the short side, but there wasn't anything boyish about him, nor was there an extra ounce of flesh to be seen.

"You must be a cyclist," he said, eyeing her short skirt.

"Yes."

"It's quite popular in Nashville."

"You ride?" she asked.

"It was forbidden."

He pulled a saddle off a rack, threw it over the mare's back and began to cinch it up. The horse swiveled her head around and bit him.

"Rosebud, no!" Jumping back, he rubbed his arm and shot Essie a glance. "I told you she didn't like me."

Suppressing a smile, Essie hugged herself to keep warm.

"Push the barn door open for me, would you?" he asked, slipping a bridle over the horse's head.

They walked the horse to the front gate, where she retrieved Cocoa and mounted up.

"It sure is good to be home," he said, inhaling deeply.

"You didn't like Nashville?"

"I loved it. Never seen a prettier place. But it gets mighty cold in the winter. Mighty cold." He pulled up short. "Shhhh. Listen."

She stopped.

"You hear that? You hear that beetle?" he asked.

A noise much like a squeaky hinge sounded over and over again.

"That's a pine sawyer," he said. "You know how I know that?"

She shook her head.

"You taught me."

"I did?"

"Yes, ma'am. You taught me to listen to all the night creatures."

"I was probably just trying to get you to hush up."

He chuckled. "You cut me to the quick, Miss Essie."

They rode in silence, she with a new ear to the nocturnal. The animals and insects of the night were as familiar to her as breathing. She had no recollection of teaching their identities to Ewing.

"So what have you been doing with yourself since I've been gone—besides bicycling, that is?" he asked.

"Nothing much, I suppose."

"Now, why is it I don't believe that?"

She didn't respond and he allowed the conversation to lag. Something she'd never known him to do before. Maybe that school had taught him a thing or two, after all.

They arrived at her house and he would have gone all the way to the stables with her, but she stopped him.

"Let me put her away for you," he said.

"No. Don't you remember? Cocoa doesn't like you, either."

He huffed. "I'd forgotten."

"Good night, Ewing. And thank you for seeing me home."

He tipped his hat. "My pleasure, ma'am. I'll see you tomorrow."

"What?"

"You said you were going to check on Harley. I'll be there, too."

"Oh. Of course. Well, tomorrow, then. Good night."

He made no move to leave, so she left him staring after her as she guided Cocoa round back.

———

"I wanna take some flowers to the rope-walker's grave," Harley said, pulling a gooey handful of pulp and seeds from inside a pumpkin.

He and Essie were cleaning them out for Lester, the orphanage's cook. He'd set them up in the dining hall, now empty apart from the two of them and their pumpkins. She scraped the sides of hers with a spoon.

"I'll take you," she said, "but you'll need a bath and a haircut first."

Scrunching up his nose, he paused. "The feller's dead. Why should he care what I look like?"

The screen door at the front of the dining hall squeaked open, then slapped shut. "If Miss Essie says it's time for a bath and haircut," Ewing said, entering, "then you don't argue. You simply do it."

"Howdy, Ewing," Essie said, then turned back to her task. "Harley, have you met Mr., um, Preacher Wortham?"

Harley shook his hand, trying to dislodge a pumpkin seed. "I met him," he said, accidentally slinging the seed off of his hand and onto her cheek. "I didn't know he was a preacher, though."

Ewing spun a chair backwards and straddled it. "Ewing is fine."

Her hands were a mess, so she brushed the seed with her shoulder but could not get it off. Ewing leaned his chair forward on two legs and plucked the seed from her cheek.

"Thank you."

He smiled.

"Cook's gonna make some pumpkin soup," Harley said.

"Y'all need any help?" Ewing asked.

"Not with the pumpkins, but Harley might need some assistance with his bath."

"I don't need no help. I can do it."

"Just the same, will you help him, Preacher?"

"Be glad to. And don't call me Preacher. Doesn't sound right coming from you."

"But neither Ewing nor Mr. Wortham is the correct form of address."

"Ewing will be fine."

She wasn't so sure about that, but calling him by anything other than his given name did seem a bit bizarre.

She shot a surreptitious glance in his direction. Wouldn't the girls in town be agog when they saw how he'd changed? It wouldn't be long before he'd marry one of them. She wondered which one it would be.

"I'm all done with mine," Harley said. "What about you, Miss Essie?"

"I've still got a little ways to go. Why don't you and Ewing go on to the creek and wash up. When you return, I'll be finished here and ready to cut your hair."

Ewing stood.

"You gonna wash, too?" Harley asked him.

"Might as well." He picked up a rag and wiped the boy's hands off. "We'll be back shortly."

"Take your time."

———

The water was cold as a Tennessee winter. Ewing dove under, then shot back up with a roar. Harley stood naked and shivering at the edge of the creek.

"Come on in. Feels great."

"Preachers ain't supposed to lie."

"I'm not lying. It does feel great. It feels great to be clean and to smell nice. Now, come on."

"How 'bout we just say I did. Nobody'll know."

"Miss Essie will know. And then we'll both be in trouble." He could see the boy wasn't going to make it in past his ankles. Striding out of the water, he swooped Harley up.

"No, no! I'm gonna freeze." The boy kicked and screamed.

Ewing kept right on walking. Harley put up such a fight that by the time Ewing managed to dunk him, they were both warm from the effort.

But it didn't last long. He had to soap the boy's hair and body two or three times to remove all the dirt. His lips turned blue before they were finished.

He toweled them off with worn fabric that was too old for someone's rag basket and had therefore been donated to the orphanage.

"Here's some clean clothes. They might not fit just right, but they'll keep you warm for now."

He'd never heard someone's teeth actually chatter, but Harley's were clacking up a storm. He'd known all along that they'd need a fire after their swim, so he'd laid some kindling in advance. Now he bent to light it, then pulled on his trousers, shirt, and jacket.

Harley huddled in his oversized clothing and fed the flames with dead leaves and pine needles.

"You must be something special to have Miss Essie looking after you this way," Ewing said.

He shrugged. "Me and Miss Essie is friends, is all. We go fishin' together. She ain't never made me take a bath before, though."

"Well, she's taken a shine to you. Anybody can see that."

"I akst her to marry me."

Ewing lifted his brows. "Did you? What'd she say?"

"She said I had to wait 'til I was taller. Then I could ask her again."

The smell of freshly burned pine spread throughout the clearing. Ewing blew on the flames and they surged upward. "Has she had many beaus?"

"Lots o' fellers like her."

"Who?"

"The sheriff. The peddler. The shopkeeper."

"What shopkeeper?"

"Mr. Crook."

"Never heard of him."

"He runs the Slap Out. So did Miss Essie for a while. That's where she took the king snake we caught. You shoulda seen it. His name was Colonel."

"What happened to it?"

"Me and Miss Essie and Jeremy let it go free."

"Jeremy? Jeremy who?"

"You know. His granddaddy's the drunk?"

Ewing nodded. "Gillespie. You're talking about Jeremy Gillespie?"

"I don't know. He works on Miss Essie's oil well. Him and that cowboy fella by the name o' Adam. The one what likes Miss Essie. 'Cept he cut outta town real quick-like."

"Who did? Jeremy or Adam?"

"Adam. Ain't you payin' attention?"

"I'm trying." Ewing scratched his jaw. "So this Adam fellow. He was sweet on Miss Essie?"

"She liked him, too. She never came to see me once when he was in town. I saw her plenty o' times, but she was always with him and didn't even know I was there. She even let him ride her bike. He crashed it and ever'thing and she still let him kiss her. I saw."

Kiss her? And he'd left town in a hurry? But Ewing let those questions go unspoken and instead asked another, more important one. "Does Miss Essie know you saw her kissing this man?"

"Nope."

"Have you told anyone else what you saw?"

"I tol' Jeremy."

"Anybody else?"

"Well, I tol' you just now."

Ewing rested his elbows on his knees. "Harley, there are some things a man does, and some things he doesn't. He does protect the womenfolk. So if you were spying on Miss Essie—"

"I wasn't spyin'!"

"Excuse me. If you accidentally saw Miss Essie with a man and feared for her safety, then it would've been okay to have kept your eye on her. But once you realized she wasn't in any danger, keeping an eye out for her changed into spying. And that's something a man doesn't do."

"How can ya tell she ain't in danger?"

"When she kisses him back."

"Now, how am I supposed to tell who's kissin' who?" Harley said, clearly exasperated.

"Was she struggling, Harley?"

The boy looked off into the distance as if recalling what he'd seen. "No. Can't say that she was."

"Then she was kissing him back and it was time for you to leave. All right?"

"All right."

"And one more thing."

Harley looked at him.

"A man never, ever, kisses and tells. And not just when he's doing the kissing, but when he sees someone else doing the kissing. I don't want you to ever, and I mean *ever*, breathe a word about Miss Essie and this cowboy to anyone else. You understand?"

"Yes, Preacher."

Ewing ruffled the boy's head. "All right, then. Let's put this fire out and go get you a haircut."

———

Something had happened at the creek. Essie could sense the change in Harley and Ewing immediately. A camaraderie. An easiness.

She tied a sheet around Harley's neck, glad to know he had a new friend, especially one who would be so close by.

They were once more in the dining room, but this time it held a handful of children doing chores. A girl about ten years old in a tattered brown sack dress wiped grime from the windows. A boy a little older than Harley placed chairs on top of the tables while another followed behind with a mop.

Ewing had just finished stacking the chairs closest to him, when he twirled one around and straddled it.

"That crick was cold, Miss Essie," Harley said. "I don't ever wanna do that again."

Thank you, she mouthed to Ewing.

He winked.

The gesture so startled her, she dropped her scissors. He grinned and did it again.

"You ever cut a fella's hair before?" Harley asked.

"What? Oh. Yes. Of course. I've cut my father's many a time. Now, sit still."

She picked up the scissors and concentrated on her task. She couldn't fathom why in the world Ewing would wink at her. That would be like, like *Jeremy* winking at her. She shook her head. Ewing might have grown up some, but she couldn't think of him as anything other than a tagalong that never shut up.

"I hear you've been drilling oil wells," Ewing said.

"Yes. Papa has a rig over on Twelfth, though it has yet to produce."

"How far down are they?"

"I'm not really sure."

"Who's working the rig?"

She pulled a section of Harley's hair up with her comb, trapping it between her fingers before snipping off its ends. "Jeremy Gillespie and a man by the name of Cal Redding."

"Redding? Who's that?"

"He's new to town. Only been here a month or so."

"Who worked the rig before that?"

"A drifter."

"Adam, that cowboy I was tellin' ya about," Harley piped in.

Essie froze, wondering what Harley had said about Adam. She caught herself with idle hands and immediately resumed her cutting.

The silence was heavy and uncomfortable. But no, she was just imagining it. Ewing had no reason to suspect anything out of the ordinary about Adam. The girl washing the windows headed back to the kitchen with her bucket and rag.

"Tell me about him, Essie," Ewing said, his voice soft.

She glanced at him briefly, then began to cut a section around Harley's ears. "There is nothing to tell, really. He was a drifter. Came to town, worked for a while, then left."

"Golly, Miss Essie, that ain't true. He petted Colonel. He helped us catch them mice. He bought me sarsaparillas. He could rope anything that moved. And you ran over him with your wheeled feet. Remember?"

She swallowed. "Put your chin down, Harley, and quit talking so I can even out the back."

She cut the back, the silence worse now. Much worse.

"Okay. You can raise your chin."

He lifted his head and she parted his hair, combing it to one side.

"There," she said. "All done." She untied the sheet from around his neck.

Harley jumped off the stool. "How do I look?"

"Handsome," she answered. "You look very handsome."

"Handsomer than Adam?"

Her lips parted. "Yes."

He puffed out his chest. "Thank ya, Miss Essie. Can I go now?"

"Yes."

He raced out the door, letting it bang closed behind him. She stared at it, the sheet hanging limp in her hand.

"Adam was handsome?" Ewing asked.

Essie lowered her gaze. "Yes," she whispered.

He stood. "I'll go get the broom so we can sweep up this mess."

CHAPTER | TWENTY-TWO

I T FELT FUNNY ENTERING the Slap Out from the front door instead of the back. Essie paused a moment just inside the threshold, inhaling the familiar scent of molasses, leather, and grain. She took in the store and the changes that had been made.

The corner shelf and table she had once arranged to hold sewing and millinery items now held a hodgepodge of goods—sewing notions, cookware, even farming supplies. The medicinals were no longer grouped according to ailments, nor even grouped alphabetically. She could not tell if there was any rhyme or reason whatsoever to their order on the shelf.

No items had been set out on the front porch to lure customers in, nor did the windows hold anything of particular interest.

The stove at the back was still there, though, with a hot pot of coffee and cups hanging in invitation. Huddled over a barrel, Mr. Vandervoort jumped his black disk across the checkerboard, spit into a spittoon, then gloated while Mr. Owen crowned him. Hamilton displayed an array of grommets for Mr. Bunert, the harness maker. Heads together, Katherine and Sadie Tyner studied the catalog.

Essie took a close look at Sadie and wondered, not for the first time, if she was the mysterious owner of the "mouse catcher." If she was, it hadn't done the girl much good.

"Essie," Hamilton exclaimed, looking up. "It's good to see you. Come on in. You know where the coffee is." He smiled. "And I guess you know where everything else is, too. Katherine or I will be with you in a moment."

"I'm fine, Hamilton, take your time." She glanced at Katherine.

The petite woman, wearing a stiff white apron Essie had donned many a time, was whispering to Sadie. The girl giggled and glanced over her shoulder, then turned back to Katherine, leaning close to give her response.

"Miss Essie," Mr. Vandervoort boomed. "This is the third time today I've beaten Lafoon. Come over here and give me some competition."

She draped her cloak on a hat rack, then wove around barrels, crates, and tables. "Is he cheating, Mr. Owen?"

"I believe he is, Miss Essie, I just cain't quite figure out how. He always straightens up when you come round, though. So maybe my luck will improve now."

She picked up the coffee kettle, but only the dregs remained. She moved to the coffee grinder, poured in some beans and cranked the handle, the potent aroma soothing and familiar.

Katherine hurried to her side. "That's my job. If you'll just wait until I'm through with Miss Tyner, I will take care of this."

Essie released the grinder and took a step back.

"Oh, let her do it, Katherine," Hamilton said from across the room. "Nobody can brew a pot of coffee the way Essie can."

"What do you want?" Katherine hissed.

"Some fabric."

She waved her hand in the general direction of the cloth. "Well, when you find what you are looking for, *I* will cut it off the bolt. Is that clear?"

"Certainly," Essie said, averting her gaze. "Please, excuse me." She moved to the alcove housing the cloth. The selection had diminished considerably. Replacement bolts should have long ago been ordered.

Katherine returned to help Sadie. The men resumed their game. Hamilton filled out a credit slip for Mr. Bunert.

A few moments later, the bell on the door jingled and the harness maker left. She fingered a corner of some black India lawn.

"Find what you're looking for?" Hamilton asked softly, slipping up behind her.

"Didn't we used to have some brown worsted wool?" she asked.

"Why, yes." He scanned the stacked bolts. "Hmmm. I don't see any, but I'd have ordered it if we'd been low."

He rummaged through the cloth, lifting up a bolt here and there. Finally, he straightened and sighed. "I'm sorry. We must be out. I had no idea."

"It's all right."

"It's not all right. This never used to happen when you were here." He flashed a glance at Katherine, then stepped farther into the alcove and out of his wife's view. "Would you consider coming back, Essie? Things haven't been the same since you left."

"It's not even been a full three months, Hamilton," she said, lowering her voice. "Give her some time."

"It didn't take you more than a week to have this place running like clockwork."

"She's had a lot to adjust to. A new husband, a new baby, a new town. You must be patient."

"But look at this place. It's a mess."

"Hamilton, please. You're embarrassing me."

"Well," Katherine said, causing both of them to jump. "Isn't this cozy?"

The woman stood just outside the alcove, her body stiff, her lips pursed.

"Where's the brown worsted wool?" Hamilton snapped.

"Why don't you ask Miss Spreckelmeyer? She seems to know where everything is, now, doesn't she?"

Hamilton's cheeks flushed, and Essie felt the heat rising to her own, as well.

"I believe the men are in need of coffee," he said. "Why don't you go and make it, Katherine?"

She jerked loose the strings behind her waist and yanked off her apron. "Why don't you?" She shoved the apron against his chest. "I'm going upstairs to check on Mae and Mrs. Peterson."

She marched away, leaving the two of them alone in the alcove. Her bootheels cracked against the wooden floor, heralding her path from the store to the stairs, until finally a door slammed in the distance.

"Do not ever put me in such an awkward position again, Hamilton."

"I'm sorry." His glasses magnified his brown eyes and the distress within them.

"Comparing your new wife with another is the height of foolishness."

"I haven't said anything."

"You've done nothing but sing my praises since the moment I walked through the door. I'd thank you not to let it happen again." She stormed to the front, grabbed her cloak, and left without even saying good-bye to the men in the back.

Furious, Essie strode toward the Flour, Feed and Liquor Store. She could not decide who she was more irritated with—Hamilton for being so clumsy or Katherine for being unhappy with the man she had stolen right out from under Essie's nose.

Crossing the street, she dodged horse droppings, swatted at flies, squinted against the dust kicked up by traffic, barged into the Feed Store, and ran smack into a solid male body.

"Whoa!" the man said, encircling her with his arms to keep them both from falling. He quickly released her and stepped back. "Why, Essie. Are you all right?"

She took a deep breath. "I'm sorry, Ewing. I wasn't watching where I was going."

"Well, if I'd known it was you, I might not have let go so fast."

She frowned. She understood exactly what he was implying but couldn't reconcile the fact that it was Ewing talking to her this way.

The teasing glint in his eye was not at all patronizing, but instead glowed with obvious male interest. Her first thought was exasperation, followed by a bit of panic. There was simply something amiss about being admired by a man whose nappies she used to change when his mother was too busy.

"I think you must have jarred something loose in our collision," she said.

He chuckled. "I assure you, ma'am, I am in full use of my faculties."

She gave a short huff.

"What are you doing here?" he asked. "Is it anything I can assist you home with?"

"No, I was just going to pick up some wool. I wanted to make Harley a few pairs of pants and a shirt or two before winter set in."

"Did you, now? How very good of you."

She waved her hand in a dismissive gesture. "He's a sweet boy. Now, if you will excuse me?"

He tipped his hat. "Of course. Good afternoon." He opened the door, glanced back at her and winked.

She gave him a frown, but he smiled in return—completely unrepentant.

———

Essie stepped into the kitchen, cold from the walk home but anxious to start on Harley's trousers.

Mother came around the corner, pulling up short when she saw Essie. "Where have you been?"

"At the Flour, Feed and Liquor Store," she said, setting her cloth and cake on the table. "Then I stopped by Mr. Weidmann's bakery. What's the matter?"

"Your father wants to see you."

She paused in the unbuttoning of her cloak. "Why?"

Mother unfastened the final button for her, then slipped the cloak from Essie's shoulders. "Go on, dear. He said to send you in the moment you arrived home."

"Why?"

"You never used to question me when he wanted to see you."

"He hasn't asked to see me since Adam's desertion and since he banished me from the oil fields."

"Nevertheless, you'd best not tarry."

Essie turned around.

Papa stood in the archway separating the hall from the kitchen. "I need to speak with you," he said quietly. "Please."

Was he going to reinstate her in his oil business? He'd mellowed somewhat since he'd been reelected, but she hadn't expected him to give into her wishes quite so soon.

He stepped back from the archway, allowing her to sweep past and precede him into his office. When the door clicked shut behind him, he placed his hands on one of the upholstered chairs designated for guests and pulled it back slightly.

She sat, expecting him to circle around his desk. Instead, he sat in the matching chair beside hers.

For a long time he said nothing. She did not squirm. Nor did she make eye contact, choosing instead to look straight ahead in an effort to appear nonchalant.

"Ewing Wortham came by to see me."

She whipped her head around. Ewing? Papa called her in here to talk about Ewing?

"It's not public yet, but our church board has asked him to be its pastor as soon as Preacher Bogart retires at the beginning of the year. Now that Ewing has a means of support, he asked me for permission to court you."

She didn't know which alarmed her more—the idea of Ewing being her pastor or of Papa giving him permission to court her. "You told him no, I trust?"

"I did not."

She sucked in her breath. "Why not?"

"Because he's a good man."

"Which is precisely why you should have refused his request." Her eyes widened. "Please do not tell me you *accepted* on my behalf? Surely, if you did not refuse him outright, you told him you would think about it, knowing full well you would refuse him later?"

"I didn't need to think about it."

She shot up from her chair. "Papa, what are you saying? Are you saying you said yes?!"

"He came all the way back for you."

"He *what*?"

"He came back home from Tennessee because he wanted you. He said he'd been confident God would keep you available for him."

She shook, unable to believe this was happening. "If I have remained unmarried all these years because that snotty-nosed brat has been praying that I be here for him when he returned, then I will personally go and wring his sorry neck!"

"Come now, you can't be surprised. He's been infatuated with you since he was ten. He's written you every quarter since his departure and you've answered his letters."

"His letters were no more than two paragraphs long and I only answered him three times. And I only did that out of courtesy. Out of friendship. Never once did he intimate any romantic feelings for me. I thought he'd outgrown all that!"

A hint of humor touched Papa's face. "Apparently not."

"This is not the least bit funny. Have you forgotten that I am ruined? *Ruined.*"

Papa surged to his feet. "You are nothing of the kind."

"How can you even say that? You know I am."

"You made a mistake, as has many an innocent girl."

"I'm not a girl. I'm a full-grown woman and I certainly am no longer innocent!"

"God is merciful. He gives second chances."

"Well, *God* is not asking to court me."

"Are you sure?" Papa set his jaw.

Heaven help her, he could not be serious. "Think, Papa. Ewing is going to be a preacher. *A preacher.* That would make me a preacher's wife. A preacher's wife does not go to her marriage bed soiled!"

He slammed his fist on the desk. "Do not speak of that again."

"But it *happened.* You cannot pretend it didn't simply because you want to."

"You have been forgiven. In God's eyes you are as pure as snow."

She pressed a hand to her forehead. "Perhaps that is so, Papa. But in Ewing's eyes, I'd be used goods."

"Enough!" he roared. "I gave him permission to court you. He will be here at five o'clock to take you for a ride."

"Well, I hope you and he enjoy your little outing, then, because I am not going."

He took a menacing step toward her. It took every bit of self-control she had to hold her ground.

"You are going, Esther Spreckelmeyer. Make no mistake. Your bread, your butter, and the clothes on your back are provided by me. And if I say you go, you go. Do you understand?"

An overwhelming fury consumed her.

"Do you?!" he shouted.

Mother burst into the room.

Essie whirled toward her. "Did you know about this?"

"Of course."

"And you *agreed*?"

"I did."

"How could you?"

"Because your father is correct. You have every right to be courted by a man."

"I do not! I gave up that right to Adam Currington. Are you suggesting I conceal that truth from Ewing? That I, in essence, lead him on some merry chase all the while knowing he thinks I'm untainted?"

"Well, no, of course not. But there's no need to be rash. No need to put the cart before the horse."

"And what happens if the cart and horse line up? What happens if the courtship progresses to the point that he makes an offer? What then?"

Mother wrung her hands. "Your father will handle that when the time comes."

"I won't do it." Essie rushed past her mother. "I'm not going," she cried, running up the stairs and slamming herself into her bedroom.

CHAPTER | TWENTY-THREE

ESSIE COULD NOT SIT still. She paced round and round the perimeter of her room, stunned at her parents' maneuverings. Papa should never have accepted Ewing's request. It was nothing short of dishonest.

In her heart of hearts, she still wanted to marry and have children, but she knew that was no longer a possibility. No matter what Mother and Papa thought, no decent man—especially not a preacher—would want a woman who'd lain with another.

She stopped at her window, looking out at the myriad of leaves covering the ground. What on earth was she going to do? If she outright refused to accompany him today as she threatened, he'd no doubt take it personally. She didn't want to hurt Ewing's feelings. Nor did she want to encourage him.

Papa had said Ewing came back for her. All the way from Nashville. She shook her head. He'd hung on to his feelings for her all this time? It was simply too preposterous to comprehend.

She began to circle her room again. Finally she decided she would go on that ride today. And she would tell Ewing the truth. About her and about Adam. She would not wait as her parents suggested.

And after that, perhaps Papa would think twice about granting anyone permission to court her. Not that anyone would be asking.

Sighing, she went to her wardrobe and tried to decide what a woman should wear on her first outing with a man who was about to be given the shock of his life.

———

At five o'clock, Essie opened her door, stepped to the top of the stairs, and made her way down. Papa stood at the entryway with Ewing. Both turned when they heard her descending.

Papa looked ready to collapse with relief.

Ewing looked like Harley when someone gave him a sarsaparilla. "Hello, Essie," he said.

"Ewing," she responded. His clay worsted frock coat was a perfectly respectable jacket but would have been better suited to someone with more height, what with its hem coming down to his knees and all.

"You look lovely," he said.

She tugged on the edge of her carriage cloak. The black satin was trimmed with black marten fur that descended down the front and about the hem like a round boa. Rather than a hat, she wore a simple beaded clip above her Empire twist.

He held out a bouquet of white chrysanthemums.

It was the first time in her life a man had brought her flowers. She faltered. "Oh. My goodness. Why, thank you. I . . . well, how very thoughtful. Thank you."

"You're welcome."

She touched her nose to the flowers, inhaling their light, refreshing scent.

"Here, my dear," Mother said, joining them. "Shall I put those in some water for you?"

"Yes, please."

Ewing made a small bow. "Good evening, Mrs. Spreckelmeyer."

"Hello, Ewing. It's good to see you again. Welcome home."

"Thank you, ma'am."

The four of them stood in the foyer, awkward and uncertain.

Ewing put his hat on. "Shall we go?"

He held out his arm. Essie placed hers atop it, feeling like an actress in a performance.

"I'll have her home before dark, sir," he said to Papa, then they stepped out of the house and headed to the fence where his rig was waiting.

She was surprised to see it was an actual top buggy as opposed to a road wagon and wondered if the church had given him an advance on his salary. He placed a hand beneath her elbow and helped her up before moving around to his side of the rig. The seat creaked and tilted when he pulled himself up.

He did not reach for the reins right away but instead sat looking at her, a smile on his face. "I can't believe I am here, with you, in this carriage. I cannot tell you how many times I have dreamed of this moment."

She flushed, knowing she'd had no such longings for him.

He searched her eyes. "You take my breath away. You always have. Did you know that?"

No.

"I know you'd probably rather go fishing than riding in a carriage, but now that we're courting, I don't think it would be wise. I'm afraid being alone together like that might damage your reputation."

She gave him a weak smile, wondering if there had been some gossip to prompt his statement. Gossip from Katherine Crook, perhaps?

"Well," he said, rubbing his thighs, "I suppose we ought to get going."

He unwound the reins, gave the horse a "giddy-up" and headed toward downtown. His gift of gab had been perfected and honed over the years he'd been gone. He elaborated on his letters, entertaining her with stories of his train rides to and from Tennessee, his adjustment to living so far from home, and the pranks he and his schoolmates had played upon one another. She'd never dreamed Bible college could be so rambunctious.

The familiarity the two of them had shared as children made a resurgence, but this time she found herself laughing and chattering and teasing. They'd circled all the way through town before she even took note of her surroundings. Once she did, however, she became conscious of the townsfolk.

They openly stared. What on earth was an old maid like her doing with a youth like Ewing? That's what they were wondering, she knew. Her cheeks burned under the scrutiny, and she couldn't bring herself to meet their gazes.

As the buggy swayed, the two of them inched unconsciously toward the center of the bench, until finally their shoulders touched. Shocked by the contact, Essie reached for the wing and pulled herself to her side of the seat.

He pinched a corner of her cloak and tugged it softly toward him. "Where ya going?"

"We were, I didn't realize—"

"I did. And it was nice."

"Ewing, I . . . well . . ." She sighed. How in the world did you tell a man you'd been ruined and he ought to turn his attentions elsewhere? She couldn't exactly blurt it out right here in the middle of town.

"Let go, Essie," he said, his voice quiet, persuasive, full of invitation.

She didn't answer, just intensified her grip on the arm rail.

"Don't be scared."

"I'm not scared."

"You look scared."

"Well, I'm not." She turned her attention to the street and saw Mrs. Lockhart standing on the walkway, handkerchief in hand. She waved it at Essie, a delighted smile on her face, a knowing look in her eyes.

Good heavens. "I'm ready to go home now, please."

"What's the matter?"

"Nothing."

"No, it's something. What is it?"

She tucked her chin.

The next opportunity he had, he guided the buggy in a northwesterly direction, pointing them toward home. The route took them right past the Merchants' Opera House.

The orchestra gathered at the grand entry, and Essie realized with a start that it must be ten-cent night. She remembered the way the "society belle" had flashed her ankle and bare foot in front of the braying crowd, and how she'd allowed Adam to embrace her in the balcony. Then kiss her, touch her. Were his intentions dishonorable even back then?

They reached the railroad tracks on the edge of town, but instead of turning north, Ewing prodded the horse to cross them.

"Where are we going?" she asked.

"Somewhere we can talk."

"I thought you said we needed to avoid being alone."

"We do, but there's something wrong and whatever it is, I don't want to sort it out on your front porch with all the windows open."

She made no protest, for she, too, abhorred the thought of telling him about her sordid past within earshot of her parents. That he could read her so well was unsettling and comforting all at the same time.

They traveled in silence, twilight beginning to fall. With its approach came the sounds of nature and her inhabitants—some preparing for bed, others just awakening. He turned into an unobtrusive break in the tangled growth that lined the road. It quickly led them to a copse of trees just wide and long enough to completely conceal their vehicle from casual passersby.

"Whoa," he said, stopping the horse.

In front of them was an opening that overlooked a pond she'd fished at many a time. Yet she had never noticed this spot. A spot perfect for lovers who did not want to be discovered.

"You've been here before," she said.

He turned. "Is that an accusation?"

"No! No, of course not. Just an observation, I suppose."

He wrapped the reins around the dash rail, then rested his elbows on his knees. Bullfrogs made their low, vibrant call of *jug-o-rum, jug-o-rum.* Crickets buzzed and trilled. A gathering of ducks squawked, loud and out of sync.

She moistened her lips, having no idea where to begin.

"Are you angry with me?" Ewing asked.

"No," she whispered. "Not at all."

"Then what's the matter?"

The pond picked up the pinks and purples touching the sky and duplicated them on its shimmery surface.

"Ewing, I . . ."

He studied his fingernails. "You don't like me."

"No, no. I do, I like you just fine, but . . ."

"But what?"

"But Papa has not been completely honest with you."

He sat up, frowning. "What?"

"He should never have granted you permission to court me. He should never grant permission for *anyone* to court me."

Confusion traveled across his features before alarm replaced it. "Essie, are you ill? Are you . . . dying?"

"No, no." She shook her head. "Nothing like that."

"Then, what?"

O Lord, help me. Her throat filled, requiring force to push the words out. "I am not marriageable, Ewing. Not to you, not to anyone."

He grasped both her hands and turned her toward him. "You are barren?"

She slid her eyes closed and shook her head.

He briefly tightened his hold. "If you aren't dying and you aren't barren, then what are you?"

"Ruined," she choked, a tear splashing onto their intertwined hands.

His grip relaxed, then withdrew.

She couldn't bring herself to look at him at first. But she decided that, whatever else she might be, she was no coward. She wiped the tear from her cheek and lifted her gaze—only to wish she hadn't.

His jaw was tight with shock, a tremor running under his skin. His eyes sparkled dully, like they'd been forced to see too much and then had stopped seeing altogether.

He looked away, running a hand over his mouth. His Adam's apple bobbed. He stared at the pond as if mesmerized. "Who all knows?"

"My parents and the sheriff."

"No one else?"

"No one else."

He pinched the bridge of his nose. "Do I know him? Is he someone I will see at church, at the store, at the club?"

"No. You never knew him."

"Was it the drifter?"

She sucked in her breath but said nothing. Finally she touched his sleeve. "I'm sorry."

He jerked away from her touch. "I waited for you, Essie," he said, anguish coating his words. "Do you have any idea how many opportunities I've had to be with other women? Yet I never betrayed you. Not once. I held myself back. For you. For *us.*"

"I didn't know," she said, the tears coming more rapidly now. "We had no understanding between us."

"You shouldn't need one. You should have waited on principle alone for whatever man God had for you."

"I know, I know. I'm sorry."

He jumped from the buggy, striding down the slope to the pond, kicking a log here, a rock there. At the bottom of the hill, he plopped down and propped his head in his hands. She watched his shoulders bounce.

I'm sorry, Ewing. I'm sorry, Lord. It wasn't worth it. The few moments of bliss I shared with Adam, they weren't worth all the torment I have caused my parents, my friend, myself, and you. Oh, if I could do it over, I would make a much different choice. Forgive me, Lord. Forgive me.

But even if He granted such a thing, she would never forgive herself.

It was dark before Ewing climbed back up the hill and joined her in the carriage. She could no longer see his face, but the stiffness in his body spoke for itself.

He drove her home with unbearable slowness, keeping the buggy at a sedate and calm pace. He didn't say a word to her or even glance her way. She kept religiously to her side of the seat. When they finally pulled up in front of her house, she prepared to jump down.

He touched her arm. "No."

He circled around and helped her to the ground, then took her elbow and walked her clear to the door.

"Good night, Essie," he said in a pleasant voice plenty loud enough to be heard through the windows.

"Good-bye," she whispered.

He tipped his hat and returned to the rig.

Papa was standing in front of his office door when she entered. "He said he would have you home before dark. Where have you been?"

Resentment surged through her, momentarily overshadowing her fragile bid toward repentance. "Where do you think I've been?"

"I have no idea."

She released the ties of her cloak, letting him think what he would.

"What is it?" Mother asked, stepping into the hall. "Has something happened?"

"I told him."

She hurried forward. "What do you mean, you told him?"

"I mean, I told him." Essie looked her father in the eye. "I told him I was ruined."

Mother gasped. "You didn't."

"I did."

"Why on earth would you do such a thing?"

Instead of answering, she slipped off her cloak, smoothed it over her arm, then returned her attention to Papa. "Do not accept another request for courtship on my behalf. I will never marry and I do not want to have to go through something like that ever again."

———

Katherine Crook knelt beside a bucket of oatmeal, carefully packing a half-dozen eggs inside. Lizzie was a careless girl, and Katherine didn't want the eggs to crack before they made it home to the child's mother. She glanced up when Hamilton entered the storage room and lifted the long, wooden bar from their barn-like door.

"Quickly," he said, "Mrs. Bogart has brought in a box of butter, but I need to receive a delivery."

Katherine placed the final egg in the bucket, then scrambled to her feet. The preacher's wife made the best butter for miles around. Not every woman scrubbed her churn out before each use or washed the buttermilk out of the butter. Mrs. Bogart not only did that but she also churned her butter twice a week while the cream was still fresh. Her trays would sell for double the normal price before the day was through.

Brushing oatmeal off her hands, Katherine picked up the bucket and entered the store. "Here are your eggs, Lizzie."

"Thank you, ma'am."

She nodded to the girl, then made her way to the preacher's wife, who had placed her butter chest on the counter.

"Good morning, Mrs. Bogart. How are you?"

The elderly woman's face and chin above her collar held as many wrinkles and sags as a mastiff. Her eyes were barely visible beneath the folds of her skin, but her smile was warm as ever. "I'm fine, dear. How is that beautiful baby?"

"Growing every day."

"I'll just bet she is."

Katherine opened the chest and began to remove trays of butter from inside. Each tray was dovetailed together and made with white wood, which kept its contents free from taint or smell. "I heard Preacher Bogart will be retiring soon?"

The woman rested her clasped, gloved hands against her waist. "Yes. I still can't quite believe it."

"How long has Preacher Bogart been at the pulpit?"

"Nearly fifty years now. And did you know that the young man the elders are bringing in as our new shepherd is barely out of school?"

"No. I hadn't heard a thing. Who is it?"

"Ewing Wortham. The son of the couple who run the orphanage?"

Katherine hesitated. "Yes, of course. I met him for the first time last week."

Mrs. Bogart tugged a handkerchief from her sleeve and dabbed at her eyes. "I just don't know how in the world I'll be able to sit in those pews and listen to someone my grandson's age give the message." She shook her head, sending the flaps along her chin to swinging. "I can't imagine what the elders were thinking to entrust our flock to such an untried fellow. Can you?"

Katherine covered the woman's hand and squeezed. "I cannot. And a couple of days ago I saw him driving Essie Spreckelmeyer through town. He's not thinking to court her, is he?"

A poignant smile stacked the wrinkles on each side of Mrs. Bogart's mouth. "If he is, that is his saving grace. Anyone smart enough to snatch up that sweet little thing clearly has more intelligence than most of the other men in this town."

Katherine stiffened. Was that a hidden inference to Hamilton? She was so tired of hearing people speak of Essie with such regard. Oh, many made remarks about her choice of hats and her fancy attire and her penchant for pursuits more suited to men.

But there were many more—including her husband—who were quick to defend the brazen woman, and Katherine had had about all she could take.

She closed the chest and opened their accounting book. "Well, I wouldn't say this to just anyone, but I'd hate for young Mr. Wortham to assume such an important position in town, only to find out he'd been led astray by the woman he was considering for marriage."

Frowning, Mrs. Bogart cocked her head. "What do you mean?"

Katherine moistened her lips. "I want you to understand I'm not gossiping. I just thought you might want to, um, pray about this."

"Pray about what?"

Katherine scanned the store, then moved around the counter to Mrs. Bogart's side. "Do you remember when that cowboy who worked for the judge left town in a hurry?"

"No. Not particularly."

"Well, he did." She lowered her voice. "And I have it from a good source that it was because he compromised Miss Spreckelmeyer."

The woman regarded Katherine at length before exasperation transformed her face. "Of all the ridiculous . . ." She tugged her gloves more tightly into place. "I wouldn't believe everything I heard if I were you, Mrs. Crook."

The censure of the preacher's wife stung. Katherine straightened. "Think what you will, Mrs. Bogart. Hamilton told me Essie was so desperate for a husband that she threw herself at him—right here in this very store when no one else was around. Why, she even wrote down the names of the men in town she'd decided to try her wiles on. Hamilton saw it with his own eyes. As a matter of fact, he was one of the men on her list."

A troubled frown puckered Mrs. Bogart's brows.

Katherine lifted her chin. "And the cowboy I was telling you about told Hamilton she did the same thing to him. Only he was not as discerning as my husband, and when the sheriff caught that man and Essie in an, um, unfortunate encounter, he and the judge ran the fellow right out of town—as if he were the one at fault."

Mrs. Bogart searched Katherine's eyes. And though Katherine couldn't be certain of the details, she knew she wasn't far from the mark. Jeremy and Harley were as close to Essie as anyone and not nearly so guarded with their tongues. It didn't take much to put two and two together.

She picked up a pencil and handed it to the preacher's wife. "Your signature, Mrs. Bogart?"

The woman scribbled down her name, and for all her earlier bravado, her disorientation was such that she left the store without her butter box. No matter. Katherine would see that it was delivered to her before the next batch of cream was ready for churning.

CHAPTER | TWENTY-FOUR

HARLEY PRESSED HIMSELF AGAINST the arm of Essie's chair and watched every stitch she took. The fire popped, filling the parlor with warmth.

"Cain't ya take bigger stitches? Then you'd finish quicker."

"Smaller ones are better," she answered. "You want these trousers to hold up through the winter, don't you?"

"Well, shore. But I ain't never had brand-new pants before. Not even at Christmas."

"Well, in another hour or so, you will."

Pushing away from the chair, he wandered throughout the room. But instead of admiring the scenic painting above the secretary or the bronze cherub on the mantel, he squatted down and smoothed the tangled strands at the edge of their Axminster rug.

"Go into the kitchen and ask my mother for a fork," she said. "Tell her you are going to rake the fringe in the parlor for her."

He raced out to do her bidding, returning shortly with fork in hand. She expected him to tire of the chore, but he gave it his full attention, lining the threads up like teeth on a comb.

"Ewing's gonna take me hunting," he said without deviating from his task.

"Is he?" She paused, picturing Ewing's carefully controlled expression when he'd escorted her to the door last week after her confession. "Hunting for what?"

"Dove."

"Dove? But you'd need a gun to bring down one of those."

"I know. He's gonna teach me how ta shoot. I already know how to load."

"But you're only seven."

"Ewing says his daddy gave him his first gun when he was six."

She tried to remember when Grandpa had taught her to shoot, but she couldn't recall. Surely she'd been older than six or seven.

A knock at the front door interrupted her musings.

"Want me ta get it?" Harley asked.

"Please."

The boy loved to answer the door. Such a simple, ordinary thing, unless you were an orphan and had no door to open.

"Howdy, Ewing," she heard Harley say. "Come on in."

Essie stiffened. She'd been to the orphanage several times this past week but had not seen any sign of him there or anywhere else in town.

He stepped into the parlor, hat in hand, his strawberry blond hair neatly combed. A moment passed before it dawned on her how he was dressed.

He wore a black cutaway, black vest, black necktie, light-colored trousers, and pale gloves. The consummate dress for a gentleman caller.

"Hello, Essie."

She felt heat rush to her cheeks. "Ewing." She put down her sewing and stood. "My goodness. I . . . well, can I offer you something to drink?"

"No." He swallowed. "Actually, I was wondering if I could interest you in a carriage ride?"

Perplexed, she studied him. His face had cleared of all expression. She couldn't imagine his motive for asking such a thing. "Why?"

"Because that's what courting couples do."

Her lips parted. Surely he didn't still want to court her? Yet his rust-colored eyes were intense and determined.

"What are you saying, Ewing?"

"I'm saying my feelings haven't changed." He looked to the side, floundered a moment, then returned his gaze to hers. "Well, that's not exactly true."

She stood mute and completely caught off guard. Never in all her imaginings had she expected him to show up on her doorstep.

She glanced at Harley. The boy had stopped combing the fringe and placed his full attention onto them, his brown eyes alert.

"Harley?" Ewing said. "Run along to the kitchen for a moment and let me speak to Miss Spreckelmeyer. Would you?"

"She cain't go with ya right now. She's makin' me some pants."

"Go on, Harley," she said. "Tell Mother I said you've worked so hard you deserve a cookie."

His eyes lit up. "A cookie? Right now? Before supper?"

"Yes."

He raced from the room, his rapid footfalls echoing in his wake.

Essie indicated her father's chair on the opposite side of the hearth from hers, and the two of them sat down.

Ewing crinkled the brim of his hat and stared at the fire. "I'm not going to pretend I'm not devastated. I am. But my feelings, the ones that count, haven't changed."

She had no idea what to say. Those stolen moments beneath the magnolia tree had not been forced upon her. She'd been a willing participant. Not for one second had she considered how her actions might later affect Ewing or any other man. Of course, she hadn't thought there would ever be any other man. Yet now an honorable one sat before her, his heart in his hand.

"I've been doing a lot of thinking," he said, "and a lot of praying. I came to the conclusion that I wouldn't be much of a preacher if I held against you something God has already forgiven."

Forgiven? How could God forgive her when she hadn't even forgiven herself, not to mention Adam? Disbelief warred with shame and regret. "I'm unworthy of it," she whispered.

His expression softened. "None of us are worthy of it. That's not the point. The point is, I'm not perfect and you're not perfect. But that doesn't mean I don't have strong feelings for you, because I do. And I'd still like to court you. If you'll have me, anyway."

She could not reconcile the boy she'd known with this man. This amazingly gracious, poised, well-spoken man. He deserved better.

"But I'm so old."

"Old?" A hesitant smile lifted one corner of his mouth. "Are you telling me you have some gray hairs tucked up in that bun of yours?"

"Certainly not."

"Well, then. Let's not worry over trivialities such as how old you are and how old I am."

"Seven years is not trivial."

"It is to me."

And, of course, it probably was to him. Anyone who could overlook her unchaste life would certainly be able to overlook her advancing age.

"What's the matter?" he asked.

I don't know, she thought. This was what she'd always wanted. Ewing might not send her pulse skittering, but he was a good man and a cherished friend. He'd be an excellent father and provider. If he was willing to accept her the way she was, how could she turn him down?

He shifted in his chair. "We would, of course, need to be very circumspect in how we proceed."

She frowned, unsure of his point.

"What I mean to say is, now that I am aware of your, um, weakness, I think it is essential that we do everything we can to guard you from yourself." Both his tone and posture stiffened.

"Guard me from myself?" she asked.

"Yes." He cleared his throat. "As you know, I have been offered the position of pastor at our church. And as such, my actions and those of the woman I court must be above reproach."

A spurt of defensiveness leapt to the forefront. What exactly did he think she was going to do? Drag him to the nearest tree and have her way with him?

With effort, she squelched her uncharitable thoughts. After all, she was the confessed sinner here, not him. And if he was willing to overlook her transgression, she could at least remember he was only trying to do what he thought best. Still, he needn't sound so self-righteous about it.

"First," he said, "any . . . um, extravagant feelings we have must be carefully repressed."

The image of him as a youngster jumping from a tree in an effort to fly flashed into her mind, along with the shockingly coarse words he'd exclaimed after his subsequent fall. She pushed the memory aside.

"If we wish to express affectionate fondness in our visits," he continued, "then we must keep it a sentiment, not debase it with animal passions."

Animal passions? She might have regretted her tryst with Adam. She might have felt profound remorse for squandering the most precious gift she had to offer. But never once had she considered her actions with him *animal passions.*

"Also, a woman's dress," he said, "is an expression of her inner soul and should serve to heighten her charm, not draw attention to her . . . to her garments."

What on earth? Ewing was suddenly so stiff and upright, spouting rules as if he'd memorized them along with his Bible verses. She sighed. Had his Bible college impressed these ideals upon him? Was he trying to act the way he thought a preacher should?

She became conscious of her plain wool gown and gloveless hands. Not exactly an outfit she would have chosen to receive callers in. But she didn't know she was going to have any callers.

"Do you have some objection to the way I dress, Ewing?"

"Your hats are very extravagant," he answered with a gentle tone. "I think it might be best to tone them down a bit. Quite a bit."

She slowly straightened her spine. Tone down her hats? But they were her pride and joy. "You think they are excessive somehow?"

"I don't mind them, Essie. I'm just not sure they are fitting for a preacher's wife to wear."

"Well, I don't happen to be a preacher's wife," she snapped.

"Yet," he said softly.

Her breath caught. Well. If she'd had any question about his intentions, they were certainly clear now. But for heaven's sake, what could possibly be wrong with wearing a pretty hat?

"And though we have known each other for our whole lives," he continued, "I think it best to start using a more formal form of address. From now on, I will call you Miss Spreckelmeyer and you must call me Mr. Wortham."

She stopped just short of snorting. Hadn't he been the one to insist upon first names when he'd returned home? Still, she knew he was right, but it seemed so absurd. When he was a toddler, she'd slapped him on his backside for sticking his tongue out at her. She'd kissed his knee when he fell and scraped it raw. She'd quizzed him on his multiplication tables. She'd helped him place his first worm on a hook.

And now she must call him Mr. Wortham?

"Anything else?" she asked, trying to keep the exasperation out of her voice.

"Just one more thing."

She folded her hands in her lap and waited.

"You must give up bicycle riding."

She sucked in her breath.

"I know this is difficult for you," he said. "But there are doctors, well-respected doctors, who claim that the bicycle will ruin the feminine organs of matrimonial necessity." Color rushed to his face. "And it is believed to greatly increase the labor pains of childbirth. And it will develop muscular legs, which would be an unsightly contrast to underdeveloped feminine arms. Forgive me for mentioning such delicate subjects, but I wanted you to understand how serious this is and why I am so opposed to women riding."

His color remained high, attesting to his embarrassment.

Her high color had nothing to do with embarrassment and everything to do with total and complete outrage. "You cannot possibly believe that bunch of poppycock. *Cosmopolitan* trumpeted the benefits of riding for women just last month."

"*Cosmopolitan* is a magazine, Essie. Hardly the same as a doctor."

"You are to call me 'Miss Spreckelmeyer,' if I am not mistaken." She sat stiff, her fingernails making indentations in her hands as she clasped them tightly.

He sighed. "You are angry. I knew this last one would be a touchy one."

"Touchy? It is outrageous. And you are living in the Dark Ages."

"Lower your voice," he whispered. "You know good and well that the leaders of God's church have a completely different set of expectations to adhere to."

"Are you now going to try and tell me the Bible says I cannot ride a bike?"

He searched her eyes. "You yourself have admitted to stumbling, Essie—Miss Spreckelmeyer. I am merely trying to keep us both on the straight and narrow."

Sputtering, she strove to collect her thoughts but could think of no polite way to express them.

He sighed. "The honest truth is that the elders were very reluctant to appoint someone my age to such an important position in the community. But it was either that or hire someone who was less qualified or who'd not been born and raised in Corsicana."

She held herself still, neither encouraging nor discouraging him.

"I can't afford to do anything the least bit controversial," he said, combing his fingers through his hair. "I have to show them my age is nothing to be concerned about. And while I am courting you, everything you do reflects back on me."

She pictured Preacher Bogart and the church elders. They were indeed an intimidating force and should not be taken lightly.

Her heart pounded as her mother's words came whistling back through her mind. *"Is that bicycle so important you'd rather have it than a man? Than babies of your own?"*

She wouldn't, of course. It wasn't really the bike, though, so much as what it represented. Freedom. Independence. Progress.

On the other hand, if she did sacrifice those things, she would reap a harvest of untold value. She'd have a husband, a home, a place in the community, children.

Wilting a little, she lowered her chin. "All right, Mr. Wortham. I will put away my wheels for now—but not necessarily forever."

"Thank you." He stood and offered her a gloved hand. "I'd like to take you for a carriage ride, Miss Spreckelmeyer. Will you do me the honor?"

After a charged moment, she allowed him to assist her to her feet. "If you would excuse me for a moment, I must go and change first."

She made her way to her room, telling herself this was exactly what she'd been wishing for. But instead of a weight being lifted, she felt heavy and burdened.

―――――

The sun provided Essie with warmth, while Ewing provided her with conversation. He kept the carriage close to the sidewalk, restraining the horses from using undue speed.

Making their way down Eleventh Street, the false fronts of town began to be replaced with quiet homes and picket fences. A scattering of crimson clover lined the road.

Ewing pointed to a flock of birds flying in V formation. The lead bird dropped off to the back of the line, allowing another to take its place.

"I wonder how they know when their turn at the front of the line is up," he said. "I wonder if some birds are lazier than others and don't fight the wind as long as they should. What would the other birds do, do you think?"

Essie followed their progress across the blanket of blue overhead. "I have no idea. I never thought about it before."

"Look," Ewing said, spotting some black huckleberries in a vacant lot and pulling over. "Want some?"

It took them ten minutes to pick a handful and less than a minute to eat them.

"I wish they weren't so tedious to harvest," he said. "I haven't had any of those since before I left."

"They don't have any huckleberries in Tennessee?"

"In the mountains they do."

"You've been on a mountain?"

Shaking out his handkerchief, he laid it across his hands and presented it to her. She placed her hand inside and allowed him to wipe her fingers clean of huckleberry juice.

"I didn't like being on it," he said. "Those misty mountains are beautiful from a distance, but when I got up on them, I felt surrounded and hemmed in." He began to wipe her other hand. "No, I prefer wide-open spaces."

He'd cleaned four of her fingers and reached for her thumb. She immediately moved it and tried to pin his down. Within seconds the handkerchief had floated to the ground and a thumb war began in earnest.

He pinned her thumbs in record time.

"Oh no!" she squealed. "I always used to win."

"I've grown up some since the last time we played."

"Don't get mouthy with me, youngster. I bet I can still beat you at the hand-slap game."

Grinning, he held out his hands. She lightly touched her palms to his and held fast his gaze. Quick as lightning, she struck and just barely caught the tips of his fingers.

They reversed positions. It took him four tries before he could catch her. But instead of slapping her hands, he grabbed them and did not let go. They stood in the middle of the lot, the breeze cold against their faces, the laughter of a moment before melting away.

"Your cheeks are all red," he said, studying her.

"My nose, too, I'd wager."

"Yes. But it's becoming. You have a lovely nose."

She gave a short huff.

He moved his gaze to her lips and she felt a moment of panic.

Gently tugging her hands free, she glanced at the carriage. "We should probably be getting back."

He walked her to the rig. And though he took her elbow, he did not immediately help her up. "Can I see you tomorrow?"

"The Ladies' Garden Club is cleaning the Methodist church sanctuary tomorrow."

"What about during the evening?"

"I'm substituting for Mrs. Quigley who can't make it to Mrs. Lockhart's whist game."

"Wednesday?"

"I'm helping Mother with the washing and ironing."

"Perhaps the following day, then?"

"Yes. Thursday should be fine."

"Good."

No words were spoken on the rest of the ride home. He pulled to a stop in front of her gate, then alighted. Placing her hands on his shoulders, she allowed him to assist her to the ground, his hands under her elbows.

"I'll see you Thursday." Touching his hat, he returned to the carriage seat.

She watched as he turned the rig and disappeared around the bend. It had been a lovely afternoon and an invigorating ride. She headed toward her front door, wondering what she would do if Ewing tried to kiss her.

She enjoyed his company, but she had no desire whatsoever to introduce anything physical into the relationship. It wasn't because she didn't enjoy those intimacies. She did. Very much.

She just couldn't muster up any enthusiasm for sharing them with Ewing. He was a pleasant-looking man. Amiable. Easy to get along with. She just wasn't attracted to him in that way.

Maybe that would come. Maybe the feelings she had for Adam weren't a one-time thing. Or maybe Ewing would be too fearful of arousing her "weakness" to risk kissing her.

Sighing, she entered the house. She needed to finish those trousers of Harley's.

CHAPTER | TWENTY-FIVE

EIGHT LADIES FROM THE Garden Club had gathered early in the morning to clean the First Methodist Church. The noon hour found the sanctuary's leaded windows sparkling, the floor pristine, and the choir and amen corners shining. Only the pews were left.

Three more and they'd be done. Essie rubbed her polishing cloth against the varnished oak, praying the task would soon come to completion.

The church held the distinct honor of having housed the first democratic convention in Texas after the Civil War. At the time, a host of hogs had made their home beneath the building, and the convention had to be stopped several times due to the ruckus the hogs had made.

Essie fervently wished those hogs were still present today. Anything to stop the direction of today's conversation.

"I always knew the Lord had someone for you," Mrs. Owen sighed. "And didn't that Ewing turn out to be the most handsome thing you ever did see? Even if he's not very tall."

"The thing to remember, Essie," Shirley Bunting's mother interjected, "is a happy courtship promotes conjugal felicity more than anything else. So don't spoil it."

"She's right, dear," said Mrs. Shaw. President of the Garden Club, she never took a wrong step or had a hair out of place. Even now, after a morning of scrubbing, her apron was still stiff and her coif tidy. "So of course you want to look your best when he's courting you, but keep in mind that ornamentation that has no use is never, in any high sense, beautiful."

Essie frowned in confusion. Then why did Mrs. Shaw put so much effort into her ornamental flower garden, which, after all, had no purpose but beauty?

"What she means is," said the undertaker's wife, "buttons that fasten nothing should never be scattered over a garment. And bows, which are simply strings tied together, should only be placed where there is some possible use for, well, strings tied together."

Known as a woman of few words, the blacksmith's wife added, "In short, Esther, anything that looks useful, but is useless, is in bad taste."

Essie resumed her polishing, wondering if these women had bothered to look at *Godey's Lady's Book* sometime in the last few decades.

"More important than your attire, though, is your general treatment of each other." This from Mrs. Richie, who harangued her poor husband so much that he spent most of his waking hours at the Slap Out whittling and playing checkers. "You must tell

Ewing that you should like to be treated thus, but not so, and that he must let you do this, but not that. It is much better to arrange these things now than for them to be left for future contention."

"Love will not bear neglect, however," said Mrs. Lockhart, settling herself on the first pew while the rest of the ladies finished up. "It should not be second in anything. You must spend a great deal of time together. Once love's fires have been lit, they must be perpetually resupplied with their natural fuel, or else they die down, go out or . . . go elsewhere." She looked over the rim of her glasses meaningfully.

The other matrons nodded in agreement. The only person who had yet to offer any advice was Mrs. Bogart. A worried frown puckered the woman's brows as she collected the dirty rags and dropped them into a bucket. The members of the Garden Club were set to clean her church at the beginning of the year. By then, though, Ewing would be their preacher.

Essie sighed, wondering what these ladies would do if she were to tell them how troubled and unsure she was over her blossoming relationship with Preacher Wortham.

———

Pumping the handle above the kitchen's washbasin, Essie filled a bowl with water, then splashed her face. She was glad to be finished with the cleaning and with hearing unwanted advice.

"Oh, thank goodness you're home," Mother said, entering the room and handing Essie a towel.

"What's the matter?" she asked, dabbing her face.

"Nothing. Your father is in his office with Melvin. They have something they'd like to, um, show you."

"I thought Uncle Melvin was out of town," she said, hanging the towel over a rod.

"He's back."

Essie frowned. "Is anything wrong?"

"No. Nothing at all."

Essie sighed. All morning she'd felt like a carcass that had been pecked and gouged. She wasn't sure she was up to facing Papa or even Uncle Melvin. Squaring her shoulders, she took a deep breath and headed toward the hallway.

"Perhaps you should freshen up a bit first," Mother said.

"No, I'm sure they won't mind either way."

Mother grabbed her hand. "Actually, I insist. Come on, I'll help you change."

Too tired to argue, Essie allowed her mother to pull her up the stairs and assist her in replacing work clothes with a simple white shirtwaist and wool skirt. Mother took the pins out of Essie's hair, brushing it with long, slow strokes.

Essie closed her eyes, relishing the unexpected treat of having someone else see to her needs. "The church cleaning this morning was awful."

"Awful? Why? What happened?"

"Every single one of those women had advice to offer me on my courtship with Ewing. Seems the entire town has us married already."

"Oh dear. I'm sorry I wasn't there."

"It's all right. I'm just glad the morning's over."

She opened her eyes. Mother had styled her hair in a loose bun at the back with soft tendrils framing her face.

"There." Her mother set the silver brush on the toilet table. "Ready?"

Essie met her gaze in the mirror. "Ready for what?"

"For your, um, meeting with your father and uncle."

Essie swiveled around on her stool. "What is going on, Mother?"

"Nothing. Now come along." But she was blushing and Essie found herself reluctant to follow.

Still, they made their way down the stairs and Mother opened the door to Papa's study. "She's home."

Essie stepped through the door. The neat and orderly office provided an unlikely backdrop for Uncle Melvin's slouching form. Covered with dust and dirt, he looked as tired as she'd ever seen him—eyes bloodshot, shoulders wilted, mouth sagging.

"What happened?" she asked, going straight to him. "Are you all right?"

"Just a little tuckered out."

"Where on earth have you been? You look like you rode clear to China and back."

He pushed a smile onto his face, but it didn't stay there long. She turned to ask Papa what this was all about and froze.

Behind her and leaning against the north wall, one hip cocked, was Adam Currington, hat in hand. He was just as filthy as Uncle Melvin, the starch long since gone from his handkerchief and blue shirt.

His eyes stayed on her face, never once venturing to places they ought not go. They were as clear and pretty as ever, but their sparkle had dulled.

"How's your nose?" she asked.

It was a ridiculous question, all things considered, but his nose was so crooked and bruised. Even after six weeks, hints of purple still hovered in the circles beneath his eyes.

He gave a slight smile. "It's fine. How's yours?"

She smiled back, but her good humor slowly dissolved as she remembered his perfidy. "Where have you been?"

His gaze dropped and he pulled away from the wall. "I owe you an apology, Essie."

An apology? He thought to waltz in here with an apology and all would be forgiven?

"Would you like to sit down?" he asked, pulling out one of Papa's chairs.

"No, thank you." She held herself still and straight.

"You're angry. And I can't say I blame ya." He swallowed. "I've come back to do right by ya. I've offered fer your hand, but your pa won't give it without your consent."

She sank into the previously offered chair, her eyes locking with Papa's. He'd erected a wall of indifference around him, refusing to let her see what he was thinking. She had no idea if he was angry, relieved, or anxious. But one thing was certain. He wasn't indifferent, no matter what he pretended.

She turned to Uncle Melvin. "You went after him, didn't you? That's where you've been."

He said nothing.

"Where did you find him?"

No one answered.

Adam pulled out the chair next to hers and sat down facing her, his spurs jingling. "None of that is important. What matters is that I'm back. And I'm back for good. Ready to do the honorable thing."

"Did Uncle Melvin have to threaten you?" she asked. "Cuff you and force you here by gunpoint?"

Hurt and irritation mingled, providing her heart some protection against the shock of seeing him again. She'd dreamed so often of his return that she could hardly credit the fact that he was actually here. Still, she'd never considered he would have to be tracked down and dragged back.

"No, Essie. Not at all. I'm here of my own free will."

He must think she was an idiot. And not surprisingly, considering the poor decisions she'd made concerning him. "Really? What took so long?"

He glanced at Melvin.

"Don't look over there for help," she said. "It's me who's asking and me whom you'll be answering to."

"Essie," he said, rotating his hat round and round in his big, bronzed hands, "I have no excuse to offer other than cowardice. The thought of being hogtied by matrimonial ropes made me as nervous as a long-tailed cat under a rockin' chair. So I left in such a hurry I forgot to take my right mind with me."

She waited, but no more was forthcoming. "That's it? That's your excuse?"

He frowned. "I'm back, ain't I?"

"Oh, for heaven's sake." She jumped out of her chair. "Surely you don't think I'm going to crumple at your feet for doing me the great service of returning, do you?"

"Well," he drawled, glancing at Melvin, then back at her. "Yes, ma'am. I guess I sorta did."

He was serious. Completely serious. An initial rush of anger was quickly replaced with disappointment.

"I'd like to speak to Adam alone," she said.

"Absolutely not," Papa answered.

Her heart softened toward her father for the first time in over a month. Walking to his desk, she held out her hand. He enveloped it in his.

"If he tries anything," she said, her voice gentle, "I will break his nose again myself."

She squeezed Papa's hand. He looked at Melvin, then the two of them left the study, closing the door behind them.

Essie sat in Papa's throne, hoping the position would imbue her with the strength she suddenly needed. "Where were you?"

"Dallas."

"Doing what?"

"It don't matter."

"It does to me."

"Well, it shouldn't. What should matter is that I'm back."

"Why? Why did you return?"

"To marry you."

She leaned against the warmth of Papa's chair. The fire crackled in the hearth. "What changed your mind?"

He paused. "The sheriff changed my mind, but not how you'd think. He didn't threaten me or try to whup me. He just talked to me, is all."

"About what?"

"You."

She studied him. So serious, so solemn. "I heard you were supposed to take Shirley Bunting to the Harvest Festival."

He slowly straightened. "Who told you that?"

"Is it true?"

His gaze darted about the room.

"Before you answer, please do not insult me with a falsehood. Furthermore, remember that this is a very small town and most everyone knows everyone else's business."

He wiped a hand across his mouth. "I might've led Shirley to believe I might possibly escort her to the festival, but I wouldn't have."

She didn't miss the ease with which he used the girl's first name. "Did her father know you were calling on her?"

"I wasn't callin' on her."

Shooting to her feet, Essie pressed her hands against the giant desk, a horrible thought robbing her of breath. "Did you compromise Shirley, too?"

"No, ma'am," he said, standing as soon as she did.

Relief swept through her, but only momentarily. "Were you thinking to?"

He didn't answer. His disheveled hair grazed his forehead. Several days' worth of whiskers shadowed his jaw. His broad shoulders stretched taut the blue shirt he wore. He was such a gorgeous man, even after riding for days on end. But he was not so handsome on the inside—and she didn't need to look in his mouth to determine as much. The thought of spending the rest of her life with him was rapidly losing its appeal.

"How many others, Adam? How many other women in this town were you carrying on with?"

Tunneling his fingers through his hair, he moved to the window. "Don't ya want to get married, Essie?"

"Yes. Oh yes. More than anything in the world. I'm just not sure anymore that it's *you* I want to marry. A man who has such a voracious appetite for the female gender. A man who prefers wandering to planting down roots. A man who would run out on a woman he'd said he would marry and who might have been carrying his babe. A man who may not even believe in Jesus Christ."

He looked down at his fingernails. "I'd be true to ya, Essie. Once we was wed, I'd be true."

"How many illegitimate children have you sired?"

He looked at her then, his eyes bleak with regret. "I don't rightly know," he whispered.

Sorrow crashed through her. "Oh, Adam."

"I think about it all the time. Wonderin'." He blinked several times. "Might be none, ya know." His voice was sandpaper rough. "And I'd have done all that worryin' fer nothing."

She went to him then. He folded her into his embrace and she felt moisture from his eyes slide against her cheek.

"I want you to stop carrying on with women who aren't your wife."

Pulling back, he untied his neckerchief and wiped his eyes and nose. "I done told you already, I wouldn't cheat on ya."

She gave him a sad smile.

He stilled. "You ain't gonna marry me, are ya?"

"I'm sorry."

He searched her eyes. "Why not?"

"Marriage is a sacred and blessed thing. I'm beginning to realize entering into it only because we had relations would be a very foolish thing indeed."

"Then why did the sheriff traipse all over the state just to track me down?"

"Because he loves me and I'm sure he thought you were what I wanted. So he must have decided to go and get you for me."

He nodded. "Yer lucky to have him. And your ma and pa, too."

"You have a father and grandfather who love you. Perhaps you should go and see them."

Lifting her hand to his lips, he placed a soft kiss against her knuckles. "Maybe I'll do that, Miss Spreckelmeyer. Maybe I'll do that very thing."

She gently withdrew her hand. "Good-bye, Adam."

He put on his hat and tugged its brim. "Miss Spreckelmeyer, I'll never forget ya and I wish you nothin' but the very, very best."

———

Essie scrubbed Papa's shirt against the washboard, her hands shriveled from being in the water so long. Washing was never pleasant, but washing when the weather turned wintry was downright onerous. The hot water burned her fingers, the cold breezes chafed her skin.

She glanced at the back door. Inside, Papa sat cloistered with Mr. Davidson, the oil scout, discussing the future of the still-dry well. The well she'd been forbidden to so much as inquire about.

Mother wrung out the clothes, then hung them on the line.

The back door slammed.

"Doreen?" Papa called from the porch.

Mother stopped.

"I need you to take a message to Melvin for me. Tell him I'm with Mr. Davidson right now, but that I'll collect everyone and meet him at the jailhouse in thirty minutes."

"What's happened?" Mother asked.

"Looks like Harley's gotten himself into some trouble."

Essie released the shirt she'd been cleaning, allowing it to slide into the water. "*My* Harley? Harley North?"

"I'm afraid so."

Drying her hands with her apron, she crossed the yard. "What kind of trouble? What did he do?"

"It's a long story. Melvin's got him locked up for now."

"Locked up! He can't put a seven-year-old in jail."

"He can if the boy committed a crime. He can if he wants to scare the living daylights out of him."

Essie quickly removed her apron and flung it over the back-porch rail. "I'll go."

"Would you like me to go with you?" Mother asked.

"No. I'll send word if I need you."

She raced to the barn, not bothering to change out of her work dress or to remove the handkerchief from around her head. "When will you be done?" she hollered back at Papa.

"Hopefully within half an hour."

———

She had to hike her skirts clear up to her knees in order to keep them from tangling in Peg's chains. With one hand holding her skirts and the other on the handlebars, she couldn't go as rapidly as she wanted, but it was quicker than saddling Cocoa. Ewing would just have to understand this was an emergency. After this, though, she'd put the bike away.

She whizzed through the heart of town. Katherine Crook swept leaves from the Slap Out's porch, gasping when she saw the spectacle Essie made. Mr. Klocker's horse became spooked by the bike and pranced to the side, forcing an oncoming buggy to swerve out of the way.

Essie didn't slow so much as a mite. She had to reach Harley. She turned onto Jefferson Avenue, spotting the sheriff's office and jailhouse.

Ever since Uncle Melvin had returned with Adam in tow, things had smoothed out between her, her uncle, and her parents. Both Melvin and Papa were relieved she wasn't going to marry the cowboy and they had wasted no time in sending Adam on his way. She hoped this time he had gone home to his family.

The bike had not come to a complete stop when she jumped off and barreled up the steps leading to a small red-brick structure. An oversized, five-pointed star emblazoned with the word SHERIFF was attached to the brown wooden door she burst through.

Uncle Melvin looked up from a modest, scarred desk stacked with papers and books. A kerosene lamp cast a golden glow over his half-empty bottle of stomach bitters and a crusted mug of coffee. A pair of handcuffs and a set of keys doubled as paperweights.

"Papa said he'd have everyone you needed in thirty minutes. What has happened?"

Melvin tipped his chair back on two legs and hooked his thumbs into his vest pockets. The movement caused his impressive shoulders to expand, displaying his badge to advantage. It also disclosed the gun strapped across his waist—a waist that was perhaps even broader than his chest.

"Well, Mr. Harley North has broken the law," he boomed, combing the edge of his bushy moustache with his bottom teeth. "And folks who break the law go to jail."

Essie recognized this performance for what it was. And it wasn't for her benefit but for Harley's. She glanced over at the cell in the back corner of the room. Harley had wedged himself on the floor between the cot and the opposite wall. He sat huddled, his arms wrapped around his legs, his head resting against his knees.

"May I see him?" she asked.

Melvin stayed as he was for a moment, then dropped his chair with a thud and grabbed the keys. "I want you to be careful. He might be dangerous. If he gives you any trouble, I'll be right here within shoutin' distance."

Her heart squeezed with compassion. Whatever trouble Harley had gotten himself into, it was serious. Otherwise, Melvin would not have been so unsympathetic.

"I'll be careful."

Melvin opened the cell door, locked her in, then returned to his desk. The small cubicle had unpainted, barren plaster walls barely wide enough for a folding cot to fit between. Beneath it sat a gray enamel chamber pail with no lid. And in the corner was Harley.

What on earth had happened between yesterday, when the boy had swung by the house to pick up his new trousers, and now?

She butted the cot up against the far wall, then bent down next to him. "Harley? It's me, Miss Essie." She stroked the mop of hair on his head. "What happened, honey?"

He lifted his head, tears streaking down his face. "I ruined my new pants," he cried.

"You did? Let me see."

Straightening his legs, he pointed to a jagged tear in the fabric of his trousers. But it was the large stain of blood that captured her attention.

She gasped. "My stars and garters. Are you hurt?"

"No, ma'am. That ain't my blood. It's Mr. Vandervoort's."

"Mr. Vandervoort's?! How did his blood get onto your clothes?"

"I shot him, Miss Essie. I killed him dead."

CHAPTER | TWENTY-SIX

ESSIE TWISTED AROUND TO look at Melvin. *Did he kill Mr. Vandervoort?* She didn't say the words out loud. She didn't have to. Melvin knew what she wanted to know.

He gave a very slight negative shake with his head.

Releasing the pent-up breath within her, she turned back around and settled herself on the floor, legs crossed. "Tell me everything that happened. Start at the beginning."

"Ewing was supposed to take me huntin' today. But somebody in Cryer Creek needed a preacher to say some words over a fella who died. So he went there instead. Said he didn't know when he'd be back. Maybe tomorrow, maybe not."

"Yes, he told me the same thing. Were you disappointed you couldn't go hunting?"

"I guess so. Then I thunk to myself, I could go without him. I mean, how hard could it be to shoot a gun? You jus' point and pull the trigger. Thing is, I didn't have no gun."

"Go on."

He stuck his finger in the hole of his trousers, tugging at it. "So I borrowed one."

"From who?"

"From the Slap Out."

"You stole a gun from Mr. Crook's store?" she exclaimed.

"I didn't steal it. I jus' told you. I *borrowed* it. I was gonna bring it back."

"And the shot?"

"I borrowed that, too."

"And just how were you planning on bringing that back?"

He leaned forward and lowered his voice. "It weren't shot. It were bullets. Colts don't use shot. I was gonna dig the bullet outta the bird, wash it off, and put it back in the box."

"A Colt? You took a *Colt*? You thought to use a revolver for shooting dove?"

"What's wrong with that?"

Good heavens. "So what happened?"

"Well, I would've gotten clean away, but that Mr. Vandervoort saw me and I didn't know it." His little eyebrows furrowed with indignation. "He followed me, only when I heard him, I thought he was a big bear or somethin'. So I shot him."

"Heavens to mercy. And you hit him?"

" 'Courst I hit 'im. You just aim and pull."

"Oh, Harley. What happened then?"

"Well, he hollered, that's what. And there was blood everywhere. Lots and lots o' blood." He crooked his finger.

She leaned in close.

"And lots o' swearin'," he whispered. "Lots and lots o' swearing. Then his eyes rolled back and he died. Just like that."

"What did you do?"

"I ran, Miss Essie. I ran as fast and as far as I could. I emptied the gun and I snuck it back in the Slap Out and put it back in that glass shelf. The bullets, too. Only, I was too scared to get the one I used on Mr. Vandervoort. So the box full o' bullets is missin' one."

"Did you find a doctor for Mr. Vandervoort?"

"He didn't need a doctor, he needed the grave-man."

"Did you go to Mr. McCabe's funeral parlor, then?"

"I couldn't. Just as I was putting the bullets where they go, that mean ol' Mrs. Crook grabbed my arm and started screamin' she was being robbed. She must be dead between the ears or something 'cause she weren't bein' robbed, I was puttin' the stuff *back*."

"Oh dear."

"That's when I tore my pants. She was tryin' to take me to the sheriff. I wrestled her somethin' good."

"You wrestled with Mrs. Crook?"

"Yep. And she's a fair ta middlin' wrestler, Miss Essie. I had to work awful hard to escape her."

"You got away?"

"Shore did. But the sheriff caught up to me. And ain't nobody wrestles with the sheriff. I been in jail ever since."

Now that the telling was over, the magnitude of what he'd done seemed to hit him again. His eyes filled with tears, his lips quivered. "I didn't mean to hurt nobody. I 'specially didn't mean to kill Mr. Vandervoort."

"I know you didn't."

"They're gonna send me to the big jail or the cottonwood tree or the Poor House. Mr. Wortham, he don't put up with no funny business."

She didn't agree or disagree with him, for part of what he said was true. The State Orphan's Home was not for boys who misbehaved, but for children with no relatives. And the two did not mix.

The front door opened. Papa, Hamilton, Katherine, and Mrs. Vandervoort all crowded into the small building. Essie quickly rose to her feet, prompting Harley to do the same.

Melvin greeted everyone, then slipped a key into the keyhole, unbolting the lock with a loud thump. The door squeaked open. He stepped into the cell and reached for Harley's hands, cuffing them and squeezing the ratchets until they fit his tiny wrists.

"Is that really necessary?" Essie asked quietly.

This Melvin was not the amiable man who'd once bounced her on his knee. Nor was he the outraged uncle who had discovered her with her lover.

This Melvin was an unbending man who fought for law and order. A man who showed no weaknesses, no sympathy.

"He robbed the Slap Out, shot Mr. Vandervoort, left him for dead, and attacked Mrs. Crook. He's lucky I'm not putting him in leg irons."

Essie searched Melvin's eyes, but this was not a performance. The charges against Harley were hanging offenses, and though Essie knew it would not come to that, she was unsure of what it would come to.

"Come on, son," Melvin said, placing his large, calloused hand on the boy's head and guiding him to the center of his office.

Papa set a Colt revolver and a box of bullets on the sheriff's desk, then offered seats to Katherine and Mrs. Vandervoort. When they were settled in stark bentwood chairs, he looked at Essie.

She shook her head. She had no intention of sitting down to watch these proceedings like some spectator. She'd stand beside Harley throughout the entire thing. Her only regret was that she would do so in a worn brown work dress and headscarf. Not the best costume when needing to put her best face forward, but there was nothing she could do about it now.

A wall of accusers faced them. Her father was front and center, Melvin on his right, the Crooks on his left. Hamilton stood with his hand on Katherine's shoulder. For someone who'd been in a tussle, she looked very put together with not a hair out of place.

Mrs. Vandervoort, however, looked a mess. The barrel-shaped elderly woman had dressed in her best, but she'd obviously done so in a rush. Her clothing was wrinkled and smelled of camphor. She dabbed her eyes with a handkerchief.

"State your name," Papa said.

"Harley North." His little voice came out plenty loud, if a bit quivery.

"*Sir*," Melvin scolded. "That's the judge you're talking to."

"Harley North, *sir*," the boy corrected.

"Your full name," Papa said.

"I don't remember it and nobody else knows what it is, neither."

Papa waited.

"Oh! I mean, I don't remember, *sir*."

"Your age?"

"I think I'm seven, but I don't know fer shore, sir. Mr. Wortham just kinda guessed when they brought me to the Home."

Essie's heart squeezed. It had never occurred to her that he didn't know his real age or, she imagined, even his birthday.

"Did you rob the Slap Out?" Papa asked.

"I borrowed somethin', then put it right back where I found it, sir."

"Mr. Crook?" Papa asked without breaking eye contact with Harley. "Are you in the business of loaning out goods, or of selling goods?"

"I sell goods, sir," Hamilton answered.

"Is anyone ever allowed to take stock from your store without paying or signing for it?"

"No, sir."

"Harley," Papa said, "what's it called when a person secretly takes something that doesn't belong to him?"

"But I gave it back."

"Did you or did you not take a Colt revolver and a box of bullets out of the Slap Out in secret and without paying for it?"

"I took the Colt, sir, but I didn't take the whole box o' bullets, only a handful."

"Did you do it in secret and without permission?"

Harley glanced at Hamilton. "Yes, sir," he mumbled.

"Speak up!"

"Yes, sir," he repeated, overly loud and thus magnifying the ensuing silence.

"Then you are guilty of stealing."

Harley looked up at Essie, his expression full of distress, but there was nothing she could do. What Papa said was right, and they both knew it.

"And did you shoot Mr. Vandervoort with that same gun?" Papa asked.

The boy looked at Mrs. Vandervoort. She was watching him, her handkerchief now pressed against her mouth. And though she was clearly upset, her eyes conveyed a touch of compassion.

"Not on purpose, ma'am. I liked Mr. Vandervoort. He was always real nice and gave me a 'howdy' whenever he saw me. I didn't know it was him comin' up behind me. I thought it was a bear."

The woman's eyes flickered with the faintest amount of understanding.

"And when you shot him," Papa continued, "did you run away and leave him for dead?"

"No, sir. He died first and then I run off."

A stunned silence filled the room.

"And did you run off in order to go and get help?" Papa asked, softening his voice for the first time.

"No, sir. I run off 'cause I was scared. I didn't want the sheriff to play cat's cradle with my neck, so I decided to run away fer good. Start fresh somewheres else. But I needed to give Mr. Crook his Colt and bullets back. And I needed to tell the grave-man about

Mr. Vandervoort. But I never got to warn the grave-man 'cause that woman grabbed me and started in with her caterwaulin.'"

He'd pointed his finger at Katherine, but because his hands were cuffed, both came up together.

She stiffened in her chair. "Well, I never."

Essie gently pushed Harley's hands back down. "It's not polite to point," she whispered.

"Mrs. Crook thought you were robbing her," Papa said.

"Well, she must not have anything under that hat but hair, then, 'cause I was puttin' everything back."

Katherine sucked in her breath. Hamilton scowled. And Papa exchanged glances with the sheriff.

"Watch your tongue," Melvin said.

"Meant no offense," Harley said to Hamilton.

"She said you attacked her," Papa accused.

Harley's shock was evident. "I didn't attack her, she attacked me. Look what she done with her fingernails!" He pointed to the tear in his trousers. "She ruined my brand-new pants. And she grabbed my arms, too, shakin' me so hard I thought my eyeballs were gonna fly right outta my head. When I broke free, she jumped on me. I tried to get away, but she wrestles better than all the boys at the Home. And she cheats, too."

Katherine gasped.

"When clawin' me didn't work, she bit me." He pulled up his sleeve with his teeth. Moon-shaped punctures decorated his arm. "See? Everybody knows yer not allowed to bite when yer wrestlin.'"

Papa kept his expression firm, but Essie could tell the boy's outrage had struck a chord with him.

"A woman can do anything she wants if a man is attacking her," Papa said gently.

"But I weren't attackin' her, she was attackin' me!"

"*Sir*," Melvin interjected.

"*Sir*," Harley repeated.

Hamilton looked down at Katherine. "You bit him? Why did you bite him?"

Turning almost purple, she jumped to her feet. Harley reacted as if he'd been shot, stumbling back, then darting to Melvin and taking cover behind him.

"Don't let her git me, Sheriff. She chews up nails and spits out tacks."

"Harley," Essie hissed.

Katherine yanked her cloak together and strode out the door, slamming it behind her.

"She's overwrought," Hamilton said in a conciliatory tone.

Melvin put his hand on Harley's shoulder and nudged him back to where he had been.

Papa studied the boy for a long, quiet moment. Harley looked down, scuffing the floor with the toe of his boot.

"You see those pictures there?" Papa asked, pointing to the Wanted posters tacked up on the wall behind the sheriff's desk. "That fella on the left? He stole something that didn't belong to him. When he's caught, he'll be hanged."

Harley's eyes grew large.

"The one toward the middle? He shot a man. When he's caught, he'll be hanged."

Tears rushed to the boy's eyes.

"The one next to him? He attacked a woman. When he's caught, he'll be hanged."

"I didn't mean nothin' by it. I didn't." Tears spurted from his eyes, and he covered his face with his cuffed hands.

Essie felt her own eyes water.

"Lock him up, Sheriff. I'll have a decision before nightfall."

CHAPTER | TWENTY-SEVEN

WHAT ARE YOU GOING to do?" Essie asked, following Papa out of the sheriff's office.

The activity on this end of the street was minimal, with an occasional carriage or pedestrian passing by. Papa's rig sat parked beside the building. The town stray, Cat, darted out from underneath it, startling Essie. Meowing, the tabby wove a figure eight between her ankles.

"I don't know what I'm going to do," Papa answered. "I haven't decided."

"He's only a child."

"If he's old enough to steal, he's old enough to suffer the consequences."

"Reasonable consequences."

"I'd like to think all my decisions are reasonable."

The door opened. Hamilton escorted Mrs. Vandervoort down the steps.

"How's Mr. Vandervoort?" Essie asked her.

"Worried about Harley," the woman said, the space between her thin gray eyebrows crinkling. "He feels worse about all this than the boy, I think. I told him he should have known better than to sneak up on a hunter like that."

"It wasn't Ludwig's fault," Papa said.

"Well, he could have gone about it differently, is all."

"He's mending all right, though?" Essie asked.

"Yes, dear. Don't you worry. The bullet merely winged him. The doc says he'll be fine in no time." She nodded to the two of them, then allowed Hamilton to walk her to the judge's chaise.

"Papa?" She touched his sleeve, stalling him.

"I won't discuss it with you, Essie. And I don't want you telling the boy that Vandervoort is alive."

"Why not?"

"Because he could have been killed. I want Harley to remember for a long, long time what it feels like to rob someone of his life."

Much as she hated to burden Harley with such heavy thoughts, she knew Papa would brook no argument from her. "All right, then. If you think it's best. But you'll be lenient with your verdict?"

He put on his hat. "I'll see you at supper." Then he headed to his shay and left her standing on the street with no clue as to how he would handle the matter.

———

Uncle Melvin locked the cell door behind Essie. Frigid temperatures from the rugless floor seeped through the soles of her boots as she approached the cot. There was no blanket, no pillow, no nothing. Only Harley, curled up tightly and facing the wall.

She didn't know what to say, yet she understood what it was like to feel all alone. Sitting on the edge of the makeshift bed, she stroked his hair, his arm, his back. Slowly, tension eased from his little body.

He rolled over, his eyes swollen and red. "I hope they hang me."

"Don't say that."

"I mean it. The only thing worse than a orphan is a cracksman. And now I'm both."

"Listen to me." She gathered his hands in hers. "You did something you weren't supposed to and you'll have to suffer some consequences. But once you've fulfilled your obligations, you'll get to start over, fresh and new."

"There ain't no such thing as startin' over. Folks got long memories. Everywheres I go, they'll be whisperin', 'That there's Harley North, the murderin', area-sneak.' See if they don't."

No matter how badly she wanted to argue with him, she knew there was some truth to what he said.

"What other people think doesn't matter."

He rolled his eyes. " 'Course it matters."

She propped her hands on either side of his prone form, bracketing him. "You are very mistaken, Harley North. All that matters is what Jesus Christ thinks. Remember all those Bible stories you've heard in Sunday school, where Jesus met up with sinners? Do you recall what He told them?"

The boy said nothing, but he was listening.

"He told them that what had happened in the past was not of consequence. It was their new relationship with Him that mattered. You are just as valuable to Christ right this moment as you were before any of this happened."

As are you.

The thought was so strong, so powerful, that Essie stilled, listening to her own words echoing in the silence.

"Not of consequence . . . just as valuable . . . before any of this happened."

What Harley had done was nothing compared to what she had done, though. Or wasn't it? Didn't the Bible say one sin was no worse than another? Was she really as valuable to Christ now as she was before?

An overwhelming sense of peace and affirmation poured through her. And she knew. She knew she most certainly was.

"Jesus don't care nothin' about me. If He did, He would've gave me a mama and a papa."

"He did give you a mother and father. They just went up to heaven sooner than most parents do. But He cares about you, Harley. And if you tell Him you're sorry and you truly mean not to steal or sneak again, then He'll forgive you. Completely and totally."

"I *am* sorry," he whispered. "And I *won't* never do that again."

She pulled him up and into her embrace. "Then tell Him, Harley. In the quiet part of your heart, tell Him what you just told me."

And while she hugged him against her, she, too, confessed and repented. After a few moments, she opened her eyes, basking in the unfathomable knowledge that in the only way that really mattered, she was no longer "ruined." But was instead as pure and as white as the newly fallen snow.

And if that was how the God of the Universe saw her, then who was she to argue?

———

Melvin cut short her visit with Harley. He didn't give any reasons, but she guessed he wanted the boy to have a taste of life behind bars.

Papa shut himself in his office, asking that he not be disturbed. At suppertime, instead of joining Mother and her, he put on his coat and hat, then left without sharing his destination.

Essie quickly finished her meal, put on a simple woolen jacket and skirt, then went down to the State Orphan's Home to find something clean for Harley to wear. Ewing had not yet returned from Cryer Creek, and the Worthams displayed concern over what was to be done with "that North boy."

Back at the jail, Essie dipped a comb into a basin of water, slicking down Harley's black hair. He wore ill-fitting pants and a blue percale blouse she had brought for him. It showed little wear, and no wonder. No boy in his right mind would want to be dressed in it. The blouse had a ruffled sailor collar, a double-ruffled front, and ruffled cuffs.

"I look like a girl," he said, tugging at the collar and poking himself with the ruffles on his cuff. The tension in his face suggested he was worried about much more than his attire, however.

"It is a very becoming blouse," she said. "Any mother would be proud to have her son wear it."

"Then how come she gave it to the orphans?"

Ah. Smart boy. "You be sure to answer with respect when you address the adults. Understand?"

"Who all's comin'?"

"Same as before, I imagine."

She smoothed down his collar just as the sheriff's door opened. The Crooks, Mrs. Vandervoort, and Papa entered. The ladies wore the same costumes they'd had on earlier, though Mrs. Vandervoort had taken the time to iron hers.

Both women immediately sought Harley out with their gazes. Katherine looked him up and down but gave no indication of her thoughts.

When Mrs. Vandervoort saw his shirt, though, she pressed a hand to her heart and said, "Awwwww. Doesn't he look precious?"

Papa assisted the ladies into chairs while Melvin unlocked the cell and handcuffed the boy, ruffles and all.

"Essie," Papa said, "you will sit here with the other ladies."

She stiffened, not wishing to leave Harley to face everyone alone. "I'm fine, thank you."

"It was not a request."

Melvin placed a bentwood chair next to Mrs. Vandervoort. Essie gave Harley's shoulder a reassuring squeeze, then settled herself into the proffered chair.

"Harley North," Papa began, "I have found you guilty of stealing, guilty of shooting a man, and guilty of manhandling a woman. Any one of those offenses would be plenty serious on its own, but all three put together are very condemning, indeed."

Essie clasped her hands in her lap and held her breath. Harley swallowed.

"When considering my options for your sentence, I did take into account that you returned the goods you'd stolen, minus one bullet, and that you did not intend to harm Mr. Vandervoort and that you felt you were acting in self-defense with Mrs. Crook."

Katherine gasped and, with face flushing, frowned up at Papa. He didn't even notice.

"As it turns out," he continued, "Mr. Vandervoort did not die."

Harley's mouth fell open. "Are ya sure?" he asked, his voice cracking.

"Quite sure. He could have, but the Lord spared him."

The boy immediately turned to Mrs. Vandervoort. "He didn't take off his boots at the Pearly Gates?"

She shook her head.

"I'm right glad about that, ma'am."

"Me too, son," she answered quietly. "Me too."

"Does this mean you ain't gonna hang me?" he asked Papa.

"I am not going to have you hanged."

Harley sneaked a glance at Essie. She wanted to give him a wink, but she didn't dare.

"Thank ya, sir," he said, returning his attention to Papa.

"There will be consequences for your actions, though."

He puffed out his little ruffled chest. "I'm ready, sir. Just say it straight out."

"Very well." Papa slipped his hands into his trouser pockets. "With Mr. Vandervoort incapacitated, his missus will need help around their place. So from sunup to sundown, every Monday through Friday, you are to take care of anything and everything that Mrs. Vandervoort asks of you, for as long as it takes for Mr. Vandervoort to recover."

"Yes, sir."

"And on Saturdays, you will do cleaning and sorting and running for the Crooks at the Slap Out."

The boy was not nearly as quick to respond to this sentence. He looked at Katherine, then at Hamilton. Neither offered him any encouragement.

"Yes, sir," he repeated, a bit more subdued this time.

"On Sundays, you will go to church, then finish out the day doing chores at the Orphan's Home."

Harley frowned. "When do I get to go fishin'?"

"There will be no free time. In addition, until further notice, you will spend your nights in the jail."

His eyes widened and he glanced at the cell. "By myself?"

"By yourself."

He looked at Essie, his eyes full of fear. Her heart squeezed, and she gave him a reassuring nod.

"Yes, sir," he whispered.

"At the end of your sentence, it will be up to the Worthams to decide if you will be welcomed back at the Orphan's Home or if you will be reassigned to the Poor House. I imagine much of their decision will be based on how well you do your duties for the Vandervoorts and the Crooks."

Harley's lip quivered, but he did not cry.

"Do you have any questions?" Papa asked.

"How long am I punished fer?"

"Until Mr. Vandervoort is completely healed."

"Am I supposed to go to the Slap Out and play checkers fer him, too?"

Mrs. Vandervoort gave a hint of a smile.

"No," Papa said. "That will not be necessary."

"I don't have no more questions, then."

"Very well. You will spend the rest of this day and night in the jail, and come morning you will report to Mrs. Vandervoort's house. Do you know where it is?"

"Yes, sir."

"Then these proceedings are over."

———

Essie began again at the top of the page, trying once more to concentrate on the words of *Robinson Crusoe*. But her eyes kept straying to the parlor windows closed tight against the night air. The brocade drapes were parted, allowing the glass panes to reflect back a wavy image of the room.

She thought of Harley in that dark cell all by himself. She'd taken him a pillow and several quilts, but she still wasn't convinced he'd be warm enough without a stove or fire.

So far away was she in thought, that she had no notion of Ewing's presence until he was standing before her.

"Oh! My goodness. You're back." She put the book aside and stood, looking to see who had shown him in, but the two of them were alone.

He took both her hands. "I returned as soon as I heard."

"Heard? You mean word has traveled all the way to Cryer Creek about Harley?"

"No. Father sent me a telegram."

She nodded. "How long have you been home?"

"About an hour. I went straight to the jailhouse."

"How is he?"

"Putting up a good front but scared to death underneath."

"Oh, Ewing."

He squeezed her hands. "Come sit on the porch with me?"

"Let me grab my cloak."

She had planned to sit in one of the rattan rockers, but Ewing steered her to the porch settee, then settled in next to her.

"Tell me what happened," he said.

She relayed the story, ending with Papa's all-work-and-no-play determination. They sat knee-to-knee, Ewing's arm stretched along the back of the two-seater. During the telling, he had captured a tendril of her hair at the nape, coiling it and uncoiling it with his finger.

"I think having Harley work at the Vandervoorts' will be just as good for them as it will be for the boy," he said.

"Yes, I had that same thought."

"He's not going to like working for the Crooks."

"That will be good for him, too, though. He needs to learn he can't charm everyone."

His finger strayed from her hair to her neck, grazing it lightly. "How are you holding up?"

Light from the parlor window behind them sliced his features in half, revealing only the right side of his face. The shadowing accentuated the angles and planes of his visage, calling attention to his masculinity.

The feathered caress of his finger began to coax a response from her that had heretofore been absent. Was it simply because her body now knew what it was missing and any man could rouse a reaction from her? Or was it Ewing himself that prompted this feeling?

"It's been a long day, that's for certain," she answered.

"You rode your bike through town."

She stiffened. "It was an emergency. I had to get to Harley as soon as I could and I didn't have time to saddle Cocoa."

"I heard that you weren't even wearing a split skirt. That you hiked up your hems, exposing your ankles and calves."

"Who told you that?"

"Is it true?"

"Well, yes," she sputtered. "And I'm sorry, but I only did it that once. When I went to the jailhouse later for the sentencing, I rode Cocoa."

"I want you to give me your bike."

She gasped. "What?"

"I want you to let me keep your bike in my barn so it won't tempt you anymore."

She glanced toward her own barn, where inside Peg was lovingly draped with a protective blanket. "I won't ride her again. I promise."

"Then you shouldn't mind giving it to me."

"*Her*. Her name is Pegasus."

For the longest time he said nothing. Just continued to finger her hair before finally urging her again. "Will you give her to me?"

"Do you really think that's necessary?" she asked, clasping her hands.

"It's for your own good."

She held her reaction in check. *It's just a machine,* she told herself. *It's not even a real animal, like a horse or a parrot or a snake.* And, truly, she probably would be tempted to ride again.

Sighing, she swallowed. "Yes, Mr. Wortham. I will hand her over to you for safekeeping."

He laid his palm on the side of her face, sliding his thumb from her cheek to the corner of her lips and back. "I missed you."

Pushing her thoughts of Peg aside, she considered him seriously for the very first time. The very first time since she'd dismissed Adam from her life and since she'd felt God's forgiveness for her sin. And she realized that she might never be *in* love with Ewing, but she could certainly love him. In fact, she was sure she already did.

"I'm glad you're back." And she meant that. Not just because Harley now had another staunch supporter close by, but because she really did enjoy his company.

He hesitated, then slid his hand to the back of her head and pulled her toward him. The kiss was tender, chaste, and very precious.

"Can I see you tomorrow?" he asked, the cold air making their breath visible as it blended together.

"Yes. I think I would like that."

He kissed her again, allowing a little intensity this time, but couching it with restraint.

CHAPTER | TWENTY-EIGHT

ESSIE ONLY SAW HARLEY on Sundays when he escorted Mrs. Vandervoort to church. This past Sunday, Mr. Vandervoort's health had improved enough for the three of them to attend together.

It was clear the older couple adored the boy, and he blossomed under their attention. On Thanksgiving, Mr. Vandervoort asked Papa if Harley could spend the nights at their home instead of in jail.

"He's so lonesome there," Mr. Vandervoort had said. "It's not right. A boy his age, all alone in a cell like that."

So Papa relented, and had the elderly man been able to dance a jig, she felt sure he would've. She wished she could have seen Harley's reaction. It must have been something to behold.

Meanwhile, Ewing had pressed his suit to the point that he came by the house every day, sometimes twice. So she had curtailed her visits to the State Orphan's Home. She didn't want to accelerate their courtship any further by going out to where he lived.

But it looked as if their connection was gaining momentum regardless of what she did or did not do. He had been very deliberate in his pursuit of her, going to great efforts to ensure the townsfolk saw them as a couple—carriage rides down Main Street, now decorated with a series of berried Christmas garlands spanning its width. Sitting beside her family at church and sharing a hymnal with her. Showering her with flowers, candy, and books of poetry he'd purchased from the Slap Out.

And the town was all abuzz with the news. Just yesterday, Mrs. Lockhart had loaned Essie a novel by Mrs. Bertha Clay called *On Her Wedding Morn*. A little something she thought Essie might like to read.

However, one of Mrs. Clay's books was enough. Essie had no intention of ever reading another. But as she stared at its slate blue cover decorated with red medallions, its pages called to her, like a siren singing with bewitching sweetness. She picked it up off her nightstand and opened it to the middle.

How was I to warn Miss Dalrymple? To tell her bluntly that her lover was a scamp, simply would not do. Did she still love him? Had she ever really loved him?

I was inclined to answer no *to both questions. I believed that as of yet she had really loved no one.*

"Essie?" her mother called. "Ewing is here."

Slamming the book closed, Essie shoved it under the bed. Ewing was supposed to take her to Keber & Cobb's Confectionery for a sweet. Grabbing her cloak, she hurried to the stairs, only to pull up short, halfway down.

Ewing looked absolutely splendid. He wore a brown wool dress suit richly piped with satin. The pattern fit him with meticulous precision, showing off his young, muscular physique. He had a tan cassimere coat tucked in the crook of his elbow and a derby tucked under that same arm. His smile was warm, his gaze possessive.

He'd told her that in between his classes in Nashville he'd worked for a tailor. At first he'd wrapped up the orders, made deliveries, and swept the store. Then, little by little, his employer had taught him how to measure, how to cut, and how to construct their customers' garments.

He'd had free use of any of their damaged fabrics or spares. She was certain the fine clothes he wore now were of his own making. Otherwise, he'd never have been able to afford them.

He plucked off one of his gloves. "You are beautiful. What a lovely hat."

She smoothed the twist at the nape of her neck. The hat was decidedly dull, but her reservations were soothed by his obvious appreciation.

He took her hand in his and brought it to his lips. "Good evening." His breath was warm, his lips smooth. "Allow me to help you with your wrap."

After draping it over her shoulders, he shrugged on his jacket, set his derby at a jaunty angle upon his head, and escorted her to his buggy.

The drive to the confectionery was slow and easy as Ewing pointed to the Big Dipper and Orion's Belt. Then the two of them made up constellations of their own, connecting some of the brilliant dots God had strewn across the night sky. They discovered an umbrella, a boot, and a sled before arriving at the confectionery.

The bell on its door ting-a-linged as they entered. The aromas of chocolate, nuts, and melted sugar lay heavy in the air. Mr. Keber welcomed them and suggested they look around while he finished serving his current customer.

The glass display cases were lined with every kind of candy imaginable in an assortment of colors. All looked heavenly. She decided on a cherry walnut divinity. Ewing ordered a cream caramel.

"Would you put them in a box for us, please? We'll not have time to enjoy them here, I'm afraid."

Startled, Essie looked at Ewing but said nothing.

Mr. Keber's eyes held a twinkle as he winked and handed Ewing their order. "You two have a good evenin', now, ya hear?"

When they were back inside the buggy, she slipped her hands inside an ermine muff she had brought with her. "Where are we going?"

"It's a surprise," he said.

He placed his arm along the back of the buggy seat, content to move slowly through town while guiding the horse with one hand.

At Twelfth Street, they left the busy part of town behind and passed Papa's oil field and cable-tool rig, sitting silent and still in the quiet night. The magnolia tree's silhouette was barely discernable.

Images filled her. Adam, bandanna around his neck, sleeves rolled up as he hung suspended in the stirrup and kicked down the rig. Adam practicing tricks with his lasso. Adam admitting he had no idea how many children he might have fathered along the way.

"Where are we going?" she whispered.

"Just a little farther."

She rolled the muff back and forth against her skirt. "I thought we needed to avoid being alone."

He gave her shoulder a squeeze. "Just this once I think it'll be all right."

But instead of being reassured, she grew increasingly more alarmed as he turned the buggy off the road and headed toward Two Bit Creek. He pulled to a halt in front of the slope where she'd taught Adam to ride a bicycle.

Ewing jumped from the seat, then reached up for her. Grasping her elbows, he lifted her to the ground, his hands lingering before finally releasing her.

He swiped the box of confections from the floor of the buggy, took her hand and guided her down the slope. The evening rang with sounds of crickets, frogs, and woodcocks. The temperature had dropped with the approach of winter, but Essie loved the crispness of December's air. Always had.

Beside the giant tree stump where Adam had crashed her bike was a blanket. Open, waiting, and all spread out on the ground. Ewing lit two lanterns that held down the corners of the cloth. A handful of mums lay on top of it, scattered from the breeze.

He gathered them and handed them to her. "Would you join me?"

She hesitated. The last time a man had spread a blanket in advance of her arrival, things had turned out disastrously.

But this was Ewing, not Adam. And this was the new Essie, not the old one. Accepting the flowers, she settled onto the blanket. He lifted the lid to the confections and picked up her divinity.

"Open up," he said, his large, tanned hand dwarfing the tiny delectable.

Keeping her hands burrowed inside the muff, she took a bite, her teeth grazing his fingers. The brown sugar dissolved in her mouth, leaving behind candied cherries and walnuts. With his intense gaze on hers, he took the other half of the divinity into his mouth.

Her stomach quivered in response.

"Do you like cream caramels?" he asked.

She nodded. They shared it in the same manner, but once she took her half into her mouth, she bit down on something hard and inedible. He handed her a handkerchief.

Frowning, she used her tongue to clean the candy from the object within her mouth before transferring it to the handkerchief. Opening the crumpled cloth, she discovered a gold band.

"Will you do me the honor of becoming my wife?" he asked.

Her lips parted, confusion gripping her. She had no idea what to say.

Ewing took the ring, handkerchief and all, wiped it off, then tugged on her right hand, removing it from the muff.

It was acceptable for a man whose means were limited to offer a gold band as an engagement ring. It was worn on the third finger of his intended's right hand until the wedding, at which time it was transferred to her left.

"May I?" he asked, holding the ring in readiness.

Her throat swelled. "Don't you think you should speak with my father first?"

"I have."

"And he approves?"

"He does."

"He didn't say a word to me."

"I asked him not to."

She stood transfixed by the shiny sparkle of lantern light glancing off the gold ring. The gold ring she'd been longing for her whole entire life.

She curled her hand around his and brought it against her waist. "I'm scared."

"Don't be scared."

"Can I think about it?"

He slowly lowered the ring. "You have to think about it? Surely you knew I was going to ask you."

Licking her lips, she nodded. "Yes. Yes, I knew. I just, well, I wasn't expecting this panic, this uncertainty." She pressed his fist more solidly against her stomach. "Can you feel it? Can you feel the mayhem going on inside of me?"

He stretched his fingers, freeing himself from her grip, and flicked her cloak open. He pressed his hand flat against her shirtwaist, covering as much of her stomach as he could. The gesture was possessive and terribly intimate.

"All I feel is a woman I want very much. A woman I have wanted almost my whole life."

"Oh, Ewing." She clamped her lower lip between her teeth.

He placed a kiss on the palm of her hand, then held it against his cheek. "Please say yes, Essie. Please. I need you. I love you. Please."

"You must give me some time."

"How much time?"

"Two days? Three?"

"Not a minute more."

"All right."

Leaning forward, he kissed her. But she did not open her lips or lean into his chest. She knew now where that led and she'd committed to wait. And wait she would.

———

The next day, Essie sat at the kitchen table, polishing silver fruit spoons, trying to sort out her feelings.

Papa stepped through the back door, a blast of cold air wafting through the kitchen and causing the fire to gutter. He hooked his coat on a peg, along with his hat, then poured himself a cup of coffee from the stove.

"Are you trying to shine those or obliterate their engravings?" he asked.

Essie looked up.

"You've been working on that same spoon ever since I came in."

"Have I? I wasn't paying attention."

Each spoon held on its bowl depictions of the fruit to be consumed. This one was for strawberries.

Papa pulled out a chair and settled himself into its rickety form. The sound of her rubbing was drowned out by the brisk winter wind whistling past their window and back door.

"Is something wrong?" he asked.

She shot him a quick glance. "Why do you ask?"

"Because you seem distracted. Quiet. You shut yourself in your room last night—"

"I was reading *Robinson Crusoe*."

"And Ewing hasn't come by all day."

"He had some things he needed to do." She dipped the spoon she was working on in a bowl of water, swishing it around before drying it off. "What do you think of Ewing, Papa? I mean what do you really think?"

"I think he is an excellent young man with a great deal of potential. Always has been." He paused. "What do you think of him?"

"The same, I guess."

He took a sip from his cup. "You guess? You don't know?"

"He's asked me to marry him."

Papa nodded. "Well. I had wondered. He'd requested my permission nearly a week ago."

Essie picked up the next spoon. This one had peaches on it.

"What did you say?" he asked.

"That I had to think about it."

"I imagine that wasn't the answer he was hoping for."

"No. I'm afraid it wasn't."

"Do you have some objection to him?"

Essie sighed. "That's just it, Papa. There is nothing wrong with him. He is perfect. He is a man of God. He has forgiven me for giving myself to Adam. He is nice-looking. He has a good heart. What, then, am I waiting for?"

"Perhaps someone you are in love with? Someone who isn't trying to mold you into being something you are not?" His words were quiet, gentle, yet very potent.

"But I've been waiting for this opportunity my whole life. Ever since I was a little girl, all I ever wanted was to grow up and be someone's wife, the mother of someone's children. Now here is a perfectly fine man being handed to me on a silver platter, and I am hesitating."

Papa set down his cup. "Sounds like you are trying to convince yourself that if you could just marry Ewing—any man, really—you would be fulfilled. But you won't, Essie."

"But if Ewing had asked me this past summer, I'd have said yes without a moment's hesitation. It's what I want and what I've been praying for."

"You've been praying for something you *thought* would make you happy. But God may have something else in store for you. Remember, an 'eye has not seen, nor ear heard . . . the things which God has prepared for those who love Him.' "

Essie nodded and picked up another spoon. "But I could easily make my life with him. I could. We have been friends for years. I'm sure that over time my feelings for him would grow."

"You're still justifying. Is it because you're trying to convince me—and yourself— that a man and marriage will make you complete and happy?" He placed his large hand over her delicate one, halting her ministrations. "They won't, you know. Nothing can truly fill you other than Christ."

"Can't I have both? A man and Christ, I mean?"

"Not if you prefer marriage above all else. God must come first. He must be even more important to you than marriage."

"But God's not flesh and blood." She felt her eyes pool. "And I'm lonely."

Papa removed the cloth and spoon from her fingers, then clasped her hands. "Essie, my girl, there is no aloneness like being married and alone."

"How could that be?"

"It is that way for many, many couples, I'm afraid. There is no rapport between the partners. Or the man makes decisions the woman can't walk in. Or the woman henpecks the man to death. Or the man spends his time east of Beaton Street while the woman is left at home and alone with the children."

"None of that would happen to Ewing and me. And many folks say that friendship is the very best basis for marriage."

"Friendship is important, very important, I'll grant you that. But am I wrong in my estimation when I say that Ewing is trying to press you into some mold that you don't fit into very well?"

"What do you mean?"

"I mean, why have you quit bicycling? Quit practicing on your wheeled feet? Quit hunting and fishing? And why have you quit wearing those hats that suit you like no others?"

"Ewing is afraid the church will rescind their offer if I don't maintain the strictest of standards in ladylike behavior."

"So you are giving up the very things that make you *you*?"

"Only temporarily."

"Don't fool yourself, Essie. If that's what those elders require now, they will most assuredly hold you to those same restrictions and more after Ewing is their preacher."

"But Mother says a bicycle shouldn't be more important than getting married and having children. Besides, this is what I've been praying for, crying out for, hoping for."

Sorrow etched the lines in Papa's face. "You do not need a man to be a whole person."

"Then why would God send me Ewing if not for the purpose of marrying him?"

"Perhaps because the Lord wants to see if you will trust Him. If you will choose Him over being married."

"But marriage was His idea. He sanctified it."

"Marriage is a good thing, but it may not be the highest and best for you. Are you willing to give it up for Him, if that is what He wishes?"

Moisture once again rushed to her eyes. "But I don't want Him to wish that for me. Why would He?"

"I don't know. All I'm saying is, if you truly trust God, and if He is the most important thing in your entire life, then you will accept and believe that He knows what is best for you. And you will accept it joyfully. Willingly."

She pulled her hands away, propping an elbow on the table and resting her head against her palm. "Who will hug me in my old age? Who will eat at my table when you and Mother are gone?"

"Christ will meet your needs, Essie. If you let Him."

"But I can't touch Him with my hands or see Him with my eyes or hear Him with my ears."

Papa sighed. "So you would pretend to be something you aren't and marry a man you're not in love with?"

"I don't know," she whispered. "Maybe. Except . . . except I want something more."

"Of course you do. So, for now, why not embrace Christ fully and with abandon? Then see how you feel about marriage to Ewing?"

"How? How do I *embrace* Christ?"

"You obey Him. Dwell on His Word. Do every single thing for His glory. And I'm not talking about serving the church or caring for orphans. I'm talking about everyday things. When you ride your bike, do it for His enjoyment. Talk to Him, praise Him, delight in His creation. When you wear a hat, do it for His pleasure. When you polish the silver, sing to Him. Make Him the love of your life."

Those words were so easy for him to say. He had a wife. And a child. How could he possibly understand what he was suggesting?

He drained the last of his coffee. "Whatever you decide, honey, your mother and I will support you."

Standing, he squeezed her neck and left. Leaving her to decide if Christ as her lifelong groom would truly be enough.

CHAPTER | TWENTY-NINE

EWING TRIED NOT TO study Preacher Bogart's office too closely. He didn't want the old man to think he was coveting—though, in all likelihood, he was.

He took quick note of the open bookshelves along the north wall, the fireplace adjacent to the man's substantial desk, and the small prayer table holding an open Bible. Not much had changed—other than his age—since the last time he'd visited this office. The last time he'd stood here he was a youngster who, during church, had shaped his fingers into a gun, pointed them at an elder collecting the offering, and said, "Stick 'em up."

Ewing shook the memory free and cleared his throat.

"Come in, son," the preacher said, looking up and placing his pen in a holder. Nose and ears dominated a kind face framed by a head of pure white hair so thick he was the envy of many men half his age. Large blue eyes that missed nothing conveyed pleasure as he offered Ewing a seat.

Other memories of old flashed through Ewing's mind. Preacher Bogart shooting BBs at him the night he stole a watermelon from the man's garden. Arm wrestling him after rendering a hog to see who would keep the animal's bladder for a game of catch. Squaring off with him at age fifteen when—tired of being asked to do more than his share of chores around the church—he hollered, "My name is *not* 'Get Wood!' "

Removing his hat, Ewing settled into the wooden chair the preacher had indicated.

"You're looking well, Getwood."

Ewing smiled. "Thank you, sir. As are you."

"I haven't had a chance to tell you privately how pleased I am the elders chose you as my replacement."

"Thank you, sir. I'm still trying to decide which I'm feeling more—anticipation or terror. You've left some mighty big shoes to fill."

"No need to put on these old things when you have an excellent pair of your own." He leaned back in his chair. "Many of your professors at the Nashville Bible College are colleagues of mine. They had very complimentary and remarkable things to say about you."

"I learned a lot while I was there, sir. I'm anxious to do God's work here at home."

They spoke of the church's mission. They discussed the differences between Bible college now and when Bogart had attended. They debated about closed communion and whether or not nonmembers of faith should be allowed to receive communion.

As the conversation wound down, Bogart moved aside some papers on his desk. "The elders and I have noticed you courting our Miss Essie rather doggedly these last few weeks."

"Yes, sir. It is my hope she will agree to be my wife."

He nodded. "She's a strong woman from a good family, and the two of you have been friends a long time."

"My whole life, actually. Some of my earliest memories hearken back to her."

"I assume you have discussed your intentions with her father?"

"Of course."

Bogart rested his arms on top of his desk. "As you well know, the Lord has revealed to us through His Word that His expectations for His leaders are higher and more stringent than for those in His congregation."

"Yes, sir. First Timothy."

"Then you'll remember one of those qualifications is that their wives be above reproach and worthy of respect."

He nodded.

"Son," the preacher said, steepling his fingers, "it has come to the attention of myself and the elders that Miss Spreckelmeyer might not be as above reproach as one might think."

Ewing stiffened. "I don't understand."

"There is an unconfirmed rumor concerning an illicit affair she supposedly had with one of her father's employees."

His first reaction was outrage, followed swiftly by a need to vehemently deny the accusation. His third was panic. He forced himself to remain calm.

"Rumor?" he asked, putting as much disparagement on the word as he dared. "Well, I would venture to guess that, depending upon who you talk to, there are rumors about every person in this town."

"You're probably right. But not everyone in town is being considered for a position as our pastor."

"What are you saying?"

"I'm saying that before we can move any further in our dealings, we must first verify the rumor."

"How do you plan to do that?"

"We plan to ask Miss Spreckelmeyer to either deny or verify it."

He shot to his feet. "I won't have it. I will not subject her to such a thing simply because some busybody is spreading falsehoods about her."

"Calm down, Ewing. If they are falsehoods, all she need do is tell us and we will accept her word as absolute truth."

Ewing lowered himself back into his chair. "But don't you see how humiliating that will be for her?"

"Yes, yes I do. And it is unfortunate. But there is no other way. Too much is at stake."

"And if I refuse to subject her to an interrogation?"

"It won't be an interrogation, just a simple question put to her."

"The question will be anything but simple."

He acknowledged Ewing's statement with a nod. "Be that as it may, we must put it to her."

"We? Who is we?"

"The elders and myself."

"You cannot be serious. She would die of mortification. I will not permit it."

"Then our offer to you will be revoked."

Had the preacher walloped Ewing in the stomach, he'd have been less shocked. Revoked? The elders planned to revoke their offer if Essie didn't come in for questioning?

"What if I speak on her behalf?" he asked.

"I'm sorry. We must hear it from her."

He swallowed. "And what if it is true, this whatever it is? What if it did happen and she has confessed and repented and been forgiven?"

Bogart's eyes widened in alarm. "If it is true and you intend to marry her, then you'd best look for another profession. We cannot in good conscience allow you to pastor this church or any other if your wife is less than what she should be."

"You've known her longer than I," Ewing spat. "You know her family. She is a wonderful, good, wholesome woman."

Bogart's expression softened. "Then there should be no problem. But we must speak with her first."

"How prevalent is the rumor?"

"We have only heard the accusation from one source."

"Who?"

He shook his head. "That is not of importance."

"And if Essie is guiltless, what then? Will this person spreading malicious gossip be permitted to continue?"

"We will talk with her."

"Her?" He tightened his lips. "Figures."

Bogart's eyes became troubled.

Ewing reined in his anger and gentled his tone. "Miss Spreckelmeyer hasn't even consented to be my wife yet."

"Perhaps, then, you should have a talk with her before she does."

―――――

Curled up beneath the feather coverlet on her bed, Essie stared through the darkness. Beams of orange shot from the grate of her heating stove before dissipating into thin air. She wondered what time it was—other than well past bedtime and well before sunrise.

Still, she was wide awake. No longer able to hide from her thoughts. Could she really be so selfish as to marry Ewing just for the sake of achieving a state of matrimony? She moaned.

The outline of her Bible was barely discernible on her nightstand. Reaching over, she lifted the Book and plopped it beside her on top of the coverlet.

The cushioned leather was cool to the touch.

I've read this from front to back. I've memorized verses. Entire chapters, even. I've given my time to the widows and orphans and church. I've honored my parents—for the most part. I've not stolen or murdered or taken your name in vain. I have committed fornication, yes, but you pronounced me clean.

Grasping the volume tightly in her hand, she hurled it across the room. It crashed into the wall with a loud *thunk* before banging to the floor.

So where's my man? A man whom I not only like, but whom I love? And who loves me in return? And who doesn't ask me to be something that I'm not?

Anguished sobs burst from her. She smothered her face within the downy embrace of her pillow. *Why? Why?!*

You shall have no other gods before me.

It's not a god, she insisted, addressing in her heart the powerful, non-audible voice resonating inside her soul. *It's a dream. A desire. A hope.*

Your hope is not in me.

It is!

But she knew that wasn't entirely true. From the moment she had turned thirty, she'd decided she was through "waiting on the Lord" for a husband. She'd decided to take matters into her own hands.

And what a fine muck she'd made of things. She'd packed more heartache into six months than she'd experienced in a lifetime.

Rubbing the edge of the soft, unbleached bedsheet against her lips, remorse swept through her.

She slithered out from under the covers and onto the wool rug surrounding her bed, then hurried to the wall, picked up her Bible and cradled it within her arms. She placed it back on the nightstand where it belonged and stroked its cover, thanking God for providing it for her. Then she crouched over, face to the floor, tears of sorrow rushing to her eyes.

Forgive my pride, Lord. I'm willing to deny myself of the things I desire most—a man, a marriage, and children.

She sobbed, the ramifications of her prayer squeezing her with grief. For though she desperately wanted to please God, she'd been holding fast to this particular dream since childhood. The thought of living her entire earthly life without a man, without children, broke her heart.

Especially when she knew there was nothing wrong with wanting a man and marriage. The problem had occurred when she'd allowed it to consume her, rule her, orchestrate her every action.

Yet she was determined to have no other gods before Him. To be satisfied with whatever He had for her. No, not just satisfied or content. She wanted to rejoice in His plans for her.

She took a trembling breath. *I will embrace the life you have laid out for me, Lord, and I will live it joyfully so that I may be a witness to how great you are.*

Her tears slowed to a trickle, leaving her cheeks slick and salty. She wondered if she really could live the life of a spinster with joy.

Images of herself old and gray, of this house empty and quiet, rattled her resolve. How could she embrace such a thing?

Help me be joyful, Lord. I'm afraid. Afraid of being alone.

I will never leave you.

What if that wasn't enough? She scoured her memory for characters in the Bible who had been alone or isolated. Joseph immediately came to mind, for he had been abandoned by his loved ones and sold into slavery. David had been unaccompanied as he faced Goliath. Rahab had single-handedly risked death to shelter two spies. Daniel had been thrown into a lion's den.

Yet they'd not really been alone. God had been with them. And every one of them had experienced victory. Great victory. Her determination resurfaced.

I want to do your will, Lord, and I want to do it with joy. Use me for your glory. I am yours. Amen.

Slipping back into bed, she tarried in that place with Him. But this time she let Him do the talking. And what He had to say was the very last thing she expected.

But she acquiesced and promised to speak with Papa as soon as she had everything prepared.

You will need to soften his heart, though, Lord. And if this is not your will—close the doors. Amen.

CHAPTER | THIRTY

EWING GAVE ROSEBUD HER head as he made his way to Essie's home. It had been three days since he'd proposed. Two days since Preacher Bogart's ultimatum.

He'd prayed. He'd fasted. He'd railed at God. But he was no closer to a palatable solution than he was before. He was going to have to choose between his calling and Essie.

He supposed he could marry her and then move somewhere else. But it would have to be outside the county, maybe even outside the state. But Essie had lived here all her life. He couldn't imagine her being willing to move away. And truthfully, he didn't want to live anywhere else, either.

He drug his hand down his face. If he were really honest with himself, he'd admit that Essie wasn't everything he'd remembered her to be. He'd left home a child and had carried with him an image of Essie that didn't quite translate into reality when he'd returned.

He realized now that all the things he'd loved about her were from a child's perspective. She'd fished with him. Swam with him. Climbed trees with him. Hunted with him. Played ball with him.

He'd absolutely adored her. Worshiped her, even. And had decided at a very early age that he wanted to spend the rest of his days with her.

Looking back, he realized now how unorthodox her behavior really had been. Shocking, even. She thought nothing of hiking up her skirts or soiling her clothing or barreling headlong into danger.

She thought only of adventure. What boy wouldn't fall in love with her?

But he was a man now. A man who desperately wanted to fulfill the Great Commission that Christ had given him. And when it came time for him to stand before God Almighty, what would he say?

That he had given up his calling so he could marry a woman whose everyday behavior bordered on the scandalous? Whose secrets were so shocking that the church would revoke their offer if and when they found out?

And what would he do for a living? He'd spent all his adult years preparing to be a pastor. How would he provide for Essie if he couldn't preach? Especially when that's all he wanted to do. He had a burning desire to serve God. The thought of not preaching was simply not to be borne.

Pulling Rosebud to a stop in front of the Spreckelmeyer house, Ewing stared at the two-story Georgian, shaded by giant pecan trees on a spacious lot and surrounded by a white picket fence. He'd banged in and out of that house more times than he could count. The Spreckelmeyers been more than tolerant of him over the years and had acted as surrogate parents in many ways.

He sighed. A proposal of marriage was almost as binding as speaking the actual vows. What would the Spreckelmeyers think of him if he withdrew his offer? What if word got out? Would the elders decide that any man who broke his word was unworthy of pastoring a church?

If they did, he'd have to tell them the truth about Essie. And he did not want to do that. The risk of those men telling their wives and those wives telling others was too great.

Lord, help me, he prayed. Because as he swung off of his horse and tied her to a rail, he knew that the only thing he could do was to take back his offer of marriage. And it would very likely ruin lifelong friendships that he treasured.

"It's Ewing," Mother said, returning to the kitchen after answering the door. "He's in the parlor, waiting for you."

Essie slowly removed the apron from around her waist. It was all well and good for her to give up her wants and needs to the Lord. It was something totally different to refuse Ewing his.

She re-pinned a loose piece of hair. How on earth would she tell him she couldn't marry him? Especially after he'd extended her such grace?

He'd be so hurt. And she knew all too well what that particular kind of hurt and rejection felt like.

Yet she also knew that if she tried not to hurt him, she'd end up hurting him even more. So she'd have to tell him the truth.

Still, she couldn't admit he had been the means to an end for her. Though, he had.

She couldn't say the Lord had called her to give marriage up as a sacrifice to Him. Though, He had.

She couldn't say she wasn't in love with him. Though, she wasn't.

So what could she say? That he was asking her to pretend to be something she was not?

She shook her head. No. There was nothing. No easy, pat answer she could offer without injury.

Give me the words, Lord.

He stopped his pacing when she entered. He'd dressed more casually today in a pair of wool trousers and a navy hand-knit pullover sweater that suited him quite nicely.

"Hello," she said.

"Hello." He crushed the hat in his hands. "You look lovely."

She smiled. She'd been filling lamps in the kitchen and wore an ordinary black serge skirt and white shirtwaist. But she could see he meant his words and they warmed her.

"Thank you."

"We need to talk," he prompted.

"Yes. Yes, we do. Won't you sit down?"

He joined her on the settee and must have read the distress in her eyes.

"What is it?" he asked. "What has happened?"

"Ewing, I'm so sorry, but I'm afraid I won't be able to marry you."

His face registered shock. "You won't?"

"It's nothing you've done," she quickly assured him. "Nothing at all. You have been . . . wonderful to me." She swallowed. "I just do not have the kind of feelings for you that a bride should have for her groom."

"You don't?"

She slipped her hand between his clasped ones. "You are truly one of my dearest and most beloved friends and I treasure you beyond belief, but . . ."

"But . . . ?"

"But," she said, taking a deep breath, "I don't think I would make a very good preacher's wife. I'm too, too . . ."

"Impulsive?"

"Yes. And outdoorsy. And independent. I'm afraid my impetuousness would provide the gossip mill with so much material that it could hurt the church. And you. And your work. I really don't want to do that."

They sat in silence, the fire in the hearth crackling. The sounds of Mother's puttering in the kitchen now and again reached them.

He opened his palm, entwining their fingers together. "Do you love me, Essie?"

"Yes, of course. But I don't believe I'm *in* love with you. And there's . . . well, there's a difference."

"Yes," he whispered, "there is definitely a difference."

She squeezed his fingers.

He lifted their interlocked hands, resting his lips upon her knobby knuckles. "You are an amazing woman."

"Oh, Ewing."

"Can I make a confession?" he asked.

Blinking, she nodded.

"I think you are right."

She sucked in her breath. "You do?"

"Yes." He rubbed his cheek with their clasped hands, his closely shaven whiskers like the mildest of sandpaper against her fingers. "Yes, I do. And I would hate to see you have to suppress your vivaciousness. It wouldn't be right."

"You aren't angry with me, then?"

"Not at all." Kissing her knuckles one more time, he swallowed, then relinquished his hold.

She walked him to the door. "We can still be friends?"

"Of course," he said, tugging on his gloves. "I would consider it an honor."

But as she watched him stride down the sidewalk and swing up onto Rosebud, she knew that the relationship they'd shared since childhood would forever be altered.

————

Journal in hand, Essie knocked softly on Papa's door.

"Come in."

She slipped in, then closed the door behind her but did not advance.

Twilight streamed in from the big bay window, casting shadows about the room. An assortment of rugs covered the polished wooden floor, and a fur skin provided warmth for Papa's feet. Gilt-backed books lined rows upon rows of shelves without glass or coverings of any kind so Papa could remove his books without key and lock. The uppermost shelves had been designed for easy retrieval of his volumes with an outstretched arm.

The fire had recently been stoked, combating the end-of-the-day chill brought on by the setting sun and tingeing the air with smoke.

Papa's eyes displayed deep circles beneath them. Putting his pen back in its holder, he indicated a chair.

"Am I disturbing you?" she asked. "I can return later."

"No, it's almost time for supper anyway. What's on your mind?"

Smoothing her skirts beneath her, she sat and addressed the subject she'd not yet broached with him. "I, um, have a business proposition for you."

"You may not go back to the oil field, Essie. You can do all the paper work you want here in my office, but no field work. I won't change my mind on that."

"Oh." She looked toward the window. "That's not what I was going to ask, but I have wondered how it was going. You never talk about it at the supper table."

"It was a dry hole."

"No! You mean there was not any oil in that well at all?"

"Not a drop."

"Oh, Papa. All that work. How disappointing. I'm so terribly sorry."

He shrugged. "That's the way it is in any prospecting venture. I finally called the boys off the rig today and am moving them to another location Davidson suggested."

"Are you sure you trust his scouting instincts after this?"

"We'll give him another try before I call in somebody else. Now, what proposition did you have for me?"

She had dressed carefully for this meeting, wearing her green-and-gray tailored suit, blazer-style. Her hat was modest, decorated only by an ostrich demi-plume for some added height.

Straightening her backbone, she looked him directly in the eye. "I'd like to use my dowry to purchase the abandoned seed house, please."

He sat nonplussed for a moment. "Your dowry?"

"Yes. I'm through waiting for a husband. It's time to move forward."

"Now, Essie—"

"No, Papa. I'm officially setting my cap on the shelf. But if it's all right, I'd still like to invest my dowry. Just not in a husband."

"What if one comes along?"

"Then he'll have himself a very nice seed house."

"A seed house." It wasn't a question but a statement. A confirmation that he understood her correctly.

"Yes."

He rubbed his temples. "You want to go into the cotton business?"

"No. I'd like to found a bicycle club."

"A bicycle club?" he asked, clearly puzzled.

"That's right. I'd like to renovate the seed house and use it one night a week for members to ride in while a band plays. During the days, I'll give lessons."

"But you're the only person in town who owns a bicycle."

"I know. I'll have to rent or sell bikes to any members who don't have one of their own."

"So you want to buy not only the seed house but several bicycles?"

"For starters."

"Why? Why now?"

"Because I'm good at both teaching and bicycling and I can use the talents the Lord blessed me with to bless others."

He leaned back in his chair.

If you were serious about this, Lord, you will have to see it done.

"I believe," Papa said, "I had deferred these kinds of decisions to your mother."

"She's all for it."

He blinked. "You've discussed this with your mother?"

"At length."

He placed his arms on the desk. "What did she say?"

"That she'd like to sign up for lessons."

"Doreen wants to ride a bike?" Stiffening, he scowled. "I won't have it. She'll break her neck."

"No, she won't. I'm an excellent teacher."

"What would she wear? I will not have her riding about town in those short skirts."

Essie smiled. "You let me."

"That's different. Entirely different. I can't even fathom what Doreen was thinking."

Crossing her arms, Essie cocked her head. "She was thinking it looked like fun. And she's right. It is. I cannot believe you are being so stuffy about this."

"I'm not being stuffy."

She lifted an eyebrow.

"What would she wear?" he repeated.

"A costume with a series of drawstrings that will convert her skirt into bloomers while riding and can then be released to re-create the skirt."

He frowned. "Where would she get that?"

"She'll have to buy or make one. But that will be no problem. You see, I'm also going to sell patterns and bicycle-wear in my club."

"A seed house. Bicycles. Patterns. Ready-made clothing. Anything else you want to purchase while you're at it?"

"Quite a bit, actually."

He shook his head. "You are talking about a great deal of money. Your dowry is generous, but not that generous. I cannot see myself investing such a sum. Not for a business that is doomed to failure."

Picking her journal up off the floor, she set it on the edge of his desk. "Inside here I have a list of several hundred *profitable* bicycle clubs from all around our country. I have marked a section that lists what my club will entail, how it will work, and what it will cost to convert the seed house. I've gone into great detail about what I will charge for membership, bike rentals, and lessons. I have inserted an article from one of your old *New York Times* that cites, 'The bicycle is of more importance to mankind than all the victories and defeats of Napoleon, with the First and Second Punic Wars thrown in.'" She slid the bound book closer to him. "I have also listed my costs and how I will pay them back to you with interest."

He didn't even look at the journal. "Are you concerned with how you will live once I am gone? You needn't be. I have listed you as beneficiary in all my dealings, including Sullivan Oil. You will be well taken care of."

"Thank you, Papa. And I am most appreciative. But in the meanwhile, I'd like to have something that is mine." She leaned forward to emphasize her point. "The bicycle is the way of the future. Don't you see? It is better than a horse because it costs almost nothing and is never tired. It will take its rider three times as far as a horse in the same number of days or weeks. The *Times* says that the value of horseflesh will drop to almost nothing within the next twenty years."

"I'm sorry, Essie, but that is rather hard to imagine. Wheels may be a mode of transportation for some, but not the majority. Consider Mr. Fouty or Mrs. Vandervoort. Do you really believe they would give up their horses for a bike?"

"Yes, I do. Did you know in Brooklyn they have a Fat Man's Bicycle Club, where members must weigh over 250 pounds to join?"

He looked at her with skepticism. "But so many doctors and churches are against it. You won't be able to drum up enough business to support your venture."

"The folks in town are simply uninformed. I can show them article after article by doctors and clergymen who are not only proponents of bicycling for both men and women, but who actually make their rounds on bikes."

He harrumphed. "And will you tell me next that you'll pull a wagon with it?"

"Of course not, but the papers say you can make fifty miles a day as comfortably as twenty miles on foot while carrying all the clothing you need, besides a camera and other traps. And the exercise is more invigorating than walking."

He opened her journal and perused the first few pages. "What's this about social activities? I thought the main focus was bicycling."

"It is, but other clubs around the country offer banquets and bicycle debating societies and cycle races. In order to increase my yield, I thought I should do the same."

He continued to read, and after a while she quietly let herself out of the room, but not before she caught the slightest sparkle in Papa's eyes as he turned the pages of her journal.

CHAPTER | THIRTY-ONE

Five Months Later

ESSIE TOOK PEG FOR another turn around the Corsicana Velocipede Club. After an adjustment to the frame of her bike, the blacksmith had been able to eliminate the click that had resulted from Peg's fall. Now the wheels of her machine hummed with each rotation of the pedals.

Light poured in from long, narrow windows lining the ceiling of the one-hundred-fifty-foot structure, spotlighting her ride. The plank flooring offered an escape from the dirt roads outside, though the smell of cottonseed still tinted the club's air.

Today was to be her grand opening. She had, so far, seventy-eight paying members, and private lessons would start this morning. This would give her two months to teach her members the rudiments before the Fourth of July when she would host their inaugural "group ride"—band and all.

Shirley Bunting and Sadie Tyner entered from the back, their giggles and excited whispers echoing throughout the vast room. Essie steered her bike toward them.

She still marveled at Papa's cleverness in soliciting Mr. Bunting as an investor. He and Shirley had evidently been in Dallas and had seen for themselves the bicycle craze that had begun to grip the big city, and they were eager to participate.

With one of the town's most prominent bankers not only blessing her venture but backing it, the rest of the community responded in kind, many of them signing up for a membership.

Shirley lifted her arm and waved. "Helloooooooooooo."

. . . *helloooo . . . helloooo . . .* echoed in the vast space.

What a surprise the lovely young blonde had turned out to be. In many ways, she was as lonely as Essie had been. But her loneliness was due to an overabundance of suitors, who—attracted superficially to her beauty—offered her no real companionship.

Her closest chum, Sadie Tyner, was as sharp as they came but had been suppressed by a mother who had convinced the poor girl she was unattractive and too smart and would, therefore, never land a husband if she didn't do something about it.

Essie had hired the girls as a personal favor to Mr. Bunting. And what a gift from God they were. Both were quick, enthusiastic learners and had blossomed under her tutelage. For she had not only taught them the thrill and exhilaration of mastering a bicycle but also the sense of freedom and accomplishment a woman could achieve through it.

Of course, convincing Shirley to wear simple, lightweight clothing had so far been the most challenging task. She'd wanted to wear a fancy bicycle suit and hat, but Essie forbade it. The men and women in town were not yet comfortable with such fashions and she did not want to alienate them.

She drew up next to the girls. "Are you ready for a long day of work?"

"We can't wait," Shirley said. Sadie nodded her agreement.

She hoped that would still be the case at the end of the day. Once word had gotten out that the charming Miss Bunting would be assisting in lessons, the youth of Corsicana—male and female alike—had signed up in droves.

Gliding to a stop, Essie jumped from Peg.

"I'm wearing my bicycle corset," Sadie whispered, smoothing down the front of her shirtwaist, "just like you told me to. Can you tell?"

"Not a'tall. What about you, Shirley?" Essie asked.

"I feel downright scandalous. I cannot imagine how you are going to convince our mothers to do the same."

"We won't have to. They won't be able to breathe if they don't."

The door at the front of the building opened, and an elderly woman with a cane entered.

"Hello, Mrs. Lockhart," Essie said. "You are right on time. Welcome to the Corsicana Velocipede Club."

"A bunch of foolishness," she answered. "I'm going to break every bone in my body."

"Nonsense." Essie hugged the woman, the smell of lilacs teasing her nose. "Tumbling off your bicycle is inexcusable. All you need do is decide you won't fall and you won't."

"I had better not."

"Shall we begin right away?" she asked, taking the woman's shawl.

"If we must."

"Very well. First, let's watch Miss Bunting demonstrate."

Shirley mounted a Ladies Yukon with grace and ease, pedaling it away from them and toward the back wall of the building.

"By July Fourth you will know how to sit, pedal, balance, steer, turn, and dismount," Essie said. "Do you see that black thing attached to the front of the machine that looks a bit like bat wings?"

"Yes."

"That's called a Cherry Screen, and its purpose is to block the view of Miss Bunting's ankles and feet and to prevent her skirt from blowing about."

Shirley turned and headed back toward them, as pretty and engaging a sight as ever. There wasn't a woman under ninety who wouldn't want to look just like her.

"Notice how she isn't looking down," Essie continued, "but is looking up and off, on and out. Her forehead and feet all in line."

Shirley waved.

Mrs. Lockhart gasped. "Good heavens. Hold on, child."

. . . *child* . . . *child* . . . Her exclamation bounced off the walls throughout the building.

Swinging her legs to the side, Shirley jumped to the ground and jogged to a stop while still holding the handlebars.

Mrs. Lockhart turned around. "That is it. Never in all my days will I be able to do that. I'm leaving."

Essie took her elbow and brought her back. " 'Except ye become as little children,' " she quoted.

"I'm too old to remember that far back."

"We will be beside you the entire time."

Shirley turned the wheel around and waited.

Sadie took Mrs. Lockhart's cane. Essie expected the woman to lean more heavily into her, but that did not occur. Why, the woman didn't need the cane at all. She obviously carried it for effect—or as a tool to whack misbehaving boys.

Essie suppressed her smile. "You remember Miss Tyner?"

"Of course. It's my body that's old. Not my mind."

Sadie placed a step stool next to the bike.

"For now, you will use a stool to help you mount. Are you ready?"

The woman tightened her grip on Essie. "I don't believe I can do it."

"It is all right," Essie said. "All three of us will be right beside you. You needn't ride today, just mount and dismount. That's all."

She placed her right foot on the stool.

"Other foot. You will need to straddle the seat."

Pressing a hand to her throat, Mrs. Lockhart stared at the machine as if it were the devil himself. "I've never done such a thing in my life. What will people think?"

"Princesses Louise and Beatrice both ride at Balmoral. You will be in fine company indeed."

The woman's eyebrows raised just a mite before she lifted her chin and placed her left foot on the stool. With Shirley on one side, Essie on the other, and Sadie holding the seat, they assisted her onto the saddle.

"Good heavens. Don't let go. Don't let go."

The grip she had on Essie's arm cut off her blood flow and crushed Shirley's leg o' mutton sleeve.

"We're not going anywhere, Mrs. Lockhart," Essie said, "but you must release us and take hold of the crossbar. Letting loose of the handles is the equivalent of dropping the bridle of a spirited steed. If you remember nothing else, you must forever keep your main hold, else your horse is not bitted and will shy to a dead certainty."

Mrs. Lockhart grasped the handlebars.

"Excellent work. Now, rest your feet on the stirrups, but do not exert any pressure on them."

She placed her black pointed boots on the pedals.

"This is downright wicked," she whispered.

Sadie giggled.

"It most certainly is not," Essie insisted. "Your position equally distributes your muscles so that when the exercise begins you will not overuse any one muscle. Now, would you like to move forward or sit awhile longer?"

"I'll just sit awhile, thank you."

"Of course."

She waited for Mrs. Lockhart to become accustomed to sitting astride the animal. Black draped the woman like a mantle—black shirtwaist and skirt, black gloves, black hat, black boots. Yet Essie knew behind all those morose clothes lived a heart that loved intrigue and risk.

The extra folds of skin below the woman's brows gave her eyes a beady look, but they were alight with anticipation.

"Better?" Essie asked.

Mrs. Lockhart gave a slight nod.

"All right, then. Shall we give her a try?"

Squeezing the handlebars, she nodded again.

"Excellent. Now, there are two things that must occupy your thinking powers at all times: the goal and the momentum required to reach it."

"What is my goal, again?" she asked, voice trembling.

"Today your goal is to ride, with our assistance, six feet. The momentum required will be one turn of the pedal. Are you ready?"

A fine sheen of perspiration gathered along her white hairline. "I am ready."

Essie signaled the girls and they walked several feet. Mrs. Lockhart exerted pressure on the pedals for one rotation, propelling her forward.

"Oh heavens," the woman said, surprise and delight transforming her wrinkled face. "Oh my. Goodness gracious. Don't let go."

"You did it," Essie exclaimed. "That's all there is to it. Congratulations. You have taken your first ride on a velocipede."

Sadie grabbed the stool, and the three of them helped Mrs. Lockhart dismount.

Pulling a handkerchief from her sleeve, she patted her hairline, cheeks, and lips. "That was the most exciting thing I have done in years. When can I do it again?"

"Miss Tyner keeps track of our lessons. If you will go with her to the front, she will tell you when your next appointment is."

They'd gone several yards before Essie stopped her. "Oh my. Don't forget your cane."

Mrs. Lockhart turned around and walked in perfect form back to Essie. "Thank you, my dear." She squeezed Essie's hand. "For everything."

———

July 4, 1895

Uncle Melvin pressed his tongue against his teeth and let loose a piercing whistle that bounced off the walls of the Corsicana Velocipede Club and silenced the excited mumblings of the crowd. All eyes turned to the source of the noise—a platform in the corner of the building. Members of the Merchants' Opera House orchestra shifted in their chairs.

Uncle Melvin offered Essie a hand up onto the platform. She wore a new pink-and-white-spotted taffeta dress with wide, leg o' mutton sleeves and elbow-length gloves, bracelets dangling over the top.

Her wide-brimmed hat of straw was one of the most spectacular she'd ever owned with pleated chiffon, ribbon loops, a steel buckle, and a bouquet of American beauties turned up slightly at the back.

"Ladies and gentlemen," she projected across the assembly. "Welcome to the Corsicana Velocipede Club's inaugural Group Ride."

The crowd applauded, whooped, whistled and stomped. Essie smiled, waiting for them to settle down. Her students had worked long and hard in preparation for this event. She felt like a mother watching her offspring perform in the annual school play.

Splashes of color from the ladies' garments were juxtaposed with the men's brown and black suits. Though a few of the younger, more fashionable men were wearing red-and-white striped jackets with white trousers.

Her pupils stood scattered around the track, bicycles in hand, while spectators lined the perimeters of her building.

"Ladies," she said, "prepare your skirts."

The crowd murmured as the men held both their bikes and the women's. A rustling of fabric ensued and her female students pulled up the drawstrings in their hems, transforming their skirts into bloomers. When all stilled, she turned her back to the audience and faced the band.

"Are you ready?" she whispered, raising her hands.

They lifted their instruments into place, poised and waiting.

She gave them four counts, then swept her hands down and up. The strains of "A Bicycle Built for Two" filled the cavernous room. She nodded to the director, Mr.

Creiz, and he took her place. Spinning around, she watched the bicyclists mount and ride. The crowd cheered, then sang with gusto to the band's tune.

"Daisy, Daisy,
Give me your answer do.
I'm half crazy,
All for the love of you.
It won't be a stylish marriage,
I can't afford a carriage
But you'll look sweet upon the seat
Of a bicycle built for two."

Mr. Vandervoort whizzed by, with his newly adopted son, Harley, balanced on the handlebars and squealing in delight. He was followed by Mr. Baumgartner, Mr. Pickens of the Flour, Feed and Liquor Store, Miss Lillie Sue, the doctor's daughter, and Mrs. Peterson, the Crooks' nanny.

Shirley looked as if she were being escorted by an army of men as they flanked her on all sides with their machines. Mayor Whiteselle and his wife sang and wheeled in time to the music.

Mrs. Lockhart reigned over all, though. Her head high, her bearing regal. She commanded her wheel with ease, but it was her new bicycle costume complete with wide knickerbockers and colored stockings that garnered the most attention.

Essie moved from the platform and made her way toward the front of the building. Mr. Weidmann handed out free samples of his fruitcake, along with some new items on his menu of sweets. Mother poured punch for those with parched throats. Young Lawrence passed out flat fans to the ladies, the backs of which had been printed with *The Corsicana Velocipede Club*.

The song came to a close and the roar of the assembly momentarily deafened Essie's ears. Some of her pupils parked their bikes and went in search of family. Others continued to ride.

In the center, Sadie and Shirley began free instruction to the lucky two winners whose names had been drawn earlier. Jeremy Gillespie had been one of them. He'd made no delay in getting to Shirley's side.

She scowled at him and Essie stiffened. It hadn't occurred to her that Shirley would resent teaching the town drunk's grandson. Jeremy leaned over and said something to the girl. Her eyes widened.

He smiled, winked, and straddled the bike. Long hours kicking down the oil rig had broadened his shoulders, chest, and legs. It had also given him a confidence and cockiness he'd not had before. He wore a smart suit and straw boater. The transformation from boy to man boggled the mind.

". . . the conclusion that bicycles are just as good company as most husbands."

Essie recognized Mrs. Lockhart's voice at once and turned to see her waving her cane at a group of elderly widows.

"Why, you can dispose of it and get a new one without shocking the entire community," she concluded.

The band reached the chorus of "Say 'Au Revoir' But Not 'Good-Bye,'" and the crowd's voices in song drowned out whatever response the women had to Mrs. Lockhart's sentiment. But their expressions of horror and disbelief were enough.

Essie choked back a snort.

"Looks like your big debut is a success," Papa said in her ear.

She looked over her shoulder and smiled. "I think so, too. I had no idea folks would turn out in such numbers."

He gave her waist a squeeze. "Perhaps I should have you pick the location of my next well."

"You hit oil this last time."

"I don't know if I'd call twenty-two barrels of oil a day hitting much of anything."

"Pishposh. You can't expect to find a gusher the first couple of tries. Where will you drill next?"

"I'm open to suggestions."

"Essie?" Ewing said, touching her elbow.

"Ewing! I didn't expect to see you." She grasped his hands and touched her cheek to his. He was dressed in black, as befitted his station, his hair neatly combed, his jacket crisp and neat.

"Almost the whole town is here," he said, "including a good portion of my flock." Leaning forward, he winked, a teasing note entering his voice. "I thought I'd best come to make sure some calamity didn't befall them."

Papa extended a hand. "Hello, Preacher. I must admit you do a mighty fine job in the pulpit. Mighty fine."

"Thank you, sir."

Someone called Papa's name and he turned.

Ewing squeezed Essie's elbow. "Congratulations. I'm exceedingly proud of you."

"Thank you."

He searched her face. "You look as fetching as ever. I particularly like your hat. Is it new?"

"It is."

"Will your box supper have ribbon to match it?"

"It will."

"Then I'll be sure to watch for it."

She shook her head. "I'm not entering it in the auction."

"Not entering it?" His crestfallen expression surprised her. "But why not? Surely—"

"Miss Spreckelmeyer?" Mrs. Fowler called. "Where can I sign up for membership?"

Essie glanced at the blacksmith's wife, then back at Ewing. "I'm sorry. Would you excuse me?"

He reluctantly released her and she hurried to Mrs. Fowler's side, guiding her to the front desk.

The rest of the two-hour event passed in a blur as she handed out membership cards, answered questions, accepted compliments on her club, and calmed naysayers.

After the final song, Uncle Melvin informed the crowd the box-supper auction would begin at the park in thirty minutes' time. The building emptied as fast as it had filled.

Essie thanked the band, picked up some fans that had been trampled upon, and locked up.

———

A large oak at the crest of a hill offered both shade and a view. Essie shook out her blanket, set her box supper on top of it and sat down.

Oh, it felt good to get off her feet. Mr. Roland's voice floated up the hill as he enticed the crowd with Miss Lizzie's basket. Bidding began in earnest.

Pulling the covering from her basket decorated with pink-and-white polka-dotted ribbon, she withdrew her journal, a pencil, and some cheese.

Jesus Christ

She formed the letters of His name with careful script.

Points of Merit:

- *Will never leave me*
- *Nothing can separate me from His love*
- *Took my sins upon himself*
- *Forgave me*
- *Turns my darkness into light*
- *Cares about everything I do, even knows how many hairs are on my head.*

Drawbacks:

She took a bite of cheese, then tapped the top of her pencil against her lips.

- *Can't see Him, touch Him, or hear Him with my physical body*

  Yes, but blessed are those who have not seen and yet have believed.

- *Is always right about everything*

True. But if you depend on me and trust me, I will take care of you.

- *Expects absolute obedience*

I have warned man that it is better to live in a desert than with a quarrelsome and ill-tempered woman. It's in Proverbs, in case you've forgotten.

She took another bite of cheese and suppressed a smile.

- *Has a droll sense of humor*

A feeling of shared warmth and amusement washed over her. She giggled. Wrapping her arms around herself, she basked in the warmth of His love. It was more fulfilling than she had ever thought possible.

She knew, of course, that she would still go through difficult times. But she also knew she would not be alone. Smiling, she closed the journal and bowed her head before partaking of her meal. She thanked the Lord for her daily bread, for blessing the bicycle club and, most of all, for being her One and Only.

Corsicana, Texas, is passionate about its history. They have preserved it, celebrated it and made it extremely accessible for us to enjoy. They have a historic section downtown, a Pioneer's Village—that, in my opinion, ranks up there with the best I've seen in our entire country—and a Petroleum Park commemorating the location where oil was first discovered in Texas—by accident while drilling a water well. If you find yourself on that patch of road between Dallas and Houston, set aside some time to spend in Corsicana exploring all it has to offer while dining on some fruitcake from the historic Collin Street Bakery.

That said, the folks of Corsicana will notice that I bent their timeline in places in order to fit things into my novel that didn't really take place in 1894. For example, Adam's story of the Cowhead Trail was true—but it happened in 1860 and the trail boss was a fella by the name of Tom Hester. Oil was struck in 1894, but not in August. It was struck on June 9th. I needed my novel to start on the Fourth of July, though, so I bent the dates a bit.

Also, over a year passed before the second oil well was drilled (two hundred feet south of the original water well). Again, my story only spanned eight or so months, so I had to speed up the drilling process.

The peg-legged rope walker was true, but I found conflicting dates for the actual occurrence. Some sources said it was 1884, some said 1898. Either way, it didn't happen in 1894, but again, some events in history call to be included even if we have to bend the timeline a little bit.

And before I get emails from all those snake lovers out there who know that snakes can go for quite some time without eating—please forgive my rush to release Colonel. I just couldn't bear to leave him at Katherine Crook's mercy, and it would have been too cumbersome to the story for Essie to take him home with her.

I look forward to spending another year with Essie in Corsicana as I write *Deep in the Heart of Trouble*, the sequel to *Courting Trouble*. It will take place four years later (1898) and in that time, Corsicana's population exploded—becoming the first oil boomtown in Texas, complete with derricks in almost everyone's backyard.

DEEP IN THE HEART OF TROUBLE

"When I saw you on your wheel, sweet Lenore
Oh my brain did never reel so before.
You were clad in knickerbocks
And you wore such brilliant sox
I could see 'em twenty blocks, maybe more.

"I but gave a passing glance, sweet Lenore
At the natty sawed-off pants which you wore,
Then the cruel ground I hit
I had fallen in a fit,
And I've not recovered yet, sweet Lenore."

—Anonymous

Central Park, New York
June 2, 1898

ESSIE SPRECKELMEYER DIDN'T HAVE a man, nor did she need one. She had her own arms and legs, a head full of sense, and a hearty constitution. Furthermore, if she'd married and multiplied—thus fulfilling her moral and physiological destiny—then she'd never have been able to travel to New York City alone and enter her bicycle costume in the *Herald*'s competition.

Hundreds of people had gathered to celebrate this first day of New York's cycling season. The stately grounds of Central Park contrasted sharply with the hustle and bustle of the city's streets, yet Essie found herself unable to enjoy her surroundings. Moisture collected on her palms, and her stomach tensed, for the newspaper editor on the podium was winding down his speech and preparing to announce the contest winner.

With one hand, she smoothed the full yellow bodice of her costume, which fastened on the right side under a ruffle of cream lisse. With the other, she plucked at bloomers that drooped deeply upon gaiters of cloth to match.

Glancing at the crowd of bicycle enthusiasts packed in and around her, she took a deep breath. Her solo train trip across the country had scandalized everyone back home in Corsicana, Texas. If she won this competition, though, it would go a long way in soothing their sense of propriety. There was nothing Texans liked more than to prove they could do things better than their northern compatriots. In Essie's mind her only real competition was a woman from Boston, whose costume was both appealing to the eye and extremely practical. But the lady's plain brown hat fell quite short of the mark.

Essie checked the hat perched atop her tightly twisted blond tresses, hoping the extravagant design of her own invention would tip the scales in her favor. The straw confection held two lines of yellow roses, with a frill of laced leaves towering well above the crown.

The speaker recaptured Essie's attention. "So without further ado, ladies and gentlemen, the winner of the *New York Herald*'s contest for Best Bicycle Costume goes to . . . Miss Esther Spreckelmeyer of Corsicana, Texas!"

At the sound of her name, Essie trembled with a mix of elation and disbelief. Excusing herself, she wove through the murmuring crowd and toward the festooned podium. Heads craned to catch a glimpse of her approach. The masses parted like clouds making way for a tiny beam of light.

"Congratulations, dear," said an elegant woman wearing a hat of rose-pink chiffon with a sheer polka-dot veil. A swarthy man in white knickerbockers and matching jacket touched his beret. A young police officer took Essie's elbow and waved the crowd back.

And then she was at the podium, where the newspaper editor, who couldn't weigh more than a hundred twenty pounds soaking wet, handed her the giant first-place wreath. It was half again as big as she and almost as heavy.

A bouquet of luscious aromas from the roses, gardenias, and carnations decorating the wreath filled her nose.

"Thank you," she said.

The editor beheld her prizewinning costume, then turned to the crowd with a flourish of his elegant little hand. "I give you Miss Spreckelmeyer, owner and president of the Corsicana Velocipede Club."

Straightening her posture, she slipped the pleated cuff of her gigot sleeve through the wreath and held it to the side so the crowd could take another look at the costume that had been voted to victory.

Men cheered. Women clapped, their gloved hands sounding like the rapid flapping of birds' wings. Out of the corner of her eye, she caught sight of an illustrator just as he flipped back a page in his sketchbook.

He poised his charcoal on a fresh sheet of paper and shouted, "Miss Spreckelmeyer, look this way!"

Startled, she glanced at him, amazed as he quickly swept his charcoal pencil in large arcs across his pad, his movements culminating in a rough outline of her holding the wreath. The crowd quieted and she returned her attention to the waiting audience.

The confident words she had rehearsed in her daydreams fled from her mind. In a panic, she looked to her right and left as if she might miraculously discover the content of her acceptance speech hanging from the grand oaks lining the park.

She cleared her throat. "Ladies and gentlemen wheelers. I, um, I cannot begin to find the words to express how very much this honor means to me."

A smattering of applause.

"I wish to thank—"

"Hey, lady!" A large man in a black summer jacket, black Derby, and black boots pushed his way to the front. "I'm a member of the Anti-Bloomer Brigade, and we don't approve of this emancipation movement you lady wheelers are pushing on our female population. We believe that a lady should look like a lady. What are you thinking to parade in an outfit like that, and in front of an assembly like this? Why, you're shaming God, our country, and the entire fair sex."

The crowd hushed and the illustrator hastily flipped over a new page, sketching the heckler.

"I do not belong to any special dress-reform movement, sir," she said. "I simply wear bloomers because they are the most sensible attire for a lady cycler."

"Well, you might as well be wearing men's trousers!" He leaped up onto the stage.

Essie stumbled back. Gasps rose from the crowd.

The diminutive editor-in-chief would be no match for the burly man, and she saw no sign of the officer who had escorted her to the podium.

"I've taken an oath," the man said, lumbering toward her. "An oath to do everything I can to put a stop to this immorality. And I intend to do just that!"

He grabbed Essie's arm. Three men standing close to the front scrambled onto the platform.

"Now, see here," shouted one of them. "Unhand that woman!"

His words had the effect of a battle cry. And the most defining moment of Essie's cycling career reduced itself into an all-out brawl.

Beaumont, Texas
One Week Later

THE YEARS HADN'T BEEN good to Norris Tubbs. His back curved like a bow. Long white hairs grew from his ears in a tangled mess. His nose had increased in width and depth. And his eyes were glassy—but earnestly focused.

"Your father told me I could have Anna," he said.

"Have Anna?" Tony Morgan asked, taking a sip of coffee.

"Yes. As my wife."

Tony sucked in his breath, taking the coffee down the wrong pipe, choking himself and burning his throat.

Tubbs thumped him on the back. "Everything was settled."

"Everything?" he asked, eyes watering.

"Except for informing Anna, of course."

"Of course." Still regaining his composure, Tony scanned the group of mourners filling his family's parlor and caught sight of his sister accepting condolences from the governor of Texas.

Though she wore black from head to foot, the cut and style of her gown was anything but harsh, particularly on her. A modest hat sat upon piles of dark hair, and the form-fitting bodice accentuated her feminine assets.

Tony sighed. With her nineteenth birthday just a week or so away, he wasn't surprised his father had been considering offers for her hand. But, Norris Tubbs?

Tubbs followed Tony's line of vision. "I assume you will honor your father's wishes?"

Pulling his attention back to the part owner of the H&TC Railroad, Tony tried to rein in his exasperation. Once his father's will was read, he expected to be placed at the helm of Morgan Oil while his older brother ran the more profitable Morgan interests. Therefore, it wouldn't do to alienate Tubbs.

"Dad never said a thing to me about this."

"No? Well, I'm sure he intended to, but he just didn't figure on dropping dead last week."

Tony smoothed the edges of his moustache. "No, I imagine he didn't. Nevertheless, Anna will be in mourning for a year, so there's no need to rush into anything."

"Now, Tony, it's almost the twentieth century. Folks aren't nearly as particular as they used to be about that kind of thing."

"Maybe some folks aren't," he said. "But I am."

Tubbs stiffened. "Well, perhaps it's Darius I should be speaking to about this anyway. He's the oldest, after all."

Tony set his cup on the tray of a passing servant and reminded himself there was more than one railroad coming through Beaumont.

"You can speak to Darius all you want to, Norris," he said, "but you're forgetting that he is only her half brother. I'm her full brother, and I can assure you that her hand will not be awarded to anyone without my express permission."

———

The Morgans' longtime friend and family lawyer, Nathaniel Walker, murmured a few words of condolence to Mother, then ushered her inside his office. Tony led Anna by the arm, leaving Darius to bring up the rear. His half brother crossed to the far side of the room and installed himself in a wing chair. Tony, along with his mother and sister, made do with a small, uncomfortable black-and-white cowhide settee. Horns from about six steers acted as a cushion for their backs.

Walker fished his watch from a vest pocket, confirmed the hour, then pulled a sheaf of pages from a drawer in his grand mahogany desk. The silence, while he fixed a pair of gold-rimmed spectacles to his nose, was awkward and charged.

"I will now read the Last Will and Testament of Blake Huntley Morgan," he announced.

He began in a strong, even voice, but the farther he went, the slower he read. After a while, the words began to recede into the background, supplanted by the thumping in Tony's head.

"There must be some mistake," he finally blurted out, interrupting Walker.

The lawyer looked up. "I'm sorry, Tony. There's no mistake."

"But what you've read makes no sense. It sounds as if Dad only married Mother to have someone to take care of Darius. Like Anna and I don't even matter. Or Mother either."

"Yes," Walker said softly.

Mother whimpered. Anna placed a black handkerchief to her mouth.

The smell of leather, musty books, and tobacco pressed against Tony's lungs. He caught his nails against the grain of the settee's coarse hair. Darius shifted in his chair but showed no visible reaction to the news.

"I don't understand," Mother whispered.

Walker cleared his throat. "Leah, you will be allowed to reside in the mansion and awarded a generous stipend for the duration of your life. Anna may also remain at home until she weds, at which time she will receive a respectable dowry."

"What about Tony?"

"I was just getting to that." Peering through his spectacles, he looked down at the papers on his desk and took a deep breath. " 'I bequeath to my son, Anthony Bryant Morgan . . . nothing. No portion of my estate, real, personal, or mixed is bequeathed to him.' "

Nothing? Tony thought. *Nothing?*

Mother squeezed his hand. Bit by bit, her grip tightened until he was sure her wedding band would leave an imprint on his fingers.

" 'Anthony will be endowed with the most valuable gift of all: an education. I charge him to take his knowledge and go higher and farther than even I have.' "

The windows were barely cracked, leaving the room stuffy and hot. A droplet of sweat trickled down Tony's back.

" 'I hereby declare that after Anthony has reached his majority, my wife is not to share her bequest with him or she will forfeit all monies and inheritance provided herewith.' "

After he reached his majority? At twenty-eight, he was well past that.

As Walker read on, Tony tried to comprehend how his father could have intentionally left him penniless. Unless his brother died, that is, in which case Tony would be the subsequent beneficiary. But the likelihood of that happening anytime soon was extremely improbable. Darius was thirty-one and in excellent health.

Tony glanced at his mother, noting a fine sheen of moisture around her graying hairline. Both she and Anna had worn black serge suits. Mother was prone to fainting, and given the situation and the extreme heat, he was surprised she'd not succumbed already.

Walker finished, turned over the last page of the will and looked at Tony. "Are you all right, son?"

Tight-chested, he kept his voice calm and level. "When? When did he change it?"

Walker straightened the stack he'd made in front of him on the desk. "He didn't change it. It has been like this for years."

Tony nodded. "How many years?"

"Since you children were born." He hesitated. "Well, no, that's not quite true. He did revise it that time Darius had the fever as a boy. He wasn't sure Darius would survive and wanted provisions in place."

Since they were born? His father had disinherited him from the moment of birth? Only making provisions for him in the case of Darius's premature death?

Bile rose in the back of Tony's throat as he thought of the countless times he'd tried to earn his dad's approval. How pathetic.

"Why didn't you tell me, Nathaniel?" Mother asked, choking.

"It was not my place."

"Our families have known each other for three generations."

He removed his glasses, then slowly folded them. "I took an oath, Leah. Would you have me break it?"

"Couldn't you have convinced him to offer Tony some kind of settlement, to give him a start?"

Walker rubbed his nose where his glasses had been, then directed his answer to Tony. "I'm sorry. Blake said he started with nothing. He wants you to do the same. I will say, however, that as the years passed, he had every faith you would rise to the occasion and then some."

The tick in Tony's jaw began to pulse. "I see."

Darius, who had observed the proceedings in cold silence, finally rose. "Is there anything else, Mr. Walker?"

"No, I believe that is all."

Tony watched his half brother cross the room. Apart from Darius's lack of facial hair, the two brothers looked alike. The same olive skin, the same brown eyes, the same tall, lean, and hard physiques.

But they could not have been more different in temperament. Darius had no time for other men's ethical codes. From the start, he'd been out to please himself. Leaving the Morgan Oil enterprise in his hands was as good as feeding it to the wolves.

But his father had loved his first family and merely tolerated his second. No matter how hard Tony had tried to measure up, obviously nothing had ever changed that.

Beads of sweat glistened above Darius's mouth. "Thank you for your time, Walker. I'll be in touch. Would you give us a moment?"

Walker nodded, gathered his papers and stepped out of the office.

Darius moved behind the desk. "Anna," he said, leaning back in the cavernous calf-skin chair, "clearly there was no love lost between you and Dad. So you should have no objection to cutting the grieving process short. Moping about in unrelieved black will do nothing to advance your chances for matrimony."

Mother paled even more. "You mean to marry her off before the mourning period has been observed?"

"I most certainly do. You, Tony," he said, shifting his focus, "will be gone by morning."

Mother gasped. "Darius! Don't be ridiculous. He must have time to make a plan, to prepare."

Tony took several slow, deep breaths.

Darius looked at his stepmother with neither malice nor cruelty, merely disinterest. "I'm afraid you have nothing to say about the matter. Everything now belongs to me, and no one is welcome unless I say he is welcome."

Tony jumped up from the sofa. "Mother, Anna, leave us."

Anna immediately stood, slipping her arm around Mother and helping her vacate the room. Their skirts rustled, muffling his mother's sobs. But Tony heard them. And his anger swelled.

As soon as the door clicked shut behind the women, he advanced toward the desk. He had not struck Darius in years. Not since childhood.

Tony spread both palms on top of the massive desk and leaned over as far as it would allow. "If you try to marry Anna off before a year has passed, or if anything happens to her or Mother while I'm gone, you will answer to me."

Surprise brightened Darius's eyes for a moment, then he relaxed. "Don't be melodramatic, Tony. I have no ill will toward Leah or Anna. We hardly see each other as it is, what with them in the opposite wing of the house."

"That will all change when you take over Dad's rooms. Mother has been in the chamber that connects to his for thirty years. Where are you going to put her?"

Darius pursed his lips. "Well, if it will ease your mind, I'll allow her to choose whatever room she likes for herself."

"Very generous of you." The bite in Tony's tone belied the charitable words.

"Thank you."

Tony did not remove his hands or his bulk from the desk.

Darius cocked an eyebrow. "Do you mind?"

With slow deliberation, Tony straightened, turned and strode from the room.

———

Standing on the porch of the dilapidated gable-front house, Tony knocked again. The wooden door opened a crack, revealing a small blond girl shorter than the doorknob.

"Hi there, Miss Myrtle. Is your papa home?"

She said nothing. Just stood there, looking through the crack with big brown eyes.

"How 'bout your mama? Can you tell your mama Uncle Tony's here?"

She stuck her thumb in her mouth.

He rubbed his jaw. He usually brought Russ's kids a licorice stick, but with all that had happened, he'd come empty-handed.

Setting his suitcase down, he squatted so he'd be eye level with her, then crossed his arms over his chest, slapped his thighs and clapped his hands to the rhythm of his words. "Miss Myr-tle . . . ?"

He extended his hands, palms up, in front of her. Smiling around her thumb, Myrtle slipped out the door and tapped her free hand against one of his at each repeating word.

" . . . Mac, Mac, Mac," he continued. "All dressed in black, black, black. With sil-ver buttons, buttons, buttons. All down her back, back, back."

Opening his arms, he waited. She came into them and he kissed her downy hair, the smell of dishwater and milk bringing a smile to his face. The door opened behind her.

"Mercy, Tony. You oughta know you can come right on in without waiting for an engraved invitation. How long has she kept you out here for?"

Tony stood, ruffling Myrtle's head. "I just got here, Iva. Is Russ home?"

"Sure, sure. Come on in." Shifting the baby boy on her hip, she widened the door, hollered for her husband, then frowned at his suitcase. "You all right?"

He slipped his hands into his pockets. "I've been better, I guess."

He'd known Iva all his life, though she was closer to Anna's age than his. Russ had claimed her just as soon as her red braids had been released and twisted up in a bun, and then wasted no time in filling up his house with their little ones.

The apron she had tied around the waist of her linsey-woolsey might have started out white but now held smudges of dirt across its entire breadth. Her strawberry hair stood in disarray, long since coming loose from its pins, but her cheeks were rosy and her eyes bright.

The little one on her hip blinked at him and blew bubbles through his lips. Tony reached out and tickled the boy's chin, causing him to giggle and swat at Tony's hand.

"You shaved off your moustache," Iva said.

He swiped his hand across his mouth, still trying to get used to having a clean-shaven face. "Feels funny."

"Looks nice, though. You have a right handsome face, Tony."

He smiled.

"I'm sorry about your pa," she said.

"Thanks."

"Well, are you comin' in or not?"

Picking up the suitcase, he crossed the threshold just as his best friend rounded the corner, his large body filling the hall. Russ had one boy wrapped around his leg, the other on his shoulders.

"My turn, Pa! My turn!" the one on his leg yelled.

Russ's face sobered and he lifted Grady off his shoulders. No sooner had Grady's feet hit the floor than they pumped as fast as they could to Tony.

"Unk Tony! Unk Tony!"

Tony lifted him up, throwing him high into the air before catching him and lowering him to the ground. Tony briefly remembered jumping into his own dad's arms once, but his dad hadn't caught him.

"Let that be a lesson to you, boy," his father had said. *"Never trust anybody. Not even me."*

Tony felt a tug on his trouser.

"Me too! Me too!" Jason had released Russ's leg and now stood beside Tony with arms up. Tony repeated the ritual with Jason amidst squeals of not exactly fright, but not exactly delight, either.

"Okay, you two," Russ said. "Go on to the kitchen with your mama."

Iva shooed the boys toward the back. "Step lively, now, I've just sliced up some juicy peaches."

All but Myrtle ran to the kitchen.

Russ glanced at the suitcase. "It's true, then?"

"What have you heard?"

"That your daddy left you with nothing but the clothes on your back."

"That about sums it up."

Russ ran his fingers through his sandy hair. It had begun thinning at an alarming rate, leaving him with half the amount he'd had just last year. "I can't believe it. Why?"

Tony shrugged. "Darius has always been the favorite. We've known that from as far back as our memories take us."

And the memories stretched clear back to their one-room school days, when during lunch Tony had miss-kicked a ball outside, nearly knocking a painter off his ladder. The teenaged painter had come after Tony, cursing and whacking him with his paint paddle.

Darius had done nothing more than watch and laugh. Russ, big even then for his age, grabbed the teener and shoved him clear to kingdom come, promising more if the fella didn't leave Tony alone.

They'd been inseparable ever since. Didn't matter that Russ's family lived across the tracks. The two boys were either at Russ's place or Tony's or somewhere in between.

"I came to say good-bye," Tony said.

"Good-bye?" Russ's eyebrows lifted. "You in a rush or do you have time to sit a spell?"

Tony checked his pocket watch. "I've a ticket on the noon train. That leaves me a little less than an hour."

"Well, come on, then."

The two men stepped onto the front porch and settled into a couple of rockers, Myrtle right behind them. She crawled up into her daddy's lap and curled into a ball, sucking vigorously on her thumb.

"What are you going to do?" Russ asked.

"I'm not sure, really." Pulling out his pocketknife, he flipped it open and began to clean his fingernails. "I bought a ticket up to Corsicana. Thought I'd try to see if I could get hired on as a cable-tool worker for Sullivan Oil."

"A toolie! For Sullivan Spreckelmeyer? You gotta be joshing me. You don't know the first thing about it. Do you have any idea how the boys treat rookies? They'd eat you alive."

Tony looked out over the yard. Iva kept it swept, neat, and orderly. No grass, but the azaleas around the house's foundation would rival any in the pampered gardens around the mansion he'd built for his father.

He sighed thinking about all the work he'd put into supervising the construction of that monstrosity, hoping to earn his father's approval. Instead, his father made him pay rent just to live within its walls.

"Are you listening to me, Tony? You know nothing about working in the oil field."

Closing the knife, he returned it to his pocket and set his chair to rocking. "I've been doing the bookkeeping for Morgan Oil since its inception. I've handled its shipments, inspected deliveries, corrected bills, paid bills, recorded payments. If I can do all that, I figure I can manage working in the fields."

"It's nothing like sitting behind that desk of yours. A driller is judged on his ability to fight first and hold his liquor second. What do you think those boys are gonna do when they find out you don't drink?"

"Fight me?" Tony hooked his hands behind his head, leaning back as far as the rocker would allow. "Sure am glad you taught me how to fight, Russ. 'Course, I can't handle a bullwhip the way you can, but I'm plenty good with my fists. So, if that's what they judge a man on first, maybe I'll be exempt from the other. Besides, I'm not qualified to be a driller. I'll have to start on the bottom rung. Nobody's gonna pay any attention to some lowly rope choker."

Russ rested his chin against Myrtle's head. "They will if his last name is Morgan."

"My last name isn't Morgan anymore. I'm going by Mother's maiden name. From here on out, I'm Tony Bryant." He rubbed the skin below his nose. "Besides, I shaved off my moustache. Nobody will recognize me."

Russ shook his head. "I saw that, and ridding yourself of that colossal mess must have taken a good ten pounds off of ya. But moustache or no, it's a small world, the oil business. Everyone is gonna know who you are."

"I don't think so. I never went out to Dad's fields. I spent my time either behind my desk or at the rail station."

"Which brings us back to my point. You aren't cut out for this kinda work. We work from can-see to cain't-see. It's brutal, dangerous, rough, and dirty. You talk like an educated man, but the boys have a vocabulary all their own."

Tony smirked. "You think because I spent my youth sweeping out the church and my adulthood adding up numbers that I don't have the stamina for outdoor labor?"

"I think *you* think you can."

"I'm not afraid of hard work, Russ. And it's not like I can't tell the difference between a Stillson wrench and a pair of chain tongs. Morgan Oil doesn't own one single tool that I haven't inspected and logged in first."

"But do you know what they're used for?"

"I'm a fast learner."

Myrtle began to squirm. Russ set her down, pointed her toward the door and gave her bottom a soft pat. "Go on, Myrtie. Mama's in the kitchen."

They watched her toddle to the door, then struggle to open it. Russ got up, opened it for her and let her inside before returning to his seat. "Maybe I better go with you."

"No, Russ. Thanks, but I need to do this on my own. Besides, you have Iva and the kids. You can't be leaving them."

"And just how long do you suppose Darius will keep me on, do you think? Not long, I'd wager."

Tony popped open his pocket watch and stood. "You're the best driller in the entire state of Texas. And Darius may be a shoddy businessman, but he's no fool. He's gonna need somebody in charge who knows what he's doing."

"But don't you resent it?" Russ asked. "Wouldn't you like to see Morgan Oil go down in flames and Darius with it?"

Not a question Tony wanted to examine too closely. "What I want is to build a bigger and better oil company than Darius ever dreamed of. To do that, I need to know all there is to know about the business. Starting with how to work a rig."

"Maybe I oughta give you my hat. It's splattered with slush from the pits, and no decent driller would be seen without one."

Tony laughed. "I may be a six-footer, but your hat would still swallow me whole. Besides, what would a toolie be doing wearing a driller's hat? Wouldn't be right, somehow." He stuck out his hand.

Russ grasped it. "Do you suppose you'll meet Spreckelmeyer's daughter?"

"What daughter?"

"The bloomer-gal," Russ said, rolling his eyes. "The one that caused such a ruckus up in New York City and had her name plastered in all the papers."

"Bloomer-girls," Tony scoffed. "They are nothing but a roly-poly avalanche of knickerbockers."

Russ chuckled. "You better not let your new boss hear you say so. I hear he sets quite a store on that gal of his."

"I figure that unless bloomer girls have suddenly decided to roustabout in those trousers of theirs, then I won't be running into much of the fair sex—seeing as I'll be working from dawn to dusk." He picked up his suitcase.

"Well, you take care of yourself, you hear?" Russ said, slapping him on the shoulder.

"Will do." He'd made it halfway to the gate when Russ's deep bass voice came floating to him in a parody of a popular nursery song.

> "Sing a song of bloomers out fer a ride,
> With four and twenty bad boys runnin' at her side,
> While the maid was coastin', the boys began to sing,
> 'Get on to her shape, you know,' and that sort of thing."

CHAPTER | TWO

TONY CHECKED UP AND down Bilberry Street. This had to be it. The fellow at the train station had said Sullivan Spreckelmeyer lived northwest of town in a two-story Georgian, shaded by giant pecan trees on a spacious lot and surrounded by a white picket fence.

It was nothing like the ostentatious Morgan mansion, but the place had all the makings of a well-to-do, respectable family home.

Giving his Stetson a determined tug, Tony opened the gate and approached the front porch that ran the entire width of the house, its cedar posts enhanced with carved appliqués. He paused a moment to admire the work, then took the steps two at a time and allowed himself a quick peek through the screen door.

An open dogtrot ran clear to the back of the house, with rooms on either side and a set of stairs just inside the threshold. He raised his hand to knock, then paused, noticing in the darkness at the top of the stairs a creeping figure looking to the left and right.

Tony jumped back out of sight, then peered around the edge of the door. The figure at the top of the stairs straddled the banister and rode it down, flying off the end and landing with a thump on both feet, arms flung into the air.

Tony lunged forward instinctively, pushing open the screen door, expecting to cushion the fall of a misbehaving boy, but stopped in shock when he found himself facing the back of a woman.

Her infernal knickerbockers—along with the means by which she'd decided to descend the stairs—initially misled him as to her gender. But this was no young lad. This was a fully grown woman. Complete with hat, pinned-up hair, tiny waist, and pointy boots.

Her landing looked perfect at first, but then something on her left side gave, an ankle maybe, and with a squeak, the woman crumbled.

She hit the floor before he could react. Kneeling down, he helped her to a sitting position. "Are you all right, ma'am?"

"My stars and garters," she said, a feather from her hat poking him in the eye. "Would you just look at this?"

Repositioning himself, Tony watched as she propped her left foot onto her right knee, wiggling the heel of her boot. It hung like a loose tooth that should have long since been pulled.

"These are brand-new," she said. "Straight out of the Montgomery Ward catalogue. Can you even imagine?"

What he couldn't imagine was how that hat of hers stayed attached. One-and-a-half times as tall as her entire head, this haberdasher's nightmare had steel buckles, looped ribbons, feathers, foliage, and even a bluebird. The only evidence it gave of her fall was a slight tilt to the left.

She thrust out her arm for assistance. He took her hand and placed his other beneath her elbow, helping her stand.

"Well, you'd think a pair of boots that came clear from Michigan Avenue could hold up a little better than that." She brushed the front of her skirt, then raised her gaze to his.

Thou shalt not covet thy neighbor's wife.

The commandment popped into his head just as he noticed the blue of her eyes, the dimples carved into her cheeks, and the peach color of her heart-shaped lips. He'd thought Spreckelmeyer's wife was deceased. But clearly he was mistaken, for here she was—alive, healthy, and fine looking. He'd had no idea she was so young. And a wheeler, as well. Though it made sense, since the daughter was such an avid cyclist.

He whipped off his hat. "Are you all right, ma'am?"

Narrowing her eyes, she brushed off her backside and glanced at him, the screen door, and back again. "How long have you been standing there?"

"I was just fixing to knock when you, uh, fell."

She touched her hand to her mouth. "You saw me?"

"I saw you fall, ma'am."

She studied him for several seconds before a smile crept up. "I reckon that's not all you saw, is it?"

He answered her smile. "I have no idea what you mean."

She chuckled. "Well, sir. I do apologize and thank you for helping me up."

" 'Twas no trouble. Are you all right?"

"Fine, fine. Heavens, I've taken much worse tumbles than that. Now, is there something I can help you with?"

"Yes, ma'am. I was here to ask your husband if he had any need for a cable-tool worker."

"Ah." Her grin widened. "If you're wanting to speak to my husband, you're going to have one *loooong* wait. But, now, if you wanted to speak with my father, well, you'd find him right through there." She indicated a closed door along the wall.

He felt a surge of blood rush to his face. "I beg your pardon, miss."

"No need to worry yourself." She twirled her hand in a dismissive gesture. "Now, what's your name, son?"

Son? "Tony Bryant, miss."

"Come on, then, Mr. Bryant, and I'll introduce you to Papa." She hobbled a few steps, then came up short and turned back to face him. "You, uh, you won't tell, will you?"

"Tell?"

"About . . . you know." She nodded toward the banister, the bird in her hat coming perilously close to losing its perch.

"I didn't see a thing." He licked his finger, crossed his heart and winked.

"Oh, thank you," she said, her laugh sounding like bell chimes.

She knocked and poked her head inside a door, mumbling something, then threw it open, inviting Tony in with a sweep of her hand.

"Papa? This is Mr. Tony Bryant of . . . ?"

"Beaumont," Tony offered.

"Beaumont," she repeated. "Mr. Bryant, this is my father, Judge Spreckelmeyer."

"Judge?" Tony asked.

"Of the Thirty-fifth Judicial District," she confirmed.

"Come in, come in," Spreckelmeyer said. The robust man with a full gray-and-white beard, and blue eyes just like his daughter's, placed his pen in an ornate brass holder. If his brown worsted suit had been red, the man could have been Santa Claus.

"Would you fetch us some coffee, Esther?" Spreckelmeyer asked.

"I'll bring it right in," she answered, then turned to go.

"Essie?"

She paused at the open door, her hand on the knob.

"Are you limping?" her father asked.

She glanced quickly at Tony before looking down at her feet. "Oh, it's my new boots. The heel snapped right off. Just as I was about to answer the door."

"Those bicycle boots you ordered?"

"Yes. Can you imagine? They just don't make things the way they used to."

"Well, you must take it to the cobbler at once."

"And so I shall. Now, if you will excuse me?"

She backed out of the room and closed the door.

Judge Spreckelmeyer stared after her for a long moment, his frown becoming more and more pronounced. "Surely she didn't slide . . . naw," he muttered, then with a shake of his head, he stood and offered Tony a hand. "Mr. Bryant, please have a seat."

Tony settled into a heavily stuffed wing chair and glanced out a large bay window. The view outside was blocked by a massive oil derrick taking up almost the entire backyard. Nearly every home he'd passed had one.

Corsicana couldn't be more than two square miles, yet it was full to bursting with thousands of oilmen and at least that many derricks, allowing no relief from the pungent odor of gas.

"Now, what can I help you with, young man?"

Tony set his hat on the chair beside him. "I'd like a job as a toolie, sir."

"You ever worked in the patch?"

"Only on the supply end. Never in the actual field. But I've a strong back, a quick mind, and you won't find a harder worker anywhere in the state."

Spreckelmeyer glanced down at some papers on his desk, then moved them to the side. "What do you mean, 'the supply end'?"

"I used to oversee the ordering and shipping of tools and supplies for Morgan Oil."

"What happened?"

"Mr. Morgan died last week and the younger Morgan decided he no longer needed my services."

"You said your name is Bryant?"

"Yes, sir. Tony Bryant."

The judge looked up over the rim of his glasses. "Is that short for Anthony?"

"It is."

"And your age?"

"Twenty-eight."

"Really." He leaned back in his chair. "Interesting."

Before Tony could ask him what he meant, Miss Spreckelmeyer entered with a tray of coffee. Gone were the broken boots, replaced by bicycle shoes covered with gaiters. Tony and Spreckelmeyer rose to their feet.

"Oh, please, sit down. I'll just be a minute." She placed the tray on an oak sideboard and began to pour.

Spreckelmeyer sat. Tony remained standing.

"Do you take cream, Mr. Bryant?" she asked, her back still to him, the bird in her hat wobbling.

"No, thank you."

"Sugar?"

"Yes, ma'am."

"One lump or two?"

"Two, please."

"Ahh. Seems we have us a man with a sweet tooth like yours, Papa."

The affection on Spreckelmeyer's face while he watched her surprised Tony. No wonder people talked about how he doted on his daughter. His own father never would have allowed his feelings to be so transparent.

She turned and handed Tony a cup. "Tsk, tsk. I thought I told you to sit, sir."

"I don't mind standing." He wondered how he ever could have mistaken her for Spreckelmeyer's wife. She was far too young. But it was hardly unheard of for a man to marry a much younger woman. Hadn't his father done the same?

Sipping the coffee, he tried to gauge how old she was but found it difficult. Well past marrying age, that was for certain. Yet she had a fine figure. Barely any lines around the eyes, and none at all around her mouth. He felt sure she was somewhere in her thirties, but beyond that, he couldn't tell.

She set her father's cup and saucer on the desk.

"Why don't you join us, Essie," Spreckelmeyer said. "Mr. Bryant here is interested in working in our fields."

Our fields? Did the man actually include his daughter in his business dealings?

She poured herself a cup—with three lumps, he noticed—picked up his hat and carried it to a coatrack before settling herself in the upholstered chair next to his. Only then did he sit back down.

"What kind of experience do you have, Mr. Bryant?" she asked.

He hesitated, taken aback by her question. Yet Spreckelmeyer seemed perfectly willing to let her take over the interview. "I was just telling your father that I'd cataloged tools and supplies for Morgan Oil before Morgan Senior died."

Her brow furrowed. "We heard about his death. So unexpected. Did you know him at all?"

"I knew him, though we were never close."

"No, of course not." She blew on her coffee. "So you have no experience in the field whatsoever?"

"No, ma'am. Not yet. But I aim to—whether with Sullivan Oil or somebody else."

She exchanged a glance with her father. "Your lack of experience is going to be a problem, I'm afraid. Working in the field is quite a bit different from cataloging tools."

He narrowed his eyes. It was one thing for Russ, an experienced driller, to doubt his abilities, but to sit here and be questioned by a female with birds in her hair was something else altogether.

"Does it look to you like I can't handle it?" he asked, his tone sharper than he'd intended.

And though he'd meant the question rhetorically, she gave him a thorough sizing-up, like she could appraise his merits then and there. In spite of his irritation, he straightened his shoulders.

"You needn't get defensive, Mr. Bryant. There is nothing lacking in your physique. It's your gumption that I'm concerned about."

"I beg your pardon?"

"The fields require a man who can keep calm in the face of danger. I can tell by looking that you're strong, but I've no way of measuring your courage."

He set his cup on the edge of the mahogany desk, careful not to rattle the china. "Are you questioning my manhood, Miss Spreckelmeyer?"

She sighed. "It's nothing personal, just a requisite for the job."

His jaw began to tick. In spite of his troubles, he'd still grown up a Morgan. He might have his hat in hand right now, but he had more mettle in his little finger than this gal could possibly have from the top of her ridiculous hat to the tip of her bicycle shoe-clad toes.

All those newspaper articles he'd read about her came back to him now. He leaned toward her. "There is a difference," he said, "between wearing trousers and being a man."

Her breath hitched, and for the first time since he'd met her, she seemed at a loss for words. She recovered almost at once, however, dabbing at the corner of her mouth with her handkerchief.

"Nevertheless, the oil field is no place for novices. Seasoned oilmen can be killed or crippled in a day's work." She shrugged. "I'm afraid we can't help you."

Tony speared Spreckelmeyer with a questioning stare. Surely the man wasn't going to allow her to make such a decision for him?

But the expression on the old judge's face was unreadable. He held Tony's gaze a moment, then shifted in his chair to address his daughter. "What about that well out on Fourth and Collin, Essie? We could use another man out there."

Her head was shaking before he got the words out. "But he has no experience at all."

"Neither did Jeremy, and look at him now. A derrickman at the ripe old age of eighteen."

"That was different," she said. "That was back in the old days."

Spreckelmeyer chuckled. "Four years ago hardly qualifies as 'the old days.' "

"In the oil patch it does."

The judge said nothing. Tony could not believe this woman held the kind of power she did. Oh, but he'd like to take her down a peg or two. Instead, he kept quiet and waited.

She cocked her head to the side. "Do you really wish to give him a try, Papa?"

Spreckelmeyer shrugged. "He's certainly a strapping fellow."

"And yet he would have us believe he did desk work for a major competitor. He'd have to have had schooling for that."

Tony leaned back in his chair, forcing himself to assume a casual air. Clearly, his trouser comment had hit its mark. He knew he ought to leave well enough alone, but temptation overrode caution.

"Would you like to see my grade-school cards, Miss Spreckelmeyer?" He patted his pockets as if he always kept them at hand. "Or perhaps you could write for references to the schoolmarm from my hometown?"

It was on the tip of his tongue to reveal he'd learned Spencerian penmanship, bookkeeping, banking, and business ethics at no less an establishment than the Bryant & Stratton Commercial College. But those kind of credentials didn't measure an oilman's fortitude.

She stood imperiously, like she was ready to shake the dust of Tony Bryant off her fancy bicycle shoes. He rose politely in response.

"Do what you want, Papa," she said. "But I won't take responsibility for hiring this one."

There was no mystery now as to why this woman had never married. He watched her bloomer-clad body stride out of the room, the blue bird in her hat quivering.

Good, he thought. Now he and the judge could talk man-to-man.

As soon as the door clicked shut, Spreckelmeyer smiled. "Think you could work for a woman, Mr. Bryant?"

"That one?"

The glint in the judge's eye spoke volumes. "None other."

"How much will you pay me?"

CHAPTER | THREE

S WEAT DRIPPED INTO TONY'S eyes but he never slowed his pace on the grindinvg wheel. Pumping his foot to keep the grindstone spinning, he pulled the drill bit across the wheel's surface again and again, raising a burr on the stone that set off an explosion of sparks.

The wheel sat within calling distance of the rig but far enough away to quit grinding if the crew smelled gas. All it would take to blow them to smithereens was a single spark. Over his shoulder, Tony could see the cable-tool boys bailing out the hole. Soon they'd be finished and would need the drill he was sharpening.

Pulling his foot from the pedal and the chisel-like bit from the stone, he dipped the tool in and out of a water bucket to cool the steel. The grindstone whirred almost to a stop before he started it up again and laid the chisel flat on the stone, rubbing it side to side.

After a week on the job, he'd been expecting to have his mettle tested any time, but according to the others, "Grandpa" didn't allow any hazing, harassing, or fighting on the oil patch.

Grandpa, the driller in charge of the rig at Fourth and Collin, was thirty years old and got his nickname from the way he hunched over when he walked. Skilled and proficient, he was a patient teacher, and Tony had made up his mind to be the best hand Grandpa had ever brought up through the ranks.

Most of the other men working the rigs were boomers—here today, yonder tomorrow. All they wanted was a place to sleep, food to eat, and plenty of good whiskey to wash it down. He smiled to himself. A couple just wanted the whiskey.

Not me, he thought. He had a business to build. A mother and sister he still felt responsible for. It killed him that they had to rely on his half brother's mercy, so Tony was determined to provide for them as soon as he could. He would work harder than any man in the patch and move up the chain of command accordingly.

Just a few more rubs and the bit would be ready.

"Ain't ya through with that drill yet, Rope Choker?"

"I'm coming, Gramps," Tony hollered over the sound of the wheel, giving the chisel a couple more swipes before dousing it in water.

"Wall, whatchya been doin' all this time?"

Once the steel cooled properly, Tony jogged to the eighty-two-foot rig, holding the bit in two hands. Three cables ran up and over a pulley system in the crown block at the top of the derrick. One cable was the drilling line, one was for the bailer, and the third to lower and pull casing.

Jeremy Gillespie stood high up on the double board about thirty-five feet above the derrick floor. The eighteen-year-old was wiry, quick, and exceptionally strong. What impressed Tony most, though, was the boy's sense of timing.

Grandpa worked fast, expecting Jeremy to handle those cables and to run or pull pipe without missing a stand. The youth took his trips with a semi-controlled madness that made him as competent an attic hand as a person could be. Not surprisingly, he was no boomer, but a local Corsicanan.

Below him on the derrick floor stood a structure that looked like a giant seesaw. An upright post acted as fulcrum for a horizontal timber. One end of the timber extended over a band wheel. The other end extended into the derrick as far as the center of the floor. Grandpa waited there to inspect the bit.

"Good as new," Tony said, holding the bit while Grandpa attached it to a drilling cable suspended from the timber.

"There we are. You can let her go now."

Tony pulled his hands back and watched Grandpa gently lower the bit into a hole until it rested on the bottom. Once the cable showed some slack, he put a mark on the line three or so feet above the floor and put the rocking beam in motion, raising and dropping the bit as it pounded away at the bottom of the hole.

The chisel would only break up three feet of the black gummy soil before they'd have to stop and bail out all the rock and shale. It was nigh on noon and they'd only drilled about twenty feet.

Tony rubbed the stubble growing on his jaw and thought again of the water-well drillers from the Dakotas. The men were brothers and claimed their rotary drill could go a thousand feet in three days.

They'd set up their contraption in Beaumont and given Tony a demonstration. From all accounts, it looked as if the thing just might be as good as the brothers claimed, but before Tony could commission them, his father had died.

He couldn't help wondering, though, if Darius had followed up. Or if Spreckelmeyer had even heard of them. Maybe he'd go to the judge's house after work and ask him about it.

A man dressed in black with a boy in tow approached Paul Wilson, who was stacking pipe on the north side of the rig. The salty old roughneck was stout in the back, weak in the head, and had the biggest hands Tony had ever seen. He stretched one of them out and shook with the stranger.

"That's Preacher Wortham," Grandpa said, taking hold of the drilling line in order to judge what was going on down in the well. "Good fella."

"Kinda young for a preacher, isn't he?"

Grandpa glanced over at him. "Same age as us, I reckon."

"Exactly."

The driller shrugged. "Don't see why God cain't use him same as some old geezer."

Tony studied Wortham more carefully. Nothing about him looked like any preacher he'd ever known. This one was quick to smile, broad as an ox and probably just as strong.

"That his kid?"

"He's not married. That little fellow's an orphan who was adopted by a local couple a few years back."

The preacher caught sight of the derrickman up in the attic and gave a wave. "What's the weather like up there, Jeremy?" he hollered.

"Purty near perfect, Preacher. You wanna come up and see for yourself?"

"That's a little too high for my liking, I'm afraid."

"Shoot. You've climbed plenty o' trees in your day. This ain't no different."

"The difference is I got older and wiser and prefer to keep my feet planted on solid ground."

Jeremy grabbed the casing line and leaned out over the men, dangling above them. "Well, I got older, too."

"What about wiser?" Wortham asked.

"Married me the prettiest gal in the county, didn't I?"

The preacher chuckled. "That you did, Jeremy Gillespie. That you did."

"Hey there, Harley. What you doin' out here?" Jeremy asked the kid.

The boy cracked a smile, revealing a chipped front tooth. He hooked his thumbs in the straps of his overalls and squinted up at Jeremy. "Preacher's gonna take me fishin' after he's done savin' a few souls."

"It's a good day fer it. Bet they'll be biting."

"The fish or the souls?" Harley asked.

Jeremy laughed. "Both, I reckon."

Stepping up onto the derrick floor, the preacher nodded at Grandpa and offered a hand to Tony. "Howdy. I'm Ewing Wortham, pastor of the First Christian Church on Sixth Street."

"Tony Bryant."

"You're new around here. Where you from?"

"Beaumont."

"Well, welcome to town. You have a wife? Kids?"

"A mother and sister, sir."

"Well, I'd sure like to see y'all join us on Sunday morning. Mr. Alfrey here attends our services. I'm sure he'd make room for you on the pews."

"Sure, Bryant. You come on out with me and the missus." Grandpa adjusted the drilling line, taking up some of the slack so it wouldn't spring up and kink.

"Where's your family staying?" Wortham asked. "I'd love to call on your mother and sister."

"He don't have no family here," young Harley said. "He stays in Mrs. Potter's boardinghouse and keeps purty much to himself. I ain't never seen him go to a saloon even once."

Tony gave the youngster a closer look. He appeared to be about ten, well fed, and with big brown eyes that, apparently, didn't miss much.

"I don't believe we've met," Tony said, extending a hand.

"Howdy. I'm Harley Vandervoort." He pumped Tony's hand. "I have a ma and pa. If'n you come to church, you'd be able to meet 'em."

Tony looked up at the preacher, but Wortham simply smiled.

" 'Courst," Harley continued, "if'n you ever go to the Slap Out, you'd see my pa there. He plays checkers near every day. 'Cept Sunday, of course. You play checkers, Mr. Bryant?"

Tony nodded. "I've been known to play a time or two."

"Well, if'n you come out to the store after supper tomorrow, I'll play you a game. But don't feel bad if you lose. I'm the second-best player in town."

The preacher chuckled and slapped Tony on the back. "Well, then. It's all settled. Checkers on Wednesday. Church on Sunday." Leaning in, he gave Tony's shoulder a squeeze. "Though I'd wager you'll find Sunday more to your liking. We got us some right pretty women all dressed up in their Sunday-go-to-meeting clothes and smelling of rose water. That's sure to be a nice change from looking at these crusty old fellows."

Grandpa shook his head. "Everybody's old to you. Except maybe Jeremy up there. Now go on with you. I got me a rig to run."

Smiling, Wortham tugged on his hat. "See you Sunday." He sauntered across the field toward the rig next door, Harley skipping behind him.

Tony had seen the mercantile called the Slap Out over on Collin Street. A game of checkers would get him out of that cramped boardinghouse and maybe even help clear his mind. He supposed it wouldn't hurt any to visit the First Christian Church either, but he had no intention of tangling with the young ladies there. His mother and sister were counting on him. He had no time for distractions.

"Quit yer squinting at the sun, Rope Choker," Grandpa said. "I've got me some tools over there that still need sharpening."

Taking his cue, Tony returned to the grindstone and started on the next drill bit.

———

Marrying "down" had certainly agreed with Shirley Bunting Gillespie. The banker's daughter had always been an attractive girl, but after her nuptials to Jeremy—a boy from the other side of the tracks—she'd come into full bloom.

Essie moved away from the refreshment table and signaled the girl with a slight nod.

Immediately, Shirley rapped her gavel on the lectern to get the group's attention. Although she'd dressed in a no-nonsense shirtwaist of starched white cotton, trying to look more the authority figure, nothing could disguise her youthful exuberance. "It is time to resume the meeting of the Corsicana Velocipede Club, ladies."

After making announcements, having the minutes of the last meeting read, and receiving the balance sheet—which showed the club to be in a flourishing condition both financially and numerically—Shirley had adjourned for a short break. At the sound of the gavel, the women began to make their way back to their chairs in the seed-house-turned-bicycle-club.

When the club held its weekly meeting, chairs were arranged facing the bandstand on the north wall of the massive structure, just overlooking the wooden rink that dominated the room. Bleachers flanked the rink down the length of the western wall, and on the opposite side of the building were small rooms set aside for selling bicycles and bicycle parts, along with ready-made clothing and patterns. There was also a small repair shop and an office for the staff.

"As you are all aware," Shirley said, watching the ladies settle, "Mrs. Crook is unable to attend this evening's meeting due to the birth of her twin baby boys a few weeks ago."

A swelling of voices ensued as the ladies shared comments about that celebrated event.

It was sometimes difficult for the women to get away in the evenings, but with the discovery of oil, Corsicana had gone from a quiet farming community to an oil boomtown. And with that growth had come a swell of new "businesses" on the east side of Beaton Street.

And though the bicycle club had many male members, they'd not been able to attend any of the daytime meetings. In an effort to accommodate the men's schedules— and to lure them away from the public houses—the Velocipede Club changed their Tuesday morning meetings to Tuesday evenings. Yet no men came, and the women had long since quit expecting them to.

Shirley struck the lectern three more times. "Please."

They quieted.

"Since Mrs. Crook isn't here to make the introductions, it is my pleasure, as your treasurer, to present our teacher, the founding member and owner of the Corsicana Velocipede Club, Miss Essie Spreckelmeyer. She is going to lead us today in a discussion about a rather delicate matter."

The ladies tittered behind their gloved hands, not daring to speculate aloud as to what that matter might be. Shirley gave Essie an encouraging smile.

When she reached the front of the assembly, Essie placed a basket at her feet. She hadn't braved the topic of bicycle fashion since that debacle in New York. In spite of the effusive compliments she'd received from club members for winning first place, Essie knew many of the ladies had been shocked by the newspaper accounts, most of which were grossly inaccurate.

There were only three reasons a woman's name should ever appear in the Corsicana newspaper: being born, getting married, and keeling over dead. To provoke a full article not just in the *Corsicana Weekly* but in newspapers scattered across the country was nothing short of appalling.

So instead of coming home a reigning queen, she had slinked back with her tail between her legs. But it had been almost three weeks now. She decided it was time to quit her cowering. Steeling herself, she faced her peers.

"Life in a corset is one long suicide," she began. "But nothing short of death will get us to admit it."

The fidgeting stopped. As if everyone were playing a game of freeze tag, no one breathed, or even blinked.

"Ours is a living death, though. Fainting. Indigestion. Restriction of movement. Shortage of breath." She placed a hand against her stomach. "Worse, it can endanger not only a woman who is quickening, but it can harm her unborn child, as well."

She paused to make eye contact with several women in the audience. "Is an hourglass figure really worth all that?"

The murmuring started in the back, and before long many of the women were leaning sideways to whisper with a neighbor. Shirley pretended not to notice and gave Essie another encouraging smile.

Usually, Essie addressed this topic individually with her students during private lessons. Never before had she spoken so openly to the group.

Whether their rumblings were due to the injustice of the corset or the boldness of the topic, she did not know.

"Dr. Weller Van Hook of Chicago recommends cycling for women because it requires the discarding of 'the murderous corset,' as he calls it."

She heard an audible gasp. Glancing over, she saw Mrs. Bogart, the retired preacher's wife, turning an alarming shade of red.

"I'm not suggesting we throw our corsets out altogether," Essie continued. "I do, however, strongly recommend the use of a modified corset while riding."

She reached into her basket and held up a white eyelet bicycle corset. At the sight of the garment, several matrons in the audience covered their mouths and lowered their eyes. Mrs. Bogart sat rigid with shock.

Essie paid them no mind. "Notice its shortened length for easy bending at the waist?" She pulled until the side panels began to stretch. "See that? These panels are made of a new stretchable fabric called elastic, so it's even more flexible. The American Lady Corset Company is offering free bicycle accident insurance for every garment purchased."

At the sound of a bargain, some of the murmuring stopped and a couple of the ladies in the back craned their necks for a better look. Essie continued as if she were discussing something as ordinary as how to fry a chicken. She unfurled a new advertising poster that read, "Pretty Women Who Ride Should Wear Smith's Corsets."

She quoted excerpts from medical journals cautioning women not to cycle in traditional corsets. She even went to the dress form she'd brought from the back room and demonstrated how to lace the corset so it wouldn't cut off the wearer's breath.

"An article in *Lady Cyclist* last week cautioned that a host of sufferings arise from 'interference with the circulation of the blood and the prevention of the full play of the breathing organs,'" she said.

In conclusion, she offered ten percent off any bicycle corsets purchased at tonight's meeting. By the time the evening was over, she had sold a half dozen new corsets.

Mrs. Lockhart approached her afterward and gave her a pat on the arm. "Quite an informative lecture, my dear."

A few short years ago, the petite, elderly widow had worn unrelieved black from head to toe. A more traditional lady couldn't have been found. Since learning to ride the bike, however, she had embraced the modified corset and split skirt—going so far as to wear them even when she wasn't out cycling.

"Thank you, ma'am," Essie said.

"What do you plan to discuss next week?"

"Bicycle Etiquette for Courting Couples."

"Excellent. I shall look forward to it. And how is our young racer coming along?"

Essie smiled. "Splendidly. Mr. Sharpley trains with me five evenings a week. He is quite proficient on the wheel and I think this might be the year for Sullivan Oil to claim the trophy. Wouldn't it be something if Corsicana's hometown oil company won?"

"The townsfolk would be ecstatic. Might even name a street after you."

Essie flushed with pleasure.

Mrs. Lockhart paused in the midst of pulling on her gloves and peered at Essie over the rim of her glasses. "But you're training Mr. Sharpley five evenings a week, you say? That is quite a bit of time to be spending with a young man without chaperone."

"He's barely eighteen," Essie said, reining in her exasperation. "I hardly think it qualifies."

Mrs. Lockhart buttoned her gloves thoughtfully. "Jeremy married our little Shirley this year, and he's eighteen."

"And Shirley is twenty," Essie whispered, hoping none of the other ladies could overhear. "I, as you well know, am almost twice that."

"Tut-tut. You're merely thirty-three. Plenty of time left yet for breeding."

Essie rolled her eyes. She'd turn thirty-four next week but did not feel inclined to mention that fact. "Good night, Mrs. Lockhart. I shall see you later in the week for your lesson."

After the last of the women shuffled out, she and Shirley began to place the chairs against the wall. They'd barely cleared the first row when Jeremy stuck his head inside the door.

"Is it safe?" he asked in an exaggerated whisper that echoed off the cavernous walls.

"Jeremy!" Shirley squealed, hurrying to him. "We were just straightening up."

The young man strode in with a cocky grin and eyes for nothing but his bride. "I came to walk you home."

"How long have you been out there?"

"Long enough to be glad I wasn't in here with all them harpies."

Shirley swatted his arm. "For shame. Those ladies are the life and soul of this place. Now, come help me and Miss Essie."

"Howdy, Miss Essie," he said, tipping his mud-caked hat. As an oilman's point of honor, his hat stayed filthy, but the rest of him was clean as could be. His starched and pressed blue cotton shirt fit taut across his wide shoulders. He'd cinched his denim trousers with a store-bought belt—which was a good thing, since there was nothing in the south end of his frame to hold those pants up. With the young man's help, they quickly finished storing away the tables and chairs.

"I'll do the sweeping," Essie said. "You two go on."

"Are you sure?" Shirley asked.

"Of course."

"Thank ya, Miss Essie," Jeremy said, grabbing Shirley's hand. "Good night."

She watched the two hurry out, a smile on her lips. Such an unlikely couple. One just never could tell.

Humming to herself, she began to sweep the yawning floor when the hinges on the door squeaked once more.

"Did you forget something?" she asked, looking up.

But it wasn't Jeremy or Shirley or even one of her club members in the doorway. It was the new toolie her father had hired the previous week.

CHAPTER | FOUR

WHY, MR. BRYANT. WHAT brings you here?" Essie asked. The new hire stood in the threshold of her clubhouse, dressed much the way Jeremy had been, but the effect was entirely different. Jeremy had the shoulders, but this man had the chest, forearms, and legs to go with it.

"May I come in?" he asked.

"Yes, of course."

Closing the door behind him, he took off his hat and revealed a thick mat of brown tousled hair. She noted that this past week in the sun had added a bit of color to his face.

"Is there something I can do for you?" she asked.

He glanced over the rink as he moved toward her, obviously impressed by the size of the place. His black boots tracked mud across her floor, but she knew better than to scold him. Oilmen put as much stock in slush-marked boots as they did their hats.

At least she hadn't swept that part of the floor yet. Perhaps she'd make him do it. The thought made her smile.

He took stock of her Parisian toque hat and the cherry velvet bows decorating her chest, elbows, and waist. Stopping at the edge of her skirt with its full four-yard sweep, he tapped his hat against his thigh.

"Miss Spreckelmeyer, are you aware your operation is just about ready for the boneyard? All the boys in Pennsylvania have switched from cable-tool rigs to rotary drills. If you don't make improvements, you'll be obsolete before the year is out."

Her lips parted.

"I've already spoken to your father about it," he continued, giving her no chance to reply. "But he said you were in charge of deciding what supplies he needed and when. So I've come to discuss it with you."

Staring at him, she had no idea how to respond.

He put his hat back on his head and rested his hands on his hips. "You do know what a cable tool and rotary drill are, don't you?"

Good heavens. "Mr. Bryant. How on earth did those Morgans let a man of your qualities slip through their fingers?"

"They shouldn't have."

She arched a brow. "Perhaps I'm mistaken, but last time I checked, you were a toolie with no field experience."

"It doesn't take much experience to see the obvious."

"Well, it's pretty obvious to me that a newly hired employee with nothing to recommend him should know better than to challenge the boss his first week on the job."

"It's not the boss I'm talking to," he said. "It's his daughter. Besides, this isn't a challenge. I'm trying to help you."

She drew up to her full height. "I regret to inform you, sir, that I am not only your boss, I am also part owner of Sullivan Oil and have all the power that goes along with it. Furthermore, we don't need any help."

"You need more than help," he said, looking her over from top to bottom. "You could use an entire overhaul."

She clenched the broom handle. "Just what is that supposed to mean?"

"It means that a rotary can drill almost a thousand feet in three days."

A thousand feet? In three *days*? Impossible. It took their cable-tool rigs at least three weeks to go that deep.

"How would you know?" she asked.

"I've seen them."

"In Pennsylvania? You've been to Pennsylvania?"

"No. I saw a demonstration down in Beaumont."

"A demonstration. I see. And what guarantee would I have that this rotary could drill into the black Corsicana soil? It's nearly unbreakable and gummy, to boot."

He shrugged. "Those Baker boys up in the Dakotas have been using rotaries to drill for water in all that hard rock they call ground. I don't know how successful they were at finding water, but I can tell you they were plenty successful at drilling."

"And what magical principle makes this rotary drill bore so quickly?"

"A mule."

"A mule?"

"Rotaries are completely different from cable tools," he explained. "It's kind of like a giant screw. Here, give me your broom." Plucking it from her hand, he clamped his fist around the handle. "You attach a gripping device to a very strong rod with a cutting tool at its tip." Spinning the broom upside down, he ground it against a knot in the floorboard. "Then rotate it. The tip cuts into the ground as it turns."

"Where does the mule come in?"

"You put an extension on the rod, then attach it to the mule. The mule goes round and round and round in the same small circle. Basically, he rotates the cutting tool."

What he said made sense. Her grandfather used to have a maple syrup mill that ran much the same way. And she could see Bryant believed in this new method. But a thousand feet in three days? That was awfully hard to take seriously. "How much are they?"

"Around six hundred dollars, I believe."

"Six hundred dollars! Do you have any idea how many wells Sullivan Oil has? We can't replace all our cable tools at that price when there is absolutely nothing operationally wrong with the rigs we have."

"If you don't, then you're done for. Morgan's just a couple hundred miles away with money and slow-producing wells. If he commissions the Baker boys first, his wells will start producing at a rate you couldn't possibly compete with. But if Morgan hasn't hired them yet, you could. Morgan's oil isn't as pure as yours, and if you convert to rotaries, you'll leave him and everybody else in the dust."

She pursed her lips. With her trip to New York and then the accompanying scandal, she'd had her mind on other things recently. Sullivan Oil's competition had never been a big concern and, therefore, made his dire predictions rather hard to believe.

She studied his face. For all his exasperating presumption, he at least seemed honest. But for a clerk to hire on for field work, then come back a week later with news like this . . . something just didn't add up.

"And why exactly are you so bent on Sullivan Oil having the upper hand?" she asked.

He shrugged. "Because it's in my best interest for you to succeed."

"Oh really?"

"Keeps my belly and pockets full."

"Well, if we spend all our money and have to borrow more just to buy all these new drills, then more bellies than yours will go empty. Pockets too."

"Don't you understand what I'm saying? This decision isn't something that can be put off. It could make or break Sullivan Oil's entire future." He tunneled his fingers through his hair. "I cannot believe your father is leaving this up to you."

"Be careful, Mr. Bryant, lest you find yourself with no job at all. Then what will happen to your belly and pockets?"

"What's the matter? Is your feminine constitution too fragile to take a business risk?"

"That is quite enough, sir."

He stepped back, letting go of the broom. Too late, she reached out to catch it, but it slapped to the floor, the sound echoing off the walls.

"You're the one trying to move within a man's world, *Miss* Spreckelmeyer. And men don't sugarcoat the facts or run away from a chance to grow and expand their businesses. We face challenges head on. And we do so without fear of losing our jobs. If you don't want to take this small-time operation and turn it into something that rivals the companies up in Pennsylvania, then get yourself back in the kitchen where you belong."

She bent down and snatched up the broom. "I won't be going back to the kitchen, sir, but you will be looking for a new employer. You're fired."

His eyes darkened with anger. "Now, that's exactly what I'm talking about. You let a woman wear the britches and she gets way too big for 'em."

She took a step forward, but he did not retreat. "I will have you know, Mr. Bryant, that Sullivan Oil is the largest producer of oil in this entire state."

"Not for long. Not if you refuse to recognize progress when you see it."

"Get out."

"No. You need me. Now, get off your high horse and let's talk about this—man-to-man."

"You don't seem to have grasped the situation, sir. You are no longer an employee of Sullivan Oil. So there is no need for us to talk. Man-to-man or otherwise."

He stared at her for several seconds. The patch of skin under his sunburned nose was burned more than the rest of his face, making him look like a child who'd drank too much cherry juice.

But there was nothing childlike about his thick neck. His piercing gaze. His lips and square jaw. Nor the hollow beside his mouth that formed a deep groove when he smiled.

He heaved a sigh, his animosity falling away like a collapsing crinoline. "I can't afford to lose my job."

"You should have thought about that earlier."

"Your father is too busy with his judicial duties to give the oil company the attention it needs, and you spend most of your time in here," he said, stretching his arm out in a gesture that encompassed everything from the wooden floor to the rafters above.

"You've worked in the fields for one week, Mr. Bryant. You barely even look the part. How can you possibly presume to know enough to advise me?"

"And just how many hours have *you* worked in the field?"

Ignoring him, she returned to her sweeping.

"It's not only the rotary drills, Miss Spreckelmeyer," he continued, following behind her. "There's other changes that need to take place, as well. And soon."

"My stars and garters," she mumbled.

He gently clasped the broom handle, stopping her. "Don't let your pride stand in the way of the good of your father's company. 'Dare to be wise.' "

Was he quoting Horace to her? Surely not.

" 'It is not wise to be wiser than is necessary,' " she responded.

He raised his left brow. " 'Some folks are wise and some are otherwise.' "

Jerking the handle away from him, she touched the bristles of her broom against his boots as if she could perhaps sweep him away. "The door is that way, Mr. Bryant. Good night."

He bucked the bristles with his foot, a tick in his jaw setting up a rapid pace. After the slightest of hesitations, he strode to the door and slammed it behind him.

———

The following afternoon, Sheriff Melvin Dunn and Deputy Billy John Howard stepped through Essie's back door and into the kitchen.

"Hey, darlin'," the sheriff said. "How's my girl?"

Cracking an egg into a small bowl, Essie looked at her uncle. "I'm all right. I suppose you came by to check on Papa?"

"I did. How's he holding up?"

She began to whip the egg, thinking of how surprised the lawbreakers would be to discover their big, husky sheriff had a heart as soft as butter. It was the two-year anniversary of Mother's death, and grief over her passing continued to plague Papa. And though Uncle Melvin came by on the pretense of seeing him, she knew he grieved for his only sister as well.

"He's sequestered himself back in his study," she said.

He hung his hat on a peg, revealing a head of hair with more gray than brown. "Something smells mighty good in here," he said, giving her a kiss on the cheek. "How come you're doing the cooking? Where's Mrs. Carmichael?"

"Her rheumatism was bothering her again, so Papa sent her on home. I was just whipping up some veal soup. Would you like to stay for supper?"

He patted his belly, which had grown rounder over the last couple of years. "Better not. I'm watching my girlish figure. Besides, Verdie's expecting me home any minute." He headed toward Papa's study. "Be back in a minute."

The clacking of her eggbeater sounded loud in the sudden quiet. She knew she should acknowledge Deputy Howard, but she was loathe to encourage even polite conversation.

He stood just inside the door, tracking her every move. He was small in stature and had the face of an angel, but in the six months since Uncle Melvin had deputized him, he'd enjoyed the power of his badge just a little too much for her liking.

Her uncle was blinded to the deputy's shortcomings, though, for Billy John Howard was grandson to a close friend—who also happened to be the Texas secretary of state.

Without bothering to remove his hat, Deputy Howard sauntered to the stove and lifted the lid off her cast-iron pot. "Ummmm. I sure do love veal soup." He dipped his finger in the broth, then licked it off. "And I'm not growing soft in the middle like your uncle."

The thought of his grimy finger fouling her supper curdled her stomach. She strode to the stove and poured the egg into the pot, ignoring his attempt to finagle an invitation.

He leaned in toward her and inhaled deeply. "I do believe I smell dessert. I always like a little something sweet after my meals, don't you?"

She placed her fingertips on his chest and pushed. "You're crowding me. Do you mind?"

Capturing her hand, he brought it to his lips. "Not at all. I don't mind in the least little bit."

She snatched her hand out of his grasp. "Deputy Howard, you are making me uncomfortable."

"Call me Billy John. Come on now, sweetheart, let me hear you say my name just once."

"That is quite enough!"

"Uh-oh," Uncle Melvin said, coming back through the archway. "What've you gone and done now, Billy John?"

Deputy Howard took a casual step back and removed his hat. "Oh, I'm just teasin' her some. Telling her how a bowl of veal soup would cure me of my ailment, but she got mighty prickly about it."

Uncle Melvin chuckled. "Now, Essie, don't be so hard on him. It's been a month of Sundays since that boy's had himself a home-cooked meal."

"I thought that *boy* had dinner with you and Aunt Verdie last week?"

"Well, that's not quite the same, is it, Deputy?"

Howard turned up his smile. "I do enjoy Mrs. Dunn's cookin', sir, but having a meal put together by Miss Spreckelmeyer surely does sound right nice."

She poured a cup of milk into the soup. "Perhaps another time."

Replacing his hat on his head, he nodded. "I'll be countin' on it, ma'am."

Uncle Melvin opened the door. Deputy Howard passed through it, his footfalls heavy as he made his way off the porch.

When the door remained open, she looked back over her shoulder.

Uncle Melvin stood puzzled, his hand on the knob. "What is it about him that rubs you so raw?"

"How much time do you have?"

He chuckled. "Oh, I know you told him to leave you be, and if he doesn't, you just tell me and I'll talk to him. But, girl, he really has taken a shine to you."

"I'm not interested."

"You're nearly thirty-four, Essie. He's a good man, and if you don't take him, you might not ever—"

She slammed the lid on the pot. "I'm not interested."

He held up his hands. "All right. All right."

Sighing, she wiped a spot of milk off the stove with her apron. "How was Papa?"

"Struggling. Tonight's supper won't be easy." He gave her a sad smile, retrieved his hat and quietly closed the door behind him.

Essie slumped against the stove. When it came to his deputy, Uncle Melvin wore blinders. She couldn't understand how such a shrewd judge of character could be as deluded as Melvin was to Mr. Howard's true nature. She'd begged Papa to intervene, but he always demurred.

"If you've heard rumors about the man, then you can be sure Melvin has, too. If he chooses not to credit them, then we ought to respect that. No amount of arguing will change his mind."

"So you won't say anything?"

"Essie," he'd said. *"Is it the stories about the deputy that bother you, or is it the fact that he's intrigued by you?"*

She moved to the washbowl, dipped a rag into it, then wrung out the water. Perhaps her father was right. If the townsfolk told tales about Deputy Howard, goodness knows they told more about Essie herself. Perhaps the rumors about Howard were as false as the ones about her.

But why couldn't the deputy pursue some other woman? As Uncle Melvin had reminded her, she was well into her thirties and had another birthday fast approaching. She might not have a man, but she didn't want one, nor did she need one.

Her work in the bicycle club brought great satisfaction, and she enjoyed helping Papa with Sullivan Oil. Her neighbors and friends had known her all her life and loved her. She attended a thriving church. She had a wonderful God.

No, she didn't need a man to make her whole. She was whole already. Picking up the egg bowl, she wiped it clean, then placed it on the shelf.

Her only wish was for a close female friend. She knew plenty of women and most all of them cared for her and would help her if she were in need. But she didn't have a confidante.

Now that her mother was gone, she found herself longing for another woman who could give her an opinion on which hat would best suit her new outfit. Or someone she could play a duet with on the piano. Someone to go bike riding with. Someone to share a cup of coffee with.

For a while, Essie thought perhaps Shirley would fill that role. But her helper at the club was almost fifteen years younger than she, a new bride and a bit too whimsical to suit Essie's taste. They were friends, but the intimate rapport she longed for had yet to materialize.

She gave the soup a stir and tried to recall ever having a girl chum. But even as a child, her friends were always boys. And she got along with them famously.

Didn't matter the age, the occupation, or even how long she'd known them. If they were male, she had something in common with them.

Boys loved the outdoors. They didn't play catty games with each other. They spoke their minds. They were everything she'd ever wanted in a friend. Even now, in spite of the many women who had embraced the Velocipede Club, she was closest to Mr. Sharpley, the young man she was training for the Corsicana Oil & Gas Bicycle Invitational.

Yet lately she found she'd rather stitch a sampler than climb a tree. Or read a book of poetry instead of hunt snakes. Oh, she still enjoyed the outdoors, but having a man for a chum simply wasn't practical at this juncture of her life. Besides, she couldn't whisper secrets and press flowers or discuss facial creams with a man. There were some things only a woman could understand.

Picking up a teakettle, she put some water on to boil. It didn't do to dwell on such thoughts. God knew her heart's desire for a friend. She would wait on Him, and He would bring it to pass. It was only a matter of time.

CHAPTER | FIVE

ESSIE DISHED VEAL SOUP into two bowls, then called her father to the table. She hoped Uncle Melvin's visit had brought Papa some comfort. He stepped into the kitchen, his eyes puffy.

She set down their ice tea glasses and walked into his arms. He wrapped them clear around her shoulders, squeezing her so tightly she couldn't breathe.

"I don't think I can eat in here tonight, Squirt. Would you mind if we ate on the porch instead?"

She patted his back. "Of course not, Papa. We're having soup, so it'll be no trouble to move outside."

He released her and pinched a napkin against his tea glass in one hand, then tucked his spoon and bowl in the other.

From the porch, they could look across the flat, coastal plain of East Texas where the town of Corsicana resided. Black silhouettes of derricks too numerous to count stretched to the sky, the smell of oil riding on the breeze. Dusk coated the blue above them, frosting it with deep navy clouds. Magenta fired the clouds out on the far horizon and glazed those closer to them.

Crickets chattered, toads bleated, whippoorwills sang out their names over and over. The creaking of Papa's rocker joined in, his napkin riding the slope of his stomach, his bowl resting in his lap, untouched.

A large, broad man, he held a commanding presence and had earned the respect of most everyone in town, garnering their votes election after election. Essie hated to see him in such a dolorous state.

"I heard you fired the new toolie last night," he said finally.

She hesitated a moment before finishing her bite. "Yes."

"Grandpa was none too happy when he found out. According to him, Bryant was the soul of courtesy—fearless, punctual, and hardworking."

She scooped up slices of potato and onion.

"You gonna tell me about it or not?" he asked.

She dabbed her lips. "You gonna eat or not?"

He placed a spoonful of soup in his mouth.

"Mr. Bryant barged into the club after everyone had left and started ordering me around," she said.

"Ordering you around? How so?"

"He demanded we convert all our rigs to rotaries, or else."

"Or else what?"

"Or else we'd become obsolete."

"He said that?"

"More or less." She waved her spoon at his bowl.

He took another bite. "I talked at length about the rotary drills with Mr. Bryant before I sent him out to see you. I'd been reading about them and was actually toying with the idea of updating."

She set her empty bowl on the small round table between them. "Well, heavens. You've not said a word. Why didn't you tell me?"

"I was going to, but I've been . . . distracted." His gaze roved over the sky. There was only the barest hint of magenta left.

Her heart squeezed and she laid a hand on his arm. "I'm sorry, Papa. I know this month has been hard on you."

His beard quivered.

"The rotary drills are terribly expensive," she said, "but if you'd like for me to write up an assessment, I can."

"Please," he whispered, rubbing his eyes with his thumb and finger.

She placed her napkin on the table, gathered her skirts and knelt before him. His hand now rested against his entire face.

She removed the bowl from his lap and placed it on the table. "I'll write up a report first thing tomorrow."

He nodded. "Would you re-hire Bryant also, please?"

She bit her lower lip. "I'd rather not."

Papa lowered his hand and looked at her, his expression turning protective. "Was he fast with you?"

"No, no. Just . . . officious."

"I imagine he's not very used to discussing business with a woman."

"What's he doing discussing business with either one of us? He's a toolie, for heaven's sake. And a novice at that."

"Don't kid yourself, Essie," he said. "He knows the oil business. Somehow he secured a higher-up position for himself in Morgan Oil without ever having to get his hands dirty. He's a pencil pusher, not a rope choker. Doesn't mean he's ignorant."

"I don't like him."

"I don't think he much likes you, either."

"I stopped caring a long time ago what men think of me," she said. "Anyway, he's probably already left town."

"I saw him at the Slap Out playing checkers with young Harley just before I came home for supper."

She took his hands into hers. "Why is he so important to you, Papa?"

"Why's he so repugnant to you? It's not as if you've never had to tangle with a fella who didn't like the idea of taking orders from a female."

Full dark had descended and she could no longer distinguish his features. "He said I was too big for my britches."

Papa chuckled. "And so you are."

She started to pull away, but he squeezed her hands. "Now, Squirt, you know there's a bit of truth to that. And what does it matter one way or the other? Bottom line is, you're his boss. He'll come around."

If he'd asked on any other day, she'd have put up more resistance. But she simply didn't have the heart to argue with him tonight. "Will you hire him back, Papa, so I don't have to?"

Standing, he brought her to her feet, as well. "I'd rather you do it. I'd like to be alone for a while, if it's all right with you."

She frowned. "You mean, you want me to go find him right now? This minute? And leave you alone in the house?"

"Yes, please."

"Can't it wait until tomorrow?"

"He's leaving at first light."

"But what if he's left the Slap Out already? I wouldn't have a clue as to where he might go. He could be anywhere."

"You'll find him." The words came out a croak. And she realized Papa truly did need to be alone with his memories without worrying she might overhear him grieving.

"Very well," she sighed. "You sure you'll be all right?"

He pulled her into another hug but gave her no assurances.

———

Tony could not believe he was being trounced in checkers by a ten-year-old. They'd been playing for best out of five, but when Tony went down early by two games, he'd convinced Harley to play the best out of seven. It was three to one. Harley.

The child's shiny black hair had been parted on the side but would not stay slicked down. The barrel that the checkerboard rested on came up to his chest.

He jumped two of Tony's pieces before landing on his king row, then leaned against his cane chair. "Crown, please," he said with a smirk.

The door to the Slap Out—where Corsicanans came if they were slap outta something—was propped open by a basket of oranges, giving Tony a view of the darkening sky. The smell of stale coffee, tobacco, and vinegar wrestled for dominance over the mercantile. Mr. Crook, the slim and fastidious man who owned the store, began to prepare for closing.

"How'd you learn to play checkers so well?" Tony asked.

"Miss Essie taught me."

"Miss Essie?" Tony asked, his finger poised on the checker he was fixing to move. "Miss Essie Spreckelmeyer?"

"Yep."

The boy's grin irritated Tony. Because of that pompous, short-tempered woman, he'd be heading over to Powell's oil patch in the morning looking for another job. "You play checkers with her?"

Harley shook his head. "Not if I can help it. I cain't hardly ever beat her."

Tony slid his piece into a position to jump one of Harley's blacks.

The boy leaned forward and studied the board. "Me and her go way back."

Way back? The boy was only ten. "You're friends, then?"

"Thicker 'n calf splatter."

"She fired me yesterday." Tony couldn't keep the edge from his voice.

Harley snorted. "What'd ya do? Kick a dog or somethin'?"

"No. I told her she needed to update her father's rigs."

The boy looked up from the board. "Told her or askt her?"

"Told her."

The shopkeeper, sweeping between two tables, began to chuckle.

Harley shook his head. "She don't like to be told what to do. But she's a square shooter and once you're her friend, she'd back you 'til Sittin' Bull stood up."

"That a fact?"

"Sure is." Harley moved his piece out of harm's way.

The unmistakable sound of a lady's bootheels approached the open door, then stopped. Tony looked up. Speak of the devil.

"Good evening, Hamilton," Miss Spreckelmeyer said to the shopkeeper. "I was afraid you might be closed already."

Crook set his broom aside. "No. Katherine has ladies from the Benevolent Society upstairs fawning over the twins. I thought I'd hide out here for a while longer."

Tony couldn't help staring, though she paid him no mind. She could pretend all she wanted that she hadn't noticed him there, but he knew better.

She wore a simple skirt and white shirtwaist with a relatively plain straw hat. Her entire countenance had mellowed the moment she'd seen Crook, and mention of the babies had provoked a tender expression.

"They're so adorable, Hamilton," she said. "I could gobble them right up."

Crook pushed his spectacles farther up onto his nose. "Yes, they're something special, all right." His expression sobered. "I've been thinking about you today. How's your father?"

The softness about her melted into melancholy. "It's been a difficult day for us both."

"I'm sorry," Crook said. "What brings you to the store at this hour?"

She looked somewhat at a loss, then noticed the basket of oranges holding open the door. "I'd like one of these, please."

"An orange? You came all the way out here for an orange?"

"Yes, please." She picked one up and gently squeezed it. "Can you put it on our tab?"

Crook eyed her curiously but didn't argue.

"Your turn, Mr. Bryant," Harley said.

Tony turned his attention back to the board, but he could see Miss Spreckelmeyer out of the corner of his eye. She made a show of noticing them for the first time, then approached the barrelhead slowly, her boots tapping the floorboards.

"Good evening, Harley," she said.

"Hey, Miss Essie. Sorry you're havin' a bad time. What's the matter?"

She gave the boy a sad smile. "My mother died two years ago today."

Harley's face collapsed. "I'd forgotten it was today. The judge all right?"

"As good as can be expected, I suppose."

Tony had learned Mrs. Spreckelmeyer was deceased, but, of course, had no idea this was the anniversary. The anger he felt toward Essie dulled a bit in light of the circumstances.

She turned to him. "Mr. Bryant."

He stood, snagging Harley by the shirt collar and lifting him to his feet, as well.

"Miss Spreckelmeyer," he said. "I'm sorry for your loss." Harley squirmed away from Tony's grip.

"Thank you," she said. "And, please, don't mind me. Go ahead and resume your game."

He grabbed a chair from beside the potbellied stove and brought it to the barrel, holding it in readiness. Smoothing her skirts beneath her, she sat. He and the boy followed suit.

"Who's black?" she asked.

"I am," Harley replied.

"Hmmm." She and Harley exchanged a smile.

Tony frowned at the board.

"Shouldn't you be home having supper?" she asked Harley while cutting into the orange's skin with her thumbnail.

"Ma, Brianna, and a couple of ladies are upstairs fussin' over Mrs. Crook's babies. Ma told me to wait here for her."

"Brianna's here?" Essie asked, glancing at a curtain that led to a back room. "Brianna Pennington?"

"Yep."

"I heard you've been teaching her how to fish."

Harley scratched his chest. "Reckon you heard right."

Essie cocked her head. "How's she doing?"

"She won't put worms on her hook. Thinks it's mean. So I'm gonna take her snake hunting. No killin' involved in snake hunting."

Tony glanced at Essie, waiting for her to raise an objection to Harley doing something so foolhardy—particularly with a girl in tow. But she didn't so much as bat an eye.

"Who's Brianna?" he asked.

"You know," Harley said. "She's one of them Pennington girls. There's a whole passel of 'em, aren't there, Miss Essie?"

"There sure are." She turned to Tony. "Bri's the youngest of the cooper's eight daughters. Her mother died about three years ago."

Nodding, Tony moved his piece. Essie paused in the peeling of her orange to assess his move and again gave Harley the slightest of smiles.

"We're playing best of seven," Harley said. "I've already won three out of four."

Tony stiffened. Essie might have been irascible last night due to her distress over her mother's anniversary, but that was no call to fire him, nor to gloat over him being beaten by this kid in knee pants.

She split open the orange, and its fresh smell filled their corner of the store.

"Hadn't seen ya around much lately," Harley said.

She offered him a sliver of fruit. "I've been busy training Mr. Sharpley for the bicycle race."

She offered Tony a piece, too, but he declined with a wave of the hand.

Harley popped his slice into his mouth. "How come you're not trainin' him tonight?"

"I had planned to spend the evening with Papa, but he retired early."

"I hear Sharpley's purty fast." He slid a black piece onto a square that would allow him to jump one of Tony's, unless Tony jumped him first.

Tony propped his elbows on his knees, trying to figure out if it was a trap.

"I have high hopes for Mr. Sharpley," she said. "You should come by one evening and see him for yourself."

"Sure. That is, if Ma will let me."

"I'll speak to her for you."

The boy beamed. "See?" he said to Tony. "I done told you she was a good egg."

Her gaze touched Tony's before skittering away. Just then, several chattering women poured through a curtained partition at the back of the store, disrupting their concentration.

Essie moved to greet them. Tony stood.

"Hello, Essie, dear. Have you seen the babies yet? Precious, simply precious."

"Yes, Mrs. Vandervoort. They are indeed adorable. How do you do, Mrs. Tyner, Mrs. Whiteselle?"

The women greeted Essie with warmth, then swept past her and Crook, pulling on their gloves while continuing to extol the virtues of the babies they'd been to visit.

"Hey, Harley," said a girl of about eight with reddish brown braids. "Whatchya doin'?"

"Climbin' a tree. What does it look like I'm doin'?"

Scrunching up her nose, she stuck her tongue out at him.

Mrs. Vandervoort, a woman with salt-and-pepper hair and shaped like a cracker barrel, signaled the children.

"I gotta go, Mr. Bryant. Miss Essie can take my place for me."

"Oh, I'm sure—" he began.

"I'd be glad to finish up the game for you, Harley," Essie said.

Smiling, the boy nodded. "Come on, Bri." He waved to Tony and ran out the door to catch up with Mrs. Vandervoort, who looked better suited to be his grandmother than his mother. Brianna scampered behind him, braids bouncing.

Essie settled into Harley's seat and took a small bite of orange. A drop of juice formed at the corner of her mouth. Without ever taking her attention off the board, she pressed the butt of her hand to the liquid, stopping its descent.

"I'm afraid Harley has you in a pickle, Mr. Bryant. Would you like to cry uncle?"

He had no interest whatsoever in playing checkers or anything else with this woman. But he'd be hornswoggling something fierce before he gave up, especially to her. "I'm not sure all is lost just yet."

"Whose turn is it?"

"Mine." Reclaiming his chair, he jumped the disc Harley left open.

She quickly moved a piece on the other side of the board. The store owner carried the carton of oranges inside, allowing the door to slam shut behind him.

"Your turn," she said.

She studied him with eyes the color of bluebells, disconcertingly direct. Having a ten-year-old flounce him was humiliating enough. He wasn't about to let Essie Spreckelmeyer do the same. Tony needed time to examine the board, but after she'd moved her piece so quickly, he'd look like a fool if he dawdled.

He slid a disc into her king row. She crowned it and moved one of her pieces toward the center.

"I'm calling it a day, Essie," Crook said, removing his apron. "Will you turn down the lantern when you're done and go out the back?"

"Of course." She twisted around. "Are you sure you don't mind?"

He smiled. "You know I don't. Just make sure this fella goes with you when you leave."

"Will do. Good night, Hamilton."

"Good night, Essie." He nodded toward Tony. "Bryant."

Crook's footsteps clunked on a set of stairs behind the partition before the sound of a door opening and closing sealed off the silence in the mercantile.

"You and Mr. Crook must be pretty good friends for him to let you stay in here after hours."

"I used to work here, is all. He knows I'll leave everything in its proper place. It's your turn."

Of his four pieces left, he could only move his crowned one safely. He headed it in the direction of one of her more vulnerable blacks, trying to figure out why she had offered to finish out the game for Harley. From all indications, she didn't care for his company any more than he cared for hers.

She slid her king into an attacking position. Tony would have no choice but to move out of her way or be jumped.

"Why did you stay just now, Miss Spreckelmeyer? Why didn't you leave when Harley and the others did?"

Her lips flattened a bit. "Actually, I was looking for you."

"Me?" Surprise tinted his voice.

"Yes." She struggled for a moment, clearly unhappy with whatever it was she had to say, then straightened her spine and gave him her full attention. "Papa wants me to reinstate you."

Leaning back in his chair, he hooked an arm over the backrest. *Well, well, well. What do you know about that?* "He was in here just before sunset. Why didn't he say something?"

"He wanted to discuss it with me first."

"And what happened when the vote was one in favor and one against?"

She rent the last two slivers of orange in two. "I conceded under duress."

"Duress?"

"I didn't want to upset Papa by arguing with him tonight. But rest assured, had it been any other night, you would be on your way out of town."

He leaned his chair back on two legs. "What makes you so all-fired sure I still even want to work for Sullivan Oil?"

Hope kindled within her eyes. "You don't have to if you don't want to."

He dropped his chair to the floor and slid his checker to a safer square. She finished off her orange, then bullied another of his discs with a different king. Their pieces danced for several more moves—hers charging his, then his charging hers.

"Are you going to switch to rotary drills?" he asked.

She took so long to answer, he thought she was going to ignore the question.

"We're considering it," she finally conceded.

The woman clearly did not like to eat crow. And if he were a betting man, he'd guess she didn't do it often.

He faced off his king against hers. "I'll expect a raise, of course."

Her mouth slackened. "A raise? Don't you think that's a bit precipitous?"

"I think it's the least you can do."

She puckered her lips. "You may have your old job back, Mr. Bryant, at the same rate as before." Reaching for a single black disc, she jumped all four of his remaining markers. "Take it or leave it."

TONY STOMPED ON HIS shovel, sinking it into the gummy soil, then hoisted up a load of dirt. As soon as he'd returned to the rig, Grandpa promoted him from toolie to roustabout, and he'd spent the morning picking up broken rods, junk pipe, and connections so the men wouldn't stumble as they scurried around the well. He'd discharged the lines to safeguard against leaks. He'd put new clamps on a broken sucker rod. And now he was digging a ditch for the saltwater that had accumulated in the stock tank. Once he filled the ditch with the water, he'd have to figure out how to make the liquid evaporate.

Arching his back, he glanced up at Jeremy on the double board. The boy was juggling elevators—resting one pipe on a device used to lift and lower drill pipe while fitting a collared pipe to a second device, pulling some pipe, then shifting a giant hook back to the other elevator. The process was tedious and the greatest crusher of fingers ever invented, yet Jeremy never missed a beat.

Paul Wilson, their roughneck, had made a visit out to the old pecan tree thirty yards east of the rig and was hotfooting it back. Tony smiled, thinking that what the old fellow lacked in brain power, he made up for in brawn.

Instead of returning to the pipe he was stacking, though, Wilson snatched up his knuckleduster and bullets, then hurried back to the tree.

Tony tossed down his shovel and jogged after him. "What is it, Wilson?"

"I spotted a squirrel up in that there pea-can tree and I mean to get me a piece of it," he hollered over his shoulder.

Tony slowed, coming to a stop several yards behind Wilson. Toolies, roughnecks, roustabouts, and pipeliners from the surrounding rigs left their posts. All work came to a standstill as they watched Wilson shoot up a box of twenty shells.

For ten minutes he and the squirrel played chase. Men cheered poor Wilson on while simultaneously making bets against him. When he'd fired his last shot, the untouched squirrel eyeballed him from the edge of a branch, flicked his tail, then jumped to another tree and darted out of sight.

Throwing down the empty box of ammunition, Wilson cursed the varmint. Red-faced, he plowed through the crowd and headed back toward the pipe he'd been stacking.

The fellas slapped him on the shoulder as he went through their gauntlet. "Didn't know you was such a crackshot, Wilson."

"Where'd ya learn to shoot? At Lady Pinkham's School of Charm?"

"I'm thinking ol' Crackshot would've had a better chance of finding hair on a frog than pullin' that squirrel's picket pin."

"Maybe you oughter join up with Miss Spreckelmeyer's shootin' class fer ladies. Now, there's a gal that could fill a hide so full o' holes it wouldn't hold hay."

Tony tried to pinpoint who'd called out that last remark, but the crowd was too dense.

"Back to work, fellas," Moss hollered. "We ain't being paid to laze around in the sun."

As tool pushers go, Moss was a whopdowner—hard, mean, and ugly. He didn't put up with any lip or lollygagging. No one openly criticized him, though, because he had a few loyalists who would frail your knob if you low-rated him. He looked after all of Sullivan Oil's rigs and had the stroke to hire and fire.

Catching Tony's attention, he motioned him over. "I see the old bicyclette changed her mind about you."

"It's the judge who's responsible for me being here."

"I wouldn't put any money on it if I were you." Moss had a laugh that sounded more like a growl. "The lady of the house wields a mighty sword and you'd best be remembering it."

Someone from a rig up the way called for Moss, and the tool pusher headed his direction.

"He's right, ya know," Jeremy said, falling into step beside Tony. "Miss Essie pretty much runs the place. Even Moss reports directly to her."

"Why?" Tony asked. "Why doesn't the judge manage it?"

"He kinda lost interest when his wife died. So Miss Essie took over and it's been that way ever since."

They reached the sump Tony was digging and paused. "Is it true what that fellow said?" Tony asked. "About Miss Spreckelmeyer being an accurate shot?"

Jeremy smiled broadly. "It shore is."

"And she teaches other women how to use a gun?"

"My missus takes lessons from her every Thursday mornin', " Jeremy said, "along with a passel o' others."

"What possible use could a woman have for shooting?"

Chuckling, Jeremy placed a hand on Tony's shoulder. "Don't let Miss Essie hear ya askt such a thing. She'll wear yer ear out giving ya reasons."

Grandpa barked out Jeremy's name. The boy hustled up the rig to his spot on the double board leaving Tony to try and make sense of Miss Spreckelmeyer. Checker champion. Marksman. Wheeler. Banister-slider. And worst of all . . . boss.

————

By the time Tony had been to the bathhouse and washed off all the drilling mud, the shale, the ditch, and the compound used to grease the pipe with, he'd barely made it to Castle's Drug Store for dinner. He took his time over the meal, though, regardless of the fact that the "boss" wanted to see him first thing after work.

Taking a swallow of genuine Coca-Cola, he listened along with the other men as

Mr. Castle read aloud the latest news of the war. The boys cheered and whistled upon hearing the marines had captured Guantánamo Bay and seventeen thousand troops had landed just east of Santiago.

Setting his coins on the counter, Tony wiped his mouth and slipped out. The streets were congested with men heading east toward the saloons. A ninety-foot gas tower at the corner of Beaton and Collin threw out enough illumination to get by on, though from here he couldn't see the abandoned seed house Miss Spreckelmeyer had converted into a bicycle club. Still, he'd have no trouble finding it in the dark. It was just northeast of town, not far from Whiteselle's Lumber Yard.

He skirted the red-light district, passed Frost's Wagon Yard and the Central Blacksmith Shop. He wound behind the city pound and set a few dogs barking until he was a good distance away.

When he got within sight of the club, gaslight from its high horizontal windows guided him to the doorstep. He knocked, but no one answered, so he pushed the door open.

"Quicker, Mr. Sharpley. You must keep your eye on the ball. Now, let's try again."

In the middle of the vast room, Miss Spreckelmeyer faced a young man who wore a quarter-sleeve shirt with exercise tights as snug as a pair of long johns.

Bunching her skirt in her fists, she raised her hem and tapped a ball back and forth between her booted feet as she moved toward Mr. Sharpley. The full skirt and white shirtwaist she wore were more suited to a stroll through town than a ball drill.

It was the first time he'd seen her without a hat, though. Her hair had wilted, its twist no more than a suggestion of its former glory. Hunks of blond hair swirled across her face, over her shoulder and down her back.

Sharpley crouched, bounced on his toes, and kicked at the ball when she drew near, but only succeeded in stirring her skirts.

She easily passed him, then stopped the ball with her toe. "You lunged again. I'll get by you every time if you jump in like that."

"I don't see what this has to do with ridin' bikes. Just put me on the bicycle and I'll go faster than any of the rest of 'em. I swear I will."

She brushed a strand of hair from her eyes. "There is a difference between being fast and being quick. I will admit you are fast. But if something happens during the race that requires you to respond quickly, you will not fare well."

Tony settled his shoulder comfortably against the south wall, ankles crossed and hat in hand. They went through the exercise two more times, and he could see their frustration mounting. Sharpley did lunge, but she also outplayed him. Even if the boy used proper technique, he'd be hard pressed to win the ball from her.

"Perhaps I can be of assistance?" Tony suggested.

Miss Spreckelmeyer squeaked and whirled around. "What are you doing here?"

"You sent for me."

"I sent for you hours ago."

"And here I am." He pulled away from the wall and gave a mock bow.

"Well, I'm busy now. You will have to come back in a hour or so."

He strode onto the court. "Surely that won't be necessary. I can't imagine you needing me for very long and it looks like your young charge could use a rest."

"He can't have a rest. I'm trying to build up his stamina."

"By trouncing him at football?" He extended his hand toward the boy. "You must be Sharpley. My name's Bryant."

Sharpley grinned. "You work with Crackshot."

Tony smiled at the mention of Wilson's new nickname. "I surely do."

"Who's Crackshot?" Essie asked.

"Nobody," Tony answered, turning toward her. "If you'd like, I would be glad to help you show Sharpley what it is you want him to do—with the football, that is."

He bent over and pulled off his cowboy boots.

"Mr. Bryant! Stop that at once. What do you think you are doing?"

"You can't very well expect me to play football in my boots." He removed both socks and stuffed them in his boots.

She stared at his feet. He wiggled his toes.

"Oh, my goodness." She clasped her hands together, red flooding her face. "This really isn't at all proper, and I'm not dressed for an actual match. I was merely demonstrating."

He walked to the ball, flipped it high into the air with his feet, juggled it with his knees, dropped it in front of him and passed it to her. "Watch closely, Sharpley, and I'll show you how to tame your opponent."

She trapped the ball with her instep, a spark firing her eyes. "I'm really not dressed for this," she said again.

He neither encouraged nor discouraged her, just held her gaze.

She worried her bottom lip, then looked from him to the ball and back up to him. "Where's the goal?" she asked.

"I'll take the bandstand, you can have the entire south wall."

She rolled the ball back to him. "I won't need the entire wall."

Allowing himself a slow grin, he again passed the ball to her. "Oh yes, you will. And . . . ladies first."

She didn't stop the ball as he'd expected, but lifted her skirts, kicked the ball as it slid past her, then sprinted after it. He had no trouble catching up and stealing it back.

Instead of racing to his goal, though, he toyed with her—changing directions, faking a kick, cutting across the ball. But when he tried to backheel it, she intercepted the ball and skirted around him.

He took her on again. Planting her left foot, she lunged to the right, then abruptly to the left, catching him off balance. She attempted a shot on the goal, but he managed to knock the ball into the bleachers before she made contact. Sharpley ran after it.

"Here!" she cried, jogging south. Sharpley threw it her direction.

She pulled the ball back toward her body, forcing Tony to step up and open his legs, then she kicked it between his feet, maintaining possession.

They parried for another minute before Tony acted as if he was going to turn, but stepped over the ball instead and headed in the other direction, breaking away. A few feet short of the bandstand, he struck the ball and scored his goal.

Essie held her waist and tried to catch her breath, droplets of moisture clinging to her skin. Playing football in a tight corset was not terribly wise, but she took satisfaction in the fact that Mr. Bryant was panting just as hard as she. Sweat plastered his shirt to his chest and back, accentuating the muscles beneath.

A smile played on his lips. "A good match, Miss Spreckelmeyer. I'm impressed. Too bad you lost."

She wondered how well he'd fare running up and down the length of the building strapped into a corset, but, of course, she could not plead her case.

"What?" he said. "Nothing to say?"

Inhaling, she squeezed her side. "That was fun."

His eyebrows shot up and his smile grew. "So it was. How is it that a judge's daughter knows how to play a game popular only with the lower, working classes?"

"It's a beautiful game," she breathed. "A couple of years ago we had a group of oilmen who used to play every Sunday. I'd go and watch them—from a distance, of course."

"Of course."

"Then I secretly played here with Jeremy Gillespie and practiced until I could duplicate what they did. But this is the first time I've ever played with anyone other than him or Mr. Sharpley." She propped her hands on her knees, trying to suck in more air.

His smile began to fade. "Are you all right?"

She nodded.

"Sharpley, go get some water for Miss Spreckelmeyer."

"No, no. I'm fine." She straightened and the room began to spin. "Uh-oh."

Tony rushed to her and grasped her elbow. "Perhaps you should come sit on the bleachers."

Her vision dimmed. The room began to fade.

Tony scooped her up into his arms. "Keep your eyes open, Miss Spreckelmeyer." He glanced at Sharpley. "Is there somewhere she can lie down?"

"Over here," Sharpley answered. "There's an office."

Weak. She felt so weak.

"Do not faint. Do you hear me? I won't have it."

Chagrined at the panic in his voice, she tried to keep her eyes open and focused, but all went dark.

CHAPTER | SEVEN

TONY FOUND THE OFFICE door ajar and kicked it wide. "Get everything off that desk, Sharpley, and be quick about it."

The tiny office held an old teacher's desk, a bookshelf, a stove, and two ladder-back chairs. Sharpley grabbed the books littering the desk and pushed all the papers to the side so Tony could lay Miss Spreckelmeyer on top. He glanced around for something to prop her head on.

"There's some ready-mades two rooms down," Sharpley said, reading Tony's mind.

"Good. Grab the first thing you see."

She lay still and limp. He gently squeezed her wrist, relieved to feel a strong pulse, yet wondering what he would do if she didn't come to.

What had he been thinking to challenge her to a game of football? If she suffered some serious injury and word got out that he had pitted himself against her in a one-on-one match, a scandal would follow for sure and he would permanently lose his job. The men in the patch might think she was eccentric, but they were protective of her.

He combed his fingers through his hair, admitting to himself exactly why he had challenged her. Because he knew he could beat her. He, Russ, and a group of immigrant boys from across the tracks used to spend many an hour playing football. When his father had found out he'd participated in that "workingman's game," he'd taken a strap to Tony. But it hadn't kept him from playing.

It wasn't worth losing his job over now, though. Instead of trying to prove himself to this woman, he needed to start focusing on his goals.

He glanced at the door. What was taking Sharpley so long? A B. F. Goodrich Company advertisement tacked on her wall caught his eye. *Cycling produces Health. Health produces Honesty. Honesty impels Cyclists to ride licensed SINGLE TUBE TIRES!*

Sharpley returned with two pairs of bloomers. "It's all I could find."

"You're kidding me," Tony said, but took them anyway. "Now go get a pitcher of water and some cloths."

He wadded up one pair of bloomers and put them under her knees. The other pair he placed beneath her head.

Blond hair spilled over the navy fabric and across her face. Hooking a tendril with his finger, he pulled it free of her mouth. Then brushed another strand from her forehead.

Her sandy-colored eyebrows arched gracefully above her eyes. Long, long lashes lay still against her pale cheeks. Cheeks that usually held such color and life. Her perfect, rosebud lips were bleached white.

"Miss Spreckelmeyer?" He ran his thumb along her brow. "Wake up. You need to wake up."

Sharpley zoomed around the corner with a bowl of water. "I can't find any cloths."

Tony grabbed Essie's left wrist and slipped his finger inside her cuff, snagging the handkerchief hidden within its folds. Taking the bowl, he dipped the frilly piece of cotton inside, then brushed it against her forehead, cheeks, and lips.

"Can you hear me, Miss Spreckelmeyer?"

Her eyelids quivered.

"I think she's coming around." He dipped the hanky again and bathed her chin, the back of her neck, and up behind her ears.

She blinked her eyes open, then let them fall closed again.

"No," he said, his voice clipped. "Do not go back to sleep. Open your eyes, Miss Spreckelmeyer. This instant!"

She opened her eyes, her brows crinkling.

He took a deep breath. "That's better. Now keep them open."

She obeyed, though the blue orbs were clouded with confusion and fatigue. Her body was still as flimsy as jelly.

"Go see if you can find a glass or at least a smaller bowl than this, Sharpley, and fill it with water so I can give her something to drink."

Wrapping the hanky around two fingers, he dipped it again. "You about scared me to death."

Her expression didn't so much as flicker. He slid his cloth-encased fingers down each side of her nose, beneath her cheekbones, and across her upper and lower lips.

The wet fabric provided no barrier between his skin and hers. She was so soft. As soft as a goose-down pillow. Swallowing, he glanced up and suspended his ministrations. Her blue, blue eyes had cleared and were fixed on him.

They held waves of royal blue and sky blue and a blue so light it was almost white, all captured within a fine ring of deep navy.

"Found one," Sharpley said, entering the room with a glass of water.

Tony jerked his hand away from her mouth. "Good. That's real good." He slid his hand beneath her head. "I want you to take a little sip now."

He brought the glass to her lips, tipping it slightly. She swallowed. A tiny rivulet missed her mouth and plunged down her chin and neck.

He captured it with the handkerchief. "Your color is starting to come back. Do you feel any better?"

"Yes," she whispered. "I've never fainted before in my life. I'm so terribly sorry."

"It wasn't your fault, it was mine. Are you able to take a proper breath yet?"

A splash of color momentarily touched her pale face. "Yes, thank you. I'd like to try to sit up now."

He placed a staying hand against her shoulder. "Not so fast. There's no rush." He looked over at Sharpley. "I think the danger's passed, son. It would probably be best if you called it an evening, though. I don't think she'll be up to training you any further tonight. Were there any laps you needed to do or anything?"

"No, sir. We usually do the football drill last."

"Very well. Report back here tomorrow night as usual unless she sends word otherwise. I imagine she'll be back to herself within the hour, though."

"Yes, sir. You'll make sure she gets home all right?"

"I will."

He turned to leave.

"Sharpley?"

The boy paused.

"You're not to say a word about this to anyone. As part owner of Sullivan Oil it would cause her a good deal of embarrassment if the boys were to blow this thing all out of proportion. I'll have your word that you'll keep your trap shut about both the football match and her fainting."

"You have it, sir. I wouldn't never do nothin' to hurt Miss Spreckelmeyer."

"Thank you, Sharpley." He gave the youth a nod of approval and listened as he moved to the entrance and let himself out.

The lantern in the room hissed. Retrieving the water glass, Tony propped her up again. "Let's have another sip now."

She brought her hand to the glass, her fingers resting against his as she swallowed.

"Excellent." He laid her down and smoothed the hair away from her forehead. "How are you feeling?"

"Lethargic."

"That will pass."

"I'm terribly embarrassed. I'm not some weak, simpering female."

"And nobody thinks that you are. As a matter of fact, I heard today that you're one of the best shots in town."

"Who told you that?"

He relayed Crackshot's story, pleased to see the color return to her lips and cheeks as she smiled over the tale. She had a nice smile, with white teeth and dimples on both sides.

"If today is any indication, I'm afraid Wilson's gonna be forever known as Crackshot," he said.

She started to push herself up, and Tony reached to support her shoulders.

"Are you sure you're ready?" he asked.

"I'm feeling much better."

"Sit here on the desk for a minute before you try to stand." He removed the bloomers propping up her knees and took hold of her calves, gently swiveling her around so her legs dangled off the side of the desk before realizing what he'd done.

Snatching his hands back, he slid them into his pockets, looked at the floor and discovered he was still barefoot. "Do you recall why you sent for me today?"

"Yes, of course," she said, catching her breath.

He glanced up to make sure she wasn't faint again, but her cheeks weren't pale, they were burning with embarrassment. He felt his own begin to heat. What in the blazes had he been thinking to manhandle her just now?

"It was just a small thing, really," she said, "but I didn't have time to get out to the fields today and didn't want to wait until tomorrow."

He said nothing, not sure how to respond.

"I, um, I wanted to find out the names again of the men who sell those rotary drills and how to contact them," she said.

"Baker. M.C. and C.E. Baker. I'm not sure where they are, though. I know someone I can telegraph over in Beaumont to find out if they're still there or if they've taken a job out of town."

"Would you mind?"

"Not at all."

"If they are there, do you think you could ask if they would come to Corsicana and give me a demonstration?"

"Yes, ma'am."

"I'd appreciate that, Mr. Bryant. Thank you."

"You're welcome."

He waited, but she said nothing more.

That's it? he thought. *That's all she wanted? All of this for one simple question?* He suppressed his irritation, then realized that as a female, she probably avoided coming out to the fields if she could.

She'd only shown up at his rig once since he'd started, and all work had come to a complete standstill. If she tried to do anything, someone would jump in and do it for her. All the while, Grandpa and Jeremy did what they could to get her away from the patch. He wondered if she was aware of the effect she had on them.

He curled his toes beneath the hem of his denims. "Do you think you'll be all right if I go out and get my boots?"

"Oh yes. I think I'm ready to go now, actually."

Frowning, he pointed a finger, stopping her. "No, ma'am. Don't you move from there until I get back."

"I'm fine, Mr. Bryant."

"I mean it, Miss Spreckelmeyer. I want you to stay put. Tell me you'll stay put."

She shooed him out with her hands. "I'm fine."

He didn't budge. "Say it."

"Oh, for heaven's sake." She sighed. "All right. I'll stay put."

He wasted no time in grabbing his boots and heading back to her office. She'd stayed where he'd left her, as promised.

Plopping down into a chair, he pulled on his socks and boots, then slapped his hands on his knees.

"Well," she said. "I guess we'd better call it a night."

He jumped up to help her off the desk, holding tightly to her elbow.

"I'm really all right, Mr. Bryant. You can let go now."

"I'll just hang on awhile longer, if you don't mind."

When they left the office, he tried to guide her toward the exit, but she tugged in the opposite direction.

"Where do you think you're going?" he asked.

"I need to turn out the lights."

"I'll do it. You want to sit down?"

"No. And please, all this mollycoddling is not necessary."

"Listen, you plum scared the living daylights out of me and I'm not anxious for a relapse. Now, can you stand on your own or do you want a chair?"

"I can stand on my own."

He eyed her skeptically, but her color was better and she seemed to have her wits about her. Still, he wasted no time turning out all the lights except for the one by the front door.

"Okay, nice and slow, now," he said, returning to take her elbow.

At the entrance he lifted her shawl off a hook, draped it over her shoulders, turned out the final lamp and locked the door behind them.

Essie had become so used to the smell of oil permeating town that she hardly ever noticed it anymore. But now, as she and Mr. Bryant stepped outside the club and the familiar fumes rushed up on her, her stomach lurched and her knees wobbled.

He pulled her close, allowing her to lean more heavily onto him. "There's a wagonyard just around the corner," he said. "Would you like to go there instead and get something to ride home in?"

"No, thank you. Walking is fine."

"Are you sure?" he asked, slowing their pace to a stroll.

"Yes. I'm positive."

Darkness shrouded them. With the sun gone, the worst of the heat had dissipated, but its stickiness lingered, leaving the air thick with humidity.

Her pride urged her to pull away from Mr. Bryant, but common sense insisted otherwise. She was not as surefooted as she'd pretended, and she didn't want to risk humiliating herself again. Though his ministrations had been swift and efficient, thrusting him into the role of caretaker had been too unsettling by half.

She was his boss. His superior. But now he'd beaten her at her own game and had also taken charge of her. To make matters worse, she'd participated in a rather physical match with a man—a barefooted man—and then allowed him to see to her personal needs. If anyone found out, there would be the devil to pay.

His parting words to Mr. Sharpley had surprised her, though. The field men loved telling tales, and tonight's episode would have been embellished, laughed over, and retold for weeks. It could have damaged her standing in the community and embarrassed Papa. That Mr. Bryant had made certain her privacy and reputation remained intact had taken her completely off guard.

She risked a surreptitious glance in his direction, but it was too dark to see more than a faint silhouette. Cowboy hat. Straight nose. Defined chin. Powerful chest.

A few years back she might have pretended they were a couple. A young married couple strolling for the sheer pleasure of enjoying each other's company.

But she'd learned the hard way that ill-founded fantasies and manipulations brought nothing but pain and heartache. No, she knew exactly who she was and who she was walking home with and why. She had no illusions whatsoever.

Still, the man no longer fit so neatly into the mold she'd originally placed him in. "Do you have a family, Mr. Bryant?"

The muscles supporting her arm tensed slightly, then eased. "Yes, ma'am. A mother and a sister."

"In Beaumont?"

"That's right."

"Have you lived there all your life?"

"More or less. What about you? Have you lived here all your life?"

"Yes. I used to go out to my grandparents' farm in Quitman every summer as a child. Other than that, I've been right here in Corsicana."

"Guess it's changed a lot in the last few years."

"Oh my, yes. We went from being a small, struggling cotton community to an overpopulated oil boomtown almost overnight. We are still trying to adjust to the growing pains."

To reach her house, they would need to cross through town. Instead of taking her the shortest—and more public—route, Mr. Bryant kept them on the abandoned streets that edged the city limits. It would double their walking time but would keep curious eyes from speculating about her disheveled appearance and her choice of escort.

"I heard you give shooting lessons to the ladies in town every Thursday morning," he said, interrupting the quiet. "Is that true?"

"Yes, it is."

He said nothing for the longest time, their leisurely footfalls muffled by the dirt in the street.

"Why would a bicycle club offer shooting lessons?"

She allowed herself a small smile. "Women are unaccustomed to being without escort or chaperone. I think it wise, therefore, to give my students the skills needed to protect themselves from any threats they may encounter while out bicycling alone."

"Threats of the four-legged kind or the two-legged?" he asked, a touch of humor in his voice.

"Both, I suppose."

"Are you telling me, then, that the ladies of Corsicana ride their wheels with six-shooters strapped to their bloomers?"

"No, of course not," she said with a short huff of amusement.

"Then, why learn how to shoot a gun if you aren't going to carry one?"

"I never said we weren't carrying pistols. Just that we don't strap them to our bloomers."

He pulled her to a stop, clearly appalled. "Are you packing a pistol right now?"

"I am not."

He took a moment to absorb her answer. The moonlight behind him silhouetted his head, hiding the nuances of his expression, but it did not disguise his thorough perusal of her. "Where do you put it when you are carrying, then?"

She shook her head. "I shall not discuss such a delicate matter with you, Mr. Bryant."

"Delicate?" he asked, a hint of astonishment in his voice. "You carry it someplace delicate? Do you think that wise? What if it went off?"

She started toward home again. "I cover safety precautions in my instruction."

He caught up to her and recaptured her elbow.

"I feel steadier now," she said. "I can walk without assistance."

"All the same." He held her firmly. "Who is allowed to take lessons?"

"Any of my club members."

"Are all your members female?"

"No, no. I have a vast number of men in my club. But their work keeps them from utilizing as many of the privileges as the women."

"What other privileges do you offer?"

"Our members can receive private instruction on bicycle riding and repair, etiquette, fashion, health, and a number of other things. We also have weekly lectures, monthly group rides, service projects, and an annual ball and supper. We are going to have a huge group ride on the Fourth of July that is open to the public, regardless of membership status."

They turned in a westerly direction toward the residential part of town. The clouds hovering earlier in the day had dispersed, leaving a palette of stars too numerous to count.

"You do all that and run Sullivan Oil, too?"

She hesitated, wondering if it was surprise or appreciation she detected in his tone. "Papa makes all the major decisions for the oil company. I have more of an administrative role."

"That's not what I heard."

She glanced up at him. "What have you heard?"

"That you pretty much run the company."

"That's not true. Papa is the majority owner and I couldn't possibly manage it without him."

A scream rent the air. It came from somewhere deep in the woods, a long, piercing wail that stopped Essie in her tracks, then sent her racing toward the sound, skirts lifted just high enough to clear the ground.

She forgot about her earlier ordeal as a surge of energy shot through her. Whoever was screaming was either terrified or in a great deal of pain—perhaps both.

She'd spent the better part of her childhood cavorting in these woods and knew them backwards and forwards. The lack of light didn't slow her down, but she could hear Mr. Bryant stumbling through the underbrush behind her.

Harley Vandervoort burst through some trees in front of them. "Miss Essie! Brianna got bit by a snake!"

"Lead us to her," Mr. Bryant said, catching up to them. Harley wasted no time. He turned and bolted deeper into the forest.

"What kind of snake?" Essie shouted, racing after him.

"A rattler!"

They found the girl writhing on the ground in a damp clearing lit by a full moon. She grasped her wounded leg and kicked out frantically with the other.

"My foot! My foot!" she screamed.

Several yards away lay a three-foot rattler with a severed head and a bulge in his middle from a recent meal.

CHAPTER | EIGHT

TONY KNELT IN THE damp leaves to lift the girl up. He wasn't sure exactly how far from town they were, but he'd run the whole way if he had to, with the struggling girl in his arms. He slid his arm under her, but Essie pushed him back.

"Leave her be," Essie said.

She crouched over the girl's hurt leg, trying to grab the calf, but the little thing kicked free.

"*Hold still!*" Essie snapped.

"I can't. I can't." The girl whimpered, tears coursing down her face, her reddish brown braids mussed and filled with leaves and dirt.

"Grab hold of her, Tony, and keep her from thrashing."

"We've got to get her back to town," he said.

"There's no time! Hold her!"

He pulled the girl onto his lap and wrapped his arms around her, crushing her to his chest. "Hush, now," he said. "It'll be all right."

Essie reached across to him. "I need a knife."

"No!" Brianna screamed, twisting frantically and almost breaking free of his hold.

"Keep her still, I said!"

Anchoring the girl against him with one arm, he quickly pulled his knife from his pocket and tried to open the larger blade, but Brianna kept jostling his hold.

"Here," Essie said. "Let me." She took the knife from his hand and flipped it open.

Brianna fought with renewed vigor, screaming, squirming, and kicking her feet. A spot of blood stained the girl's stocking above the ankle.

"Shhhhh," Tony said, tucking the girl's head and knees against his chest. "Hold still, honey, and let Miss Essie have a look."

"I'm just going to cut your shoe off, Brianna," Essie said, her voice a little calmer now that she had the knife in hand. "But you must hold still so I don't cut you instead."

"We were snake hunting," Harley said, his thin voice choking on the words. "Not fer rattlers, o' courst, but that's what we found when we poked under that bush over yonder."

"Snake hunting?" Tony asked. "With a girl? And at this time of night? What were you thinking?" And what were her parents going to say when they found out, he wondered, though he didn't say so aloud.

Harley puffed out his chest. "The snake wasn't expectin' us to go peeking in its hidey-hole or it would've warned us away with its rattle. But we didn't know it was there 'til Bri lifted that branch. She started screamin' and carryin' on and scared the blasted thing so bad that it bit her. I killed it right quick, then ran fer help."

The boy sounded defensive, and Tony regretted saying anything. He watched Essie slice the buttons off the girl's shoe and rip open her stocking. Amid the cuts and scratches on the girl's ankle, he spotted two oozing fang bites.

Essie took one look at the injury and turned to the boy. "Go get a horse, Harley, and bring it to the edge of the woods."

Harley tore off in the direction of the nearest house. Tony tried to maneuver Brianna so that a beam of moonlight fell across her ankle. He knew what was coming. They'd need all the light they could get.

"It's burning, it's burning," she sobbed.

Tony kissed her head and stroked her hair. "I know, honey. Try to take some deep breaths, if you can."

She took a shaky breath, then moaned.

Essie tossed up her own hem, ripped the ruffle clean off her petticoat, then split it into two strips. She quickly tied one strip above the bite and one below.

"You need me to tighten those?" he asked.

She shook her head. "I'm just trying to slow down the venom, not cut off her blood flow." She wedged two fingers beneath the cotton bands, making sure the strips weren't too tight.

He'd seen plenty of snakes in his day but had never actually seen someone who'd suffered from a bite. He had a gleaning knowledge of what had to be done but wouldn't have trusted himself to do it when he could just as easily have taken her to a doctor.

But Essie had no hesitation in her actions. Picking up his knife, she pantomimed a firm, rigid hug.

Nodding, he gathered Brianna to him and clamped down. "Hold real still now, sweetheart. Essie's gonna have a look at the bite and I don't want you to kick her. All right?"

Brianna moaned in answer and stiffened in his arms.

With quick proficiency, Essie made an incision across each wound. Brianna screamed. Tony held her firmly in place.

Tossing the knife down, Essie grabbed the girl's leg like it was a piece of corn on the cob and began to suck at the wounds, then spit out blood.

The girl cried out in protest, struggling anew, but Tony held her secure, watching in wonder as Essie sucked and spit, sucked and spit.

He knew of grown men who wouldn't have the stomach to do what she was doing, yet there was no wavering in her task. On and on she went. How long would she continue?

"Stop, stop. Please. It hurts!"

He buried his nose in Brianna's hair, shushing her, whispering to her, all the while Essie tried to pull the venom from the girl.

"You need a break?" he asked. "You want me to do that for a while?"

She swiped her mouth with her sleeve. "I won't be able to hold her still. Besides, every minute counts. We've only a few left for this to be effective."

Essie checked the tightness of the bands, then bent to her task again. The girl was trembling all over and sobbing uncontrollably now. Her leg was beginning to swell.

Wasn't it dangerous for Essie to suck the venom into her mouth like that? What if she swallowed some of it? Could both she and the girl die?

His stomach started to gurgle and he took several deep breaths.

Harley exploded back into the clearing. "I got two of Mr. Peeples' horses tied to a tree. He said he'd get word to Doc Gulick to meet you at the Penningtons."

Essie surged to her feet. "Come on. We need to hurry."

As Tony ran with the girl in his arms, he could feel all the fight bouncing out of her. When they reached the horses, Essie held out her arms for Brianna. The girl was no longer thrashing but lay limp, sweating profusely and keening in a high, mournful voice.

Tony grabbed the mane of a cinnamon-colored horse and pulled himself onto it. He hadn't ridden bareback since he was a kid. At least Harley had taken the time to bridle her.

Slipping off his jacket, he wrapped it around Brianna and took her from Essie's raised arms. Harley made a stirrup with his hands, giving Essie a boost up onto her mare.

Without so much as a word, she straddled the horse like a man and kicked the animal's sides.

———

The Penningtons lived in a house on West Jackson Avenue. It had three large rooms, a kitchen, and a center hall leading to a back porch, where Tony and Harley waited for word about Brianna.

A full moon hanging high in a bed of stars threw muted light onto the yard. Nearby crickets performed a syncopated symphony.

"You should see this place in the day," Harley said, sitting on the top porch step, his back against a post. "Miss Katy loves to work in the garden and she has flowers almost solid from here to the fence out front. Blue ones, purple ones, red ones, pink ones, every color you could name."

Tony set his chair to rocking. After arriving, he remembered what Essie had said back in the Slap Out about there being no Mrs. Pennington. She'd died and left behind a husband and eight girls. The cooper and his oldest daughter had met them at the door and whisked Brianna into a room off the central hallway. The doctor and Essie followed, but Tony and Harley had been consigned to the back porch. Which was just fine with Tony.

"Which one is Miss Katy?" he asked.

"One of the older ones."

Tony had seen four of the sisters since arriving. The one that had greeted them at the door and three others running between the kitchen and the room they had taken Brianna into.

"Did Brianna's father know you'd taken her snake hunting?"

"O' courst. My pa would whup me good if'n I took her without permission."

"Aren't your parents wondering what's keeping you now?"

"They might be. But I ain't leavin' 'til I know Bri's gonna be all right."

A distant coyote gave a yapping howl, ending with a shrill, scream-like sound. Harley repositioned himself on the step.

"You do this often?" Tony asked. "Snake hunting, I mean?"

"Yeah, I guess. I caught me a yellow-bellied water snake a few weeks back out by the old watershed. It was a good four feet long and this big around." He made a circle the size of a silver dollar with his fingers.

Tony whistled in appreciation. "You still have it?"

"Naw. My pa made me let it loose 'cause I snuck up on Lexie Davis and scared her with it." Harley gave Tony a conspiring grin. "She shore did squeal something fierce, though."

Tony chuckled. "How do you know which snakes are poisonous and which are friendly?"

"Miss Essie showed me."

Tony stopped his rocker. "Essie? Our Essie?"

Harley gave him a funny look. "You know any others?"

"She *showed* you?"

"Well, at first, she just tol' me that if it had a flat head instead of a round, pointy one, that it would be poisonous. Then when we would run acrost a copperhead or cottonmouth or something, she'd tell me what it was."

"Do you and Essie make a habit of running across snakes?"

Harley laughed. "Well, yeah. Wouldn't be much use in huntin' snakes if we never ran acrost any."

"You and Essie hunt snakes?"

"Why, shore. She's the one what taught me how."

Tony rubbed a hand across his mouth. He didn't know why he was surprised. Nothing about that woman should surprise him anymore. "How often do you go hunting with her?"

"Not so much anymore. She's always busy with her bicycle stuff."

The screen door opened and Essie stepped outside. Tony and Harley came to their feet.

"She's going to be fine," Essie said.

Tony let out his breath and Harley slumped against the porch rail.

"What did the doctor say?" Tony asked.

"That the swelling should go away in another two or three weeks and then she'll be back to normal."

"You extracted all the venom, then, when you were, um, treating her?" Tony asked.

"Well, I don't imagine there was all that much to begin with. It was apparent the snake had eaten recently, which would have used up most of its poison."

"No, Miss Essie," Harley said. "You saved her life." He pitched himself against her skirts and hugged her tightly. "I don't know what I would've done if somethin' had happened to Bri."

Essie smoothed her hand over his head. "Well, she's fine now, so no need to worry yourself. And I'm surprised you're still here. Hadn't you better be getting on home?"

He pulled away from her and swiped his nose with his sleeve. "Can I see Bri?"

"Not tonight, Harley. Maybe tomorrow."

He glanced at the back door, then slumped his shoulders. "Well, if yer sure she's gonna be all right?"

"I'm sure. Now go on with you."

He waved good-bye to Tony, clomped down the steps, then disappeared around the corner and into the night. Essie moved to the porch railing, leaned her hands against it and looked out at the moonlit sky.

Tony wished he had a lantern. Her hair had come completely unbound. It was wild and thick and clear down to her waist. Her blouse was twisted, its sleeve stained with blood. Her torn skirt fell limply about her slim hips.

"You okay?" he asked.

"It's been a long night," she said, looking at him over her shoulder. A breeze swept across the porch, stirring her hair and causing her to shiver.

"You left your shawl in the woods," he said, slipping off his jacket and hooking it on her shoulders. The coat trapped her hair beneath it, cutting all but the top from his view.

She pulled the collar tighter around her neck. "I left your knife behind also," she said.

Patting his pockets, he realized she was right. "I'll have Harley fetch them for us tomorrow. I'd do it myself, but I don't think I could find the spot."

"I hope your knife doesn't rust being left out overnight. It was such an unusual one."

"It'll be fine. I'm more worried about you."

She waved her hand in a gesture of dismissal. "I'm just tired, is all."

"Why don't you let me walk you home, then. Surely you've done all you can."

Keeping her back to him, she scanned the yard and the shadows beyond it. "Yes. Dr. Gulick is almost finished, and Brianna's sisters will take good care of her. But you needn't walk me home. I'm sure you're just as anxious to get some rest as I am, and morning will come awfully early for you."

Moonlight gilded her hair, and his jacket hung on her like a burlap sack, shrouding her form. He tried to recall the reasons he'd held contempt for her just a few short hours ago, but could not. Instead, he kept seeing her in his mind's eye crouched over that little girl, desperately trying to save her life—and succeeding.

Then he pictured her sliding down a banister, playing football, hugging Harley, smiling.

He took a deep breath. He was no stranger to the feelings stirring inside him. But this time they were unwelcome. He had a purpose to fulfill, a mother and a sister to provide for.

There was no room in his life for distractions. Essie had offered an excuse, and he knew he should accept it and put as much distance between them as he could.

She lowered her chin and began to pick at the wood on the railing. Her hair bunched along the back of the jacket's collar. Reaching up, he scooped the golden mane into his hand and pulled it free from its confinement. The silky strands glided through his fingers and fell against her back.

She spun around, her skirts catching against the railing and twisting round her legs. She lifted her hands to her hair, causing the jacket to fall off, then swiftly fished out some pins from a skirt pocket and placed them in her mouth. She finger-combed her hair, banded it together, and twirled it against her head with quick, efficient movements.

While her hands were full and occupied, he drew the pins from her mouth. She stilled and lifted her gaze to his.

He handed her a pin. She took it from him, careful to keep her fingers from brushing his, and tucked it into her hair. He doled the pins out one at a time until she reached for the last one. He squeezed it, keeping her from taking it.

They stood suspended, linked not by touch, but by opposite ends of the pin. What would she do if he tugged on his end? Would she let go or would she come to him?

Releasing the pin, he stepped away, retrieved his jacket from the floor of the porch and held it open. "Ready?"

Patting her hair, she presented her back to him. He hooked the jacket on her shoulders and offered her his arm.

After a slight hesitation, she slipped a hand out from the folds of his jacket.

On the street, he adjusted his stride to hers. The fabric of her skirt swished when she walked and brushed against his leg. Neither of them uttered a word the entire way home.

At Bilberry Street they took a right and she gently removed her hand from his arm. He opened the gate leading to her house. There were no lights coming from the windows. Hadn't her father wondered where she was? Did she come home late so often that he didn't even bother to wait up for her?

The giant pecan trees on either side of the walkway shadowed the porch, making it almost impossible to see. Taking her elbow, he guided her up the steps, then reached for the door.

She placed a restraining hand on his arm. "Thank you for seeing me home, Tony."

He straightened. "You're welcome."

Darkness surrounded them. He could make out her silhouette, but little else.

Shrugging his jacket from her shoulders, she handed it to him. "Thank you."

He nodded and slung it over his arm, but made no move to leave. A lonely bird some distance off called out, but received no answer.

"Well," she said.

"Well," he repeated, backing up a step. "I guess I'd better be going."

"Yes." But she made no move to go inside. "When do you think the Bakers will be able to come to Corsicana?"

"Who? Oh! The Baker brothers. Yes, well, I'm not sure. It depends on whether or not they're still in Beaumont. I could shoot my friend a telegram first thing in the morning, but it would mean I'd be a little late for work."

"I'll tell Mr. Moss."

"Then I'll take care of it and let you know when I hear from them." He backed up another step.

"Be careful. I think the stairs are right behind you."

He glanced over his shoulder. "Right. Yes. Thank you. Don't suppose it would be good if I fell down the stairs after everything else that's happened tonight."

She made no response. He wished he could see her expression, then thought better of it. After another second's hesitation, he tugged the brim of his hat, then strode down the steps, across the yard, out the gate and back toward town.

CHAPTER | NINE

ROLLING PEGASUS OUT OF the shed, Essie walked her bike to the street, pointed it toward town and smoothly mounted. The cloudless day offered no breeze or relief from the sun's intense rays, but Essie took little notice of it, her mind fully occupied with thoughts of Mr. Bryant.

Something had changed, though she couldn't pinpoint what exactly. When he'd gathered her hair into his hands, she'd briefly remembered another man doing the same thing. And much as she'd enjoyed those moments, there was a wealth of hurt in the memories, too.

Turning onto Fourth Street, she waved at the men working a series of Sullivan Oil rigs. Work on the derricks ceased. The men doffed their hats, waved back and waited for her to pass before resuming their duties.

When she'd first met Tony, he had bristled with resentment. When had his feelings changed, she wondered. After she re-hired him? After the football match? Brianna's tragedy? Whenever it happened, there was no question the animosity had slowly melted away like bubbles in a washtub. What troubled Essie was what the change meant.

Approaching Collin Street her heart began to hammer. In another minute or two, she'd be passing the rig Tony worked on. Releasing one handlebar, she touched her hair and hat, assuring herself all was in place. She smoothed her collar, pinched her cheeks, then ran a hand across her stomach.

Turning the corner, she immediately spotted his rig several hundred yards ahead. Should she look for him? Pretend she didn't notice him? Wave? Smile? Do nothing?

Before she could decide, she was upon them. Again the men stopped and she raised a hand to wave. Her tire hit a rut in the road, throwing her off-balance. She grasped the handlebars with both hands as if they were the horns of a bull wrenching its head from side to side.

The bike pitched to the left, and she only kept upright by kicking out her foot and pushing against the road. But she overcompensated and had to do the same with her other foot before regaining control.

Heat rushed to her face. Were they still watching her? Had Tony seen? She knew the answer without looking.

Mortified, she kept her eyes straight ahead and did not wave to any other rigs or acknowledge them in any way. Experienced wheelers fell off of their machines all the time, she told herself. It was part of the sport. Nothing to be embarrassed about.

Her stomach refused to calm, however, so she cleared her mind of all thoughts and concentrated on reaching the sanctuary of the jailhouse.

At the south end of Jefferson Avenue, she rolled to a stop, jumped off Peg and leaned her against the red bricks of the sheriff's office. The handlebars of her bike knocked loose a bit of grout, sprinkling the boardwalk with flakes of gray.

Adjusting her straw hat, she took a moment to compose herself, then tiptoed underneath the oversized five-pointed star hanging above the open door and peeked into a building that was as familiar to her as her own home. She could tolerate the deputy if Uncle Melvin was there to run interference, but she didn't relish being caught alone with the man.

Nothing stirred inside the vacant room. "Uncle Melvin?"

Two desks filled the space between the door and the empty cells running along the back wall. Moving to the desk closest to the door, she fingered a Wanted poster frayed at the edges, and examined the vacant eyes of Saw Dust Charlie, horse thief, wondering what led a man into a life of crime.

Oil leases, tax records, and licensing documents littered the left side of the scarred wooden desk, rings of black ink stained the other. A hollowed-out groove cradled her uncle's Easterbrook pen.

Accidentally brushing his papers, she recoiled at the discovery of a postcard with the corpse of a badly beaten man in shredded clothes hanging from a rope while onlookers gawked. She flipped the offending card over, but its image still branded itself in her mind.

She scanned the printed inscription, *Wichita, Texas*. A note scribbled in coarse letters slashed the expanse above it.

Melvin,

    If this can happen in my town, it can happen in yours. When my deputies interrupted the proceedings, they were imprisoned by the mob. Something's got to be done.

Herbert

Covering the note back up, she tried to quell the sickness in her stomach. She'd heard of lynchings in neighboring counties, but nothing like that would ever happen in Corsicana. And the local merchants certainly wouldn't sell postcards glorifying them.

Her gaze moved to a delicate china figurine tucked beside an unlit kerosene lamp, the sight of it bringing a touch of normalcy and comfort. The six-inch woman was lifting her porcelain face to the sun while hugging a basket of wild flowers to her waist with one hand. The other hand was plastered to her head in an attempt to keep a hold on her wide-brimmed straw bonnet. Her back was arched, her laughing face enchanted.

Essie remembered the first time she'd seen it prominently displayed in the window of the Flour, Feed and Liquor Store. She couldn't have been more than eight or nine years old. The figurine had captured her imagination and she'd saved up her money for weeks. Not for herself, but for one of the most important persons in her young life. She'd never forget Uncle Melvin's surprise when she proudly presented the little statuette to him on his birthday.

The following morning, she'd all but burst from pride upon entering the jailhouse to see her gift prominently displayed on his desk. And it had been there ever since.

She smiled at the memory, then started as the town stray, Cat, jumped up onto the wooden surface, scattering a stack of oil leases to and fro.

Picking up the tabby, she curled it against her chest and rubbed her nose against its head. "Where is everybody, hmmmm?"

Cat raised her chin, and Essie obligingly scratched it. "What's the matter? You looking for Uncle Melvin, too?"

The words had hardly left her mouth before she sensed someone else in the room. She glanced behind her.

Deputy Billy John Howard leaned against the open doorframe of the storage room where all weapons and supplies were kept under lock and key. She wondered how long he'd been standing there.

His petite frame never failed to surprise her, especially considering how quick he was with his fists—too quick. In the six months he'd been deputy, those fists had made many enemies and actually killed a man who'd challenged his authority. All in the name of maintaining law and order.

"Have you finally come to your senses, Essie?" he asked. "Come to accept my suit?"

"I'm afraid not."

"I promise not to disappoint."

"All the same, no thank you."

"As you wish," he said, his eyes hooded.

"What were you doing in there?"

"We got us a leak and had to move all the spare rifles to your uncle's house. So he's been pestering me to fix the ceiling."

Pushing away from the doorframe, he locked the storage room, sauntered to her and reached for her arm. She jumped back, dropping Cat between them. Howling, the animal streaked out the front door.

Deputy Howard's hand veered to Uncle Melvin's top drawer—as if that had always been his destination—and dropped the key inside. "A bit jumpy, aren't we?"

"Where's Uncle Melvin?"

"Here and there."

She edged back, keeping the desk between them, but he followed her step for step.

"What brings you here?" he asked.

"I have a message for my uncle."

Howard hooked one hip on the edge of the sheriff's desk. "You can leave the message with me. I'll be sure he gets it."

She began backing toward the door. "If it's all the same to you, I'll just check back later."

"The Fourth of July celebration is next week," he said, standing, then hitching up his trousers. "I figured I'd pick you up around ten."

"My bicycle club sponsors a group ride that morning. And even if it didn't, I'm afraid I would have to decline. Now, if you'll excuse me?"

She didn't have time to so much as turn around before he'd closed the distance between them and grabbed her arm.

"You goin' with somebody else?"

"No," she said, trying to pull away. "Now, let me go. You're hurting me."

He increased the pressure on her arm ever so slightly before releasing her. "My apologies. I'm just gettin' a little tired of your excuses."

"They aren't excuses, Mr. Howard. They are outright refusals. I am not going to the celebration with you or anyone else. Is that clear?"

His eyes flickered. "Clear as a bell, Miss Spreckelmeyer. I guess if you won't let me escort you, then I'll just have to settle fer seein' you there."

———

Tony pushed away a plate piled with chicken bones, then pulled the napkin from his neck. He caught Castle's eye and laid a nickel on the counter. The proprietor strolled over, wiping his hands on his apron, and snatched the coin up with a nod of thanks.

A boomer two stools down from him pointed a drumstick at the man sitting beside him. "I'm tellin' ya, pulling all this oil from the ground ain't gonna do a lick o' good lessen we have a refinery of our own. Just ain't right the way we send all our slick up to them Yanks."

"It'd take a lot o' cartwheels to do it ourselves," his partner responded. "Why, we'd need to build a refinery first, along with gatherin' lines, pipin', heavy steel, and I don't know what all."

The door jingled, signaling the entrance of two young women. The men draped along the counter straightened, tracking the ladies' progress. Those wandering about the drugstore removed their hats.

Tony didn't recognize the girls, but he smiled politely, then slipped out the door. Harley had promised to return Tony's pocketknife to him at the Slap Out in exchange for a game of checkers, and he didn't want to be late.

The sun had long since set, and oilmen filled the walkways and road, jostling Tony and kicking up dirt. Pulling his handkerchief from his pocket, Tony sneezed and wiped his nose. The dirt never settled in this town, coating him with a film of grime every time he stepped outside.

Like a trout moving upstream, he wove through the press of men and crossed Main Street, then over to Collin Street. A man in overalls and a straw hat strode into the store while another man stepped out of the mercantile, swung up onto his horse and headed in the opposite direction.

Tony climbed the steps and made his way back to where the stove was. Harley leaned against the chair of an old man whittling on a piece of wood, a pile of shavings between his feet. Two other gaffers divided their attention between the game of checkers they played and the man whittling. The carver held up his piece of wood and said something Tony couldn't quite catch, causing the group to guffaw.

"Howdy, Mr. Tony," Harley hollered, noticing him. "Come look here at what Pa's a-whittlin'. "

The man stopped working and greeted Tony. His nose was as wide as it was long and the texture of tree bark. Bushy gray eyebrows shaded little bitty blue eyes.

"I'm Ludwig Vandervoort. Harley's pa. That there is Owen and Jenkins." He looked Tony up and down. "You the feller what left his knife exposed to the elements?"

Tony flushed at the censure in his tone.

"I done told ya, Pa," Harley said, "we was helping the womenfolk after Bri got bit. And womenfolk is way more important than knives. Ain't that so, Mr. Tony?"

The three old-timers waited for Tony's response.

"A knife is an important tool, Harley," Tony said, "and a man shouldn't be leaving it behind like that."

The men nodded.

"But what about the women?" Harley asked.

Tony put his hand on the boy's shoulder. "In my book, the women are definitely more important than a pocketknife."

Harley gave his father a triumphant look, but the man had propped his elbows on his knees and continued to whittle . . . with Tony's knife.

"You keep 'er good and sharp," Vandervoort said, making no apologies for testing it out. "I'll give ya that."

From what Tony could tell, the carving was almost finished. Vandervoort shaved very small pieces around the figure's shoulders, then blew on it. "Well, that just about does it."

Pressing the back of the blade against his trouser leg, Vandervoort snapped the knife closed and handed it to Tony. "Much obliged."

Tony ran his fingers along the stag handle, then slipped it into his pocket. He wanted to inspect it for damage from the previous night but decided to do that without an audience.

Harley held out his hands and his father placed the figure into them. The boy turned the carving over, a smile splitting across his face.

"Lookit," he said, handing it to Tony.

The real-life features of the three-inch figure impressed him. A hat hid the eyes of the statue and rested on an oversized nose. Thin lips formed a smile that looked more like a leer.

"Turn it over," Harley said, delight in his voice.

Tony flipped the figure over, expecting to find its back but instead discovered it was another man. The eyes on this one, though, were visible with eyebrows drawn into an angry V. The lips were curled and the hands formed exaggerated fists.

"It's the deputy!" Harley exclaimed. "See?" He took the carving from Tony, holding up the smiling side. "This is how he acts in front of the sheriff and the ladies." He flipped it over. "But this is what he's really like. Ain't he, Pa?"

Vandervoort shot a stream of tobacco into a spittoon. "It's just a carving, son. Not meant to be anybody in particular."

Harley's face registered shock. He started to say something, then must have thought better about contradicting his father.

"Where'd ya get a knife like that?" Vandervoort asked.

"My father gave it to me."

"How come the top of it's shaped like a dog bone?"

Tony hesitated, recalling the long-ago day a mean-looking dog had chased him home from school. After outrunning the beast, he'd burst into his father's study with tears streaming down his face.

"*Come 'ere,*" his father had said, laughing at the tale and motioning Tony forward. He rummaged through his desk and produced the oddly shaped knife. "*Here's a weapon fit for you, Dogbone.*" He chuckled at the nickname, amused at his own joke. "*If that dog comes looking for you again, you can throw this at him.*"

Tony fingered the memento in his pocket. "My dad liked unusual things, I guess."

Vandervoort spit again. "Well, I ain't never seen nothing like it."

Tony nodded. "Me neither, sir. Me neither."

"Guess what I did, Mr. Tony?" Harley asked.

"What's that?"

"I got to watch Miss Essie train Mr. Sharpley."

"That a fact?"

"Sure is. And you should see 'im. He takes off like the first rattle outta the box. Everybody's saying we're gonna win the race this year, ain't they, Pa?"

Vandervoort cracked his knuckles one at a time. "If what the peddler man says is true, then we just might have a shot."

"The peddler man said the fella over at Alamo Oil is purty fast," Harley explained, "but he thinks Sharpley might have the edge on him."

Owen jumped his opponent's checker, then looked up from his game. "The boys have a kitty going if you want in on it, Bryant."

Tony smiled. "I'll keep that in mind, sir."

Jenkins rubbed his bald head and slumped back in his chair, having lost his last checker. "Well, that's it fer me."

He and Owen stood.

"Y'all leavin'?" Vandervoort asked.

"Reckon so."

Vandervoort pushed himself into a standing position. "We'll go with ya." He looked at Harley. "You ready?"

"I was hopin' to play a game with Mr. Tony first. Can I stay a little longer?"

"I dunno, son," he said, scratching his cheek. "Yer ma's gonna want ya home soon."

"I won't go easy on him this time, Pa, so it won't be a long game."

Tony frowned.

"Well, all right, then," Vandervoort said, patting Harley's back. "But come straight home when yer finished."

"Yes, sir. I will."

The men shuffled out and Harley began setting up the game.

"How's Brianna?" Tony asked, pouring himself a cup of coffee.

"Madder 'n a hornet."

"Mad? What about?"

"Her pa ain't gonna let her go to the Fourth of July celebration."

Tony settled into the ladder-back chair. "That's a pity. How's she doing otherwise?"

"Okay, I guess. She doesn't have to do no chores."

"Ah. A silver lining." Tony took a sip of coffee.

Harley moved first. "I still feel bad for her. The whole town will be there and we're gonna have sack races, a marble contest, and everything."

"Brianna plays marbles?" Tony asked, pushing his piece forward.

"Naw. She's all upset about that dumb box-supper auction. You know, where the fellers buy up food they could get fer free if they'd just eat with their ma instead o' some girl?"

Tony chuckled. "Isn't Brianna a bit young to be putting her box up?"

"Oh, she don't do it yet, but she wants to somethin' fierce. She still likes to see who buys whose, though. It's all her and her sisters been talkin' about." He jumped two of Tony's pieces.

"Maybe you could bring a bit of the celebration to her."

"How do you figure that?" Harley asked, moving onto Tony's king row.

"Well, you could ask your mother to help you make a box tied up with some little gewgaw of Brianna's. Then, when the auction starts, you could take it to her house, pretend like it was hers, bid on it, and then share it with her."

Harley smiled, positioning his king so that it threatened three of Tony's pieces. "She'd like that fer shore. And I bet my ma would like makin' a box, too."

Tony refocused on the checkerboard, dismayed to see any move he made would put him in harm's way. He looked at Harley.

The boy shrugged. "You gotta learn to talk and play at the same time."

In the next few minutes of silence, Harley claimed all of Tony's pieces.

CHAPTER | TEN

WITH A TELEGRAM FROM driller M.C. Baker in his pocket, Tony headed to the Corsicana Velocipede Club. He'd sent a message to Russ and received a reply from Baker himself. The brothers were still in Beaumont and free to come to Corsicana in a couple of weeks.

He lengthened his stride, wondering what kind of paces Essie was putting Sharpley through this time and if he could coax her into letting him participate.

He'd thought of her often over the last few days and had tried to glean a bit of information by covertly pumping the boys in the patch. But he hadn't learned anything new, other than a few specifics that confirmed what he already suspected. If the judge was head of the company, then Essie was its hands and feet.

Reaching the club, he knocked, then pushed open the door. Instead of Sharpley, though, he found a group of about twenty-five women gossiping around a table with cookies and punch. Some were young and in their twenties, but most were matrons. Essie was not among them.

He scanned the building and spotted her up on the bandstand, flipping through a sheaf of papers. She wore a blue gown with poofy sleeves that narrowed sharply to a skin-tight fit outlining elbows and lower arms. An extremely wide sash hugged her tiny waist, emphasizing curves both above and below. The brim of her hat protruded well past her forehead, while the back was pinched up, her blond hair piled underneath with a collection of curls at its center.

With her head bent over her papers, he noted for the first time the length of her long, lovely neck.

"Well, now, who have we here?" a petite, elderly woman asked, approaching with a cane.

He stifled his surprise at the woman's attire. She was wearing bloomers rather than a gown. Her trousers were baggy at the knees, abnormally full about the pockets, and considerably loose where one strikes a match.

He doffed his hat. "I was wanting to speak with Miss Spreckelmeyer, ma'am."

"Were you, now?" Through wire-rimmed spectacles, she looked him up and down with frank appreciation.

He felt his cheeks warm. "I can see she's busy, though. I'll just come back another time."

"Are you a member, Mr. . . . ?"

"Bryant." He nodded. "Tony Bryant. And you are?"

"Mrs. Penelope Lockhart."

"A pleasure, Mrs. Lockhart. And, no, I'm not a member."

"Would you like to be?"

He hesitated. "I'm . . . Is it . . . Are visitors allowed?"

Her skin folded like an accordion as she smiled. "Indeed they are. But in order to attend a meeting, you must come as a guest of one of the members."

"Well, I didn't really come to attend the meeting."

"Of course you did." She glanced quickly over her shoulder. "But we're supposed to register our guests ahead of time," she whispered. "We could just pretend I forgot all about that. Would you like to attend as my guest?" Her eyes were alight with appeal.

Despite his better judgment, he found himself responding to her less-than-subtle petition. "Won't your husband mind?" he asked in mock undertone.

She looked at him over her spectacles. "Not likely. He's been dead almost twenty years now."

He choked back a laugh, having no notion of what to say.

"Tonight's topic is Bicycle Etiquette for Courting Couples," Mrs. Lockhart said, then leaned in close. "I do not believe Miss Spreckelmeyer has ever discussed this particular topic in front of a, um, mixed crowd."

The touch of mischief in her eyes was unmistakable. He glanced again at Essie. She was giving lessons on *etiquette*? But the woman on the stage was not the ball-playing, snake-hunting, disheveled tomboy he'd walked home earlier this week. This Essie was every inch the proper, elegant, refined lady, and he found himself wondering what this side of her was like.

Returning his attention to the old woman before him, he offered her his arm. "It would be my honor to have such a lovely lady at my side this evening, Mrs. Lockhart."

Her eyes lit up. Hooking her cane over her elbow, she placed her hand on his arm. "Come, I'll introduce you to the girls."

Satisfied with the arrangement of her notes on the lectern, Essie decided it was time for Shirley to call the meeting of the Corsicana Velocipede Club to order. As she looked for Shirley, the sound of deep male laughter filled the room.

She moved her attention to the refreshment table. Tony, with a coffee cup in one hand and Mrs. Lockhart on his arm, stood surrounded by the ladies of the Velocipede Club.

He looked up, caught her watching him and telegraphed her a private hello. She experienced a quick rush of pleasure.

After careful consideration over the last few days, she finally realized why Tony had bucked her authority before. When she'd looked at him, all she'd seen was a toolie, not a man.

She smoothed the hair at the nape of her neck. She admitted to herself that she'd definitely noticed the *man* the other night, though. And she was sure he knew it—just like she knew he'd taken notice of her.

At the moment, Mrs. McCabe, the coroner's wife, held Tony's attention. She was a jolly, large-chested woman with a wicked sense of humor that did not suit her husband's occupation. Essie could not hear what the woman was saying, but her eyes were glowing and when she finished speaking, she whipped open her fan and put it to rapid use.

Tony threw back his head in laughter. The younger ladies giggled, though their eyes were downcast. The matrons, chuckling good-naturedly, exchanged knowing looks with one another.

Essie quickly left the stage and headed toward the group.

"You'll find Mr. Bunting a fine, civic-minded banker," Mrs. Blanchard, secretary of the bicycle club, interjected. She was a stout woman of fine form and looked as if she'd come right out of a Rubens painting. "Now, were you to visit Mr. Delk's bank, he'd say that he'd be happy to help carry the load. But what he means is for you to carry the piano and him to carry the sheet music."

Tony smiled. "Sounds as if Mr. Bunting's bank is the place to entrust my money, then?"

"I think so, yes."

"Ah," said Mrs. Lockhart, "here comes our teacher."

The ladies made room for Essie.

"My dear, this is my guest, Mr. Bryant. Mr. Bryant, this is the owner of the Velocipede Club, Miss Spreckelmeyer."

He tipped his head. "I've had an opportunity to become acquainted with Miss Spreckelmeyer already, as I'm a roustabout for Sullivan Oil."

The women *ahhhhed* in understanding.

"Hello, Mr. Bryant," Essie said. "Was there something you needed to see me about?"

"No, no," Mrs. Lockhart answered for him. "He is considering membership in the club and wanted to attend tonight's lecture on bicycle courtship."

Essie looked at him in surprise. Mrs. Lockhart was a consummate matchmaker. Had she decided he would do nicely for one of the younger girls and brought him here to promote her agenda? Was he party to her shenanigans?

"I don't recall seeing any guests listed on the register," she said.

"Oh my." Mrs. Lockhart brought a gloved hand to her lips. "I confess I completely forgot to sign him up in advance. Will you forgive me, dear?"

Something wasn't quite right, but Essie couldn't determine what it was. "Of course. Had I known he was coming, though, I might have chosen a more suitable topic."

He covered Mrs. Lockhart's hand with his. "Perhaps it would be best if I came another time."

"No, no," the woman responded. "We wouldn't hear of it. Would we, Essie?"

"Don't answer, Miss Spreckelmeyer," he said. "I have no wish to make you uncomfortable." He kissed Mrs. Lockhart's cheek. "Thank you, ma'am. It's been a pleasure."

"Tony," Essie said, stopping him before he could withdraw. "Don't be silly. You are more than welcome to stay."

He shook his head. "Thank you, but—"

"I insist."

Mrs. Lockhart latched on to his elbow. "There. All settled." She gave Essie a pointed look. "Isn't it time we start?"

"Yes, ma'am." She made eye contact with Shirley, and the girl hastened to the stage.

Tony glanced at Essie and, with a pained look, mouthed, *I'm sorry.*

She waved her hand in a dismissive gesture, but Mrs. Lockhart had already commandeered his attention as she directed him to the spot she sat every week. Right on the very first row.

Having a gentleman in the house electrified the women. Some tittered, some preened, while others laughed a little too loud. The younger women cast inviting glances Tony's direction, but he had eyes for Mrs. Lockhart alone.

Leaning much closer than was proper, he whispered something in her ear, earning himself a wicked chortle and a halfhearted slap on the arm.

Essie's stomach fluttered. How on earth would she convey tonight's message with Tony sitting directly in her line of vision? He towered almost a foot above the women.

She sighed. It could be worse, she supposed. He could have come to last week's lecture on corsets. She felt ill just thinking about it.

A spattering of applause commenced and Shirley looked at her expectantly. Essie jumped to her feet. Good heavens. She'd missed her own introduction.

Stepping up to the lectern, she silently read the first line of her notes. She believed her opening statement would set the tone for the entire evening and she'd given careful thought to its wording.

The charming and fascinating power of serpents over birds is as nothing compared with what a woman can wield over a man.

She couldn't say that now. Not with Tony sitting right there. She scanned down to the next paragraph.

A woman who once starts a man's love can get out of him, and do with him, anything possible she pleases.

Warmth began to bedevil her cheeks. She'd lifted that statement right out of the Social Manual her mother had given her. But how could she, a thirty-four-year-old unmarried woman with more failed relationships than she cared to admit, present such an argument? She'd thought nothing of it before when she wrote her speech. But having a man present changed everything.

Perhaps she should skip the introduction and move directly to the point at hand. She flipped her first page over. The ladies began to fidget, disrupting the stillness of the vast room with a slight fluttering of skirts as they shifted in their chairs.

Panicked at how long she'd been standing there without saying a word, Essie simply picked a sentence and started. "Marriage very rarely mends a man's manners."

Good heavens. She took a calming breath and pressed forward. "Goldsmith says that 'love is often an involuntary passion placed upon our companions without our consent, and frequently conferred without even our previous esteem.' "

She knew only too well that statement was true.

"The first point to be considered on this subject is a careful choice of associates, which will often, in the end, save future unhappiness and discomfort."

Memories of the drifter who had stolen much more than her heart the summer of '94 swept through her, giving an urgency to her message. There were young, impressionable girls in her audience who could become the next ne'er-do-well's victim.

"An unsuitable acquaintance, friendship, or alliance is more embarrassing and more painful for the woman than the man. Wealth, charm, and genius mean nothing if the character of the man is flawed."

She looked from her papers to her club members. "The bicycle is responsible for much promiscuous acquaintanceship. Many elderly chaperones find it too difficult to keep up with their young charges. And if we are not very, very careful, the people lobbying to have bicycling outlawed for females will get their way."

She had them now. Every eye was focused on her. No outdoor pastime could be more independently pursued than bicycling. None of these women wanted to give up that freedom.

Tony, however, gazed back at her, not with rapt attention but with a touch of amusement, and it hurt her feelings, then ignited her sense of injustice. Men could walk away unscathed from a licentious relationship. Women were left ruined. Stripped of their reputations, their options, their very virtue.

"Just remember this, ladies," she said. "You cannot come to any harm unless you get *off* your bicycle."

Murmurs of agreement flitted through the room. Faint laugh lines formed at the corners of Tony's eyes.

Had she been wrong about him? Was he, in fact, simply passing through town, looking for a woman desperate enough to believe his quiet words and soft gestures?

Old wounds long since buried rose to the surface, surprising her with how swiftly and painfully they struck.

She made her next statement looking straight at him. "A man's duty to the woman who rides could be turned into a long sermon. But long sermons are never popular. So I will briefly state that he must always be on the alert to assist his fair companion in every way possible."

Mrs. Lockhart looked at him and he nodded at her with mock sobriety.

"He must be clever enough to repair any slight damage to her machine. He must assist her in mounting and dismounting. Pick her up when she has a tumble. And make himself generally useful. Incidentally ornamental. And quintessentially agreeable."

He chuckled. Not out loud, of course, but he bit the insides of his cheeks, and his shoulders shook. Mrs. Lockhart gave him a stern frown.

Essie gripped the lectern. "Lastly, he is to ride at her left in order to give her the more guarded place."

She stomped down from the bandstand and grabbed one of the two bicycles she'd had waiting in readiness for her demonstration. The wheels stood side by side, center front.

Originally, Shirley had agreed to assist her, but now that they had a bona fide "gentleman" in their midst, there would be no need for Shirley's help.

"In mounting, he holds her wheel." She thrust the machine toward him. "Mr. Bryant? Would you be so kind?"

He jumped to his feet. "It would be my honor." He turned to Mrs. Lockhart. "Please excuse me."

Mrs. Lockhart nodded and he stepped to the front, taking hold of the bike's handlebar.

Essie lifted her chin. "The lady stands on the left side of the machine and puts her right foot across the frame to the right pedal, which at the time must be up." Her skirts were far too long and full for riding. She'd never meant to actually mount, just to take the women through the steps verbally. But her entire speech had gone awry.

Giving him a brisk nod, she shooed him away. "You may see to your wheel now, Mr. Bryant." She edged the hem of her skirt up so it wouldn't get caught in the spokes or chains. "The lady rider starts ahead."

She pushed the right pedal, causing her machine to start and then with her left foot in place began to move forward. "She must go slowly at first, in order to give her cavalier time to mount his wheel, which he will do in the briefest possible time."

She glanced over her shoulder, hoping against hope that he would be slow and clumsy. But he was already upon his bike and taking up his position on her left side.

They kept to the perimeter of the seated assembly. She clutched at her skirts to keep them from becoming entangled. He made no effort to avert his gaze from the show of her ankle.

Halfway around the circle, she turned her attention to her members. "When the end of the ride is reached, the man quickly dismounts and is at his companion's side to assist her."

The women twisted and turned, trying to keep Essie and Tony within their view. Approaching the final leg of her journey, she prepared for dismounting.

"The most approved style of alighting from one's machine is when the left pedal is on the rise, the weight of the body is thrown onto it, and the right foot is crossed over the frame of the bike. Then, with an assisting hand, the rider easily steps to the ground."

Before she had finished speaking, he was there. Hand out, seeing her smoothly to the ground.

They stood facing each other, the silence in the room palpable.

He grazed her gloved knuckles with his thumb. "The pleasure was all mine, Miss Spreckelmeyer."

A collective sigh issued forth from the audience.

Essie snatched her hand from his. "Thank you for your assistance, sir."

He took her machine, parked it next to his and returned to his seat. The women started chattering at once, sharing their thoughts on what they'd seen and learned.

Essie reached the lectern and noted with a start that Tony's attention had never strayed from her. Mrs. Lockhart was speaking to him, but he paid her no heed. Instead, he stared intently at Essie.

It was not a flirtatious look he gave her. Or even a suggestive look. It was the look he'd given her when they played tug-of-war with her hairpin.

She swallowed and tugged her gloves more securely onto her hands. One thing was certain: His intentions toward her, honorable or otherwise, would be discernable soon enough.

CHAPTER | ELEVEN

MRS. LOCKHART PEDALED HER bike slowly, allowing Tony to keep up as he walked her home.

"So, Mr. Bryant," she said, her bloomers rustling, "why did you *really* come to the bicycle club tonight?"

He shot her a glance. "I had some business to discuss with Miss Spreckelmeyer."

"Business?" The wheels of her machine crunched against the gravel and dirt. "What kind of business?"

"Oil business."

"At such a late hour?"

"I work until sundown, ma'am. By the time I clean up, eat, and walk out to the club, the hands on the clock have done some spinning."

"Why not speak with the judge?"

Tony adjusted his hat. He wasn't sure if the townsfolk knew exactly how involved Essie was in the running of things. "I probably should have done that, now that you mention it."

A smile flitted across her face. "No. You did the right thing. Whatever you wanted, I'm sure Sullivan would have told you to go ask Essie."

They took a right on Decatur Street. A door closed in the distance. As they passed a house on the corner, the lantern hanging in its window went out.

"You like Essie, don't you?" Mrs. Lockhart asked.

He missed a step. "Uh, yes, ma'am. The Spreckelmeyers are good folks."

"That's not what I meant, sir."

He remained silent, wondering how much farther it was to her home.

"Well, then, where are you from, Mr. Bryant?"

"Beaumont."

"Beaumont. A very nice town. Do you still have family there?"

"Yes, ma'am. A mother and sister."

"I have family there, too. A daughter and a son-in-law."

He smiled in acknowledgment.

"I don't rightly recall any Bryants, though." She squinted her eyes, searching her memory. "Of course, there's Leah Bryant. You know, Blake Morgan's widow?"

He kept his face carefully blank.

"Would you be related to those Bryants?"

He pulled a handkerchief from his pocket and wiped his neck. "I imagine we're all related one way or another. What's your daughter's married name?"

"Otter. Mrs. Archibald Otter."

His heart began to hammer. Archie Otter was Morgan Oil's tool pusher. His wife, Leslie, was an intimate friend of Anna's, and the couple often sat with Tony's family on the porch while Archie picked his banjo.

He cleared his throat. "Do you have opportunity to visit your daughter very often?"

"Yes. Quite often. Her husband works for the Morgans. Who did you work for while you were there?"

"The same."

"Really? Then you must have known Archie." She lowered her voice. "He's very high up in the company, you know."

"Yes, ma'am. Everybody knows who Mr. Otter is."

She hit a hole in the road, causing her bike to wobble.

He reached out and steadied her.

"My son-in-law was always singing the praises of Tony Morgan, one of Mr. Morgan's sons." She sighed. "According to Archie, though, Mr. Morgan disappeared after being disinherited by his father. Actually, that happened right about the time you arrived in town."

He studied her face, trying to decide if she was baiting him.

She slowed in front of a hipped-roof bungalow surrounded by a white picket fence. "I shall have to tell Archie I've made your acquaintance." She looked him directly in the eyes. "He never forgets a name or face."

She knew who he was. No question about it. Perhaps they had even met when he was with the Otters, but he could not recall one way or the other.

He assisted her off her bike.

"Won't you come in for a refreshment, Mr. Bryant?"

He handed her cane to her and opened the gate. "I'm afraid I can't, ma'am. It's awfully late and I have to be out on the fields at first light."

She walked through, then waited while he retrieved her bike and brought it inside the yard.

"Where would you like me to put this?" he asked.

"Come, I'll show you."

The grass crunched beneath his boots as they headed to the back of her house.

"Are you returning to the club to discuss . . . *business* with Essie?"

"I might swing by on my way home and see if she's still there."

Mrs. Lockhart nodded. "She wears her spinsterhood like a suit of armor, you know."

"I beg your pardon?"

"It'll take a man with great skill to find the chinks."

He stopped, but the old woman kept going. She was much more intuitive than he'd given her credit for and in order to keep her quiet about his identity, he would need to cultivate a relationship of some sort with her.

That aside, he was willing to admit he wanted to find the chinks in Essie's armor but didn't think it wise. Not while his family relied on the goodwill of Darius. Instead, he should be working his way up through Sullivan Oil, learning everything he could about the business.

He'd been working hard during the day, sleeping hard at night. He'd been keeping an eye out for men who would make good partners and good investors. He'd been saving every penny he earned. And when the time was right, he planned to branch out on his own, build up his business and send for his mother and sister.

But that would take months yet. Years, even. His mother would probably be all right, but what about Anna? He decided to write another letter home. His sister must observe the customary year of mourning. Not just because it was the respectful thing to do, but because her very future depended on it.

"Take Monday, for example," Mrs. Lockhart said, pulling Tony back into the present. He quickly caught up to her.

"If you were wanting to escort Essie to the Fourth of July celebration, you'd certainly have your work cut out for you."

"You think so?"

"I know so."

They rounded the house and came face-to-face with the silhouette of a giant derrick in her backyard. For houses in these parts, derricks had become as common as chimneys over the past few years—he'd seen the same thing happen in Beaumont, though he was a little surprised to find Mrs. Lockhart living under the shadow of such a monstrosity.

"You can prop Hilda right there," she said.

Hilda? He leaned her machine against the derrick's legs. The familiar smell of oil enveloped them. He figured he could find every derrick in Corsicana blindfolded just by sniffing for fumes.

"Are you going to ask our Essie to the celebration?"

A rabbit leaped from underneath a bush, then disappeared into the tree line. He cupped Mrs. Lockhart's elbow and helped her onto the back porch. "I hadn't thought much about it."

"Perhaps you should."

He considered her suggestion. Essie was already disrupting his schedule and his efforts to remain focused. He thought about her constantly. And tonight she'd looked so, well, pretty. Maybe taking her to this one event would relieve some of his pent-up tension.

"You think Miss Spreckelmeyer would tell me no?" he asked.

"I'm sure of it."

He removed his hat. "You have any suggestions?"

Mrs. Lockhart smiled. "Yes. As a matter of fact, I do. Would you like to come in?"

He hesitated. "Only for a minute, ma'am."

———

After such an unsettling evening, Essie wanted nothing so much as to be alone, so she had sent Shirley home. Without help, it would take twice as long to close up, but the quietness of the club at night never failed to soothe her.

She loved the vastness of the room and the way it magnified even the slightest of sounds. In the lamplight, the vaulted roof seemed closer somehow, and the stillness reminded her of church. Staying here when everyone else had gone gave her a sense of keeping vigil, and she loved sharing her thoughts with God when no one else was around.

One by one she began to extinguish the sconces along the far wall, each sputtering as she snuffed out their amber glow. At the sound of the door opening, she turned. Tony stepped through, searched the shadows until he found her, then pushed the door shut behind him. The latch clicked into place.

Light from the remaining lamps glazed the left side of his silhouette with gold. He tipped his hat back, then swaggered toward her, his footsteps echoing through the building.

As he approached, he studied her from hat to head, shoulder to waist, waist to toe, and back up again. The slow survey awakened in her long-forgotten—and certainly forbidden—desires.

He came to a stop just inches from her.

Not wanting to be in the dark with him, she twisted the metal knob on the lamp at her shoulder until the hissing flame bathed them both in light. His eyes shone, his whole face seemed to glow.

"I didn't expect to see you again this evening," she said. "Was there something you needed?"

"I received a telegram from the Baker brothers."

He spoke quietly, his words saying one thing but the look on his face another. She hardly knew which overture to answer.

"What did it say?" she asked.

He slipped his hand behind his lapel, digging inside his shirt pocket. The blue cotton stretched tight across his chest, until he found and withdrew a crumpled piece of paper.

Pinching the edge with one hand, he unfurled it between the thumb and finger of his other, one slow stroke at a time. The parchment crackled, opening like a flower.

"M.C. is going to come in a few weeks," he said, handing her the telegram.

She took hold of the message, but when she tried to draw it near, he didn't let go. She waited, eyes down. He'd released her hairpin that night on Brianna's porch. Surely he would release the paper now.

But he did not.

She tugged again.

"Essie?" he whispered.

She let go and took a step back.

He held the telegram suspended between them before finally reaching for her hand. He pressed the crumpled paper in her palm and gently squeezed before releasing her.

She curled her fist around the telegram, the paper rough against her skin. "What else does it say?"

"Read it."

She opened her hand, but the note remained crumpled. Placing it against her stomach, she flattened it, then made the mistake of looking up.

She wished she'd left the lantern off. Tony's eyes were dark. Intense. His nostrils flared.

She held the telegram up to the light, confirming that M.C. Baker would be here the fourteenth of July. "Thank you for arranging this."

"You're welcome."

She handed him back the telegram. "Would it be too much to ask you to accompany me to the train station when he comes? That way you could point him out and make the introductions?"

He folded the paper into fourths, creasing each fold between thumb and fingernail. "It would be my pleasure."

She moistened her lips. "Yes. Well. Thank you again."

"You're welcome again."

He tucked the paper back into his shirt pocket.

She waited, but he said no more.

"Was there something else?" she asked.

He hesitated, then took a deep breath. "Is anyone taking you to the Fourth of July celebration?"

Her lips parted. "No."

"I'd like to take you, Essie. Will you go with me?"

She ran her fingers along the skirt pleats at her waist. "My father usually escorts me to such events."

He removed his hat, then tapped it against his leg. The light caught and highlighted the richness of his hair.

"Tony, I . . . How old are you?"

He lifted his brows. "Twenty-eight. Why?"

"Because I am a good deal older than you." She gave a quick twist to the knob of the lamp, plunging them into darkness. "I'm afraid I must respectfully decline."

She headed to the next sconce.

He followed. "I'm only six years younger. That's nothing."

She spun around. "How do you know my age?"

"Mrs. Lockhart told me."

"Mrs. Lockhart told you? Why would she do a thing like that?"

She started toward the sconce again, but he touched her arm, stopping her. "She said you still have plenty of years left in you."

"Mr. Bryant!"

He held up his hands. "She said it, not me."

She yanked on her cuffs. "The two of you gossiped about me?"

"Not in the way you mean. Mrs. Lockhart has a way of getting a fella to spill out more information than he has a mind to. By the time I got her home, she'd learned I was planning to ask you to the festivities." He pulled on his ear. "Once she found that out, she gave me all kinds of tips and advice."

Essie stiffened. "Like what?"

"She said you'd hide behind your spinsterhood—"

"I'm not hiding!"

"She said you'd worry over what people would think—"

"Well, of course I'd worry what people would think. I have a business to run and a reputation to uphold. I can't be acting like a schoolgirl. Every one of my business acquaintances will be there."

"She said you'd not want to step out with an employee—"

"And she's absolutely right! That would be the height of stupidity."

"She said your eyes shoot out sparks when you feel passionately about something." His voice dropped and he took a step closer. "I can see she's right."

Essie retreated a step. "The answer is still no. Thank you for asking."

She continued turning out lanterns all the way around the room. He didn't move or say a thing. One more sconce left. The one at the entrance.

"Are you coming, Mr. Bryant?" Her voice sounded shrill, even to her own ears.

He settled his hat on his head. "Yes, ma'am."

He took his time, then instead of heading to the door, he removed her shawl from its hook and held it open for her.

Swallowing, she turned her back. He draped it across her shoulders, turned out the final lamp, opened the door and waited.

"You are not walking me home."

He said nothing. Just held the door.

She hurried outside, but no matter how fast she walked, he stayed by her side. She suppressed a groan, chagrined that she'd allowed things to come to this.

She was still shocked by the objections he'd heard from Mrs. Lockhart. No doubt he had expected her to disown them, coming from his lips, but they had the opposite effect. Whatever attraction she might have felt for him, whatever scruples she'd been thinking to set aside before, the objections made perfect sense. After all, she was the boss and he was the worker. She had wealth and standing in the community, he had nothing.

What would people say if they saw him courting her? They would laugh at the difference in age and station. They would whisper behind her back about how desperate she'd become. They'd say he was after her wealth or, worse, her virtue.

And for all she knew, they'd be right. She could hardly trust her own judgment when it came to matters of the heart.

No. She had long since reconciled herself to being unmarried. Once she had finally embraced singleness, she found it suited her quite nicely. She must keep that at the forefront of her mind.

Tony never would have made his offer if Mrs. Lockhart hadn't put him up to it, and now that Essie had refused, he ought to be grateful. It went against all his principles to complicate his personal mission by pursuing a woman. Instead, however, her refusal roused a deep-seated instinct to hunt, capture and conquer.

Essie was churning up dust just ahead of him, dragging him along like a fish on a hook. He lengthened his stride to keep up with her. The faster she bolted, the more he wanted to stop her, but they were almost halfway to her house and he still didn't know what he'd say if he did.

Still, he reached out, gently grabbing her elbow. "Slow down. You're moving faster than a deacon taking up a collection."

She yanked herself free and spun to face him. "I wouldn't be going so fast if you would leave me be."

Her chest was heaving. A few bits of hair had slipped loose of the fancy twist decorating the back of her head, and he wondered what she'd do if he reached over and took the pins out to let it fall.

"I like your hat," he said.

A bit of the starch immediately left her. "Th-thank you."

"You're welcome."

She touched the back of her head and discovered her disheveled hair. With jerky movements, she stuffed bits and pieces into place.

"Why won't you go with me?" he asked.

She closed her eyes for a moment before answering. "Because I'm your boss. It is simply out of the question."

"I don't believe you."

Surprise followed by a look of wariness crossed over her face.

He clasped her hand. "Why won't you go with me?"

Her eyes welled up. "I can't," she whispered. "I can't do this again. Please don't ask it of me."

He stroked her inner wrist with his thumb, catching part glove and part skin. "Can't do what again?"

She tugged on her hand.

He interlocked their fingers. "Tell me."

"We've an entire town of young, pretty girls much more suited to your age. I'm sure any one of them would be thrilled to accompany you."

"I don't want to go with them."

"Why not?"

"Because I want to go with you."

"Why?"

"Why?" He hesitated, stumbling over his thoughts. "Why do I want to go with you? You're asking me why?"

"Yes." She looked straight at him, a touch of confusion in her expression and not a little vulnerability.

In a whoosh, his pulse calmed, his vision cleared, the tension left him. "Because, Essie, you have real pretty eyes. You're nicely put together. You're not flighty and giggly like all those young girls you seem so anxious to thrust upon me. You showed an incredible amount of strength and character when Brianna was bitten by that snake. And when you smile, you have two dimples that I noticed the very first time I saw you. Remember? You'd just fallen off the banister."

She'd gone stone still. "I didn't fall off. My heel broke."

"Go with me, Essie."

"No."

"Why?"

"It's . . . complicated."

"It's not. It's the simplest of things and it's done every day by men and women all over God's creation."

"Not by me. And I won't change my mind. So will you please let me go?"

He studied her. She meant every word. He dropped his hold.

She tucked her arm against her waist, well out of his reach. "Good night, Mr. Bryant."

"I'm walking you home, Essie."

"Please don't."

He swept his hand in an "after you" gesture.

The pace she set was not exactly breakneck, but it wasn't leisurely, either. He wanted to take her elbow but reconciled himself to simply walking beside her. They approached her house and he opened the gate.

"Thank you for seeing me home, Mr. Bryant. I believe I can make it to the door by myself."

He tugged the rim of his hat. "As you wish, ma'am."

She backed through the gate, then spun and raced up her sidewalk and into the safety of her home.

CHAPTER | TWELVE

THE FOURTH OF JULY dawned full of promise. After breakfast, Tony went out on the streets, which were already packed with people. The whole of Corsicana was outdoors, basking under sunny skies punctuated by the occasional cloud.

He set a jaunty pace, falling into step with the people around him. Children darted through the crowds, and a morning breeze blew down the lane, rustling ladies' skirts. At Beaton Street, he paused while a marching band passed through the intersection, serenading the town with patriotic tunes.

He eyed a taffy vendor urging him to buy, but he shook his head. He couldn't afford such frivolities. Every penny counted.

A pang of homesickness washed over him and he wondered if his mother and Anna would be attending Beaumont's celebration. In years past, he'd always been their escort. Now they'd be adrift in the crowds—or worse, they would be under Darius's thumb.

He'd only received one letter from them, a quick note conveying Mother's relief that he'd found some work and her chagrin over Darius's disregard for showing proper respect for the dead. At the time, though, both she and Anna were still in black.

A stray tabby wove between Tony's legs. He stroked its matted fur, then followed the band as they made their way to the Velocipede Club. Essie was hosting a public ride and he aimed to witness the spectacle firsthand.

On the way, he saw familiar faces from the rigs. Most of his working buddies had started their celebration in the saloons and would not find their way out for at least another hour. A few of the oilmen, however, had already imbibed and were ready to commence with the day's activities.

Females of every age, size, and shape came bedecked in all their finery. He watched them kick up the back of their skirts as they strolled on the arms of their husbands, fathers, and beaus.

He wondered what Essie was wearing and how much it would cost to win her box supper. Slipping his hand in his pocket, he ran his fingers over the coins jingling there. He'd have to set himself a limit—not so low as to be insulting, but not so high he couldn't part with the money.

If someone else outbid him, he'd just have to live with it. He would bid, though, for as long as he could, on whatever basket matched her clothing.

———

The care and planning that went into a woman's Fourth of July outfit was second only to her Easter attire. For Essie, the burden was greater, because she had a reputation to maintain, and she no longer had her mother to conspire with. As she approached the bandstand of the Velocipede Club, she glanced down at her white dotted-swiss gown one last time hoping she had achieved her desired effect. The front of her skirt was pleated in, its folds caught with a series of blue bows, each held by a fancy button.

She smoothed her bodice of blue accordion-pleated mousseline de soie and straightened her fancy straw hat. It held a cluster of red roses on the left side, surrounded by loops of blue ribbon and white lace.

The club was filled to capacity. Looking out at the crowd, she saw new members, established members, and plenty of adventurers, too, willing to give the bicycle a try just this once. The bleachers burst with spectators in an array of colorful attire, calling down cheerfully to the riders as they prepared.

The Collin Street Bakery provided refreshments at a table in the back. Bicyclers stood about the rink visiting with each other as they waited for the music to start. Attendance this year was even higher than the last. She decided she would most likely have to hold two public rides in '99.

"The band's about settled there on the platform," Uncle Melvin said, his sheriff's badge winking. "You ready to get this thing goin'?"

"I'm ready," she said, tucking her hand into his elbow and noting he'd curled and waxed the ends of his bushy gray moustache.

He assisted her onto the stage, then let out a piercing whistle that cut through the crowd, silencing them.

"Here's the rules," Uncle Melvin shouted. "No chewin'. No spittin'. No walkin' across the rink. Food and drinks are free. If you're of a mind to give one of these machines a twirl, then don't cut anybody off. Don't run anybody over. And don't park in the middle o' the track. Any questions?"

None were forthcoming.

"Essie-girl?" he said. "You got anything you wanna say?"

She stepped to the front. "Welcome to the Fourth Annual Corsicana Velocipede Club's Group Ride. We're so very glad you're here." She turned to the band director. "Mr. Creiz?"

The conductor held up his baton, bringing the band to attention, then commenced on the downstroke, starting the event off with their traditional "Bicycle Built for Two."

The wheelers mounted their bikes and began whizzing around the track, singing to the music while friends and family joined in from the bleachers. Mr. Peeples, an employee of the Anheuser-Busch Brewing Company, wobbled back and forth on his machine, had a near miss but, to his credit, kept his balance and avoided taking a spill.

"You go on ahead, honey," Melvin hollered in her ear. "I see Deputy Howard signaling me."

He gave her a peck on the cheek, then headed to the other side of the stage. Lifting her skirts, she started down the stairs, accepting a hand that shot out to assist her before realizing it belonged to Tony.

His appearance made her pause. Gone were the blue denim trousers, rawhide boots, and cowboy hat. In their place stood a gentleman in the very latest of summer fashions.

He wore a blue pincheck four-button coat that fit his broad shoulders so well it could not possibly have been borrowed. She'd developed an eye for such details after working in Hamilton Crook's mercantile.

She noted at once that the fine dress shirt, celluloid collar, and cuffs Tony wore were of the very best quality. The silk tie around his neck had been knotted by an experienced hand. Even the brown Derby on his head seemed particularly fine. How could a roustabout afford such fine clothing? What's more, how could he wear them with such ease?

He said something to her, but the music swallowed his words.

From the corner of her eye, she saw Mr. Peeples accidentally cut off Mr. Davis. Essie couldn't catch Mr. Davis's words as he swerved to the side, but she had an inkling as the man's face turned red and he shook his fist.

Mr. Peeples smiled and waved, fully confident in his newfound ability.

She continued down the steps, then stood before Tony. His gaze traveled over her hat, her new gown, her face.

"You look beautiful," he said, bending close so she could hear him.

"Thank you." She kept her voice neutral.

"Will you ride with me?"

"I'm sorry. I've hostess duties to attend to."

As if verifying the truth of her words, a loud shriek, followed by a sharp, "Look out!" caused her to whirl around.

Mr. Peeples jerked his handlebars sharply to the left to avoid running into one matron, only to, instead, broadside another.

Lifting her skirts just above the toes, Essie hurried to the collision.

———

Tony stood on the periphery of the bicycle club watching Essie welcome guests, soothe ruffled feathers, manage crises, calm drunks, enroll new members and sell bicycle accessories. He was content to watch her work until Deputy Billy John Howard approached her.

The crowd drifted away as the deputy moved in. People in Corsicana tended to give the small man a wide berth. All the rumors Tony had heard about Howard came back to him.

He was surprised at how familiar the man was with Essie. As a protégé of her Uncle Melvin, it was natural that they'd be acquainted, but the way she stiffened as he hovered near her—and the way she bobbed and weaved to avoid his covertly straying hands—put Tony on his guard.

What was the deputy playing at? If he'd been courting Essie, Mrs. Lockhart would have said, and it was obvious from Essie's reactions that Howard's attentions were unwelcome.

Several times, Tony started forward to intervene, then stopped himself. It was none of his business, after all. And if Essie was a distraction from his purpose, then trouble with a deputy was even worse.

Howard settled his hand on Essie's waist, and all Tony's reasoning evaporated. He headed toward them. She twisted from Howard's touch, but he immediately returned it to the curve of her back and leaned over to whisper something in her ear.

He couldn't tell what the man was saying, but whatever it was caused Essie to flush.

The band finished up the last chorus of "A Hot Time in the Old Town." Spectators clapped. Wheelers continued to ride.

" . . . so what do you say?" Howard asked.

"If you would excuse me, I have things to attend to," Essie said in undertones, once again shoving aside his hand.

He grabbed her wrist, careful to keep it hidden in the folds of her skirt. "You listen here, missy. I've had just about enough—"

"Miss Spreckelmeyer?" Tony said, joining them. "Mrs. Gillespie needs your assistance."

The deputy puffed out his chest, making sure Tony saw the star pinned to his vest. "She'll be along in a minute."

"She's needed now." Tony kept his posture relaxed but allowed a bit of steel to enter his voice.

Howard narrowed his eyes. "I don't believe we've—"

"Billy John," said Preacher Wortham, stepping to their circle and extending his hand.

The deputy had no choice but to let go of Essie or leave Wortham's hand hanging in the air.

"I've been meaning to talk to you about the appalling amount of liquor consumed within our town," the preacher said, placing a hand on Howard's shoulder and turning him toward the door. "You don't mind if I steal the deputy for a moment, do you, Essie?"

Tony saw a look pass between the preacher and Essie, leaving him no doubt as to Wortham's motivations. The preacher had done what Tony could not.

"Mr. Bryant here said Shirley was in need of me." She turned to Tony. "Lead the way."

Cupping Essie's elbow, Tony escorted her toward a table in the far corner where a German man and his partner were giving out slices of fruitcake.

"What was all that about?" Tony asked.

"Nothing."

"Didn't look like 'nothing' to me. How long has he been bothering you?"

"Just a bit longer than you have."

He let go of her. "You view me the same way you do him?"

She paused, looking startled at the suggestion. "No, of course not. I meant no offense." She looked around. "I don't see Shirley over here."

Taking a deep breath, he decided to ignore the sting of her careless remark. "Mrs. Gillespie doesn't need you. I made that up."

"*Did* you?" She took a moment to study him, her guard slipping a bit as she considered his gesture. "Well, thank you, then—for coming to my assistance. I appreciate it."

He picked up a slice of fruitcake, broke a piece off and handed it to her.

She popped it into her mouth. "Ummm. That's good. I didn't realize how hungry I was."

He started to ask her about Howard again but realized this wasn't the place.

"Well." She brushed the crumbs from her fingers. "I'm afraid you'll have to excuse me. I see Mrs. Tyner is waving me over."

He nodded his head in acknowledgment, but she had already walked away, slipping him as quickly as she had the deputy.

———

Beneath an old wooden pavilion, Tony strolled past the tables lining the auctioneer's dais, each of them bowed with the weight of box suppers. Not a one of them held frippery to match Essie's outfit. Tony once again surveyed the collection of baskets, ribbons, bunting, bows, and gewgaws. Where in the blazes was her box?

"Quite a selection, isn't it?" the preacher said, joining him. "Do you see one that takes your fancy?"

"Not just yet, I'm afraid," Tony answered.

The preacher stuck out his hand, and Tony clasped it.

"Good to see you again," Wortham said. "What did you think of the service on Sunday?"

"I enjoyed it very much."

The preacher wasn't the only one of Essie's patrons to have arrived at the red-white-and-blue-festooned pavilion. Most of the others, having concluded their group ride, milled about the fairgrounds with other locals in anticipation of the box-supper auction.

"So," Wortham said, "are you looking for any basket in particular?"

"Matter of fact, I am. What about you? Is your wife's box somewhere in here?"

Wortham smiled. "I'm afraid hers might be a bit difficult to find seeing as how I haven't got a wife."

Tony nodded, remembering Grandpa had mentioned that the time Wortham and

Harley came out to the patch. Tony didn't think he'd ever met a preacher with no wife. Those two things just went together like ham and eggs.

"Which one are you going to bid on, then?" Tony asked.

"Oh, I don't have a particular one in mind this year. What about you?"

Tony scanned the box suppers. "I was looking for Miss Spreckelmeyer's."

"Were you, now?" Wortham lifted his brows. "Well, what do you know about that. Is she aware you want to bid on it?"

"She might have some inkling. How much competition do you think I'll have?"

A mischievous smile grew on the preacher's face. "Considering who she's been sharing her basket with for the past four years, I'd say you have some mighty big competition."

Tony's chest tightened.

Chuckling, Wortham slapped him on the shoulder. "Don't worry. It's nobody you need concern yourself with."

"It's not the deputy, is it?"

"Goodness, no." Wortham's frown made his distaste for the deputy plain, but he disguised it quickly enough.

Tony rubbed his mouth. "Do you know what was going on this afternoon when you interrupted Howard and her?"

"I aim to find out."

"You interested in Miss Spreckelmeyer?" Tony asked, narrowing his eyes.

The preacher gave him a long look. "I was at one time. But she turned me down."

She seemed to make a habit of rebuffing suitors, Tony thought. He wondered if Wortham had given up on her yet.

"You bidding on her box supper today, Preacher?"

"No, I'm not."

Tony released a pent-up breath. He'd never been one to share his thoughts with strangers, even if they were preachers, but he figured Wortham could answer some of the questions rattling around in his head. "So how long have you known her?"

"Essie? A long time." Wortham smiled. "We've been friends for as far back as I can remember."

"That so?"

"She was a grand playmate. She taught me how to fish, shoot, swim, climb trees, and gig frogs. I was half in love with her before I ever reached adolescence."

Gig frogs? "So what happened?"

"She turned me down flat. Said I was too much like a little brother. Kinda takes the starch out of a fellow, if you know what I mean."

Tony smiled. "Well, don't feel bad. She's fighting me tooth and nail, as well."

As soon as he said the words, he regretted them. He hadn't meant to make light of his feelings toward her, even if he didn't exactly know what they were.

The preacher picked up on the false note in Tony's voice. The man's posture never changed, but his tone turned colder than a well chain in December.

"Just make sure you don't hurt her, Bryant, or else you'll answer to me."

Tony shook his head. "I'd never hurt her, sir."

For the first time, he sized Wortham up as a man, not a preacher. He was short, but he was no weakling. The way he filled out his jacket was nothing to scoff at. Tony figured he could throw a good punch if he had a mind to.

The crowd had grown in anticipation of the auction, gathering tightly within the pavilion. A group of young ladies clustered together, giggling and trying hard not to see if the fellow of their choosing was lingering nearby. Essie was nowhere in sight.

Wortham took Tony by the shoulders and turned him so he was facing east. "She's up there. Under that big oak tree."

A couple hundred yards away on the crest of a green hill, a massive oak tree dwarfed Essie while providing an abundance of shade beneath its outstretched branches.

"And her basket isn't for sale," he added. "It's been off the market for a long time. If'n you want to share it with her, you'll have to do some mighty slick talking. Good luck."

Pushing the rim of his hat back, Tony took in the sight. Young boys rolled down the slope, racing to see who could reach bottom first, with no regard for the clumps of yellow wild flowers they crushed along the way. But Essie kept her head down, paying them no attention.

He wove through the crowd, greeting several of the men he worked with. To his surprise, many of the women he'd met at the Velocipede Club last week stopped and introduced him to their husbands. Mrs. Bunert was married to a harness maker. Mrs. Fowler, the blacksmith. Mrs. Garitty, the Opera House president. And Mrs. Whiteselle, the mayor. By the time he made it to Essie's hill, the auction in the pavilion was in full swing.

The farther up the incline he moved, the better he could see. With her white skirt billowing out around her, she scribbled in a journal of some sort that she'd propped on her lap. Beside her lay her gloves, hat, and box supper. She'd decorated her basket to match the ribbons in her hat and the bows on her skirt.

As he drew closer, he half expected to be overtaken by a rival. He looked around and saw no one, but his imagination still ran rampant. What would he do if a man stepped out from behind the tree and took his place beside Essie, neatly edging Tony out?

A blue-checkered cloth covering her meal had been nudged aside, and she occasionally removed bits and pieces of the basket's contents, absently nibbling on them. So caught up was she in her writings that she didn't hear him approach. Didn't know he was there until his shadow fell across her blanket.

Shading her eyes, she looked up. "Mr. Bryant!" She slammed her journal shut. "I didn't expect . . . I thought you were . . ." She took a deep breath. "How do you do?"

He removed his hat. "How do *you* do?"

"I'm fine. Thank you."

"May I?" he asked, indicating the blanket.

"Well, um, actually, I was, um, saving it, sort of."

"Saving it?" He looked around. "For whom?"

She placed her pencil atop her journal. "For the person I usually share my box supper with."

Disappointment gripped him. "And who would that be?"

"Christ."

He blinked. "Christ? You mean, *Jesus* Christ?"

"The very same."

"You share your box supper with Jesus Christ?"

"Yes. I do."

Relief poured through him. No suitor would intercept him, after all. He knelt on the blanket, then settled down beside her.

"As it happens," he said, "the Lord and I are very close. I'm sure He wouldn't mind if I were to join the two of you."

"I'm sure He wouldn't."

He placed his hat next to hers.

"I, on the other hand, mind very much."

He froze.

"I cherish this time I spend with Him. The nice thing about all this is that if you would like to take your meal with Him, He can be in two places at once."

He could not believe he was having this conversation. "Essie, it's you I want to have supper with."

"I'm sorry. Perhaps if you hurry, you can acquire one of the boxes up for auction."

"I don't want any of those boxes. I want yours." He sighed. "Is my company really that repulsive?"

She looked away. "It's not you personally, Tony."

"Then what is it?"

"You're my employee. It would be unseemly."

Couples began to trickle out from the pavilion as suppers were auctioned off. Mothers put their youngsters down on blankets for naps. A group of older men sharing stories and a liquor jug clustered together on the edges of the fairgrounds. Up on the hill, it all seemed so far away.

Rubbing the back of his neck, he glanced at her lap. "What were you writing?"

She kept the pages of her journal firmly closed within her grip. "Nothing."

"Something, surely?"

"Nothing that need concern you."

His stomach growled. He glanced at her supper. "You know, I was really looking forward to today because I haven't had anything to eat since I arrived other than the fare Mr. Castle serves up in his drugstore."

Her brow crinkled for the briefest of moments.

He picked up his hat and started to rise.

"Mr. Castle's meals aren't so bad," she said.

"Not if you like to eat the same thing over and over every three days."

"There are other restaurants in town."

"Not that a roustabout can afford."

After a slight hesitation, she moistened her lips, then gently tugged the covering off her basket. Fried chicken, green corn patties, cheese wafers, potato croquettes, hard-boiled eggs, two fluffy biscuits, and a broken-off fig tart. His mouth watered.

"Somebody's sampled the dessert already," he said, making no effort to disguise the teasing in his voice. "Was that you or the Lord?"

She studied him for a moment, then moved the basket between them. "Just remember, Eli's sons both dropped dead when they ate food prepared for God."

He smiled and settled back down on the blanket. "That was a consecrated offering. And made before Christ came to fulfill the law. Besides, I've already sent up a quick prayer asking if He'd mind."

She gave a slight smile. "And what did He say?"

"To help myself."

She huffed, but he could see her heart wasn't in the resistance. He peeled a bite off a chicken breast with his teeth, the crispy crust a perfect foil for the tender meat.

Back in the pavilion, a heated competition had commenced, the shouting so loud it nearly drowned out the auctioneer's voice. At the climax of the proceedings, everyone burst into applause.

Tony ate another piece of chicken, plus a sampling of corn, cheese, and potatoes before Essie finally joined in.

"Harley tells me Brianna is doing better," he said. "Have you seen her?"

"Yes. And every day the swelling goes down a little bit more. Today will be hard on her, though. Her father wouldn't let her come to the festivities."

"That's what Harley told me," he said. "But he and I came up with a scheme to cheer her up."

"What scheme?" she asked.

"Harley had his mother make up a box supper for him. He's going to take it over to Brianna's and pretend like it's hers, then 'buy' it from an imaginary auctioneer." He scanned the park. "As a matter of fact, I haven't seen him in a while, so it wouldn't surprise me if that's where he is now."

Essie's lips parted, her eyes softening. "I know Harley didn't think of that. Was it your idea?"

He shrugged. "It was the only thing I could come up with."

"It was wonderfully sweet."

He chuckled. "It oughta earn Harley a star or two." He reached for the half-eaten fig tart.

"What are you doing?" she asked.

"Having my half of dessert."

"That's not your half. That's my half."

He removed the partially eaten confection. "There were at least two portions of everything but the fig tart. So either you've eaten one and a half tarts, or you forgot to provide Christ with dessert."

"I made Him one."

"Then where is it?"

She didn't answer.

He wagged his finger at her. "You ate it already, didn't you? You ate the Lord's dessert and half of your own, and now you want the rest of mine?"

She eyed the tart longingly. "They're my favorite. And I didn't know you were coming."

"All right, then," he said, winking. "What will you give me for it?"

Her back went ramrod straight. "I'll not play those games with you, Mr. Bryant."

He started to laugh, but her stern, unwavering glare said she was serious.

"You may take the fig tart and go." Her voice was sharp, clipped.

"Whoa, there, girl. I was only kidding." He placed the tart back in the basket, then motioned for her to take it, but she remained stubbornly still.

"I was just teasing, Essie. I didn't mean anything by it."

"Didn't you?" She held up her hand, cutting off his denial. "I know exactly how men like you work. A charming word. A gallant gesture. Then you cast out some harmless bait—only it isn't harmless once it is taken. But by then it is too late. The damage is done."

She wadded up the checkered cloth and tossed it into her basket, along with her journal and pencil.

Tony sat still, stunned by the force behind her words, by the anger that surged up like a newly tapped well. And like a gusher, it had drenched everything around it, including him.

He placed a hand on her gloves before she could reach for them. "I'm sorry. I meant no offense. I have no idea what you thought I intended, but it wasn't dishonorable. You have my word."

"And just how do I know if your word is any good?"

He sucked in his breath. "Now, wait just a minute. What's that supposed to mean? You think I'd lie?"

She plucked up her gloves.

"Don't leave," he said, standing. "I'll be on my way. I never intended to chase you from the celebration. I know you've worked really hard today with your group ride and all. And I want you to enjoy yourself. Please."

She stilled, her hand on the basket handle, never once meeting his gaze.

"Thank you for the meal, Essie. It was the best I've had in a long while. You have a nice evening, now."

Placing his hat on his head, he headed down the hill without a single backward glance.

CHAPTER | THIRTEEN

SNAPPING THE BLANKET IN the air, Essie shook loose the dirt and debris. She should never have shared her lunch with Tony. She loved spending this time with the Lord and had no desire to replace it with a man simply because he couldn't afford a decent meal.

Folding the blanket in half and then fourths, she glanced at Tony's retreating figure. He'd reached the bottom of the hill and was making his way toward a game of horseshoes. Even from here the expensive cut of his clothes struck her.

His was no new outfit purchased for the holiday. The jacket, though brushed and well taken care of, draped his shoulders like a dear old friend. Only a man accustomed to wearing costly clothes could move in them with such ease.

She recalled Mr. Zimpelman attending his daughter's wedding in a suit clear from New York City, his work boots peeking out from the wool trousers puddling at his feet. His jacket had ridden too low, his vest too high. He'd tugged on his collar, tripped on his pant legs and soiled his ascot.

She smoothed the creases along the folds of her blanket. Tony didn't even seem to notice his fine clothes. He wore them with casual indifference, as if he were born to them.

Not for the first time, she wondered who his kin were and why he wasn't with them. She sighed. Whomever he was, he'd obviously come down in the world.

Perhaps she should have been a bit more sensitive to his plight, though she didn't regret sending him on his way. She'd celebrated her thirty-fourth birthday with her father, aunt, and uncle just last week. She had no interest in romantic pursuits.

Tony handed his jacket to another man, rolled up his sleeves and pitched a horseshoe. From where she was, she couldn't see how close he'd come to the stake, but judging by the amount of backslapping the other men gave him, he'd come mighty close.

She studied him for a moment more. The townsfolk were usually very reticent about accepting newcomers into the fold. Even with the boom, there was a clear delineation between the boomers and the native Corsicanans. Yet Tony had won over Mrs. Lockhart, the women of the Velocipede Club, and, if the game of horseshoes was any indication, several of the old-timers, as well.

Picking up her basket, she shook Tony from her thoughts, turned her mind to the many tasks awaiting her in her father's study, and made her way toward the sanctuary of home.

———

Darkness ushered in the much-anticipated Fourth of July dance. Crowds began drifting in the direction of the pavilion around dusk, but Tony hung back until the sound of fiddlers sawing on their instruments to foot-stomping music became irresistible.

He ducked inside. Strings of Japanese lanterns lined the covered area, splashing light on the festivities and attracting every bug in Corsicana. Tony tapped his toe, unused to attending a dance where he didn't know most everyone present.

He tried to stick to the sidelines, but no place was safe from the dancers. He jumped out of the way as an enthusiastic couple whirled by.

In their wake, a grandfatherly man glided with smooth finesse around the floor, his arm unable to reach around his partner—a large, elderly woman as wide as she was tall. A father stood in the center of the dancers, swaying to the music, his baby daughter in his arms. And a young man with a day's worth of beer in his belly coaxed a flushed young lady into an intimate embrace as he spun her across the floor.

The novelty of being just another oilman, as opposed to a "mighty Morgan," was both refreshing and disconcerting. Tony's anonymity provided him with a viewpoint he'd never experienced before. Still, he missed his family and the camaraderie of friends and neighbors who had known him for years.

"Good evening, Mr. Bryant."

Tony smiled at Mrs. Lockhart's greeting, tugged on his hat, and made room for her beside him. "Ma'am."

"I saw you shared a supper with Miss Spreckelmeyer."

His jovial mood dimmed a bit. "Yes, ma'am."

"How did it go?"

"Not too well. She ran me out on a rail, then left the celebration by herself and never came back."

"What happened?"

"I'm not exactly sure." He scratched the back of his head. "One minute we were carrying on a conversation, the next she was as sore as a frog on a hot skillet."

"Tell me exactly what you said."

"I can't really remember." He watched the dancers without seeing them, trying to recall what had caused Essie to ignite. "I just wanted my half of the fig tart and she started screeching at me."

Mrs. Lockhart tapped her finger against her cane, deep in thought. "Come by my house tomorrow night after dinner. I'll serve you up some coffee and sweets and we'll see if we can piece together where you went wrong."

"Sweets? Well, ma'am, you have yourself a date." He removed his hat and bowed. "Until then, may I have this dance?"

Hooking her cane on her elbow, she stepped into his arms and looked at him over her glasses. "Just try to keep up."

With that, she attempted to lead him around the floor, but he admonished her with a stern look and stiff arms, until, laughing, she acquiesced and followed his lead.

"Please come in," Mrs. Lockhart said, pulling the door open.

She smiled, causing the rice powder frescoing her face to congregate in the hollows of her wrinkles. A cameo brooch decorated her throat. The pearl gray gown she wore was dated but very finely made with gold-embroidered trim. Long, tight sleeves covered her arms, bracelets jangling against one wrist. No cane in sight.

Swiping his hat from his head, Tony offered up a quick prayer of thanksgiving that he'd "dressed" for the occasion. On a hunch that Mrs. Lockhart would entertain in high style, he'd taken special care with his toilette. Then he'd thoroughly brushed his clothes, blackened his shoes, and attached spotless cuffs, collar, and handkerchief.

Taking her hand, he raised it to his lips. "How enchanting you look this evening, ma'am."

She took his hat and hooked it on an ornate hall tree, then beckoned him inside. When she turned, he was surprised to find a bustle swinging from side to side. He couldn't remember the last time he'd seen anyone wear one.

Entering the drawing room, he took note of the ornaments, bric-a-brac, and gadgets covering every inch of available space. Framed photographs lined the walls as thickly as wallpaper. A piano sat at the far end of the room, bookcases on either side.

She led him to two upholstered easy chairs with fringe skirting their arms and feet. A tray with china cups and a sterling coffeepot graced the table next to her chair, along with two small plates of fancy cake. She poured him a cup and he settled in across from her.

"Do you play, Mrs. Lockhart?" he asked, indicating the piano.

"Certainly. But I won't be persuaded to do so this evening. We've much more serious pursuits planned." Picking up a tiny pair of silver tongs, she looked at him. "Sugar? Cream?"

"Sugar, please," he answered, willing to let her lead the conversation. She obviously knew who he was, and his main purpose for the visit was to ensure no one else did. If he had to endure her instruction on how to woo Essie in exchange for silence about his identity, he could think of worse prices to pay.

"First," she said, "I think it's time you come clean."

Leaning forward, he accepted the cup and plate of fancy cake she offered. "I'm Tony Bryant Morgan. Son of Blake and Leah Morgan."

Her facial features relaxed, losing some of their sternness. "And why are you pretending to be otherwise?"

"My father disinherited me, so I have dropped his name and carry my mother's instead. I'm not pretending to be anything other than who I am."

"Dropping your father's name does not make you any less a Morgan than you were before."

The tick in his jaw began to pulse. "It does to me."

She poured a dollop of cream into her coffee. "Who all knows?"

"About my being here? My mother, my sister, and my best friend in Beaumont."

"No one here in town?"

"No, ma'am. Not unless you've told them."

She shook her head. "No, no. I haven't said a word."

Relieved, he began to relax. "I'd like to keep it that way, if you don't mind."

"You're going to be found out."

"Eventually, perhaps. For now, though, I'd like to remain anonymous."

Picking up a spoon, she swished it in her drink, then tapped it against the edge of her cup. "Very well. We'll talk about that later. Tell me, instead, exactly what happened yesterday with Essie."

He hesitated. "The whole thing was a mistake, actually. I'd really rather not talk about it."

"Nonsense. What happened?"

He took a deep breath. "Do you know who Essie usually shares her box supper with?"

"Yes, of course. The whole town knows. And though no one would say anything to her face, plenty is said behind her back."

Mrs. Lockhart's words evoked an unexpected surge of protectiveness in Tony. It was one thing for him to think of Essie's picnic with the Lord as a bit unconventional. It was another thing for the townsfolk to make fun of her over it.

"The fact that she shared her supper with you did not go unnoticed, though," Mrs. Lockhart added.

"How long has it been since she put her box up for auction?"

"Three—no, four years now. But that's neither here nor there. I want to know why she chased you off."

"Like I told you last night, I'm not really sure. And it doesn't really matter anyway." He took a bite of cake.

"You had to have said or done something."

He shrugged. "I teased her a little bit about eating most of the dessert, then asked her what the last fig tart was worth to her. That's all I can remember."

"Ahhhh. You hinted that you'd let her have the last tart if she were to pay some kind of forfeit?"

"I never said that at all."

"No. Of course you didn't. But games of forfeit are a risky gambit. Take, for example, *Repented at Leisure,* where Mr. Flexmore robbed Miss Kite of her innocence through clever games. Perhaps Essie was simply being cautious."

Tony blinked. "I beg your pardon? Mr. Who did *what*?"

"Mr. Flexmore. According to Mrs. Bertha Clay, he has a face no one can look into without admiration, one that irresistibly attracts man, woman, and child alike, and he uses it shamelessly."

Tony set down his empty plate, cake crumbs decorating its surface. "And who is Mr. Flexmore?"

"He's head of one of the oldest families in England."

"And he did something to Essie?"

Mrs. Lockhart rolled her eyes. "No. For heaven's sake, he's a fictional character."

Tony rubbed his forehead. "What exactly are you talking about, ma'am?"

The elderly woman began to rise. Tony jumped up and assisted her to her feet. "Come," she said. "I'll show you."

She led him to the bookshelves on the far wall and began running her finger along the spines of books, her bracelets tinkling as she searched for one volume in particular. He scanned several of the titles. *Lady Damer's Secret. Foiled by Love. A Fiery Ordeal.*

Incredulous, he could only stare. The entire bookcase was filled with romance novels, rows and rows of them. He quickly looked for just one classic or tome of learning or even a dialogue or recitation. Instead, he found *Evelyn's Folly, A Crooked Path, A Pair of Blue Eyes.*

"Ah," she said, pulling a volume from the shelf. "Here we are. *Repented at Leisure.*" She thumbed through the book, stopped about a third of the way through and held it up to him. "There. You see?"

Looking over her shoulder, he glanced at the chapter heading. *Weaving the Spell.*

"This is where Mr. Flexmore uses his charm to engage Miss Kite's affections." She flipped to the next chapter.

Deeper and Deeper Still.

"Here he convinces her that her parents' motives for keeping them apart are self-serving." She turns to yet another chapter, sighs and shakes her head. "This is where Miss Kite's downfall occurs."

How the Plot Succeeded.

She snapped the book closed. "So you see? In order for a young lady to guard herself from such things, she must be always on the alert." She pushed the novel back onto the shelf. "Essie is a smart girl. Very conscientious. At the first hint of such shenanigans, I've no doubt she would squash the man's pursuit immediately."

Tony straightened his spine. "Are you comparing me to Mr. Flexmore?"

"No, no," she said, waving her hand in the air and making her way back to her chair. "I'm simply suggesting Essie might have."

"Essie's read *Repented at Leisure*?" he asked, appalled.

Mrs. Lockhart lowered herself into the chair, her bustle keeping her from sitting very far back on the cushion. "I'm afraid not." She shook her head with regret. "I lend my books to her all the time, but she never reads them. Prefers highfalutin authors like Mr. Dumas and Mr. Twain—though they obviously haven't taught her a thing about the human heart, or she'd have long since been married."

She poured Tony a fresh cup of coffee. "No, my books are the ticket. And since Essie won't listen to these authorities, you must. Otherwise, all hope for her is lost."

He sat down, the books once again drawing his attention. Hundreds. There were hundreds of them.

"I think what you need to do, Mr. Mor—Bryant, is to ask Essie's father for permission to court her."

Having just accepted the cup of coffee, he'd been taking a swallow and ended up singeing his tongue. "Court her?"

"Like in *The Squire's Darling*," she continued. "The squire falls in love with Lady Carline—only he isn't a squire at all. Ends up, he was in reality of noble birth, only he wanted to be loved for himself, not his position or title. So he disguised himself as a squire. Like you."

"Like me?" He was having difficulty keeping up with the conversation.

"That's kind of what you are doing, isn't it? You being a Morgan, yet pretending to be a boomer." She nodded, satisfied with her conclusion. "Yes. It's perfect. You must ask Sullivan for permission as soon as possible."

He had no notion of what to say. She was citing her romance novels the way a Latin tutor invoked Cicero. Yet he had to admit, asking Essie's father for permission to court her was something he'd already considered.

The fact that he could achieve his goals much more quickly by marrying into his empire instead of building it was not lost on him, though that wasn't his motivation. But if Essie were to learn of his identity, she might mistake his intentions completely. And it was for precisely that reason that he should suppress his interest in her.

"I'm afraid this match won't work, Mrs. Lockhart," he said. "I can't afford to pay court to Essie anyway. As I said before, my father disinherited me."

She reached over and patted his knee. "I am sorry about that, Mr. Bryant. It must be extremely difficult to go from being heir apparent one day to a nobody the next."

He raised a brow. "I'm not sure I consider myself a 'nobody' just yet."

"That's because deep down you are still a Morgan. In the meanwhile, there are many ways to court a young lady without spending money. Why, Mr. Kent courted Miss Awdrey with long walks in the park, quiet moments on the porch, and Sunday dinners with her family."

"Are they married now?"

"Oh my, yes. And very happily, I might add."

"Do they live here in Corsicana?"

"No, no. They were the two in Mrs. Barrie's *When a Man's Single*."

He cleared his throat. "I see." Finishing his drink, he stood. "Thank you for the refreshments and the . . . enlightening conversation, ma'am. I'm afraid, however, I must take my leave now."

He assisted her up. Before she walked him to the door, she moved to the bookcase and pulled out a novel.

"Essie will be extremely easy to court without money." She made her way to the entry hall and handed him his hat. "All you need do is ask her to go fishing, and you'll win her heart for certain. Meanwhile," she said, tucking the novel into his hand, "it would profit you to study Mr. Chester's speech in chapter five and meditate on his words."

Out of politeness, he accepted the volume. Once he made it down her sidewalk and onto the street, he glanced at the title.

When False Tongues Speak.

CHAPTER | FOURTEEN

PAPA BLESSED THE FOOD, served himself up a portion of mashed potatoes, then passed them across the kitchen table to Essie.

"Tony Bryant asked if he could court you," he said.

Essie plunked the bowl of potatoes on the table. Papa paid her no attention, just kept piling his dinner plate with food as if he'd merely mentioned what the phase of tonight's moon would be.

"I beg your pardon?"

"You heard me."

"And how did you respond?"

He sawed a piece of roast beef on his plate, jabbed it with his fork and stuck it in his mouth. "Said it was up to you."

"Well, then." She took a sip of ice tea. "You can tell him I'm not interested."

"You'll have to tell him yourself." He dunked his bread in his gravy.

She looked up. "What do you mean?"

"You're old enough now to make up your own mind about such things," he said around his mouthful. "No need for the fellas to be coming to me anymore. And that's exactly what I told Bryant. So I guess it's you he'll be asking permission from next. You can tell him your decision then."

"He's our employee."

"Yep."

She set down her glass. "Papa, you know how I feel about this subject."

He met her gaze for the first time. "What's past is past, Essie. Let it go. And in the meanwhile, I'm getting too old and soft to keep breaking these boys' hearts. You can just do it yourself if you're so bent on it."

"I hardly think anyone's heart has been broken on my account."

"Just the same, I've made my decision."

She crinkled the napkin in her lap. "But don't you see? By giving no answer at all, you are in essence giving your permission."

"If you tell him no, I'll stand behind you."

"I don't want you to stand behind me, I want you to stand *in front* of me. It's the father's job to refuse suits of this sort, not the daughter's."

He shook his head. "If you want to get particular, the father's job is to decide what's best for his daughter. So if you want me to do the answering, you'll have to let me do the deciding, too. And you may not like my decision."

"That's blackmail."

A shadow from the oil rig in the backyard moved across the room as the sun began to set, casting her father in momentary darkness as he softly burped into his napkin, then continued to eat.

"Papa, I'm too old. If I step out with a young, handsome man like Mr. Bryant, the whole town will laugh."

"Yep."

Her jaw slackened, stung that he hadn't contradicted her. "Don't you care?"

"Nope. And you don't, either, when it suits you. If you want to wear bloomers or ride a train to New York City by yourself, you don't seem bothered by what the townsfolk have to say about it. So don't go picking a fight with me just because you're scared of anything that wears trousers."

She shoved back her chair. "I'm not scared."

"No? Then where are you running off to?"

Her stomach tightened. "All this talk has made me lose my appetite, is all."

"You needn't eat if you don't want to, but I'd like you to stay and keep me company. I get lonesome when I have to eat by myself."

She forced herself to take a deep breath. Wearing bloomers and going to New York City were nothing like being courted by a man. Papa was comparing apples to oranges. But she would not disrespect him by running to her room like a spoiled child. She scooted her chair back up, picked up her fork and glanced across the table.

He smiled politely. There would be no changing his mind. He really was going to make her be the one to turn Tony down.

———

Tony looked up from the grindstone and saw that work all around him had stopped. Up in the derrick, the men stood still, shielding their eyes from the sun to glance off to the west, and on the ground they left what they were doing to wander in that direction. Tony stepped back, placed his hands on his head and twisted from side to side before jogging over to see what the fuss was about.

"What is it?" he asked a man in back.

"They're saying somebody fell from the Tarrant Street rig."

"Is he all right?" Tony asked, but no one seemed to know.

He pushed his way through to where Grandpa stood wiping his brow with a soiled handkerchief.

"Who was it?" Tony asked him.

Grandpa frowned. "Sharpley," he said, "the derrickman over on Tarrant Street. Lost his footing and plunged from the double board to the ground."

Just then Jeremy came running from the direction of Sharpley's rig. He pulled up next to Grandpa out of breath.

"Is he dead?" Grandpa asked.

"Naw," Jeremy said with a shake of his head. "But the ones who seen him land said his leg was all stuck out like this." He laid his arm over his leg, forming a hideous contortion. "They stopped the work and Moss is bringing him this way in the wagon."

A few moments later, the wagon creaked by with the company's tool pusher on the buckboard and the pitiful Sharpley laid out back.

Tony couldn't get a good look at him, but he could hear the boy's moans, then an outright shriek when Moss hit a rut in the road. The same rut that had caused Essie to lose her balance before and thus reinforce the nickname the men had long since given to her: Errant Essie.

A few minutes later, Essie herself zoomed by on her bike. She stood in the stirrups of her machine, her skirt and petticoats flapping as she pumped the pedals.

The men stopped again, but she paid them no mind. Her straw hat bounced against her back, held on by the ribbons straining at her neck. Snippets of long blond hair slapped her shoulder as she circumvented the pothole.

Tony remembered her racing to Brianna's rescue and doing everything she could to keep the girl alive. He knew she'd do no less for Sharpley.

Tony tracked Essie's progress down the road until she was swallowed by dust and the other traffic.

"He'll be all right," Grandpa said, squeezing Tony's shoulder.

Tony roused himself, realizing the driller was referring to Sharpley. But Tony was every bit as worried about Essie as he was the derrickman. She'd take the boy's injury hard and it didn't set well with Tony that Moss would be the one at her side.

"Does Sharpley have family here?" Tony asked.

"Not that I know of," Grandpa answered. "But the Spreckelmeyers take care of their own. He'll be in good hands."

Tony strengthened his resolve to win a higher position in Sullivan Oil. If he were tool pusher, it would be him driving that wagon, him making sure that boy was all right, and him comforting Essie in her distress.

———

Essie pounded on the lectern with her gavel, calling the emergency meeting of the Velocipede Club to order. Townsfolk had turned out in grand numbers, forcing most of the gentlemen to stand at the rear due to lack of seating.

Only Mrs. Lockhart had taken time to dress for the meeting. Most of the women wore their linsey-woolsies along with simple straw hats. The men wore their denims. Essie had done no more than splash water on her face and re-twist her hair. All were frantically conferring with one another, bringing the volume to horrendous heights.

The one person whose attention she held was the one whose she didn't want—Mr. Tony Bryant. He stood in the back, his white shirt unbuttoned at the collar, his hat in hand, his eyes on her. This was her first sight of him since the Fourth of July celebration three days earlier.

She looked away and rapped again on the wooden lectern. "Ladies and gentlemen. Please."

They shushed each other, which ended up being even louder than their talking. Finally they began to settle.

"As you know," Essie began, speaking over them, "we have convened this evening to discuss what action to take concerning our entry in the Corsicana Oil & Gas Bicycle Invitational. It is but one month away, and as a club we voted to sponsor the Sullivan Oil rider, Mr. Lucas Sharpley."

Murmurs of agreement filtered throughout the room.

"This morning Mr. Sharpley fell from the double board of his rig, snapped his leg in two and broke three ribs. The Benevolent Society has set up a schedule for visitations with Mr. Sharpley as he recovers in the home of Mr. and Mrs. Blanchard. Ladies, if you haven't had a chance to sign up, please see Mrs. Whiteselle after our meeting."

Essie tucked a loose piece of hair behind her ear. "Sullivan Oil has asked the Velocipede Club to find a replacement for their bicycle race. And though we mean no disrespect to Mr. Sharpley's circumstances, we dare not delay our decision for even a day or our team will be in jeopardy of forfeiting."

Old Widow Yarbrough raised her hand. "My son, Finis, could stand in for Mr. Sharpley."

"Finis Yarbrough is sixty years old if he's a day," one of the men from the back yelled. "He'd be no match for those young fellas the other oil companies have."

Barks of agreement followed.

Essie banged on the lectern. "Thank you for that nomination, Mrs. Yarbrough. And may I remind the gallery that comments are restricted to Velocipede Club members only." She wrote Finis's name on a piece of octavo amidst the grumbling of the townsfolk who'd yet to join the club. "Does anyone else have a name they'd like for us to consider?"

Victoria Davis stood up—young, fresh, and pretty as spring. "What about Preacher Wortham?"

Victoria had been sweet on Ewing for two summers now, and though many of the men her own age had expressed interest in her, she'd set her sights on the preacher.

Mrs. Bogart struggled to her feet, her skin drooping in folds about her eyes, cheeks, and neck. "Impossible," she said, out of breath from either the effort of standing or from outrage. "Neither the elders nor the congregation will stand for it. I insist Preacher Wortham's name be stricken from the list."

Ewing, having taken the pulpit from the retired Mr. Bogart, stepped forward. "Though I appreciate the nomination, I'm afraid any free time I have will need to be used for more charitable pursuits."

Essie scratched Ewing's name from the list. Victoria sent him a smile, then resumed her seat.

Several more names were offered up, but the members found fault with every recommendation. The man in question was either too old, too young, too unfit, too reckless, too lazy, too unfamiliar, too free with his liquor consumption, or too something.

Essie had just about given up when Mrs. Lockhart stood. "What about Mr. Bryant?"

The crowd twisted around to look at him.

He was clearly stunned.

"He ain't even from Corsicana," someone yelled.

"Neither is Mr. Sharpley," Mrs. Lockhart said. "But Mr. Bryant lives here now, he is an employee of Sullivan Oil, he is in excellent physical condition and, from what I understand, handles himself very well on a bicycle."

One by one, the members—particularly the women members—began endorsing the nomination. They praised Mrs. Lockhart for seeing what was right before their noses and encouraged Tony to step up for the good of the club.

Essie began to panic. True, he was the best candidate so far, but if the club elected him as their racer, they'd expect her to train him. Five evenings a week. More if she were to get him ready in time.

Mrs. Lockhart smiled. The proverbial cat who got the cream. Essie tamped down a groan. The old biddy was nothing more than a frustrated romantic who didn't have enough sense to fill a salt spoon.

Essie frantically searched her mind for another, more suitable candidate. None came to mind.

A speculative gleam entered Tony's eye. Had he, too, realized he'd be forced to spend most every minute of his time off with her?

The men around him pushed him toward the bandstand, encouraging him to accept the nomination. He circled around and made his way to the front.

Stepping up onto the platform, he addressed the crowd. "I would be most honored to represent the Corsicana Velocipede Club and Sullivan Oil in the Corsicana Oil & Gas Bicycle Invitational. That is, unless there is some objection?"

He directed this last question at Essie. And what could she say? That he was an employee? Well, so was Sharpley. That he didn't have the physical stamina? Anyone with eyes could see he did. That she wanted a chaperone during their training sessions? They'd think she was a delusional old maid and laugh behind their hands.

A swelling of excited voices filled the room.

"Take a vote, Miss Spreckelmeyer," Mrs. Lockhart said over the crowd, punctuating her demand with a thump of her cane. "And start with Mr. Bryant's name. I have a feeling you won't need to go any further on your list."

Silence fell like a guillotine.

Essie cleared her throat. "Were there any other nominations?"

Not so much as a murmur.

She swallowed. "Very well, then. All in favor of electing Mr. Tony Bryant as Sullivan Oil's representative in the Corsicana Oil & Gas Bicycle Invitational, please raise your hand."

Unanimous amongst the women. Well, almost unanimous. Mrs. Yarbrough was still holding out for her son. And a majority of the men members voted in the affirmative, as well.

Essie gripped the lectern. She must not let anyone—most of all Mrs. Lockhart or Tony himself—see her distress.

Pasting a smile on her face, she turned to him. "Congratulations, Mr. Bryant. It seems you are our new contestant."

CHAPTER | FIFTEEN

ESSIE WORKED TONY TWICE as hard as she'd ever worked Sharpley. She made him do twice as many laps, twice as many sit-ups, twice as many push-ups, twice as many bell pulls, twice as many sprints, twice as many jumps of the rope, twice as many everything.

She wanted to make certain that when the session was finished, he didn't have enough energy left for amorous pursuits.

He took to the regimen without complaint. How he had the strength after putting in a full day on the rig, she could not imagine. But he did.

As the days passed, and she observed his remarkable stamina, she grew optimistic. They just might have a chance of placing in the bicycle race, after all. They might not take first, but they certainly had a shot at the second- or third-place trophies.

Holding Tony's feet to the floor, she gave the final countdown for his three hundred sit-ups. "Five, four, three, two, and one."

He fell back, flinging his arms above him. Sweat saturated his sleeveless shirt, his chest pumping as he sucked in air. The lightweight navy fabric stuck to his torso, outlining the shape beneath it. Even relaxed, his muscles bulged.

Dark hair matted the pits of his arms. Skin a few shades paler than the rest lay bare along the underside of his outstretched limbs. His fingers curled in repose.

She released his feet. He'd refused to wear the tights so many men preferred when exercising and she'd been extremely relieved. Those tights left little to the imagination.

She unscrewed the lid of a water canteen and handed it to him. Pushing himself up, he lifted it to his mouth, the muscles in his arm flexing. He guzzled the liquid, ignoring the rivulets seeping from the corners of his mouth. They streamed around his jaw, down his neck and into his shirt.

"Not too fast, Tony," she cautioned. "I don't want you getting sick."

He lowered the canteen, swiping his mouth with his forearm, his chest still heaving. The richness of his deep brown eyes struck her again.

He hadn't said a word about what had happened after their meal on the Fourth or what he'd talked with her father about. And though the words had remained unspoken, she'd caught him staring at places he oughtn't. He tried to cover his indiscretions, but he made no apologies for them.

"You ready for our football drill?" she asked.

He scratched the stubble on his jaw. "I dunno if I want to waste my time kicking the ball with some female who doesn't have the constitution to play a match without fainting."

After her embarrassing episode with him and Sharpley, she'd been careful to dress more appropriately for the training sessions. But Tony never ceased to tease her about her one lapse.

"Careful, sir. Don't you know that pride is the never-failing vice of fools?"

He rose to his feet and offered her his hand. " 'If we had no pride we should not complain of that of others.' "

She allowed him to help her stand, then fetched the ball. At first they passed it back and forth, giving her a chance to get her blood flowing.

"M.C. Baker's coming in on the three-o'clock train tomorrow," he said. "If you'd like, I can come round and pick you up at the house on my way."

She leaned back, giving the ball a lift. He caught it with his knee, allowed it to drop, then passed it back.

"That'll be fine," she said.

"I'll pick you up at two, then."

"Don't you think that's a bit early?"

"I told Moss I'd take some tools to the smithy for repair on our way." Putting a spin on the ball, he kicked it past her and took off running.

For the next fifteen minutes they raced up and down the building, fighting for advantage. And though Essie tried to keep up, Tony was not only better with his foot skills, but he also outmatched her in size and speed. The fourth time he scored, he lifted his fists in the air like a pugilist and bounced up and down.

She propped her hands on her waist. "That's not very gentlemanly of you. The conduct of the winner should be modest and dignified."

He slowly lowered his arms. "Modest and dignified? Who was it that stuck her tongue out when she scored a few moments ago?"

"I wasn't gloating. I was trying to see which way the wind was blowing."

A slow grin crept onto his face. "Inside the seed house?"

"This is not a seed house, Mr. Bryant. It is a bicycle club."

"And your undue liveliness during our match, Miss Spreckelmeyer, was improper by anyone's standards."

She picked up the ball and returned it to its bin. "Well, maybe it was. I almost scored two off of you tonight, though. You're slipping, sir."

Without asking, he helped her put away jump ropes, dumbbells, Indian clubs, and his bicycle. Mr. Sharpley had never thought to do that for her.

After they put the lights out, he draped her shawl over her shoulders and followed her through the door. He locked it, then handed her the key.

Their walks home were her favorite part of the evening. She had protested at first, but Tony wouldn't hear of any objections. He would walk with her whether she consented or not.

"Suppose some snakebitten child should need assistance," he said, "and there you'd be without a knife."

"Yes, but I usually pack a pistol, don't forget," she teased.

"A pistol's not much use to a snakebite victim."

So she had acquiesced and then grown to enjoy the company. Something Mr. Sharpley had also never offered.

Earlier in the week they had talked of the transatlantic steamers filled with Americans sailing to Europe. Last night, of Napoleon Bonaparte's invasion of Egypt a hundred years ago, a subject on which Tony seemed remarkably well informed. Often they discussed the latest developments in the war with Spain, but when he fell to discussing tactics, he lost her entirely.

Tonight they deliberated over Thomas Stevens' three-year trip around the world on his Columbia highwheeler back in 1884, a trek Essie had researched for a recent lecture.

"Can you even imagine?" she asked. "Velocipedes were so cumbersome and heavy back then."

"And the roads rough and poorly formed."

"How marvelous to be a man, though," she sighed. "To embark on such an adventure. Meeting princes. Seeing the Taj Mahal. Riding alongside a caravan of three hundred camels."

Tony shook his head. "You forget his supplies were limited to socks, a spare shirt, and a slicker that doubled as a tent and bedroll."

"Still, I'd give anything to do something like that."

They reached her house and he placed his hand on the gate's latch. "For what it's worth, Essie, I'm glad you're not a man."

She pulled herself out of her musings. He stood close. Too close.

The hinges squeaked as he pushed open the gate. "I'll pick you up at two o'clock. Don't forget."

"I won't forget." Slipping past him, she hurried into the house.

———

Mrs. Lockhart opened the door before Tony had a chance to knock. She took one look at his exercise clothes and frowned.

"Quickly," she said. "Before someone sees you."

He slipped into the darkened entry hall. Mrs. Lockhart clasped his hand and led him blindly down a hall and into another room before releasing him. He stood where he was while she lit a lantern.

Light spilled onto a square table, revealing a typical kitchen with a braided rug, a woodburning stove, and a water pump in the corner. The smell of coffee coming from the stove filled the room. Two mugs sat in waiting beside it.

Grabbing a towel, Mrs. Lockhart poured coffee into the cups. She wore a black shirtwaist and skirt, no bustle, no rice powder. She'd twisted her white hair up so tightly, bits of pink scalp peeked through.

He glanced at the red-checkered curtains hanging still as stone above the water pump, indicating a secured window and explaining why no breeze circulated through the room. The tightly closed curtains would also keep light from seeping out and curious eyes from peeking in.

"Why all the secrecy?" he asked.

She added sugar to his cup, cream to hers. "A gentleman caller at this hour? What would people say?"

He came up behind her and pecked her cheek. "They'd say I was sparkin' my favorite gal."

Blushing, she pushed him away and indicated he take a seat. "Get on with you, now."

She picked up their cups and he followed her to the table, then pulled out her chair.

"I received your note," she said, settling herself. "What has happened?"

Sitting across from her, he grabbed the corner of his shirt-sleeve and wiped his forehead. "Sorry I didn't have time to clean up before I came."

She waved away his concern. "You did the right thing. If you'd gone back to Mrs. Potter's and then left again all spruced up, eyebrows would have raised for certain. Now, tell me what has brought you to my doorstep at this late hour."

He took a sip of coffee. "Am I keeping you from your beauty rest?"

She leaned forward, light capturing the sparkle in her eyes. "I haven't had this much fun since Mr. Dubois ran off with Lord Wynton's daughter."

He suppressed a smile. "How shocking. And when did this perfidy occur?"

"Several summers ago in *A Young Girl's Love*."

Tony leaned back onto two legs of his chair. "I read *When False Tongues Speak*."

Mrs. Lockhart glowed with delight, the pleasure taking ten years off her face. "And what did you think of Mr. Chester's speech?"

"The man was a fool."

"Never say so!"

"He'd have completely gotten away with his scheme if he'd simply kept his mouth shut. That speech was his undoing."

Mrs. Lockhart raised a finger in protest. "But what of Miss Laura?"

He gave a disgusted snort. "Miss Laura? She led him around like a bull with a ring in his nose. What did he see in such a spoiled little miss anyway? Mrs. Neville of Neville's Cross, however—" He smiled with lazy appreciation. "Now, that is what I call a woman."

Mrs. Lockhart sat stunned. "You are deceived, Mr. Bryant. You have completely turned things around. Why, I never would have suggested you read the book if I thought—" She slowly narrowed her eyes. "You are teasing me."

He took a sip of coffee.

She chuckled. "You are a wicked man, Mr. Tony Bryant Morgan."

Dropping the legs of his chair on the floor, he placed his mug on the table. "I received a letter from my mother."

Mrs. Lockhart sobered. "What's happened?"

Tony hesitated one last time, questioning the wisdom of sharing confidences with Mrs. Lockhart. He'd stopped by her home several times now and discovered she knew much more about his family situation than he'd first realized. Though, it wasn't all that surprising, what with her daughter being such an intimate friend of Anna's and her son-in-law, Morgan Oil's tool pusher.

He took a deep breath. "Darius had all of Anna's mourning clothes removed from her armoire and replaced them with gowns suited for a debutante's first season. She has no choice but to wear them or remain hidden in her room indefinitely."

"Why would he do such a thing?"

"He wants to marry her off."

"Why?"

"To increase his wealth and standing in the community."

"But the Morgans are already wealthy and quite powerful in these parts."

"Not enough to suit, evidently. Mother said he has been parading Anna in front of senators and railroad men." He combed a hand through his hair. "Including old Norris Tubbs."

Mrs. Lockhart removed her glasses. "Anna simply cannot marry for at least a year. It would be downright scandalous."

"I agree. But there is no one who has the gumption to stand up to Darius other than me. Yet I don't know what to do. Knocking his teeth down his throat would be extremely satisfying but won't really solve anything."

She rubbed her eyes. "What if you brought Anna here to Corsicana?"

"How? I can barely support myself. And if I brought her here, the Spreckelmeyers would find out I'm a Morgan and I'd lose my job." He shook his head. "Not only that, Darius would find some way to sabotage her inheritance and keep it for himself. Then where would Anna be?"

"Let's tackle one thing at a time. First, Judge Spreckelmeyer is a reasonable fellow. And he knew Blake quite well, so he'd be sympathetic to your situation."

Tony blanched. "He knew my father?"

"Oh my, yes. When the railroads first started coming into Texas, your father tried to use his influence to push regulations through the state congress that Judge Spreckelmeyer opposed." She held her glasses up to her mouth, huffed onto their lenses, then wiped them with a napkin. "The judge didn't have the money your father did, but he had the support of many who, combined, were quite powerful. I don't remember the particulars other than the regulations your father was pushing for were not passed."

Propping his elbows on the table, Tony dropped his head into his hands. "Spreckelmeyer knows. He has to. I'm the spitting image of my father."

Mrs. Lockhart put her glasses back on. "I think it is quite possible you are correct."

He jerked his gaze up. "Do you think Essie knows?"

She shook her head. "I doubt it. She's not nearly as good at hiding her feelings as the judge. If she knew who you were, she'd have been much more antagonistic toward you."

"Why do you think Spreckelmeyer hasn't said anything?"

She considered his question. "You could always ask him."

Tony tapped his fist against his mouth. "It just doesn't make any sense. If Spreckelmeyer knows who I am, why would he have granted me permission to court Essie?"

Mrs. Lockhart lit up. "You're courting Essie? Why, no one has said a word!"

"That's because I haven't stepped out with her yet. I'm still undecided about the whole thing."

"Why? She'd be a wonderful catch for any man."

"It's not that."

"Then, what is it?"

Lowering his gaze, he ran his finger along the rim of his cup. "She's Spreckelmeyer's sole heir."

"So?"

"So don't you think it looks a bit suspicious for the disinherited son of Blake Morgan to suddenly take an interest in the spinster daughter of the largest producer of oil in Texas?"

Mrs. Lockhart pursed her lips. "In *Wooed and Married*, Mr. Tayne pursued the Lady Conyngham. She, too, was a spinster—and every bit as attractive as our Essie. Yet all of England opposed the match, claiming the second son of the new baron simply wanted to increase his family's lands and wealth. But it was a love match, and after Mr. Tayne had slain a dragon or two—figuratively speaking, of course—"

"Of course," Tony said.

"—love conquered all and the young people married and went on to live a full and happy life."

He drained the last of his coffee. "That's all well and good, Mrs. Lockhart, but I can't court Essie simply because Mr. Tayne courted Lady What's-Her-Name."

"Conyngham."

"Exactly."

"What if you confess all to the judge and reassure him that your motives are honorable?" she asked.

"Why? He's already given me permission, of a sort, to court Essie."

"What do you mean, 'of a sort'?"

Tony rubbed his neck. "He said I had to ask Essie directly for permission and if she agreed, he would be favorable to the match."

Mrs. Lockhart rolled her eyes. "For the love of Peter. That man has not been the same since Doreen passed." She picked up their cups and moved to the washbowl. "Tell me this, Mr. Bryant. Are your motives pure?"

He stiffened, then sighed. "The advantages of marrying her are not lost on me. But my . . . interest . . . has nothing to do with that. I intend to earn my position in life and not have it handed to me—by inheritance or marriage."

Mrs. Lockhart nodded. "Well, I recommend you court her as planned and if you find yourself more interested in the inheritance than the woman herself, then you can simply bow out gracefully."

"That would hardly be fair to Essie."

"It would be better than marrying her for the wrong reasons."

He nodded. "What about Anna?"

The elderly woman picked up the lantern and headed out of the kitchen and over to the parlor, Tony following.

"I think it is too early to make any moves on that front," she said. "So long as nothing official has been announced, you still have time." She slipped a book from the shelf. "Now, I'd like you to read this and we will discuss it when next we meet."

He glanced at the title. *Marjorie's Fate*.

"Mrs. Lockhart, I really don't think—"

"Pay particular attention to the strategy employed by the down-on-his-luck earl who thwarted his wicked brother's scheme to steal his lady love."

She handed him his hat. He took it, knowing he'd read her book, if for no other reason than to have an excuse to come back and spend time with someone who knew who he was and liked him anyway.

Squeezing her elbow, he whispered, "Next time we meet, I'll come in the back door."

Her eyes sparkled with delight just before she extinguished the lantern and shooed him out the door.

CHAPTER | SIXTEEN

ESSIE TOLD HERSELF SHE chose her Worth gown and her favorite tall walking hat to make a favorable impression on Mr. Baker. But it wasn't Mr. Baker's reaction she pictured in her mind.

She checked her gown in the mirror. The stamped linen fit her close as a sheath, the maroon design standing out on the lighter background. A wide revers of white plush narrowly massed on her shoulders, then knotted in the middle of her back above full pleats. Tasteful, yet eye-catching.

A week had passed since Tony asked for Papa's permission. Yet he'd said nothing at all to her about courtship. Had he changed his mind?

She ran her finger over a new wrinkle between her eyebrows that she didn't remember seeing before, then sighed. The more time she spent with him, the more she enjoyed his company, his wit, and his willingness to discuss anything with her—whether it be politics, gas versus electricity, or Mr. Ford's motorized carriage.

He was courteous, hardworking, and attractive, and he could ride a bike with the best of them. Most of all, he didn't seem to mind her independent ways anymore. If he truly did want to step out with her, what could it hurt?

But she knew all too well what it could hurt. The real question was if courting him was worth the risk. Worth the risk of rousing talk in town. Worth the risk of making herself vulnerable. Worth the risk of being rejected.

The clock chimed two. Pinching her cheeks, she headed down the stairs. Tony crossed the porch just as she reached the entryway. He wore a silk vest, gray trousers, and summer jacket. They stared at each other through the screen door.

"The first time I saw you through this door, you were sliding down the banister," he said.

"Shhhhh." She glanced over her shoulder, then quickly opened the screen. "Papa might hear you."

"You were wearing knickerbockers and a hat that reached clear to here." He held his hand level with his nose. "And then you looked at me and I thought you were just about the prettiest thing I ever had seen."

She raised a brow. "You thought I was married to my father."

"And I was jealous of him."

Her stomach somersaulted.

"You ready?" he asked.

"Yes. Let me just poke my head into Papa's study and tell him I'm leaving."

When she returned to the entryway, Tony stood holding the door open. She stepped out onto the porch and hesitated at seeing a Studebaker carriage parked in front of the house. The buckboard held a front and backseat with a natural wood finish and green cloth trimmings.

"We aren't walking?" she asked.

Riding through town all dressed up like this would look too much like courting, and she certainly didn't care to have her employees or the townspeople misinterpreting the reason for her excursion.

"I'm taking some tools to the Central Blacksmith Shop," he said. "Plus, M.C. will have a trunk with him. I figured a carriage would be best."

She glanced at the boot of the vehicle. Sure enough, a box of tools had been stowed there behind the second seat. Not seeing any way around it, she allowed him to escort her down the sidewalk and assist her into the buckboard.

Shaking out her skirts, she noted he'd replaced his mud-splattered work boots with his Sunday boots. The expensive kind the cowboys called Wellingtons.

Once again she wondered what had happened to change his circumstances. He enjoyed playing a card game or two with the boys, but she couldn't imagine him gambling away his life's fortune. He simply didn't strike her as the type. But looks and charm and good manners meant nothing, really. It was what was on the inside that counted.

"You look awfully fetching, Essie. Is that a new hat?"

She glanced at him. "No. It's not new, exactly. I just don't wear it too often."

"Well, it's very nice."

Despite herself, she was pleased. With its tall, willowy plumage, maroon satin ribbon, and butter-colored lace, it was one of her very favorites.

She tipped her face up to the sky. It offered no clouds to temper the sun's penetrating rays, but a steady breeze kept her from getting hot in the open carriage.

Mr. Drake's towering pecan tree—whose branches had provided her with hours of quiet reading as a child—spread beyond his yard and stretched out over the road. Warblers and songbirds that had poured into town after crossing the Gulf of Mexico flitted through its branches, each trying to outdo the other in song. Mrs. Davis's rose garden thrived, showing off blooms of white, yellow, and pink.

They reached the smithy's in no time. Tony jumped down from the seat, instructed her to stay put and toted the box inside. Moments later he rejoined her.

It couldn't be more than ten after two. What in the world would they do for the next fifty minutes while they waited for the train to arrive?

Clicking his tongue, Tony pointed the buckboard south.

"Where are we going?"

"We've some time to kill, so I thought a ride out to Two Bit Creek would be nice."

"Why?"

He looked at her. "Why not?"

"I'm not sure it's such a good idea, is all."

"Why not?" he asked again, making no move to redirect the horses.

"Because in order to get there we will have to pass many of my rigs and the men will see us together."

"So?"

"So," she said, scrambling for a delicate way to point out the obvious. "It might produce some talk."

"What kind of talk?"

"You know exactly what kind of talk."

Pushing up the rim of his hat, he leaned back against the seat. "Yes, ma'am. I guess I do."

Now, what is that supposed to mean? "Well, I'm not sure I care to stir up any talk."

He chuckled. "Essie, there isn't a woman in town who defies convention more than you. You own one business. Run another for your father. Wear bloomers. Travel clear to New York City by yourself, only to get your name plastered in the papers from here to kingdom come. You ride all over Corsicana on that bicycle and hold weekly shooting lessons for the women in this town. And now you expect me to believe a little ride out to Two Bit Creek is gonna upset your apple cart?"

Good heavens. Put like that, she sounded like an eccentric old maid. But what some thought of as eccentric, others took for something else entirely.

"It doesn't mean I'm loose, Tony," she said, fiddling with the gathers in her skirt.

He yanked the horses to a stop. Right there in the middle of Fifth Street. She had to grab on to the rail to keep herself from pitching forward. She glanced up and down the street, relieved to find no one else coming or going.

The muscles in his forearm swelled against his sleeve as he held the reins tightly wrapped in his right fist. "Look at me."

She lifted her gaze.

His brown eyes conveyed acute displeasure. "I never, ever, for one single minute thought that you were anything other than the respectable woman you are."

Swallowing, she nodded.

"Furthermore," he continued, "I was not taking you out to Two Bit Creek for some prurient purpose. The train's not due in for almost an hour, and you were looking so pretty in your dress and gloves and hat that I just wanted to take you for a ride."

She opened her mouth to reply, but he wasn't quite through.

"And you wanna know something else?" he asked, whipping off his hat. "I'm sick and tired of you assigning motives to me that I don't have. First you question my integrity. Now you question my morals." He twisted to face her. "I don't know what makes you think otherwise, but let me assure you I'm not about to risk my job by playing fast with the boss's daughter."

She moistened her lips, refusing to be cowed. "I see. And if I wasn't the boss's daughter? Would you play fast with me then?"

"Take the deuce, woman!" A tick in his jaw hammered. "Sometimes you make me so mad I could strangle your pretty little neck. And no. I do not make a habit of playing fast with *any* women. Boss's daughters. Farmer's daughters. Any kind of daughters. You got that?"

The very fact that he was so insulted soothed many of her concerns. "Yes. I believe I do."

"Good." He slammed his hat back on his head. "Now. Do you think you can ride out to Two Bit Creek without finding fault every step of the way?"

She bit the insides of her cheeks. Never had she heard a more hostile invitation from someone who, she was beginning to realize, truly didn't have some ulterior motive. "I shall do my best to steer my thinking in a more positive manner."

"Fine." He slapped the reins, and the buckboard lurched forward. "You do that."

The horses shook their heads in protest and slowed to a walk after only a few yards. Essie's mind backtracked, filtering through Tony's exasperation and honing in on what he'd actually said.

"You were looking so pretty in your dress and gloves and hat that I just wanted to take you for a ride."

She allowed his words to wash over her, seep inside and settle. In the past, she'd have waved off a declaration of that sort, assuming the speaker was simply being polite.

But Tony hadn't been spouting platitudes. He'd meant what he said. He was attracted to her and wanted to ride out with her. So simple, yet so complicated.

She'd already admitted to herself that she found him attractive, as well. But so far she'd been very careful not to dwell on it.

She glanced at his hands as they loosely held the reins. Blue veins crisscrossed his tan skin, drawing her eyes to defined knuckles, masculine fingers and nails that, though scrubbed, still held a slight stain of oil.

"I'm sorry I lost my temper," he said.

She pushed a tendril of hair back up into her hat. "It's all right. I seem to have that effect on people."

Squinting, he searched the horizon. "You have no idea of the effect you have on me."

She lifted her gaze.

He swallowed, causing his Adam's apple to jump up, then roll back down his throat. "I'd like to court you, Essie."

She caught her breath.

"I asked your father, but he said I must appeal to you directly."

"Why?"

"I don't know. That's just what he told me."

"No, I mean, why do you want to court me?"

He frowned. "What kind of question is that? The same reason any man goes courting."

"Why *do* men go courting?"

He appeared at a total loss. "Because."

"Because why?"

"Because they just do." He turned the team west, taking the long way around in order to avoid passing any of Sullivan Oil's rigs.

She grabbed on to the wing to steady herself. "Let me rephrase it, then: What are your intentions?"

"Are you trying to make me mad on purpose? This is the last time I'm going to tell you. They're completely honorable."

She sighed. "I don't want to know what *kind* of intentions you have. I want to know what they *are*. If you can't tell me, then the answer is no."

He slipped a finger in his collar and gently tugged. She understood his discomfort but did not want to misinterpret or mistake what he was asking her. At this point in her life, there was only one acceptable reason for a man to go courting, and that was if he was considering marriage.

The longer he took to respond, the more she realized she had her answer.

"It's all right, Tony," she said. "Let's forget you ever mentioned it."

"No," he said, panic lining his voice. "I just don't know what to say."

"It's a simple question."

"It's not."

On the outskirts of town he guided the horses off the road and onto a lightly worn trail that led to the creek. Sand and grass muffled the horses' hooves. The wheels creaked with each turn.

He sat up straighter. "I would like to see you more often in a more intimate setting so that I can get to know you better." He let out a *whoosh* of air.

"You're all alone with me every night."

"That's different. We're working. Training. You're bossing me around the whole time." He shook his head. "I want to take you somewhere. Like the soda shop or fishing, even. I want to pick you up at your house knowing that you'd put on your finery for me—and only me. I want to go where there is no boss or trainer. I want to go somewhere with just you and me."

The trees grew thicker. The sound of water churning reached her ears. Loamy smells stirred from the earth.

She toyed with her gloved fingers. "And what," she whispered, "would all that lead to?"

The creek came into view, its contents chafing against the banks, racing toward an unseen goal.

He pulled the carriage to a stop, anchored the reins and turned toward her, placing his arm along the seat back. "Well, ideally, I suppose it would lead to marriage. Occasionally, however, I've seen it lead to heartache."

She nodded. "Tony?"

"Hmmm?"

"What if I knew right now that it would lead to heartache. Would you still want to pursue this, um, courtship?"

He frowned in confusion. "What makes you so certain our courtship would lead to heartache?"

"Because," she said, taking a deep breath. "If your feelings for me were to grow to the point of making an offer, I would be honor bound to reveal some things about me that might cause you to change your mind. And that would then lead to heartache."

An expression of skepticism crossed his face before he realized she was serious. After a moment of thought, he rubbed his mouth. "Would you like to tell me about them now and get it over with?"

She clasped her hands together. The last time a man had asked to court her, she'd laid all her past transgressions on the table before proceeding. But she wasn't the same person now as she'd been then.

For the past four years she'd learned to embrace her singleness. Enjoy it. Be proud of it.

Mrs. Lockhart's words to Tony flitted through her mind.

"She hides behind her spinsterhood. . . . She worries about what people think. . . . She won't want to step out with an employee."

A fish jumped above the surface of the creek, the sun catching its silver scales in a moment of brilliance before it disappeared back into the safety of its home. She scanned the water, waiting for some of its companions to do the same, but no other fish appeared.

Was she like that? Did she stay below the surface where it was safe? Never risking a journey out into the sunlight?

"Essie?" he said, placing a finger beneath her chin and bringing her face around. "How 'bout we just take our chances and see how it goes?"

She worried her lip.

"It'll be all right. If things progress, there will be time enough for you to tell me your secrets and for me to tell you mine."

She searched his brown eyes and found no censure there.

Long ago she'd learned that she was a whole person without a man. That all she needed was Jesus Christ. Had she somehow taken that blessing and pushed God out of it? Made it about her instead of Him? About her being single and successful?

She thought of the virtue she'd so carelessly gifted to a man who wasn't her husband. Had she accepted God's forgiveness, then subconsciously built a wall around herself that no man could possibly scale? What if God had a man for her after all?

Is this your will, Lord?

She waited, but He gave no answer. Not so much as an inkling as to what His thoughts were. Her heart began to hammer. Was she willing to let Him knock down that wall?

Tony ran his thumb along her jaw. "What do you say, Essie? Will you accept my offer?"

It was a risk. A huge risk. But deep down, she wanted to tell him yes. This time, however, she wanted to do it the Lord's way.

Will you show me how to knock down that wall, Lord? Will you show me how to court a man?

But she didn't need an answer. She knew He would.

Taking a deep breath, she nodded. "Yes, Tony. Yes, I will."

A gorgeous grin split across his face. His fingers tightened on her chin.

He's going to kiss me.

After the slightest hesitation, however, he let her go and pulled his watch from his pocket. "We need to head back. With all the stopping and starting and detouring, it took longer to get here than I estimated."

"All right."

He gave her a sideways look. "If we take the more direct route back, we'll pass all the boys."

Her palms dampened.

"I can't think of an easier way to announce our courtship," he said. "Can you?"

Arranging her skirts, she shook her head.

"Well, then. Let's make it official."

CHAPTER | SEVENTEEN

TONY CUT THEIR BUCKBOARD right through the heart of the oil patch, passing rig after rig after rig. Most of them belonged to Sullivan Oil.

The men stopped their work. They pulled off their hats and waved, then shouted a greeting and glanced speculatively between Tony and Essie.

He kept one arm along the seat back, so there'd be no mistaking his claim. Essie looked neither left nor right but sat rigidly beside him, face flushed, eyes on the road.

For an awful moment back there, he'd thought she was going to refuse him. He wondered what social faux pas she'd committed in her past to make her think he would back out. Any woman who'd been so outlandish as to have been in the newspapers was sure to have made a spectacle of herself more than once.

But if he reached the point of wanting to marry her, he couldn't fathom this imagined sin of hers being something he wouldn't be able to overlook. How bad could it be?

Besides, any secrets she had would pale in comparison to the fact that he'd lied to her about his identity. No telling what her reaction was going to be when he revealed himself as a Morgan. When he revealed that just a train ride away his own flesh and blood owned and operated Sullivan Oil's most adverse competition.

He clucked at the horses, urging them to pick up their pace. He really ought to go ahead and tell her. But if she found out now who he was, she might question his motives. He needed to keep his identity a secret at least a little while longer. But time was running out. M.C. knew who he was, as did Mrs. Lockhart and quite possibly Judge Spreckelmeyer. He only hoped he could convince M.C. to keep his knowledge to himself.

Essie squirmed, becoming even more agitated now that they'd reached town. The boomers gave them no more than a passing glance, but the more established citizens gaped, tracking their progress down Main and making even Tony uncomfortable. What was the matter with everybody?

He removed his arm from behind her and urged the horses onward. "Giddyup, there."

When they finally reached the railroad station, he felt as if he'd run a gauntlet. "What in tarnation was that all about?"

"What?" she asked, placing her hands on his shoulders while he lifted her from the seat by her elbows.

"You can't mean you didn't notice," he said, indicating the town with a nod of his head.

"Oh. That." She took a step back. "Well, what did you expect? You're now courting the town's old maid."

He cringed. "Don't call yourself that."

"It's true. I'm not ashamed of it."

"Well, I don't want you saying it anymore. You hear?"

She shrugged and started toward the train platform.

He grabbed her elbow. "Whoa, there. We're together. Remember? That means so long as you're with me, you don't go anywhere unless it's on my arm."

"Even during the day?"

"Especially during the day." He extended his bent arm.

"Why especially?" she asked, slipping her hand in the crook of his elbow.

"Because there are only three reasons a man would give his arm to a lady during the day. If she was a close relative, if her safety required it, or if she was the gal he was sparkin'. "

She swallowed. "I see. Well, you needn't worry. I'm perfectly aware of how to conduct myself on the street."

He let her rebuke pass. She might know the proper etiquette, but she'd been going her own way for a long time. He wondered just how willingly she'd give up that independence.

A train whistle pierced the air while the rumbling of the oncoming locomotive shook the ground. Metal screamed as the conductor put on the brake, the smell of burnt wood and clashing steel reaching the depot even before the railcars did.

A blue-green iron boiler with gleaming brass handrails, silver road assemblies, and ornamental stag's horns barreled toward them, pitch black smoke pouring from its cabbage stack.

Tony would need to get M.C. alone before introducing him to Essie. He wanted to make sure the rotary man didn't accidentally give him away.

He ran his gaze down the rainbow-colored cars. The russet baggage car rolled by first, pulling a red car behind it, where the nicer compartments were housed. A yellow car held the express passengers, and the Jim Crow section brought up the rear in a bright green car.

The train stopped with a smoky sigh. Corsicana's depot provided a wooden plat-form for passengers so they wouldn't have to step out onto the dirt beside the tracks like so many other train stops Tony had seen. Men, women, and children milled about, searching the railcar windows for friends and loved ones.

Tony spotted M.C. jumping off the express car. He wore a baggy ready-made suit one size too big, the sleeves falling clear to his knuckles. His short blond hair stuck out in sporadic tufts across his balding head.

"You stay put," he said to Essie. "I'll be right back."

Weaving through the crowd, he hollered out to M.C., capturing the man's attention.

"Tony! Good to see you. Where in the world did your moustache run off to?"

Shaking hands, Tony clapped him on the shoulder. "I shaved her clean off. What'd you think?"

"Doesn't look right. Doesn't look right a'tall. And say, I'm sorry about your pa."

"Thank you." Tony never quite knew which of M.C.'s eyes to look at because one went to the east and the other went to the west and he never could tell exactly which one was looking at him. "Speaking of my father, I need to ask a favor. After he disinherited me, I dropped the name Morgan and started going by my mother's name, Bryant."

M.C. scratched the back of his neck. "Well, I'd heard what your pa did and couldn't quite credit it. Strange doings, that's for sure."

"Be that as it may, I'm sure you can imagine that in Sullivan Oil country, having the last name of Morgan wouldn't earn a body any trust. So no one knows who I am and I'd like to keep it that way."

"You're fooling me."

"I'm deadly serious."

"How could they not know? You look just like him."

"I don't think Corsicana was a place he frequented, if at all."

"Well, I'll be." M.C. shook his head. "I don't much like the idea of hoodwinking people, Tony. Even ones I don't know. I'm a God-fearing man and it just don't sit well."

"He disinherited me, M.C. As far as I'm concerned, he's not my father anymore, so you wouldn't be hoodwinking anybody."

"Your pa is Blake Morgan, son. Ain't no piece o' paper or different last name that can change that."

"Doesn't mean I have to claim him."

"You're gonna be found out. Cain't keep a secret like that. It's too big."

"I agree. I'd just like for folks to find out later rather than sooner. So will you hold your tongue?"

Sighing, M.C.'s shoulders slumped. "Well, all right, then. I won't go volunteerin' the information, but if somebody asks me straight out, I ain't gonna lie about it, neither."

"Fair enough, and I appreciate it, M.C. I surely do. Now, where's your trunk?" Tony looked around and caught sight of Deputy Howard talking to Essie.

"I imagine it's over by the baggage car."

"What? Oh. Right. Well, you head on over there. I'm going to fetch Spreckelmeyer's daughter."

M.C. swiveled his head around. "*The* daughter? The one that was in the papers?"

"Watch yourself, buddy. I've taken a shine to her and I won't take kindly to any disparaging remarks."

The man's eyebrows shot up, his right eye zeroing in on Tony. "Does she know who you are?"

"Not yet."

M.C. let out a slow whistle. "I don't envy you the telling of that tale."

"All the more reason for you to keep your knowledge to yourself. Now, go on. I'll meet up with you in a minute."

Tony, tall enough to see over most everyone else's head, kept Essie and the deputy in clear view. The man stood much closer to her than propriety allowed, and every time she took a step back, Howard took a step forward.

Tony was still too far away to hear their conversation, but there was no mistaking Essie's displeasure. Pressing through a clump of people reuniting with their loved ones, Tony finally reached them.

"Does your uncle know about this?" Howard was saying.

Essie caught sight of Tony and looked at him as if she were drowning and he was the only life preserver around. Howard glanced back over his shoulder and scowled.

"Pardon my interruption, Essie, but our guest has arrived." Tony slipped his arm around her, then touched his hat. "Deputy, would you excuse us?"

Not waiting for an answer, he applied pressure to Essie's waist and moved her toward the baggage car. "You okay?"

"Yes. I'm fine."

"What did he want?"

"Nothing. He saw us riding through town and wanted to see why we appeared so 'cozy.' His word."

"What'd you tell him?"

"That you'd received permission to court me."

"What did he say?"

"He was not pleased."

Tony frowned. "Why not?"

"Because a few months back I refused his suit. But I made it clear to him that I'd accepted yours. Really. So there's no need to hold me so close."

"We'll talk about it later," he said, keeping his hand right where it was. If the deputy was watching, Tony wanted to make sure he knew which way the wind blew.

―――

Essie took a liking to M.C. Baker right away. He was around the same age as Uncle Melvin—younger than Papa but older than herself—and he didn't seem to mind that she was the one representing Sullivan Oil instead of her father.

They'd dropped his trunk off at the front desk of the Commercial Hotel and were now sharing a meal in its large dining room. Used to be, Essie would have known every person in the place, but with the way the town had grown over the last couple of years, most of the patrons were unfamiliar to her.

M.C. picked up his final roasted rib and peeled some beef off with his teeth. "How much you producing?"

"In '96 we produced only about fourteen hundred barrels," Essie said, dabbing the sides of her mouth with her napkin. "But by the end of last year, we'd produced almost sixty-six thousand—all within the city limits."

"They've since moved out of town," Tony said, "and have expanded their producing wells to three hundred forty-two."

"All cable-tool?"

"Yep." Tony sliced off a portion of chicken-fried steak. "And all flush production—no pumps whatsoever."

M.C. lifted his brows. "How far down's the oil?"

"Anywhere from nine hundred to twelve hundred feet," Essie said. "Between us and that oil, though, is black, gummy clay and soft rock. So it takes us a good bit of time to break it up."

M.C. swiped his plate with his bread. "My rotary will bust through that in no time. And we can speed everything up even more by pouring water outside the drill pipe."

"What good would that do?" Essie asked.

"The water will come back to us through the pipe. But it'll be carrying rock and mud with it."

She took a sip of tea, realizing the wisdom of what he was saying. "How long do you think it would take you to drill me a well?"

M.C. dragged his napkin across his mouth and leaned back in his chair. "I can drill a thousand feet in thirty-six hours for six hundred dollars."

She and Tony exchanged a glance. A frazzled woman Essie had never seen before took away their plates and replaced them with bowls of suet pudding, then hurried off to her next customer.

"When can you give me a demonstration?" Essie asked.

"I'll need a third down and Tony's help. That going to be a problem?"

She shook her head.

"Well, then. You show me where and I'll start assembling everything as soon as I can get a crew here."

"That would be wonderful."

With their business concluded, the talk turned more personal. M.C. caught Tony up with news of Beaumont. The two men had obviously become well acquainted while Tony was with Morgan Oil.

"Just heard yesterday that Miss Morgan's been betrothed to Norris Tubbs."

Jerking his head up, Tony stopped his spoon halfway to his mouth.

"You might remember her," M.C. said. "She's the old boss's daughter? Name's Anna, I believe. You know her?"

Tony narrowed his eyes. "I believe I've run across her a time or two."

M.C. nodded. "Nuptials are set to take place within the month."

Tony paled, and Essie wondered at his reaction.

"But she can't get married this month," Tony said. "Her father hasn't even been in the grave for six weeks."

"You know Darius—" M.C. leaned in as if imparting a secret. "He's the new boss-man now."

Lips thinning, Tony gave a succinct nod.

"Anyhow, he's not one to give much nevermind to any social conventions."

The tick in Tony's jaw began to beat. "This is a bit more serious than a society rule. He's marrying Anna off with undue haste and to a man three times her age."

"Appears so."

Tony set his spoon down on the table. His easy use of the girl's first name surprised Essie. Had they been sweethearts? Had she broken his heart? Was that why he had left Beaumont without so much as a reference?

"That's not what has the tongues wagging, though." M.C. shook his head and scraped his spoon along the sides of his pudding bowl. "Nope. The really big news is that Finch Morgan's new wife died."

Tony fell back against his chair.

Essie looked between the two men. Who was Finch Morgan?

M.C. lifted his gaze. "Don't ya wanna know what the cause of death was this time?" He pulled his napkin free from where he'd tucked it into his collar. "Gastric fever."

Tony's lips parted.

M.C. turned to Essie. "This will be the second one in just over a year."

She frowned. "Second wife to die?"

"Yes, ma'am."

Sympathy filled her. "Childbirth?"

"No, ma'am. They died of gastric fever."

She blinked. "*Both* of them?"

" 'Fraid so." He pointed his spoon at Tony. "I believe our boy here knew the family, didn't you, son?"

Tony rubbed the strip of skin just beneath his nose. "When did she die?"

"Last week."

Folding her napkin, Essie wondered again at Tony's familiarity with these Morgans. First Anna, then Finch, and now his deceased wife?

"Who exactly is Finch Morgan?" she asked.

"I'm not right sure of his exact connection to the family," M.C. said. "Tony'll know, though."

Tony combed his fingers through his hair. "He's first cousin to Darius Morgan."

"Maternal or paternal side?" M.C. asked, his eyes sparkling with mischief.

"Paternal," Tony ground out.

"I see," Essie said. But truth was, she didn't see. She didn't at all understand how Tony had such intimate knowledge of the Morgan family. Intimate enough to call them by their first names and intimate enough to know who was related to whom.

Then a more disturbing thought occurred to her. If Anna was Darius Morgan's sister, then she was in line to inherit Morgan Oil. And Essie was in line to inherit Sullivan Oil.

Her heart sped up. Was Tony a modern-day fortune hunter? Was he looking to woo the beneficiaries of oil tycoons until he found one gullible enough to fall for him?

Papa might not have old money the way the Morgans did—and therefore was not a tycoon—but in Texas, Sullivan Oil was by far the biggest producer.

She studied Tony's drawn face. One thing was certain. Anna Morgan was much more to Tony than the daughter of his old boss.

CHAPTER | EIGHTEEN

TONY HAMMERED MRS. LOCKHART'S kitchen door with his fist. In the twilight, he could see the backyard was not kept nearly as nice as the front. Weeds filled the gardens, vines rode up the derrick's legs, a loose board shifted beneath his feet, and paint peeled off the porch railings.

The door swung open. "What are you doing here?" Mrs. Lockhart asked, ushering him inside. "Aren't you supposed to be training for the bicycle race?"

"I decided to stop here first. Is it a bad time?"

"No, no. Come in. Have you had your supper?"

"Yes, ma'am. I ate down at Castle's."

She tsked. "Sit down. I'll slice you up some fruitcake." She served them both a piece, poured two cups of coffee and joined him at the table. "Now, what's wrong?"

"Have you heard from your daughter?"

"Goodness, Tony, there hasn't been enough time for a response. Why?"

"I found out that Darius has arranged a marriage between my sister and Norris Tubbs."

"What! Who's Norris Tubbs?"

"Part owner of the H&TC Railroad. Both my father and Darius have been trying to get him in their back pocket for some time now. The man is old enough to be Anna's grandfather."

"Is there any chance whatsoever that your sister is amiable to the match?"

Tony scoffed. "She cannot stand the man."

Mrs. Lockhart drummed her fingers on the table. "Well, don't panic. Your father's not been in his grave even two months. Anna's betrothal is nothing short of scandalous, but she won't be able to marry for at least another ten months or more."

"They are to marry before the month is out."

"Impossible! How do you know?"

"I heard it today from a driller by the name of M.C. Baker."

She touched her throat. "Good heavens."

"I've got to do something." He jumped up from the table. "But short of kidnapping her, I can't think of a thing."

"Dear me." She watched him pace, a worried frown on her face. "In *Her Martyrdom*, Lady Charlewood sequestered herself in a convent. Perhaps—"

Tony whirled around. "This is not some senseless romance novel! This is my baby sister we are discussing, and I'll thank you to treat the topic with the seriousness it deserves."

The elderly woman straightened her spine. "How dare you take that tone with me, sir."

His shoulders slumped. "Mrs. Lockhart, please. I meant no offense. I'm merely trying to point out that—"

"If you want my assistance, you'd best watch both your tone and your tongue."

He said nothing.

"Sit down."

He returned to his chair.

"I see you brought my novels back," she said, eyeing the two books he'd set on the table upon his arrival.

"Yes, ma'am."

"Did you read *Marjorie's Fate*?"

"Yes, ma'am, I did."

"And what did you conclude?"

"That Dr. Letsom was a scoundrel."

"I see." She folded her hands on the table. "And what brought you to that conclusion?"

"He loved no one more than himself. He acted out of turn without thinking through the consequences. He ruined the woman he professed to love."

She took a sip of coffee. "And what of Miss Marjorie?"

"She was taken advantage of. How could a young, naïve thing like her have been expected to know what he was up to?"

"She knew the difference between right and wrong. She knew she was breaking the rules of society. She knew she was lying to her parents."

He leaned back in his chair. "What are you saying? It was her fault?"

"I'm saying they both made poor choices."

"All right. I'll agree with that."

"Good." She dabbed her mouth with a napkin. "Now, about your sister. I will wire my daughter and tell her I am coming to Beaumont on tomorrow's train. Meanwhile, can you get word to Anna to meet me at the First Baptist Church on Pearl Street two days from now at ten in the morning?"

He put his chair down. "What are you going to do?"

"I'll see for myself how Anna feels about this match. If she is as reticent as you say she is, I will tell her to sit tight for now, but to be ready for action the moment you or I send word. In the meanwhile, I am going to do some research."

"Research?" he asked. "What are you going to research? Your romance novels?"

"The very same."

Rubbing his eyes, he checked his irritation. "Have you ever met Anna before?"

"Of course, but only briefly."

"I'll give you a letter to take with you, then. Now, what about your daughter's husband, Archie? He's Darius's right-hand man."

Mrs. Lockhart frowned. "Archie is not anyone's 'right-hand man.' He is an employee of Morgan Oil. No more. No less."

"I didn't mean to imply Archie would be involved in anything untoward."

"I should think not. Nevertheless, I don't wish to jeopardize his job, nor put his loyalties to the test. So you can be assured I will be very discreet." She stood. "Now, I need you to go so I can begin my research."

"Mrs. Lockhart, I'm not sure that romance novels—"

She handed him his hat. "You may pick me up tomorrow morning and carry my bag to the train station for me. By that time, I will have several options for you to consider."

He stood with indecision. What other choice did he have? He could go to Beaumont himself and confront Darius, but that would solve nothing. His brother would go to great lengths to protect this coveted connection with Norris Tubbs, just like Tony would go to great lengths to protect his sister.

But Darius had the upper hand. He was Anna's legal guardian and had the ability to keep Tony from getting anywhere near her or Mother until it was too late. Darius would also have Tubbs' power and support behind him.

But he would never suspect Mrs. Lockhart. Tony doubted Darius even knew who she was. If he got wind of it, though . . .

Tony gave her arm a gentle squeeze. "You must be very careful. Darius isn't evil, but he's greedy. If you were found out, no telling what he'd do. At the very least, Archie would lose his job."

She nodded. "I'll be careful."

"You won't do anything without discussing it with me first?"

"Of course not."

"All right, then." He settled his hat on his head. "I'll come by for you first thing tomorrow morning."

———

With Mr. Baker in town, Essie had to forgo Tony's bicycle training. Instead, she and Papa had Baker, Uncle Melvin, Aunt Verdie, and Preacher Wortham over for supper.

Papa had wanted Tony to join them, now that he was officially courting her, but she'd insisted that Tony train instead, even if she wasn't there with him. But what she really wanted was an opportunity to speak with Mr. Baker without Tony present.

Slicing an apple pie at the sideboard, she served up six plates while Aunt Verdie placed them on the table. The sheriff's wife was a handsome woman, her blond hair highlighted with silver. Having never had children, she had the hourglass figure that every woman in town coveted—a tiny, tiny waist with extremely generous proportions both above and below.

"My crew should get here within a couple of days," Mr. Baker said, "and then we'll be able to get started."

"I'll take you through the fields tomorrow, then," Papa replied. "We've started drilling outside the city limits now."

"That's what Tony was sayin'."

Essie slid back into her chair. "Have you known Mr. Bryant for long?"

Mr. Baker looked at her with confusion, before his expression cleared. "Oh, you mean Tony? Well, I guess that depends on what you'd call 'long.' I've been in Beaumont off and on for a couple of years."

"Off and on?"

"Yes, ma'am. My brother and I have been drillin' water wells all over the state, but our families are in Beaumont and so we always return there between jobs. That's how I got to know Tony."

"I see." She scooped up a bite of pie with her fork. "You know his family, then?"

"Oh, I know who they are, but I don't know them personal-like the way I do him."

She frowned. How could he know Tony and not his family? That didn't make a bit of sense. Not in a small town like Beaumont. But she couldn't think of a graceful way to ask such a question.

"I'm surprised Morgan Oil didn't hire you to drill for them, what with you right there and all," Uncle Melvin said.

"Well, I reckon we were so busy with our water business that we didn't really think about drillin' fer oil until here recently when we heard they was using rotaries up in Pennsylvania—and very successfully, I might add. But once we got wind of it, we went straight to Tony."

"And did Mr. Bryant contract your services?" the preacher asked.

"No, sir. Before any firm plans were made, Mr. Morgan passed. And now, well, the new boss is still sorting out which end is up."

"Tony knows the Morgans quite well, then?" Essie asked.

Color rushed to Mr. Baker's cheeks. "I'd say that's a safe assumption, ma'am."

"Oh?"

He swallowed. "Yes, ma'am. He, uh, he worked for them." He glanced at Papa, then back at her. "You did know that, didn't you?"

"Oh yes, of course," she replied. "He said he ordered their equipment and such."

Mr. Baker visibly relaxed. "That's right. That's why I went to him about the rotary drill."

"And what about you? Do you know the Morgans?"

"No, ma'am. Just . . ." His voice tapered off.

"Just . . . ?" she prompted.

"Just from a distance, ma'am."

She dabbed her mouth with her napkin. "Mr. Bryant seemed upset about Miss Morgan's betrothal to Mr., um, Tubbs, I believe?"

Mr. Baker's eyes darted in two different directions. "Did he?"

"He certainly did. Were he and Miss Morgan close?"

With a large, stubby finger, the driller pushed the last bite of dessert onto his fork. "They went to school together, I believe."

Before she could continue her line of questioning, Aunt Verdie interrupted.

"The pie was delicious, dear," she said. "Every bit as good as your mother's."

The others at the table echoed her sentiments and Essie smiled her thanks.

Papa pulled his napkin from his neck. "Mr. Baker? Preacher? Melvin? Would you care to join me for a cigar?"

The driller shoved back his chair. "I'd be much obliged, sir." He turned to Essie. "The meal was mighty fine, ma'am. Mighty fine."

Thanking him, she stood and gathered their plates while the men retreated to the front porch. She realized many of her questions about Tony and his relationship to the Morgans could have been answered if her father had simply thought to ask Tony when he first brought up the idea of courting her.

But Papa had relegated that discussion to her and now it seemed a bit late to start inquiring about it. Or maybe it wasn't. Now that they were officially courting, it was only natural she'd want to know about his family and his past and, certainly, his connection to Morgan Oil.

"You have somethin' on your mind, Essie-girl?" Aunt Verdie asked.

Essie glanced out the window, trying to judge the time. "I was just thinking about Tony. Perhaps if we hurried with these dishes, I could still catch him before he left the bicycle club."

Her aunt's expression softened. "You run on, now, and see to that man of yours. I'll take care of these dishes."

"Oh no. I couldn't."

"It would be my pleasure."

Essie shook her head. "No, really. I wouldn't feel right."

Without further argument, Aunt Verdie cleared the table, and Essie made short work of the dishes. She was just finishing up when she spotted Ewing and Mr. Baker through the window. They'd come around from the front and moved into the backyard, deep in discussion.

Mr. Baker was clearly distressed. Ewing placed a hand on the man's shoulder, stopping him. The preacher glanced at the house, frowning, then said something to Mr. Baker. Both men bowed their heads.

———

Essie slipped into the clubhouse, surprised to see Tony was only on the Indian clubs. He should have finished with those long ago. He juggled them in the air with much more precision than Sharpley ever had.

Pushing aside thoughts of Anna Morgan, Essie allowed excitement over the upcoming race to fill her. She only wished she had more time to prepare Tony.

She'd been training riders for four years now, ever since she opened the club. She'd originally organized the race to bring in new members, but after reading everything she could get her hands on concerning the art of racing and training, she'd come to covet a winning trophy for Sullivan Oil, for her club, and for her town.

Tony caught the clubs, returned them to their bin, then dropped to the floor for push-ups. She stayed in the shadows, telling herself she just wanted to see if he did all one hundred of them. But she lost count after the first fifteen, distracted by the sight he made aligning himself parallel to the floor.

He lifted his body with quick, powerful movements. Arms flexing, legs stiff, toes together. Light from the sconces splashed onto him, highlighting the sweat glistening on his skin. With a final grunt, he lowered himself to the floor and lay on his stomach, unmoving.

She stepped from the shadows.

"Essie," he said, raising his head. "I didn't hear you come in." He pushed himself up and stood, leaving an imprint of moisture the length of his body on the wooden floor.

His dark hair fell in abandon around his face. His chest heaved with each breath, stretching the wet shirt across his shoulders and delineating his muscles in sharp relief.

Arms hanging limp, he rested his weight on his right leg, throwing his hip slightly off to one side. She pulled her gaze and thoughts from their wayward paths, only to be caught short by the intensity of his stare.

"I . . ." she began. "We . . . Papa and Mr. Baker . . . they, uh, they retired to the porch, so I thought I'd come check on you."

His breathing was the only sound in the quiet of the building. "I'm glad you did."

She swallowed. "I thought you'd be almost finished by now."

"I got a late start."

"Oh?"

"I stopped by Mrs. Lockhart's on my way."

She blinked in confusion. "Mrs. Lockhart's?"

"Have you seen her backyard, Essie? It's a mess. I think I might go by and clean it up some while she's gone."

"Gone? You went by her house and she was gone?"

"No, not yet. She's leaving tomorrow for a short visit with her daughter."

Essie shook her head. "I don't understand. Why were you at Mrs. Lockhart's to begin with?"

He shrugged. "I've been by to check on her several times since that night I first escorted her to your lecture. She's rather up in years and has no family in town."

Essie absorbed that bit of information. Mrs. Lockhart had been such a pillar of the community for so long, it had never occurred to her to think of the elderly woman as fragile or lonely. But she could understand how a newcomer might view her that way.

"Oh," she said. "Well, that's very thoughtful of you. And, no, I had assumed her front yard was a reflection of her back."

"Well, it's not. But I'll take care of it."

She nodded absently, trying to gather her scattered thoughts. "So what all have you done?"

"The first three sets of laps and some of my exercises. I was just fixing to do my last set of laps now."

"I see," she took a step back. "Well, go ahead. Don't let me stop you."

Nodding, he retrieved the bicycle leaning against the wall, swung into the saddle and began his regimen. The wheels whirred slowly, then picked up momentum with each passing lap. The faster Tony went, the more he crouched down, like a jockey riding a horse.

She soon found herself caught up in his progress, shouting encouragement and urging him to even greater speed. When he completed his final lap and crossed the imaginary finish line, she cheered. It was one of his best runs by far.

Releasing the handlebars, he sat up, a smile wreathing his face. Clasping his hands together, he shook them in the air like a winner, then continued to glide around the track once more before pulling to a stop beside her.

"Oh, I wish I'd had my stopwatch!" she exclaimed. "You were splendid!"

He sat straddling the bike, his feet planted on either side. "I do better when you're here watching." His voice was low, pleased.

"Well, it's no hardship to watch you, I can tell you that."

His expression changed immediately. Reaching out, he clasped her hand and drew her close. Her skirts bunched around his leg. The bike's crossbar pressed against her hip.

"You smell good. Like cookies," he said, raising her hand to his mouth.

Shivers raced up her arm. "Cookies?"

"You know, the kind with cloves. Icebox cookies." He turned her hand over and rubbed his lips against her palm. "They're my favorite."

She stared, fascinated with the difference between her white fingers and his tanned ones, while the dark stubble on his cheek caught against her fingernails.

"Unfortunately, I smell like I've been training for a bicycle race."

She felt his smile while watching the skin beside his eyes crinkle, his expression turning rueful. And though he did smell of a man who'd been laboring, she did not find the odor unpleasant. She managed to refrain from saying so, however.

"Would you like to go fishing?" he asked.

"Right now?"

His smile widened. "Tempting, but I was thinking of after church on Sunday."

She flushed and tried to step away, but he put a hand against her waist, staying her.

She lowered her gaze. "Yes, thank you. I'd love to go fishing."

Closing his eyes, he planted a kiss onto her palm. "Sunday it is, then."

Pulling her hand away, she pressed it against her stomach—whether to capture the kiss and keep it close or to calm the jitters inside, she didn't know.

She took a step back. "It's late. I suggest we call it a night. Why don't I start putting out the lights while you take care of the bike?"

He nodded and she turned, making her way to the far wall, all the while disconcerted to know that he stayed right where he was, watching her.

It wasn't until much later that night when she was home and tucked safely in bed that she realized she'd totally forgotten to ask him about his family and the Morgans.

Rolling over, she bunched up her pillow. No need to fret. There would be time enough for that while they were fishing.

CHAPTER | NINETEEN

ESSIE COULDN'T REMEMBER THE last time building a rig had caused such a stir. Every boomer in the patch kept one eye on his job and the other on the Bakers' marvel.

Two days after M.C.'s arrival, his brother, C.E., descended on Corsicana with their crew of rig builders. Essie watched them with fascination. A tougher, stronger, meaner group of men would be hard to find.

Whiteselle's Lumber Yard delivered pre-sawed roughs, and M.C.'s crew attacked them like ants on a picnic lunch. They worked at a fast and furious pace, putting every other able-bodied man to shame.

Skillful, ambidextrous, and exceedingly strong, they laid down a derrick floor, then began to nail together the rig's legs. Dirt clouds churned so thick around the crew that she had to squint sometimes just to see.

When Essie made an appearance, the Sullivan Oil hands invariably stopped their work, but there was no stopping M.C. Baker's crew. They paid her no mind at all. She wasn't even sure they realized she was there.

As the derrick went up, the men raised their timbers with a pulley they called a "gin pole." Muscles bulged, sharp commands abounded, and a good deal of hazing occurred without anyone missing a step.

Essie watched one sweat-soaked man as he steadied a three-by-twelve-inch board in a corner of the derrick, then sank in a spike with three quick blows. Instead of a hammer, he used a long-handled hatchet with a round, serrated head opposed to the blade, hammering spike after spike with first his right hand, then his left.

Tony stood below him, then pointed up and shouted something, but she couldn't make out his words. In conjunction with M.C.'s arrival, Papa had pulled Tony from his roustabouting and promoted him to tool pusher for the rotary rigs, while Moss would remain tool pusher for the cable rigs.

Tony knew his tools backwards and forwards, but she didn't think he came close to deserving such a high position. He was, after all, a very recent employee, and they had several other men who had worked longer and were more deserving—if not, perhaps, as qualified.

She also didn't want people thinking the job had been given to him because of his relationship with her, though she worried that might have indeed factored into Papa's decision. And until she could find out exactly what had happened to him at Morgan Oil and what his connection to Anna Morgan was, she was determined to maintain an employer–employee relationship with him while in the patch. It wouldn't be easy, though.

The rig builder shouted something down to Tony, who, in response, threw back his head and laughed. The two shared a smile before Tony turned away from the derrick and caught sight of her. His face registering surprise, then panic.

He quickly glanced around to see if anyone was near her, then bore down on her, scowling. "What are you doing here?"

"I beg your pardon?" she said.

"You heard me." He snatched his hat off belatedly, pinching the crown between his fingers. "What are you doing here?"

His vehemence shocked her.

"I'm here to watch the construction of our new rig, Mr. Bryant. Was there something you needed?"

He shooed her with his hat. "I need you to leave. This is no place for a woman, and you are distracting the boys."

"Nothing seems to distract these boys. And even if I were, I own the company. Which means I can go wherever I please—and without having to explain myself."

"Lower your voice," he said. He grasped her elbow and propelled her toward the edge of the field where she'd left her bicycle. "I don't want you challenging me in front of the men."

She tugged against his hold. "Let go. I want to watch the rig builders."

He tightened his grip. "I'm afraid that's out of the question."

"It is not. Just who do you think you are?"

They reached the street and he jerked her bike up off the ground. "I am overseer of the rotary rigs. And I do not allow females of any sort around the patch—even part owners."

"You work for me, Tony, not the other way around. You do not have the authority to tell me where I can and can't go."

"I told your father I would not accept this position unless I had absolute power on the field. He agreed to my terms. If you have a problem with that, then take it up with him. But for now, you are to put your pretty backside on this bike and ride well out of harm's way."

"No."

He narrowed his eyes. "If you don't want me to sling you over my shoulder and bodily carry you all the way to your front door, then I suggest you get on this machine, and right quickly."

"You wouldn't dare."

He leaned in close. "Try me."

She didn't make any move to take the bike from him.

"You have to the count of ten. One . . . two . . ."

She could not believe he would actually do it. But, then, maybe he would. And if he did, the men would talk about it all over town, and any respect she'd garnered over the years would go up in a puff of smoke.

"Seven . . . eight . . ."

She grabbed Peg's handlebars. "I am going straightaway to discuss this with my father. We will see just exactly who is boss and who is not. I expect you to be in our office the moment your shift is over."

Without another word, she mounted the bicycle and, with all the dignity she could muster, rode toward home.

———

Papa was not at home. Nor at the courthouse. Nor at the attorney's office. The longer she looked for him, the more irritated she became. He'd promoted Tony without consulting her. He'd excluded her from discussions with the Baker brothers. He'd contracted for three rotary rigs before even seeing if the first one was going to work.

Pulling to a stop in front of the jailhouse, she jumped from the bike, then stormed up the steps and through the door, bumping square into Deputy Howard.

"Whoa there, girl," he said, clasping her around the waist to keep her from falling. Warm breath from his mouth and nose touched her cheek.

She shoved against him. "Let me go."

He held up his hands in mock surrender. "Now, what's got you cross as a snappin' turtle on this fine summer day?"

"Men in general. You in particular." She scanned the room and found her uncle and father standing beside the sheriff's desk, staring at her in surprise.

She knew she was behaving badly, but she couldn't seem to rein in her temper. "I've been looking all over for you, Papa."

"Well, I'm right here. Has something happened?"

"Nothing catastrophic. Just a few things I'd like to get straightened out."

"Can it wait a minute? Deputy Howard is leaving for Austin this afternoon, and Melvin and I need to finalize a few things before he leaves."

"Austin? Why?"

"The annual Texas Sheriff's Association Convention starts Monday, and Melvin is going to send Howard in his stead."

"Oh." She tugged the bow under her neck and removed her bonnet. "Very well. I'll wait."

Howard moved away from the doorway. "I think I'll pick up those records from the courthouse on my way to the train station instead of getting them now."

"Fine," Uncle Melvin said, then turned back to Papa.

Howard sidled up to Essie, winking at her. She stepped to the right, putting distance between them.

"I like the opening sentence much better than the way we had it before," Melvin said. "Do you think the petition is strong enough now?"

"Oh, I think it's plenty strong. The question is whether or not the Association will back it."

Essie moved to the desk. "What is it?"

"Take a look," Melvin said, turning the document so she could see. "We want to ride the tide of the anti-lynching crusade led by that newspaper editor in Tennessee. If Billy John can get members of the Sheriff's Association to sign this petition, the state congress will be hard-pressed not to pass a law punishing those responsible for lynching in our state."

She glanced at the other papers on his desk but saw no evidence of the postcard she'd seen before. "You can't arrest an entire mob, can you?"

"Naw," he said. "But we could arrest the ringleaders and make an example of them."

Papa checked his pocket watch. "Well, if you don't need me any further, Melvin, I guess I'll see what it is Essie wants."

"No, no. You go on. Billy John and I can take it from here."

Papa ushered her out the door and to her bicycle. "Now, what is it that has you all worked up?"

She recalled the sting of Tony's dismissal afresh. "Tony refused to let me watch the rig builders. He practically forced me onto my bike and made me leave."

"Oh, I'm sorry, honey. I forgot to tell you to quit going out there."

"What?" She stopped pushing her bicycle to stare at him. "You agreed to that without talking with me first?"

He shrugged. "There wasn't time. Besides, he's the one running the site now. If he doesn't want any women out there, then that's his prerogative."

They continued down the street. "I'm not just *any* woman. I'm part owner and his boss, to boot."

"That may be so, but surely you see his point, Essie. The fields are getting rougher and rougher. Tony said you interrupt the work and distract the men, and depending upon what they're in the middle of, that can be extremely dangerous."

"What are you saying? That I'm never to go out to our fields again for the rest of my life?"

He chuckled. "I don't think we have to go quite so far as that. Just lay low for now until Tony has a chance to establish himself in his new position."

She blew out a huff of breath. "I wish you would consult with me before making decisions like this. You promoted Tony without due consideration. Grandpa or some of our other men should have been offered the position first."

"I don't know why you keep harping about this. If we were replacing Moss, then you'd be right." He shook his head. "We needed a tool pusher for our rotary rigs. None of the men but Tony had ever even seen one. Like it or not, he's the man most suited for the job."

She sighed. "That may be true, but something just isn't quite right. I can't put my finger on it. But he left Morgan Oil so suddenly, and he knows the Morgan family more intimately than he let on at first."

"You think he's lying to us about something?" Papa asked, clearly surprised.

"Withholding, maybe. He knows too much about that family not to have some personal tie."

Papa considered her words as they turned onto Eighth Street. "Well, let's put the shoe on the other foot for a moment. Moss or any of the men who report at the house know plenty about our personal lives."

She supposed he was right. But would Mr. Moss use her Christian name in casual conversation the way Tony had with Miss Morgan's? She couldn't imagine him taking such a liberty. Not unless theirs was a more . . . intimate acquaintance.

No, if Mr. Moss were to call her something other than Miss Spreckelmeyer, it would undoubtedly be in the form of a nickname. Thank goodness she'd escaped that unpleasant designation.

———

Essie showed Tony into the study. She'd forgotten he was coming by the house right after work. When she'd instructed him to do so, she'd thought to tell him in no uncertain terms that she would go out to the fields whenever she pleased. To have to concede defeat on the matter did not sit well.

He'd not taken the time to bathe or change. His clothes were splattered with mud. His face was covered in dirt. His brown eyes, however, shone brightly.

"I'd ask you to sit, but, well . . ."

He smiled. "I understand. You go ahead, though."

Papa was not at home, so she took his place behind the desk.

Tony moved to the window, leaning back against the sill. "The judge told me y'all bid on some land south of town."

"That's right."

"I went down there and looked it over. Looks like a ripe field."

"I certainly thought so."

"When will you know if you won the bid?"

"Anytime now."

An awkward silence settled over them.

Tony cleared his throat. "The rig builders should finish the derrick within another day or two, but that's going to cut into our fishing time. Would you mind if we postponed our date until next Sunday?"

She moistened her lips. Her plans had been to ask him about Anna Morgan while they were fishing, and she wasn't sure she could wait another week to satisfy her curiosity. Perhaps an opportunity would present itself between now and then.

"No, of course I don't mind," she answered. "Next Sunday is fine."

He hesitated. "Did you have a chance to talk with your father?"

"Yes," she said, clipping the word.

"Good. He told you about the masks, then?"

"Masks?"

"Yes. The cup masks."

"What cup masks?"

"I thought you talked to your father?"

"I did, but we discussed your request that I stay away from the fields."

He nodded as understanding dawned. "I am sorry about that. It's just that women—"

She held up her hand. "I'd rather not rehash it, if it is all the same to you. Now, what about these masks?"

"When we swab the wells, the sulphur gas that rushes up out of the hole is so strong it can knock a fella clean out. We waste a lot of time waiting for that gas to blow before letting the bailer down. So I was thinking, what if we got us some of those cup masks they use in the factories up north? We could just wear those and then we wouldn't have to worry about anybody keeling over. And it would save time, too."

She leaned back in her chair. "You know, Tony, you come up with more creative ways to spend money than anyone I've ever met. You just talked Papa into investing in three rotary rigs and now you want me to order masks?"

"Not just any masks. Cup masks. You know, the kind that look like pig snouts?"

"Pig snouts."

"Yes. They fit over the nose and mouth and prevent noxious gases from getting into your throat and lungs. For us, they'd also save time."

She sighed. "I appreciate what you're trying to do, but if the sulphur gas is truly as dangerous as you are suggesting, then cup masks would be used up in Pennsylvania.

But no one uses them. No one. They simply get out of the gas's way when it starts to blow."

"So your answer is no?"

"I have to consider both the benefit and practicality of them," she explained. "And though they might help the men breathe, I cannot imagine the boomers wearing them. Think of how uncomfortable and hot they would be."

"They wouldn't wear them all the time. Only when the gas starts to blow."

She shook her head. "They could just as easily clear out of the way. I'm sorry. I simply can't justify the expense of masks for every man in my employ."

"Not every man. The drillers."

"We have over three hundred drillers, Tony. We can't just up and buy masks for all of them. Besides, we don't even know if they would work."

"Yes, we do. I had one sent out already and tried it. Works great."

She frowned. "Where did you get it?"

"I'm not sure where it came from. Your father ordered it."

Her lips parted. "When did he do that?"

"Couple of weeks ago."

"Good heavens."

"So what do you say?"

"I say we've been doing just fine for the last four years. I imagine we'll continue to do so."

"You don't even know what they cost and haven't seen them in action."

"I'm afraid I won't have the pleasure of seeing them in action, Mr. Bryant, since I'm no longer allowed on my own fields."

His lips thinned. "Is that what this is about? You're mad because you got your nose tweaked, so you're going to risk the health of the men for the sake of your pride?"

She shot up out of her chair. "That is quite enough. I don't know what makes you think you can address me in such a manner, but let me assure you that you cannot."

"Those masks can be a matter of life or death."

"I hardly think so. As I pointed out before, every oil patch in America has managed just fine without them."

"Does your father know you are refusing to buy them?"

"You go right ahead and run to him, since that seems to be your wont. But I guarantee you, this time he will say the decision is mine and mine alone."

Tony put on his hat. "Well, I guess we'll find out, won't we?"

"We certainly will. In the meantime, I expect to see you at training tonight. Be prepared for a vigorous workout."

"Not to worry, Miss Spreckelmeyer. I can handle anything you care to throw my way." Spinning around, he stalked out of the office and slammed the door behind him.

CHAPTER | TWENTY

ESSIE PLACED SUGAR COOKIES in a tin, the buttery aroma filling the room. The door opened and she glanced over her shoulder.

"Ewing," she said, smiling. "It's been a while since you've come in the kitchen door. And just in time for cookies. Would you like some?"

Hanging his hat on a peg, he nodded. "Don't mind if I do."

His reddish blond hair fell in abandon across his forehead, but his black clerical suit fit him with the precision of a well-tailored garment.

She handed him the tin. "Papa's in his study. I'd walk you back there, but I need to get to the clubhouse."

He set the cookies on the table. "Actually, I didn't come to see your dad. I came to see you."

"Me?"

"Yes."

She glanced out the window. "I'd love to visit, but Tony's expecting me."

He held out a chair. "He can wait."

She slowly untied her apron and hung it over the oven-door handle. "What's the matter?"

"Please, have a seat." Tension tightened the lines on his face.

Smoothing her skirts, she took the chair he offered, then watched as he settled in across from her.

"We've been friends a long time," he began.

"My stars and garters, Ewing. What on earth has happened to make you so morose?"

He took a deep breath. "How well do you know Tony Bryant?"

She blinked. "What kind of question is that? I'm courting him, for heaven's sake."

"Yes." He cleared his throat. "But what I'm trying to determine is, um, just how much you know about him."

"Who's asking?" she said, cocking her head. "My preacher, my friend, or my former suitor?"

His face filled with color. "I'd like to say your preacher, but I'm not sure that's the case."

"Then which is the case?"

"Your friend. Your friend is asking. Though, I don't think I'd have agonized over it quite so much if I hadn't been a former suitor."

She digested that bit of honesty, then pushed the tin of cookies toward him. "You've heard something you think I need to know. And whatever it is, it's unpleasant. Am I right?"

He nodded, breaking a cookie in half, then putting it in his mouth.

"Well, let's hear it."

He finished chewing and swallowed. "Tony Bryant is actually Tony Morgan. As in the Morgan Oil Morgans."

"What?" she asked, frowning. "What are you saying?"

"I'm saying he's the late Blake Morgan's younger son."

As she tried to sort through her confusion, one thought rose immediately to the surface. *That would mean Anna Morgan's his sister.* She slid her eyes closed, a sense of relief flowing through her.

"Oh, Ewing. I'd suspected his ties to the Morgans were more than he'd let on, but I'd imagined he was a spurned suitor of Anna Morgan's and that he had ulterior motives for courting me." She shook her head. "And now to find out Anna's his sister, of all things."

She smiled at her foolishness and at Ewing, but his face did not reflect her relief.

"I don't think you're seeing the big picture, Essie. He's been lying to you. To the entire town."

"Oh, I'm sure there's a perfectly reasonable explanation. Just look at how I mistook his interest in me, thinking it was due to my being an oil heiress—just like Anna—when all the time she was his sister."

"I don't know. I mean, we both know your first instinct has always been to see the best in people—even when it's not there."

He gave her a pointed look, and she knew he was referring to a beau of hers from a few years back whom she'd grossly misjudged.

"That aside," Ewing continued, "why would a Morgan pass himself off as a nobody unless he wanted something?"

She gave him a cautious look. "Like what?"

Ewing rubbed his forehead. "Like a position with Sullivan Oil."

She hesitated. "Come to think of it, why would he need a position with Sullivan Oil when he has his own company?"

Ewing held her gaze. "Perhaps he was figuring to learn firsthand his competition's strengths and weaknesses."

She swallowed, her calm suddenly eclipsed by impending dread.

Setting his elbows on the table, Ewing linked his hands together and rested his chin on his fists. "And what better way to do that than by courting the owner's daughter and infiltrating the company at its highest and most vulnerable level?"

Her mind balked. She tried not to think the obvious, but it was becoming all too clear.

"Are you absolutely certain about this?" she asked.

"I'm not at all certain of his motives. Only that his real name is Tony Morgan."

"How long have you known?"

"I was told a couple of days ago," he said, lowering his hands.

"By whom?"

"Does it matter?"

She cringed. If Ewing had heard it from some busybody, then no telling how many others were whispering behind their hands about Essie Spreckelmeyer being courted, once again, for all the wrong reasons. "Who all knows?"

"I think only me and the person who told me."

"But I thought you heard it through the gossip mill?"

"I never said that. I was given the information in the strictest of confidences from an outsider. You have no idea how much I have struggled with whether or not I was at liberty to tell you."

"And no one else knows?"

"If they do, I've not heard a word. And I feel sure I would have. This would be way too juicy a piece of meat not to have every jaw in town gnawing on it."

She nodded, dreading the time when Tony's identity was eventually discovered. Not only would she be at the center of the townsfolk's speculations, but now that she had time to consider it, she realized they would not take kindly to being duped. Particularly not by a Morgan.

Ewing looked out the window. "I wonder if he had some nefarious reason for using a false name."

"What do you mean?"

He shrugged. "Well, a fella doesn't hide his identity for good reasons, that's for sure."

She frowned, then rose to her feet. "You did the right thing, Ewing. It would have been horrible if I'd been the last to find out."

"That's what I finally decided, too," he said, standing. "So what are you going to do?"

"Tell Papa."

"Would you like me to come with you?"

"No, I think it's best if I do it myself." She reached out with her hand. Ewing slipped his around it.

"Thank you," she said, squeezing.

"You all right?"

Nodding, she bit her lower lip. "I'll be fine."

"You don't have to put on a brave face for me."

"I know."

Hand-in-hand, they walked to the door.

He retrieved his hat. "Well, thanks for the cookie. And remember, I am your preacher. If you ever need a shoulder . . ."

She kissed him on the cheek. "If I ever need a shoulder, I think I'll come visit my friend Ewing, not Preacher Wortham. That is, if it's all right with you?"

"You know it is."

Closing the door behind him, Essie swallowed the hurt pushing against her. She would save that for later. Right now she needed to tell Papa.

———

Essie knocked on the door of her father's study, then poked her head inside. "Can I come in?"

He waved her in without bothering to look up from the paper he was writing on. His gray hair looked as if it had been plowed into distinct rows. Even as the thought occurred to her, he ran his fingers through it again, reinforcing the furrows.

His jacket hung on the back of his chair. His four-in-hand tie lay in a puddle on the corner of his desk. The cuffs of his white shirt were smudged with ink.

She seated herself in one of the wing chairs across from him. After a few minutes, he put his pen in its holder and blotted the page. "Don't you have bicycle training tonight?" he asked, still skimming whatever it was he'd written.

"Yes, but I needed to talk with you first."

"Well, if you plan on hounding me again about Tony's position as tool pusher, I'm not up to it," he said, reaching for his pen and dipping it in the ink well.

"No. It isn't that."

"What is it, then?"

"I've just received some rather disturbing news."

He scribbled something on the bottom of the paper. "Go ahead."

"Tony Bryant is actually Tony Morgan, Blake Morgan's son."

Papa stopped writing mid-sentence and looked up. Being a judge, he was a master at disguising his feelings. But she knew him well and saw the surprise light his eyes before he quickly shuttered it.

"How did you find out?" he asked, returning the pen to its holder.

"Ewing told me."

"How did Ewing find out?"

"He wouldn't tell me."

Papa leaned back, the brown leather upholstery creaking. "Who else knows?"

"I don't think anyone, yet."

"Well, somebody does or else Ewing wouldn't have found out."

"He said it was an outsider who asked him to keep the information private." She hesitated. "Perhaps it was Mr. Baker? I saw them talking out in the yard that night they were over for dinner."

"Isn't exactly reassuring to find out our preacher can't keep his mouth shut, is it?"

Essie stiffened. "He was wanting to protect me. Surely in this case, breaking a confidence was the lesser of two evils. And why are we talking about Ewing when we should be talking about Tony and what to do about this?"

Papa rubbed his mouth. "I'm not planning on doing anything about it."

"What?"

"I like him. I always have. He's a hard worker. He's knowledgeable. He's innovative. And he had the good sense to court you."

She threaded her fingers together. "Papa. Surely you can read between the lines here. He isn't courting me because he has feelings for me. He's courting me to worm his way into our company."

"I don't think so, Essie. And it disturbs me that you do."

"It's the only thing that makes sense. What other possible motivation could he have for pretending to be someone he's not?"

"I'm not sure he sees it as pretending, exactly."

She raised a brow.

"His father disinherited him. Completely. Didn't give him so much as a penny. Left just enough for his wife and daughter to get by on and gave the rest to his first son."

"Oh, Papa. That can't be true. Mr. Morgan had plenty of money to spread around. It doesn't make sense for him to disinherit anyone, especially not his own son."

"All the same, that's what he did."

She frowned. "How could you possibly know all that?"

"The content of Blake's will is common knowledge among the men in my circle."

She tried to process what he was telling her. "But how do you know Tony is the son that was disinherited?"

"He's the second son."

"How can you be sure?"

Papa took a deep breath. "I've known who he was from the moment he stepped into my office that first day."

"What? He told you and you didn't tell me!"

"No, no. He never said a word about it. But I knew his father, Essie. We were on opposing sides of a bill I wanted passed once, back when you were just a little girl. He was a hard man with a lot of money. When the bill went in my favor, he took it personally and I found, through no fault of my own, that I'd made a formidable enemy."

"But that doesn't explain how you knew Tony."

"The Morgan men all bear a striking resemblance to one another. Tony looks like his father. And his father like the father before him. There was no mistaking him. And even if I'd had any doubts, they were put to rest when he used the last name Bryant."

"Why?"

"His mother was a Bryant. I'd known her father for years. He hated the Morgans and refused to grant Blake permission to court his daughter. But Blake was still stinging from the loss of that bill and wasn't about to be told no a second time. So they eloped."

"Good heavens."

"And if that weren't enough, she was barely out of the schoolroom and he was twenty years her senior and still grieving over his first wife."

"What are you saying?"

"It wasn't a love match—at least, not on his part. He wanted a mother for his baby son and a wife to . . . well, he wanted a wife. And to be perfectly honest, I think his main reason for choosing Leah was because Alfred told him he couldn't have her."

"Oh, that poor girl."

He shrugged. "It was a long time ago. In any event, she gave him another son and then a daughter, but Blake left his fortune and his business to Darius, his first son, and nothing to Tony."

"Why? What did Tony do to warrant his father's wrath?"

"He had the unfortunate distinction of being the product of a loveless marriage. Blake didn't care any more for Leah's offspring than he did for Leah."

Essie couldn't begin to comprehend something so reprehensible, particularly when it was the man's own flesh and blood.

"What happened to Mrs. Morgan and Anna?"

"He marginally provided for Leah and Anna, though Darius holds all the power and the purse strings."

"But that doesn't explain why Tony would pretend to be someone he's not."

"Let me ask you this: If you'd known he was Blake Morgan's son, would you have hired him on?"

"I never wanted to hire him to begin with."

"Exactly. If he had any chance of getting a job in the oil patch, he had to be someone other than Tony Morgan."

She rubbed her forehead. Tony, her Tony, was the cast-out son of Blake Morgan? She tried to imagine her parents disinheriting her. The hurt and betrayal alone would be devastating.

"Why didn't you tell me?" she asked.

"I didn't mind his being a Morgan. I wasn't about to hold a grudge against him simply because his father hadn't cared for me. At the same time, I didn't want to show my hand too soon, just in case his motives were questionable. So I decided to sit tight and see what happened."

"And when he asked to court me? It didn't occur to you that I might like to know the identity of the man I was stepping out with?"

"I thought about telling you. But after praying about it, the Lord told me to be still. So that's what I did. You'd have found out here pretty quick, though."

She frowned. "Why do you say that?"

"I just learned that Darius Morgan outbid us on the mineral rights for that chunk of land south of town."

"No! You can't mean it. I didn't even know he was interested in it."

"Me either."

"And we lost?" She tightened her lips. "I can't believe it. And not only that, but now we're going to have to deal with Morgan Oil doing business right here in our own backyard."

Papa shrugged. "He has just as much right to it as we do."

"But . . . but we were here first!"

A sparkle entered his eyes. "Would it soothe your sense of injustice if I bought up some mineral rights in Beaumont?"

She thought about it, then smiled. "Actually, I think it would. You want to?"

He chuckled. "We'll see. In the meanwhile, Morgan's men will be pouring into town pretty soon and they'll be all too happy to tell everyone within hearing distance just exactly who Tony is."

She bit her lip. "Is Tony aware that you know he's a Morgan?"

"He has no idea."

"And you think it's really as simple as he wanted a job?"

"I do. From everything I've seen and heard, he's a fine man. I've been most impressed."

She hoped he was right. Oh, how she hoped he was right. "Do you think he knows about Morgan Oil's plans to move in?"

"I doubt it. It's my understanding he's been completely cut off from them. Besides, I just found out myself a couple of hours ago."

"Did you tell Uncle Melvin about Tony?"

"The very first day the boy arrived."

Slapping her hands against the arms of the chair, she pushed herself up. "Well. I guess I'll go on to the clubhouse. I'm sure Tony's wondering what's keeping me."

"What are you going to do?"

"First I'm going to train him for the bicycle race. Then I'm going to ask him straight out who he is."

CHAPTER | TWENTY-ONE

TONY JUGGLED THE FOOTBALL with his thighs and feet, trying to see how long he could keep it in the air. The door to the clubhouse squeaked open and he caught the ball.

"Where have you been?" he asked.

Essie removed her shawl and hat and hung them by the door. "Something came up and I couldn't get away."

He pushed the hair out of his eyes. "Is it because you're still mad at me?"

"Mad at you about what?"

He hesitated. If she wasn't dwelling on their argument about her going to the fields, he wasn't fool enough to bring it up. "You aren't wearing your bloomers."

She glanced down at her brown skirt and white shirtwaist. "I didn't have time to change."

"What is it? What's happened?"

"We lost our bid for the mineral rights south of town."

"You're kidding." He frowned, yet took time to appreciate the sway of her hips as she approached. "Who outbid you?"

"Morgan Oil."

He froze. "Morgan Oil? Why would they bid on rights clear up in Navarro County?"

She stopped in front of him and took the ball from his hands. "You tell me."

Dragging his hand across his mouth, he looked around the clubhouse, trying to make sense of what she'd told him. "I have no idea. I didn't even know they were interested in it."

"No? Well, I'm glad to hear that, anyway."

He glanced at her sharply. "What's that supposed to mean?"

"Nothing," she said, moving to the bin against the wall and dropping the ball inside. "Did you put yourself through all the paces?"

"I did."

"You're completely through with your workout?"

"Except for our football match."

"Well, we won't be having that tonight." She turned around, facing him, then clasped her hands in front of her. "Just when were you planning on telling me your real name is Tony Morgan?"

Take the deuce. One of M.C.'s crew must have inadvertently said something. He'd been afraid of that. He'd hustled her off that field just as quick as he could. But it obviously hadn't been quick enough.

"I don't know, exactly," he said. "How did you find out?"

"That hardly matters, Tony."

"No, I don't suppose it does." He cleared his throat. "I've been wanting to tell you for quite some time."

"Then why didn't you?"

"I was afraid you'd question my motives."

"Motives for what?"

"For working for Sullivan Oil. For," he swallowed, "for stepping out with you."

"And what are your motives, Mr. Morgan?"

He started toward her, but she held up her hand. "Stay right where you are, sir, and answer my question."

"It's a really long answer. Can we go to your office over there and sit down?"

"I don't think so. Why don't you just give me the short version."

He massaged the back of his neck. "My interest in you is genuine, Essie. Very genuine. And asking for permission to court you was not something I did lightly."

He gave her a chance to respond, but she remained silent. The sconces cast a glow over her features. Her expression gave nothing away.

"I think about you all the time," he continued. "I think of all the places I want to take you and all the things I'd like to do with you, then I remember I have no money. No secure future. Not even a real name anymore." He blew out a huff of air. "Then I start worrying about how I'm going to support you. I've been scared out of my mind that if you ever found out who I was, you'd think I was using you to gain a foothold in your father's business. And I'm not. I swear I'm not."

She remained stoic. "What are you doing, then, Tony?"

"I'm trying to learn everything I can about the oil industry. I know a lot about the business side of it, but not as much about the everyday field work. So that's why I came here. To get a job with the largest producer of Texas oil so I could learn the ropes."

"Well, you've certainly managed to move up the chain of command rather quickly, haven't you?"

He crossed the floor, ignoring her attempts to keep him at bay. "I earned those positions fair and square," he said. "My success in the fields has had nothing to do with you and me."

"I'm part owner and sole heir to the Sullivan Oil enterprise. Of course it has to do with you and me. Do you take me for a fool?"

He grasped her arms. "Don't, Essie. Don't believe the worst, please."

"How can you expect me not to when you've done nothing but lie from the moment I laid eyes on you?"

"That's not fair. I've not lied about everything. Only about my name. It's just a name."

She pulled free of him. "Don't patronize me. It's much more than a name and you know it."

"All right. I was wrong to have lied. And I've known that for quite some time now. You have no idea how many times I've wanted to push the clock back and knock on your door for the first time as me. The real me."

She swallowed, her poker face disintegrating, the distress in her eyes apparent.

"Why didn't you just tell me?" she asked. "At least when we began to court. Couldn't you have told me then?"

He reached for her again, but she flinched, so he contented himself with lightly rubbing her arms.

"I wanted to," he said, "but don't you see? If I'd told you at that point, you would have sent me packing. You know you would have."

She turned her face away, and he could not resist pulling her to him. She felt so good. So soft. Whiffs of clove and sugar teased his senses.

He nuzzled her hair. "If you don't believe me, ask Mrs. Lockhart."

She jerked out of his arms and stumbled back. "Mrs. Lockhart? *Mrs. Lockhart!* What has she to do with this?"

"Well, she, she knows who I am," he answered, confused at her reaction.

"You told Mrs. Lockhart who you were and you didn't tell me?" she screeched.

"Not on purpose. She recognized me. What was I supposed to do?"

Essie spun around, no longer willing to face him. "Oooooh, I cannot even believe this is happening."

"What's wrong with Mrs. Lockhart knowing who I am?"

Essie covered her face with her hands. "Don't you see how humiliating this is? 'Poor little Essie Spreckelmeyer, the wallflower of Corsicana, finally gets herself a man because she comes part and parcel with the biggest oil company in Texas.' "

"Now, just a minute," he said, grabbing her arm and jerking her back around. "That's about the stupidest thing I ever heard and not a single soul would ever believe it. You're smart, you're pretty, you have a zest for living that others only dream about. You've accomplished more in your short life than most could accomplish in two lifetimes, you think nothing of risking your own skin to save somebody else's, and you make the best green corn patties I've ever tasted in my life. That oil company is nothing compared to you."

Her jaw slackened. "When have you had my green corn patties?"

"On the Fourth of July."

She stared at him, completely befuddled. "You think I'm pretty?"

"What fool kind of question is that? You're bound to own a mirror, so you know good and well you're pretty."

By slow degrees, her expression softened. "Thank you." Her gaze swept over him. "I think you're pretty, too."

He frowned. "Men are not pretty."

A smile crept onto her face. "Tony Bryant's pretty," she crooned in a soft, whispery voice.

It took him a moment to register she wasn't baiting him but was instead teasing him. And smiling. She wasn't angry anymore.

He let out a sigh of relief, then smoothed a tendril of hair behind her ear. "My name is Tony Morgan. Tony Bryant Morgan."

"Ahhh. That's right. I forgot. Tony Bryant *Morgan* is pretty."

"He is not."

"He is, too."

The light picked up the laughter in her eyes, the peaches in her skin.

"I'm sorry," he said. "I promise you this: I'll never, ever be anything but completely honest with you henceforth and forevermore."

Her amusement was slowly replaced with a touch of vulnerability. "Is there going to be a forevermore, Tony?"

Slipping his arms around her waist, he gently drew her close. "There will be if I have anything to say about it."

He lowered his lips to hers and kissed her. Not the way he'd have liked to, but the way he ought to. He tucked her more tightly against him, inhaling her scent, testing the way she felt in his embrace. Her arms snaked up around his neck, her fingers stroking the hair at his collar as she returned his kiss with the same enthusiasm she brought to most everything else she did.

Desire rushed through him and he forced himself to pull back. The yearning he saw in her eyes nearly undid him. Groaning, he pressed his face against her neck and helped himself to the tiniest of tastes before setting her at arm's length.

"I think we'd better head on home, Essie," he said, breathing heavily as he waited for the fog in her expression to clear. When it did, she gave him a tender smile, not at all embarrassed by her passion or his.

———

For the next two weeks, Tony hardly saw Essie outside their training sessions. Even then, with the date of the bicycle race drawing near, all her energies were focused on the track, not the courtship—though he did manage to steal a kiss or two.

Still, she broke their fishing date when an argument flared up amongst her organizers over who was to be the grand marshal for the bicycle parade. Some thought it should be the mayor, others thought it should be a wheeler.

He tried to take her to the soda shop, but she insisted she didn't have time; race headquarters needed to be set up downtown instead. On Saturday, the hospitality committee had proposed to greet guests at the front door of the Commercial Hotel with a white porcelain bathtub filled with punch and large cakes of ice. The preacher was none too happy about it.

He'd nodded coolly to Tony. And though Tony was careful to acknowledge the preacher's greeting, he accepted the fact that some folks were not as friendly as they used to be now that they'd discovered he was a Morgan.

"My congregation is scandalized at the very idea of using a bathtub in public," Wortham said to Essie.

"But a bathtub is perfect," she argued. "Think of all the filling and refilling of punch bowls we'd have to deal with otherwise, not to mention the chipping of ice."

"How 'bout using a horse trough?"

"A horse trough! I can't have our guests drinking out of the same thing their horses do."

"A coffin?"

"Ewing, would you please be serious?"

"I am. All my elders are breathing down my neck and a coffin is where I'm gonna end up if you insist on using that bathtub!"

"Listen, if you're so concerned with propriety, why don't you and your elders park yourselves in front of Rosenburg's Saloon and save a few souls instead of pestering me?"

In the end, she got her way, but it caused a strain between her and Ewing, and various members of her church took her to task on Sunday morning, though she didn't seem too terribly concerned.

Tony's relief at no longer having to hide his identity had filled him with an unprecedented sense of freedom—regardless of the censure bestowed by a few Corsicanans. Judge Spreckelmeyer had told Moss that he'd known all along Tony was a Morgan—which turned out to be the case—and that he'd thought it best if the boys judged him on his own merits before finding out who he was.

There was a bit of awkwardness among the Sullivan Oil hands for a few days, but M.C.'s crew had no such reservations. Since the other men on the patch held them in awe, their obvious respect went a long way in restoring Tony's standing in the fields.

Mrs. Lockhart returned from her second trip to Beaumont in just as many weeks, catching up to him on her bike in front of Castle's Drug Store.

"I need to talk to you," she said.

He assisted her off her wheel, took hold of the handlebars, then glanced up and down the street. "Shall we walk?"

As soon as they were out of earshot, she stopped. "Anna is being most uncooperative. She refuses to enter a convent. She doesn't find the idea of being swept out to sea by a pirate the least bit intriguing. And she claims you are the only relative she has that would be willing to stand up to Darius."

"You found a pirate?" he asked, shocked.

"Well, no. But I'm sure I could have."

He blinked. "I see. Well, Anna's got the right of it. Convents and pirates are not at all how I would have her proceed. And Grandfather Bryant would have taken her in, but he passed several years ago."

He turned the bike in the direction of Mrs. Lockhart's home and started walking again. "How's Mother holding up? Did Anna say?"

"Your mother has taken to her bed. She'll be of no help whatsoever."

"No. That doesn't surprise me."

"And I've a bit more bad news, I'm afraid."

He glanced at her. "What?"

"Morgan Oil is entering the bicycle race."

He stopped. "Our bicycle race?"

"The very same."

"But, Morgan Oil has never once accepted the invitation. It was only extended to us out of courtesy. Everyone knows we wouldn't accept."

She said nothing.

He narrowed his eyes. "Darius is clearly meddling. He's only entering because he knows I'm racing for Sullivan Oil."

"That was Anna's opinion, too."

"Has a wedding date for her been set?"

"August thirteenth."

The tick in his jaw began to pulse. "Come on. Let's get you home. For now, I've got to get through this race. But after that, I'm taking care of Anna. And Darius, too."

Half an hour later, he stormed into the bicycle club. A large group of women sat in a circle, hemming blue-and-white sashes for the assistant parade marshals.

Their chattering came to an abrupt halt at his entry, but he couldn't have cared less. He walked directly to Essie and snatched the sash she was stitching out of her hands.

"You're coming with me," he said.

"What's happened?"

"I'm sick and tired of playing second fiddle to a bicycle race. I want to go to the soda shop, and I want to go right now."

She pulled the sash back into her lap. "Don't be ridiculous. I've got more to do than I can possibly finish before Saturday arrives. I can no more go to—"

He reached down, pulled her to her feet, then leaned so close he could count her eyelashes. "Put that sash down, Esther Spreckelmeyer."

She narrowed her eyes. "Don't you bully me. I will not leave my members in their time of need."

"You wanna make a bet?"

Shirley Gillespie stepped beside them and reached for the sash. "Go on, Essie. You've been working ten times harder than the rest of us. A walk to the soda shop will do you wonders."

Essie tightened her hold on the sash. "I don't want to go to the soda shop. I want to hem sashes."

Shirley began to peel Essie's fingers away from the fabric. "We'll be fine. Won't we, girls?"

A chorus of affirmations filled the room, urging Essie to go. He could see it was a matter of pride now, and if nothing else, Essie had more than her fair share of pride.

He placed his lips next to her ear and whispered, "I want a kiss and I'm not waiting one more minute. So you can either come outside and give me one or I'll take it right here in front of God and everybody."

She immediately let go of the sash. "Good heavens." She glanced at her members. "Ladies, I'm afraid I must—"

"Go on, honey," Mrs. McCabe said. "You give that young man of yours a little attention."

"That's right," Mrs. Bunert said. "You'll find your man has to roar like a lion and posture and establish himself as king of the jungle. But don't let it trouble you none. We all know it's the lioness who's really in charge."

"It's the lioness who does all the work, you mean," Mrs. Gulick said. "While the 'king' lounges around and waits for his supper to get hunted, caught, killed, and laid at his feet."

Shirley gently pushed them toward the door. "Perhaps y'all had better get going."

Tony glanced around. "Actually, I'm thinking about changing my mind and helping with the sashes. The conversation has become rather . . . enlightening." He winked at Mrs. Zimpelman.

The women tittered. If they had been surprised to find out he was a Morgan, they'd been quick to come to his defense when townsfolk had a cross word to say about it. He didn't know what he'd done to earn their loyalty, but he was sure glad he had it.

Even still, he didn't linger. Clasping Essie's hand, he pulled her out the door, down the steps and around to the side of the building lickety-split.

Pressing her against the wall, he covered her mouth with his. Their kiss was long, wet, and pure heaven.

"I thought you were taking me to the soda shop," she murmured against his lips.

"I am." Holding her face with his hands, he kissed her again, running his thumbs along her jaw, her ears, her neck. "I've missed you."

"Mmmm."

When his passion began to outpace his good sense, he buried his fingers into her hair and pulled back, resting his forehead against hers.

"I can only afford one soda," he said. "You want a Coca-Cola or a Dr. Pepper?"

She smiled. "I like them both. It makes no difference to me."

"Let's go, then." Tucking her hand in the crook of his arm, he headed toward town, looking forward to sharing a drink in one glass with two straws.

CHAPTER | TWENTY-TWO

TIPPING HIS HAT, TONY stepped off the boardwalk, allowing two women to squeeze past. Town was always crowded, but with tomorrow's parade and race, the streets, hotels, and restaurants teemed with people.

A wheeler darted between an oncoming carriage and a wagon. Drivers cursed and horses whinnied, but the rider gave them no heed. Turning south, he hugged the edge of the street, heading straight for Tony.

Tony jumped back onto the walkway and out of the way, accidentally jostling a farmer and his son.

"Excuse me."

The man had no time to respond before he was caught up in the movement of the crowd. The bicyclist whizzed past.

Glancing over everyone's heads, Tony spotted the Commercial Hotel another block up the road. In conjunction with City Hall, Essie's club was hosting a reception for the oil companies participating in the race. He'd received a telegram from his mother. She, Anna, and Darius would be attending. Fortunately, Anna's betrothed planned to stay behind in Beaumont.

Tony looked both ways, then loped across the street, avoiding horse droppings and dodging traffic. At the steps leading to the hotel, he paused to brush off the front and shoulders of his jacket. It would be the first time he'd seen his family since being disinherited.

"What's the matter? Worried they won't allow a field worker into the party?"

Recognizing his brother's voice, Tony glanced sharply over his shoulder. Darius approached the steps, sporting a new goatee, carefully shaped and trimmed. His Prince Albert suit, however, fit a bit too loosely. Seemed he'd lost some weight. On his arm, Mother stood in her widow's weeds. She frowned up at Darius before sending a sympathetic smile in Tony's direction.

"Tony!" Anna gasped, drawing his attention. A vision in white and yellow, she wore the diametrical opposite of Mother's black clothing.

He barely had a chance to take it all in before his sister launched herself into his arms. Managing to stay upright, he clasped her tightly while her feet dangled above the boardwalk.

"You have my word," he whispered, "you'll not marry Tubbs or anyone else unless you want to."

"Oh, Tony," she responded, her voice cracking.

He gave her a reassuring squeeze.

"I absolutely adore Mrs. Lockhart," she said quietly in Tony's ear. "Thank you for sending her."

"Anna," Mother hissed. "Would you please conduct yourself with at least some semblance of decorum. Get down. Tony, release her at once."

He lowered her to the ground and brought his mother's gloved hand to his lips, her familiar scent of lavender teasing his nose. "You are looking well, ma'am."

His words contradicted his thoughts, though. The severe black gown accentuated her drawn appearance and sallow coloring. Even the powder she'd used could not disguise the circles beneath her eyes. Were they testament to her grief or to her distress over the events following Dad's death?

"If you would, Dogbone," Darius said, his tone sarcastic, "be a good boy and follow a few steps behind us. I don't want anyone to think we're together."

"Enough of that, now," Mother said.

Darius placed his hand under her elbow and guided her up the stairs.

Tony watched them pass, then looked at Anna.

She rolled her eyes, holding Tony back out of Darius's hearing. "He's been an absolute beast. For a while now I've been wishing Dad had disinherited me, too. Then I wouldn't have to put up with our charming brother day in and day out."

———

For a split second, Essie thought Tony had grown a goatee overnight. Then she realized it wasn't Tony at all, but his brother. She stood at the hotel's parlor door, receiving guests with Mayor Whiteselle on her left and his wife on her right. A good many folks had arrived already, and the pleasant hum of conversation drifted about them.

She was so caught up in studying Darius, she failed to notice the person ahead of him in line until the woman spoke.

"How do you do?"

Essie jerked her attention to the task at hand. "Ma'am. Thank you so much for coming, and welcome to the Corsicana Oil & Gas Bicycle Invitational. I'm Essie Spreckelmeyer."

"Miss Spreckelmeyer, at last. So nice to meet you. I've heard a lot about you."

Essie felt her face heat, silently cursing that blasted newspaper article. She never knew how to respond to references of this sort. Saying "thank you" didn't seem quite right, yet ignoring the comment wasn't acceptable, either.

"Ma'am. And you are?"

"Leah Morgan. I've heard my Tony is courting you?"

Essie's lips parted. This was Tony's *mother*? Good heavens. She was clearly much younger than Essie's parents, yet she looked so tired and downtrodden. Did she mourn for a man who never saw fit to love her back? Did she mourn for him the way Papa mourned for Mother?

She squeezed Mrs. Morgan's hand. "Yes, ma'am. Tony and I are indeed courting. I am delighted to make your acquaintance. I would very much like to find a few moments to visit later, if you are able. For now, however, please allow me to introduce you to our mayor's wife."

She made the introductions, noting that while Mrs. Morgan's black silk gown was fashionable, the style was quite severe.

"Would you look at that?" Tony's brother said, drawing Essie's regard. "Punch served out of a bathtub." He smiled at her. "How quaint."

His eyes were the same coffee color as Tony's. Same broad shoulders, same height, same hair, no dimple.

"You must be Mr. Morgan," she said. "Welcome to the Corsicana Oil & Gas Bicycle Invitational. I'm Miss Spreckelmeyer."

"Not *the* Miss Spreckelmeyer?" he asked, taking a step back and looking her up and down. "The one who is so well known for her participation in a bicycle, um, *competition* up north?"

He might look like Tony at first glance, but his skin had a distinctly yellowish tint to it, giving him an unhealthy appearance. And the warmth of his voice did not match the coolness of his eyes.

"Even more important, though," he continued, "the Miss Spreckelmeyer whom my half brother has taken such keen notice of?"

She glanced down the line. Tony and a lovely young woman were conversing with the mayor. He must have felt her regard, though, because he looked over and winked.

It was all the fortification she needed. She turned back to Darius with a genuine smile. "You are quite correct, sir. I am indeed being courted by your brother."

"I must confess," he said, taking note of the exchange between her and Tony. "I'm a bit surprised. Tony's interests have always run to girls fresh out of the schoolroom. Strange that he would suddenly acquire a taste for the more matronly type. Wouldn't you say?"

Shock momentarily held her silent before she realized he was deliberately trying to discomfit her. She smiled to herself.

"Well, Mr. Morgan," she said, leaning toward him conspiratorially, "you know what they say . . . there's no accounting for taste."

He lifted his brows.

"Please, might I introduce you to our mayor's wife?"

She handed him over to Mrs. Whiteselle, then turned as Tony and the young girl beside him finished with the mayor.

Tony reached out to her. She placed her hand in his as he leaned over and kissed her cheek.

"You look stunning," he said.

So do you, she thought. He had on his dark alpaca jacket, but the silk four-in-hand tie with a paisley pattern was one she hadn't seen before.

She tried to picture what changes his family might see in him after his summer away from home. His shoulders and chest had filled out from his work in the fields and their training in the clubhouse. The sun had added warmth to his skin, and though his trim waist wasn't visible beneath his suit, it would be in evidence tomorrow at the race.

A spurt of pride rushed through her. This handsome, wonderful man was *her* beau.

"I'd like you to meet my sister, Anna," he said.

The young woman smiled and Essie caught her breath. Flawless skin, large brown eyes, long, long lashes, and rich brown hair conspired together to form nothing short of perfection. And as if that weren't enough, she'd accentuated it all with a fabulous hat heaped high with white trim, yellow posies, and blue ribbons.

"It is so very nice to meet you, Anna. Welcome to the Corsicana Oil & Gas Bicycle Invitational."

"Thank you. Mrs. Lockhart had nothing but the nicest things to say about you."

Essie glanced at Tony, then back at Anna. "You know Mrs. Lockhart?"

"Oh my, yes. We are fast friends. Has she ever loaned you any of her books?"

Frowning, Essie lowered her voice. "Oh dear. I hope she hasn't been foisting those awful things off on you. They are a bit frivolous and not a little shocking."

"Do you think so? I hadn't really noticed. What do you think, Tony?"

He shrugged. "*Thorns and Orange Blossoms* wasn't so bad."

Essie stared at him, aghast. But before she could ask why in the world *he* had read Mrs. Lockhart's books, the next person in line stepped up.

———

"So then the mortician says, 'Yes sir, sheriff. It was a grave undertaking.' " Laughing, the mayor looked around at the men in their circle. "Get it? Grave undertaking?"

Tony smiled, beginning to see why the man was so well liked. Judge Spreckelmeyer, the sheriff, and a fella by the name of Mudge from Alamo Oil chuckled.

A burst of appreciative male laughter from across the hotel's parlor drew their attention.

"Appears your sister is the belle of the Welcome Reception," the judge said, clapping Tony on the shoulder.

Taking a sip of punch, Tony looked over the rim of his cup to where Anna sat surrounded by men. A couple of wheelers from some of the smaller oil companies, along with Preacher Wortham and Deputy Howard, all vied for her attention.

"Their efforts are doomed to failure, I'm afraid," Darius said, joining them.

"Oh?" Spreckelmeyer said, stepping back to make room for him. "And why is that?"

"She's betrothed."

"Betrothed?" Dunn asked. Tony could see the sheriff mentally counting up the three short months since his father's death.

"Yes. To Norris Tubbs."

"Norris Tubbs!" Spreckelmeyer exclaimed. "Of the H&TC?"

"The very same."

"But he's my age."

Darius pulled on his cuffs. "So he is."

The sheriff, the judge, and the mayor exchanged glances, then looked at Tony, but before he could say anything, Harley tugged on his coat.

"Hey, Mr. Tony."

"Well, howdy there, Harley. Where did you come from?"

"Me and some o' the boys have been helpin' Miss Essie lug ice and such. I was telling 'em about what happened that night when Bri was bit and wanted to show 'em your knife. Do ya mind?"

"Of course not." He pulled it from his pocket and handed it to the boy, watching as he raced over to a small group of schoolmates. The gangly youths in their Sunday-go-to-meeting clothes pulled at their collars and scratched their starch-covered chests while hovering near the refreshment table.

"Ah, looks like Finch has finally made it," Darius said.

Tony turned his attention to the entryway. Essie excused herself from the group she was attending and welcomed the newcomer. Finch made a show of bowing deeply and bringing her hand to his lips.

He didn't look like a man who was grieving over the loss of his second wife. He held Essie's hand too long, no matter how gracefully she tried to extract it, and then bent close, whispering something before pulling back, clearly amused by his own words.

Essie freed her hand and unobtrusively wiped it against her skirt.

She scanned the room, smiled at Tony, then proceeded to escort Finch toward the group of men. His suit was black with lace at his cuffs, accented by an elaborately tied ascot and patent leather bals. He always had been a bit of a dandy.

"Gentlemen," Essie said, "I'd like you to meet Mr. Finch Morgan. Blake Morgan was his uncle." She introduced her father, the sheriff, the mayor, and Mr. Mudge from Alamo Oil. "And you, of course, know these two."

Tony extended his hand. "I was sorry to hear about Rebecca."

Finch clasped his hand. "Thank you. I still can't quite believe she's gone."

"I confess to feeling the same way."

Finch pulled out a quizzing glass and peered at Tony more closely. "I see you finally stripped yourself of that ghastly moustache. When did you do that?"

"He did it the same day he was stripped of his inheritance," Darius answered. "Both lightened his load a bit, didn't they, Dogbone?"

Essie gasped and an awkward silence followed.

Tony rubbed the skin above his lips. "Funny how something that was such a part of me is so easily discarded. I find I hardly even notice its absence anymore."

Chuckling, Finch reached into his jacket and withdrew a silver cigarette case. Flipping it open, he offered mechanically rolled cigarettes to the men. Darius and Mudge each withdrew one from the holder, but the others declined.

"Well, if you gentlemen would excuse me?" Essie was wearing her blue gown, the one that had a really wide sash that hugged her waist and emphasized her curves. He'd first seen it the night she lectured her club on bicycle etiquette. It was one of his favorites.

Pink filled her cheeks at his obvious admiration before she excused herself again and turned away.

Finch struck a match against the wall, held the flame for Darius and Mudge, then himself.

"I'm afraid I haven't quite decided what to think about those pre-rolled cigarettes," the mayor said. "Do you really think the taste is worth the extra expense?"

"I find them far superior to the handmade ones," Finch answered. "What about you, Darius?"

"Oh, I'll not turn them down when offered, but in truth, a smoke's a smoke. They're all pretty much the same to me. Kinda like women. Right, Tony? It appears women are all pretty much the same to you, too, no matter how old they are."

Spreckelmeyer pulled his hands out of his pockets. The sheriff slowly straightened.

Darius had been trying to rile Tony since he'd arrived. Tony wasn't sure of his brother's game, but until he figured it out, he would hold on to his temper. Still, if Darius wasn't careful, it would be Spreckelmeyer's wrath he'd be facing and right soon if he kept it up.

Harley reappeared at Tony's elbow and handed him the knife. "Thank ya. The fellas liked it real well."

"Anytime, Harley."

"Hey, that's some kind of knife there, Mr. Morgan," Mudge said. "Can I see it, too?"

Tony handed it to him.

"Look at this, Mayor," he said, holding it up. "It has a fancy stag handle with the top shaped like a dog bone."

Spreckelmeyer and the sheriff also leaned in for a better look.

"I'm surprised you still have that old thing, Tony," Darius said. "I remember when Dad gave it to you." He laughed. "Now, there's an amusing story for you—"

Jeremy Gillespie busted through the parlor door covered in slush and skidding to a stop. He quickly scanned the room, spotted Tony and started toward him. He'd just reached their circle when he noticed Darius.

"That your brother?"

"Yeah. What's the matter?"

Jeremy returned his attention to Tony. "It's Crackshot."

"What about him?"

"Well, we'd tied a gunnysack around the top o' the bailer and let it down real slow-like, when the sulfur gas started to blow. So we all backed off, but Crackshot, he got a little impatient. I tried to tell him that sulfur'd knock him out. But he goes right back over there and starts swabbing all the while that gas's rolling down his throat."

Tony shook his head. "You'd think he'd have known better."

"Aw, you know what a loose screw he is."

Essie joined them, and Tony slipped his hand under her elbow. "Is Wilson all right?"

Pulling off his hat, Jeremy gave Essie a brief nod, then turned back to Tony. "He stood it for a while. Even started up with another jag when his knees just up and buckled."

"Oh no. What did you do?" Essie asked.

Jeremy shrugged. "I grabbed that cup mask Tony takes such stock in." He shook his head. "You should've seen me wearin' that thing all the while I was wrestling with that load o' human being, trying to get him far enough away so's I could push up and down on that big set o' lungs he has and pump some o' that stuff out of him."

"Where is he now?" Tony asked.

"Still lying there. But he's breathing."

Tony looked at the sheriff. "Can you find the doc and have him meet me out at the Agarita well?"

"Both me and Howard will look for him, but in this mess there's no telling where he is. You'd be better off takin' him to the doc's house before dark sets in. We'll meet you there."

"I'll go with you, Tony," Judge Spreckelmeyer said.

"No, sir. I don't want you out around that sulfur. And you'd be of more use looking for the doc."

The judge nodded and headed off with Sheriff Dunn.

"Jeremy, go get Ewing," Tony said. "He's over there with my sister, that woman in white and yellow."

"You think you'll need the preacher?" Essie asked, concern lacing her voice.

"I just want to be prepared. Either way, I'll come by the house tonight and let you know how he's doing. Harley, you stay clear of the field, you hear? I don't want you near the gas, either."

He started to leave when Essie grabbed hold of his hand.

"Be careful, Tony. That sulfur is . . ." She swallowed.

It wasn't just worry he saw in her eyes. It was something bigger. Something deeper. Something so sweet he couldn't possibly resist it.

And right there in front of his brother, his cousin, and the entire oil industry of Texas, he grasped her chin and kissed her flush on the lips. "I'll be careful."

CHAPTER | TWENTY-THREE

IT WAS ALMOST MIDNIGHT when Essie finally headed toward home. At the Welcome Reception, some of her club members had uncovered the plans of a small group of automobile advocates. They intended to overrun tomorrow's bicycle parade with their horseless carriages.

With a great deal of effort, Essie managed to track down this faction only to discover they had but one automobile between them. They were, however, quite intent upon using it.

"I'm a firm believer in progress, Mr. Roach," she'd said. "It is my opinion that though your automobiles are slow and prone to break down, they will one day be as common on the street as horse-drawn vehicles."

"Darn tootin', " he replied, spitting a wad of tobacco at his feet.

"I suggest a compromise."

His eyes narrowed. "I'm listenin'. "

"Your vehicle can bring up the rear of the parade, and after you have passed, the crowd can fall in behind you, cheering you all the way to the racetrack."

"No, ma'am. I wanna be at the front."

"I'm afraid that is quite impossible. The entire event is centered around bicycles and they must lead the way. However, we could arrange for one of our city councilmen to ride in the vehicle with you, making your automobile our grand finale and hinting of our bright and prosperous future."

Scratching his chest, he considered her for a moment, then thrust out his hand. "You got yerself a deal, little lady."

She spent the next hour trying to find a councilman who was still awake and who would be willing to miss the parade so he could ride in the caboose.

Opening her gate, she stepped through. The city had coordinated the race with the cycle of the moon to ensure as much light as possible during the evening hours of the event weekend. That full moon now shone down on Tony Bryant Morgan lounging on her porch steps. Her fatigue fled.

He didn't say a word as she moved forward, just patted the spot beside him.

"How's Mr. Wilson . . . er, Crackshot?" she asked, settling on the step.

"In a minute," he said, then gathered her in his arms and kissed her.

The scent of sandalwood and shaving soap surrounded her. He splayed one hand on her back, the other squeezed her waist. She tried to inch closer, but they were as close as their position would allow.

"Come here," he said, slipping his arm beneath her legs.

But before he could lift her onto his lap, she placed her hands against his chest. "Absolutely not."

He stilled, and she softened her words with a smile. "Much as I'd like to, it's improper and we both know it."

"Nothing will happen," he murmured, shifting over onto one hip so he could hold her flush against him.

She shook her head, the brim of her hat knocking against his forehead.

"Will you take off your hat, at least?"

She pulled back. "You don't like my hat?"

"I love your hat, but it's in my way."

"Which, in all likelihood, is just as well."

He brushed her cheeks with his knuckles. "It's also hiding your eyes from me and I want to see your eyes."

She tried to scoot back, but he was having none of it.

"Don't," he said.

"I wasn't going far. Just to the other end of the step, at least until my heart slows down a little bit."

He ducked under her hat and trailed kisses along her jaw. "It won't do you any good. I'll simply follow you over there."

"Tony, if we don't stop I'll have a difficult time staying, um, unmoved. So either you let me put some space between us or I will go on inside and we can talk about Crackshot tomorrow."

Sighing, he moved his hands from her back to her face. "All right. Just one more, then we'll talk."

And what a kiss it was. By the conclusion of it, Tony was the one who stood and put distance between them. Standing a few feet away, with his back to her, he tilted his head up toward the sky.

Millions of stars glittered against its black backdrop. Was this what Abraham saw when God made His promise? Stars so brilliant and numerous no one could doubt His omnipotence?

"Will you marry me, Essie?"

She jerked her attention back to Tony. He'd turned to face her, his hands jammed in his pockets.

"What?" she said.

He stepped forward, bent down on one knee and took her hand in his. "Will you do me the honor of becoming my wife?"

Her heart sped up. Her hands turned clammy. Her eyes filled.

The answer was on the tip of her tongue when she realized he'd never mentioned his feelings for her. Not ever. Not even once. Oh, she knew he enjoyed her company and that he was attracted to her. But she wanted more. Much more.

"Why?" she asked.

He seemed taken aback by the question. "Because I love you. Don't you love me?" His grip on her hand loosened and he started to pull away. "I thought you . . ."

She squeezed his hand and fell to her knees in front of him. "I do, Tony. I love you very much. And, yes. I would absolutely love to be your lawfully wedded wife."

A huge grin split his face. Scooping her up against him, he kissed her again. She wrapped her arms around his neck, answering his delight with her own.

When he finally pulled back, they were both having trouble breathing.

"Now will you take off your hat?"

"No," she said, smiling. "Not yet. Not until the deed is done."

He groaned. "What if I can't wait that long?"

Placing a tiny kiss on his chin, she removed herself from his embrace and returned to the step. "Now . . . how's Crackshot?"

And though her tone was casual, she could not calm the excitement and exhilaration she felt within. After all the years of singleness and all she'd been through, for the Lord to drop this man from the sky when she was least expecting it made her somewhat speechless.

Tony settled himself on the sidewalk, facing her. "He's not good, Essie. He woke up, and he can breathe all right, but he can't see."

She sucked in her breath. "What do you mean? Are you saying he's blind?"

"Yes, but we're hoping it's temporary. The doc has potatoes against his eyes and is keeping him in a dark room. As soon as Crackshot's kin can get here, though, Doc wants them to take him down to Galveston where he can swim around in the ocean with his eyes open."

"Will that cure him?"

"That's what they say. Only time will tell, though."

She covered her mouth. "I should have listened to you. If we'd had those cup masks, none of this would have happened."

"No, it has nothing to do with the masks. If Crackshot had stayed back like the rest of 'em, he wouldn't be laid out right now. My guess is, even if he had a mask, he would've been too cocky to wear it." Tony shook his head. "He has nobody to blame but himself."

She still couldn't help but feel guilty. "Will you make sure any doctors settle up with me?"

"I will." He stretched out his leg, then tapped her toe with his. "You sure were a long time coming home."

"Last-minute details."

He yawned.

"Goodness," she said, rising to her feet. "You need to get to bed and get some rest. I need you in tip-top shape for tomorrow's race."

Standing, he brushed off his backside. "Don't worry, ma'am. I'll be ready." He joined her on the porch. "I have a ring for you, Essie."

A ring? She clasped her hands together, still struggling to comprehend how she could go from organizing parade details to becoming betrothed in the span of an hour.

He fished inside his pocket, then removed a bit of cloth. Unfurling it in his palm, he cradled a diamond ring, barely distinguishable in the shadows of the porch.

"I don't need a ring, Tony," she said, her throat closing.

"Yes, you do. All the Morgan women wear a diamond." He reached for her left hand. "This one was my grandmother's."

She frowned. "I thought you were disinherited?"

"It belonged to my mother's mother and had nothing to do with my father."

He tried to take her ring finger, but she closed her hand around his.

"Don't you think we should wait?"

"For what?"

"Well, to, to talk with Papa. And the truth is, there are still some things we need to talk through. After the bicycle race is over and things calm down will be soon enough."

He frowned. "I don't want to wait until then. I want everyone in Texas to know you're mine and I want them to know it while they're all here in town."

She hesitated. "I do, too, Tony. But not until we've talked."

"About what?"

"Things."

"Well, you sure don't sound like a very excited bride-to-be. Are you sure you even want to do this at all?" His tone was sharp, wounded.

"I *am* excited. You can't imagine how thrilled I am."

He said nothing.

"Tony, it's just that, well—"

"Are you gonna marry me or not?"

"I am."

"Then give me your hand."

Biting her lip, she slowly lifted her left hand. He slid the ring on, the metal smooth, his fingers rough.

"It fits perfectly," she whispered. "Thank you."

"You're welcome." But his voice was clipped.

"I really am excited, Tony, and the ring is lovely."

"You can't even see it. It's too dark."

"I don't need to see it. Just having you give it to me makes it everything I'd ever want."

He stood stiffly for a moment. "Well, good night, then."

She clasped his hand. "I love you."

After a slight hesitation, he pulled her against him. "I love you, too. So much it scares me."

He kissed her thoroughly, then rested his forehead against her hat's brim.

"I didn't mean to be so clumsy in the asking, Essie. The question just kind of popped out."

"It was perfect."

"A fella only has one chance to ask his woman to marry him. He's supposed to have flowers and poetry and stuff like that. The only reason I had the ring with me was because Mother gave it to me tonight at the reception."

"She did?"

He nodded. "I asked her to bring it."

Essie stilled. "When?"

"When I knew I wanted to marry you."

"And when was that?"

"For a while now."

She laid her hand against his chest. The diamond on her finger caught the moonlight. "I loved your proposal and I love the ring. I'll cherish them both forever."

He brought her hand to his lips and kissed her palm. "Good night, love."

"Good night, Tony."

―――――

The diamond was huge. And beautiful. And hers.

Essie knelt beside her bed in her nightdress, moving her finger this way and that, watching the facets of the stone capture the candlelight and reflect it back at her.

She wondered if it would make rainbows on the walls when the sun hit it just right. Her grandmother used to have crystal prisms hanging in her front window. As a girl, Essie would jiggle them just as the sun was beginning its descent, then stand as tiny rainbows danced across the walls and the floor and even herself.

Tony said his mother had given the ring to him. That pallid woman she'd met briefly at the reception and who had innocently asked if Tony were courting her had, all the time, knowingly carried an heirloom that she would, by evening's end, relinquish forever to another woman. A woman she didn't even know.

What had she thought when Essie brushed her off so easily on to the mayor's wife? When Essie had been too busy filling a bathtub up with punch to sit down for a proper visit? Did she know Essie was thirty-four years old, ran a bicycle club, and was part owner of Morgan Oil's biggest rival?

She worried over Tony's earlier refusal to hear her confessions. At the same time, she wondered how critical it was for her to share those transgressions with him. She'd already confessed them to the Lord. He'd forgiven her and pronounced her clean.

Did that mean she wasn't obligated to ask for pardon from her fiancé? Was the Lord's forgiveness truly enough for her and Tony both? Maybe she wouldn't tell Tony anything. Maybe she didn't need to.

She folded her hands together.

Dear Lord, thank you for giving me Tony. I love him. I want him more than life itself. But I do not want him more than I want you. Give me wisdom. Guide me. Show me what you would have me do.

Opening her eyes, she admired her ring one more time before blowing out the light and crawling into bed.

CHAPTER | TWENTY-FOUR

THE MORNING OF THE parade dawned clear and beautiful with a smattering of clouds scattered like dandelion puffs in the sky. Essie fastened a cropped white jacket with large red buttons over her bicycle costume. She'd considered wearing her award-winning outfit but decided against it—not wanting to invite any questions about that unfortunate event.

Besides, there were still those who frowned upon the use of knickerbockers. Her shortened white skirt and matching gaiters were much more acceptable to the masses.

Lifting her latest purchase from its box, she settled the lacy white toque onto her head, then secured the hat with pearl-headed pins. Inspecting herself in the mirror, she fluffed the scarlet silk trim, the red ribbon roses, and the white ostrich tips spilling over the crown.

But it was her ring that again and again captured her attention as it flashed in the light. Lowering her hand, she held it out. With delicate craftsmanship, the platinum mounting displayed a rose-cut diamond encircled by eight tiny ones. She still couldn't quite believe it was hers.

The grandfather clock chimed nine. She quickly pinched her cheeks, then skipped down the stairs. Tony was already waiting in the parlor.

He held a beret, his brown hair mussed and windblown. The new racing outfit he wore hugged his tall, athletic form and left Essie short of breath.

"Good morning," he said, his voice low and intimate. "Is that a new hat?"

She nodded.

"I like it." He looked her up and down, his gaze snagging on her hands. "Somebody forgot her gloves."

She clasped her hands behind her, hiding them from view. "I didn't want to cover up my ring."

His eyes grew warm. "I like seeing it on your finger."

"So do I."

"Has your father seen it?"

"This morning at breakfast."

"What did he say?"

"He said it took you long enough."

Tony let out a breath and smiled.

"Didn't he mention anything about it when you arrived?" she asked.

"No. He just opened the door, told me 'good luck' and instructed me to wait for you in the parlor. I didn't know if he meant good luck with the race or good luck with you."

She laughed. "Probably both."

"I'd told him I was going to ask you, about the same time I asked my mother about the ring. Yet now he seems upset. Did he change his mind, do you think?"

"No. Believe me, I'd know if he didn't approve. I think his reticence is due to his just now realizing that once we marry I'll belong to you and not him."

They stared at each other across the parlor floor, thinking about her words and what they meant. Her heart began to hammer. It was really going to happen. She was really going to marry this man.

"The day's going to be extremely long and hectic," he said.

"Yes."

"This will probably be the only opportunity we have to be alone until late tonight."

"Probably."

"Would you mind terribly if I kiss you, then?"

Her eyes darted to the clock.

"I know it's early, Essie, but—"

She held up a finger, stopping his words, then closed the parlor door behind her and leaned against it. His Adam's apple bobbed.

She waited, but he made no move to close the distance between them. Apparently, if they were going to share a kiss at the shocking hour of nine o'clock, he didn't mind asking permission, but he wasn't going to start it.

Pushing off the door, she walked across the Axminster rug and slid her hands up onto his shoulders. "Don't mess up my hat."

After a long kiss, he placed her at arm's length. His face was flushed, his breathing ragged, his eyes dark.

She smiled. "Perhaps we'd better go?"

He nodded.

She let herself out of the parlor.

A bicycle built for two leaned against the white picket fence. Squealing with delight, Essie ran down the porch steps.

"Tony, look! Is it yours? Where did it come from?"

Catching her by the hand, he hauled her back. "It's not mine. It's on loan from Flyers. They agreed to lend it to us for the parade as an advertisement. I thought it would be the perfect solution to your grand marshal dilemma. I'm just glad it arrived in time."

"But there is no dilemma. The mayor is going to be the grand marshal. We've already decided."

"It might have been decided, but there's still dissension in the ranks. Those ladies of yours want a wheeler as the grand marshal and are only agreeing otherwise because you asked them to."

He opened the gate.

"So what did you have in mind?"

"The mayor on one seat, his lovely wife—and prominent member of the Corsicana Velocipede Club—on the other."

"Oh, Tony, that's perfect," she said, running her hand along the machine's sleek red frame. "I've never ridden one. Have you?"

"I rode it over here and I have to tell you, it's deuced embarrassing to ride without a partner."

"Oh, I hadn't thought of that."

He grasped the front handlebar and held out his hand. "Ma'am?"

She gazed longingly at the backseat. "You get to steer?"

"It's the gentlemanly thing to do. Plus, it gives you the better view. I only hope I can see over your hat."

She took his hand, then hesitated. "If I start, how will you mount? Plus, I can't steer. How are we going to do this?"

"You're the etiquette expert."

She worried her lip. "I don't see any way other than starting together."

He glanced up and down the street, then gave her a quick peck on the lips. "Together's my favorite way."

Being in the back not only allowed Tony to steer, but it also gave him an opportunity to admire a view he didn't get too often. He greedily took in Essie's long neck, gently sloping shoulders, and trim waist. His inspection continued and though her skirts ruffled in the breeze, he was able to make out enough of an outline to be pleased with what he'd discovered.

As they drew closer to town, activity picked up and he was forced to focus on his surroundings so as not to hit any potholes or run anybody over. Friends hollered out greetings. Others stopped and pointed, admiring the unusual machine.

All along Jackson Avenue, from Thirteenth Street on down, the people of Corsicana congregated in anticipation, even though the parade was still a good hour away. Tony and Essie weaved through a sea of brown suits and white dresses. Flags hung from second-story windows, red-white-and-blue banners draped from building to building along the parade route. The oil companies had strung up signs endorsing their riders in the upcoming race. Tony smiled at the sight of the Morgan name on the hand-lettered Sullivan Oil sign.

By the time they reached the starting point, a majority of the parade entrants had already gathered. Tony slowed the bike but before he could stop, Essie jumped off and began to organize the event.

She sent the city council members and the Corsicana Commercial Club off to clear the streets and stand along the parade path. She corralled the assistant marshals and asked Mrs. McCabe to give them the white duck caps the Slap Out had donated, along with the blue-and-white sashes her club members had hemmed.

She asked the bugle corps to warm up their trumpets, then attempted to organize the rest of the club according to bicycle brands. Mr. Sharpley arrived in a cart pulled by a wheeler, his leg cast wrapped in red-white-and-blue bunting. Essie spent several moments visiting with him before being called back to her task.

She was positioning a "giraffe" tricycle with its rider nine feet above the street when a group of about twenty young men, led by Jeremy Gillespie, rode up wearing bloomers.

Essie propped her fists on her waist. "Just what do y'all think you're doing?" she asked over the laughter of the crowd.

"Why, we're joinin' the parade," Jeremy said. "And don't you try and stop us, neither. We call ourselves the Bloomer Brigade and it's our mission to make sure any anti-bloomer fellas out there will behave, or else!"

She was no match for Jeremy's charm and after her experience in New York, she realized his mission might indeed be warranted. She sent him and the others on down the line, where the boys made a show of batting their eyes and calling out to the fans in falsetto voices.

She had most everyone where she wanted them and was arranging the women of the Corsicana Velocipede Club at the front of the line when Shirley Gillespie screamed, bringing silence to the immediate vicinity.

"Essie! What on earth is this?!" She grabbed Essie's left hand and held it in front of her.

Essie, already flustered from the activity, turned a deeper shade of red and pulled her hand from Shirley's grip. Shirley looked around her, locked eyes with Mrs. Lockhart and hoisted Essie's hand up again.

"Look!"

Every man, woman, and child within fifty yards looked at the diamond on Essie's finger. The women of her club swooped in around her, exclaiming, babbling, and vying for a better look. One by one they turned to Tony, wide-eyed.

He stood grouped with the other five racers and tugged on his beret. Smiles replaced the women's questioning expressions and they turned back to embrace their leader. She might never have broken free if the automobile hadn't chosen that moment to drive up, blast its horn and scatter her entire parade to the edges of the street.

It took her another twenty-five minutes to reorganize everyone before finally approaching Tony's band of racers.

"We're ready to begin, gentlemen," she said, careful to avoid his eyes, though her face again filled with color. "If you would fall in right behind the buglers, then you will be the first to reach the track and will have time to rest before this afternoon's race. Are there any questions?"

There were none. She glanced at him briefly. He winked. She blushed again, turned to the trumpet players and gave the signal to start.

———

Mr. Mitton's racetrack at the fairgrounds was one of the best mile tracks in Texas. It was run by the Navarro County Jockey Club and leased by the oil companies for the annual bicycle race.

Wandering through the pasture outside the gate, Tony perused the wide variety of exhibits. Bicycle manufacturers had every kind of bike on display: sociables, trikes and quadricycles, Warthogs, Spauldings, and Panthers.

He picked up a new racing bicycle to judge its weight, then spun the pedals to see if the wheels wobbled.

"A finer machine you'll not find anywhere in the country," the salesman assured him.

Tony tapped the steel tubing with his fingernail and listened.

"Mr. Tony!" Harley Vandervoort hollered, running up to him. "Howdy-do."

The boy's lips had turned blue from eating some kind of berry and he smelled like he'd been hanging around Mr. Mitton's thoroughbreds.

"Howdy-do to you, too. You having a good time?"

"I surely am. You gonna win that race fer Miss Essie today?"

"I'm going to try."

"I hear tell you're mashed on her and done asked her to wed up. That true?"

"Sure is," he said, chuckling, then looked around. "Where's your folks?"

"Ma's over there selling husk rugs with them other women, and Pa's whittling up stuff for the Men's Bible Group. What're you doing with that there bicycle?"

"Listening to its ring." He tapped it again with his fingernail. "Hear that? That flat sound means the tubing's not seamless but has been made from a strip of steel rolled and brazed along the seam."

The salesman sputtered.

Tony tipped his hat and guided Harley away. "You don't want a wheel with brazed tubing."

Brianna ran up with a saucer of ice cream piled on top of a waffle. "Howdy, Mr. Bryant."

"It's Mr. Morgan," Harley corrected.

"Oh yeah. I keep forgettin'. "

"Mr. Tony will be fine," Tony said. "You all recovered from your snakebite?"

"Oh yes, sir. I got me some fang marks on my ankle, though." She looked around, then leaned in close. "I charge the fellers at school a nickel to see 'em. I done saved up sixty-five cents already."

Tony frowned. "I don't know that you need to be showing off your ankles like that, Miss Brianna. That's not exactly proper."

"Shoot," Harley said. "It ain't like she's wearin' her hair up yet. Besides, she don't let just anybody have a peek. I got to give 'em the nod first."

Another youngster called out Harley's name, and the two took off before Tony could think of a response. He recalled Brianna didn't have a mother and made a note to himself to ask Essie to have a talk with her.

The League of American Wheelmen motioned Tony over to their booth and persuaded him to sign a petition demanding better roads, as well as laws protecting cyclists from teamsters and cab drivers who waged an unrelenting war against the machines.

Local citizens and merchants had set up tents to sell garden vegetables, fruits, breads and honey, floor rockers, agricultural implements, hops, boots, shoes, harnesses, and leather.

He was surprised to find Mrs. Zimpelman inside a booth filled with sterling vest chains, watch fobs, and buckles. He'd never met her husband and therefore didn't realize she was married to the silversmith. Before he could offer a greeting, however, a customer approached asking to see her selection of cuff pins.

Tony passed by M.C. Baker's booth and waved but didn't interrupt the brothers as they gave a demonstration of their rotary drill to curious onlookers. The rotary had been so successful in drilling through Corsicana's gummy clay soil that the boys had christened it the "Gumbo Buster."

A few of those very same boys just outside the Anheuser-Busch tent were trying to subdue one of their own who'd had more than he could hold. Deputy Howard shoved them aside, grabbed the rowdy and dragged him a few yards away, where he locked him up in what had become known as Howard's Hoodlum Wagon. Tony noted there were already a few others inside the mobile jailhouse sleeping it off.

The *aroogha* of an automobile's horn signaled the arrival of the final parade participants, followed by a wave of spectators. Tony headed back toward the track, making a point to stop at each oil company's exhibit on his way, even Morgan Oil.

"Well," Darius said as Tony approached, "if it isn't the cast-off who's doing everything he can to land on his feet."

Tony ignored him and offered a hand to Morgan Oil's racer. "Duckworth, good to see you again."

"Morgan." The man was small, like a horse jockey, but with thighs as big around as a woman's waist.

"I saw you practicing yesterday," Tony said. "Should be a good race."

Before Duckworth could reply, Darius interrupted.

"I hear felicitations are in order," he said, drawing deeply on a hand-rolled cigarette, the fire at its tip consuming the tobacco.

"That's right."

Darius flicked ashes onto the ground. "I know what you're doing," he said, his words and tone slicing through any previous pretense.

"And just what is it that I'm doing, Darius?" Tony asked with a sigh.

"You're placing yourself into a position of attack, with your sights on me and your gun cocked and loaded." Smoke trickled out of his nose. "I'm here to tell you you're wasting your time. I must say, though, you managed to insinuate yourself into Sullivan Oil rather quickly. Dad would have been proud—if he'd cared enough to be."

Tony turned to walk away and bumped chests with Finch. The man had sidled up behind him, blocking his path. And though his cousin gave the appearance of being soft, he had the Morgan brawn hidden beneath his dandified clothes.

Tony didn't excuse himself. Nor did he ask Finch to move. Just stared at him eye to eye.

Finch finally stepped back. "Care for a smoke?"

Tony ignored him and headed to the hospitality tent, hoping to find Essie. He wanted to check over his bike one more time before the big event.

C H A P T E R | T W E N T Y - F I V E

S TUMBLING ALONGSIDE THE SHERIFF, Harley prayed his pa wouldn't hear about this. It was bad enough to be hauled across the fairgrounds by his collar, but if Pa were to find out, it'd be a whupping for sure.

"Crook?" the sheriff hollered, frog-walking Harley up to the Slap Out's booth. "I'm in need of a bar of soap, if you please."

But it wasn't Mr. Crook who approached the table. It was that spiteful ol' Mrs. Crook. She'd not been around much lately. Not since she'd whelped them two babies. And Harley hadn't missed her at all.

She didn't look like the witches he'd read about in some of them storybooks. No big nose with a wart or nothing. No stringy hair. No evil laugh. Matter of fact, she didn't look so bad for an old lady . . . until you got to know her.

"Any particular kind of soap, Sheriff?" she asked, eyeing the two of them.

"Whatever you got at hand will do—nothin' that tastes too good, though."

Her mouth formed a little o. "I see. Just one moment and I'll fetch you some."

"Mama?"

Harley could just make out the top of Mae Crook's head as she skipped over to her ma. "How come the sh'ff wants to eat soap?"

"It's not for him, Mae. It's for Harley," she said, heading toward the back of the tent.

The four-year-old girl grabbed the edge of the table and rose up on tippy-toes, her big brown eyes peeping over the top. "Won't ya rather have a licorice, Harley?"

"Not today, Mae," he said, making his voice sound real natural-like. "Today I think I'll have me a nice big bar o' your daddy's most expensive soap. Sheriff's treat."

The sheriff gave Harley's collar a twist, choking him some. Mae let loose of the table and climbed up into her mama's chair.

"I got me two baby brothers," she said. "Chester and Charlie."

"Sound like a couple o' crooks to me."

Keeping the grip he had on Harley's collar, the sheriff used his other hand to pinch the tender spot between Harley's shoulder and neck. Hurt like the devil, but Harley made sure he didn't flinch.

"Here we are, Sheriff," Mrs. Crook said, making a show of setting out not only a yellow ball of waxy soap but a tin cup of water to wash it down with.

The sheriff slapped a nickel on the table.

Mrs. Crook slid it back and gave Harley a look colder than a dead snake. "No charge."

Picking up the ball of soap, Harley tossed it in the air and caught it one-handed. "Why, thank ya, Mrs. Crook. That's right neighborly of ya. Ain't it, Sheriff?"

The sheriff pocketed his nickel, then grabbed the tin of water. "Let's go."

Harley had hoped to do this someplace private, but Sheriff Dunn just took him out behind the Slap Out's tent and handed him the cup of water. No doubt he wanted to make sure that soap lathered up but good.

"Swish."

Mae Crook lifted the back hem of their canvas tent and stuck her head out like some puppy dog. She might only be four, but Harley'd be jiggered before he'd carry on in front of her. He swished, lifted his chin and spewed the water out in a big ol' arc that spread out just enough to catch the sheriff in its wake.

Sheriff Dunn grabbed Harley's cheeks and squeezed. "Stick out your tongue."

He was tempted to "stick out his tongue," all right, but didn't dare. He opened wide. The sheriff didn't give him any quarter as he rubbed soap all over Harley's tongue and mouth.

The longer the sheriff scrubbed, the more Harley fought back the desire to gag.

The slimy stuff smelled bad and tasted worse. Finally he couldn't stand it anymore and began choking.

The sheriff let go but didn't offer up any water. Harley leaned over, spitting out what he could.

"You gonna curse anymore?" the sheriff barked.

"No, by jingo, I'm not!"

The sheriff growled. Harley slapped his hand over his mouth, realizing what he'd said, but it was too late.

Dunn grabbed him and scoured his mouth all over again. When the sheriff finally let go, Harley fell onto all fours, choking, spitting, gagging.

"Any man worth his salt can make his point without using foul language," Dunn said. "If'n you wanna grow up to be half the man your pa is, you'd best be acquiring some better manners. You got that?"

"Yes, sir," he said.

Dunn tossed out the water and stalked away. Harley sat back on his feet, raking his fingernails over his tongue, trying to get the soap off. Residue trickled down his throat, mixing with the berries, ice cream, and taffy he'd eaten earlier. His stomach began to rebel.

A pair of very small, brightly polished boots entered his range of vision. He tamped down his bile.

"I brung ya some water, Harley," Mae said.

Accepting her offering, he rinsed and spit until he'd drained the cup. "Thanks."

"How come the sh'ff done that to ya?"

Harley stood and made his way to a shade tree. The little girl followed. "Your ma know you're out here?"

"She's gone home with the babies."

"Your pa, then? He know you're not in the tent?"

She nodded, making her black curls bob up and down like springs on a buggy seat. "I askt him fer these." She opened her fist. Two buttons of licorice nestled inside. "I knows ya like 'em."

He scrutinized her, surprised she'd asked her pa on his account. "You sure ya don't mind sharing?"

"I ain't sharing 'em with ya, Harley. I'm a-giving 'em to ya." She extended her chubby little hand.

He knew if it had been him who had the licorice, he wouldn't be sharing them with anybody, much less giving them away lock, stock, and barrel.

He took one of the candies. "You eat the other, Mae. Wouldn't be right fer me to take both."

They popped the candies into their mouths and sucked on them. The licorice went a long way in covering up the taste of the soap, though it still lingered.

They continued to suck, trying to make the treat last as long as they could, when four men slipped behind the hatmaker's tent a few yards away. Harley'd snuck around enough to recognize it when somebody else was doing the sneaking. He put his finger to his lips, warning Mae to keep quiet, inched the two of them behind the tree trunk, then peeked around the edge.

One of them was Mr. Tony's brother. Everybody was talking about how the two of them looked alike, but Harley disagreed. This fella had eyes that reminded Harley of the Wanted posters in the sheriff's office, and his hands were cold and clammy when you shook them. Mr. Tony was nothing like that. The other three men wore racing outfits and had been in the parade. One wore a black sash, one a blue, and one a yellow.

"We ain't so sure we still wanna do this, Mr. Morgan," the one in the black sash said. He wasn't puny or nothin'. He just looked it standing next to Mr. Morgan. "I askt around and yer brother's well liked in these parts."

"Not only him," another piped up, "but the judge, too. Did ya know the sheriff is his brother-in-law? If'n we pocket Sullivan's man, it'll be more than the bloomer-gal and yer brother who'll be upset."

The third one nodded his head. "We want more money."

Mr. Morgan eyeballed the fellers one at a time, real slow-like. "I'm sure it would interest the League of American Wheelmen to find out you boys failed to ride the full and exact course in Kickapoo Creek's Six-Day Race."

The men exchanged glances. The one with the yellow sash took off his hat and scratched a bald spot that had previously been hidden. "You can't tell 'em that without implicatin' yerself."

"You think not?" Mr. Morgan pulled out his watch and popped it open. "The purse will remain the same. You pocket Sullivan Oil's wheeler, my man will take first, and we'll split the winnings between us, just as planned."

Baldy straightened his shoulders, puffing out his chest some. "We ain't doin' it, then."

Quicker than scat, Morgan grabbed the feller, yanked him close and read him the Scriptures.

Mae tugged on Harley's overalls. "I'm hot. Can—"

He clamped his hand over her mouth, shaking his head and hammering his finger against his lips. Her eyes widened, but she hushed up.

Harley held real still but didn't hear any signs they'd been nicked. Still, he didn't risk taking a look. Just kept him and Mae hidden behind that tree until he heard the fellers break up and leave.

After a minute of quiet, he pressed his hands against the bark and leaned just a wee bit over—just enough for one eyeball to have a look-see. Nobody there. He poked his head out. Still nobody.

Taking Mae by the hand, he hustled her back toward her daddy's tent. "You done real fine fer a girl, Mae. Shoot, fer a boy, even. Maybe when ya get a little older, if ya promise not to act like a girl, I'll take ya out fishin'. "

She jumped up and down. "Yes, by jingo! Take me fishin'. "

He pulled up short. "Don't ya be swearin' none, Mae. A feller worth his salt can say what needs to be said without swearin', fer gosh sake." Lifting the bottom of the Slap Out's tent, he shooed her under. "Go on. I gotta find Miss Essie."

She fell to her knees and scurried under.

"Mae?" he said.

She poked her head out.

"Thanks fer the licorice."

———

"Now, remember," Essie said, tucking in the ends of Tony's red sash, "keep your body as close to the bicycle frame as you can. Legs in, chest down, head up."

"I will."

"Don't let the others run you wide on the curves or foul you with their elbows."

"I'll be careful."

"Pace yourself. Don't start out too fast, but don't let anybody get too big a jump on you, either."

Tony clasped her hand and squeezed. "Quit worrying, Essie. Everything's going to be fine."

"I'm not worrying. I'm just reminding you of a few things, is all."

He smiled. "Well, how about this, then: How about I go win this race for you?"

Butterflies churned in her stomach. "Do you think we have a chance?"

"More than a chance. A good chance." He looked over at the other cyclists talking with their trainers. "When I was watching them yesterday, Ethey Oil's man started out slow, then took off like a shot, but it was too little, too late."

"That may be, but Ethey Oil's not the one I'm worried about, nor El Filon de Madre Oil or even Tyler Petroleum. It's Alamo and Morgan Oil that will be your real competition."

"Mudge is known for launching a series of attacks, but he doesn't have the leg strength to endure it. He'll start falling behind toward the end."

"Maybe, maybe not. Some men accomplish feats in a race that they can't ever achieve during their training."

"Not this one."

"What about Morgan Oil?"

"Duckworth's good, but I think I can beat him. No, I know I can beat him. You wanna watch me?"

"I sure do."

"Then go on to the stands, woman. I'm fixing to win Sullivan Oil a race and me a hefty little purse." He leaned close and whispered, "If you kiss me real sweet, I might treat you to a soda with my winnings."

She lifted an eyebrow. "If I kiss you real sweet, you're likely to lose your head and not concentrate on what you're doing. Now, quit your lollygagging and go win me a race."

———

Everywhere Essie looked, she encountered the anxious faces of spectators who had placed their final bets and filled the stands to root for their champion. Excusing herself, she wove through a press of men, women, and children wearing scarves and hats with their oil company's colors.

A group of rowdies wearing Alamo Oil's orange sang the "Texas War Cry" to the tune of "Anacreon in Heaven." Another group, who smelled as if they'd made one too many trips to the Anheuser-Busch tent, booed the Alamo singers and a shouting match ensued. Essie hurried past, hoping to be well out of the way if their shouts turned into something more physical.

She finally reached the section of stands designated for the Corsicana Velocipede Club. Mrs. Zimpelman stepped back, allowing Essie room to move toward the front.

"Why, Miss Morgan," Essie said, surprised to see Tony's sister beside Ewing and Mrs. Lockhart. "You're wearing Sullivan Oil colors."

The girl had secured a charming straw hat to her head with a red scarf tied fashionably off-center underneath her chin. "Please, call me Anna. And I hope you don't mind, but I was afraid Darius might lose his temper if I started cheering for Tony while sitting in the midst of Morgan Oil supporters."

Essie grasped Anna's hand. "It is our pleasure to have you, and I know Tony will be touched. Will it upset your mother, do you think?"

"None whatsoever. It wouldn't do for her to stand here with me, though, so she chose not to come at all."

The Merchants' Opera House band began to play the "Flag of Texas" as two flag bearers marched onto the track, one carrying the Stars and Stripes, the other carrying the Lone Star. The six bicyclers followed, their wheels beside them.

A deafening cheer rose, then the grandstands swelled with song as the crowd robustly sang along with the band.

> "Among the flags of nations,
> There is a place for thee,
> Flaunt up, thou bright young banner,
> Flaunt proudly o'er the free."

The racers' bright silk sashes glistened in the late-afternoon sunlight. The man from Alamo lifted his hand and waved to the fans. But it was Tony who captured Essie's attention. He looked like a giant among the other men. Tall, self-assured, and singing the well-known song with gusto.

Her heart filled with pride and pleasure and excitement. These races had always been important to her, but this one was by far the most significant. Not only because Tony was Sullivan Oil's man but because he was *her* man.

The song ended and the crowd roared their approval. An official began to line the cyclists up. The anticipation in Essie slowly built with the sweetest suspense imaginable. What a week it had been. The frantic preparations. The Welcome Reception. The heart-tugging moment when Tony proposed. The bright, color-splashed parade. And now these last few precious, nerve-jangling moments.

"For heaven's sake, Essie," Mrs. Lockhart said. "Wave to that Vandervoort boy before he falls."

Essie looked in the direction Mrs. Lockhart indicated and saw Harley several sections over, leaning across the barricade and madly waving his arms. She waved back and held up crossed fingers.

He pointed to the track and shouted, but of course she couldn't hear what he was saying. She assumed he was pointing to Tony, so she smiled and waved to the boy again. His face turned frantic. He began squeezing past people in an effort to get to her, but when he tried to push past Katherine Crook, she pulled him up short.

Essie held her breath. Harley had a history with the Slap Out's proprietress and did not always think before he acted where she was concerned. But there was nothing Essie could do about it from here.

A quietness settled over the crowd, pulling her attention back to the track. Each man placed his right leg over the bicycle bar and rested his foot on the pedal. The official raised a gun toward the sky.

"One!"

Essie's hands grew clammy.

"Two!"

Her heart thundered.

"Three!"

Bang.

The sound reverberated through her. Spectators shouted and whistled. The riders shot forward and immediately converged on the inside line. Tony settled down over his handlebars and focused on the track ahead of him.

The riders took turns leading and falling behind, but Tony did exactly what they'd decided on in advance. He moved forward early and pushed a moderate pace rather than stay amidst the pack and fight off attack after attack.

Morgan and Alamo Oil would eventually bridge. When that happened, it would be survival of the fittest and she wanted Tony right up there with them.

At the halfway mark, the riders for Morgan and Alamo Oil began to pull forward, then suddenly became embroiled in a shoving match. Essie couldn't tell who pushed whom first, but their antics threatened to unseat Tony, who rode on their left.

Mr. Duckworth, the Morgan man, grabbed Mr. Mudge by his sash and nearly jerked him off his machine.

Mudge lost his balance and zigzagged, while Tony, Mr. Duckworth, and the three other competitors whizzed by him. The remaining group of five stayed fairly close until about three-quarters of the way around. Duckworth, in a green sash, began to push toward the front.

Get ready, Tony, she thought. *Get ready.*

In a burst of speed, Ethey Oil pushed ahead of both Tony and Duckworth, but neither of those men gave chase, knowing the man would never be able to sustain his lead.

Sure enough, the Ethey man began to slow and pulled directly in front of Tony. Before Tony could go around him, however, Tyler Petroleum came up on Tony's immediate right.

No! Essie thought, as El Filon de Madre Oil rode up behind him, the three men pinning Tony in a box. Duckworth came around on the outside and took the lead.

Utter pandemonium broke loose in the stands. Spectators screamed, banners waved, whistles pierced.

"What's happening?" Anna asked.

"Tony's been pocketed," Essie shouted over the noise, frustration welling inside her. "The other riders are conceding the race to Morgan Oil and are trapping Tony to keep him from competing."

"But why? Why would they do such a thing?"

"The usual reason," Essie answered. "For a percentage of the purse."

Anna sucked in her breath. "Can't the official do something? Surely he realizes what is happening."

"Yes, he knows. And though pocketing may be unethical, it isn't illegal."

Essie rode the wave of her emotions along with the Sullivan Oil supporters around her as they alternately expressed shock, anger, and, finally, fury.

"Is there anything Tony can do?" Anna shouted.

"Yes," Essie said helplessly, "but it's very dangerous and we never trained for it. I just never expected such a thing to happen."

Grabbing the railing in front of her, she watched the racers continue to move in a clump. Never had she felt so impotent. And with a knot of concern in her throat, she turned to the one source she knew could do anything, no matter what the situation.

Help him, Lord. Please. Won't you please help him?

CHAPTER | TWENTY-SIX

OUTRAGED, TONY GRIPPED HIS handlebars more tightly. He'd seen a jockey pocketed once in a horse race, but it hadn't occurred to him it could be done in a bike race.

He wasn't about to concede defeat now, however. Breaking out of the pocket would require a cool head, and he was running out of time.

Pushing his anger aside, he quickly assessed the men surrounding him, then began to shore up his nerves. If he was willing to gamble with his good health, he just might manage it. He had to. Essie had never won before and he wanted to be the first man to win it for her. Just like he'd be the first man—the only man—she'd ever know in the biblical sense.

The Tyler man on his right eased off to the outside, presenting an enticing opening. But Tony checked his impulse to shoot through, realizing Tyler could close the pocket at any time and dump Tony in the dirt.

Instead, with heart hammering, he inched forward until his front wheel just barely overlapped Ethey Oil's rear wheel. Maintaining a constant rate of speed, Tony gave a quick twist on his handlebars, slapping Ethey's wheel and knocking it toward the inside of the track.

The Ethey man responded just as Tony anticipated, involuntarily overcompensating to the outside and momentarily swerving out of Tony's path. Accelerating, Tony shot through on the inside and escaped.

The crowd exploded with noise. Duckworth glanced over his shoulder, then hunkered down. Shutting out as much of the world as he could, Tony settled into a crouch, zeroed in on Duckworth's rear wheel and concentrated on catching up to it.

Help me catch him, Lord. Help me win this for Essie.

The gap between them shortened, but his legs burned, his back ached, and he was running out of track. He pedaled harder, his feet flying, his wet shirt clinging to his back. The finish line came into view. Duckworth glanced back again, giving Tony an opportunity to gain a few more rotations of the wheel.

His front tire pulled within inches of Duckworth's. Tony veered to the outside. *Faster. Faster.* The only sound that came to him was the purr of tires.

He passed Duckworth's back tire, his pedals. Closer. Closer. Almost even with him. The finish line hurtled toward them. Tony curled up and pushed as hard as he could.

They were so close, Tony didn't know who'd won and was going too fast to stop. People poured over the barricade and onto the track, sprinting toward the two riders. Those left behind shouted, whistled, stomped their feet and rattled cowbells.

No political rally, prayer revival, or holiday parade ever sounded so loud. The wooden beams supporting the grandstand trembled. Tony finally managed to slow enough to stop. He jumped off the bike just as hordes of men bedecked with green ran past him and surrounded Duckworth, congratulating him, patting him on the back, hefting him up onto their shoulders.

Disbelief, disappointment, and frustration crashed down around Tony, threatening to buckle his knees. He'd lost. He couldn't believe it. He scanned the stands for Essie but, of course, couldn't find her.

Instead, he found Darius. On the track, not ten yards away, accepting handshakes and congratulations as if he'd earned the privilege.

Tony should have known Darius wouldn't leave the outcome to chance. Too much was at stake—for both of them. Darius wanted to demonstrate his supremacy over Sullivan Oil in general, and Tony in particular. Tony had wanted to win the thing for Essie and the town of Corsicana.

Anger at being stripped—again—of something that rightfully belonged to him burst through the tight control Tony had heretofore been able to manage. Like a bull who'd been teased with a red cape one too many times, he charged, a war cry bursting from his throat.

Darius's startled expression before Tony slammed into his gut gave a momentary bit of satisfaction. But not nearly enough. Following his brother into the dirt, Tony made the most of his advantage and drove his fist into Darius's jaw. Blood spurted from his brother's mouth.

Hands from countless strangers pulled Tony off of Darius and up onto his feet.

He flung them off. "Get back!" he shouted. "This is between me and him. *Back away*, I said."

Whether no one wanted to be the first to persuade him otherwise or if the men had simply found something new to bet on, Tony didn't know and didn't care. All that mattered was that the crowd formed a circle around the two men, leaving Tony free to even the score with his brother.

Pushing himself into a sitting position, Darius touched a hand to his mouth. "You knocked out one of my teeth!"

"I've barely begun, big brother."

Darius removed a hanky from his coat pocket and pressed it against the place where his tooth used to be.

Tony nudged Darius's boot. "Get up. And for once in your life do your own dirty work instead of paying somebody else to."

Folding his feet underneath him, Darius began to rise. "Look, Tony. I'm not going to fight you just because you haven't learned how to lose with grace."

Tony grabbed Darius's lapels and snatched him close. "I didn't lose. You cheated."

Darius grinned, the black gap in his teeth giving Tony great satisfaction.

"I didn't do anything illegal," his brother said. "And let's admit it, that's not what has you so riled up. It's that I, once again, have come out on top."

Tony shoved him. Hard. Pedaling his feet, Darius stumbled back and would have fallen if the crowd hadn't been there to catch him.

"There isn't a person present," Tony said, "who doesn't know you won because you stooped to chicanery."

The crowd propped Darius back up. With great nonchalance, he dusted the dirt from his sleeves. "And there's not a person present who doesn't know the only reason you're in a higher-up position with Sullivan Oil is because you got underneath Essie Spreckelmeyer's skirts."

Tony exploded with fury. Leaping forward, he slammed another fist into Darius. Before he could follow him to the ground, though, strong hands grabbed Tony and jerked him back.

"What the blazes do you think you're doing?" Sheriff Dunn roared. He gave Tony a hard shake. "You better get out of my sight, Tony Morgan, and stay out before I throw you in Howard's wagon and keep you there until you rot."

Tony's vision cleared. He stumbled back, taking stock of his surroundings. The once uproarious crowd stood in silence. Finch knelt beside Darius. Others made room for Dr. Gulick as he shoved his way to the front.

Within the circle of gawking men stood Essie, hands covering her mouth, his grandmother's ring winking in the sun.

Turning, he walked away. Away from what he had done. Away from Darius. Away from her.

———

Essie knocked on Room 314 of the Commercial Hotel, then wrapped her shawl and her composure about her. The door swung open.

"Essie," Anna said, widening the door. "Come in."

Crossing the threshold, Essie glanced around the sitting room. Tony's mother, dressed in black, stood with her back to the room, holding open a panel of blue-and-gold damask drapes at the window. Darkness obscured any view she might have had, though, and instead reflected the woman's frail image like a mirror.

The golden striped settee was vacant. One of Mrs. Lockhart's romance novels was open and flipped upside down on a side table. The wing chair beside it held an indention in its cushion.

"Tony's not here?" Essie asked.

"We've not seen him since before the race," Anna said, closing the door.

"How's Darius?"

"Cut lip. Black eye. Nothing too serious. He was complaining more about some stomach ailment that's been grieving him lately. He's really angry about his missing tooth, though."

Essie nodded.

"Do you mean to say you've not heard from Tony, either?" Mrs. Morgan turned away from the window, worry lines making deep creases between her brows.

"I'm afraid not."

"Oh dear." Anna glanced at her mother, then back at Essie. "Can I pour you something?"

"I'm sorry. I can't stay. I need to find Tony."

Mrs. Morgan stiffened. "Is he in some kind of trouble?"

"Not that I know of, ma'am. I'm just worried because he didn't come out to the house tonight. I . . ." She swallowed. "I thought he would."

The two women stared at her.

"Well," she said, backing toward the door, "if you hear from him, would you tell him I'm looking for him?"

"Of course," Anna said. "Where are you going now?"

Essie opened her mouth to answer, but tears clogged her throat. She didn't know where to go. They didn't have any "special place" just the two of them went other than the bicycle club, and he certainly wasn't there.

She'd sent Jeremy to check in all the saloons. He'd insisted it was a waste of time, convinced that Tony didn't drink, yet he still did as she bid. But with no luck.

She'd been to his boardinghouse, Castle's Drug Store, the Slap Out, and now here. Where on earth was he?

Swallowing, she took a deep breath. "I guess I'll try the jailhouse next."

"The jailhouse!" Mrs. Morgan exclaimed.

"Only because my uncle is the sheriff," Essie assured her. "It's very likely that he'll know where Tony is. I'm sure he's fine, ma'am. I just, well . . ."

"You're upset," Anna said. "And understandably so. Of course you want to find him." She grabbed her hat and tied it on. "I'll help you."

"No," Essie said. "It isn't necessary."

"Nonsense. We can cover twice the amount of territory if we work together. Just tell me where you planned to go after the jailhouse?" Anna grabbed her wrap and slung it over her shoulders. "Don't wait up, Mother. I will very likely be quite late."

She followed Essie out the door and down the stairs into the hotel lobby.

"I honestly don't know where I'll go, Anna. And I'd hate to—"

"Well, ladies. This is a surprise."

"Ewing," Essie breathed, whirling around at the sound of his voice. "Oh, I'm so glad you're here."

The preacher nodded politely at Anna, then turned to Essie. "What's the matter?"

"I can't find Tony anywhere. Have you seen him?"

"I'm afraid I haven't."

She listed the places she'd already searched. "I was just heading over to the jail to see if Uncle Melvin had seen him. Anna offered to help, but it's so late and she doesn't know the town. I don't want to send her off by herself."

"Not to worry," he said. "I'll be glad to assist. Have you tried your house?"

"Not for the last hour or so."

"Okay. Miss Morgan and I will check there while you head to the sheriff's. We can rendezvous at the Slap Out."

———

Essie leaned Peg against the railing in front of the sheriff's office. Uncle Melvin would not be pleased to see her out this late, especially with the town full of so many strangers bent on extending the day's festivities into the wee hours.

But she was desperate to find Tony. To let him know she loved him and the race didn't matter. She also needed to assure herself that he was safe and unhurt, for though Darius hadn't struck Tony with his fists, he'd delivered blows just the same. He'd simply delivered them with words.

She cringed again at Darius's coarse accusation. And she was just human enough to confess she'd been every bit as outraged as Tony. All the same, she was glad Melvin had shown up when he had.

Stepping into the office, she noted two of the cells held a handful of men sleeping off their inebriated states.

Deputy Howard dropped his chair onto all fours and rose to his feet. "Well, well. Look who's out past her bedtime."

"Where's Uncle Melvin?"

"Here and there. You need something?"

"I'm looking for Tony. Have you seen him?"

Howard circled around his desk. "What's the matter? Worried yet another man's gonna leave you high and dry?"

She froze. What exactly was he intimating? That he knew something about Tony she didn't? Or that he knew something about her past that he shouldn't?

"A simple yes or no will do, Deputy. Do you or do you not know where Tony is?"

He leaned a hip against her uncle's desk. "No, can't say that I do."

"And Uncle Melvin? Do you know where he is?"

"Nope."

"Thank you." She turned to leave.

"There is one thing before you go." His hand brushed against the figurine she'd given her uncle years ago and set it to wobbling. Making a grab for it, he snatched it up before it could fall and break. Turning it over in his hands, he examined it, then slowly scratched underneath the figure's raised arm with his dirty thumbnail. "Seems we have a mutual acquaintance."

Her first instinct was to ignore him and keep going, but some sixth sense made her turn back around to face him.

"I met him while I was in Austin at the Sheriff's Association Convention." His thumb moved to the open neckline and chin of the figure. "His name is Adam Currington."

Her breath caught. She glanced again at the men in the cells. One snored. The others lay sprawled out in various positions, either asleep or unconscious from too much drink.

The deputy looked up. "Ever heard of him?"

She said nothing.

" 'Cause he sure as shootin' has heard o' you."

Swallowing, she forced down her panic. Surely Adam would not have betrayed her deepest, most carefully guarded secret. He might not be an honorable man, but he wasn't cruel or unfeeling.

"Mr. Currington's a sheriff now?" she asked.

Howard chuckled. "No, no. I ran into him at a—while I was uptown, not at the convention."

"How do you know him?"

"I'd only just met him that evening. I entered a local establishment and settled myself down by a few friendly lookin' fellas, one of whom was Currington. When they found out I was from Corsicana, they asked if I knew that bicycle gal from the papers. Before I could answer, Currington piped up, saying he knew you . . . quite well."

She kept her expression carefully blank.

He encircled the statuette in his hand more securely and began to rub his stubby finger across its chest. "Since you and he are so, um, close, you prob'ly know liquor seems to loosen his tongue a mite. Makes him say things that would be best kept to himself."

Apprehension welled within her.

He slid his thumb down the figurine and began caressing the hem of its skirt. "When I think o' the mistake I almost made with you." He shook his head. "I can't bear the thought of lettin' another man fall into your trap."

"My trap?"

He set the china ornament back on the desk, then directed his full attention to her. "Oh yes, Essie. I know all about ya. I'd heard the rumors, o' course, but Currington, who was evidently run out of this town on a rail a few years back, confirmed every tale I ever heard and then some."

Her lips parted. She'd thought Adam Currington was beyond hurting her anymore. She began to realize, however, that was not the case, as a fresh sense of betrayal rose within her yet again.

"And I think it's my civic duty to warn your *fee-yon-say* so he doesn't suffer the same fate." Standing, Howard hitched up his trousers. "O' course, if you could convince me that Currington was lying . . . or maybe take a stroll with me one evening real soon so we could, um, *discuss* the matter . . ."

She gasped. "How dare you!"

"Oh, keep yer knickers on." He leered. "Though it won't bother me none if'n ya don't. Either way, I'm free on Tuesday. Perhaps I could meet ya out behind yer place, say, around midnight?"

Shoving the hurt aside, she straightened to her full height. "You are wasting your breath, Mr. Howard. You'll find I'm not one to quail in the face of a bully."

"That so?" He walked to the big window fronting the office. "Wonder what the townsfolk would think about both their judge and sheriff harboring a strumpet?"

She sucked in her breath.

"Wonder how many members you'd have left in that club o' yours if'n the matrons of this town learned the truth about their leader?"

Whirling around, she charged to the door. "I will not listen to this."

He sidestepped in front of her, thrusting his arm across the doorway and blocking her way. "You will listen, you uppity little tart."

"All I've to do is tell my uncle and you'll be out of a job."

"You do that and I'll see your reputation ruined before you can spit three times."

"I doubt anyone would believe you."

"You think not? Not everybody around here kisses the ground your uncle and father walk on. And you can be sure their reputations would suffer plenty. They are, after all, elected officials by the trusting citizens of this fine town. And don't underestimate what yer beau's reaction is going to be, either. Not too many men I know of want used goods."

She tried to duck under his arm.

He grabbed her and slammed her against the wall. "I want a piece of what you gave Currington."

"Release me this minute, and if you threaten me again I'll not only tell Tony, I'll tell my uncle and father, too. Just watch me if you don't believe me."

He studied her as if gauging her sincerity. "You tell Tony and you can kiss your wedding day good-bye." He ran a finger from her ear to her chin. "Besides, there's no need to tell anybody anything. It's just one little stroll I'm wantin', Essie. Which is no more than you gave Currington." He loosened his hold, stepped back and winked. "See ya Tuesday, sugar."

CHAPTER | TWENTY-SEVEN

COASTING TOWARD HOME, ESSIE took note of the late—or early—hour. The first light of dawn had touched the sky and set off a chain of events she ordinarily delighted in. A yellow-and-pink sky framed the hundreds of stark, towering derricks that formed Corsicana's landscape. Songbirds flitted from rig to rig and tree to tree, announcing that this was a day the Lord had made and all should rejoice and be glad in it.

Rejoicing was the furthest thing from her mind, however. She, Anna, and Ewing had spent the entire night looking for Tony. But without success. And as troubling as that was, it was her confrontation with the deputy that had unsettled her the most.

She refused to be blackmailed by him. But if she didn't do as he said, he'd reveal her secret to the entire town. Were that to happen, the effects on her father and uncle could be devastating—not to mention what Tony's reaction would be.

The only thing to do, then, was to call Howard's bluff and confess to Tony. And the sooner the better. That was turning out to be a bit difficult, however, seeing as she couldn't find him.

The knot in her stomach tightened. Where was he? Anna said it wasn't like him to disappear like this and not tell the family where he was going. Her mood softened a bit at the thought of Anna. What a surprise she had been. Not at all the pampered little rich girl Essie had expected. Hardheaded, passionate, and fiercely loyal to Tony, she'd been tireless in their search for him.

And Ewing. *Preacher* Ewing. Essie smiled. As a youngster, she had spent many a day with him hunting all manner of creatures. And all those hours of hunting together had come back in a rush, allowing them to work with efficiency and thoroughness. Yet even then they couldn't locate Tony.

Where is he, Lord? Where is he?

Surely he wouldn't have left town. Would he? But she could think of no other explanation. There wasn't a rock in all of Corsicana that she, Anna, and Ewing had left unturned.

Opening her gate, she dragged herself down the walkway and leaned Peg against the porch.

"Where have you been?"

Squealing in fright, Essie jumped back. She glanced up on the porch, then felt a rush of joy and relief, quickly followed by anger.

"Tony!" She raced up the steps. "We've been looking all over for you. Where on earth have you been?"

"Where have *I* been? I've been right here. For hours—once I cooled off, that is. Wondering where the devil *you've* been." He pointed at the front door. "I spent forever throwing rocks at your window, until one actually broke the glass and went all the way through. Nobody could've slept through that. And that's when I realized you weren't home. I've been waiting for you ever since."

He still wore his racing outfit minus the red sash and beret. His hair lay in disarray. A full night's growth of whiskers shadowed his face.

"Well, if that don't beat all," she said. "There we were looking every which way, and you were right here on my very porch the entire time. Anna and Ewing must have just missed you when they came by here to check."

"Anna? Anna stayed out all night, too? And in Ewing's company? She can't be doing that, Essie. What were the two of you thinking?"

She propped her hands on her waist. "Don't you dare lecture me, Tony Bryant Morgan. I've just spent the longest night of my life looking for you and I'm not about to take any sass over it. You had the three of us worried to death."

"About what?"

"About where you were. And how you were. And if you were okay." She ran her gaze over him. "Are you? Are you okay?"

"I'm hungry."

She smiled. "Anything else?"

"My knuckles are pretty sore."

She walked to him and lifted his scuffed-up hand to her lips, anointing it with a kiss. "Come inside and I'll take care of this for you." She moved to the door and held it open. "You coming?"

"It's awfully early for me to be paying a call."

"Probably so, but I think it'll be okay. Just this once."

Bone tired, Tony lowered himself into a bentwood chair at Essie's kitchen table.

She lit a fire in the stove, set a pot on to boil, then grabbed a couple of cloths and a bottle of arnica.

Placing her rag over the mouth of the bottle, she tipped it upside down, dousing the cloth with liquid, then held her palm out. "Let me see your hand."

He rested his hand in hers while she pulled a chair up beside him and began to dab the cuts and bruises.

"I'm sorry, Essie."

She looked up. "For worrying me?"

"For losing the race."

"I don't care about that silly race, Tony." She returned her attention to what she was doing.

He knew that was a lie, but he didn't feel like arguing. She moistened her rag again.

"Did Anna say anything about Darius?" he asked. "Is he okay?"

"He's mad about his tooth and has a black eye, but other than that, sounds like he'll recover just fine."

After wetting the cloth time and again, she finally upended the tincture and poured it out onto the rag.

"I haven't fought him since we were kids," he said.

She attended a particularly tender spot, but he held himself still, careful not to show any signs of discomfort.

"He never even swung back," he said. "Not once."

She gently cleaned some dried blood from his knuckles, set the rag down and blew on the places she'd doctored.

"I wish you'd say something."

She looked up at him, her blue eyes soft. "I love you."

His throat started working.

She put the stopper back on the bottle.

"Essie?"

"Hmmm?"

"I love you, too."

She smiled. Not a big, hearty smile. But a small, quiet one. Like she was being told something that she already knew.

Leaning over, he took hold of her waist and pulled her onto his lap. "Will you marry me soon? I don't want a long engagement."

"I'll marry you whenever you say the word."

Gathering her close, he kissed her. Only, this kiss wasn't hot with passion like the one yesterday morning. This one was slower. Gentler. More of a sharing. Of her heart. Of his love. And it affected him even more than the other one.

"Essie Spreckelmeyer! Get off that man's lap this *instant*!"

Essie jumped to her feet, color rushing to her face.

Judge Spreckelmeyer stood in his nightdress, his pale, white shins and bare feet poking out the bottom. He looked back and forth at the two of them. "Has he been here all night?!"

"No!" she said. "I mean, not exactly. Not like you mean."

Standing, Tony picked up the cloth and tincture of arnica and handed it to her. "I was on your porch, sir."

"All night?"

"Yes, sir."

"With Essie?"

"No, sir. Alone."

He looked at Essie. "And where were you? Why are you still wearing yesterday's clothes?"

"I was with Anna and Ewing. We were looking for Tony. I didn't realize he was here waiting on me."

Spreckelmeyer set his mouth into a stern line. "Well, I don't care what age you are or whether the two of you are betrothed. His staying on our porch all night and coming inside the house before I've even made a trip out back simply isn't done, and you know it!"

"Papa—"

"You're absolutely right, sir," Tony said, interrupting her. "I apologize. It won't happen again." He turned to Essie. "I'll stop by later to pick you up for church."

She slammed the medicinals on the table. "Now, wait just one minute. Nothing improper happened, Papa. That kiss was the first time he's so much as touched me since yesterday morning. I won't have him running off with his tail between his legs like he's done something wrong."

Tony clasped her hand. "I did do something wrong, Essie. I came inside the house while your father was sleeping and at an hour no decent fella should."

Her lower lip curled down in a sweet pout. "I was gonna make you breakfast."

The picture of her cooking for him at the brush of dawn filled his mind. "The first time you make a morning meal for me, Essie, your name will be Mrs. Morgan." He leaned over and kissed her on the cheek. "I'll pick you up at the usual time." Stepping toward the archway, he nodded at Spreckelmeyer. "Sir."

The judge stepped out of the way and Tony left the house, his spirit renewed, his step light.

————

Knocking on the Spreckelmeyers' doorframe a few hours later, Tony peeked through the screen, wondering which hat Essie would be wearing to church. He heard a door slam, then her booted feet run to the top of the stairs.

To his surprise, she jumped onto the banister, slid down on her backside, and landed square in front of him, her smile happy and wide, her hat tall and sassy.

Shoving open the screen, he stepped in, grabbed her around the waist and kissed her just as he'd been thinking about doing ever since he'd left this morning.

"I wanted to do that the first time I ever saw you sliding down that thing," he murmured against her lips.

She ran her fingernails along the nape of his neck. "I don't think you would have received the same response from me then as you are now."

He chuckled. "No, I guess not."

Spreckelmeyer's study door opened and Tony released her, putting a proper distance between them.

Essie tugged on her gloves. "Tony's here, Papa. You ready?" She glanced up at her father's silence.

He wasn't even close to being ready. He was only in shirt, trousers, and suspenders. No vest. No tie. No jacket. No hat.

"Papa? Are you feeling poorly?"

Before he could answer, the sheriff stepped out into the hall as well. He wasn't dressed for church, either. In fact, he looked as if he'd never even gone to bed.

With the town as full of rowdies as it was, it wouldn't have surprised Tony. But since he'd moved to Corsicana, he'd never known the sheriff to miss a Sunday service. Not once.

"What's the matter?" Essie asked.

Tony considered making a polite withdrawal, but whatever news they had to give, it clearly wasn't good and he wanted to be with her when she received it.

Spreckelmeyer must have guessed as much, because he indicated the four of them should move into the parlor and take a seat.

Tony escorted Essie around a green-and-gold ottoman before settling her on the settee beneath a huge painting of an English fox hunt with hunters in full riding habits, restraining their anxious horses.

Joining her, he threaded his hand with hers.

Spreckelmeyer and Dunn sat in chairs opposite them. Neither said a word for several moments. The sheer white curtains along the front wall stirred, but the breeze was not sufficient enough to be felt inside the room.

"You're scaring me, Papa," Essie said as the silence stretched on. "What is it?"

Spreckelmeyer rested his elbows on his knees, then looked up at Tony. "Son," he said, "your brother was found dead in his hotel room this morning."

Essie gasped.

"What?" Tony asked, frowning and confused.

Spreckelmeyer said nothing, just looked at him with compassion and sympathy.

Tony turned to the sheriff. "I don't understand."

"He's dead, Tony."

Shock, disbelief, and bewilderment stacked up so fast, he couldn't even think of where to begin. "How? He's in excellent health."

The older men looked at each other, their glances telling.

White-hot panic shot through Tony. "Sweet saints above." His breath stuck in his throat. "From that punch? He died from that punch I gave him yesterday?"

"No, no," Spreckelmeyer said.

Relief poured through Tony, but he still felt sick to his stomach. "Then how? How did he die?"

"He was murdered."

Tony's lips parted. "Murdered? What are you talking about?"

The sheriff cleared his throat. "He was stabbed."

"Stabbed?" Tony shook his head. "That can't be. How did that happen? Who did it?"

"I don't know yet."

Essie squeezed Tony's hand. He felt the blood drain from his face. "My mother and sister? Were they harmed?"

"No."

He expelled a breath. "Have they been told about Darius?"

"Yes."

He released Essie's hand and stood. "I need to go."

The sheriff stood, as well, and put a hand on Tony's shoulder. "They're all right. Preacher Wortham is with them."

Tony frowned. "But Wortham has church this morning." The absurdity of him worrying about who was going to preach the Sunday service sounded strange even to his own ears. But if the others in the room thought so, they didn't give any indication.

"Bogart's gonna take care of it for him."

Tony stared at him.

"Bogart was our preacher before Ewing," Dunn said. "He retired a few years back."

Shaking his head, Tony made another effort to pass the sheriff. "I still need to get to my family."

Dunn increased the pressure on his shoulder. "In a minute. I think it would be best if you got all the details now. No need to upset the women with this kind of talk."

Desire to comfort his mother and sister pulled at Tony, but he saw the wisdom of the sheriff's words. He looked at Essie.

Nodding, she patted the spot beside her. He sat back down, trying to make sense of what the sheriff had told him. Stabbed? Darius had been stabbed? To death? But how? Why? By whom?

He knew Darius had enemies. Knew his brother could be underhanded. Still, he couldn't imagine Darius doing something so nefarious it would motivate someone to kill him in cold blood.

But someone had. And whoever it was would have to be mighty strong. His brother might not have fought back yesterday when Tony was going after him, but he'd most assuredly have fought back if someone was trying to kill him.

"Do you have any suspects at all?" Tony asked.

Dunn slowly nodded. "One."

"Who?"

The sheriff swiped his thick gray moustache with a leathery hand. "You."

Essie gasped a second time.

"*Me?*" The idea was so preposterous, he couldn't even process it. "Why? Because of that stupid race?" His anger started to build. "You think I'd kill somebody—my own flesh and blood—over some stupid bicycle race?"

"No. I don't think it had anything to do with that race."

"Then what possible reason can you have for suspecting me?"

"You mean besides the fact that you have now inherited the entire Morgan fortune and the oil company that goes along with it?"

All powers of speech fled from Tony.

"Besides the fact," the sheriff continued, "that you can save your sister from a marriage you've been very vocal about opposing but had no way of stopping—before now, that is?"

None of what the sheriff was saying had even occurred to Tony. But, of course, Dunn was right. Tony was next in line to inherit. And with that inheritance came all the power, resources, and privileges he needed to take proper care of his loved ones. And Essie, too.

Dunn leaned back in his chair. His blue eyes sharp. Perceptive. Intelligent. Deep grooves surrounded them from years of squinting into the bright Texas sunlight.

"I'm not gonna pretend like I don't want it," Tony said. "I do. I'd always assumed part of it would be mine." He drew down his eyebrows. "But I don't want it so badly that I'd kill a man for it. Especially not my own brother. We had our differences, but I never wished him dead. Never."

"Uncle Melvin," Essie said, her voice soft, calm, "I do not for one minute believe that you think Tony did this awful thing. And even if you did, there is no crime in inheriting the Morgan fortune. Granted, it doesn't look good, particularly on the heels of the scuffle the two of them had yesterday. But it isn't enough to accuse him of murder, and I'm devastated to think you would stoop to doing so."

Her voice cracked on the last few words. Tony slipped his hand back into hers.

Dunn moved his attention to her, his distress evident. "You know I would move a mountain for you if I needed to, but this is not something I have total control over. I have rules to abide by. Procedures to follow."

"You have no proof that he did it," she said, anger and hurt edging her voice.

Dunn and Spreckelmeyer exchanged a glance.

"Essie," Spreckelmeyer said, "Darius was stabbed with a stag-handled knife shaped like a dog bone."

CHAPTER TWENTY-EIGHT

ESSIE'S BREATH CAUGHT.

Tony fell back onto the cushions of the settee. "My knife? Darius was stabbed with *my* knife? The one my father gave me?"

Uncle Melvin's cheeks sagged, weighing his frown down even farther. "I'm afraid so."

"But I haven't seen my knife since I showed it to that Alamo fellow, Mudge, at the reception Friday night." He sat up. "You were there. Harley had just borrowed it and given it back, when Mudge asked to take a look at it."

Uncle Melvin gave no indication as to whether he recalled the incident or not.

Tony looked over at Papa. "Before I had time to get it back, Jeremy came in with news of Crackshot and I left without it." He scooted forward, sitting on the edge of the couch. "I missed it almost immediately because I needed it out at the rig when we were tending Crackshot."

"You never asked Mudge to return it to you?" Melvin asked.

"Of course I did. The very next morning when I saw him at the parade. But he said he'd left it at the Commercial, thinking I'd go back there to retrieve it."

"And did you go back to the hotel?"

"Yes, but no one there had seen or heard a thing about it."

Essie had held her peace for as long as she was going to. She knew her father and uncle didn't really suspect Tony killed his brother. She also knew they were elected officials and had to follow the due course of the law.

So she had sat there and let them accuse Tony, interrogate him and scare him half to death. Enough was enough.

"What are we going to do, Papa?" she said. "Both of you know he didn't do it. Anyone could have picked up his knife."

Papa rubbed his forehead. "It's not that simple."

"It is."

"No, it's not. Besides, the decision isn't mine to make."

"You're the Thirty-fifth Judicial District Judge. If you say there's not enough evidence, then that's an end to it."

He lowered his hand. "Not this time. Not when the accused is my future son-in-law. Maybe if the two of you weren't already betrothed, I could do something. But now, if we don't make this arrest, no one will believe in Tony's innocence. They'll think Melvin and I manipulated the facts to suit ourselves. And that's just the type of thing that incites lynch mobs."

Her heart jumped into her throat. "You're going to arrest him?" She swerved her gaze to Melvin. "You are thinking to actually take him to the jailhouse and put him in a cell?!"

"Where were you in the wee hours of last night?" Uncle Melvin asked Tony.

A tick began to hammer in Tony's jaw. "Sitting on the front porch there."

"This front porch?"

"Yes, sir."

"For how long?"

"From about midnight to dawn."

Melvin shot Essie a quick glance before returning it to Tony. "Alone?"

Essie stiffened.

"Yes, sir."

"Did anyone see you there?"

"No, sir."

"The whole night long? Not one single person happened by?"

"A straggler or two happened by. But it was dark and I was sitting in the shadows. I wasn't about to holler out a greeting. It would have ruined Essie's reputation."

Her uncle stood and approached the fireplace. His back to them, he propped his hand on the mantel. "Where were you before that?"

"I walked down to Two Bit Creek to cool down after my fight with Darius. Then I came here."

"What did you do then?"

"Threw rocks at her window."

He whirled around. "What?"

"I was trying to wake her up. I hadn't seen her since my fight with Darius and I knew I'd never get to sleep unless I talked to her first."

"So you snuck around back and threw rocks at her window?"

"Yes, sir."

Melvin took a step forward, pointing his finger. "Don't you ever do that again!"

Papa heaved a sigh. "Melvin, you are digressing."

"Are you forgetting what happened last time, Sullivan?"

"Melvin—" Papa growled.

Essie jumped to her feet. "Can we please just stick to the issue at hand?"

Her uncle looked at her. "Did you go out there and meet him?"

"I wasn't even home!"

"Has he done that before?"

"Of course not."

"Well, if'n he ever does it again, I assume you will not dignify him with a response?"

She stormed around the chairs. "I most certainly will respond. Nothing short of desperation could motivate Tony to wake me up in the middle of the night, and I'd answer his call like *that*," she said, snapping her fingers.

"Desperation? Desperation for what?" her uncle barked.

Papa surged to his feet. Tony jumped clear over an ottoman and shoved her behind him, placing himself between her and her uncle.

"Listen here, Sheriff. You got something to say, then you say it to me, but you leave Essie alone. I don't care if you're the sheriff, her uncle, or her last living relative. Nobody talks to my woman like that. *Nobody.* You understand?"

"And just what're ya gonna do about it, Morgan? Stab me with your knife?"

Essie gasped.

"That is enough!" Papa roared.

Her uncle and Tony stood chest to chest.

"Stop it, Melvin," Papa said. "I mean it."

Melvin took a step back but didn't relax his stance.

"You too, Tony."

Tony fished around for her hand. She slipped it inside his. He took a step back, keeping her partially behind him.

"Say what you have to say, Sheriff," Tony said. "But I'm done chitchattin.' "

Uncle Melvin hardened his features. "You wanna know what I have to say? I say you're under arrest, Anthony Bryant Morgan. For the murder of your brother, Darius Morgan."

———

Essie lay curled up on her bed, crying to the Lord for help. Her first instinct had been to go out and do something. Anything. But what could she do?

Melvin had forbidden her to go to the hotel until they'd removed the body. He wouldn't even let her go and offer condolences to Anna and her mother.

Tony didn't want to make any more of a spectacle than necessary as he went to the jailhouse and asked her to stay behind.

Papa had gone to send a telegram to a judge from another district. It would be unethical for Papa to sit in judgment on a case that involved his future son-in-law.

And Mother was gone, of course. Out of reach.

Essie pressed a handkerchief to her mouth. *Oh, Lord. I need my mother.*

Aunt Verdie had tried to be there for Essie since Mother's death, but Essie was closer to Uncle Melvin. She ran her finger over the Florentine stitches on her pillow slip. Going to her uncle now, though, was out of the question—particularly when she was so disappointed in him.

She had many women friends from church and the bicycle club, but what could they do? Nothing. Not one blessed thing.

And then, she realized, Christ was still her groom. He hadn't left her simply because she and Tony had decided to get married.

But as she lay on her bed, no words of prayer came to her. No Scriptures. No memorized verses. No nothing. So she'd simply cried, beseeching the Lord and repeating the only prayer she could think of.

Help. Please, Lord. Help.

She was so tired. So empty. When had she last been to bed? At some point she must have dozed off, for the sound of someone knocking on the front door downstairs jolted her awake.

Too tired to move and not up for visitors, she stayed in her bed.

The door opened. "Essie?"

It was a woman's voice.

"Are you home, honey?"

She heard the creak of the stairs, but she still didn't answer. The footsteps came down the hall and stopped at her bedroom door.

She rolled over and tears engulfed her eyes. "Mrs. Lockhart."

The elderly lady came in, sat on the edge of the mattress and opened her arms. Essie moved into them and sobbed. The slightest hint of camphor rose from Mrs. Lockhart's clothing.

"There, there, dear," she said, patting Essie on the back. "That's it. You have a good cry, then I'll tell you what we have planned."

Essie took a trembling breath and leaned back. "We have a plan?"

"Well, of course. But finish your cry first. You'll feel much better for it."

Essie dragged the hanky across her eyes. "I want to hear our plan."

Mrs. Lockhart stood up and held out her hand. "Come, let me do your hair first."

"For what?" Essie swung her legs over the side of the bed.

"For the emergency meeting of the Velocipede Club."

"But I didn't call an emergency meeting." Essie sat down on her vanity stool and began to remove the pins from her hair.

Mrs. Lockhart picked up the brush. "Shirley called it. We are due to convene in thirty minutes."

———

Wearing a white shirtwaist, brown skirt, and simple straw hat, Essie entered the Velocipede Club with Mrs. Lockhart. Afternoon sunlight streamed in through the windows lining the upper edge of the building. It appeared as if the entire female membership was present and every single one of them was talking at once.

Mrs. McCabe and Mrs. Zimpelman caught sight of her first. One by one the women quit speaking until the earsplitting noise trickled into total quiet. Essie looked over the sea of faces regarding her with concern and affection.

When she'd asked the Lord for help, she never imagined He'd send angels disguised as bloomer-girls. Tears piled up in her throat, making it almost impossible to swallow.

Shirley strode to her and clasped her tight. "Oh, honey. Don't you worry about a thing. We'll figure something out."

And in a rush, the entire group crowded about her, reassuring her and pulling her to the chairs that had been set up.

Shirley moved to the podium and hammered on the gavel. "Order, please."

The women settled and gave their attention to Shirley.

"As you know, our beloved member and Essie's much-anticipated fiancé has been placed in the jailhouse for something we all know, beyond a shadow of a doubt, our Mr. Morgan would never do."

"He certainly wouldn't."

"Don't know what the sheriff was thinking."

"Inexcusable is what it is."

Shirley rapped the gavel again. "Because of Mr. Morgan's relationship with Essie, the sheriff and judge don't have the legroom they usually do under these circumstances."

"Such a mess."

"Poor Mr. Morgan."

"We've got to get him out of there."

"Verdie, can't you do something about the sheriff?"

Aunt Verdie was here? Essie twisted around but was unable to find her in the crowd.

"Ladies!" Shirley said, shushing them. "Please. We are wasting time."

The women quieted.

"Now," Shirley continued, "leaving Mr. Morgan's fate to some strange judge or, worse, Deputy Howard, simply will not do." She lifted her chin. "Therefore, I move that we, the women of the Corsicana Velocipede Club, take on the task of rescuing our Mr. Morgan."

A beat of concern broke through Essie's daze. Rescue? They were going to break Tony out of jail?

"I second the motion," said Mrs. Gulick.

"All those in favor say 'Aye.' "

"Aye."

"Opposed?"

Essie opened her mouth, but before she could interject a bit of caution, the door opened. Anna, Mrs. Morgan, and Ewing stepped inside.

Shirley smiled. "Mrs. Pickens, as Membership Chair, would you please go and welcome the Morgans and Preacher Wortham?"

The proprietress of the Flour, Feed and Liquor Store jumped to her feet and escorted Anna and her mother—both in black—to some vacant chairs, Ewing close behind them.

"We appreciate your coming," Shirley said, "and we offer our condolences. However, I feel compelled to warn you, our conversation today will be open and frank and perhaps upsetting to you as we discuss the circumstances surrounding Mr. Morgan's death. Are you sure you're up to staying?"

Anna looked at her mother, who dabbed her eyes with a handkerchief, then nodded.

"Very well. Then, as there was no opposition to our motion, the floor is open for discussion. Before we start, however, I respectfully suggest that the most effective and upright way to accomplish our goal is to find out who really did kill Darius Morgan. So we must first try to ascertain who would profit from his death." She scanned the audience. "The floor recognizes Mrs. McCabe."

The coroner's wife stood, her usual jolly expression nowhere in sight. "Mr. McCabe has laid out many a man in his day. Those who died in a similar fashion to Mr. Morgan were most often the victims of," she held up her fingers, ticking off the reasons, "explosive anger—due to cheating at cards and such. Or accidents—cleaning out guns and that sort of thing. Reckless behavior while under the influence of intoxicants. Sometimes jealousy—usually involving a woman. And occasionally, premeditated, cold-blooded murder."

"Have you spoken to Mr. McCabe since he's seen the body?" Shirley asked.

"I have."

"And what is his opinion?"

"Premeditated, cold-blooded murder."

Fans fluttered and whispers ricocheted throughout the room.

"The floor recognizes Miss Davis."

Young Victoria stood, casting a quick glance at Ewing, then blushing prettily. "Mr. Morgan was quite wealthy. Isn't it possible that someone who worked for him or who had unsatisfactory business dealings with him might have held a grudge of some sort?"

"Excellent point. Are you recording all this, Mrs. Blanchard?"

The club secretary nodded, busily scribbling in her record book.

"The floor recognizes Mrs. Lockhart."

"In *The Shadow of Sin*," she began, using her cane to push to her feet while those in attendance suppressed a groan, "Mr. Goodenough found his young wife in the arms of Mr. Huffstutter and planned an elaborate scheme to murder them both in their sleep. Of course, he ran into difficulty when—"

"Thank you, Mrs. Lockhart," Shirley said, gently interrupting. "As Mrs. McCabe pointed out earlier, jealousy can, indeed, be a powerful motivator. Mrs. Vandervoort? I believe I saw your hand next."

Essie listened as each woman had an idea for motive, and as the list lengthened, her optimism wavered. The possibilities were endless, but of all those presented, none were as compelling as the motives assigned to Tony.

"Last one," Shirley said.

Anna Morgan rose. "I believe that there is one motive we are overlooking, and that would be my motive."

The women stilled.

"Darius was forcing me into a marriage I did not want. I had just as much motive to kill him as Tony did. Anyone who knows our family well knows that Tony and I are very close. If something were to happen to Darius, and Tony were to inherit, that would solve all my worries."

Ewing jumped to his feet. "Miss Morgan, though your hypothesis sounds reasonable at first, there isn't a soul who would actually believe you capable of such a thing. The idea is ridiculous."

"No more ridiculous than believing Tony did it."

Ewing scowled at Shirley. "I will not permit that ludicrous supposition to be entered into the minutes."

"If we are going to do this right, the list needs to be thorough," Anna argued. "Keep it in the books."

Essie glanced back and forth between the two.

Shirley cleared her throat. "There are no right or wrong suggestions, Preacher Wortham."

"Then I did it!" he said, slamming his fist against his chest.

Mrs. Bogart gasped.

"Don't be absurd, Ewing," Anna said. "You'd never even met Darius before Friday."

"Well, I can tell you this: I don't want you to marry that old boiler you're betrothed to. So that gives me just as much motive as you, now, doesn't it?"

Anna's features softened. "You don't want me to marry Mr. Tubbs?"

"Well, of course I don't."

She bit her lower lip. "Well, I don't believe I'll have to."

Ewing blinked in confusion. Essie smiled.

Shirley folded her arms. "Are you two quite through?"

After a slight hesitation, Anna nodded, slid a hand beneath her skirts and sat. Befuddled, Ewing plopped down beside her.

"Now," Shirley continued, "I suggest we try to gather a bit of evidence based on some of these suggestions. Mrs. Blanchard? Let's start from the top and begin making assignments."

The secretary stood. "Number one. Someone who worked for him or who had unsatisfactory business dealings with him."

Shirley tapped the lectern with her fingernail. "That's going to be difficult. We'll need access to Mr. Morgan's personal files and records." She looked at Anna. "Would that be something you or your mother could get your hands on somehow?"

"Yes," Anna said. "That part would be easy. We simply take a train back to Beaumont and raid Darius's desk. The problem will be what to do with the papers once we have them. Neither Mother nor I would know where to begin."

"Essie?" Shirley asked. "You would be able to, wouldn't you?"

"Perhaps," Essie said. "But is there any reason we can't have Tony go through them? He's apt to be much more familiar with the Morgan ventures."

"Excellent idea. And it would make him look less guilty and more a martyr to have him resort to doing his work within the cell."

"I agree," said Mrs. Zimpelman. "As a matter of fact, I recommend he also continue his work for Sullivan Oil. The men he oversees could go to him daily with their reports and for their assignments."

"Will the sheriff allow that, do you think, Mrs. Dunn?" Shirley asked.

Aunt Verdie smiled. "You leave the sheriff to me."

Ewing stood. "That's all well and good, but Miss Morgan and her mother cannot do what you ask of them. If the murderer really is a business acquaintance, he will not allow these women to simply walk off with the evidence. No, the scheme is much too dangerous."

"Oh dear," Shirley said, then looked at Anna. "Don't you have a cousin who could escort you?"

Anna shook her head. "Finch is determined to stay here. He doesn't think Sheriff Dunn and Judge Spreckelmeyer will be impartial and he wants to make sure 'Tony gets his due.' So we wouldn't want Finch to accompany us or even to hear of our plans. He's very loyal to Darius."

"But all the Morgan papers are rightfully Tony's," Essie said. "Your cousin wouldn't have any choice in the matter."

"It would still be best to keep our plans to ourselves."

"I'll go with them," Ewing said.

Essie lifted her brows.

"Not only can I provide them with escort and protection," he said, "but I can help them carry the documents back here."

"That's very generous of you, Preacher Wortham," Shirley said. "Thank you. Mrs. Blanchard? What's the next motive on our list?"

"Jealous husband."

"Oh my." Shirley scanned the crowd. "Miss Morgan? Can you or your mother shed any light here?"

"I'm afraid not," Anna said. "Darius was not stepping out with anyone. As far as him seeing someone he oughtn't, I'm afraid I have no idea about that."

Mrs. Lockhart rose. "I have a daughter in Beaumont. I will contact her and see if I can determine who Mr. Morgan's romantic interests were."

By the end of the hour, several women had been assigned a motive to investigate. The rest compiled a schedule for delivering meals to Tony.

Before the meeting adjourned, all members pledged themselves to secrecy. Even Aunt Verdie and Ewing. In order to keep the women's plans from being hindered, the menfolk needed to be kept in the dark.

As the meeting broke up, Essie stayed in her seat and looked down at her ring. A ring worn for over four decades by another woman, yet even still it sparkled. She wiggled her finger, allowing the sunlight to catch in the diamond's prisms.

Somewhere long, long ago, this stone had been nothing more than a lump buried in the ground. But with hard work and great perseverance, it was mined, cleaned, cut and polished. Then treasured by the woman who wore it.

And now the man God had prepared for Essie had placed it on her finger. A good man. An honest man. A man who'd been forsaken by his father.

But he would not be forsaken this time. Not by her. Not by his friends. And not by his heavenly Father.

She stood. There was work to be done and she aimed to do her share.

CHAPTER | TWENTY-NINE

M.C. BAKER STEPPED INTO the jailhouse. "Howdy, Sheriff. I'm here to see Morgan."

Melvin slapped his pen on the desk, splattering ink all over his papers. Tony'd had more visitors in the last two days than any one prisoner in the history of Melvin's entire tenure as sheriff. He'd spent so much time letting folks in and out of Tony's cell that he hadn't accomplished one single thing.

Grabbing up the keys, he strode to the back of the building. Tony sat behind an old table, pen and ink in hand, lantern sputtering in the breeze. Melvin couldn't believe he'd let Verdie talk him into allowing all that stuff into Tony's lockup. She never interfered with his work. Never. Until now.

Yet Verdie and every other woman in town was treating Morgan as if he were a native Corsicanan or something. And it was all due to the fact that he was Essie's betrothed. Melvin had at first figured the women would try to convince Essie to break the betrothal. Instead, they'd aimed their displeasure at him, the man who had kept them safe and secure for the past three decades.

Oh, he didn't think Tony had done the killing. He'd merely lost his temper back at the Spreckelmeyers' house and as a result had treated the boy a bit harshly. Still, he couldn't outright ignore the evidence that pointed to him or it would bring down censure from every man in town and many of those in the state's capital. That might be preferable, however, to the censure of the women of the Corsicana Velocipede Club.

He drove his fingers through what was left of his hair. If he had any prayer of finding out who did the actual killing, though, he was gonna have to be allowed to get some work done.

Unlocking the cell, he jerked it open and scowled at his prisoner. "I'm getting mighty tired of jumping up and down like a jack-in-the-box every other minute. If'n I leave this durn thing open, will you stay put?"

The average person might have missed the momentary surprise on Tony's face, but Melvin had made a career of watching for subtle nuances in a man's expression.

"Yes, sir," Tony answered. "I give you my word."

Melvin nodded once. "Well, all right, then." He turned to Baker. "Go on. Everybody else has."

Baker entered the cell and began to review the day's business with Tony.

Melvin returned to his desk and looked over his notes. A vast number of the folks who had entered town for the bicycle race had left, leaving behind the locals and the oilmen. For all he knew, the killer had come and gone, too. But until he knew for sure, he'd do everything he could to piece together what had happened. He didn't want to be known as the sheriff who'd allowed the killer of one of the wealthiest men in Texas to get away without a trace. He also didn't want Essie's fiancé hung if he wasn't the guilty party.

He again examined the list of every guest at the Welcome Reception, where Tony'd left his knife, along with every employee of the Commercial Hotel. He'd questioned the men who'd attended the reception, particularly Mudge, who'd been knocked out of the race by Darius's man.

But after the race, Mudge had nursed his disappointment in Rosenburg's Saloon and passed out, spending the whole of the night in plain view. The other men in the race had plenty of folks confirming how they'd spent their evening, as well. Melvin scratched through name after name on the guest list. Those who had a motive didn't have an opportunity, and those who had an opportunity didn't have a motive.

He had a few more people at the Commercial Hotel he wanted to talk with, though. Not only the ones who were working the night of the reception, but those who'd discovered Darius's body in his room early that morning. He also wanted to find out if anyone had seen Darius's sister and mother coming or going during the time in question.

Baker bid good-bye to Tony, then tipped his hat to Melvin before leaving. Darkness fell and crickets took to serenading his small office.

Melvin turned up the flame of his lantern. "So what do you think, Morgan? Anything new occur to you as far as your brother's concerned?"

Tony looked up from his papers. "I really don't know what to think, Sheriff. My mother and sister brought a bunch of Darius's papers back from Beaumont today and I've been studying them. Everything looks to be in order. He's let go of an employee here and there, but nothing that would incite a person to murder."

"How recently have those folks been dismissed?"

"Since my father's death at the beginning of the summer."

Melvin nodded. "Well, make me a list of their names and I'll send it over to the sheriff of Jefferson County and have him look into it."

Howard walked in, saw the cell door open and quickly palmed his gun. "What's goin' on?"

Melvin shook his head. "Put your gun away before somebody gets hurt. I was just tired of opening and closing his cell a hundred times, so I decided to leave it open."

Keeping his gun trained on Tony, Howard stealthily made his way to the back of the office. Tony lifted his hands.

"Would you put that thing away?" Melvin repeated.

Howard ignored him until he had the cell door firmly closed and locked. Releasing the hammer on his pistol, he returned it to his gun belt. "Seems a mite careless to leave his door open like that, Sheriff."

Shrugging, Melvin stood. "Suit yourself. Now that you're here, though, I'm gonna make a run over to the Commercial."

"You find out something new?"

"Nope. Just snoopin'. I'll be back directly." Grabbing his hat, he strode through the door.

———

Essie stepped into the sheriff's office, then stopped cold at seeing Deputy Howard alone with Tony. Her hands grew clammy. For the past two days, she'd wrestled with herself about whether or not to tell Tony about Howard's threats and the reason behind them. But that was a discussion she preferred to have in private. Something sorely lacking under the present circumstances.

She'd debated telling her father or even Uncle Melvin but found that for the first time in a long, long while, it wasn't either of them she wanted to share her troubles with. Instead, she wanted to go to another man. Her man.

She smiled at him through her worries and he rose to his feet. Circles shadowed his eyes and some color had faded from his sun-washed skin.

"I've brought you a little something to eat," she said.

Howard stepped around his desk. "Why, thank you, Essie. I appreciate that."

She stiffened. "I was talking to Mr. Morgan."

Hitching up his trousers, Howard sauntered over to her. "Well, I don't reckon he's hungry right now. Them women from yer bicycle club have been making sure he's the best-fed fella in all of Navarro County. Me, on the other hand, I've not had me so much as a bite to eat since noon." He stepped into her space. "You got something fer me, Essie?"

"My name is Miss Spreckelmeyer."

He lifted the corner of the napkin covering her basket. She swatted his hand.

"Easy, now. I was only taking a peek." He lowered his voice to a level Tony wouldn't be able to hear. "But I don't mind waiting, Essie. It is Tuesday, after all, and if'n you wanna give me a peek of what you got later on tonight, well, that's just fine by me."

"Step aside," she said.

"Not just yet, sweetheart." He grasped the napkin and whipped it off. "I can't let you take that into his cell without making sure of its contents. Wouldn't want you to slip our prisoner a weapon or nothin'." He rifled through the basket, then picked up a peach and took a bite out of it. "Ummm. That tastes mighty sweet. You sure you wanna waste all your sweet stuff on him?"

She slipped out from between Howard and the wall, then walked over to her uncle's desk and snatched up the keys.

Howard followed and grabbed her wrist. "I'm not sure you should be goin' in there."

The prisoner might be dangerous and I'd hate for something to happen that would, um, compromise you in the town's eyes."

"I believe I'll take my chances," she said, shaking off his grip.

Howard smiled, removing the keys from her grasp. "That's what I'm countin' on, girl. That's what I'm countin' on."

Tony stood at the bars, frowning as he looked at the two of them.

"Get back," Howard said, approaching him.

Tony moved to the back of the cubicle. Howard opened the door, then locked it behind Essie when she stepped inside.

Instead of returning to his desk, though, Howard leaned a shoulder against the cell and ran his finger along one of the bars.

"Would you excuse us, please?" she said.

"Don't mind me, Miss Spreckelmeyer. I'm only doing my job and standing guard. Just carry on. You know, like you would if nobody was around to see."

His words hung in the air and she didn't know what to say or do. She couldn't tell Tony about Adam with the deputy standing there. And she couldn't not tell him, either.

"Maybe I should come back when Uncle Melvin's here," she said to Tony.

He took her hand and pulled her to the other side of the table. Putting his back to Howard, he leaned against the table, his broad form blocking her from the deputy's view.

"What is going on?"

"Long story," she whispered.

"You're gonna need to speak up," Howard said. "I can't hear ya. Unless, of course, you want me to join you." His chuckle made her skin crawl.

Tony studied her a moment. "Your uncle's at the Commercial Hotel," he said quietly. "Find out when he'll be here and come back then. And from now on, only come when he's here."

Her shoulders wilted. "But I don't want to go. I just got here."

"Quit your whispering," Howard said.

She heard the keys rattle in the lock. "Here," she said, handing Tony the basket of food. "I'll be back later."

He squeezed her hand. "I love you."

Howard threw open the door.

Essie hustled around the table. "Thank you, Deputy. I'm ready to leave now." She sailed through the door of the cell and out of the office before he had a chance to waylay her.

———

Essie waited until nearly midnight, then made her way to the sheriff's office, careful to stay under the cover of the wooded areas, even though it was a more circuitous route. She knew it was the deputy's turn to spend the night at the jailhouse. She also knew he'd be slipping out in hopes of meeting her behind her house.

With any luck at all, his absence would give her enough time to tell Tony everything. About Howard blackmailing her. About Adam. About her past.

Give me the strength, Lord. Give me the words.

The jailhouse was dark when she arrived.

"Who's there?" Tony said when she opened the door.

"It's me." She struck a match and lit the lantern on Melvin's desk.

Tony rose from his cot, his hair tousled. "What are you doing here?"

"We need to talk."

"Has something happened?"

"Howard's blackmailing me." She grabbed the keys to the cell.

"No," Tony said. "Don't open the door. If someone were to come in, I don't want them to think you're trying to bust me outta here or, worse, that we were doing something that would compromise your reputation. Just leave those where they are and we'll talk through the bars."

She returned the keys to Melvin's desk.

Tony held out his hand. "Come here."

Running to the cell, she slipped her hands into his. The bars separated their bodies but not their hearts. Not their souls.

"I miss you," he said.

"Me too." She leaned against the door. "I don't like being barricaded from you. I want to be in there with you or you to be out here with me."

He brought her hands to his lips. "You better tell me what's going on. I expect Howard to be back any minute and I don't want you here when he arrives."

She nodded. "While Howard was in Austin a couple of weeks ago, he ran into a man who used to work for Sullivan Oil." She stopped, unsure of what to say next.

"Who was he?"

She moistened her lips. "Just a man. A man who, um, makes a habit of going from town to town and preying upon women who can't see that his charm has but one goal. A very unsavory goal."

Tony nodded. "I understand. What has that to do with Howard?"

"Well, this man told Howard some things—private things—about me . . . and him."

"What do you mean?" Tony asked, frowning.

Her heart tripped. *Help me, Lord.* But no words came. Only incredible remorse and shame and fear. Before she could summon up a gentle way to say what needed to be said, his jaw slackened and his eyes widened.

"What are you saying, Essie?" he whispered.

She swallowed. "I'm saying that this man seduced me and told Howard about it, and Howard is using that to blackmail me."

Tony's hands relaxed their hold, but he didn't completely let loose of her. "What do you mean by 'seduced' you?"

Moisture rushed to her eyes. "I mean that he ruined me."

"By force?" he asked.

She slowly shook her head.

He let go of her and stumbled back. "You—you've been with another man?"

"Once. It was a long time ago. He means nothing to me. I was foolish—"

Tony turned his back, braced his hands on the table and hung his head.

"I'm sorry, Tony. I, he, it was . . ."

Tony gripped the edge of the table, his knuckles turning white. "Why didn't you tell me?"

She didn't know what to say. Explaining there had never been an opportune time sounded hollow even to her ears. "I should have."

"You're right, you should have." His voice was hoarse.

Oh, don't cry, Tony. Please don't cry.

"Tony—"

"Go away."

"Please. I tried to tell you. Not once, but twice. Yet each time—"

He whirled around. "You should have tried harder. Insisted, in fact—*before* I put that ring on your finger." He pointed toward the west. "You gave that man something you can never give again, Essie. Something that rightfully belonged to me. Why is it that every important thing that belongs to me—my inheritance, my father's approval, my woman's virtue—is given to someone else?"

"Tony, I—"

"Get out!" he shouted. "Get out now!"

Tears flooded her eyes. "Just like that? You don't even want to give me a chance to explain what—"

"There is nothing you can say, Essie, to change the fact that you will come to our marriage bed soiled."

She sucked in her breath. "Oh yes, there is." She removed his grandmother's ring from her finger and held it out to him. "If there is no marriage bed, I can't very well come to it 'soiled,' now, can I?"

He slapped the ring, knocking it from her grasp and onto the floor somewhere. Though his hand had barely grazed her fingers, the sting of his rejection went much deeper.

She longed to explain, to make amends, but his eyes were shuttered and a barrier much more formidable than a few steel bars now stood between them.

Fortifying herself with calm resolve, she picked up the lantern and returned it to her uncle's desk. She could feel Tony's gaze boring into her, but she resisted looking at him. She blew out the flame, plunging the room into darkness. After a bit of fumbling, she found the door.

"Good-bye, Tony," she whispered. "I'm sorry." Then she clicked the door shut behind her.

CHAPTER | THIRTY

ESSIE WENT STRAIGHT FROM the jail to Uncle Melvin's house, staying well away from the streets east of Beaton. Tony might think her loose, but she wasn't. And she may have to accept his condemnation, but she needn't put up with Howard's perfidy in the meanwhile.

She knocked and didn't have to stand on the Dunns' front porch for very long before Melvin swung open the door. "Essie! What's happened?"

"I need to talk to you."

"It's the middle of the night."

"Your deputy is blackmailing me and has asked for sexual favors in exchange for his silence."

His face registered shock. "He *what*?!"

"May I come in now?"

He widened the door.

"Mel?" Aunt Verdie said, her voice filtering down from upstairs somewhere.

"It's business, Verdie," he hollered. "Go back to sleep."

Essie followed him to the kitchen. A room she'd spent many hours in as a child, a haven that held memories of laughter and love.

Lighting a lantern, he looked up and saw her tear-streaked face. He sucked in his breath, anger flushing his face. "I'll kill him. I'll kill him with my own hands. Sit down, baby, while I get Verdie to come down here with you."

She touched his arm, stopping him. "Please. Can we just talk for a minute?"

"He's hurt you and he's gonna pay. There's nothing to talk about."

"I've been able to hold him at bay. Nothing's happened . . . yet."

"He hasn't touched you? Hurt you?"

"No."

"Then why are you crying? Why are you here at one in the morning?"

"I'm here at one in the morning because the deputy said he would be waiting for me behind the house tonight and I was afraid to go home. I was crying because I went to the jailhouse and told Tony what was happening. Which then led to me telling him about Adam. Tony, he, he—" The tears came again.

Melvin reached for her, enfolding her in his embrace. "Oh, honey."

"He doesn't want me anymore. He told me to get out of his sight."

She couldn't believe this was happening again. *Why, Lord? Why? After everything I've been through. After accepting my singleness and living in it joyfully. Why would you dangle Tony in front of me only to snatch him away? Haven't I been tested enough?*

After a few minutes, Melvin released her, built a fire in the stove, then put a pot on to boil. She laid her arms on the table and rested her head within them.

Moments later, Melvin put a handkerchief in her hand and joined her at the table.

"Start at the beginning," he said. "Tell me everything."

———

After seeing Essie safely to her house and checking the grounds surrounding it, Melvin headed to his office. All was dark and quiet when he arrived. He lit the lantern, hoping to wake his prisoner from a sound sleep. But Morgan sat on the edge of his cot, elbows propped on his knees, his head in his hands.

Just the sight of him caused Melvin's anger to rise all over again. Unlocking the cell door, he flung it open. Tony raised his head, the splotches on his face giving evidence to the young man's devastation. But Melvin hardened his heart. Tony wasn't the only one devastated this night.

"You've got some kinda nerve," Melvin said. "Sitting in here accused of murder like a common criminal, yet passing judgment on one of the sweetest angels God ever placed on this earth. And did that angel pass judgment on you when I hauled your lousy backside to this jail? No. No, she did not. That gal never doubted you for a minute. And how do you repay her?" Melvin took a step inside the cell. "By throwing her love right back in her face because she made a mistake."

"A mistake?" Tony asked, incredulous. "Do you know what she did?"

"I know all about it."

"And you call that a *mistake*?"

"Yes, I do."

"Well, I'd call it a lot worse than that."

"Is that so?" Melvin narrowed his eyes. "Well, sir, let me ask you a thing or two: Are you without sin? Can you throw the first stone?"

Tony didn't answer.

"I didn't think so."

A tick in Tony's jaw pulsed. "And that's supposed to make everything all right? Because I'm human and haven't led a sin-free life?" He jumped to his feet. "She was mine, Melvin. *Mine*. And she gave that no-account something that belonged to me and nobody else. She had no right!"

"She had every right. I'm not defending what she did. I'm not saying it was honorable, but it was her gift to give and she gave it. Are you so puffed up with yourself that you can't come down off that high horse and forgive her?"

Tony scrambled around the table.

Melvin drew his gun. "I wouldn't."

Tony froze. The two stood facing each other, both breathing hard.

"I'm gonna put away my gun," Melvin said, releasing the hammer, the sound loud in the quiet room, "but while I got your attention, let me remind you of something.

Everything you have belongs to God Almighty. Your inheritance. Your freedom. Your family. Your woman. Your very life. So quit whining about losing what 'rightfully belongs to you,' because the truth of it is, ain't none of it belongs to you. It belongs to Him. And the sooner you realize it, the sooner you'll quit wallering around in this sorry state you're in and start being thankful for whatever blessings He's decided to bestow on you." He shook his head. "And one of those blessings, son, is a sweet little gal by the name of Esther Spreckelmeyer. Heaven knows you don't deserve her, but for whatever reason, you got her. And you might wanna think long and hard before you go throwin' my baby out with the bathwater."

The door to the office opened.

Howard entered, paused, then closed the door behind him. "Sheriff. This is a surprise. What are you doin' here? Is everything all right?"

Melvin unbuckled his gun belt and set it on Tony's table, gun and all.

Howard frowned. "What're ya doing? Morgan can reach those from there."

Melvin walked toward Howard, rolling up his sleeves. "Give me your gun, Billy John. And your badge."

"What?"

"You heard me. Let's have 'em."

"What are you talking about?"

"I'm talking about the fact that you're fired and I want your gun and badge before I beat the tar outta you for threatening one of the finest citizens of this town."

Howard chuckled. "Come on, Melvin. Quit foolin'."

"Do I look like I'm foolin' to you, Billy John?" Melvin stopped in front of him.

Howard glanced at Tony. "Listen, I don't know what lies Morgan's been feedin' you, but I haven't threatened anybody."

Melvin swiped Howard's gun from its holster, cocked it and pressed it against the deputy's chest. "Give me your badge."

"You do this, Dunn, and I'll tell my grandfather. You sure you want to cross the secretary of this fine state? You sure you want me to tell him how you risk the safety of this town—our entire county—by favorin' murderers?"

Nudging Howard's jacket aside with the gun's nozzle, Melvin raised his other hand and ripped the star off the deputy's shirt. "You tell your grandpa anything you like. Now, take off your gun belt."

Howard hesitated, then unbuckled his belt and let it drop to the floor.

Melvin stepped back, opened the pistol's cylinder and emptied it.

"You even gonna tell me who I supposedly threatened?" Howard asked.

Melvin set the empty weapon on his desk. "Yes, sir. I'm firing you because you had the audacity to threaten a woman in my town. But this," he said, swinging his fist around and planting it deep into Howard's gut, "is for making the mistake of threatening my niece."

Howard was younger and prided himself on being fast with his fists, but Melvin hadn't been sheriff for thirty years without learning a thing or two about how to handle himself in a fight.

The boy didn't have a prayer. Melvin's size, strength, and experience overpowered him in no time. Howard shielded his face and head with his arms, then curled up against the wall.

"That's enough, Melvin," Dunn heard someone say. He felt himself being pulled away.

"No more, Sheriff," the voice said. "No more."

Winded, Melvin looked over to find Tony holding him back.

"No more," Tony repeated.

Melvin nodded, his own body immediately cataloging all the places Billy John's fist had connected with during the scuffle. His eye, his jaw, his shoulder, his ribs.

Tony knelt beside Billy John. "Howard? You okay?"

"Leave me alone," he slurred, pushing Tony away and bringing himself to his feet. He sneered at Melvin through eyes beginning to swell shut. "You've made a big mistake, Dunn. A big mistake."

"Get outta my town, Billy John," Melvin said.

"I'll leave when I'm good and ready to leave. Maybe that's now. Maybe it ain't. But you can't kick me out. I haven't broken any law." He glanced briefly at Tony. "But then, you don't care about that, do you, Sheriff? You only care about protectin' the criminals and running off the upstanding citizens, don't ya?" Without waiting for an answer, he stumbled out the door.

———

Sunlight poured through the jailhouse window. A breeze that carried a hint of lilac on it rustled the papers on Tony's table. Rubbing his forehead, he tried to concentrate on his work, but his grandmother's ring—Essie's ring—kept distracting him.

He'd found it in the corner of his cell and had set it on his desk. Picking it up for the hundredth time, he discovered he enjoyed touching it simply because she'd touched it, too.

Melvin's words kept ringing in his head, but he had a hard time accepting them. Because if what Melvin said was true, then Tony had nothing and God had everything.

And there were some things Tony wanted. He wanted to be proven innocent and freed from jail. He wanted his inheritance. He wanted his father to be proud of him. He wanted his wife to be pure. No, he wanted *Essie* to be pure.

But he would never have his father's approval and he would never be Essie's first. He might never win his freedom and, thus, never be able to enjoy his inheritance.

So he was back where he started. With him having nothing and God having everything.

Don't you have enough already, Lord? Do you have to have what belongs to me, too?

But deep down he knew no matter what he did or didn't do, he had no control over any of it. But God did. And the only viable solution was to give it up to Him.

And why not? How much worse could it get? He swallowed, immediately realizing it could get a whole lot worse. He could lose Essie for good. Lose his life for good.

But even if he didn't get her back, or if he hanged for the murder of his brother, he would at least have the comfort of knowing he'd left the decision-making up to God and not to himself.

Blowing out a breath, he silently relinquished his control and laid it at Christ's feet. And in doing so, realized he might not ever have made his earthly father proud, but perhaps he had his heavenly Father.

The knot he'd been carrying around in his chest eased some. A shadow crossed the door to the sheriff's office. He glanced up.

"Russ!" he exclaimed, jumping to his feet. "Walker!"

With his cell wide open, it was hard to stay put, but he did, allowing Dunn to greet the men first.

"Sheriff," Tony said, "this is one of Morgan Oil's finest drillers, Russ O'Berry, and my family's attorney, Nathaniel Walker."

Dunn shook the men's hands. "I'll need you to leave your weapons out here, fellas."

Tony lifted his brows but said nothing. Men had been coming and going for days now without being relieved of weapons. Shoot, Dunn had even let Tony start shaving with a razor blade every morning.

Still, he could understand the sheriff's caution. Not only were these fellas strangers, but Russ was a virtual giant. With his driller's hat and boots, shoulders like an ox, and a chest like a locomotive, he'd give anyone pause.

Tony smiled. He hadn't realized how much he'd missed Russ until just this moment.

Russ handed over a pistol and a bullwhip. Walker wasn't carrying.

"Won't you come into my parlor?" Tony asked, indicating the two ladder-back chairs in front of his table.

Russ chuckled, extending a hand. "Here I been picturing you in some dark, dank cell and look at ya. Even jail cain't keep you down. How are ya?"

Tony clasped his best friend's hand and slapped him on the shoulder. "Well, I've been better, but I'm mighty glad to see you." He turned to Walker. "Good of you to come, Nathaniel."

"You shaved your moustache."

"I did."

"Yes, well." He pushed his spectacles farther up on his nose. "I'm sorry it took me so long to get here, but there were a lot of papers to draft and prepare."

"I understand."

The three of them settled.

Tony looked at Russ. "How are Iva and the kids?"

"Iva's sassy as ever and the kids are missin' their 'Unk Tony.' "

"Well, don't you leave town without letting me give you some sarsaparilla sticks for 'em. I'll send out for some today."

"They'll love that."

Tony smiled. "How are the fields?"

"They're pretty much running themselves these days." He proceeded to give Tony a rundown on the wells in Beaumont—which were producing, which were drying up, and which were still being drilled. Throughout the conversation, Walker removed some papers from his satchel, fidgeted and cleared his throat.

Finally Tony turned to him. "You have something there for me?"

"Yes, I do." He handed Tony the papers. "You need to sign in all the places I've indicated."

Tony nodded. "I'll read them today and have 'em ready for you in the morning."

Walker hesitated. "Well, I was hoping to get them back right away."

"Oh?"

"Yes, I, um, need to return to Beaumont."

Tony thumbed through the documents. "I'd like to oblige you, Nathaniel, but it'll take a while for me to sort through these. Even if I could finish them by tonight, it'd be after the evening train's already left."

"They're just standard papers, Tony, transferring everything from Darius's name to yours."

"I understand. I'd still like to read them, though, before signing."

"I see. Well," he said, clearly affronted. "I guess I'll have no choice but to come by first thing in the morning, then."

Tony nodded. "I appreciate your understanding, sir. Meanwhile, Finch is staying at the Commercial. I know he'd love to see you."

"Tony Bryant Morgan!" Mrs. Lockhart marched into the office, slamming her cane down with each step. "Just what in the Sam Hill is going on?"

She was wearing her bloomers. The really poofy ones. And charging into the jailhouse like a schooner in full sail.

The men quickly rose to their feet.

She pulled up short and gave Russ the once-over. "Well, now. Aren't you the kind of fellow who could carry his bride out of a fire? You married?"

"Yes, ma'am," he said, casting Tony a sideways glance.

She sighed. "Well, of course you are."

"Mrs. Lockhart, may I present my friend Mr. O'Berry, and my attorney, Mr. Walker."

She waved her cane at Tony. "Don't you try to distract me, young man. I want to know where Essie's diamond ring is."

"I'm a bit occupied right now," he answered. "Perhaps you could come back a little later?"

"It's all right, Tony," Russ said. "We don't mind. Besides, we'd like to know about this diamond ring, too. Wouldn't we, Walker?"

Walker blinked. Tony groaned.

Russ placed a hand on the back of his chair and held his other out to Mrs. Lockhart. "Please, ma'am?"

Accepting his hand, she settled herself in the chair as if it were a throne. "Now," she said. "Where's her ring?"

"Right here on my desk."

"Don't you know whether you're on your head or your heels? It's supposed to be on her finger. Why isn't it?"

"Mrs. Lockhart—"

She slammed the end of her cane on the floor. "Do not patronize me, sir. In *Love's Chain Broken*, you will remember Mr. Tittle and Miss Vermilyea treated the elderly Mrs. Coughenburger with disdain, yet if they had just taken but a moment to heed her words, much of their pain and misery would have been avoided. Tell me you remember that part?"

Tony felt his face heat. "Yes, ma'am. I remember."

Russ's eyebrows shot up to his hairline.

"Then you will also recall that in *Her Only Sin*, Miss Klingenfluss was gravely misunderstood?"

"Yes, ma'am."

"And Mr. Longanecker had to do a great deal of groveling to get back in her good graces?"

"Yes, ma'am."

She folded her hands on top of her cane. "So what are you going to do about that, then?"

Russ, Walker, and the sheriff all stared at him.

He cleared his throat. "Grovel?"

She smiled. "I think that would be the best course of action."

Tony nodded. He'd already come to terms with the Lord and had planned on coming to terms with Essie—even before Mrs. Lockhart arrived. He still loved his fiancée and wanted his ring back on her finger. Wanted her as his wife. The question was, did she still want him?

CHAPTER | THIRTY-ONE

FIVE DAYS HAD PASSED since the Velocipede Club last convened. In the meanwhile, Essie's members had taken quite a shine to sleuthing. No need for Mr. Holmes or Dr. Watson in this town—not when they had the ladies of the Corsicana Velocipede Club. But now the novelty had worn off a bit, and the women found themselves hitting one dead end after another.

Graying clouds blocked out the morning sunlight but produced a cooling breeze through the clubhouse's high windows. Members filed in, their voices quiet, their expressions gloomy. Shirley called the meeting to order and one by one the women stood and reported what they'd discovered about Darius—or rather, what they *hadn't* discovered.

Essie smoothed her glove over each of her fingers. Since she'd given Tony his ring back, she'd begun to wear her gloves again, thinking it would keep her from noticing her bare left hand. But it hadn't. She missed his ring. And she missed him.

All the women knew she and Tony had had a "tiff," as they called it, but none knew the reason. Most assumed it was due to his being in jail, and they were none too happy with her for not standing by his side. Little did they know it was Tony who'd renounced her, not the other way around.

She was sorry she'd given the ring back, though. If she'd realized it would create such turmoil and division in the club, she wouldn't have. Her decision to break their engagement was in no way a reflection of her belief in his innocence.

So she'd minimized their estrangement. Told the ladies it was her way of teaching him a lesson. They shook their heads and explained there were plenty of ways to do that without removing the ring, but now that the deed was done, they advised she not take it back too quickly, else all would be for naught.

So when Tony sent her a message via Harley Vandervoort requesting she come by at her earliest convenience, she'd prevaricated. Not just because the ladies expected her to, but because she wasn't quite ready to face him again.

"Mr. Tony wants to see ya," Harley'd said as he waltzed into her office at the Velocipede Club.

"He does?" she'd asked, putting down her pen.

"Yep. Said fer you to come by soon as ya could."

She'd glanced at the door, resisting the urge to leap to her feet and run all the way to the jailhouse. But what would she do when she arrived? Nothing had changed and they couldn't say what needed to be said with anyone else listening in.

Howard wouldn't be there, of course, not since Uncle Melvin had dismissed him, though she'd heard he was still in town. And he'd wasted no time in announcing to any who would listen that she'd had an affair with Adam.

She hoped no one would believe him—that they'd attribute his tales to sour grapes over losing his job. But with all the new people in town, not everyone knew her. So he might be able to persuade some.

Still, she couldn't discuss the matter with Tony. Not under the current circumstances, for even her uncle's presence would embarrass her. And with Howard spreading rumors, she dare not sneak out at night to rendezvous at the jailhouse.

Besides, it was a little irksome to be summoned in such a high-handed manner. As if Tony did, in fact, expect her to drop everything the moment he crooked his finger.

She'd picked her pen back up. "I'm not sure I can go, Harley. I have an awful lot of work to do."

His eyes widened. "But he has somethin' powerful important to tell ya. He ain't gonna like it if'n you don't come."

"Tell him to write it down, then."

That had been two days ago. He'd sent Harley around three more times, but with nothing more than further curt invitations. She'd politely, but firmly, declined.

"He's gettin' kinda testy about all this, Miss Essie," Harley'd argued. "He says I weren't to leave unless I had ya in tow."

"In tow?" she asked, stiffening. "He expects you to *tow* me down there? Were those his exact words?"

Harley started backing up out of her office. "Don't worry none. I ain't gonna make ya do nothing you don't wanna."

"You most certainly aren't. And let me give you a little advice, young man. If you ever decide to woo a lady, you do it with gentle persuasion. You do *not* demand she do this or that, and you definitely don't have her towed somewhere."

"What's pur-sway-shin?"

"When you try to make someone change their mind about something."

"Now, how's Mr. Tony supposed to do that when ya won't even talk to him?"

She blinked. "Well, I don't know. With a kind note? Maybe something poetic? Seems to me he could figure it out, considering all those silly romance novels he reads."

She sighed. She should have known better than to lose her patience. Harley was far from discreet, so every person in town knew she'd not only refused his requests, but that, according to him, she'd demanded romance.

It wasn't romance she wanted, however, but divine intervention. So she hadn't quit praying. Or quit loving him. Or quit trying to help find the real murderer.

"We've come full circle, then," Shirley said to the group. "We're no closer now than we were on Sunday."

Essie reined in her thoughts and looked around the room, but no one had observed her inattention. Mrs. Bogart worked her fan. Young Miss Davis picked at a snag in her skirt. Mrs. Owen shooed a fly.

"Perhaps we're taking too much for granted," Anna Morgan said. Her mother had not returned with her to Corsicana but had stayed behind in Beaumont, too distraught to venture out again. So Anna had taken up residence with Mrs. Lockhart.

"What do you mean?" Shirley asked.

"I don't know, really," she said, sighing. "What do you think, Mrs. Lockhart? Has there ever been a horrific state of affairs in one of your books where things were not as they seemed?"

Essie closed her eyes, trying to suppress her exasperation. They were not going to find the man who murdered Darius Morgan by examining romance novels.

"Well," Mrs. Lockhart said, tapping her cane, "in *From Out of the Gloom*, everyone thought Mr. Bumpus had been strangled, when, in fact, he'd been poisoned. But the killer made it look like strangulation to confuse the authorities."

Essie gripped her hands together and kept her mouth firmly closed, reminding herself it was Mrs. Lockhart who had comforted her in her hour of need. Mrs. Lockhart who'd taken in Anna. Mrs. Lockhart who'd made sure meals were delivered to Tony on a regular basis. Essie would, therefore, be still and let the dear woman refer to as many books as she wanted to.

"Actually," Mrs. McCabe said, "it's interesting you should bring that up. When my husband laid Mr. Morgan out to rest, he mentioned to the doctor that the deceased's stomach was inflamed and his skin rather yellow."

Shirley frowned and turned to the doctor's wife. "Is that normal for someone who's been stabbed, Mrs. Gulick?"

"Indeed, it isn't."

"What was Dr. Gulick's response to your husband's remark, Mrs. McCabe?"

"Well," she said, "he sort of laughed and jokingly said perhaps Mr. Morgan had been poisoned with arsenic. I thought nothing of it at the time, because it was so clearly obvious that Mr. Morgan had been stabbed. I mean, blood was everywhere."

Moaning, Mrs. Bogart turned white and swooned. The ladies sitting next to her exclaimed and jumped up, one supporting the elderly woman's head, another putting her fan to vigorous use and yet another patting the woman's cheek.

"Oh dear," Shirley said. "Seems our conversation has upset Mrs. Bogart's sensibilities. Does anyone have smelling salts?"

The next few minutes were spent reviving Mrs. Bogart, while Essie's heart began to hammer. Even though the basis for Mrs. Lockhart's suggestion was a romance novel, Essie could not dismiss it out of hand. Not after hearing the comments of the doctor and coroner.

"For argument's sake," Shirley said, continuing even though Mrs. Bogart had not yet fully recovered, "let's pretend Mr. Morgan's death was due to poisoning. Well, if that were the case, why in the world would the killer go to the trouble of stabbing him?"

"Because he needed to implicate Tony," Essie said, eagerness stirring inside her. "And that meant using his knife and leaving it where the sheriff would be sure to find it."

Mrs. Zimpelman shook her head. "Then why not just stab Mr. Morgan to death and leave the poison out of it?"

Mrs. Bogart fainted again. Miss Davis alternately fanned the elderly woman and wiped her brow with a handkerchief.

"Perhaps the killer is of small stature," suggested Mrs. Pickens, her bug eyes overwhelming her reedlike face. "Mr. Morgan was a very large man and, I would imagine, rather hard to subdue in a fight."

"But doesn't it take a while to poison someone?" Shirley asked.

"Not necessarily," said Mrs. Gulick. "There was that woman over in Walker County who put arsenic in her husband's eggs. He died within the hour."

Excitement began to buzz throughout the room.

Shirley rapped the gavel on the lectern. "Mrs. Pickens? Who's purchased arsenic at the Flour, Feed and Liquor Store lately?"

"Well, heavens to Betsy, any number of people. Mr. Flouty bought some rat poison. Mr. Pennington, some paint. Deputy Howard, some paste." She lifted her bug-eyed gaze to the rafters as if visualizing the patrons who visited her mercantile. "The Buntings are putting up new wallpaper."

Shirley gasped.

"Oh dear," she said, wringing her hands. "I didn't mean to—"

Shirley held up her hand. "It's all right, ma'am. I'm quite sure my parents didn't poison Mr. Morgan with their wallpaper." A smattering of giggles flitted throughout the room. "Still, it is best to be thorough with your recollections. Please continue."

Mrs. Pickens listed at least a half dozen more names, none of whom were at all likely to have murdered Darius.

"We need to ask the Crooks," said Mrs. Vandervoort. "Perhaps someone bought something from the Slap Out."

Mrs. Pickens stiffened. "I'm sure if there was arsenic to be had, the person in need would have come to the Flour, Feed and Liquor Store. As a matter of fact, even that Mr. Morgan bought soap and arsenic to kill the bedbugs in his mattress."

Essie's lips parted. Silence blanketed the room.

"What?" Mrs. Pickens asked, looking from one woman to the other, then her eyes all but popped right out of her head. "Good heavens, I don't mean *our* Mr. Morgan. I meant the other one."

"The dead one?" Shirley asked, confused.

"No, no. The other one. The Frenchified one."

"Finch?" Anna asked. "Finch Morgan?"

"Yes, I believe that's his name."

Anna shook her head. "It wouldn't have been him. He was Darius's constant companion. They were more like brothers than cousins. He would never have wanted Tony to inherit."

"What about Deputy Howard?" Aunt Verdie asked.

"An unpleasant man, for certain," Shirley said, "but what possible motive could he have?"

"It is no secret he's been sweet on Essie," Mrs. Lockhart said. "Maybe he implicated Tony to get rid of his competition?"

The ladies murmured to one another.

Essie cleared her throat. "Mr. Howard knew full well he had no chance with me even had Tony never stepped foot in our town."

"Well," Shirley said, "let's meet again tomorrow morning to discuss this further. In the meanwhile, we will ask Mrs. Pickens to check with Mr. Pickens so we can be sure we haven't overlooked anyone. And Mrs. Vandervoort? If you would visit the Slap Out and see what you can find out from the Crooks, we'd be most appreciative." She struck the lectern with her gavel. "Meeting adjourned."

———

Essie opened the door to find Harley on her front porch. His boots were scuffed, one of his stockings had slid all the way down, and dirt-encrusted knees peeked out from beneath his short pants.

"This is fer you, from Mr. Tony," he said, handing her a note card, now smudged with dirty fingerprints.

"Tony wrote this?"

"Yep. And he made me cross my heart, hope to die, that I'd not let anybody read it but you."

"I see." She slid her finger under the wax seal, breaking it open, then unfolded the piece of paper.

Dearest Essie,
> In the tale of *Lord Birmingham's Daughter,*
> Miss Dye thought her beau didn't want her.
> He exclaimed, "That's not so!"
> She said, "Tallyho,"
> Then came back and he did like he oughter.
>> Yours, ABM

She bit her lip but was unable to suppress her smile.

"Uh-oh," Harley said. "Yer not gonna give in to him, are ya?"

She tilted her head. "I thought you wanted me to. Don't you like Mr. Tony?"

"Oh yes, ma'am. I like him plenty. But I just figured out that if you go see him, he'll quit payin' me two pennies to bring you messages, and I've made ten cents in three days. Besides, my ma said you wouldn't give in easy. She says the fellers in Miz Lockhart's books like stuff better when they hafta work fer it."

"Good heavens." She widened the door. "Come on in and wash your hands. I've some warm cookies on the cooling tray."

"Yes, ma'am!"

He ran to the kitchen, but she slipped into Papa's study, sat down at his desk and took up his pen.

Dearest Tony,

I enjoyed your limerick very much. However, I have it on good authority that Lord Birmingham's daughter never appeared too eager. Since you hold this tome in such high esteem, I will maintain my distance but look forward to future correspondence.

ES

———

"You needn't stay in Corsicana any longer, Russ," Tony said a few days later, leaning his arms on the table. "Spreckelmeyer says it looks like he's going to have to take me up to Fort Smith for a trial sometime next week and we should be able to clear everything up then."

"Fort Smith?" Russ replied, spinning his chair around and straddling it. "Isn't that where Hanging Judge Parker presides?"

Tony hesitated. "You know, I think it is. But Melvin didn't mention it."

"Well, that's not good. Darius is still dead. He was killed with your knife. You're the only one with a motive. So how exactly do ya figure this judge—or any judge, for that matter—will let ya go free?"

"Because I didn't do it."

"Sure looks like ya did, though."

Tony rubbed his eyes. "There's talk now that Darius was poisoned and the knife was just a decoy."

"Yeah, I heard that. I also heard it weren't true. Heard instead, the sheriff made the whole poison thing up on account of his niece." He shook his head. "That Howard fella's done nothing but harp about how Dunn treats ya more like a guest in here than a prisoner, and there's plenty of roughs who are willing to listen to him."

Tony looked around his cell—the pillows and quilts on his cot, his shaving implements on a stool, the table covered with books and papers, a basket of cookies from the women, the cell door wide open. The only things lacking were curtains for the barred window and a rug for his feet.

"What are you suggesting?"

"I dunno, Tony. I just got an uneasy feelin', is all. There's a trace o' unrest in town. And Finch ain't helpin' any, either, what with the way he's making Darius out to be a candidate for sainthood."

Tony sighed. "That can't surprise you."

Heavy footfalls clumping up the stairs outside drew Tony's attention. An oilman with skin leathered from the sun stepped into the jailhouse, the slush from his boots leaving imprints. He was one of the men brought up from Beaumont to begin work on the new piece of land Darius had bought. Crossing the room, the man glanced at the sheriff, looked Tony up and down, then turned to Russ.

"The boss is lookin' fer ya."

"Finch?" Russ asked.

"Yep. And he ain't gonna be none too pleased to find out yer in here with Mr. Darius's killer."

Russ rose slowly to his feet. "Finch isn't my boss or yours. Mr. Morgan here is. And he's no murderer. Once he's had a trial, that'll be clear enough."

"That ain't the way we see it." He lifted his hand to keep Russ from speaking. "Now, we ain't holdin' it against ya, Russ. Not with you and Tony goin' back as fer as you do. But ever'body knows he done it."

The sheriff rounded his desk, stepping between the oilman and the cell. "You've said your piece. Best move on outta here now."

The man pushed a plug of tobacco from one cheek to the other with his tongue. "The boys don't like it, Sheriff. Man like him killing his own blood. He don't deserve to live, much less be treated like some highfalutin guest." He spit, missing the spittoon by a good foot. "Don't imagine they're gonna put up with it fer much longer."

"They're gonna put up with it until the law takes its due course, and you can tell 'em I said so."

He took Melvin's measure, then spit again. "Whatever you say." Moving his gaze past the sheriff's shoulder, he locked eyes with Russ. "You comin'?"

"I'll be there in a minute."

Russ and Melvin didn't move until the oilman retraced his steps and was well out of sight.

Melvin let out his breath.

"How long's that been going on?" Tony asked.

"Been like that since I arrived in town and is only gettin' worse." Russ turned to face him. "So if it's all the same to you, I'd like to stick around awhile. Keep my eye on things."

"What about the wells back in Beaumont? What about Iva?"

"Iva and the kids'll be fine. And don't you worry none about Morgan Oil. Archie's top-notch. He'll keep everything going back home."

————

Dearest Essie,

    I dream of the girl in big hats.

    Who hunts frogs and snakes but not rats.

    Will she slide down the rail

    And visit the jail,

    And stay for a nice little chat?

                    Forever yours, ABM

CHAPTER | THIRTY-TWO

ESSIE SAT WITH THE other members of the Velocipede Club, content to let Shirley run the meeting. Being the banker's daughter had always given the young woman a place of distinction within town, but it wasn't until she married Jeremy that she had gained the confidence she displayed now.

Gone were the frilly ruffles and flounces and oversized bows. In their place were sensible and modest shirtwaists and skirts. Some of that, Essie knew, was due to the fact that Jeremy refused to take money from his father-in-law, so Shirley couldn't afford to dress as she had before. Yet Shirley had never been happier. And there was no denying she was still the prettiest girl in the county.

Essie glanced at Anna sitting beside her in her mourning attire. If there was ever anyone to rival Shirley's beauty, it would be Tony's sister. But she was so different from Shirley. Her brown hair and olive complexion were in stark contrast to Shirley's blond hair and pale, pale skin.

Anna looked at Essie and smiled. They'd spent quite a bit of time together this past week. Enough for Essie to recognize that the girl came alive as soon as Ewing appeared on Mrs. Lockhart's doorstep. It hadn't gone unnoticed in town, either, that he'd become a frequent visitor of the elderly woman now that the girl was staying there. Essie slipped her hand into Anna's and squeezed.

Perhaps the girl would one day become Essie's sister by marriage. That is, if Essie and Tony reconciled. And with the poems he'd sent, a kernel of hope had begun to stir within her.

Even if he was willing to forgive her indiscretions, however, they had the murder charge to face. What if the new judge pronounced Tony guilty?

Please, Lord. Even if he doesn't marry me, I don't want to see him condemned for something he didn't do. Please help us find the culprit, Lord. Please.

She drew her attention back to the meeting at hand.

"Do you have a report for us, Mrs. McCabe?" Shirley asked, nodding to the coroner's wife in the second row.

Mrs. McCabe stood. "Mrs. Gulick and I both checked again with our husbands and we are quite certain now that Mr. Morgan was poisoned. When he and our Tony Morgan got into fisticuffs, Dr. Gulick was called in to treat Darius Morgan's injuries."

"That's right," said Mrs. Gulick. "But my husband said he spent more time treating things that weren't the least bit related to the fight."

"Like what?" Shirley asked.

"All kinds of things," Mrs. Gulick answered. "The man complained of severe stomach cramps, burning pains in his hands and feet, dizzy spells, and irritating rashes. My husband didn't know what to think of it at first."

"But after he was killed," Mrs. McCabe said, "and my Percy brought up the yellow color of his skin and the swollen stomach, that's when they started to suspect poisoning."

Shirley frowned. "Then he died of arsenic poisoning?"

"No, no," Mrs. McCabe answered. "The stabbing is what killed him. But Dr. Gulick said that even if he hadn't been stabbed, he wouldn't have been much longer for this life."

A sudden outburst of conversation buzzed throughout the room.

"Do you suppose it was the same person who did both?" Mrs. Vandervoort asked over the noise, silencing the exchanges.

"I don't know," Mrs. McCabe answered.

The women once again began to discuss the possibilities amongst themselves.

Shirley hammered with her gavel. "Does the sheriff know about this?"

"He does."

Mrs. Blanchard stood. "I suggest we try to find out how the arsenic was administered. That may give us a clue as to who was doing the poisoning."

Aunt Verdie rose, her simply cut gown highlighting her exaggerated hourglass figure. "I had the same thought earlier this week. Melvin rarely discusses his work with me, especially when it concerns such unpleasantness. But now that Deputy Howard is no longer about, I was able to look through Melvin's desk at the jailhouse." She slipped her hand into the hidden pocket of her skirt and pulled out a small bound book. "I managed to find his notes."

A smattering of applause circulated.

"He made a list of the items he'd found in Mr. Morgan's hotel room. I tried to narrow it down to items that might have had arsenic in them. Unfortunately, I couldn't find a thing. No cup, no whiskey bottle, no food, no nothing." Aunt Verdie licked her finger and flipped through several pages. "Would you like me to read what all he found? The list is quite lengthy."

Shirley bit her lower lip. "Before you do that, let's consider the different ways arsenic can get into a person's body, other than swallowing it. Anyone have any ideas?"

"What if it gets on your skin?" asked Miss Davis. "I mean, could the murderer have put it in Mr. Morgan's shaving cream?"

"I'm not sure," said Shirley. "Do you know, Mrs. Gulick?"

She shook her head. "I'm afraid I don't. I know it can be inhaled, though."

Shirley turned back to Aunt Verdie. "Is there anything on the sheriff's list that could be inhaled?"

Aunt Verdie bent the sides of the book back, cracking the spine. "Well, let's see. There were cigarettes in the ashtray."

Shirley's expression lit up. "Couldn't someone have mixed arsenic with the tobacco?"

Essie and Anna exchanged a glance as several of the members murmured with excitement.

"No," Aunt Verdie said. "No, that isn't possible. Says here they were those new mechanically rolled cigarettes. There wouldn't be any way to get the poison inside those."

"Mechanically rolled?" Anna asked. "But Darius didn't ordinarily smoke pre-rolled cigarettes, at least not unless Finch was around to offer him one."

Squinting, Aunt Verdie held the book out at arm's length. "Well, Mel's notes say there was not only an ashtray, but a silver case full of 'em inside the pocket of a jacket that was slung across a chair." She looked up. "According to this, it was your brother's jacket."

"But I don't understand," Anna continued. "Are you certain there's nothing about a pouch of tobacco?"

Aunt Verdie flipped back and forth between some pages. " 'Fraid not. It does say that Mrs. Morgan and Finch stayed by Mr. Darius's side throughout the doctor's exam, and both she and Finch stayed with Darius until he was resting peacefully—making them the last ones to see him alive."

"Excuse me," said Mrs. Zimpelman, the silversmith's wife. "Does it say what the cigarette case looked like?"

"Why, yes." Aunt Verdie ran her finger down the page, then stopped. "It says the case was: 'silver, engraved scrolls, crest with lion with ax in raised paw.' "

Mrs. Zimpelman gasped. "Why, that's the case I sold to Mr. Morgan—Mr. Finch Morgan—on the day of the bicycle race. I remember because we don't have very many cases, since very few people smoke mechanically rolled cigarettes. So when he came by our tent looking for one, I had to sort through several of our crates to find it."

"Why would Finch need another cigarette case when he already has one?" Anna asked. "And what was it doing in Darius's coat pocket?"

The women sat in silence, trying to decide if what they'd discovered had any significance at all.

"What if you rubbed the arsenic on the outside of the cigarette?" Mrs. Vandervoort asked. "You know, the part he puts in his mouth and inhales?"

"Mrs. Gulick?" Shirley asked.

"Well, I don't see why that wouldn't work," she said.

"Wouldn't he notice the powder?" Anna asked.

"Not necessarily."

"Is it possible," Shirley said, "that Mr. Finch Morgan poisoned Mr. Darius Morgan?"

"I can't imagine him doing such a thing," Anna said. "He and Tony have never seen eye to eye. Finch would never want Tony to inherit anything."

Disappointment assailed Essie, then she felt guilty about it. She harbored no ill will toward Finch Morgan. She simply wanted to find the real culprit.

"Wait a minute." Anna slowly straightened. "Now that I think on it, both of Finch's late wives died of gastric fever."

"Gastric fever?" Shirley asked. "Both of them?"

"Yes, and their sicknesses were very similar to what Darius had been experiencing these past couple of months—dizzy spells, headaches, yellow skin, a pain in their stomachs. That kind of thing."

"Well," Shirley said. "What do you think, Mrs. Gulick?"

"Sounds an awful lot like arsenic poisoning to me."

"But why?" Anna argued. "What possible reason could Finch have for wanting his wives or, more to the point, Darius dead? He and Darius were practically attached at the hip."

"I don't know," Shirley answered. "But I'd sure like to have a look at the cigarettes in that case. Is there any way you can get your hands on it, Mrs. Dunn?"

"Oh, heavens no. Melvin keeps everything like that locked up. He's already frantic about his notes being 'misplaced.' I haven't any idea how I'll get them back to him without him finding out I took them. Mr. Morgan—our Mr. Morgan—already knows I have them. He, of course, was there while I was searching Melvin's desk. He hasn't said a word, though."

"Nor will he," said Mrs. Lockhart. "Give the book to me. I'll tell the sheriff I picked it up by accident with a stack of novels I'd laid on his desk."

"Do you think he'll believe you?" Essie asked.

"What choice does he have?"

Shirley nodded. "All right, ladies. We're getting closer. I just know we are. Your assignment for today is to see if we can determine where Mr. Darius Morgan's pre-rolled cigarettes came from." She slammed the gavel onto the lectern. "Meeting adjourned."

———

Dearest Essie,
    I love you with all of my heart,
    There are things I would like to impart.
    You mean so to me.
    I beg leniency,
    For acting a fool and an upstart.
    Please come back to me.
                    Yours alone, ABM

———

The brisk wind whipped the treetops and made steering Peg a challenge. But Essie persevered. She'd wanted to look her best the next time she saw Tony, but after reading the sweet limerick she had waiting for her upon her return from her meeting, she'd simply turned right around and remounted her bike.

It wasn't until she reached town that the clouds began to gather and the wind played havoc with her hair. Her navy skirt slapped against her legs. Her hat strained against its pins. Increasing her speed, she tucked her head down, hoping to reach the sheriff's office before the rain began. She'd just dismounted when a raindrop plopped onto her sleeve.

She rushed up the steps and across the threshold, then pulled up short.

Tony jumped to his feet. "Essie. You came."

She had an unobstructed view of him through the open cell door. My, but she'd forgotten how handsome he was. So tall. So broad. So much a man. His brown hair was tousled, his shirt wrinkled. Bluish shadows beneath his eyes pointed to his weariness and the strain he'd been under.

A pang of guilt rushed through her. She should have come sooner. She should have realized what a shock her revelation had been and extended him some latitude—particularly considering all he was going through.

He took a step from behind his table and tentatively opened his arms. Lifting her skirts, she ran to him. He caught her tight against him, holding her, kissing her, murmuring to her.

"You came," he whispered. "You came."

"I'm sorry," she said.

"Shhh," he replied, kissing her again.

He slowly let her down, so that her toes touched the floor, but he didn't release her. "Don't ever leave me again."

"I won't," she said. "I won't." And this time, she kissed him.

Uncle Melvin cleared his throat.

Good heavens. She hadn't even realized he was there. Hadn't so much as greeted him. She tried to pull back, but Tony wouldn't let her go.

"Would you excuse us, Sheriff?" he asked.

Uncle Melvin stiffened. "Now, just a—"

"Please, Uncle Melvin?" she asked, looking at him over her shoulder. "Please?"

Red filled his face. "Essie, I don't . . ." He searched her expression, then sighed and pointed a finger at Tony. "You will act with the utmost decorum?"

"Yes, sir."

"Essie?" he barked, turning his frown onto her.

"Of course."

After a slight hesitation, he shuffled over, closed the door to the cell, locked it and left.

Tony scooped her up, sat on his chair and settled her in his lap. Now that the initial rush was over, his next kiss was slow and, oh, so sweet.

He pulled the pins from her hat, removed it and set it on his desk. "I have missed you."

"I've missed you, too."

"I'm sorry I said those things."

"It all came as a shock to you. I completely understand."

"Forgive me?" he asked.

Nodding, she brushed his cheek with her palm. "Do you forgive me?"

He tunneled his fingers into her hair, holding her head firmly and bringing his eyes close to hers. "Yes. Yes, I do, Essie. It is forgotten and we will never speak of it again."

Moisture filled her eyes. "I'm so sorry."

"No, I'm sorry. I was in no position to throw stones."

She kissed him again, wrapping her arms around his neck. Desire poured through her. She squirmed.

Groaning, he pulled back. "Will you still marry me?"

"Yes."

Reaching across the table, he grabbed the diamond ring sitting on his papers. He slipped it onto her finger, then kissed it. "I don't ever want you to take that off again. Not ever."

"I won't."

When their kisses were no longer enough to satisfy her, she pulled away and stood. His eyes were dark, his breathing heavy. Every fiber in her body wanted to return to his arms.

"Where are you going?" he asked.

"If I don't put some distance between us, I'll have a hard time doing what I promised myself I'd never do again—at least, not until I'm officially wed."

"Then go get Ewing and let's get this thing done."

She widened her eyes. "And what would we tell our children when they asked where we got married?"

He smiled. "That they were conceived in the jailhouse?"

Her lips parted.

Chuckling, he grabbed another chair and pulled it next to his. "I'm jesting. Sort of. Now come sit down."

"Is it safe?"

"I'm not sure," he replied.

She took the seat on the opposite side of the table. He moved his around next to hers.

"How have you been?" he asked, grabbing her hand. "What have you been doing all this time? Tell me everything."

She watched him bring her hand to his mouth and kiss each finger individually.

"I've been trying to keep from thinking about you," she said, "but didn't have much success. What have you been doing?"

"Writing poems."

She smiled. "They were lovely. I'll treasure them always."

"You will not. You will throw them away immediately. If anyone ever sees them, my reputation in the oil patch will never recover."

"Well, since your reputation in the patch directly affects Sullivan Oil's productivity, your secret is safe with me."

He hesitated. "Essie, honey, you do realize that if I'm freed I can't work for Sullivan Oil anymore, don't you?"

Shock struck her motionless. "What?"

"I'm head of the Morgan estates now. I'm no longer the second son. I'm the only son. I have to go back to Beaumont. We both do. Permanently."

She tried to pull her hand away, but he held tight.

"I can't run Morgan Oil or any of the rest of it from here," he continued. "Surely you realize that."

"But . . . but I've lived here all my life."

"I know. And we'll come back. Often. It's only a train ride away."

"My father."

"He and I have talked at length. He fully expects this, and if you'll think back, ever since we started courting—which was right about the time we began converting to rotaries—he started taking over the running of Sullivan Oil again."

"My uncle." She swallowed. "I don't know anyone in Beaumont. I'll be an outsider. An interloper."

"Folks are a little different in Beaumont. They don't expect you to have been born and bred in their town. New people come in all the time and are accepted as if they'd lived there all their lives."

"But . . ." Tears began to sting her eyes. "What about . . ." She took a trembling breath. "What about my bicycle club?"

His face filled with compassion. "I'm sorry, Essie. You can maintain ownership of it, but you can't bring it with you. You'll have to leave it behind."

She placed a fist against her mouth, blinking rapidly. But she could not hold the tears at bay.

He reached for her waist and pulled her back onto his lap. "I'm sorry, love. I'm truly so very sorry."

She turned into him and sobbed.

"It may never happen," he said, stroking her hair.

She hiccupped. "W-what?"

"There's a good chance I'm going to hang on behalf of whoever killed Darius."

She sat up. "You can't believe that."

"It's a very real possibility, Essie. And you should prepare yourself for it."

She shook her head, swiping moisture from her eyes. "No, I won't. I refuse to. You are innocent."

"Innocent people are hanged all the time."

"Not in my world, they aren't."

"Nevertheless, there's no sense in worrying about moving to Beaumont or even saying our vows until after the trial is over."

Her body began to tremble. "Are you saying that if you're convicted, you won't marry me?"

"I can't, Essie. Don't you see?" He rubbed his hands up and down her arms to calm her. "Even if I didn't hang, you would be marked as the wife of a criminal. You'd have to deal with that stigma the rest of your life."

"I don't care."

"I do."

"But you haven't done anything!"

"That won't matter if I'm convicted."

Giving up her club and moving to Beaumont suddenly seemed trivial compared to the possibility of losing Tony. Refusing to even consider it, she pressed the butt of her palms to her eyes to dry them. "Then we need to make sure that you're not convicted." Squaring her shoulders, she focused on that very matter. "Now, can you think of any reason Finch would want to kill Darius?"

"My *cousin* Finch?" he asked, surprise lacing his voice. "He would have nothing to gain by Darius's death. Only mine."

"Yours? Why yours?"

"Because Finch is next in line to inherit after me."

"Finch is? But what about Anna? Or your mother?"

Tony shook his head. "The will was quite clear on that. Dad wanted his fortune to remain in the hands of a man. A Morgan man, that is. Not whoever married Anna. Her husband was to receive a dowry and Mother was awarded a stipend, but neither were to inherit."

Uncle Melvin knocked—actually knocked—on his own office door before coming in.

But Essie hardly noted it and instead jumped to her feet. "My stars and garters."

Melvin moved to the cell and unlocked the door.

"What is it?" Tony asked.

"I've got to go, love." She leaned over and pecked him quickly on the lips.

"Your hat," he said.

"There's no time." Then she ran out the door and into the rain.

CHAPTER | THIRTY-THREE

SOAKED WITH RAIN, ESSIE burst into the Velocipede Club. Shirley was giving a group bicycle lesson to five older girls from the State Orphan's Home.

She took one look at Essie, then turned back to her pupils. "Please practice mounting and dismounting by riding from wall to wall five times. You may begin."

Essie tried to wipe her face with her handkerchief, but it was just as soaked as she was.

"What's happened?" Shirley asked, escorting her into the privacy of the office.

Essie grabbed a towel from the shelf and pressed it against her face and neck. "I think Finch killed Darius and made it look like Tony did."

"Why would he do that?"

"If something happens to Tony, Finch is next to inherit the Morgan fortune."

Shirley took a moment to process Essie's words. "Are you saying that Finch killed Darius in hopes that Tony would be the one hanged for the deed, leaving him as sole heir?"

"That's exactly what I'm saying."

"I don't know, Essie. It sounds awfully risky. What if he went to all that trouble and then Tony wasn't implicated?"

"Finch made sure he was."

"How?"

"By using Tony's knife." Essie shook out her skirts, splattering water onto the floor. "He was standing right there that night when Harley gave Tony his knife back and Mr. Mudge asked to see it. He could have easily slipped it into his pocket after Tony left and Mr. Mudge laid it down."

"Darius wouldn't have been an easy man to stab."

"No. But remember, he had suffered a beating in addition to those dizzy spells and things that he'd complained to Dr. Gulick about."

"What about the arsenic?"

"Like Anna said, Finch and Darius were 'inseparable,' which would have given Finch plenty of opportunity to sneak the poison into Darius's food, drink, or whatever was handy."

"We also know Finch purchased some arsenic and soap to 'rid himself of bedbugs,' " Shirley added.

"As well as buying the cigarette case found in Darius's coat pocket," Essie said. "Perhaps it had been a congratulatory gift for winning the race. Except, Finch laced the cigarettes with arsenic. Darius accepts the gift and smokes one of his new cigarettes. The poison weakens him even further. Finch kills him with Tony's knife and then leaves it where it would be found."

Shirley stared at her for a moment. "That's an awful lot of ifs. I'd hate to be hasty and accuse him unjustly."

"So would I. But you must admit, it fits."

"What should we do?"

"I think we take what we know to Uncle Melvin."

"I agree," Shirley said. "Do we wait until after our meeting tomorrow?"

"No. I think we need to do it now. Today."

"Should we call an emergency meeting first?"

Essie pulled the pins from her hair and toweled it off. "If we do that, I'd have to publicly accuse Finch. And if he didn't do it, I will have done him a grave injustice."

Shirley took a deep breath. "You're right. I guess it would be best to let the sheriff do the accusing."

———

Tony listened from his cell as Essie tried to convince her uncle that Finch was Darius's murderer. She laid out the means by which he did it, along with his motive and opportunity. Tony's initial reaction had been denial, but the more he thought about it, the more the idea had merit.

Melvin leaned back in his chair. "What do you think, Morgan?"

Essie turned toward him. Her hair was plastered to her head from being caught in the rain earlier. And though the bad weather had passed, her gown had to weigh thirty pounds as wet as it was. As far as he could tell, she didn't even realize her state of dishevelment. Her face was earnest, her cheeks rosy. Her eyes were alive with hope and trepidation.

Tony leaned against the bars. "When our family's lawyer brought me papers to sign after Darius's death, Finch had asked him to change them so that he would have the authority to run the Morgan estate while I was incarcerated."

"Doesn't make him a murderer."

"No, but he's had two wives die in two years. Both of gastric fever, which is just a fancy way of saying a swollen stomach. Doesn't arsenic inflate a person's stomach?"

"Yeah," Melvin drawled. "Matter o' fact, it does. But Darius was stabbed."

"He was also poisoned," Essie said.

"True, but it was the stabbing that killed him. You think Finch has the constitution to do something like that?" Melvin asked Tony.

He rubbed his mouth. "Not really. I'd be mighty surprised."

"Where are the cigarettes?" Essie asked.

Melvin cocked his head. "How is it that you know about the cigarettes?"

She swallowed, then stood up straighter. "I looked through your notes."

He dropped his chair legs onto the floor. "And just when did you do that?"

"This morning. Mrs. Lockhart shared them with me."

Jumping to his feet, he leaned forward. "What's she doin' with them, and who else has had a gander at my notes?"

Essie didn't respond.

"Answer me, young lady!"

The steps outside creaked and Harley burst through the door, skidding across the wood floor and stopping just short of Melvin's desk. "You gotta do somethin', Sheriff! We got trouble."

Melvin frowned. "What kinda trouble?"

"A lynch mob."

Essie gasped. Tony stiffened.

"A lynch mob?" Melvin asked, his tone questioning. "Corsicana hasn't seen one single lynching in its entire history."

"Well, look out yer window if you don't believe me."

Melvin stepped to the window. "Sweet saints above."

"What're you gonna do?" the boy asked.

Hurrying to Tony's cell, Melvin closed its door and locked it. "Harley, go to the church and tell Preacher Wortham what's goin' on. Tell him to round up as many men as he can and to get over here lickety-split."

Tony's heart jumped into his throat as Harley scurried out the door.

"And stay away from that mob!" Melvin hollered just before the door slammed shut. He grabbed his rifle and scooped up some spare bullets from his desktop. "You need to get outta here, Essie."

Yanking open the top drawer, she grabbed a key and unlocked the storage room. She disappeared momentarily, then came back out. "Where are the extra rifles?"

"Quit wasting time, Essie," Tony said, gripping the bars. "You've got to move. Now."

"I can't just up and leave y'all here. Not with a mob coming. Now, where are the rifles?"

"That blasted roof started leaking again and I had to move them out," Melvin said. "Now, I need you to go find your pa, just in case he hasn't already heard, and have him round up the Sullivan Oil men."

Standing in indecision, she glanced at Tony.

"It'll be all right," he said.

Melvin gave her a push. "Go on, girl."

She tripped across the threshold, then ran down the steps as he bolted the door behind her.

He and Tony locked eyes.

"You won't be able to hold 'em, you know," Tony said.

"I'll hold 'em. Ain't nobody lynching no prisoner of mine."

CHAPTER | THIRTY-FOUR

ESSIE PUSHED SEVERAL CARTRIDGES into her rifle. "Find as many of the women as you can, Shirley, and meet me by the hanging tree."

"You can't go out there alone," Shirley said, handing Essie another cartridge from the box.

"Nor can I spare the time it would take to get the girls." She cocked the lever, seating a round. "If we're lucky, the mob won't make it to the cottonwood tree. But if the

men can't stop them at the jailhouse, I want to be waiting for them at the other end."
She placed a hand on her friend's arm. "Don't let me down, Shirley."

"I won't, Essie. We'll be right behind you."

———

Tony heard the crowd of men well before they reached the jailhouse. The sheriff
positioned himself at the window, his rifle aimed at the crowd. "They're here, son," he
said over his shoulder, "but don't worry. Help's a-comin'."

Before Tony could respond, a voice from outside pierced the air.

"Give us your prisoner, Sheriff!"

"You know I won't do that, Howard," Melvin hollered back. "I'm under orders to
protect him and I aim to do just that. Now, you boys just go on home before somebody
gets hurt."

"We're takin' him, Sheriff. We're takin' him and seein' that justice is served."

The crowd hollered and cheered.

Melvin cocked his gun. "Not another step, Howard, or you'll be the first to go."

"That wouldn't be very smart, Sheriff, shootin' the grandson of Texas's secretary
of state."

Melvin looked down the site of his rifle. "My prisoner isn't going anywhere."

Footfalls rushed up the steps. Melvin opened fire, startling both Tony and the
crush outside. The pack fell back for a moment, leaving Howard writhing in agony
on the stoop.

Word quickly passed through the throng in front of the jail and down the street
that the former deputy had been shot. Then, as if an unseen flag had been dropped
signaling the start of a race, men stampeded the jailhouse. Some jumping through the
window, others busting through the door.

Melvin fired, wounding at least a dozen before the mob seized him by the shoulders, disarmed him and hurled him back.

The screams of the injured echoed in Tony's ears, blood pouring from their wounds.
Melvin was cut off from Tony's view as the mob surged forward, stepping on and over
the fallen men as if they were sacks of potatoes.

At first it seemed as if the crowd of roughs were strangers to Tony, but as they dragged
him from his cell, he saw their leaders were from Morgan Oil. Men who'd done Darius's
dirty work for him. Many with shady pasts. Darius had provided a haven for men of
their ilk—roughs who were loyal to his brother, even if it wasn't for edifying reasons.

Tony could smell the alcohol on their breath. He fought and kicked and bucked
but was only rewarded with beatings and rougher treatment as he was dragged down
the street toward the big cottonwood tree on the outskirts of town.

———

The two armed riders waiting for the mob gave them pause. Tony's left eye was
swollen shut, but his right still worked fine and shifted to a man and a woman on

horseback. On the left was Russ O'Berry, the best friend Tony'd ever had, sitting atop a horse at least eighteen hands tall. He sported a pistol in one hand and a bullwhip held casually within his other. To his right was Essie Spreckelmeyer, aiming a loaded rifle at the hearts of Tony's captors.

His stomach clenched. What the blazes did she think she was doing here? The crowd slowly drew to the base of the tree, becoming unusually quiet in order to ascertain the dangers posed from this unexpected quarter.

Russ scanned the crowd. "Afternoon, Horace. Norman. Paddy. I reckon you know Tony here hasn't had a trial yet?"

The mob was supposed to provide anonymity. This recital of specific names caused a disconcerting murmur to pass through the crowd.

"Our argument ain't with you, Russ," one of the roughs called out, "so just git outta the way 'fore we string you up, as well."

Faster than a striking snake, Russ stung the rowdie across his cheek with the bullwhip, leaving him with a red mark but no broken skin.

"I ain't goin' nowhere," Russ said, controlling his horse with his thighs. "And if anybody makes a move, my whip'll slice a whole lot deeper."

The man's eyes blazed while he touched his cheek, but he remained silent.

"Now, release the prisoner." Russ's voice rang with authority.

The crowd fell back in disorder, but the men holding Tony kept their grip firm.

A voice from the back cried out, "String 'im up! The woman, too!"

The mob gained a new surge of momentum. Tony's heart hammered. Where were the men Melvin had sent for? He struggled, then pitched forward, while several shots sent hats flying. A hush spread over the assembly.

Tony glanced up. Russ covered the crowd with his pistol while Essie began to reload.

Through the tight mass, Ewing pressed forward. "Stop this at once!" he cried. "Let Morgan go!"

The butt of a wooden bat descended onto the preacher's head. He crumpled to the ground. Essie gasped, momentarily losing focus.

The crowd immediately took advantage of her distraction and surged forward, pulling her from her horse. Russ couldn't shoot without the risk of hitting her. His whip lashed out, and though several men screamed, the throng managed to catch hold of the whip's tail and jerk, tearing it and the pistol from Russ's hold and spooking his horse. He inflicted some damage with his boots and fists but was no match for the number of men who dragged him from his saddle.

"We want a hangin'!" the men began to chant. "We want a hangin'!"

The atmosphere took on that of a distorted carnival. A boomer in well-worn denims slung a rope across a great limb of the giant tree while someone else slipped its noose over Tony's neck. Rough hands threw him up on Essie's horse. Others held her and Russ back.

"No!" Essie screamed. "Please! He's innocent! Let him go!"

Russ flung men from his body like a dog shaking water from its fur, only to have another swarm of rowdies wrestle him to the ground over and over until he had no fight left in him.

In that moment, a tremendous fear gripped Tony. Not for himself, but for Essie. For Russ. And for Russ's family if something happened to him.

He dared not think of what the mob had done to the sheriff. For nothing short of death would have been able to keep him away.

The sun began its descent, beating down on the ruddy faces of the rowdies who'd worked themselves into a greater frenzy than before. Nothing could save Tony, his best friend, or the woman he loved. Nothing but God Almighty himself.

Sacrifice me, Lord, but save the others. Please.

"Quiet!" someone roared. "I wanna hear his neck snap!"

The throng whooped and the ground shook with suppressed violence.

Tony braced himself. A quiet fell upon the gathering. After a couple of seconds, Tony realized the ground was still shaking, not from the agitated crowd but something else entirely.

He, along with all those present, looked to the east as over a hundred riders on horseback galloped up and quickly surrounded the rioters. A huge cloud of dust enveloped them.

When it began to settle, the silhouettes of armed men and women slowly took shape, their expressions serious, their weapons primed. Tony looked over the faces of his rescuers.

Grandpa, Jeremy, Moss, and a multitude of other men who worked for Sullivan Oil. The Baker brothers and their crew of rig builders. Men who worked for Morgan Oil but weren't in Darius's back pocket. The sheriff, the judge, and the women of the Corsicana Velocipede Club—Shirley, Mrs. Lockhart, Mrs. Dunn, Mrs. Vandervoort, and a dozen more. His gaze stopped on Anna. Did she even know how to use that weapon she was holding? But her attention was completely focused on the crowd.

"Release Miss Spreckelmeyer and Russ O'Berry!" the sheriff ordered.

The men holding Essie and Russ did not respond. Several guns swerved toward them, taking a bead on their hearts. They let go and raised their hands.

Russ quickly recovered his bullwhip. The men gave him a wide berth. Essie scrambled to Tony's horse, grabbing its reins and holding it still.

Tony looked down at her, then saw Finch for the first time. His cousin broke through the crowd and moved to the horse's flanks. He raised his hand to strike the mare when his wrist was caught midair with the whip and jerked back in an unnatural direction.

He screamed as the bones in his wrist broke, still unaware that Russ had saved his life, for several guns were seconds away from riveting Finch with bullets.

The assembly stilled, not wanting to draw the attention of the armed men—or women.

"Corsicana is a good, wholesome town," Melvin roared. "And I, for one, will not stand still while you besmirch its history with a lynching."

"But this man murdered his own brother in cold blood!" Finch shouted, cradling his broken hand.

"I have a dozen women here who say otherwise," Melvin responded.

The crowd murmured.

Tony kept his gaze pinned to Finch, uncomfortable with the man's proximity to Essie. From the corner of his eye, he saw Judge Spreckelmeyer slide off his horse and circle round Finch from behind.

"These gals have some mighty convincin' evidence that it was his cousin, Finch Morgan, who killed Darius," Melvin continued, spitting to the side. "And not just him, but he maybe killed his wives, too."

The shock of this unexpected news rippled through the crowd. Russ quietly approached Tony, while Finch and the rest of the mob were preoccupied.

"They're lying," Finch shouted, reaching across his body for a knife.

The judge pressed the barrel of his gun into Finch's back. "Raise your arms, Morgan. Nice and slow."

Finch lifted his left arm. "I can't raise the right," he said, pushing his words through clinched teeth. "My hand is hanging by a thread."

Spreckelmeyer patted him down, relieving him of his knife. Russ quickly released Tony's bound hands.

The mob's thirst for blood shifted its focus. "Hang Finch Morgan!" they began to chant. "Hang Finch Morgan!"

Tony slipped the noose from around his neck and swung off the horse. "Get Essie outta here *now*!" he said to Russ.

Russ grabbed Essie, but the crowd was already surging toward Finch. Pulling her against him, Russ readied his whip. Tony stood in front of her, effectively sandwiching her between the two of them.

The sheriff swung his horse to the front, raised his rifle toward the sky and fired.

The crowd quieted.

"I'll be taking Finch up to Fort Smith for a hearin', so you can rest assured justice will be served."

"Let's save 'em the trouble!" somebody shouted.

Melvin stilled his prancing horse. "Well, now, much as I'd like to oblige you, I'm afraid I'm bound by oath to do otherwise. If it makes you feel any better, though, Hangin' Judge Isaac Parker will be waiting for us."

The mob cheered.

"Right now, though, we'd like everybody to go on home and settle down a bit. Show's over."

There were some token protests, but being surrounded by a hundred armed men and women dampened the crowd's enthusiasm. With more encouragement from the sheriff and his posse, the gathering began to disperse, then changed courses altogether when Mr. Rosenburg hollered, "Free drinks at my place fer the first fifty patrons."

Tony turned to Essie.

"Ewing," she said.

"I'll go find him," Russ offered, then headed to the spot where Ewing had fallen.

"You all right?" Tony asked her.

"I think so," she answered, her voice shaking. "You look awful, though. Does it hurt terribly?"

He touched his cheek and eye. "I'm fine. Could've been a lot worse."

"Is anything broken?" she asked, running her hands along his chest, arms, and hands.

"I don't think so." He threaded his fingers through hers, putting a stop to her examination. "What possessed you to take on that mob with nothing more than Russ and a rifle? You about scared me to death."

"I knew the women would come as quickly as they could. I just decided not to wait on them." She smoothed a tuft of hair sticking out from his head. "On my way here, I ran into Russ and he insisted on coming with me."

He shook his head. "Well, I can tell you this, no one will ever again be able to say you're marrying a younger man."

She frowned. "What?"

"I aged ten years seeing you up there. That makes me thirty-eight and you just thirty-four."

She smiled, but before she could respond, the judge and sheriff interrupted.

"Essie?" her father said. "You all right, honey?"

"I'm fine," she said, hugging them both.

"Is Ewing okay?" Tony asked.

"He will be. Your sister, Russ, and a couple of the older women are taking him home and seeing to his injuries."

"What about Howard?"

"The mob left him for dead, but the bullet didn't hit anything vital," Melvin said. "I have him recuperatin' in a jail cell while the doc tends to the others who were wounded." Melvin looked Tony up and down. "What about you? You all right?"

Tony held out his hand. "Much better than I was a few minutes ago, thanks to you and everybody else. I wasn't sure what happened to you after the mob rushed us."

Melvin nodded. "They stuck me in a cell and left several men to guard me. You know who freed me before my men could get there?"

"Who?" Essie asked.

"Your band of bloomer-gals. That's who."

She brightened. "How'd they do that?"

"Same way them suffragettes did in *A Woman's War*."

Her jaw went slack. "*A Woman's War*? You read Mrs. Lockhart's books, too?"

"Shhhh," he said, looking around, then signaled Grandpa over. "Gather up several men and escort Essie, Tony, and the rest of the ladies home." Someone shouted the sheriff's name and he excused himself.

"I want you to go on to the house with Essie," the judge said to Tony. "I don't want you staying in the boardinghouse until things settle down."

"Yes, sir," he said. "You think they'll sentence Finch to hang?"

"I'd say it's almost certain."

The depth of Finch's misdeeds overwhelmed Tony, flooding him with sorrow. Thoughts of Darius, Finch's wives, and their shortened lives left him feeling dejected. What a waste.

Spreckelmeyer squeezed Tony's shoulder. "Well, at least one good thing came from this."

"Sir?"

"Well, Anna."

"Anna?"

"Yes. If it hadn't been for all this mess, why, she and Ewing might never have gotten married."

Tony looked at him blankly. "Married?"

"Why, sure. She was afraid if the worst happened, she'd have to honor her marriage contract with Mr. Tubbs. Ewing told her that'd be mighty hard to do if she were already wed. So I married those two up this afternoon."

"What?" He looked at Essie. "Did you know about this?"

"No," she said, eyes wide. "This is the first I've heard."

Spreckelmeyer chuckled. "Well, now, with all that's been going on, that's not so surprising."

Tony scanned the crowd, then remembered Anna and some of the others had taken Ewing home to see to his injuries.

Grandpa approached with a couple of horses. "You two ready?"

In a bit of a fog, Tony helped Essie mount, then swung up onto his horse. The Sullivan Oil men surrounded them and proceeded to escort them to the Spreckelmeyers' house on Bilberry Street.

"Where's Finch?" Tony asked Grandpa.

Grandpa spit a wad of tobacco onto the ground. "He's got him an escort, too. Straight to the jailhouse."

CHAPTER | THIRTY-FIVE

ESSIE WOKE EARLY, ANXIOUS to check on Tony. She hastily donned a shirtwaist and skirt, then hurried down the stairs. Tony and Papa sat at the kitchen table. From the looks of the almost-empty coffeepot, they'd been there awhile.

"What are you doing out of bed?" she asked Tony. New bruises had materialized and his right jaw was swollen, though both eyes were open now.

"It looks worse than it feels."

Papa stood and picked up his coffee cup. "I'll be in my study if you need me." He pecked her on the cheek and left the room.

Songbirds heralded the morning and a bit of eastern sun touched the window. She could see Tony had made good use of the bathwater she'd prepared for him last night. His hair was clean, his swollen face shaven, and she could smell a faint hint of sandalwood.

"Are you hungry?" she asked.

"Not really. I've a belly full of coffee right now. What about you?"

She shook her head, then poured herself a cup. "How long have you been up?"

"Awhile."

She leaned against the counter. "Did you sleep all right?"

"Yes. It was good to be in a real bed again."

"I imagine." She blew on her cup. "I'll have Jeremy or someone collect all of your things from the jail."

"I can do it."

"No. I don't want you near there. Not anytime soon, anyway."

He studied her. "How long you gonna make me wait for a good-morning kiss?"

A weightlessness seized her tummy. "Your jaw's swollen. Won't it hurt?"

"Not unless you plan on punching me."

She smiled.

He stood, then ambled toward her. "I like waking up in your house." He took her cup and set it down. "I'd like it even better if I were waking up in your bed."

She swallowed.

He slipped his arms around her waist. "Good morning, love." Then he kissed her. Softly. Gently. Sweetly.

It didn't take long, however, for passion to rush in and burst open the gates of desire. He clasped her more tightly against him, splaying his hands wide on her back and waist. She slid her arms around his neck.

He flinched and she jerked back.

"Oh," she said. "I'm sorry. Did I hurt you?"

"No," he said. "I guess I'm just a little more sore than I thought." He slipped his hands into hers. "Come sit down at the table with me." He held her chair, then settled in across from her. "Have you made any plans for the wedding?"

"Not yet. I've been spending most of my time trying to prove your innocence."

"And I certainly appreciate that." He squeezed her hand. "But now that we have that behind us, I was wondering if you're going to want a big wedding?"

She shrugged. "It's not so much that I want one, it's more that I'll get one by default. My father's the Thirty-fifth Judicial District Judge, and we know most every person in the county."

He nodded. "Maybe *big* wasn't the right word. I think I meant fancy. Are you going to want a fancy wedding?"

She considered his question. As a young girl, she'd imagined her wedding in a thousand different ways. Sometimes she'd seen herself wearing a lavish beaded gown fit for a princess. Other times she'd visualized a wedding in an outdoor glade fragrant with colorful blooms. She'd even imagined galloping off in the sunset with some handsome cowboy. But those childhood fantasies didn't hold the same appeal now that they did then. Since her betrothal to Tony, the details of the ceremony had become secondary to the commitment she was making to God and to him.

"You know," she began, "I think I can honestly say I don't care one way or the other. So long as it's you who I'm exchanging vows with, most any kind of wedding will do. Why? Do you want a fancy wedding?"

He took a deep breath. "You know what I'd really like?"

She shook her head.

"I'd really like to get married today."

Her lips parted.

"And not just because I'm ready to enjoy all the benefits awarded to married couples—though I'm certainly looking forward to that with great anticipation."

She felt herself blush, though he didn't suffer the same affliction.

"The other reason I'd like to accelerate the exchanging of vows is because I need to return to Beaumont. My family's business interests go well beyond Morgan Oil and have been languishing since Darius's death. I really need to go home."

She looked out the window at the legs of the oil rig in their yard. "Well, I can certainly see you needing to straighten out your affairs. And though a hasty wedding sounds extremely tempting, I'm not sure that's the best solution."

His shoulders slumped.

"Don't misunderstand, Tony. I'm impatient, too." She took both of his hands into hers. "But I have to think about Papa and all my friends. If I'm going to live away from them the rest of my life, then I think I should stay here for just a few more weeks and plan a modest wedding where everyone will have a chance to say good-bye. I also need to tie up my loose ends at the Velocipede Club and prepare Shirley to take over."

"Are you going to change your mind about marrying me?"

"No." She squeezed his hands. "In three weeks, I will be yours and I will go wherever you go."

Pulling her to her feet, he kissed her. Roughly, deeply, right there in the kitchen where anyone could walk in.

"I love you, Essie."

———

Throughout the next three weeks, she found that her hometown, the town that was as much a part of her as her right hand, no longer held the luster it once had. Not without Tony in it.

She sought out Anna's company more than anyone else's because she somehow felt closer to Tony when she was with Anna. But Anna was a new bride herself and busy settling in with Ewing, whose injury had not hindered the honeymoon at all, she guessed, considering how happy the two of them looked whenever she caught sight of them.

And this last week had been nothing short of miserable for her. Why, oh, why hadn't she told Tony to come for her sooner?

But finally her wedding day had arrived. And Tony would be coming in on the ten o'clock train. Even then, though, she wouldn't be able to see him until the ceremony. She didn't for one minute believe in bad luck or good luck or any such nonsense, but Mrs. Lockhart had been adamant. In *Clarabel's Love Story*, Clarabel had seen her groom before the wedding, and that marriage had lasted only three days.

Dragging her hope chest into the center of the bedroom, Essie ran her hand across the ornate wooden trunk. She'd been ten when her mother began filling the box with family heirlooms that would be Essie's when she married.

She slowly lifted the lid. Her grandmother's white-on-white embroidered bedspread, some lace tablecloths, and curtains all lay folded and wrapped in tissue. From her great-grandmother, she had a full set of silver tableware with engraved handles. From Aunt Verdie, a cut-crystal punchbowl and cups.

Linens hemmed and embellished by Mother and by Essie's own hands lay underneath handkerchiefs, tea towels, and hosiery. Chemises, corset covers, and dressing sacques.

And on the very top, her nightdress. Made especially for her wedding night. The tissue crackled as Essie folded it aside and lifted the gown from the chest. Tiny white rosettes were sprinkled among three rows of rice stitches decorating the neckline. Lace trim ran along the sleeveless straps. Only one delicate ribbon held the garment closed.

She slipped her hand beneath the bodice, disconcerted to find the gossamer fabric so sheer, so clingy. She swallowed. She'd only worn this gown once before. The night she'd decided to remain unmarried for the rest of her life. The night she'd decided to have her Lord and Savior as her one and only Groom.

And yet now He'd sent her a flesh-and-blood groom. One who would give her children. Who would grow old with her. Who would see her in this gown this very night.

I'm glad I wore it for you first, Lord. Because even though you've sent me a groom, you will always be first. In my heart. In my marriage. In my life.

———

Four hours later, after the ceremony and wedding meal, Tony waited for his wife at the bottom of the stairs. Her bedroom door opened, but it was Mrs. Lockhart who came out. He smiled again at her bright purple gown with pink trim, then took the steps two at a time to assist her descent.

"I'm still unhappy with you, sir," she said as he slipped his hand under her arm. "A bride should be taken on a train to Niagara Falls for her wedding trip."

"Essie didn't want to go to Niagara Falls," he said.

"Doesn't matter. You're the man. You're the one who should be deciding these things."

"And I did decide. I decided to take her to Enchanted Rock in Llano County."

"On a bicycle!"

They reached the bottom of the steps, and Tony smiled at the woman who'd taken him under her wing the very first time she'd seen him.

"Not ever," she continued, "not even in one of my novels, have the bride and groom traveled away on a bicycle." She leaned in close and whispered, "Where on earth will you spend the night? You can't think to be with your bride for the first time on nothing more than a bed of grass!"

He tweaked Mrs. Lockhart's nose. "I shall not discuss such things with you, ma'am. For shame."

"Well, someone needs to talk some sense into you. It's not too late," she said, squeezing the sleeves of his jacket. "You can send your friend with the bullwhip to the train station right quick to secure you some tickets."

The bedroom door opened again. Anna, Shirley, and Mrs. Dunn came out of the room backwards, hovering in front of Essie. Finally she came into view and his heart sped up.

Her bicycle costume was the same blue as her eyes, her straw hat surprisingly simple, with a wide ribbon band that matched her outfit. He took an involuntary step toward her.

She placed her gloved hand on the balustrade.

"Wait," he said, then patted the rail. "This way. I want you to come to me this way."

Mrs. Dunn gasped.

Smiling, Essie hopped onto the banister and, with bloomers ruffling, slid straight into Tony's waiting arms.

"Hello, Mrs. Morgan," he said, pulling her against him.

"Good afternoon, Mr. Morgan."

He kissed her firmly on the lips. "Are you ready?"

"I am."

He lowered her to her feet. She hugged the women good-bye. The sheriff, judge, and preacher stepped into the foyer. Anna kissed Tony's cheek, then moved next to Ewing while Essie's uncle enfolded her into his arms.

"Be careful, Essie-girl," he said. "Do you have your pistol?"

"Yes," she said, pulling back. "We'll be fine."

Turning to her father, she stepped into his embrace.

"Ah, Squirt," he said. "I wish your mother could have seen you today. You were the prettiest bride I ever did see."

Lifting up on tiptoes, she kissed his cheek. "I'm the happiest bride you ever did see."

He squeezed her tight, then let her go and held out his hand to Tony. "Take good care of her, son."

"I will, sir. And we'll come back through Corsicana on our return trip toward the end of the month."

"I'd like that." He sighed. "Well, you have a passel of folks out there waiting for you. Y'all'd best get going."

Tony offered Essie his arm and opened the door.

They stepped out onto the porch. The yard and street were full of wedding guests. Friends of his. Friends of hers. Friends of their families. They cheered and whistled.

Clasping Essie's hand, Tony looked at her. "Here we go."

They ran down the steps and walkway under a shower of rice. Russ opened the gate and they rushed through.

"Oh, Tony!" she exclaimed. "It's a *side-by-side* bicycle built for two!"

"That's right," he said, helping her mount. "I don't want you in front of me or behind me. I want you right beside me. On our wedding trip and for the rest of our lives."

He kissed her, amazed that if his father hadn't disinherited him, he would never have come to Corsicana. Would never have met Essie.

At the time in his life when he thought he had nothing, when he thought his cup was empty, his heavenly Father was selecting the finest of wines to pour into Tony's cup until it overflowed.

Essie pulled away slightly and flushed. The whistles and hoots of the crowd penetrated Tony's consciousness as folks on the street parted for them, waving, calling out good wishes and throwing the last of the rice.

Winking at Essie, Tony took a quick glance behind them to be sure their clothing and supplies were still secured to the machine, then jumped onto his seat and pushed off.

Beaumont, Texas
January 10, 1901

TONY CROSSED THE CURVING veranda of his three-story home and entered a side door with six-month-old Sullivan on his hip.

"Let's go find Mama," Tony said, hanging his hat on the hall tree before heading to the reception room.

Essie stood beside an easel that held a diagram of an automobile. Her new wide-brimmed hat trimmed in blue velvet slanted fashionably to one side. A number of ladies sat grouped around her.

"You're back early," she said, glancing at Tony.

The baby waved his pudgy arms and kicked his legs upon seeing his mother. Tony handed him to her, noting again Sullivan's blond hair was the same color as Essie's, though his nose was red and runny.

"How was your drive?" she asked Tony, pulling a handkerchief from her pocket and swiping Sullivan's nose.

"Exhilarating," he answered, then turned to greet Essie's guests. He recognized the senator's wife, Mrs. Lockhart's daughter, and Russ's wife among the throng. "How do you do, ladies? What are y'all up to this fine afternoon?"

"We're discussing the features of the new Locomobile," Essie answered, loosening Sullivan's coat and tickling him beneath the chin. She grinned as he squealed with laughter.

"Yes," said Iva O'Berry, smiling at Tony mischievously. "Your wife has invited us to be part of her Beaumont Ladies Automobile Club and she's going to teach us how to drive."

He snapped his attention to Essie. "What?"

"That's right," continued Iva. "Today she's explaining that the wooden body of the Locomobile rests on three full-elliptic springs. The boiler and engine are below the seat of the body, and the feed-water tank is below the rear of the body."

His lips parted.

A huge boom from somewhere outside rattled the windows of the house.

"What in the world?" Essie said, absently patting the baby's back.

Tony glanced out the tall windows facing east. "Sounded like a cannon or something."

The women stirred.

"Essie?" he asked, returning his attention to the matter at hand. "May I see you in the library for a moment?"

"Certainly." She looked at her ladies. "If you'll excuse me, I'll be right back."

With a calm he didn't feel, he escorted her beneath the majolica glass light fixture and past the gingerbread spool design portals separating the hall from the stairwell.

"You're back," his mother said, stepping into the hall.

The baby opened his mouth in a huge yawn.

"Oh dear. You've worn the poor little thing out, Tony." She held out her arms. "Come, my sweet, and let's go to the nursery, where Grandmama can get you out of your coat, then rock you to sleep."

Essie relinquished her son, and Tony marveled again at the delight his mother took in the baby. She'd regained much of her former glow and vigor since becoming a grandmother.

"Thank you, Mother," Tony said, but she was already on her way up the stairs, singing softly to Sullivan.

Tony opened the heavy sliding doors to the library, inviting Essie to enter with the sweep of his hand. Stained-glass windows with the faces of Dickens and Longfellow welcomed them.

He slid the doors shut.

"I was going to tell you," she said before he could even turn around.

"When?"

"When I knew I had enough ladies interested."

He rubbed his eyes. "Essie, women are not supposed to drive. I only taught you because you are not like most women."

"And I love it! It's fabulous. I think it a crime to forbid other women to drive. So many of my friends want to learn. That's what gave me the idea of forming a club."

"No."

"What?"

"No," he repeated. "The men of this town will ride me out on a rail if I let you teach their wives to drive."

She crossed her arms. "That's what everyone in Corsicana said about the bicycle club, too."

"Essie—"

"I'm forming the organization, Tony. I've all that money from the sale of the Velocipede Club and I want to invest it in an automobile club for women."

"Using my car as its teaching tool?"

"Using *our* car."

"They'll wreck it."

"No, they won't. I'm an excellent teacher."

He suppressed a groan. The menfolk were going to kill him. Russ, especially. He thought it a great joke that Essie was such a tomboy and took tremendous pride in ribbing Tony about it. But he would be furious if Iva took up driving.

"In *Thrown on the World*," Essie said, "Miss Moffitt became a shoe cobbler when her father lost his eyesight—a craft supposedly suitable for men alone. Yet she helped many of her lady friends make a way for themselves."

"Miss Moffitt also blew up the barn."

Essie rolled her eyes. "She was a bit careless. I'm much more levelheaded."

Someone hammered the front door's knocker with excessive force. "Mr. Morgan! Mr. Morgan!"

Tony slid open the doors and stepped into the hallway just as Iva answered the door.

A teener in dungarees and covered with oil stood dripping on the front porch. "Mr. Morgan! Come quick. One of the rigs on Spindletop Hill is gushin' clear up to the sky!"

Essie grabbed his hand, her eyes alive with excitement.

"I'll send word back as soon as I can," he said, pulling her to him and planting a kiss on her lips. "We'll talk about the auto club later."

"Be careful," she said.

Grabbing his hat and coat, he rushed out the door and headed toward Spindletop, wondering how he was going to tell the men of Beaumont that before the year was out, their wives would very likely know more about automobiles than they would.

I had such plans for incorporating all the exciting developments of the oil industry's early days—the building of the first oil refinery in Corsicana, the shipment of the first batch of refined oil in Texas, the clever marketing strategies the early oilmen used to promote their product. Yet Essie and her bicycle club simply took over the story and, before I knew it, the novel had ended and I didn't get to include all that wonderful history I'd so thoroughly researched. At least we managed to go from being rope chokers to mud drinkers! (Cable-tool boys to rotary boys.) The oil companies I used were all fictional, but the Baker brothers did, in fact, introduce their rotary drill to Corsicana, thus revolutionizing the Texas oil industry.

Being the daughter of an oilman, the wife of an oilman, a Texan, and a former resident of Corsicana, it has been a delight to write these last two books. I shall always be particularly fond of my *Trouble* books and of all the friends I made while researching them.

Next, we're off to Seattle in the mid-eighteen hundreds. So get ready to rewind back a few years and watch for a brand-new story in June 2009. Until then, come by and visit me on my Web site (*www.IWantHerBook.com*). I have a blog, a chat room, games, contests, email, and a lot of readers just like you, waiting with open arms. See you there!

ABOUT THE AUTHOR

DEEANNE GIST has a background in education and journalism. Her credits include *People Magazine, Parents, Parenting, Family Fun,* and the *Houston Chronicle.* She has a line of parenting products called I Did It!® Productions and a degree from Texas A&M. She lives with her husband, four teenagers, and two dogs in Houston, Texas, and loves to hear from her readers at *www.deeannegist.com.*

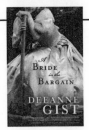